Herbert van Thal was one of the
world's most popular and successful
anthologists. Best known for his
collections of horror and suspense
stories, which sold millions of copies,
his other publications included
Landor, a biographical anthology and
The Tops of the Mulberry Trees, his
autobiography.

THE MAMMOTH BOOK OF

Great Detective Stories

THE MAMMOTH BOOK OF
Great Detective Stories

HERBERT VAN THAL

CARROLL & GRAF PUBLISHERS, INC.
New York

Carroll & Graf Publishers, Inc.
19 West 21st Street
New York
NY 10010–6805

This collection first published in the UK by Robinson Publishing 1985

This edition published by Carroll & Graf 2001

Copyright © The estate of Herbert van Thal 2001

ISBN 0–7867–0886–7

Printed and bound in the EU

CONTENTS

BOOK ONE

BOOK FOUR

The editor is grateful to the following for
permission to reprint the material in this volume:

A. P. Watt & Son for *The Inoffensive Captain* by E. C. Bentley
A. M. Heath & Co. Ltd for *The Scapegoat* by Christianna Brand
Hodder and Stoughton Ltd for *The Mystery of the Child's Toy* by Leslie
   Charteris
Curtis Brown Ltd for *The Rubber Trumpet* by Roy Vickers
A. P. Watt and Son for *The Moabite Cipher* by R. Austin Freeman
London Management Ltd for *The Scarlet Butterfly* by Dulcie Gray
David Higham Associates Ltd. for *The Cave of Ali Baba* by D. L. Sayers
Curtis Brown Ltd for *A Theme for Hyacinth* by Julian Symons

David Higham Associates Ltd for *Superintendent Wilson's
   Holiday* by Margaret Cole

The Estate of Edgar Wallace and Hodder & Stoughton Ltd for
   The Treasure Hunt by Edgar Wallace

Hughes Massie Ltd for *Sing a Song of Sixpence* by Agatha
   Christie

A. P. Watt & Son for *We Know You're Busy Writing* by Edmund
   Crispin © Edmund Crispin 1969

Mrs Dorothy Cheston Bennett for *Murder!* by Arnold Bennett

Miss D. E. Collins and Cassell & Co. Ltd for *The Eye of Apollo*
   by G. K. Chesterton

Michael Innes and Victor Gollancz Ltd for *A Matter of Goblins*
   by Michael Innes © J. I. M. Stewart 1954

Mrs Joan Orczy-Barstow for *The Woman in the Big Hat* by
   Baroness Orczy

The estate of the late Raymond Chandler and Hamish Hamilton
   Ltd for *Goldfish*

June Thomson and London Management for *The Girl with the
   Red-Gold Hair*

BOOK ONE

E. C. Bentley

THE INOFFENSIVE CAPTAIN

'INSPECTOR CHARLES B. MUIRHEAD. Introduced by Chief Inspector W. Murch.' Trent was reading from a card brought to him as he sat at breakfast. 'I had no idea,' he remarked to his servant, 'that Mr Murch was introducing a new kind of policeman. What does he look like, Dennis ?'

'He might be anything, sir. A very ordinary-looking man, I should say.'

'Well, that's the highest compliment you could pay a plainclothes officer, I suppose.'

Trent finished his coffee and stood up. 'Show him into the studio. And if he should happen to arrest me, telephone to Mr Ward that I am unfortunately detained and cannot join him this evening.'

'Certainly, sir.'

The two men who came together in Philip Trent's studio looked keenly at each other. The police officer, who did not much approve of the mission on which he had been sent, was not reassured by what he saw. Trent was at this time - it was a few years before the unravelling of the Manderson affair came to change his life - a man not yet thirty, with an air of rather irresponsible good humour and an easy, unceremonious carriage of his looseknit figure that struck his visitor as pleasing in general, but not in keeping with great mental gifts. His features were regular ; his short, curling hair and moustache, and, indeed, his whole appearance, suggested a slight but not defiant carelessness about externals.

Mr Muirhead, knowing nothing of modern painters, thought this quite right in an artist, but he wondered what could have led such a man to interest himself in police problems.

As for Inspector Muirhead, he was a lean, light-haired, upstanding man with a scanty yellow moustache, dressed in an ill-fitting dark suit, with a low collar much too large for his neck. The only noticeable things about him were an air of athletic hardness and a pair of blue eyes like swords. He looked like a Cumberland shepherd who had changed clothes with a rent-collector.

'I am very glad,' said Trent, 'to meet any friend of Inspector Murch's. Sit down and have a cigar. Not a smoker ? So much the worse for the criminal class – you look as if your nerves were made of steel wire. Now, let me hear what it is you want of me.'

The hard-featured officer squared his shoulders and put his hands on his knees. 'Inspector Murch thought you might be willing to help us unofficially, Mr Trent, in a little difficulty we are in. It concerns the escape of James Rudmore from Dartmoor yesterday afternoon.'

'I hadn't heard of it.'

'It's in the papers today – the bare fact. But the details are unusual. For one thing, he's got clear away, which has happened only in a very few cases at Dartmoor. Rudmore did what others have done – made a bolt from one of the gangs doing outdoor labour, taking advantage of a mist coming on suddenly. But instead of wandering on the moor till he was taken again, as they mostly do, he got on a road some miles from the prison, where he had the luck to meet a motor-car, going slowly in the mist. He jumped out in front of the car, and when the chauffeur stopped it Rudmore sprang at him and gave him a knock on the head with a stone that stunned him. The car belongs to an American gentleman and his wife, by name Van Sommeren, who were touring about the country.'

'Gratifying for them,' remarked Trent. 'They will feel the English are not making strangers of them – that we are taking them to our bosom, as it were.'

'Mr Van Sommeren drew a revolver,' pursued the detective stolidly, 'and shot twice before Rudmore closed with him. He managed to get hold of the weapon after a struggle, and so had them at his mercy. He was hurt slightly in the arm by one of the shots, Mr Van Sommeren thinks. Rudmore made him give up his motor-coat and cap, and all he had in his pockets ; also the lady's purse. Then he put on the coat and cap over his convict dress and drove off alone, going eastward. The others waited till the chauffeur was all right again, then made the best of their way along the road on foot. It was hours before they got to Two Bridges and told their story.'

'He managed it well,' Trent observed, lighting a pipe. 'Decision and promptitude. He ought to have been a soldier.'

'He was,' returned Mr Muirhead. 'He had been, at least. But the point is, where is he now ? We now know that he drove the car as far as Exeter, where he abandoned it outside the railway station, taking with him two large suitcases and a dressing-bag. There can be no doubt that he came on by train to London, arriving last night. He has particular business here, as well as friends who would help him. Do you remember the Danbury pendant affair, Mr Trent ? It's nearly two years ago now.'

'I don't. Probably I was not in England at the time.'

'Then I may as well tell you the story of it and the Rudmores. You must know it if you're to assist us. Old John Rudmore was for many years a doctor in very good practice in Calcutta – had been an army doctor at first. He was a widower, a man of good family, highly educated, very clever and popular. His only son was James Rudmore, who was a lieutenant in a Bengal cavalry regiment, very much the same sort of man as his father. There was a daughter, too – a young girl. Six years ago, when James was twenty-three, something happened – something to do with old Rudmore, it is believed. It was kept dark quite successfully, but the word went out against the Rudmores. The old man threw up his practice, and the son sent in his papers. All three of them came home and settled in London. The Rudmores had influential connections, and Jim got a soft job under the Board of Trade. His sister went to live with some relatives of her mother's. The father made his headquarters in bachelor chambers in Jermyn Street. He travelled a good deal and was interested in mining properties. He seemed to have amassed a great deal of money, and it was believed he made his son a considerable allowance.'

'Was there supposed to be anything wrong about the money ?'

'That we don't know ; but what happened afterwards makes it seem likely. Well, James Rudmore went the pace considerably. He got into a gambling, dissipated set, and wasn't particular about what friends he made. He was intimate with some of the shadiest characters in sporting circles – people we'd had an eye upon more than once. He was a reckless, desperate chap, with a dangerous temper when roused, and he was well on his way to being a regular wrong 'un when the affair of the pendant happened ; but he was very clever and amusing, and had a light-hearted way with him ; a gentleman all over to look at, and hadn't lost caste, as they say.'

Trent nodded appreciatively. 'You describe him to the life. I should like to have known him.'

'One day there was a big garden-party at Danbury House, and he was there helping with some sort of entertainment. Lady Danbury was wearing the pendant, which was a famous family jewel containing three remarkable diamonds and some smaller stones. It was late in the afternoon before she found that the chain it was attached to had broken and the pendant was gone. By that time many of the guests had gone, too, and James Rudmore among them. A search was begun all over the grounds, but it hadn't gone far when one of the maids, hearing of the loss, came forward with a statement. It seemed she had been philandering with one of the men servants in a part of the grounds where she'd no business to be ; the countess had been receiving people there, but it was deserted at the time. The man's eye was caught by something on the grass, and the girl, going nearer to it, recognised the pendant. Just as she was hurrying forward to pick it up, they heard steps on the path, and thinking it might be one of the upper servants, who would make trouble about her being out there, they both stepped behind a clump of shrubbery. They saw James Rudmore come round the corner of the path. He was alone and seemed to be looking for something on the ground. He caught sight of the pendant and stood gazing at it a moment. Then he picked it up and, holding it in his hand, went on toward the place where the company were. That was all that the two saw. Naturally, they thought he was carrying the thing straight to the countess ; it never occurred to them that a man of young Rudmore's appearance would steal it.'

'It was a silly thing to do,' Trent remarked.

'He was in a tight place,' explained the detective. 'It came out afterward that he was deeply in debt and had just dropped a good sum on the Stock Exchange. He wanted money desperately.'

'He had one resource,' suggested Trent. 'I have heard it described as tapping the ancestor.'

'The ancestor,' said Mr Muirhead with a hard smile, 'was away on his travels, looking into some East African mining proposition, and apparently couldn't be got at. Besides, as you'll see, tapping him might not have been much good ; and James no doubt knew that, for their relations were always very close and confidential. But as I was saying: the two witnesses told their story about the finding of the pendant. An hour afterward, I was out after James with a warrant in my pocket. About nine o'clock I arrested him as he walked into the hotel where he lived. He denied the charge with a show of astonishment and indignation, but he made no resistance. The pendant was not on him then, and it was never found. I took him away in a taxicab. In Panton Street he gave me a blow on the jaw that knocked me out, jumped from the cab, and darted round the corner into Whitcomb Street. There he ran into the arms of a constable, who held him ; he fought savagely, and was only secured by the help of two men. He didn't get away again.'

'Until yesterday,' Trent observed. 'Where had he been between leaving Danbury House and returning to his hotel ?'

'Apparently at a club in the Adelphi, where he played billiards for an hour and then dined. His story was that he'd walked straight from

Danbury House and gone straight from there to his hotel. It couldn't be shown that he'd been anywhere else ; but nobody knew exactly when he had left Danbury House. His line at the trial was that he knew absolutely nothing of the pendant and that it was a plot to ruin him. The case against him was unanswerable, and the assaults on the police, of course, made the matter much worse. He was sent to penal servitude.'

'Then you think he has his booty hidden somewhere, waiting for him to take it when he comes out ?'

'Sure of it,' the detective replied. 'Doesn't it stand to reason ? He was ruined anyway, and the assaults which his temper had led him into made a heavy sentence certain. He might as well have something to show for it when it was all over.'

'Just so. Well, then, Inspector, where do I come in ?'

Mr Muirhead drew out a pocket-book.

'Three weeks before his escape, James Rudmore, who had been a model prisoner from the first was allowed the privilege of writing a letter, in accordance with the regulations. He wrote to his father. Now it so happened that old Rudmore had then been himself in jail six months or more. I had arrested him, too. The charge was fraudulent bankruptcy, and it was as clever a piece of crooked work as ever came into court, I should think. I took him at his rooms, and he went like a lamb ; pleaded guilty and took his dose without any fuss.'

'A philosopher,' said Trent. 'So he never got the letter from James.'

'Certainly not. James Rudmore was informed, in accordance with the regulations that his letter could not be forwarded, the reason being withheld. He then asked to have it back ; and that was a mistake, for the governor of Dartmoor had already taken it into his head that there was something more than met the eye in the letter, and that made him certain of it. He believed it contained a secret message telling old Rudmore where the pendant was. Why he thought so I don't myself know ; but it was likely enough, of course. The letter was forwarded to Scotland Yard and has been gone over carefully by the experts. They can make nothing of it.'

'That is probably just because they are experts,' Trent commented. 'You want a really scatter-brained man - or shall we call him a man of tropically luxuriant mental gifts ? - such as myself, for example, to deal with the little dodges of people like the Rudmores. I know now what it is your people want of me. They think the hiding place of the jewel is described in that letter, and that if they can discover it, and mount guard over it, they will soon get James. I am to give an opinion on the letter. There is nothing I should like better. Where is it?'

The inspector, without reply, drew a folded paper from his pocket-book and handed it to Trent. He read the following, written in a firm and legible handwriting :

'MY DEAR DAD:

'I am writing to you, the first time I am allowed, to say how sorry I am for all the misery my disgrace must have caused you. When I was made a scapegoat, it was the thought of how you would feel the dishonour to our name that hurt me most.

I wish I could have seen you just once before I was put away here. But you, at least, will never have doubted my innocence, I know. It would be the end for me, indeed, if when I were free again I should find even your door closed against me.

I am strong and well ; in better health than I have been for years. Most of the time I have been set to what is really navvy's work in the open air, reclaiming waste land. At first it was fearfully hard work, and I used to wish I had a hinge in my back, and as many arms as the idol, whose name I forget, on your mantelshelf. But I soon got hardened. I have not lived an out-of-door life regularly for some years, and it has made me a new man. I feel trained to a hair. I did have one bad bout of fever, though, before I got fit. I fancy the climate here is rather hard on one if one has malaria in one's system, and isn't up to the mark ; the country looks and smells rather like the Gelderland country round Apeldijk, where you remember I was laid up three years. But this was a much worse attack. I was light-headed for days, and felt like dying. Isn't it somebody in Shakespeare who talks about "the wretch whose fever-weakened joints buckle under life" ? I felt exactly like that.

I would like to tell you about the life we lead here, and my opinion of the system, but all I write has to pass under the officials' eyes, and "Sie würden das nicht so hingehen lassen," as old Schraube used to say.

I sent this to the old rooms in Jermyn Street, trusting it will reach you. Goodbye.

Your loving son,
JIM.'

Trent read this through carefully once. Then he looked at Inspector Muirhead with a meditative eye. 'Well ?' demanded that officer.

'This,' said Trent, 'is what judges in lawsuits call a very proper letter ; meaning, usually, a letter with a faint flavour of humbugging artificiality about it. I don't like the note of its pathos and I think there's some hanky-panky about it somewhere. It contains one passage which must be an absolute lie, I should say.'

'I don't know which you mean,' the inspector replied, 'but all the statements about himself in prison are true enough. He did have a bad illness –'

'Yes, naturally all those are true ; he knew the letter would be read by the authorities, of course. I didn't mean anything of that sort. Look here, I should like to spend some time with this in a reference library. Will you meet me outside the British Museum one hour from now ?'

'Right, Mr Trent !' The detective rose quickly. 'You'll find me waiting. There may be no time to lose.'

But it was the inspector who found Trent awaiting him fifty minutes later, with a taxicab in attendance.

'Jump in,' said Trent. 'The man knows where to go. It didn't take very long after all. I even had time to dash up into Holborn and buy this.' He produced a stout screwdriver from his pocket.

'What on earth for ?' inquired Mr Muirhead blankly as the cab rushed westward. 'Where are we going ? What have you made of the letter ?'

'Inquisitive !' Trent murmured, shaking his finger at him gravely. His eyes were shining with suppressed elation and expectancy.

'What is the screwdriver for ? Well, you surely will admit that it is prudent to be armed when going after a dangerous man. I got it of Lake and Company, so I am going to call it Excalibur. Come, inspector, I ask you as a reasonable man, what else could one call it ? Then, as to where we are going – we are going to Jermyn Street.'

'Jermyn Street !' Mr Muirhead was staring at his companion as at some strange animal. 'You think the stuff is there ?'

'I think the letter says it is – or was – hidden in old Rudmore's rooms.'

'But I told you, Mr Trent, old Rudmore was hundreds of miles away when the theft took place. His rooms were locked up.'

'Yes, but isn't it likely James had a key to them ? You told me they were on terms of great mutual confidence. The father was quite likely to leave a key with his son, in case it should prove useful – and a latchkey to the front door, too, I dare say.'

The inspector nodded gloomily. 'Yes – it's quite likely. Then I suppose your idea is, he just walked round to Jermyn Street with the pendant, let himself in, went upstairs to his father's rooms, tucked the thing away, and then strolled on to the club. . . . Certainly it's possible. Only nobody happened to think of it.'

'I don't know that anything would have been found if anybody had, with all regard and reverence to you and your friends, Inspector. I doubt if anything could have been done without the indications in this letter.'

'Well, what does -'

'No ! Here we are in Jermyn Street. What number, Inspector ? 230 - right !' Trent leaned out of the window and instructed the driver. The cab drew up before a shoemaker's shop of such supreme distinction that only three unostentatious pairs were placed, as if they had been left there by accident, in the window. To the left of the shop was a closed private door for the use of those living in the chambers above.

The inspector's ring was answered by an extremely corpulent, mulberry-faced man with snowy side-whiskers and smooth, white hair. His precision of dress and manner, with a certain carriage of the body, proclaimed the retired butler.

'Well, Hudson, have you forgotten me ?' asked the detective pleasantly, stepping into the well-kept but gloomy little hall. The stout man hesitated, then said, 'Bless my soul ! It's the officer who came to take Mr Rudmore.' His face lost something of its over-ripe appearance, and he added, as he closed the door, 'I do hope it's not another business of that sort. My house will be getting the name of -'

'Now, don't you worry yourself,' the man of authority advised him. 'I'm not after anybody in your house. I only want to know if the rooms that old Rudmore had are occupied at present.'

'They are, Inspector. They were taken, shortly after that unfortunate affair, by Captain Ainger, who has them still - a military gentleman, invalided home from India, I believe ; a very pleasant, quiet gentleman -'

'Is he at home now ?'

'Captain Ainger never goes out until luncheon-time.'

'Then we want to see him. Don't you trouble to come up, Hudson ; stairs don't agree with you, I can see that. It's the second floor, I remember.'

'Second floor, and the door on the left. And I do hope, gentlemen -' Hudson withdrew, murmuring vague apprehension, and ponderously descended to the basement floor as Mr Muirhead, followed by Trent, went up the narrow stairs.

'I thought it better,' said the inspector, pausing on a stair, 'to go up unannounced. He can't say he won't see us if we just walk in and make ourselves pleasant.'

As the two men reached the first landing they heard the sound of a door closed gently on the one above and of light-stepping feet. A tall girl, in neat and obviously expensive tailor-made clothes, appeared at the head of the short stairway and, apparently not seeing them, stood for a moment adjusting her hat and veil. Mr Muirhead uttered a growling cough from below, at the noise of which the young lady started slightly and hurried down the stairs. In the half-light on the landing, they received, as she passed them, an impression of shining dark hair and barely perceptible perfume. Trent looked after her meditatively as she went swiftly along the ground floor passage and let herself out.

'Smart woman,' observed the inspector appreciatively, as the front door slammed.

'A fine example of healthy modern girlhood,' Trent agreed. 'Did you see the stride and swing as she went to the door ? From the cut of her clothes I should say she was American.'

There was a note in his voice which made the other look at him sharply.

'And,' pursued Trent, returning his gaze with an innocent eye, 'I suppose you noticed her feet and ankles as she stood up there and as she came downstairs.'

'I did not,' returned Mr Muirhead gruffly. 'What was there to notice ?'

'Only the size,' said Trent. 'The size – and the fact that she was wearing a man's shoes.'

For an instant the inspector glared at him wild-eyed ; then turned and plunged without a word down the stairway. He reached the door and tore at the handle.

'It's locked ! Double locked from outside ! Here, Hudson !' he bellowed, and swore loud and savagely as the fat man was heard shuffling across the passage in the basement below and labouring heavily up the stairs. 'Give me your latchkey !' he commanded, as Hudson, with a staring housemaid in his wake, appeared, trembling and gasping. For a few moments, filled with vivid language by the enraged officer, the man fumbled at a trousers pocket. At last he produced his key. Mr Muirhead seized it and endeavoured to thrust it into the keyhole. After half a dozen vain attempts he resigned the key to Hudson, who grasped the situation at the first try.

'I'm afraid whoever double locked it has left the key in on the other side,' he panted. 'This'll never go in till the other's taken out.'

Mr Muirhead suddenly recovered his calm and stuck his hands in his pockets. 'He's done us,' he announced. 'He could reach Piccadilly in fifteen seconds from here, without hurrying. It's a clean getaway. Probably he's bowling off in a taxi by now. Hudson, why the devil didn't you say there was a lady with the captain ? I'd never have let him pass me if I'd known he was coming from those rooms.'

'I never knew there was anyone with him, indeed, Inspector,' quavered the old man, his mind wrestling feebly with the confusion of genders. 'I expect it was this girl let her in.'

'How was I to know there was anything wrong ?' cried the domestic, bursting into tears. 'She spoke like a perfect lady and sent me up with her card and all. I never thought till this minute -'

'All right, all right, my girl,' said the inspector brusquely. 'You'll get into no trouble if you're straight. Hudson, I want your telephone. In the back room here ? Right ! And you'd better hail somebody next door and get your door opened.'

The detective disappeared into the room and Hudson shuffled down the passage to the back of the building, still in a dazed condition. 'What I don't see,' he mumbled, 'is where she, or he, or whoever it was, got the key from.' And as he said it, Trent, who had been leaning against the wall with a face of great contentment, suddenly turned and fled lightly up the stairs.

Captain Ainger's door opened easily. Captain Ainger himself, a small, crop-headed man, lay upon a sofa near the window of his tastefully furnished sitting-room. As Trent burst in a look of relief came into the captain's bewildered eyes. The rest of his face below them was covered by an improvised gag made out of a tobacco pouch and a tightly-knotted silk scarf. His ankles were tied together and his arms lashed to his sides with box cord.

He looked wretchedly uncomfortable.

Five minutes later, in answer to a call from Trent, Mr Muirhead closed his conversation with Scotland Yard and came upstairs. He found Captain Ainger sitting in an armchair, restoring his physical tone with a deep glass of whisky and soda. To Trent's account of how he had found that ill-used officer the detective answered only with a grim nod. Then, 'I suppose it was your latchkey, sir,' he said to the victim.

'Yes,' replied the little captain, 'she took my latchkey - he did, I mean. Tell you just how it was. She sent up her card - his, I should say - well, it was a woman's card, anyhow. I put it up here.' He rose and took a card from the mantelshelf.'

Mr Muirhead glanced at it with curiosity. 'Of course !' he exclaimed.

'Mrs Van Sommeren's card, is it ?' asked Trent from his chair by the window.

'It is.'

'And Mrs Van Sommeren's clothes and hat, and Mrs Van Sommeren's little bag, and Mrs Van Sommeren's own particular perfume - they all went by us just now,' Trent remarked, 'in company with, I expect, Mr Van Sommeren's shoes and Mr James Rudmore's wig. Probably he was a little excited at seeing you, Inspector, awaiting him at the bottom of the stairs. It needed some nerve for him to stand there fixing his veil without a quiver, and to trip downstairs right into your yearning embrace, as one may say.'

Annoyance, self-reproach, menacing resolve and appreciation of the comic side of the episode – all these things were in the inspector's eloquent answering grunt.

'If only he had remembered to walk along the lower passage like a lady, instead of like a champion lightweight,' Trent resumed, 'I don't suppose the meaning of the shoes would have burst upon me as it did. I daresay his hold on himself began to go when he saw the street door and safety six steps in front of him. Yet that latchkey business was pretty coolly done. Jim is certainly a gifted amateur. But you were telling us' – he turned to the obviously mystified captain – 'how she made her appearance.'

'The message with the card,' resumed Captain Ainger, who still preserved his pained expression, 'was that she would be obliged if I would answer an inquiry on a family matter. It made me feel curious, so I said I would see her. She had on a very thick veil – he had, I mean –'

'Why not stick to "she", Captain,' Trent suggested. 'We should get on quicker, I think.'

'Thank you,' said the veteran gratefully, 'I believe we should. The whole thing is so confusing, because she talked just like a woman from beginning to end. Where was I ? Ah, yes ! I couldn't see her face very well, but her voice and style were those of a well-bred woman. She told me that a year ago she had lost a brother who was very dear to her, and that on his deathbed he had laid what she called a sacred charge upon her. It seemed he had been befriended at some critical time, when he was in India, by an English officer of my name, of whom he had lost sight for many years. He wished her, if possible, to find out that officer and place in his hands a memento, something which had belonged to himself, in token of his undying gratitude. She had made inquiries and had found me in the first place, but understood there were others of my name in the army list.'

'How did Rudmore get hold of your name, I wonder ?' mused the inspector. 'He only got away from Dartmoor yesterday.'

'That wouldn't have been difficult for his sort of man,' Trent replied. 'Very likely he got it out of the housemaid who opened the door, before sending up the message.'

The captain cursed the absent malefactor feebly and took another drink from his tumbler. 'I confess I was rather touched. Of course I've usually done a man a good turn when it lay in my power, but I couldn't remember having played Providence to an American at any time. So I asked what his name was. She said their name was Smith. Well, you know, I must have run across about fifty Smiths, and I told her so. Then she said she had a photograph of him with her. She took it out of her bag. It was a picture of a good-looking, youngish chap, with the name of a Philadelphia firm on the mount.'

'Van Sommeren's photograph,' murmured Trent. 'She carried it about with her. You didn't tell me they were on their honeymoon, Inspector.'

'I felt sure I'd never seen the man,' continued Captain Ainger, 'but I took it to the window to have a good look. And the moment my back was turned she leaped on me and garotted me. There wasn't a chance for me. She was as strong as a tiger, and I'm pretty shaky from a long illness. When I was about at my last gasp she gagged me with that infernal thing, then dragged me into the bedroom and tied me up with my own cord. When I was trussed properly she went through my pockets and took my latchkey, then she carried me back to the bedroom door. She said she was so sorry to be giving me all this trouble and that she always wished women were not so dependent upon men for everything. She put her veil up a little way and helped herself to a whisky and soda and lighted one of my cigars. After that she took a screwdriver out of her bag and went to work at something behind me. I don't know in the least what she was doing ; I couldn't move. It took about five minutes, I should say. Then she skipped to the window with something that looked like a wad of cottonwool in her fingers and began gloating over something I couldn't see. She stood there a long time, smoking and looking out, and then all at once she gave a start and stared down into the street. Just after that I heard the front-door bell ring. And then she – well, she went.' The captain's bronzed face went slowly scarlet to the roots of his hair.

'She said goodbye, surely,' murmured Trent, looking at him attentively.

'If you must know,' burst out the captain with his first show of fierceness, 'she said she didn't know how to thank me, and that I was a dear, and might she give me a kiss ? So she – she did it.' Here his narrative dissolved into unchivalrous expressions. 'And then she went out and shut the door. That's all I can tell you.' He wearily resorted to his tumbler again.

Trent and the inspector, who had prudently avoided catching each other's eyes during the last part of the story, now conquered their feelings. 'What I want to know now,' the detective said, 'is where the stuff was hidden here. Can you go straight to the place, Mr Trent, or should we have to search ?'

Trent took the convict's letter from his pocket. 'Let me tell you how I got at it first,' he said. 'You will be interested, Captain, you read it.' He handed the document to the soldier and gave him a brief account of the circumstances regarding it.

The captain, now highly interested, read it through carefully twice, then handed it to Trent again. 'I don't believe I should make anything out of it in a thousand years,' he said. 'It seems straight enough to me. I should call it an interesting letter, that's all.'

'This letter,' said Trent, regarding it with a look of unstinted appreciation, 'is the most interesting, by a long way, that I have ever read. It tells us, not, I think, where the pendant was hidden, but where the diamonds of the pendant were hidden by Jim Rudmore before his arrest. What Jim did with the setting I don't know, nor does it matter much. But the diamonds were concealed here ; and they are now again, I am afraid, in the possession of Jim.'

Inspector Muirhead made an impatient movement. 'Come to the point, Mr Trent,' he urged. 'What did you pick up from that letter ? Where was the stuff hidden ?'

'I will tell you first the things I picked up, and how. The first time I read the letter – in your presence, inspector – I checked at the statement that "the country looks and smells like the Gelderland country around Apeldijk." When one reads that, it naturally occurs to one's mind that Dartmoor is practically a mountain district, whereas Gelderland is a part of Holland, most of which country is actually below sea level.'

'It didn't occur to *my* mind,' observed Captain Ainger.

'Therefore,' pursued Trent, unconscious of him, 'any similarity of look or smell would be rather curious, don't you think ? Possibly that was what struck the governor of the prison and aroused his suspicions of the letter. Well, the next thing that pulled me up was the Shakespearean reference. I knew I'd read it in Shakespeare, and yet I felt it was wrong somehow. There were some words missing, I thought. Besides, it didn't look like a prose passage ; yet it didn't fit into the decasyllabic form, or any other metre. . . . The only other notion that occurred to me at first glance was that it was an odd thing to quote a German phrase when an English one would have been just as good.

'Then I took the letter to the British Museum library and sat down to the problem in earnest. I said to myself that if there was any cipher in it, it was probably impossible to get at it. But I thought it more likely that the message, if any, was conveyed in the words as they stood. So I asked myself what were the signals that it hung out to a man who would be trying to read some inner meaning into it. What things in it were, by ever so little, out of the common, so that the reader would say to himself, "This may be a pointer" ? And I had to remember that both the Rudmores were said to be clever and cultivated men, who understood each other well.

'Now, to begin with, I thought that "the idol, whose name I forget, on your mantelshelf," was the sort of thing Rudmore *père* would have pondered over. Of course we've all seen those little images of the Hindu goddess with ten arms. Jim Rudmore, who had lived in India for years, said he had forgotten her name. That might possibly be meant to draw attention to the name.'

'It's Parvati – heard it thousands of times,' the captain interjected.

'Yes ; I found that name when I looked up the Hindu mythology. But there's another, by which she is known in Bengal, where the Rudmores had had their experience of India. There, my book told me, the people call her Doorga. So I noted down both names. . . . Very well ; now the next passage that seemed out of the ordinary was that about "the Gelderland country round Apeldijk." The first thing I did was to look up Apeldijk in the gazeteer. It mentioned no such place ; the nearest thing to it was a town called Apeldoorn, which was in Gelderland sure enough. Then I got a big map and went through Gelderland from end to end. As I expected, it was as flat as a board, and there was no sign of Apeldijk. But I found several towns in Holland ending in "dijk," which shows you what a conscientious artist Jim is. Now if he had really been ill at Apeldoorn, as I expect he had been, his father would have got a hint at once. I wrote down Apeldoorn, and then I began to see light.'

Mr Muirhead rubbed his nose with a puzzled air. 'I don't see –' he began.

'You will very soon. Next I turned to the odd-looking quotation from Shakespeare. On looking up "joints" in the *Cowden-Clark Concordance* I found the passage. It's in *Henry IV,* where Northumberland says,

'And as the wretch, whose fever-weaken'd joints,
Like strengthless hinges, buckle under life . . .'

'What do you think of that ?'

The inspector shook his head.

'Well, then, look at the German phrase. *Sie würden das nicht so hingchen lassen* means "They would not allow that", or "They would not pass that over", or something of that sort. Now suppose a man looking for a suggestion or hint in each of those German words.'

Mr Muirhead took the letter and conned the words carefully. 'I'm no German scholar,' he began, and then his eyes brightened. 'Those missing words –' he said.

' "Like strengthless hinges," ' Trent reminded him.

'Well, and here' – the inspector tapped excitedly upon the word *hingehen* – 'you've got "hinge" and "hen" in English.'

"You're there ! Never mind the hen ; she's not there on business. Lastly, I'll tell you a thing you probably don't know. *Schraube* is the German word for "screw".'

Mr Muirhead gave his knee a violent blow with his fist.

'Now then !' Trent tore a leaf from his notebook. 'I'll put down the words we've got at that were hidden.' He wrote quickly and handed the paper to the inspector. Both he and Captain Ainger read the following :

Doorga

Doorn

Hinges

Hinge

Screw

'Also,' Trent added, 'the word "door" occurs twice openly in the body of the letter, and the word "hinge" once. That was to show old Rudmore he was on the right track, if he succeeded in digging out those words. "Good !" says he to himself. "The loot is hidden under a screw in a hinge on a door somewhere. Then where ?" He turns to the letter again and finds the only address mentioned in it is "the old rooms in Jermyn Street". And there you are !'

Trent took his screwdriver from his pocket and went to the open door leading into the captain's bedroom. 'Naturally it wouldn't be the outer door, as to get at the hinges one would have to have it standing open.' He glanced at the hinges of the bedroom door. 'These screws' – he pointed to those on the doorpost half of the upper hinge – 'have had their paint scratched a little.'

In a minute or two he had removed all three screws. The open door sank forward slightly on the lower hinge and the upper one came away from its place on the doorpost. Beneath it was a little cavity roughly hollowed out in the wood. Silently the inspector probed it with a penknife.

'The stones are gone, of course,' he announced gloomily.

'Certainly gone,' Trent agreed. 'The stones were in that little piece of cottonwool the captain saw him handling.'

Mr Muirhead rose to his feet. 'Well, I don't think they'll go far.' As he took up his hat there was a knock at the door and Hudson entered panting, a sharp curiosity in his eyes.

'A messenger boy just brought this for you, Inspector,' he wheezed, handing a small package to the detective. It was directed in a delicate, sloping handwriting to 'Inspector C.B.Muirhead, CID, care of Captain R.Ainger, 230 Jermyn Street.'

Hastily the inspector tore it open. It contained a small black suède glove, faintly perfumed. With this was a scrap of paper, bearing these words in the same writing :

'Wear this for my sake. - J.R.'

Christianna Brand

THE SCAPEGOAT

'STAY ME WITH FLAGONS,' said Mr Mysterioso, waving a fluid white hand, 'comfort me with apples !' There had been no flagons, he admitted, in that murder room fifteen years ago, but there had been apples - a brown paper bag of them, tied at the top with string and so crammed full that three had burst out of a hole in the side and rolled away on the dusty floor ; and a rifle, propped up, its sights aligned on the cornerstone, seventy-odd yards away and two storeys below.

And at the foot of the cornerstone the Grand Mysterioso tumbled with his lame leg doubled up under him, clasping in his arms the dying man who for so many years had been his dresser, chauffeur, servant, and friend - who for the last five years, since the accident that had crippled Mr Mysterioso, had almost literally never left his side — tumbled there, holding the dying man to his breast, roaring defiance at the building opposite, from which the shot had come. 'You fools, you murderers, you've got the wrong man !' And then he had bent his head to listen. 'Dear God, he's saying - he's saying - come close, listen to him ! He's saying, "Thank God they only got me. It was meant for you." '

Fifteen years ago - a cornerstone to be laid for the local hospital, just another chore in the public life of Mr Mysterioso, stage magician extraordinary. But, mounting to the tiny platform, leaning his crippled weight on the servant's arm, there had come the sharp crack of the rifle shot. And in the top-floor room of the unfinished hospital wing, looking down on the scene, they had found the fixed rifle with one spent bullet. And nobody there. Up on the roof a press photographer who couldn't have got down to the window where the gun was fixed ; down at the main entrance a policeman on duty, seen by a dozen pairs of eyes, tearing up the stairs toward the murder room, moments after the shot. In all that large, open, easily searched building - not another soul.

Fifteen years ago ; and now they were gathered together, eight of them - to talk it over, to try to excise the scar that had formed in the mind of the young man whose father had been dismissed from the force 'for results of the act that day, and who now was dead.

For the young man had developed an obsession of resentment against the only other person involved, the man on the roof, who nowadays called himself 'Mr Photoze' - whose first step on the road to fame had come with the picture he had taken that day of the lion head raised, the brilliant eyes glaring, the outraged defiance. 'My father didn't fire that shot - therefore you must have,' was the burden of the young man's message, and there had been a succession of threats and at last a physical attack.

They had sent him to see a psychiatrist, and the psychiatrist had muttered darkly about paranoia and complexes and 'a disturbed oedipal pattern - the young man is subconsciously jealous of the father's domination of the mother, which seems to have been considerable. He feels guilty towards the father and now seeks to cover up the recollection of his inner hatred by an exaggerated feeling of protection towards the father, now that the father is dead and unable, as it were, to protect himself.' A long period of treatment, said the psychiatrist, would be necessary.

Half an hour of treatment, said Mr Photoze to his friend Mysterioso, would be more like it. Once convince the young man - 'Hold a little court, get together some of the people who were present and talk it out.'

'The very thing !' Mysterioso had agreed, delighted. It would be entertaining ; he was an old man now, long retired from the stage. It would give him something to do, sitting here crippled and helpless in his chair all day.

So here they were, gathered together in Mr Mysterioso's large lush apartment : Mysterioso himself and Inspector Block, who as a young constable had been on the scene of the crime ; and a lady and gentleman who had been on the hospital balcony and seen the young policeman running up the stairs after the shot had been fired ; and a lady who had been close to the site and seen and heard it all. And a once-lovely lady, Miss Marguerite Devine, the actress, who might also have something to say ; and Mr Photoze. Mr Photoze was madly decorative in dress, and a half-dozen fine gold bracelets jingled every time he moved his arm.

The young man sat hunched against an arm of the sofa, strained against it as though something dangerous to him crouched at the other end. He hated them. He didn't want their silly help ; he wanted to be avenged on Mr Photoze, who had committed a crime and got off scot-free, as a result of which his father had lost his job and his happiness and his faith in men. And his mind wandered back over the frightening, uneasy childhood, the endless bickering and recrimination over his too perceptive young head ; the indigence, the sense of failure. . . . 'I don't want to hear all this, I know what I know. Because of what he did, my father's life was ruined. I meant all those threats. I failed last time, but next time I'll get him.'

'You do *see* !' said Mr Photoze, appealing to the rest of them with outflung arms and a tinkling of gold.

'Your father was never accused of anything,' said Inspector Block. 'He was dismissed –'

' "Dismissed for negligence" - everyone knew what that meant. He lived under suspicion till the day he died.'

'We are going to lift that suspicion,' said Mysterioso. 'That's what we're here for ; we're going to clear the whole thing up. You shall re-present your father, Mr Photoze will be in the dock with you, defending himself. And here we have our witnesses – who also will be our jury. And I shall be the judge. If in the end we all come to the conclusion that your father was innocent, and Mr Photoze was innocent also, won't you feel better ?' He said very kindly, 'We only want to help you.'

The young man watched him warily. He's not doing this for my sake, he thought. He's doing it because he wants to be on a stage again, and this is the nearest he can get to it. He's just a vain, conceited old man ; he wants to show off.

A vain man, yes : a man consumed with vanity – enormously handsome once, with the tawny great mane, now almost white, a man of worldwide fame, a great performer – and not only on stage if his boast-ings were at all to be trusted – despite the fact that the auto accident at the height of the career had left him unable to walk more than a few steps unaided. It was whispered behind mocking hands that on romantic occasions his servant Tom had to lead him to the very bedside and lower him down to it. Certainly he was never seen in public without Tom : a walking stick was not enough, and as for a crutch, 'Do you see me hop-ping about playing Long John Silver ?' Close to Tom, gripping Tom's strong left arm the lameness was hardly noticeable. On stage he had continued to manage brilliantly with the aid of cleverly positioned props which he could hold on to or lean against. It was a total lack of strength only ; he suffered no pain. . . .

Mysterioso gave three knocks on the table by his side – the three knocks that usher in the judge in Central Criminal Court Number One at the Old Bailey. 'We'll take first the evidence of the police.'

Inspector Block, paying lip service to all this foolishness, was inte-rested nevertheless to see the outcome. 'May it please your lordship, members of the jury. Fifteen years ago, almost to this very day, the police were shown an anonymous letter which had been received by the famous stage magician, Mr Mysterioso. It was the first of a dozen or so, over the next six months. They were composed of words cut out from the national dailies, and enclosed in cheap envelopes, varying in size and shape, posted from widely differing parts of the country. I may add here that no one concerned with the case appeared to have had the opportunity to post them, unless of course it was done for the sender by different persons. At any rate, the letters were untraceable. They were all abusive and threatening and evidently from the same person ; they were all signed "Her Husband."

'Mr Mysterioso made no secret of having received them, and there was a good deal of excitement as each new one arrived. The police gave him what protection they could, and when in June he came down to Thrushford in Kent to lay a cornerstone, it was our turn – I was a young constable then and didn't know too much about it, but it was rather anxious work for my superiors, because he had done a brief season at the theatre there a couple of years before.

'It was arranged, therefore, to cover certain points round the site of the ceremony. The cornerstone was for a new wing ; a second wing, completed on the outside but not on the inside, lay between the cornerstone and the main hospital building.'

He drew a plan in the air, a circular movement with the flat palm of the right hand for the main building of the hospital, a stab with the forefinger of the left hand for the cornerstone, and a sharp slash with the edge of the hand for the unfinished wing lying midway between them. 'It was from a middle window on the top floor of this wing that the shot was fired.'

And he described the unfinished wing. A simple oblong : ground floor and two storeys, with its main entrance at one end. This entrance had no door as yet, was only a gap leading into a little hall out of which the stairs curled round the still-empty elevator shaft. A sloping roof of slate surrounded by a ledge with a low parapet.

'It was an easy matter to search it. Except on the top floor there were no interior walls, and up there only half a row of rooms was completed – each floor was designed to have a central corridor with small rooms leading off both sides. There was a lot of stuff about, planks and tools and shavings and so on, but literally nowhere big enough for a man to hide. It was searched very thoroughly the night before the ceremony and less thoroughly the next morning, and a man was placed at the main entrance with orders not to move away from it.'

'And he didn't move away from it,' said the young man. 'That was my father.'

Inspector Block ignored him. 'The order of events is as follows : One
hour before the ceremony, Mr Mysterioso arrived, and the superintendent explained the arrangements to him. Their way to the main hospital
building, where the reception committee awaited him, led past the
entrance of the unfinished wing. Just outside it a man was speaking to the
policeman on duty.'

'The *murderer* was speaking to the policeman on duty,' said the young
man.

'This person was well known to the police,' said the inspector, ignoring the young man again, 'as a press photographer – not yet calling
himself Mr Photoze. He wanted permission to go up on the roof and take
pictures of the ceremony from there.'

'Always one for the interesting angle,' said Mr Photoze archly.

'The Super was about to refuse him, but Mr Mysterioso recognized
the man and said he should be permitted to go up. So he was carefully
searched for any weapons, and it ended in all of them going up to the
top floor together. Mr Mysterioso, of course, had his man, Tom, help
him.'

'We'd been together so long,' said Mysterioso, 'that really in the end
we moved like a single person, always running a sort of three-legged
race. I had no pain from this thing, it was only a total lack of strength. A
couple of flights of stairs was nothing to us.'

You couldn't get on with it, with these people, thought the inspector,
They all wanted to exhibit. 'At any rate, they went up,' he proceeded,
letting a little of his irritability show. 'There was a trapdoor, the only exit
to the roof, and Mr Photoze, as we now call him, was helped up through
it with his gear. At that moment Tom came down the corridor, having
left his master standing propped up against the window-sill in one of the
little rooms, looking down with interest at the site. Tom said he didn't
like it, that he felt uneasy about the whole thing ; the man shouldn't have
been allowed up. Someone – I think in fact it was PC Robbins, the man
on the door, this young man's father – suggested that there was a bolt
which could be shot from the inside, locking the photographer on the
roof. So this was done. Mysterioso was waiting for them at the door of
the little room, and they went on to the cornerstone.

'And then – it happened. The guest of honour went up the four shallow steps that led to the platform in front of the cornerstone. There was
a shot, and both men fell. A minute later Tom, the servant, died in his
master's arms. As he died he was heard to say : "Thank God they only
got me. It was meant for you." '

'He said it over and over,' said the woman who had been near the site. 'Over and over. It was so dreadful, so touching – '

'Let us hear from our witnesses later,' said Mysterioso ; but he looked down at his hands, lying in his lap, and when she continued, he made no further attempt to stop her.

For the woman was carried away, full of tragic memories, and could not be still. 'I can see them now ! A moment before, it had all been so lovely, so sunny and pleasant, all the doctors from the hospital there and lots of guests, and Matron, of course, and some of the nurses, and Mr Mysterioso looking so magnificent, if I may say so' – she made a little ducking movement which the great man graciously accepted – 'with his top hat and flowing black cloak, as though he'd just walked down from the stage to come and lay our cornerstone for us.

'And then – they went up the steps together, he on the left. His man walked very close to him, and I suppose that under the cloak his arm was holding tight to his man's arm ; but you wouldn't have guessed that he was lame at all. They stood there in the sunshine, and a few words were spoken, and so on ; and then the man put out his hand to take the trowel, which was on a stand to his right, and pass it across to his master – and suddenly there was this sharp *crack* – and before we knew what was happening, the man fell and dragged his master down with him.' And the lifting up of the splendid head with its tawny, grey streaked hair, the great roar of defiance flung up at the window from which the shot had come.

'When you think,' said the woman, 'what a target he presented ! We had all swung round to where the shot came from, and we could see a man up on the roof. Of course, we all thought he was the murderer. And at any moment he might have taken a second shot and really killed the right man this time.'

'If he was in fact the right man,' said Inspector Block, throwing a cold pebble into this warm sea of emotion. 'Not all of us were convinced at the time that the shot wasn't meant for Tom.'

'For God's sake !' said Mysterioso. 'Who would want to kill Tom ? – My poor, inoffensive, faithful, loving old Tom. And what about the threatening letters ? Besides, he said it himself – over and over, as the lady says. He'd have known if he'd had such an enemy, but he said it himself. "It was meant for you." ' He appealed to the woman. 'You heard him ?'

'Yes, of course. You called me close. "Listen !" you said.' She shuddered. 'The blood was coming up, bubbling up out of his mouth. They were the last words he spoke. "Thank God they only got me. It was meant for you." '

'And so he died – for my sins,' said the Grand Mysterioso, and again he was silent. But he's not sorry, really, thought the young man, crouched in his sofa corner, watching the big handsome old face heavy with sadness, and yet spread over with a sort of unction of self-satisfaction. 'He's pleased, underneath it all, that everyone should know that even at that age he could still be seducing girls, breaking up homes, getting threatening letters from husbands.' And certainly in the ensuing years the aging lion had done nothing to obliterate the public's memory of that terrible, yet magnificent day. 'I was so bloody mad, I forgot all about everything but Tom. Dying for *my* sins !' In a hundred talks and broadcasts he lived it over again, mock regretful, mock remorseful (thought the young man) that a man should have died to pay for the triumphs of his own all-conquering virility. '*I* think you're pleased,' the young man said, 'I think you're proud of it. If you weren't, you wouldn't have kept telling people about it all this time.'

'He's got you there, old boy,' said the actress, Marguerite Devine, without venom. 'Literally below the belt,' she added, laughing, and then said, 'Oh, I'm sorry, love !' and laughed no more.

'I know a lot about people,' said the young man, and it was true ; the insecurities of his childhood had heightened his perception – solitary, antisocial, he paid no lip service to conventional pretences, was unde-ceived by them. Life had accustomed him to be ready for the worst.

'Well, the cheeky monkey !' said the old man in a comic accent, trying to make light of it. Inspector Block asked patiently if they might now get on with it. 'What happened next? – '

'I'll tell what happened next,' said the young man. 'Because I know it.' You could see the tense clutch of his hands, the tense pressure of his shabby shoes on the soft carpeting of Mysterioso's room ; his very skin colour had changed, strangely darkened with hollows ringed round the bright eyes. He was coming now to the defence of his father. 'My father was standing in the doorway where he'd been posted. I've heard him tell about it a hundred times ; he was always telling it. He heard the shot fired and ran to the corner of the building and sent one glance at the site and saw what had happened – and don't tell me that in that short time someone could have come out of the building and run away, because they couldn't. Could they ?' he appealed to Inspector Block.

'No,' said Block. 'In that short time, anyone shooting from the win-dow where the gun was could hardly even have reached the top of the stairs. Experiments were made.'

'Well, all right, so he saw them both fall and he saw the crowd swing round and stare up at the building, so he knew where the shot must have come from and he turned back and ran into the building and up the stairs. He didn't bother about the ground floor, because he knew the man couldn't have got there yet ; and anyway, it was just an open space, he could see that it was empty ; and so was the second floor an empty space.'

'That's right,' said Block. 'He acted perfectly wisely. Go on, you're doing fine.'

The tense, darkened face gave him no thanks. 'He went tearing up,' said the young man, 'and as he passed the first big window on the stairs looking across at the main building of the hospital, he saw people lying in beds and sitting in wheelchairs out on the balcony – '

They had sat very quiet and intent, those two who had been on the hospital balcony that day long ago – traced and brought here by the dramatic enthusiasm of the Grand Mysterioso to stand witness to what they had seen. 'Yes, I remember it well,' said the woman. 'They'd wheeled us out there into the sunshine – we were pretty sick people, from the surgical wards. Nothing to see, mind : the unfinished wing cut off the view of the park beyond, and, of course, of the cornerstone. It would have been fun to lie there and watch the ceremony, but – well, we couldn't see it. Still, it was nice to get a bit of fresh air. This gentleman was on the other side of the partition with others from Men's Surgical. We were lying there quietly, dozing, enjoying the sunshine – '

'That's right. And then suddenly we heard the shot, and half a minute later this policeman comes racing up the stairs of the unfinished wing opposite. There was a lot of glass there, at least there was going to be – now it was just a huge great open space. He went dashing past, and then something must have occurred to him, because he reappeared, hanging out of the window to shout out to us, clinging to the post with one hand, "Watch the stairs !" he shouted. "Watch that no one comes down !" We were all excited, we yelled back, "What's happened ?" and he yelled, "They've shot him !" or "They've got him !" – I don't know which – and then off he went tearing up the stairs again.'

'What a kerfuffle !' said the woman. 'Everyone squealing and hysterical, one of them fainted – we were all weak, I suppose, and I think we thought the murderer would suddenly appear and start taking shots at us from the window – '

'Or from the roof,' said the young man.

'We're coming to the roof in a moment,' said Mysterioso patiently. Don't worry about him, his look said to the rest of them ; after all, this is why we're here. 'Now – your father went tearing on up the stairs ?'

'Yes ; and came to the top and ran along the corridor. There were a few rooms with their walls up, but the rest was open space – no ceiling in yet, you could see the joists and the tiles up over your head. He ran past several of the little rooms that *were* partitioned - there were no doors or windows in yet - and suddenly in one of them he saw the rifle. A .22, rigged up, fixed, aligned on the cornerstone below.

'He took just one glance and ran out into the corridor again, to try to find someone. He knew the murderer must still be up there. But there was nobody. And then he heard footsteps coming pounding up the stairs, and it was - well, now he's Inspector Block,' Even that seemed to be an injury ; his father had never had the chance to become Inspector Robbins.

'He met me at the top of the stairs,' said Block. 'I'd been on duty at the other end of the wing. He said, "My God, there's nobody here ! They've shot him, but there's nobody here !" He looked almost - scared, as though he'd seen a ghost. "There's a rifle fixed up," he said. "Come and look !" '

In the last of the half-dozen little rooms that had so far received their dividing walls, there was a rough tripod formed of three planks. These had been shaped at their ends so that, propped against the skirting boards on three sides of the room, they met and dovetailed to form a crotch into which the butt of the rifle fitted securely. A short length of rope had been tied round the whole, and this was further reinforced by a twelve-foot length of twine, doubled for extra strength, its ends roughly tucked in as though hurriedly done. Into the wood of the window-sill two nails had been driven to form a triangle through which the muzzle of the rifle had been thrust. The whole was trained, steady as a rock, on the site below.

And spilled out of a torn paper bag, too small to hold so many, three out of half a dozen rosy apples had rolled out on the dusty boards of the wooden floor.

'We stood and stared, and as we stood, there was a scraping and scuffling overhead, a small shower of debris, and when we looked up we saw two hands tearing at the slates above us and a face peering through. And a voice said, "For God's sake, what's happening ? They've shot him !" And then added, "But, my God, what a picture !" '

The picture that had brought Mr Photoze fame and fortune : the picture of the famous lion head raised, mouth half-open in that great outraged bellow heedless of danger : 'You murderers, you've got the wrong man !'

Usually, for publication, the head was lifted out of the rest, but the whole picture showed the scene moments after the impact of the bullet. First the edge of the parapet, then an expanse of grass between the main building and the cornerstone : the smoother grass where turf had been laid for the ceremony, the flowering shrubs temporarily planted for the occasion, the tubs of geraniums ; the partially built wall with the cornerstone at its centre, the small crowd swung about to stare up, stupefied with shock.

But as the press photographer had exclaimed, in instant recognition of what he had achieved - what a picture ! A murdered man, caught in the very act of dying ; the hands that held him as famous a pair as existed in the world, and the splendid head, the magnificent, ravaged, upturned face. But the most beautiful thing in the whole photograph, Mr Photoze assured them now, had been the glimpse in the foreground of the parapet's edge. 'Because if the parapet is in the picture, then I took that picture from the roof and not from the room below, where the rifle was.'

'Anyone can fake a photograph,' said the young man.

'The police confiscated my equipment,' said Mr Photoze, 'before I had time to do any faking. And before you get any sharper and cut yourself, dear boy, there was no apparatus by which the camera could be left to take pictures all by itself. I wasn't lugging more than I had to up to that roof.'

It was a splendid room - big and luxurious, all just a bit larger than life, like Mr Mysterioso himself. But the young man sat tensed like a wild thing about to spring, and his tension communicated itself to the rest of them, meeting his sick and angry stare with eyes divided between understanding, pity, and impatience. He resumed his parrot cry, 'You were there. And nobody else was. My father didn't do it, so it must have been you.'

Mr Photoze was - understandably enough - one of the impatient ones. 'Now, look here !' He appealed to them all. 'I was up on that damn roof. I was there the whole time, anyone could have seen me there - '

'No one was looking,' said the young man. 'They were all watching the ceremony.'

'And so was I, you silly fool ! I was taking photographs, that's what I was there for. And then suddenly this gun goes off somewhere below me, and I saw the two men fall. It was like a film shot in slow motion,' he recalled, 'the two of them collapsing, but slowly, slowly. I stood there frozen, and then I saw the Mysterioso had lifted up his head and was shouting up to the window where the gun was ; and I seemed to come to life and started clicking away like mad - '

'Without a thought that a man was dying ?'

'Sort of reflex action, I suppose,' said Mr Photoze. He added simply, 'It's my job.'

Mr Mysterioso had had much cause to be grateful to the photographer who had forgotten all but getting on with his job. The photograph had kept alive the legend of that moment of bravado, of selfless courage on behalf of one who had after all been only a servant. They had remained on friendly terms ever since ; it was to him that Mr Photoze had turned for advice when the young man's foolish threats had suddenly turned into action. 'You did quite right,' Mysterioso said. 'The show must go on.'

'And so must this meeting,' said Inspector Block, tapping an impatient toe.

'I'm sorry. Yes – well, I went on taking pictures till the crowd surged in and there was nothing to take but the backs of their heads. So then I suddenly thought about the shooting, and I peeked over the parapet, and there, to my horror, I saw the tip of a gun, the barrel, just showing beyond the window-sill. To this day I don't know why I did it, but I dropped all my gear and ran along the ledge to the trapdoor, to get down and – I don't know, *do* something, I suppose. Sheer madness, because imagine if the murderer had still been there ! But anyway, I couldn't get the trapdoor open. I tugged and I kicked, but – well, we know now that it had been bolted from inside. So I ran back to where I'd seen the gun, and what was in my mind then, I think, was that here it still was, still pointing down at all those helpless people – '

'He'd have cleared out long before,' said the young man scornfully, 'while you were taking pictures and running up and down.'

'Well – ' He spread artistic, explanatory, jingly hands. 'I mean, one isn't exactly a man of action, *is* one ? I daresay what I thought didn't make much sense. But I did imagine him crouching there with that gun in his hands – of course, I didn't know then about the tripod and all that – and all those poor dear people in danger down below. And suddenly I started smashing at the slates, bashing at them with the heel of my shoe, clearing a little hole so that at least I could see what he was doing – perhaps frighten him off, make him clear out.'

But he had cleared out long ago – cleared out, vanished into thin air. Nobody was there except two policeman, staring back, astonished, into Mr Photoze's startled face. 'One said, "What are you doing up there ?" '

' "He had permission. To take photos. I know him," said PC Robbins, "he's all right." '

'My poor father – little did he think !' said the young man.

Mr Photoze collapsed into his chair with an air of giving up. '*I* don't know. What can you do ? The *facts*, you silly boy, I've just given you the *facts* ! I was up on the roof, I couldn't get down – it was your own father who pulled the bolt and locked me out. How could I have committed the murder, how could I have fired the gun ? Even if I'd *wanted* to, how could I have done it ? We've all just given you the facts.'

The trapped animal, head turning from side to side, seeking a way out, And then - the release. The young man was absolutely still, struck mindless for a moment by the immensity of the idea. He blurted out at last, 'The apples !'

'The apples ?'

'Who ties a bag of apples at the neck with string ? And - yes, there was other string in that room, wound round the tripod and the butt of the rifle, a long piece of string. What for ? The rifle was already tied into place with the rope.' He said to Inspector Block, 'Was there a nail in the wall opposite the window ?'

'There were nail holes,' said Block. 'They were everywhere.'

'The rifle fixed steady, tied by the rope, aligned on the spot.' The dark was receding from his face, he was alive with excitement. 'And tied to the rifle - to the trigger of the rifle - the string ; tied with a slip noose, easy to undo afterwards, and the other end of the string tied with a slip noose to a nail in the wall opposite the window. And a bag of apples - an innocent-looking bag of apples that no one will worry about too much. A little light refreshment for the murderer while he waits ?' he suggested to Inspector Block with a fine contempt.

'I was a plain copper in those days,' said Block, 'and not in the close confidence of my superiors. But I don't think they took it all quite so easily as that. On the other hand, murderers are funny animals, they have all sorts of cock-eyed reasons for what they do. He could, for example, have been a smoker and didn't want to draw attention to the fact - leaving ashes and stubs around. So he supplied himself with something to munch, to fill the gap.'

'Are *you* a smoker ?' said the young man nastily to Mr Photoze.

'I have no idea what either of you is talking about,' said Mr Photoze.

'A bag of apples is a funny thing,' said the young man. 'Sort of - nobbly. Of course, other things would have done as well, but the presence of a bag of apples on the scene could be explained in lots of ways - for example, something to stop the murderer from wanting to smoke.' His face, growing white and pinched now where the dark had been, stared, ugly with spite, at Mr Photoze. 'I was sure you must have done it,' he said, 'because I knew my father hadn't. But now I *know*. Because I know *how*.' And his hands described it, stretched apart, holding taut an imaginary string. 'One end tied to the trigger, one end fixed to the wall. At the right moment, something heavy falling on the string, jerking it down, yanking back the trigger, firing the shot.'

Absolute silence had fallen in the big room. Mr Photoze said at last, shakily, 'I was on the roof. How could I have dropped the bag of apples down ?'

'You admit you made a hole in the slates,' said the young man. 'You dropped it down through that.'

Silence again. Inspector Block said quietly, 'Very ingenious. But your father was in the room within two minutes or less after the shot was fired. The string was wound round the tripod when he first saw it. Who took it down and wound it there ?'

'Perhaps his precious father did,' said Mr Photoze, a trifle viciously, 'Having fixed it all up himself. He was supposed to be on duty at the entrance. But no one could see him. Who knows that he was really there ?'

'He was seen going up the stairs after the shot was fired,' said Mr Mysterioso reasonably.

'That's right. To take down the string before Block arrived and saw it.'

The young man was unafraid. 'How could he have got it to work ? He was outside the door, three storeys down – we know that, because he was seen coming up. So . . . Mr Mysterioso, you're the magician here. How could my father have got the trick to work ?'

'There are ways,' admitted Mr Mysterioso reluctantly. 'Blocks of ice and melting wax and timing machines – after all, he only had to be the first on the scene to clear the evidence away.'

'Curiously enough,' said Block, 'the police thought of some of these little ideas too. Considering the length of the string – just the width of the room – and the uselessness of it where we found it, as the young man rightly points out, just wound round the tripod, not even knotted – well, we did just think about it. Though I admit that I don't think anyone read this particular significance into the bag of apples. But I do assure you that the place was searched for candle grease and damp patches and timing clocks, till we thought we never wanted to see an unfinished building again. And Robbins, of course, was examined from head to toe, inside and out, till he couldn't have had so much as a spent match concealed about him. You can take it from me – inside and outside, both the building and PC Robbins – absolutely nothing.'

'So where does that leave me ?' said Mr Photoze, and immediately answered himself. 'On the roof, dropping a bag of apples through a hole which wasn't there until *after* the shot was fired ; when two policemen, including your own dear parent, stood there and watched me make it.'

'For the second time,' said the young man.

'Up there on the roof – out of sight, if anybody had been looking that way, which, in the nature of things, they wouldn't be – a photographer fiddling about with the tools of his trade. A slate removed, two slates or three or four – enough to allow him to slip down into the room below, fix up the tripod and the rifle and the taut string, all prepared and left ready previously. Back again, using the tripod as a step to hoist yourself up through the hole and back onto the roof ; the bag of apples in his hand. And the shot fired by dropping the bag of apples to pull sharply on the string – then down through the hole again, quickly twist the string round the tripod, and back on the roof, covering the hole over with the slates before PC Robbins even gets up the stairs. Covering the hole over roughly – anyone entering the little room will be intent on the rifle and the tripod, not looking up. And before they get around to the roof – start battering and scrabbling, smashing the slates, making the hole again –'

'Dear God !' said Mr Photoze, and caught Inspector Block's eye and said again, 'Dear *God*!'

The young man sat bolt upright in his chair, triumphant. 'Just tell me,' said Mr Photoze at last, slowly, 'Why should I have rigged up all this nonsense ? I could just have jumped down through the hole, fired the rifle, and nipped back.'

'Using what as a hoist ?' said the young man. 'It's a long way up to the roof, even to the lower bit of the slope where the hole was.'

'Oh, well, as to that, with so much ingenuity as you ascribe to me, I think I could have managed something, don't you ?'

The young man ignored the slightly teasing tone. 'There was something much more important – the photograph. You had to be there to take the photograph, the one with the parapet in it that proves you were on the roof when the gun went off.'

'So I did !' said Mr Photoze ; and it frightened the young man a little – how could the man be so easy and unafraid ? – with his mocking, half-indulgent admiration, a touch in his voice of something very much like pity. 'You knew Mysterioso,' he burst out. 'He recognized you at the main entrance, it was he who told them to let you go up on the roof. I suppose,' he added, spitting out venom, 'that . . . that, like all your kind, you revelled in having your picture taken, didn't you ?'

'I was willing to do him a kindness,' said Mysterioso mildly, 'that was all.'

'Well, it made a change then, if you were,' said the young man. 'You'd done him anything but a kindness two years before, hadn't you ?' And he looked at the rest of them with a triumph almost pitiful because it was so filled with spite. 'You want a motive ?' he said, 'Well, I'll tell it to you – the inspector could have told it to you long ago, only he protects this man like all the rest have done. All the world knew that Mysterioso had taken Mr Photoze's girl friend away from him.'

'Dear me,' said Marguerite Devine, 'would you say that this was where *I* come in ?'

There fell a verbal silence in which even Mr Photoze lost his recent poise, jangling his golden bracelets with nervous movements of his hands. Perhaps it was their tinkling that led him to say finally, 'Do I really give the impression of a man who would kill another man for taking a woman away from him ?'.

'Speaking from memory,' said Marguerite, 'I would say that the answer to that one is – no.'

'You'll confirm it, Marguerite ? All I did was to take pictures of you.' He explained to the 'court'. 'I lived in the same group of flats. I was a lodger – with this young man's parents, us in the basement, her ladyship here in considerably more comfort on the fifth floor. She was a star then, at the top of her career – '

'Not to say a little over the hill,' admitted Marguerite ruefully.

'Do you think she'd have looked at me in that way – a scruffy little press photographer without tuppence to bless himself with ? But she was an actress, she was at liberty at the time, and all actresses, all that our young gentleman here would call "their kind", like having their pictures taken. It's part of their stock-in-trade. So . . . It was good practice for me ; and in those days, what a marvellous profile – '

'For "in those days", dear,' said Marguerite, 'much thanks.' But she added, kindly, to the young man, 'However, at least an honest face, love, I hope. And in all honesty I tell you – he wouldn't have killed so much as a fly on account of *me*.'

'Well, some other reason then, what does it matter ? But he was up on that roof, he could have done it, and nobody else could, so he must have.'

Inspector Block got suddenly to his feet. 'Now, look here, my lad ! You've had a long innings, you've done a lot of very clever talking – now you listen for a change ! Your theory is beautifully ingenious, but it has one tiny flaw, and that is it won't work. The whole thing depends on a hole in the roof so big that Mr Photoze could get down through it and then up again. But the police do think of these things too, you know ; and that hole was most carefully examined, and the simple fact is that he couldn't have go his *head* through it, let alone the rest of him. The slates were securely pegged down and couldn't be removed ; the only hole was the small one he made by shattering one of the slates with the heel of his shoe.'

The young man was taken aback. It had seemed to fit so well, justify all his suspicions. And now nothing was left of it. Back to the parrot cry that had sustained him all this bitter time since his father had died. 'He was on the roof. There was only him and my father – '

'That's right,' said Inspector Block. 'Him – and your father.'

You couldn't call him slow on the uptake. The young man was there before any of them and had sprung to his feet – frightened now, really frightened. 'You mean – together ? In it together ?'

The rifle hidden away during the night – it was true that these things, the gun, the bag of apples, the string, might very easily have escaped detection during the more cursory inspection on the day of the ceremony : small enough objects to be lost among the innumerable bits and pieces lying about in a building still under construction. Up to the roof with Mr Photoze, then, searched and found free of the impedimenta of murder ; he'd have been smuggled up there without permission if none had been given, of course ; had they been surprised, these two, in the middle of their plan, when Mysterioso and the superintendent had come upon them outside the main entrance ? Up to the roof, anyway – and the bolt shot that would keep him up there, 'It was PC Robbins who suggested that the inside bolt be shot. It left his accomplice, now that he was known to be on the roof, safe from accusation of firing the gun.'

The young man did not argue. There was in his heart now a terrible fear.

Everyone gone off at last to prepare for the ceremony – a clear field. PC Robbins leaves his post at the main entrance and nips up the stairs – no patients yet, perhaps, to mark his going, or if there are, after all the passings up and down that morning, who is going to recall one more policeman checking things once again ?

Up to the murder room then ; a minute and a half to erect the prepared tripod, not more ('We experimented with that') – to fix the taut string and ('Here it comes !') to pass up the bag of apples through the small hole which meantime Mr Photoze would have been making by the removal of one slate. And PC Robbins is back at his post long before the ceremonial procession is due to pass down again to the site – and *he* can't have fired the shot because he was at the post when it was fired – any more than Mr Photoze could have fired it, known to be locked up (and taking pictures) on the roof.

The bag of apples is dropped, and the taut string pulls on the trigger, and the shot is fired ; and the one slate is replaced, to be reopened with much scrabbling and shattering when the proper moment arrives ; and the photograph is taken. And three steps at a time PC Robbins comes pounding up the stairs to untie the string and wind it – no time for knots

– round the butt of the gun, to look as though it had some purpose other than its real one ; and is ready to greet P C Block arriving, panting, 'There's a rifle fixed up. Come and look !'

The young man stared, helpless. Great tears rolled down his thin face, white now and haggard. 'I don't believe it. I don't believe it.' But to fight was better than to despair, 'Anyway, what was the reason ? My father had no reason to do it, so why should he ?'

Inspector Block said steadily, 'Mr Photoze lived in the same group of flats as this lady did. You were ready enough to accuse him of an affair with her. But your father also lived in that same group of flats; and the lady is a very pretty lady. And then – '

'Oh, come now, darling !' protested Marguerite. 'First a photographer – now a policeman as well. Have a heart ! I wasn't very fussy – *but* !'

' – along came Mr Mysterioso,' went on Block, 'and took her away from them both.'

'What a happy little threesome – not in that sense. There may be many ways of caring for a woman, needing a woman – many reasons, at any rate, for resenting her being stolen from you.'

'But I *wasn't* stolen from the policeman,' said Marguerite, half-laughing. And she looked at the young man's face and laughed no more. 'Now, look, Inspector, this is absolutely not fair. I've told you about Mr Photoze – we were both frank enough with you. So believe me when I say, when I swear to you on oath, that, as for the policeman, I never set eyes on the fellow in my life. Not till after the shooting ; then we all saw one another in connection with the case. But that was all.'

'So there !' said the young man passionately. He added with a suddenly rather sweet simplicity, 'Besides, he was married to my mother.'

'And loved your mother ?'

'Yes,' said the young man (loved her too much, to the exclusion of oneself – quarrelled with her, yes, but that was because of the failure and the poverty brooding in the home, which in turn was because of the crime and subsequent unjust dismissal).

Inspector Block did not like what he had to say next. But he said it. 'All right. He loved her. But Mr Photoze lived with them, and perhaps in his own way he was devoted to her too – enough at any rate to enter into a plot to avenge her. Because – ' It was not very nice, but it had to be said. 'Because Mr Mysterioso had been visiting those flats, hadn't he ? And one lady at a time wasn't necessarily enough for the Grand Mysterioso.'

'You flatter me,' said Mysterioso ; but nobody listened to him. For it was terrible – horrible – to see the young man. Before, it had been a young face, dark, pale, as the emotions passed across it. Now it was a man's face, a clown's face, a mask of white patched clownishly with pink. That gesture again, as though physical danger were coming close to him. He whimpered, 'Oh, no ! Oh, no !'

'We have to consider everything,' said Inspector Block, as though excusing what he did.

'It's madness,' said Mysterioso. He hauled himself straighter in his chair, but he too had gone pale. 'By all I hold sacred, I never saw her – not till after the inquiries started.' He looked with pity at the cowering young man. 'I never touched your mother, boy, never so much as saw her.'

'You could have,' said the young man, sobbing. 'You could have.' His body was bowed over till his forehead rested on his two fists clenched on the arm of the chair. 'Everyone tells lies – you have to say you didn't know her. But you could have, you may have – '

Marguerite got up from her place. She went and knelt beside him, lifted his head, pushing back the damp, soft, spiky young-boy hair from his forehead ; caught at the writhing hands and held them steady in her own two hands, so white and well-cared-for with their long, pink, manicured nails. 'Hush, Love, Hush ! Of course it isn't true.' And she looked across the room at Mr Mysterioso and said, 'A secret – between us and these kind people here who'll be too generous, I know, ever to give us away.' She glanced at the door.

'Nobody could be listening ?'

'No,' said the Inspector.

'Between these four walls then ?' She looked round at them, appealing, then back to Mysterioso. She said, 'I think we *must* tell.'

An actress 'over the hill', glad of the attentions of even a scruffy young press photographer using her as a sitter to practice his craft. Thankful beyond words for the advent of a new admirer and a rich, famous, and handsome one at that, 'good to be seen about with' at the fashionable restaurants where theatrical agents and managers would be reminded of her. Entertaining him at home, not at all secretly ; dropping naughty hints to anyone who would listen – my darling, he's fan*tas*tic ! Using it all to further her own ends, to bolster her tottering career.

And a man, larger than life size not quite like other men. Big, handsome, with his mane of tawny hair, a man who looked like a lion and must live like a lion ; a man with a reputation for affairs, in middle age still strutting in the pride of his well-publicized virility. And all in an hour, in a moment . . . The accident that had left him a crippled thing, humiliatingly powerless, had left him powerless in other ways as well. 'She was – kind,' he said, looking at Marguerite, still kneeling by the young man's chair. 'She kept my secret a secret.' To the young man he said, 'Even if I'd ever set eyes on her, my boy, your pretty young mother would have been safe from me.'

'It's true,' said Marguerite. She looked down at her hands. 'I know.'

Inspector Block helped her up from the floor and back to her chair. He said to them both, with something like humility in his cold voice, 'Thank you.'

The Grand Mysterioso stirred and sighed and came back to the present with a jerk. 'Well, now . . . My dear boy, I think you have no cause to complain. We've done what we came here to do - talked it all out, put it all before you, all the facts, the ifs and the ands, the probabilities and the just possibles - riddled out our very souls for you, so that you may save your own. So save it ! Accept the judgment of this court - who also have heard it all - and get rid of this bug that has been obsessing your mind and spoiling your splendid young life. I'll help you. I'll be your friend - you can start all over again, grow up, be a man.

'So now - you two have been the accused, you and Mr Photoze here. Go outside this room and wait ; and we will arrive at a verdict in here, all of us, me and Inspector Block and this kind and lovely lady, Miss Devine, and these three kind people who have come here as witnesses, at no small trouble to themselves, to help you too. None of us with any axe to grind, remember that. So - whatever verdict we come to, will you accept it ?' And he said kindly, 'All we want, boy, in all honesty, is to arrive at the truth and set your mind at rest.'

'Suppose,' said the young man, 'the truth doesn't set my mind at rest.'

'Then we'll tell it just the same,' said Block. He made a small-boy gesture, licking his thumb and crossing his heart with it. 'I swear you shall hear the truth. I'll tell you no lie.'

'Considering that I'm in the dock too,' said Mr Photoze, getting up and going toward the door with his accompanying jingle, 'and I'm ready to accept the verdict, I think you can too.' He opened the door. 'Come along, the jury is about to retire.'

The door closed behind them. Mr Mysterioso said 'Photoze will keep him safely out of earshot,' But he looked anxious. 'Can you really swear to tell him the truth of it ? For that matter - what is the truth of it ?'

Inspector Block went and stood in the middle of the room. He said 'The truth of it is very short, and very simple. I can tell it to you in' - he counted on his fingers - 'in fourteen words. In fact. I could reduce those words to six, and give you the whole story. Of course, I could say a lot of other words, but I'm not going to. It's not for me to accuse. Our business is to exonerate.' And he spoke the fourteen words. 'I think the rest is self-explanatory. . . . Verdict unanimous ? Let's have the young man back.'

The big lush room, curtain drawn, hushed in the evening quiet, no traffic rumbling outside, scented with flowers and the upward curl of cigar and cigarette smoke, bottles and glasses hospitably placed within reach of outstretched hands . . . The door opened, and Mr Photoze came jangling through, and the young man was standing there, wearing the dark look again, his eyes like the eyes of a frightened animal, his hands tensed into claws. Mr Mysterioso struggled his helpless limbs forward in his chair and held out a hand. 'Come over here, son. Come and stand by me.'

He came over and stood by the chair. 'It's all right,' said Mysterioso, and took the narrow brown hand and held it, strongly and comfortingly, in his own. He said, 'You see, it hasn't taken long. We all recognized the truth immediately. Verdict unanimous.' And he gave it. 'Mr Photoze - not guilty ; neither motive nor opportunity. And your father - not guilty ; neither motive nor opportunity. My hand on my heart !'

A sort of shudder ran through the young man. Tears ran down his face as he stood motionless, his head bowed. 'All go !' said Mysterioso. 'I'll look after him. We've done our job. But never again,' he said, giving a little shake to the nerveless hand still held in his own, 'any threats to Mr Photoze, let alone any violence ! You accept the verdict ? That's a promise ?'

The bowed head nodded.

'Good boy ! Well, then, good night to you all,' said the old man, 'and thank you.' And he said, again to the young man, 'I'm sure you thank them too ?'

Yes, nodded the hanging head again ; thin hand still clasped in the veined old hand, the beautiful, still mobile, veined old hand of the master magician, the Grand Mysterioso.

Mr Photoze walked away with Inspector Block. 'Well, thank God that's over ! I think I'm pretty safe from now on. He gave his promise, and he'll keep it, I'm sure,'

'Oh, yes you'll have no more trouble,' said Block. 'He meant it. I know these kids ; they only need convincing,' He walked a little farther in silence. 'What you and I now know', he said carefully, 'at least I think you know it - had better be kept secret.'

'Mysterioso and the others know it.'

'Some of it,' said the Inspector. A vain man, Mysterioso, he added, really one of the vainest he had ever known. 'Of course, as you said, it's their stock-in-trade.'

'For what he admitted tonight,' suggested Mr Photoze, 'I think much may be forgiven the old man.'

'Nevertheless, through his vanity he's obstructed the course of justice. From the very beginning – from *before* the very beginning.'

'You mean – the letters ?'

'The letters – anonymous letters signed "Her Husband." In all sorts of different envelopes, in all sorts of different type, posted from all sorts of different parts of the country – '

'Ye gods ! And who travelled all over the country constantly, with his act ? And who got all that lovely publicity ? You mean he wrote to himself ?'

'No, I think the letters were genuine,' said Block slowly. 'Genuine letters in genuine envelopes. I just think the letters didn't belong in the envelopes.'

Typed envelopes – envelopes that had previously held circulars, impossible to distinguish, even by the senders, from the myriad of similar envelopes pushed day after day through letter boxes up and down the land. 'He'd just pick one with a Birmingham postmark or a Glasgow postmark or what you will – put the letter in that, seal it up instead of merely tucking in in – the glue would be still intact ; tear it open again and then send off to the police – first taking care to arrange for the maximum publicity.'

'The publicity I understand,' said Mr Photoze. 'But for the rest – I daresay I'm dense, but why put the letters into new envelopes ? Why not just show them as they were ?' And he answered himself immediately. 'Well, but good God, yes – of course ! *Because the letters were addressed to someone else.*'

Fourteen words : The young man's father couldn't have killed Tom. Tom *was* the young man's father.

While the cat's away, the mouse will play. And why shouldn't the mouse play ? How had the indispensable servant spent the long waiting hours, while his master dallied five stories above ?

'So the letters were really addressed to Tom – Tom Cat, perhaps we should call him from now on. And shot – but good heavens, that performance at the foot of the cornerstone ?'

'A performance,' said Inspector Block briefly.

'With a dying man in his arms – his friend ?'

'I wonder if the poor neutered cat felt so very warmly towards the full Tom after all ? And think of the dividends ! The photograph – but that was a bonus – of the great, defiant gesture ; the reputation ever afterwards for heedless courage. Some defiance – he knew perfectly well there wouldn't be another shot. The murderer hadn't got the wrong man at all. It was meant for Tom.'

'But Tom himself said – '

'Just recall the way that went,' said Inspector Block, 'The man was bleeding at the mouth, hardly in good shape for clear articulation. Mysterioso listened, then he called the woman to come close. He *told* her what the man was saying : 'Thank God they only got me – it was meant for you." He told them all. The woman listened to the choked-out words and believed what she'd been told. No doubt Tom gasped out something like, "My God, they've got me. He really meant it" – something like that. Don't you see, the magician forced the card on her ; she heard what he told her to hear, that's all.'

'Some opportunist !'

'He'd shown that in the matter of the letters. This was only an extension of that.'

'He'd bring the first letter to his master – I daresay there weren't many secrets between those two. I wonder,' said Inspector Block, 'what Mysterioso's first reaction would have been ?'

'Jealousy,' said Mr Photoze.

'I think so too, especially after what we heard tonight. I think Mr Mysterioso wanted those letters for himself. So – all sorts of good reasons to the man : you're in danger ; this idiot, whoever he is, might try something funny. The police won't bother too much about you, but if I were to ask for protection – and Tom, after long years in "the business," would be the first to appreciate the value of the publicity, the anxious fans, the eager sensation-seekers, flocking to performances with the subconscious hope that something tragic would happen – as they flock to the circus.'

'Why no letters before that ?'

'I think,' said Block slowly, 'that all the way along, this was a crime arising out of opportunity. And here was the first opportunity. The months passed, the baby was born, Robbins fumed and was sick with anger ; he couldn't just go and beat up the seducer – he was in the police, and the police wouldn't stand for that sort of thing ; and more important, he wasn't going to let the world know of this shame. But then – well, Mysterioso told us that these invitations to lay cornerstones and whatnot were arranged months in advance ; and the first people to know about forthcoming events are the local police. Suddenly PC Robbins learned that his enemy was coming to Thrushford.

'Threats at first, meaningless probably, just to give the seducer a bad time, with the vague hope that when he comes to Thrushford with his master, one may be able to add some small frightening shock just to shake him up. But the seducer turns it all to his own advantage, makes a sort of public joke of it, hands the letters to another man. The rankling anger grows and begins to take on a more positive quality. And then the second opportunity presents itself.

'I don't know which came first – the rifle or the post of duty outside the unfinished wing. Either could have been fiddled, I daresay, having achieved the other. Not too difficult, for example, for a policeman to come by a weapon. Some old lady finds the rifle after her husband's death, hardly dares to touch the nasty dangerous thing, knows nothing certainly of numbers and identification marks, hands it over to the first copper, and thinks no more about it. He may have had it stashed away for years, or from the time his suspicions were first aroused ; by the time it came to be used, the hander-over could be dead or senile or have moved elsewhere – certainly it was never traced. At any rate, with it in his possession and a perfect place at his disposal for using it, he began really to think about taking action. He thought out a plan, worked on it, and brought it off. And damn near perfect it turned out to be.'

'No one guessed at the time how the thing was done ?'

'My higher-ups may have ; but it was all so tenuous. Still, he'd lived in the flats where Mysterioso had visited ; they must have had some suspicions – '

'Only, I had lived there too.'

'That's right. And been on the scene of the crime too. So how to choose between the two of you when it seemed impossible for either of you to have done it ? At any rate, they cooked up some excuse and got rid of him – I remember him as a difficult chap, brooding and touchy – well, no wonder. I daresay they weren't sorry to let him go. It wasn't till tonight – ' He laughed. 'It hit you at the same moment.'

'But you went on with the theory about possible collusion – '

'I had to run through all the possibilities. I had to leave no doubts in anyone's mind. I didn't want people coming to the young man afterwards, saying, "He never covered this or that aspect." But by then I knew. When the young man accused you of making the hole in the roof *before* I saw you apparently making it – '

'So simple,' said Mr Photoze. 'Wasn't it ?'

So simple.

PC Robbins with hate in his heart and a long-perfected plan of revenge. After the major search of the previous day, he concealed the rifle, the rope, the string, the apples, and prepared the boards for dovetailing into a tripod. Slipping up when the final inspection had been concluded and they'd all gone off to prepare for the ceremony, he erected the tripod, fixed the rifle, wound a length of twine around the butt to suggest exactly what in fact had been deduced – that some string trick had been played. (A bag of apples dropped onto a taut string, jerking back the trigger – the nonsense of it ! As if anyone for a moment could really depend on anything so absurdly susceptible to failure !) Down again, unseen because there was as yet nobody on the hospital balcony, or if observed, just another copper going about his business ; the police had been up and down all day.

And then –

The sound of a shot – in the unfinished wing. A policeman tearing up, two steps at a time, pausing only to yell out, 'Watch the stairs !' and 'They've got him !' Pandemonium, predictably, on the hospital balcony, everyone talking at once, a lot of people ill and easily thrown into hysteria. Noise and talking, at any rate, masking the sound of –

'The real shot,' said Mr Photoze.

'How do you hide a brown paper bag that you've burst to *fake* the sound of a shot ? You fill it with too many apples and leave it prominently displayed with two or three of them rolled out from the hole in the side.'

'So his father did commit the murder,' said Mr Photoze. 'But in fact he didn't. And we could all look the young man in the eye and swear to that.'

'These psychiatrists,' said Inspector Block. 'Oedipal complexes, delusions, paranoia, looking for a scapegoat for his own guilt feelings towards his father – all the rest of it. And "a long period of treatment" ! Hah ! One evening's discussion – merely convince the young man that his suspicions are unfounded, and that's all there is to it. From now on he'll be as right as rain.'

The young man was as right as rain. He was bending over the Grand Mysterioso, lying back helpless in the big armchair. 'If *they* didn't do it, then *you* must have. Of course it wasn't you who was meant to be killed – it was Tom. Because it was you that killed him, wasn't it ? You hated him because you were dependent on him, humiliatingly dependent, like a child ; I know about that, I know what that's like, to be a child and – and hate someone underneath ; and be helpless. And jealous of him – you were jealous of him because he was a man and you weren't any more ; you told us about that just now, how ashamed you were. I know about that too, I was only a child but my – my father was a man.

'I was angry with my father about that, but *you* – you were ashamed. And so you killed him. Oh, don't ask me how – you're the magician, you're the one who knows the tricks ; you said it yourself – things like melting ice and burning-down candles and a lot of others you carefully didn't mention ; but you'd know them, all right. And there you were with your big cloak, even on such a hot day – all pockets and hiding places.

'And they left you alone when they went down the corridor and hoisted Mr Photoze up onto the roof and shot the bolt after him ; quite a while they must have been there, and by the time they came back, you were waiting for them out in the corridor – out in the corridor, blocking off their view into that room with your big body and your big cloak. If you could get across that room and out into the corridor, you could do other things – oh, I don't know how, and I don't care ; you're the magician, you do tricks that nobody ever sees through, and this was just another of them. But you did it ; if that fool with his bangles and his photos didn't well then, there's no one else.

'And for what you did, my father suffered the rest of his life ; it was horrible, we were so poor, they were always fighting, and my father wasn't always – wasn't always . . . Well, sometimes he was unkind, a bloody little bastard he'd call me, and my mother would cry and cry.'

He went on and on, face chalk-white, scarlet-streaked. But he was all right now, as right as rain. He had found his scapegoat. He might love his mother and be loved by her without feeling guilty that his father was dead and could rival him no more. His father had suffered and died, and it had been – horrible – to go on resenting his memory ; but now he had avenged his father, and he was free.

The spittle ran down from his gibbering mouth and fell on the upturned face of the Grand Mysterioso. But Mysterioso made no move to prevent it. The young man's hands were around his throat, and the Grand Mysterioso was dead.

Leslie Charteris

THE MYSTERY OF THE CHILD'S TOY

GEORGE KESTRY slanted his two hundred pounds of brawn and bone back in his chair, stuck his thumbs in the armholes of his waistcoat, and spoke past a cigar that jutted out of the corner of his mouth as squarely and truculently as a cannon out of an old-time battleship.

'That's all there was to it,' he stated. 'And that's the way it always is. You get an idea – just a little one. You spread a net out among the stool-pigeons. You catch a man. And then you grill him till he comes clean. That's how a real detective does his job ; and to heck with Sherlock Holmes.'

Andy Herrick, slim and almost frail-looking opposite the Homicide Squad's toughest case-breaker, grinned amiably and beckoned the waiter for his bill. The orchestra yawned and went into another dance number. It was three o'clock in the morning, and a fair proportion of the crowd of assorted millionaires, racketeers, sight-seers, and show-girls who packed New York's most expensive restaurant had some work to think of before the next midnight.

'Maybe you're right,' said Andy, mildly.

'I know I'm right !' roared Kestry ; and then, while Andy slid green-backs on to a plate, he chuckled. 'I'm not bein' personal, kid – you know that. If you can make a living writing that detective-story stuff I'm glad about it. I wish I could do it. But when it comes to real crimes – well, it just makes me mad.' He stood up and grabbed Andy's shoulder. 'C'mon, kid – I gotta go home.'

He steered their way round the tables and up the stairs to the hotel lobby, with his stubby fingers locked round Andy's arm and his iron features set in a contented grin. It was not the first time they had had the same argument over the supper table, nor by any means the first time that George Kestry had settled it in a similar manner to his own satisfaction. He had a voice that matched his mighty build, and a belligerent crash of his massive fist on the table to go with it.

A self-made man from the soles of his shoes, self-architectured, self-educated, who had fought every inch of his own way up from a Brooklyn slum, he took an innocent and almost ingenuous delight in getting the better of anyone out of the class which he ungrudgingly ranked as 'gentlemen' – even by no sounder logic than a loud voice and a thumping fist that made the knives and forks dance and quiver. And at the same time, between those arguments, he treated Andy with a naïve respect which at times was almost comic in an unconsciously elephantine way, like a docile giant gambolling deferentially with a child. To call Andy by his first name, go about with him, clap him on the shoulder, dine with him, be introduced to his friends as an equal, gave the big, hard-boiled detective a sense of his own conquest of environment which he himself would have been the last to admit.

'Come down to Headquarters next time I'm working on a case, sir,' Kestry said in the lobby, with an abrupt return to that naïve respect which would have been humorous if it had been less completely un-selfconscious. 'You'll see for yourself how we really break 'em up.'

'I'd like to,' said Andy ; and if there was the trace of a smile in his eyes when he said it, it was without malice. He liked the big detective sincerely, enjoyed his company like a great, healthy, blustering breeze, despaired of ever carrying a point against that thunderous, dogmatic voice, and was cheerfully contented to provoke and listen to its outbursts.

Andy settled his soft hat on his straight, fair hair and glanced round the lobby with the vague aimlessness which ordinarily precedes a parting at that hour. A little group of three men had discharged themselves from a nearby elevator, and were moving boisterously and a trifle unsteadily towards the main entrance. Two of them were hatted and overcoated – a tallish man with a thin line of moustache and a tubby, red-faced man with rimless spectacles. The third member of the party, who appeared to be the host, was a flabby, flat-footed man of about fifty-five, with a round, bald head and a rather bulbous nose that would have persuaded any observant onlooker to expect that he would have drunk more than the others, which, in fact, he obviously had. All of them had the dishevelled and rather tragically ridiculous air of Captains of Industry who have gone off duty for the evening.

'That's Lewis Enstone – the guy with the nose,' said Kestry, who knew everyone. 'Wall Street man. Might have been one of the biggest financiers in the country if he could have kept off the bottle.'

'And the other two ?' asked Andy, incuriously.

'Just a coupla smaller men in the same game. Gamblers. Abe Costello

- that's the tall one - and Jules Hammel. If we put all the crooks in that precinct into our portrait gallery, Police Headquarters'd have to take over another annexe.'

Kestry chewed his cigar over to the other side of his mouth, where it stood out at the same pugnacious angle as before ; but for his surroundings, he would probably have spat expressively. 'I'd rather be seen with an honest racketeer than one of those snakes, any day.'

The detective was only one of millions who had lost money in the recent collapse of an artificial boom, and his sentiments were characteristically vehement. Andy Herrick murmured some sympathetic commonplace and watched the trio of celebrators without interest.

'You do understan', boys, don't you ?' Enstone was articulating pathetically, with his arms spread across the shoulders of his guests in an affectionate manner which contributed helpfully towards his support. 'It's jus' business. I'm not hard-hearted. I'm kind to my wife an' children an' everything, God bless 'em. An' any time I can do anything for either of you - why, you jus' lemme know.'

'That's real white of you, Lew,' said Hammel, with the blurry-eyed solemnity of his condition.

'Let's have lunch together Tuesday,' suggested Costello. 'Maybe we might be able to talk about something that'd interest you.'

'Okay,' said Enstone, dimly. 'Lush on Tooshday.'

'An' don't forget the kids,' said Hammel, confidentially.

Enstone giggled.

'I shouldn't forget that !' In obscurely elaborate pantomime, he closed his fist, with his forefinger extended and his thumb cocked vertically upwards, and aimed the forefinger waveringly between Hammel's eyes. 'Shtick 'em up !' he commanded gravely, and at once relapsed into further merriment, in which his guests joined somewhat hysterically.

The group separated at the entrance amid much hand-shaking and back-slapping and laughter ; and Lewis Enstone wended his way back with cautious and preoccupied steps towards the elevators. Kestry took a fresh bite on his cigar and squared his jaw disgustedly.

'Is he staying here ?' asked Andy.

'Lives here,' said Kestry, shortly. 'Got a terrace apartment that costs forty thousand dollars a year. There's plenty of suckers to help him pay for it.' The detective ruminated sourly. 'If I told you some of the tricks those guys get up to you'd call me a liar. Why, I remember one time -'

He launched into a lengthy anecdote which had all the decorative vitality of personal bitterness in the telling. Andy Herrick, listening with the half of one well-trained ear that would prick up into instant attention if the story took any twist that might provide the germ of a plot, but would remain intently passive if it did not, lighted a cigarette and gazed abstractedly into space.

'. . . So the word came down for me to lay off, and I laid off. It was okay with me,' concluded Kestry rancorously ; and Andy took the last inhalation from his cigarette and dropped the stub into an ashtray.

'Thanks for the tip, George,' he said lightly. 'I gather that when I really murder somebody you'd like me to make it a Wall Street financier.'

George Kestry snorted, and hitched his coat round.

'I gotta be off now. Come in an' see me again soon.'

They walked towards the street doors. On their left they passed the information desk ; and beside the desk had been standing two bored and sleepy bell-boys. Andy had observed them and their sleepiness as casually as he had observed the colour of the carpet, but all at once he realised that their sleepiness had vanished. He had a sudden queer sense of suppressed excitement ; and then one of the boys said something loud enough to be overheard which stopped Kestry in his tracks and turned him round abruptly.

'What's that ?' demanded Kestry.

'It's Mr Enstone, sir. He just shot himself.'

Kestry scowled. To the newspapers it would be a surprise and a front-page sensation ; to him it was a surprise and a potential menace to his night's sleep if he butted into any responsibility. Then he shrugged.

'I'd better give it a look-over. D'you say he shot himself ?'

'Yes, sir. His valet just 'phoned down.'

Kestry flashed his badge, and there was a scurry to lead him towards the elevators. He strode bulkily and impersonally ahead, and Andy followed him into the nearest car. One of the bell-boys supplied a floor number, and Kestry pushed his hands into his pockets and glowered in mountainous aloofness at the latticed inner gate of the elevator. Andy, the intruder, studiously avoided his eye, and had a pleasant shock when the detective addressed him almost genially.

'Say, Andy, didn't I tell you those guys were nutty as well as crooked ? Did Enstone look as if he'd anything to shoot himself about, except the head that was waitin' for him when he woke up ?'

It was as if the decease of any financier, however caused, was a benison upon the earth, in the face of which Kestry could not be anything but good-humoured. That was the impression he gave of his private feelings ; but the rest of him was impenetrable stolidity and authoritativeness. He dismissed the escort of bell-boys and strode on to the door of the millionaire's suite. It was closed and silent. He hammered on it commandingly, and after a moment it opened six inches and disclosed a pale, agitated face. Kestry showed his badge again, and the door opened wider, enlarging the agitated face into the unmistakable full-length portrait of an assistant hotel manager. Andy followed the detective in, endeavouring to look equally official.

'This will be a terrible scandal, captain,' said the assistant manager.

Kestry glared at him over an aggressive cigar.

'Were you here when it happened ?'

'No. I was downstairs – in my office –'

Kestry collected the information, and thrust past him. On the right, another door opened off the large lobby, and through it could be seen another elderly man whose equally pale face and air of suppressed agitation bore a certain general similarity and also a self-contained superiority to the first. Even without his sober black coat and striped trousers, grey side-whiskers, and passive hands, he would have stamped himself as something more cosmic than the assistant manager of an hotel – the assistant manager of a man.

'Who are you ?' demanded Kestry.

'I am Fowler, sir. Mr Enstone's valet.'

'Were you here ?'

'Yes, sir.'

'Where is Mr Enstone ?'

'In the bedroom, sir.'

They moved back across the lobby, with the assistant manager in the lead. Kestry stopped. 'Will you be in your office if I want you ?' he asked with great politeness ; and the assistant manager seemed to disappear from the scene even before the door of the suite closed behind him.

Lewis Enstone was dead. He lay on his back beside the bed, with his head half-rolled over to one side, in such a way that both the entrance and the exit of the bullet which had killed him could be seen. It had been fired squarely into his right eye, leaving the ugly trail that only a heavy-calibre bullet fired at close range can leave.... The gun lay under the fingers of his right hand.

'Thumb on the trigger,' Kestry noted aloud.

He sat on the bed, pulling on a pair of gloves, inscrutable and un-emotional. Andy Herrick observed the room. An ordinary, very tidy bedroom, barren of anything unusual except the subdued costliness of furnishing and accessories. Two French windows opening on to the terrace, both shut and fastened. On a table in one corner, the only sign of disorder – the remains of a carelessly opened parcel. Brown paper, ends of string, a plain cardboard box – empty. The millionaire had gone no farther towards undressing than loosening his tie and unbuttoning his collar.

'What happened ?' asked Kestry.

'Mr Enstone had had friends to dinner, sir,' explained Fowler. 'A Mr Costello –'

'I know that. What happened when he came back from seeing them off ?'

'He was going straight to bed, sir.'

'Was this door open ?'

'At first, sir. I asked Mr Enstone about the morning, and he asked me to call him at nine. Then he closed the door, and I went back to the sitting-room.'

'Did you leave that door open ?'

'Yes, sir. I was doing a little clearing up. Then I heard the shot, sir.'

'Do you know any reason why Mr Enstone should have shot himself ?'

'No, sir.'

Kestry jerked his head towards a door on the other side of the room.

'What does that communicate with ?'

'Another bedroom, sir. Mrs Enstone's maid sleeps there with the children.'

'Where are they ?'

'They have been in Bermuda, sir. We are expecting them home to-morrow.'

'What was in that parcel, Fowler ?' ventured Andy.

The valet glanced at the table.

'I don't know, sir. I believe it must have been left by one of Mr Enstone's guests. I noticed it on the dining table when I brought in their coats, and Mr Enstone came back for it on his return and took it into the bedroom with him.'

'You didn't hear anything said about it ?'

'No, sir.'

Kestry looked up at Andy, derisively.

'Why don't you get out your magnifying glass and go over the cigar ash ?' he inquired.

Andy smiled apologetically, and, being nearest the door, went out to open it, as a second knocking disturbed the silence. For half an hour he stood about inconspicuously in the background, while the room and the body were photographed from different angles, fingerprints developed and photographed, and the police surgeon made his preliminary examination. All the formalities were familiar to him, and after a while he drifted into the sitting-room. The hall-marks of a convivial dinner were all there – cigar butts in the coffee cups, stains of spilt wine on the cloth, crumbs and ash everywhere – but those things did not interest him.

He was not quite sure what would have interested him ; but he wandered rather vacantly round the room, gazing introspectively at the prints of character which a long tenancy inevitably leaves even on anything so characterless as a hotel apartment. There were pictures on the walls and on the side tables, mostly enlarged snapshots revealing Lewis Enstone in relaxation in the bosom of his family.

On one of the side tables he found a curious object. It was a small wooden plate on which half-a-dozen wooden fowls stood in a circle. Their necks were pivoted at the base, and underneath the plate were six short strings joined to the necks and knotted together some distance farther down, where they were all attached at the same point to a wooden ball. It was these strings, and the weight of the ball at their lower end, which kept the birds' heads raised ; and Andy discovered that when he moved the plate so that the ball swung round in a circle underneath and slackened and tightened each string in turn, the fowls mounted on the plate pecked vigorously in rotation at an invisible and apparently inexhaustible supply of corn, in an ingenious mechanical display of gluttony.

He was still playing thoughtfully with the toy when the howl of Kestry's gargantuan laughter brought him back to earth with a jar, and he realised that the photographers and fingerprint men had gone.

'So that's how the great detective works !' Kestry jeered.

'I think it's rather clever,' said Andy seriously. He put the toy down, and blinked at Fowler. 'Does it belong to one of the children ?'

'He brought it home with him this evening, sir, to give to Miss Annabel tomorrow,' said the valet. 'Mr Enstone was always picking up things like that. He was a very devoted father, sir.'

Kestry grunted.

'C'mon, kid. I'm goin' home.'

Andy nodded pacifically, and accompanied him to the elevator. On the way down he asked: 'Did you find any clue ?'

Kestry's teeth clamped on a fresh cigar.

'The guy committed suicide,' he said, addressing an obvious half-wit. 'He shot himself. What sort of clues d'you want ?'

'Why did he commit suicide ?' asked Andy, almost childishly.

'How do I know ? I told you those guys were nutty. Probably he dropped ten million while he was picking up one, and he only wanted to talk about the one. Come down to my office in the morning and I'll tell you.'

Andy Herrick went home and slept fitfully. Lewis Enstone had shot himself ; Kestry said so, and without any wild stretches of imagination it seemed an obvious fact. The windows had been closed and fastened. The valet had had the door and the lobby under surveillance from the sitting-room ; there remained the communicating door of the second bedroom . . . or Fowler himself. . . . Why not suicide, anyway ?

But Andy could run through his mind every word and gesture and expression of the leave-taking, which he himself had witnessed in the hotel lobby, and none of it carried even a hint of suicide. The only oddity about it had been the queer, inexplicable piece of pantomime – the fist clenched, with the forefinger extended and the thumb cocked up, in crude symbolism of a gun. The abstruse joke which had dissolved Enstone into a fit of inanely delighted giggling, with the hearty approval of his guests.

It was like the opening of one of Andy's own stories, a set of intriguing circumstances of which he, himself, would have to devise an explanation and a solution towards the fourth or fifth instalment ; and the psychological problem absorbed him. It muddled itself up with a litter of brown paper and a cardboard box, a wooden plate of pecking chickens, photographs . . . and the tangle kaleidoscoped through his dreams in a thousand different convolutions until morning.

At half-past twelve he found himself walking slowly down the long corridor to Kestry's office. The detective was chewing his cigar over a sheaf of typewritten reports, and he was in one of his short tempers.

'What do you want ?' he snapped.

Andy unbuttoned his coat and opened a packet of cigarettes.

'Have you found out why Enstone committed suicide ?'

'I haven't found out nothing,' said Kestry, with ungrammatical emphasis. 'His broker says it's true he cleaned up the market – sold Associated Stone Mills down to six-and-a-half and covered yesterday. Maybe he was working something else through another broker. We'll find out.'

Kestry buried himself again in his papers. Andy might have been off the earth.

'Have you seen Costello or Hammel ?' Andy asked, unabashed.

'I've sent for them. They're due here about now.'

In a few minutes Costello and Hammel were announced. Kestry 'phoned for a stenographer, and applied a match to his cigar in grim detachment while the two witnesses seated themselves. He opened the brief examination in his own time.

'Mr Abe Costello ?'

The tall man with the thin black moustache nodded.

'Yes.'

'How long have you known Enstone ?'

'About eight or nine years.'

'Ever in partnership ?'

'No. We were just friends.'

'Ever quarrel ?'

'No.'

'Have you any idea why he should have shot himself ?'

'None at all, captain. It was a great shock. He had been making more money than most of us. When we were with him – last night – he was in very high spirits. He'd made a lot on the market, and his family was on the way home – he was always happy when he was looking forward to seeing them again.'

'Did you hold any Associated Stone Mills ?'

'No.'

'You know we can investigate that ?'

Costello smiled slightly.

'I don't know why you should take that attitude, but my affairs are open to any examination.'

'Been making money yourself lately ?'

'No. As a matter of fact, I've lost a bit,' said Costello, frankly.

'What are you in ?'

'I'm controlling International Cotton.'

Kestry paused to reach for matches and Costello forestalled him with a lighter. Andy Herrick suddenly found his eyes riveted on the device – it was of an uncommon shape, and seemed to ignite the fuel by means of an electric spark, for when Costello pressed the button there was a preliminary crackle quite distinguishable from the usual grate of a flint.

Almost without realising his own temerity, Andy said : 'That's something new, isn't it ?'

Costello turned the lighter over and answered, 'I don't think you'll see one in a shop. It's an invention of my own – I made it myself.'

'I wish I could do things like that,' said Andy, wistfully. 'I suppose you must have had a technical training.'

Costello hesitated for a second. Then :

'I started in an electrical engineering workshop when I was a boy,' he explained briefly, and turned back to Kestry's desk.

After a long pause Kestry turned to the tubby man with glasses.

'Mr Jules Hammel ?'

'Yes.'

'You in partnership with Mr Costello ?'

'A working partnership – yes.'

'Were you on the same terms with Enstone ?'

'About the same – yes.'

'What were you talking about at dinner last night ?'

'It was about a merger. I'm in International Cotton, too. One of Mr Enstone's concerns was Cosmopolitan Textiles. His shares are standing high and ours are not doing too well, and we thought if we could induce him to sign a merger it would help us.'

'What did Enstone think about that ?'

Hammel spread his hands.

'He didn't think there was enough in it for him. We had certain things to offer, but he decided they weren't sufficient.'

'Wasn't there some bad feeling about it ?'

'Why no. If all the businessmen who have refused to combine with one another at different times became enemies, there would be nobody speaking to anybody on Wall Street today.'

'Do you know why Enstone might have shot himself ?'

'No.'

Andy Herrick cleared his throat.

'What was your first important job, Mr Hammel ?' he queried.

Hammel turned his eyes without moving his head.

'I was sales psychologist in a department store in Minneapolis.'

Kestry closed the interview curtly, shook hands perfunctorily with the two men, and dismissed the stenographer. Then he glared at Andy like a cannibal.

'Why don't you join the force yourself ?' he inquired heavily. 'The Police Academy's just across the street – I'll send you over with a letter.'

Andy took the sally like an armoured car taking a snowball.

'You big sap !' he retorted startlingly. 'Do you look as if the Police Academy could teach anyone to solve a murder ?'

Kestry gulped. 'What murder are you talking about ?' he demanded. 'Enstone shot himself.'

'Yes, Enstone shot himself,' said Andy. 'But he was murdered just the same. They made him shoot himself.'

'What d'you mean – blackmail ?'

'No.'

Andy pushed a hand through his hair again. He had thought of things like that. He knew that Enstone had shot himself, because no one else could have done it. Except Fowler, the valet – but that was the man whom Kestry would have suspected if he had suspected anyone, and it was too obvious, too hopelessly amateurish. No man in his senses could have planned a murder with himself as the most obvious suspect. Blackmail, then ? But the Lewis Enstone he had seen in the hotel lobby had never looked like a man bidding farewell to blackmailers. And no one else could have blackmailed him. There had been no letters, no telephone calls – Andy took that for granted ; if there had been, Fowler must have mentioned them. How could he have been blackmailed ?

'No, no, no,' said Andy. 'It wasn't that. They just made him do it.'

'They just said : "Lew, why don't you take yourself for a ride ?" and he thought it was a swell idea – is that it ?' Kestry gibed.

'It was something like that,' Andy said soberly. 'You see, Enstone would do almost anything to amuse his children.'

Kestry's mouth opened, but no sounds came from it. His expression implied that a whole volcano of devastating sarcasm was boiling on the tip of his tongue.

'Costello and Hammel had to do something,' said Andy. 'International Cottons have been very bad for a long time. On the other hand, Enstone's interest – Cosmopolitan Textiles – was good. Costello and Hammel could have pulled out in two ways : either by a merger, or else by having Enstone commit suicide, so that Cosmopolitans would tumble down in the scare, and they could buy them in. If you look at the papers this afternoon you'll see that all Enstone's securities have dropped through the bottom – no one in his position can commit suicide without starting a panic. Costello and Hammel went to dinner to try for the merger, but if Enstone turned it down they were ready for the other thing.'

'So what ?' rapped Kestry ; but for the first time there seemed to be a tremor in the foundations of his disbelief.

'They made only one big mistake. They didn't arrange for Enstone to leave a letter.'

'People have shot themselves without leaving letters.'

'I know. But not often. That's what started me thinking.'

'Well ?'

Andy rumpled his hair into more profound disorder, and said : 'You see, George, I write those detective stories : and writing detective stories is just a kind of jig-saw puzzle. For the author, I mean. You take a lot of mysterious events and a lot of mysterious characters, and somehow you have to tie them all together. And while the story's going on you have to be thinking all the time, "Now, what would A do ? – and what would B do ? – and what would C do ?" You have to be a practical psychologist – just like a sales psychologist in a department store in Minneapolis.'

Kestry's cigar came out of his mouth, but for some reason which was beyond his conscious comprehension he said nothing. And Andy Herrick went on, in the same disjointed and rather apologetic way :

'Sales psychology is just a study of human weaknesses. And that's a funny thing, you know. I remember the manager of one of the biggest novelty manufacturers in the world telling me once that the soundest test of any idea for a new toy was whether it would appeal to a middle-aged businessman. It's true, of course. If the mighty, earth-shaking business-men weren't like that they could never have helped to create an economic system in which all the fate of nations, all the hunger and happiness and achievement of the world, were locked up in a few bars of yellow gold.'

Andy raised his eyes suddenly – they were unexpectedly bright and in some queer fashion sightless, as if his mind was separated from every physical awareness of its surroundings. 'Lewis Enstone was just that kind of man,' he said.

'You still thinking of that toy you were playing with ?' asked Kestry, restlessly.

'That – and other things we heard. And the photographs. Did you notice them ?'

'No.'

'One of them was Enstone playing with a clockwork train. In another of them he was under a rug, being a bear. In another he was working a big model merry-go-round. Most of the pictures were like that. The children came into them, of course, but you could see that Enstone was having the swellest time.'

Kestry, who had been fidgeting with a pencil, shrugged and sent it clattering across the desk.

'You still gotta show me a murder,' he stated.

'I have to find it myself,' said Andy, gently. 'You see, it was a kind of professional problem – the old jig-saw puzzle with a missing piece. Enstone was happily married, happy with his family, too happy to give any grounds for blackmail, no more crooked than any other Wall Street gambler, nothing on his conscience, rich and getting richer – how were they to make him commit suicide ? If I'd been writing a story with him in it, how could I have made him commit suicide ?'

'You'd of told him he had some fatal illness,' said Kestry, 'and he'd have fallen for it.'

Andy shook his head.

'No. If I'd been a doctor – perhaps. But if Costello or Hammel had told him, he'd have wanted confirmation. And did he look like a man who'd just been told he might have got a fatal illness ?'

'It's your murder,' said Kestry. 'You go ahead an' break it.'

'There were lots of pieces missing at first,' said Andy. 'I only had Enstone's character and weaknesses. And then it came out – Hammel was a psychologist. That was good, because I'm a psychologist myself, and his mind would work something like mine. And then Costello could invent mechanical gadgets and make them himself. He shouldn't have brought out that lighter, George – it gave me another of the missing pieces. And then there was the cardboard box – on Enstone's table, with the brown paper. You know, Fowler said he thought either Costello or Hammel left it. Have you got it here ?'

'It's somewhere in the building.'

'Could we have it up ?'

Kestry looked at him and burst out laughing. Then, with the gesture of a hangman reaching for a noose, he took hold of the telephone.

'You can have the gun, too, if you like,' he said.

'Yes, please,' said Andy, hurriedly. 'I wanted the gun.'

Kestry gave the order ; and they sat and looked at each other in silence till the relics arrived. Kestry's silence explained in fifty different ways that Andy would be refused no facility for nailing down his own coffin in a manner that he would never be allowed to forget ; but Andy was only squatting on the edge of his chair and ruffling his hair like a schoolboy. When they were alone again, Andy went to the desk, picked up the gun, and put it in the box. It fitted very well.

'That's what happened, George. They gave him the gun in the box.'

'And he shot himself without knowing what he was doing,' said Kestry.

'That's just it,' said Andy. 'He didn't know what he was doing.'

'Well, for the love of a piebald mule !' said Kestry.

'But I've got an idea,' said Andy, jumping up excitedly. 'Come out and lunch with me. I know a new place.'

Kestry gathered up a handful of cigars from a drawer, thrust them into his pocket, crushed his hat on his head, and they went out to a taxi.

Kestry roared noisily on the ride. Andy sat on the edge of the seat, as he had sat on the edge of the chair in Kestry's office, and twiddled the brim of his hat awkwardly. Presently the taxi stopped in a turning off Park Avenue, and Andy looked out of the window at the numbers of the houses and hopped out. He led the way into an apartment building and into an elevator, saying something to the elevator boy which Kestry did not catch.

'What is this ?' Kestry asked, as they shot upwards. 'A new speak-easy ?'

'It's a new place,' said Andy, hazily.

The elevator stopped, and they got out. They went along the corridor, and Andy rang the bell of one of the doors. It was opened by a liveried Japanese.

'Police Department,' said Andy, brazenly, and squeezed past him.

He found his way into the sitting-room before anyone could stop him. Kestry, reviving from the momentary paralysis of the shock, followed him ; then came the Japanese manservant.

'I'm sorry, sir – Mr Costello is out.'

Kestry's bulk obscured Japan. All the joviality had smudged itself off the detective's face, giving place to blank amazement and fury.

'What the deuce is this joke ?' he demanded.

'It isn't a joke, George,' said Andy. 'I just wanted to see if I could find something – you know what we were talking about –'

His eyes were darting about the room, and then they lighted on a big, cheap kneehole desk whose well-worn shabbiness looked strangely out of keeping with the other furniture. On it was the litter of coils and wire and drilled ebonite of a radio set in course of construction. Andy ran over to the desk and began pulling open the drawers. Tools of all kinds, various gauges of wire and screws, odd wheels and sleeves and bolts and scraps of sheet iron and brass – all the junk which accumulates around an amateur mechanic's workshop. Then he came to a drawer that was locked. Without hesitation he grabbed up a large screwdriver, rammed it in about the lock, and splintered the drawer open, with a skilful wrench and an unexpected effort of strength.

Kestry let out a shout and started across the room. Andy's hand dived into the drawer, came out with a nickel-plated revolver. It was exactly the same as the one with which Lewis Enstone had shot himself. Andy turned the muzzle of the gun close up to his right eye, with his thumbs on the trigger, exactly as Enstone must have held it. Kestry lurched forward and knocked the weapon spinning, with a sweep of his arm ; then he grabbed Andy by his coat lapels and lifted him off his feet.

'If you pull any more of that stuff you're gonna have to get busted on the jaw.'

Andy looked up at him and smiled.

'But, George, that was the gun Enstone thought he was playing with !'

The Japanese servant was under a table with the telephone. Kestry let go of Andy and yanked him out, displaying his badge.

'I'm from Police Headquarters, all right,' he growled. 'When I want you to telephone I'll tell you.'

He swung back to Andy. 'Now – what's this you're getting at ?'

'The gun, George. Enstone's toy.'

Andy went and picked it up again. He put it to his eye and pulled the trigger – pulled it, released it, pulled it again, keeping up the rhythmic movement. Something inside the gun whirred smoothly, as if wheels were whizzing round under the working of the lever. Then he pointed the gun straight into Kestry's face and did the same thing. Kestry stared frozenly down the barrel and saw the black hole leap into a circle of light. He was looking at a flickering cinematographic film of a boy shooting a masked burglar. It was tiny, puerile in subject, but perfect. It lasted about ten seconds, and then the barrel went dark again.

'Costello's present for Enstone's little boy,' said Andy, quietly. 'He invented it and made it himself, of course – he always had a talent that way. Haven't you seen those electric flashlights that work without a battery ? You keep squeezing a lever, and it turns a miniature dynamo. Costello made a very small one, and fitted it into the hollow casting of a gun. Then he geared a tiny strip of film in with it. It was a good new toy, George, and he must have been proud of it. They took it along to Enstone's ; and when he'd turned down their merger and there was nothing else for them to do, they let him play with it just enough to tickle his palate, at just the right hour of the evening. Then they took it away from him and put it back in its box and gave it to him. They had a real gun in another box ready to make the switch.'

Kestry stood like a rock, clamping his cigar. Then he said : 'How did they know he wouldn't shoot his son, Andy ?'

'That was Hammel. He knew that Enstone wasn't capable of keeping his hands off a toy like that ; and just to make certain, he reminded Enstone of it the last thing before they left. He was a practical psychologist.'

Andy Herrick ran his fingers through his hair and fished a cigarette out of his pocket. 'I got all that out of a stool-pigeon, George,' he announced modestly.

Kestry swallowed painfully, and picked up the telephone.

Roy Vickers

THE RUBBER TRUMPET

IF YOU WERE TO ENQUIRE at Scotland Yard for the Department of Dead Ends you might be told, in all sincerity, that there is no such thing, because it is not called by that name nowadays. All the same, if it has no longer a room to itself, you may rest assured that its spirit hovers over the index files of which we are all so justly proud.

The Department came into existence in the spacious days of King Edward VII and it took everything that the other departments rejected. For instance, it noted and filed all those clues that had the exasperating effect of proving a palpably guilty man innocent. Its shelves were crowded with exhibits that might have been in the Black Museum – but were not. Its photographs were a perpetual irritation to all rising young detectives, who felt that they ought to have found the means of putting them in the Rogues' Gallery.

To the Department, too, were taken all those members of the public who insist on helping the police with obviously irrelevant information and preposterous theories. The one passport to the Department was a written statement by the senior officer in charge of the case that the information offered was absurd.

Judged by the standards of reason and common sense, its files were mines of misinformation. It proceeded largely by guesswork. On one occasion it hanged a murderer by accidentally punning on his name.

It was the function of the Department to connect persons and things that had no logical connection. In short, it stood for the antithesis of scientific detection. It played always for a lucky fluke – to offset the lucky fluke by which the criminal so often eludes the police. Often it muddled one crime with another and arrived at the correct answer by wrong reasoning.

As in the case of George Muncey and the rubber trumpet.

And note, please, that the rubber trumpet had nothing logically to do with George Muncey, nor the woman he murdered, nor the circumstances in which he murdered her.

2

Until the age of twenty-six George Muncey lived with his widowed mother in Chichester, the family income being derived from a chemist's shop, efficiently controlled by Mrs Muncey with the aid of a manager and two assistants, of whom latterly George was one. Of his early youth we know only that he won a scholarship at a day-school, tenable for three years, which was cancelled at the end of a year, though not, apparently, for misconduct. He failed several times to obtain his pharmaceutical certificate, with the result that he was eventually put in charge of the fancy soaps, the hot-water bottles and the photographic accessories.

For this work he received two pounds per week. Every Saturday he handed the whole of it to his mother, who returned him fifteen shillings for pocket money. She had no need of the balance and only took it in order to nourish his self-respect. He did not notice that she bought his clothes and met all his other expenses.

George had no friends and very little of what an ordinary young man would regard as pleasure. He spent nearly all his spare time with his mother, to whom he was devoted. She was an amiable but very domineering woman and she does not seem to have noticed that her son's affection had in it a quality of childishness – that he liked her to form his opinions for him and curtail his liberties.

After his mother's death he did not resume his duties at the shop. For some eight months he mooned about Chichester. Then, the business having been sold and probate granted, he found himself in possession of some eight hundred pounds, with another two thousand pounds due to him in three months. He did not, apparently, understand this part of the transaction – for he made no application for the two thousand, and as the solicitors could not find him until his name came into the papers, the two thousand remained intact for his defence.

That he was a normal but rather backward young man is proved by the fact that the walls of his bedroom were liberally decorated with photographs of the actresses of the moment and pictures of anonymous beauties cut from the more sporting weeklies. Somewhat naïvely he bestowed this picture gallery as a parting gift on the elderly cook.

He drew the whole of the eight hundred pounds in notes and gold, said goodbye to his home and went up to London. He stumbled on cheap and respectable lodgings in Pimlico. Then, in a gauche, small-town way, he set out to see life.

It was the year when *The Merry Widow* was setting all London awhistling. Probably on some chance recommendation, he drifted to

Daly's Theatre, where he bought himself a seat in the dress-circle.

It was the beginning of the London season and we may assume that he would have felt extremely self-conscious sitting in the circle in his ready-made lounge suit, had there not happened to be a woman also in morning dress next to him.

The woman was a Miss Hilda Callermere. She was forty-three and if she escaped positive ugliness she was certainly without any kind of physical attractiveness, though she was neat in her person and reasonably well-dressed, in an old-fashioned way.

Eventually to the Department of Dead Ends came the whole story of his strange courtship.

There is a curious quality in the manner in which these two slightly unusual human beings approached one another. They did not speak until after the show, when they were wedged together in the corridor. Their voices seem to come to us out of a fog of social shyness and vulgar gentility. And it was she who took the initiative.

'If you'll excuse me speaking to you without an introduction, we seem to be rather out of it, you and I, what with one thing and another.'

His reply strikes us now as somewhat unusual.

'Yes, rather !' he said. 'Are you coming here again ?'

'Yes, rather ! I sometimes come twice a week.'

During the next fortnight they both went three times to *The Merry Widow*, but on the first two of these occasions they missed each other. On the third occasion, which was a Saturday night, Miss Callermere invited George Muncey to walk with her on the following morning in Battersea Park.

Here shyness dropped from them. They slipped quite suddenly on to an easy footing of friendship. George Muncey accepted her invitation to lunch. She took him to a comfortably furnished eight-roomed house - her own - in which she lived with an aunt whom she supported. For, in addition to the house, Miss Callermere owned an income of six hundred pounds derived from gilt-edged investments.

But these considerations weighed hardly at all with George Muncey - for he had not yet spent fifty pounds of his eight hundred, and at this stage he had certainly no thought of marriage with Miss Callermere.

3

Neither of them had any occupation, so they could meet whenever they chose. Miss Callermere undertook to show George London. Her father

had been a cheery, beery jerry-builder with sporting interests and she
had reacted from him into a parched severity of mind. She marched
George round the Tower of London, the British Museum and the like,
reading aloud extracts from a guide-book. They went neither to the
theatres nor to the music-halls, for Miss Callermere thought these
frivolous and empty-headed – with the exception of *The Merry Widow,*
which she believed to be opera, and therefore cultural. And the extraordinary thing was that George Muncey liked it all.

There can be no doubt that this smug little spinster, some sixteen
years older than himself, touched a chord of sympathy in his nature. But
she was wholly unable to cater for that part of him that had plastered
photographs of public beauties on the walls of his bedroom.

She never went to *The Merry Widow* again, but once or twice he would
sneak off to Daly's by himself. *The Merry Widow,* in fact, provided him
with a dream-life. We may infer that in his imagination he identified
himself with Mr Joseph Coyne, who nightly, in the character of Prince
Dannilo, would disdain the beautiful Sonia only to have her rush the
more surely to his arms in the finale. Rather a dangerous fantasy for a
backward young man from the provinces who was beginning to lose his
shyness !

There was, indeed, very little shyness about him when, one evening
after seeing Miss Callermere home, he was startled by the sight of a
young parlourmaid, who had been sent out to post a letter, some fifty
yards from Miss Callermere's house. If she bore little or no likeness to
Miss Lily Elsie in the role of Sonia, she certainly looked quite lovely in
her white cap and the streamers that were then worn. And she was smiling and friendly and natural.

She was, of course, Ethel Fairbrass. She lingered with George
Muncey for over five minutes. And then comes another of those strange
little dialogues.

'Funny a girl like you being a slavey ! When's your evening off ?'

'Six o'clock tomorrow. But what's it got to do with you ?'

'I'll meet you at the corner of this road. Promise you I will.'

'Takes two to make a promise. My name's Ethel Fairbrass, if you want
to know. What's yours ?'

'Dannilo.'

'Coo! Fancy calling you that ! Dannilo what ?'

George had not foreseen the necessity for inventing a surname and
discovered that it is quite difficult. He couldn't very well say 'Smith' or
'Robinson', so he said :

'Prince.'

George, it will be observed, was not an imaginative man. When she met him the following night he could think of nowhere to take her but to *The Merry Widow*. He was even foolish enough to let her have a programme, but she did not read the names of the characters. When the curtain went up she was too entranced with Miss Lily Elsie, whom (like every pretty girl at the time) she thought she resembled, to take any notice of Mr Joseph Coyne and his character name. If she had tumbled to the witless transposition of the names she might have become suspicious of him. In which case George Muncey might have lived to a ripe old age.

But she didn't.

4

Altogether, Ethel Fairbrass provided an extremely satisfactory substitute for the dream-woman of George's fantasy. Life was beginning to sweeten. In the daylight hours he would enjoy his friendship with Miss Callermere, the pleasure of which was in no way touched by his infatuation for the pretty parlourmaid.

In early September Ethel became entitled to her holiday. She spent the whole fortnight with George at Southend. And George wrote daily to Miss Callermere, telling her that he was filling the place of a chemist-friend of his mother's, while the latter took his holiday. He actually contrived to have the letters addressed to the care of a local chemist. The letters were addressed 'George Muncey' while at the hotel the couple were registered as 'Mr and Mrs D. Prince'.

Now, the fictional Prince Dannilo was notoriously an open-handed and free-living fellow – and Dannilo Prince proceeded to follow in his footsteps. Ethel Fairbrass undoubtedly had the time of her life. They occupied a suite. ('Coo ! A bathroom all to our own two selves, and use it whenever we like !')

He hired a car for her, with chauffeur – which cost ten pounds a day at that time. He gave her champagne whenever he could induce her to drink it and bought her some quite expensive presents.

It is a little surprising that at the end of a fortnight of this kind of thing she went back to her occupation. But she did. There was nothing of the mercenary about Ethel.

On his return to London, George was very glad to see Miss Callermere. They resumed their interminable walks and he went almost daily to her house for lunch or dinner. A valuable arrangement, this, for the little diversion at Southend had made a sizeable hole in his eight hundred pounds.

It was a bit of a nuisance to have to leave early in order to snatch a few minutes with Ethel. After Southend, the few snatched minutes had somehow lost their charm. There were, too, Ethel's half-days and her Sundays, the latter involving him in a great many troublesome lies to Miss Callermere.

In the middle of October he started sneaking off to *The Merry Widow* again. Which was a bad sign. For it meant that he was turning back again from reality to his dream-life. The Reality, in the meantime, had lost her high spirits and was inclined to weep unreasonably and to nag more than a little.

At the beginning of November Ethel presented him with certain very valid arguments in favour of fixing the date of their wedding, a matter which had hitherto been kept vaguely in the background.

George was by now heartily sick of her and contemplated leaving her in the lurch. Strangely enough, it was her final threat to tell Miss Callermere that turned the scale and decided George to make the best of a bad job and marry her.

5

As Dannilo Prince he married her one foggy morning at the registrar's office in Henrietta Street. Mr and Mrs Fairbrass came up from Banbury for the wedding. They were not very nice about it, although from the social point of view the marriage might be regarded as a step-up for Ethel.

'Where are you going for your honeymoon ?' asked Mrs Fairbrass. 'That is – if you're going to *have* a honeymoon.'

'Southend,' said the unimaginative George, and to Southend he took her for the second time. There was no need for a suite now, so they went to a small family-and-commercial hotel. Here George was unreasonably jealous of the commercial travellers, who were merely being polite to a rather forlorn bride. In wretched weather he insisted on taking her for walks, with the result that he himself caught a very bad cold. Eucalyptus and hot toddy became the dominant note in a town which was associated in the girl's mind with champagne and bath salts. But they had to stick it for the full fortnight, because George had told Miss Callermere that he was again acting as substitute for the chemist-friend of his mother's in Southend.

According to the files of the Department, they left Southend by the three-fifteen on the thirtieth of November. George had taken first-class returns. The three-fifteen was a popular non-stop, but on this occasion there were hardly a score of persons travelling to London. One of the first-class carriages was occupied by a man alone with a young baby wrapped in a red shawl. Ethel wanted to get into this compartment, perhaps having a sneaking hope that the man would require her assistance in dealing with the baby. But George did not intend to concern himself with babies one moment before he would be compelled to do so, and they went into another compartment.

Ethel, however, seems to have looked forward to her impending career with a certain pleasure. Before leaving Southend she had paid a visit to one of those shops that cater for summer visitors and miraculously remain open through the winter. She had a bulky parcel, which she opened in the rather pathetic belief that it would amuse George.

The parcel contained a large child's bucket, a disproportionately small wooden spade, a sailing-boat to the scale of the spade, a length of Southend rock and a rubber trumpet, of which the stem was wrapped with red and blue wool. It was a baby's trumpet and of rubber so that it should not hurt the baby's gums. In the mouthpiece, shielded by the rubber, was a little metal contraption that made the noise.

Ethel put the trumpet to her mouth and blew through the metal contraption.

Perhaps, in fancy, she heard her baby doing it. Perhaps, after a honeymoon of neglect and misery, she was making a desperate snatch at the spirit of gaiety, hoping he would attend to her and perhaps indulge in a little horseplay. But for the actual facts we have to depend on George's version.

'I said "Don't make that noise, Ethel - I'm trying to read" or something like that. And she said "I feel like a bit of music to cheer me up" and she went on blowing the trumpet. So I caught hold of it and threw it out of the window. I didn't hurt her and she didn't seem to mind much. And we didn't have another quarrel over it and I went on reading my paper until we got to London.'

At Fenchurch Street they claimed their luggage and left the station. Possibly Ethel abandoned the parcel containing the other toys for they were never heard of again.

When the train was being cleaned, a dead baby was found under the seat of a first-class compartment, wrapped in a red shawl. It was subsequently ascertained that the baby had not been directly murdered but had died more or less naturally in convulsions.

But before this was known, Scotland Yard searched for the man who had been seen to enter the train with the baby, as if for a murderer. A platelayer found the rubber trumpet on the line and forwarded it. Detectives combed the shops of Southend and found that only one rubber trumpet had been sold – to a young woman whom the shopkeeper did not know. The trail ended here.

The rubber trumpet went to the Department of Dead Ends.

6

Of the eight hundred pounds there was a little over a hundred and fifty left by the time they returned from the official honeymoon at Southend. He took her to furnished rooms in Ladbroke Grove and a few days later to a tenement in the same district, which he furnished at a cost of thirty pounds.

She seems to have asked him no awkward questions about money. Every morning after breakfast he would leave the tenement, presumably in order to go to work. Actually he would loaf about the West End until it was time to meet Miss Callermere. He liked especially going to the house in Battersea for lunch on Sundays. And here, of course, the previous process reversed itself and it was Ethel who had to be told the troublesome lies that were so difficult to invent.

'You seem so different lately, George,' said Miss Callermere one Sunday after lunch. 'I believe you're living with a ballet girl.'

George was not quite sure what a ballet girl was, but it sounded rather magnificently wicked. As he was anxious not to involve himself in further inventions, he said :

'She's not a ballet girl. She used to be a parlourmaid.'

'I really only want to know one thing about her,' said Miss Callermere. 'And that is, whether you are fond of her ?'

'No, I'm not !' said George with complete truthfulness.

'It's a pity to have that kind of thing in your life – you are dedicated to science. For your own sake, George, why not get rid of her ?'

Why not ? George wondered why he had not thought of it before. He had only to move, to stop calling himself by the ridiculous name of Dannilo Prince, and the thing was as good as done. He would go back at once and pack.

When he got back to the tenement, Ethel gave him an unexpectedly warm reception.

'You told me you were going to the SDP Sunday Brotherhood, you did ! And you never went near them, because you met that there Miss Callermere in Battersea Park, because I followed you and saw you. And then you went back to her house, which is Number Fifteen, Laurel Road, which I didn't know before. And what you can see in a dried-up old maid like that beats me. It's time she knew that she's rolling her silly sheep's eyes at another woman's husband. And I'm going to tell her before I'm a day older.'

She was whipping on hat and coat and George lurched forward to stop her. His foot caught on a gas-ring, useless now that he had installed a gas-range – a piece of lumber that Ethel ought to have removed weeks ago. But she used it as a stand for the iron.

George picked up the gas-ring. If she were to go to Miss Callermere and make a brawl, he himself would probably never be able to go there again. He pushed her quickly on to the bed, then swung the gas-ring – swung it several times.

He put all the towels, every soft absorbent thing he could find, under the bed. Then he washed himself, packed a suitcase and left the tenement.

He took the suitcase to his old lodgings, announced that he had come back there to live, and then presented himself at the house in Battersea in time for supper.

'I've done what you told me,' he said to Miss Callermere. 'Paid her off. Shan't hear from her any more.'

The Monday morning papers carried the news of the murder, for the police had been called on Sunday evening by the tenants of the flat below. The hunt was started for Dannilo Prince.

By Tuesday the dead girl's parents had been interviewed and her life-story appeared on Wednesday morning.

'My daughter was married to Prince at the Henrietta Street registrar's office on 16 November 1907. He took her straight away for a honeymoon at Southend, where they stayed a fortnight.'

There was a small crowd at the bottom of Laurel Road to gape at the house where she had so recently worked as a parlourmaid. Fifty yards from Number Fifteen ! But if Miss Callermere noticed the crowd she is not recorded as having made any comment upon it to anyone.

In a few days, Scotland Yard knew that they would never find Dannilo Prince. In fact, it had all been as simple as George had anticipated. He had just moved – and that was the end of his unlucky marriage. The addition of the murder had not complicated things, because he had left no clue behind him.

Now, as there was nothing whatever to connect George Muncey with

Dannilo Prince, George's chances of arrest were limited to the chance of an accidental meeting between himself and someone who had known him as Prince. There was an hotel proprietor, a waiter and a chamber-maid at Southend and an estate agent at Ladbroke Grove. And, of course, Ethel's father and mother. Of these persons only the estate agent lived in London.

A barrister, who was also a statistician, entertained himself by work-ing out the averages. He came to the conclusion that George Muncey's chance of being caught was equal to his chance of winning the first prize in the Calcutta Sweep *twenty-three times in succession.*

But the barrister did not calculate the chances of the illogical guess-work of the Department of Dead Ends hitting the bull's-eye by mistake.

7

While the hue and cry for Dannilo Prince passed over his head, George Muncey dedicated himself to science with such energy that in a fortnight he had obtained a post with a chemist in Walham. Here he presided over a counter devoted to fancy soaps, hot-water bottles, photo-graphic apparatus and the like - for which he received two pounds a week and a minute commission that added zest to his work.

At Easter he married Miss Callermere in church. That lady had mobilised all her late father's associates and, to their inward amusement, arrayed herself in white satin and veil for the ceremony. As it would have been unreasonable to ask George's employers for a holiday after so short a term of service, the newly married couple dispensed with a honeymoon. The aunt entered a home for indigent gentlewomen with an allowance of a hundred a year from her niece. George once again found himself in a spacious, well-run house.

During their brief married life, this oddly assorted couple seem to have been perfectly happy. The late Mr Callermere's friends were allowed to slip back into oblivion, because they showed a tendency to giggle whenever George absent-mindedly addressed his wife as 'Miss Callermere'.

His earnings of two pounds a week may have seemed insignificant beside his wife's unearned income. But in fact it was the basis of their married happiness. Every Saturday he handed her the whole of his wages. She would retain twenty-five shillings, because they both consi-dered it essential to his self-respect that he should pay the cost of his food. She handed him back fifteen shillings for pocket-money. She read the papers and formed his opinions for him. She seemed to allow him little of what most men would regard as pleasure, but George had no complaint on this score.

Spring passed into summer and nearly everybody had forgotten the murder of Ethel Prince in a tenement in Ladbroke Grove. It is probably true to say that, in any real sense of the word, George Muncey had forgotten it too. He had read very little and did not know that murderers were popularly supposed to be haunted by their crime and to start guiltily at every chance mention of it.

He received no reaction whatever when his employer said to him one morning:

'There's this job-line of rubber trumpets. I took half a gross. We'll mark them at one-and-a-penny. Put one on your counter with the rubber teats and try them on women with babies.'

George took one of the rubber trumpets from the cardboard case containing the half gross. It had red and blue wool wound about the stem. He put it next to the rubber teats and forgot about it.

8

Wilkins, the other assistant, held his pharmaceutical certificate, but he was not stand-offish on that account. One day, to beguile the boredom of the slack hour after lunch, he picked up the rubber trumpet and blew it.

Instantly George was sitting in the train with Ethel, telling her 'not to make that noise'. When Wilkins put the trumpet down, George found himself noticing the trumpet and thought the red and blue wool very hideous. He picked it up – Ethel's had felt just like that when he had thrown it out of the window.

Now it cannot for one moment be held that George felt anything in the nature of remorse. The truth was that the rubber trumpet, by reminding him so vividly of Ethel, had stirred up dormant forces in his nature. Ethel had been very comely and jolly and playful when one was in the mood for it – as one often was, in spite of everything.

The trumpet, in short, produced little more than a sense of bewilderment. Why could not things have gone on as they began ? It was only as a wife that Ethel was utterly intolerable, because she had no sense of order and did not really look after a chap. Now that he was married to Miss Callermere, if only Ethel had been available on, say, Wednesday evenings and alternate Sundays, life would have been full at once of colour and comfort. . . . He tried to sell the trumpet to a lady with a little girl and a probable baby at home, but without success.

On the next day he went as far as admitting to himself that the trumpet had got on his nerves. Between a quarter to one and a quarter past, when Wilkins was out to lunch, he picked up the trumpet and blew it. And just before closing-time he blew it again, when Wilkins was there.

George was not subtle enough to humbug himself. The trumpet stirred longings that were better suppressed. So the next day he wrote out a bill for one-and-a-penny, put one-and-a-penny of his pocket money into the cash register and stuffed the trumpet into his coat pocket. Before supper that night he put it in the hot-water furnace.

'There's a terrible smell in the house. What did you put in the furnace, George?

'Nothing.'

'Tell me the truth, dear.'

'A rubber trumpet stuck on my counter. Fair got on my nerves, it did. I paid the one-and-a-penny and I burnt it.'

'That was very silly, wasn't it? It'll make you short in your pocket money. And in the circumstances I don't feel inclined to make it up for you.'

That would be all right, George assured her, and inwardly thought how lucky he was to have such a wife. She could keep a fellow steady and pull him up when he went one over the odds.

Three days later his employer looked through the stock.

'I see that rubber trumpet has gone. Put up another. It may be a good line.'

And so the whole business began over again. George, it will be observed, for all his unimaginativeness, was a spiritually economical man. His happy contentment with his wife would, he knew, be jeopardised if he allowed himself to be reminded of that other disorderly, fascinating side of life that had been presided over by Ethel.

There were six dozen of the rubber trumpets, minus the one burnt at home, and his employer would expect one-and-a-penny for each of them. Thirteen shillings a dozen. But the dozens themselves were thirteen, which complicated the calculation, but in the end he got the sum right. He made sure of this by doing it backwards and 'proving' it. He still had twenty-three pounds left out of the eight hundred.

Mrs Muncey had a rather nice crocodile dressing-case which she had bought for herself and quite falsely described as a 'gift of the bridegroom to the bride'.

On the next day George borrowed the crocodile dressing-case on the plea that he wished to bring some goods from the shop home for

Christmas. He brought it into the shop on the plea that it contained his dinner jacket and that he intended to change at the house of a friend without going home that night. As he was known to have married 'an heiress' neither Wilkins nor his employer was particularly surprised that he should possess a dinner jacket and a crocodile dressing-case in which to carry it about.

At a quarter to one, when he was again alone in the shop, he crammed half a gross (less one) of rubber trumpets into the crocodile dressing-case. When his employer came back from lunch he said :

'I've got rid of all those rubber trumpets, Mr Arrowsmith. An old boy came in, said he was to do with an orphanage, and I talked him into buying the lot.'

Mr Arrowsmith was greatly astonished.

'Bought the lot, did you say ? Didn't he ask for a discount ?'

'No, Mr Arrowsmith. I think he was a bit loopy myself.'

Mr Arrowsmith looked very hard at George and then at the cash register. Six thirteens, less one, at one-and-a-penny – four pounds, three and fivepence. It was certainly a very funny thing. But then, the freak customer appears from time to time and at the end of the day Mr Arrowsmith had got over his surprise.

Journeying from Walham to Battersea, one goes on the Underground to Victoria Station, and continues the journey on the main line. From the fact that George Muncey that evening took the crocodile case to Victoria Station, it has been argued that he intended to take the rubber trumpets home and perhaps bury them in the garden or deal with them in some other way. But this ignores the fact that he told his wife he intended to bring home some goods for Christmas.

The point is of minor importance, because the dressing-case never reached home with him that night. At the top of the steps leading from the Underground it was snatched from him.

George's first sensation, on realising that he had been robbed, was one of relief. The rubber trumpets, he had already found, could not be burnt ; they would certainly have been a very great nuisance to him. The case, he knew, cost fifteen guineas, and there was still enough left of the twenty-three pounds to buy a new one on the following day.

9

At closing-time the next day, while George and Wilkins were tidying-up, Mr Arrowsmith was reading the evening paper.

'Here, Muncey ! Listen to this. "Jake Mendel, thirty-seven, of no fixed abode, was charged before Mr Ramsden this morning with the theft of a crocodile dressing-case from the precincts of Victoria Station. Mr Ramsden asked the police what was inside the bag. 'A number of toy trumpets, your worship, made of rubber. There were seventy-seven of 'em all told.' Mr Ramsden : 'Seventy-seven rubber trumpets ! Well, *now* there really is no reason why the police should not have their own band' (Laughter)." ' Mr Arrowsmith laughed too and then : 'Muncey, that looks like your lunatic.'

'Yes, Mr Arrowsmith,' said George indifferently, then went contentedly home to receive his wife's expostulations about a new crocodile dressing-case which had been delivered during the afternoon. It was not quite the same to look at, because the original one had been made to order. But it had been bought at the same shop and the manager had obliged George by charging the same price for it.

In the meantime, the police were relying on the newspaper paragraph to produce the owner of the crocodile case. When he failed to materialise on the following morning they looked at the name of the manufacturer and took the case round to him.

The manufacturer informed them that he had made that case the previous Spring to the order of a Miss Callermere - that the lady had since married and that, only the previous day, her husband, Mr Muncey, had ordered an exactly similar one but had accepted a substitute from stock.

'Ring up George Muncey and ask him to come up and identify the case - and take away these india-rubber trumpets !' ordered the superintendent.

Mrs Muncey answered the telephone and from her they obtained George's business address.

'A chemist's assistant !' said the superintendent. 'Seems to me rather rum. Those trumpets may be his employer's stock. And he may have been pinching 'em. Don't ring him up - go down. And find out if the employer has anything to say about the stock. See him before you see Muncey.'

At Walham the sergeant was taken into the·dispensary where he promptly enquired whether Mr Arrowsmith had missed seventy-seven rubber trumpets from his stock.

'I haven't missed them - but I sold them the day before yesterday - seventy-seven, that's right ! Or rather, my assistant, George Muncey, did. Here, Muncey !' And as George appeared :

'You sold the rest of the stock of those rubber trumpets to a gentleman who said he was connected with an orphanage – the day before yesterday it was – didn't you ?'

'Yes, Mr Arrowsmith,' said George.

'Bought the lot without asking for a discount,' said Mr Arrowsmith proudly. 'Four pounds, three shillings and fivepence. I could tell you of another case that happened years ago when a man came into this very shop and –'

The sergeant felt his head whirling a little. The assistant had sold seventy-seven rubber trumpets to an eccentric gentleman. The goods had been duly paid for and taken away – and the goods were subsequently found in the assistant's wife's dressing-case.

'Did you happen to have a crocodile dressing-case stolen from you at Victoria Station the day before yesterday, Mr Muncey ?' asked the sergeant.

George was in a quandary. If he admitted that the crocodile case was his wife's – he would admit to Mr Arrowsmith that he had been lying when he had said that he had cleverly sold the whole of the seventy-seven rubber trumpets without even having to give away a discount. So :

'No,' said George.

'Ah, I thought not ! There's a mistake somewhere. I expect it's that manufacturer put us wrong. Sorry to have troubled you, gentlemen ! Good morning !'

'Wait a minute,' said Mr Arrowsmith. 'You *did* have a crocodile dressing-case here that day, Muncey, with your evening clothes in it. And you *do* go home by Victoria. But what is that about the trumpets, Sergeant ? They couldn't have been in Mr Muncey's case if he sold them over the counter.'

'I don't know what they've got hold of, Mr Arrowsmith, and that's a fact,' said George. 'I think I'm wanted in the shop.'

George was troubled, so he got leave to go home early. He told his wife how he had lied to the police, and confessed to her about the trumpets. Soon she had made him tell her the real reason for his dislike of the trumpets. The result was that when the police brought her the original case she flatly denied that it was hers.

In law, there was no means by which the ownership of the case could be foisted upon the Munceys against their will. Pending the trial of Jake Mendel, the bag-snatcher, the crocodile case, with its seventy-seven rubber trumpets, was deposited with the Department of Dead Ends.

A few feet above it on a shelf stood the identical trumpet which George Muncey had thrown out of the window on the three-fifteen, non-stop Southend to Fenchurch Street, some seven months ago.

The Department took one of the trumpets from the bag and set it beside the trumpet on the shelf. There was no logical connection between them whatever. The Department simply guessed that there might be a connection.

They tried to connect Walham with Southend and drew blank. They traced the history of the seventy-seven Walham trumpets and found it simple enough until the moment when George Muncey put them in the crocodile case.

They went back to the Southend trumpet and read in their files that it had not been bought by the man with the baby but by a young woman.

Then they tried a cross-reference to young women and Southend. They found that dead end, the Ethel Fairbrass murder. They found : *'My daughter was married to Prince at the Henrietta Street registrar's office on 16 November 1907. He took her straight away for a honeymoon at Southend, where they stayed a fortnight.'*

Fourteen days from 16 November meant 30 November, the day the rubber trumpet was found on the line.

One rubber trumpet is dropped on railway line by (possibly) a young woman. The young woman is subsequently murdered (but not with a rubber trumpet). A young man behaves in an eccentric way with seventy-seven rubber trumpets more than six months later.

The connection was wholly illogical. But the Department specialised in illogical connections. It communicated its wild guess – in the form of a guarded minute – to Detective-Inspector Rason.

Rason went down to Banbury and brought the old Fairbrass couple to Walham.

He gave them five shillings and sent them to Arrowsmith's to buy a hot-water bottle.

R. Austin Freeman

THE MOABITE CIPHER

A LARGE AND MOTLEY CROWD lined the pavements of Oxford Street as Thorndyke and I made our way leisurely eastward. Floral decorations and drooping bunting announced one of those functions inaugurated from time to time by a benevolent Government for the entertainment of fashionable loungers and the relief of distressed pickpockets. For a Russian Grand Duke, who had torn himself away, amidst valedictory explosions, from a loving if too demonstrative people, was to pass anon on his way to the Guildhall ; and a British Prince, heroically indiscreet, was expected to occupy a seat in the ducal carriage.

Near Rathbone Place, Thorndyke halted and drew my attention to a smart-looking man who stood lounging in a doorway, cigarette in hand.

'Our old friend Inspector Badger,' said Thorndyke. 'He seems mightily interested in that gentleman in the light overcoat. How d'ye do, Badger ?' for, at this moment, the detective caught his eye and bowed. 'Who is your friend ?'

'That's what I want to know, sir,' replied the inspector. 'I've been shadowing him for the last half-hour, but I can't make him out, though I believe I've seen him somewhere. He don't look like a foreigner, but he has got something bulky in his pocket, so I must keep him in sight until the Duke is safely past. I wish,' he added gloomily, 'these beastly Russians would stop at home. They give us no end of trouble.'

'Are you expecting any – occurrences, then ?' asked Thorndyke.

'Bless you, sir,' exclaimed Badger, 'the whole route is lined with plainclothes men. You see, it is known that several desperate characters followed the Duke to England, and there are a good many exiles living here who would like to have a rap at him. Hallo ! What's he up to now ?'

The man in the light overcoat had suddenly caught the inspector's too-inquiring eye, and forthwith dived into the crowd at the edge of the pavement. In his haste he trod heavily on the foot of a big, rough-looking man, by whom he was in a moment hustled out into the road with such violence that he fell sprawling face downwards. It was an unlucky moment. A mounted constable was just then backing in upon the crowd, and before he could gather the meaning of the shout that arose from the bystanders, his horse had set down one hind-hoof firmly on the prostrate man's back.

The inspector signalled to a constable, who forthwith made a way for us through the crowd ; but even as we approached the injured man, he rose stiffly and looked round with a pale, vacant face.

'Are you hurt ?' Thorndyke asked gently, with an earnest look into the frightened, wondering eyes.

'No, sir,' was the reply ; 'only I feel queer - sinking - just here.'

He laid a trembling hand on his chest, and Thorndyke, still eyeing him anxiously, said in a low voice to the inspector : 'Cab or ambulance, as quickly as you can.'

A cab was led round from Newman Street, and the injured man put into it. Thorndyke, Badger, and I entered, and we drove off up Rathbone Place. As we proceeded, our patient's face grew more and more ashen, drawn, and anxious ; his breathing was shallow and uneven, and his teeth chattered slightly. The cab swung round into Goodge Street, and then - suddenly, in the twinkling of an eye - there came a change. The eyelids and jaw relaxed, the eyes became filmy, and the whole form subsided into the corner in a shrunken heap, with the strange, gelatinous limpness of a body that is dead as a whole, while its tissues are still alive.

'God save us ! The man's dead !' exclaimed the inspector in a shocked voice - for even policemen have their feelings. He sat staring at the corpse, as it nodded gently with the jolting of the cab, until we drew up inside the courtyard of the Middlesex Hospital, when he got out briskly, with suddenly renewed cheerfulness, to help the porter to place the body on the wheeled couch.

'We shall know who he is now, at any rate,' said he, as we followed the couch to the casualty-room. Thorndyke nodded unsympathetically. The medical instinct in him was for the moment stronger than the legal.

The house surgeon leaned over the couch, and made a rapid examination as he listened to our account of the accident. Then he straightened himself up and looked at Thorndyke.

'Internal haemorrhage, I expect,' said he. 'At any rate, he's dead, poor beggar ! - as dead as Nebuchadnezzar. Ah ! here comes a bobby ; it's his affair now.'

A sergeant came into the room, breathing quickly, and looked in surprise from the corpse to the inspector. But the latter, without loss of time, proceeded to turn out the dead man's pockets, commencing with the bulky object that had first attracted his attention ; which proved to be a brown paper parcel tied up with red tape.

'Pork-pie, begad !' he exclaimed with a crestfallen air as he cut the tape and opened the package. 'You had better go through his other pockets, Sergeant.'

The small heap of odds and ends that resulted from this process tended, with a single exception, to throw little light on the man's identity ; the exception being a letter, sealed, but not stamped, addressed in an exceedingly illiterate hand to Mr Adolf Schonberg, 213 Greek Street, Soho.

'He was going to leave it by hand, I expect,' observed the inspector, with a wistful glance at the sealed envelope. 'I think I'll take it round myself, and you had better come with me, Sergeant.'

He slipped the letter into his pocket, and, leaving the sergeant to take possession of the other effects, made his way out of the building.

'I suppose, Doctor,' he said as we crossed into Berners Street, 'you are not coming our way ? Don't want to see Mr Schonberg, h'm ?'

Thorndyke reflected for a moment. 'Well, it isn't very far, and we may as well see the end of the incident. Yes ; let us go together.'

No. 213 Greek Street was one of those houses that irresistibly suggest to the observer the idea of a church organ, either jamb of the doorway being adorned with a row of brass bell-handles corresponding to the stop-knobs.

These the sergeant examined with the air of an expert musician, and having, as it were, gauged the capacity of the instrument, selected the middle knob on the right-hand side and pulled it briskly ; whereupon a first-floor window was thrown up and a head protruded. But it afforded us a momentary glimpse only, for, having caught the sergeant's upturned eye, it retired with surprising precipitancy, and before we had time to speculate on the apparition, the street door was opened and a man emerged. He was about to close the door after him when the inspector interposed.

'Does Mr Adolf Schonberg live here ?'

The newcomer, a very typical Jew of the red-haired type, surveyed us thoughtfully through his gold-rimmed spectacles as he repeated the name.

'Schonberg – Schonberg ? Ah, yes ! I know. He lives on the third floor. I saw him go up a short time ago. Third floor back –' and indicating the open door with a wave of the hand, he raised his hat and passed into the street.

'I suppose we had better go up,' said the inspector, with a dubious glance at the row of bell-pulls. He accordingly started up the stairs, and we all followed in his wake.

There were two doors at the back on the third floor, but as the one was open, displaying an unoccupied bedroom, the inspector rapped smartly on the other. It flew open almost immediately, and a fierce-looking little man confronted us with a hostile stare.

'Well ?' said he.

'Mr Adolf Schonberg ?' inquired the inspector.

'Well ? What about him ?' snapped our new acquaintance.

'I wished to have a few words with him,' said Badger.

'Then what the deuce do you come banging at my door for ?' demanded the other.

'Why, doesn't he live here ?'

'No. First floor front,' replied our friend, preparing to close the door.

'Pardon me,' said Thorndyke, 'but what is Mr Schonberg like ? I mean –'

'Like ?' interrupted the resident. 'He's like a blooming Sheeny, with a carroty beard and gold giglamps !' and, having presented his impressionist sketch, he brought the interview to a definite close by slamming the door and turning the key.

With a wrathful exclamation, the inspector turned towards the stairs, down which the sergeant was already clattering in hot haste, and made his way back to the ground floor, followed, as before, by Thorndyke and me. On the doorstep we found the sergeant breathlessly interrogating a smartly dressed youth, whom I had seen alight from a hansom as we entered the house, and who now stood with a notebook tucked under his arm, sharpening a pencil with deliberate care.

'Mr James saw him come out, sir,' said the sergeant. 'He turned up towards the Square.'

'Did he seem to hurry ?' asked the inspector.

'Rather,' replied the reporter. 'As soon as you were inside he went off like a lamplighter. You won't catch him now.'

'We don't want to catch him,' the detective rejoined gruffly ; then, backing out of earshot of the eager pressman, he said in a lower tone : 'That was Mr Schonberg beyond a doubt, and it is clear that he has some reason for making himself scarce ; so I shall consider myself justified in opening that note.'

He suited the action to the word, and, having cut the envelope open with official neatness, drew out the enclosure.

'My hat !' he exclaimed, as his eye fell upon the contents. 'What in creation is this ? It isn't shorthand, but what the deuce is it ?'

He handed the document to Thorndyke, who, having held it up to the light and felt the paper critically, proceeded to examine it with keen interest. It consisted of a single half-sheet of thin notepaper, both sides of which were covered with strange, crabbed characters, written with a brownish-black ink in continuous lines, without any spaces to indicate the divisions into words ; and, but for the modern material which bore the writing, it might have been a portion of some ancient manuscript or forgotten codex.

'What do you make of it, Doctor ?' inquired the inspector anxiously, after a pause, during which Thorndyke had scrutinized the strange writing with knitted brows.

'Not a great deal,' replied Thorndyke. 'The character is the Moabite or Phoenician – primitive Semitic, in fact – and reads from right to left. The language I take to be Hebrew. At any rate, I can find no Greek words, and I see here a group of letters which *may* form one of the few Hebrew words that I know – the word badim, "lies". But you had better get it deciphered by an expert.'

'If it is Hebrew,' said Badger, 'we can manage it all right. There are plenty of Jews at our disposal.'

'You had much better take the paper to the British Museum,' said Thorndyke, 'and submit it to the keeper of the Phoenician antiquities for decipherment.'

Inspector Badger smiled a foxy smile as he deposited the paper in his pocket-book. 'We'll see what we can make of it ourselves first,' he said ; 'but many thanks for your advice, all the same, Doctor. No, Mr James, I can't give you any information just at present ; you had better apply at the hospital.'

'I suspect,' said Thorndyke, as we took our way homewards, 'that Mr James has collected enough material for his purpose already. He must have followed us from the hospital, and I have no doubt that he has his report, with "full details", mentally arranged at this moment. And I am not sure that he didn't get a peep at the mysterious paper, in spite of the inspector's precautions.'

'By the way,' I said, 'what do you make of the document ?'

'A cipher, most probably,' he replied. 'It is written in the primitive Semitic alphabet, which, as you know, is practically identical with primitive Greek. It is written from right to left, like the Phoenician, Hebrew, and Moabite, as well as the earliest Greek, inscriptions. The paper is common cream-laid notepaper, and the ink is ordinary indelible Chinese ink, such as is used by draughtsmen. Those are the facts, and without further study of the document itself, they don't carry us very far.'

'Why do you think it is a cipher rather than a document in straightforward Hebrew ?'

'Because it is obviously a secret message of some kind. Now, every educated Jew knows more or less Hebrew, and, although he is able to read and write only the modern square Hebrew character, it is easy to transpose one alphabet into another that the mere language would afford no security. Therefore, I expect that, when the experts translate this document, the translation or transliteration will be a mere farrago of unintelligible nonsense. But we shall see, and meanwhile the facts that we have offer several interesting suggestions which are well worth consideration.'

'As, for instance – ?'

'Now, my dear Jervis,' said Thorndyke, shaking an admonitory forefinger at me, 'don't, I pray you, give way to mental indolence. You have these few facts that I have mentioned. Consider them separately and collectively, and in their relation to the circumstances. Don't attempt to suck my brain when you have an excellent brain of your own to suck.'

On the following morning the papers fully justified my colleague's opinion of Mr James. All the events which had occurred, as well as a number that had not, were given in the fullest and most vivid detail, a lengthy reference being made to the paper 'found on the person of the dead anarchist', and 'written in a private shorthand or cryptogram'.

The report concluded with the gratifying – though untrue – statement that 'in this intricate and important case the police have wisely secured the assistance of Dr John Thorndyke, to whose acute intellect and vast experience the portentous cryptogram will doubtless soon deliver up its secret'.

'Very flattering,' laughed Thorndyke, to whom I read the extract on his return from the hospital, 'but a little awkward if it should induce our friends to deposit a few trifling mementoes in the form of nitro-compounds on our main staircase or in the cellars. By the way, I met Superintendent Miller on London Bridge. The "cryptogram", as Mr James calls it, has set Scotland Yard in a mighty ferment.'

'Naturally. What have they done in the matter ?'

'They adopted my suggestion, after all, finding that they could make nothing of it themselves, and took it to the British Museum. The Museum people referred them to Professor Poppelbaum, the great palaeographer, to whom they accordingly submitted it.'

'Did he express any opinion about it ?'

'Yes, provisionally. After a brief examination, he found it to consist of

a number of Hebrew words sandwiched between apparently meaningless groups of letters. He furnished the superintendent off-hand with a
translation of the words, and Miller forthwith struck off a number of
hectograph copies of it, which he has distributed among the senior
officials of his department ; so that at present' - here Thorndyke gave
vent to a soft chuckle - 'Scotland Yard is engaged in a sort of missing
word - or, rather, missing sense - competition. Miller invited me to join
in the sport, and to that end presented me with one of the hectograph
copies on which to exercise my wits, together with a photograph of the
document.'

'And shall you ?' I asked.

'Not I,' he replied, laughing. 'In the first place I have not been formally consulted, and consequently am a passive, though interested spectator. In the second place, I have a theory of my own which I shall test if
the occasion arises. But if you would like to take part in the competition,
I am authorized to show the photograph and the translation. I will pass
them on to you, and I wish you joy of them.'

He handed me the photograph and a sheet of paper that he had just
taken from his pocket-book, and watched me with grim amusement as I
read out the first few lines.

'Woe, city, lies, robbery, prey, noise, whip, rattling, wheel, horse,
chariot, day, darkness, gloominess, clouds, darkness, morning, mountain, people, strong, fire, them, flame.'

'It doesn't look very promising at first sight,' I remarked. 'What is the
Professor's theory ?'

'His theory - provisionally, of course - is that the words form the
message, and the groups of letters represent mere filled-up spaces between the words.'

'But surely,' I protested, 'that would be a very transparent device.'

Thorndyke laughed. 'There is a childlike simplicity about it,' said he,
'that is highly attractive - but discouraging. It is much more probable
that the words are dummies, and that the letters contain the message. Or,
again, the solution may lie in an entirely different direction. But listen !
Is that cab coming here ?'

It was. It drew up opposite our chambers, and a few moments later a
brisk step ascending the stairs heralded a smart rat-tat at our door.
Flinging open the latter, I found myself confronted by a well-dressed
stranger, who, after a quick glance at me, peered inquisitively over my
shoulder into the room.

'I am relieved, Dr Jervis,' said he, 'to find you and Dr Thorndyke at
home, as I have come on somewhat urgent professional business. My

The Cipher.

name,' he continued, entering in response to my invitation, 'is Barton, but you don't know me, though I know you both by sight. I have come to ask you if one of you – or, better still, both – could come tonight and see my brother.'

'That', said Thorndyke, 'depends on the circumstances and on the whereabouts of your brother.'

'The circumstances', said Mr Barton, 'are, in my opinion, highly suspicious, and I will place them before you – of course, in strict confidence.'

Thorndyke nodded and indicated a chair.

'My brother,' continued Mr Barton, taking the proffered seat, 'has recently married for the second time. His age is fifty-five, and that of his wife twenty-six, and I may say that the marriage has been – well, by no means a success. Now, within the last fortnight, my brother has been attacked by a mysterious and extremely painful infection of the stomach, to which his doctor seems unable to give a name. It has resisted all treatment hitherto. Day by day the pain and distress increase, and I feel that, unless something decisive is done, the end cannot be far off.'

'Is the pain worse after taking food ?' inquired Thorndyke.

'That's just it !' exclaimed our visitor. 'I see what is in your mind, and it has been in mine, too ; so much so that I have tried repeatedly to obtain samples of the food that he is taking. And this morning I succeeded.' Here he took from his pocket a wide-mouthed bottle, which, disengaging from its paper wrapping, he laid on the table. 'When I called, he was taking his breakfast of arrowroot, which he complained had a gritty taste, supposed by his wife to be due to the sugar. Now I had provided myself with this bottle, and during the absence of his wife, I managed unobserved to convey a portion of the arrowroot that he had left into it, and I should be greatly obliged if you would examine it, and tell me if this arrowroot contains anything that it should not.'

He pushed the bottle across to Thorndyke, who carried it to the window, and, extracting a small quantity of the contents with a glass rod, examined the pasty mass with the aid of a lens ; then, lifting the bell-glass cover from the microscope, which stood on its table by the window, he smeared a small quantity of the suspected matter on to a glass slip, and placed it on the stage of the instrument.

'I observe a number of crystalline particles in this,' he said, after a brief inspection, 'which have the appearance of arsenous acid.'

'Ah !' ejaculated Mr Barton, 'just what I feared. But are you certain ?'

'No,' replied Thorndyke ; 'but the matter is easily tested.'

He pressed the button of the bell that communicated with the laboratory, a summons that brought the laboratory assistant from his lair with characteristic promptitude.

'Will you please prepare a Marsh's apparatus, Polton,' said Thorndyke.

'I have a couple ready, sir,' replied Polton.

'Then pour the acid into one and bring it to me, with a tile.'

As his familiar vanished silently, Thorndyke turned to Mr Barton.

'Supposing we find arsenic in this arrowroot, as we probably shall, what do you want us to do ?'

'I want you to come and see my brother,' replied our client.

'Why not take a note from me to his doctor ?'

'No, no ; I want you to come – I should like you both to come – and put a stop at once to this dreadful business. Consider ! It's a matter of life and death. You won't refuse ! I beg you not to refuse me your help in these terrible circumstances.'

'Well,' said Thorndyke, as his assistant reappeared, 'let us first see what the test has to tell us.'

Polton advanced to the table, on which he deposited a small flask, the contents of which were in a state of brisk effervescence, a bottle labelled 'calcium hypochloride', and a white porcelain tile. The flask was fitted with a safety-funnel and a glass tube drawn out to a fine jet, to which Polton cautiously applied a lighted match. Instantly there sprang from the jet a tiny, pale violet flame. Thorndyke now took the tile, and held it in the flame for a few seconds, when the appearance of the surface remained unchanged save for a small circle of condensed moisture. His next proceeding was to thin the arrowroot with distilled water until it was quite fluid, and then pour a small quantity into the funnel. It ran slowly down the tube into the flask, with the bubbling contents of which it became speedily mixed. Almost immediately a change began to appear in the character of the flame, which from a pale violet turned gradually to a sickly blue, while above it hung a faint cloud of white smoke. Once more Thorndyke held the tile above the jet, but this time no sooner had the pallid flame touched the cold surface of the porcelain, than there appeared on the latter a glistening black stain.

'That is pretty conclusive,' observed Thorndyke, lifting the stopper out of the reagent bottle, 'but we will apply the final test.' He dropped a few drops of the hypochloride solution on to the tile, and immediately the black stain faded away and vanished. 'We can now answer your question, Mr Barton,' said he, replacing the stopper as he turned to our client. 'The specimen that you brought us certainly contains arsenic, and in very considerable quantities.'

'Then,' exclaimed Mr Barton, starting from his chair, 'you will come and help me to rescue my brother from this dreadful peril. Don't refuse me, Dr Thorndyke, for mercy's sake, don't refuse.'

Thorndyke reflected for a moment.

'Before we decide,' said he, 'we must see what engagements we have.'

With a quick, significant glance at me, he walked into the office, whither I followed in some bewilderment, for I knew that we had no engagements for the evening.

'Now, Jervis,' said Thorndyke, as he closed the office door, 'what are we to do ?'

'We must go, I suppose,' I replied. 'It seems a pretty urgent case.'

'It does,' he agreed. 'Of course, he may be telling the truth, after all.'

'You don't think he is, then ?'

'No. It is a plausible tale, but there is too much arsenic in that arrowroot. Still, I think I ought to go. It is an ordinary professional risk. But there is no reason why you should put your head into the noose.'

'Thank you,' said I, somewhat huffily. 'I don't see what risk there is, but if any exists I claim the right to share it.'

'Very well,' he answered with a smile, 'we will both go. I think we can take care of ourselves.'

He re-entered the sitting-room, and announced his decision to Mr Barton, whose relief and gratitude were quite pathetic.

'But,' said Thorndyke, 'you have not yet told us where your brother lives.'

'Rexford,' was the reply '– Rexford, in Essex. It is an out-of-the-way place, but if we catch the seven-fifteen train from Liverpool Street, we shall be there in an hour and a half.'

'And as to the return ? You know the trains, I suppose ?'

'Oh yes,' replied our client ; 'I will see that you don't miss your train back.'

'Then I will be with you in a minute,' said Thorndyke ; and taking the still-bubbling flask, he retired to the laboratory, whence he returned in a few minutes carrying his hat and overcoat.

The cab which had brought our client was still waiting, and we were soon rattling through the streets towards the station, where we arrived in time to furnish ourselves with dinner-baskets and select our compartment at leisure.

During the early part of the journey our companion was in excellent spirits. He despatched the cold fowl from the basket and quaffed the rather indifferent claret with as much relish as if he had not had a single relation in the world, and after dinner he became genial to the verge of hilarity. But, as time went on, there crept into his manner a certain anxious restlessness. He became silent and preoccupied, and several times furtively consulted his watch.

'The train is confoundedly late !' he exclaimed irritably. 'Seven minutes behind time already !'

'A few minutes more or less are not of much consequence,' said Thorndyke.

'No of course not ; but still – Ah, thank heaven, here we are !'

He thrust his head out of the off-side window, and gazed eagerly down the line ; then, leaping to his feet, he bustled out on to the platform while the train was still moving. Even as we alighted a warning bell rang furiously on the up-platform, and, as Mr Barton hurried us through the empty booking-office to the outside of the station, the rumble of the approaching train could be heard above the noise made by our own train moving off.

'My carriage doesn't seem to have arrived yet,' exclaimed Mr Barton, looking anxiously up the station approach. 'If you will wait here a moment, I will go and make inquiries.'

He darted back into the booking-hall and through it on to the platform, just as the up-train roared into the station. Thorndyke followed him with quick but stealthy steps, and peering out of the booking-office door, watched his proceedings ; then he turned and beckoned to me.

'There he goes,' said he, pointing to an iron foot-bridge that spanned the line ; and, as I looked, I saw, clearly defined against the dim night sky, a flying figure racing towards the 'up' side.

It was hardly two-thirds across when the guard's whistle sang out its shrill warning.

'Quick, Jervis,' exclaimed Thorndyke ; 'she's off !'

He leaped onto the line, whither I followed instantly, and, crossing the rails, we clambered up together on to the foot-board opposite an empty first-class compartment. Thorndyke's magazine knife, containing, among other implements, a railway-key, was already in his hand. The door was speedily unlocked, and, as we entered, Thorndyke ran through and looked out on to the platform.

'Just in time !' he exclaimed. 'He is in one of the forward compartments !'

He relocked the door, and, seating himself, proceeded to fill his pipe.

'And now,' said I, as the train moved out of the station, 'perhaps you will explain this little comedy.'

'With pleasure,' he replied, 'if it needs any explanation. But you can hardly have forgotten Mr James's flattering remarks in his report of the Greek Street incident, clearly giving the impression that the mysterious document was in my possession. When I read that, I knew I must look out for some attempt to recover it, though I hardly expected such promptness. Still, when Mr Barton called without credentials or appointment, I viewed him with some suspicion. That suspicion deepened when he wanted us both to come. It deepened further when I found an impossible quantity of arsenic in his sample, and it gave place to certainty when, having allowed him to select the trains by which we were to travel, I went up to the laboratory and examined the timetable ; for I then found that the last train for London left Rexford ten minutes after we were due to arrive. Obviously this was a plan to get us both safely out of the way while he and some of his friends ransacked our chambers for the missing documents.'

'I see ; and that accounts for his extraordinary anxiety at the lateness of the train. But why did you come, if you knew it was a "plant" ?'

'My dear fellow,' said Thorndyke, 'I never miss an interesting experience if I can help it. There are possibilities in this, too, don't you see ?'

'But supposing his friends have broken into our chambers already ?'

'That contingency has been provided for ; but I think they will wait for Mr Barton - and us.'

Our train, being the last one up, stopped at every station, and crawled slothfully in the intervals, so that it was past eleven o'clock when we reached Liverpool Street. Here we got out cautiously, and, mingling with the crowd, followed the unconscious Barton up the platform, through the barrier, and out into the street. He seemed in no special hurry, for, after pausing to light a cigar, he set off at an easy pace up New Broad Street.

Thorndyke hailed a hansom, and, motioning me to enter, directed the cabman to drive to Clifford's Inn passage.

'Sit well back,' said he, as we rattled away up New Broad Street. 'We shall be passing our gay deceiver presently - in fact, there he is, a living, walking illustration of the folly of underrating the intelligence of one's adversary.'

At Clifford's Inn passage we dismissed the cab, and, retiring into the shadow of the dark, narrow alley, kept an eye on the gate of Inner Temple Lane. In about twenty minutes we observed our friend approaching on the south side of Fleet Street. He halted at the gate, plied the knocker, and after a brief parley with the night-porter vanished through the wicket. We waited yet five minutes more, and then, having given him time to get clear of the entrance we crossed the road.

The porter looked at us with some surprise.

'There's a gentleman just gone down to your chambers, sir,' said he. 'He told me you were expecting him.'

'Quite right,' said Thorndyke, with a dry smile. 'I was. Good night.'

We slunk down the lane, past the church, and through the gloomy cloisters, giving a wide berth to all lamps and lighted entries, until, emerging into Paper Buildings, we crossed at the darkest part to King's Bench Walk, where Thorndyke made straight for the chambers of our friend Anstey, which were two doors above our own.

'Why are we coming here ?' I asked, as we ascended the stairs.

But the question needed no answer when we reached the landing, for, through the open door of our friend's chambers, I could see in the darkened room Anstey himself with two uniformed constables and a couple of plainclothes men.

'There has been no signal yet, sir,' said one of the latter, whom I recognised as a detective-sergeant of our division.

'No,' said Thorndyke, 'but the M C has arrived. He came in five minutes before us.'

'Then,' exclaimed Anstey, 'the hall will open shortly, ladies and gents. The boards are waxed, the fiddlers are tuning up, and –'

'Not quite so loud, if you please, sir,' said the sergeant. 'I think there is somebody coming up Crown Office Row.'

The ball had, in fact, opened. As we peered cautiously out of the open window, keeping well back in the darkened room, a stealthy figure crept out of the shadow, crossed the road, and stole noiselessly into the entry of Thorndyke's chambers. It was quickly followed by a second figure, and then by a third, in which I recognized our elusive friend.

'Now listen for the signal,' said Thorndyke. 'They won't waste time. Confound that clock !'

The soft-voiced bell of the Inner Temple clock, mingling with the harsher tones of St Dunstan's and the Law Courts, slowly tolled out the hour of midnight ; and as the last reverberations were dying away, some metallic object, apparently a coin, dropped with a sharp click on to the pavement under our window.

At the sound the watchers simultaneously sprang to their feet.

'You two go first,' said the sergeant, addressing the uniformed men, who thereupon stole noiselessly, in their rubber-soled boots, down the stone stairs and along the pavement. The rest of us followed, with less attention to silence, and as we ran up to Thorndyke's chambers, we were aware of quick but stealthy footsteps on the stairs above.

'They've been at work, you see,' whispered one of the constables, flashing his lantern on to the iron-bound outer door of our sitting-room, on which the marks of a large jemmy were plainly visible.

The sergeant nodded grimly, and, bidding the constables to remain on the landing, led the way upwards.

As we ascended, faint rustlings continued to be audible from above, and on the second-floor landing we met a man descending briskly, but without hurry, from the third. It was Mr Barton, and I could not but admire the composure with which he passed the two detectives. But suddenly his glance fell on Thorndyke, and his composure vanished. With a wild stare of incredulous horror, he halted as if petrified ; then he broke away and raced furiously down the stairs, and a moment later a muffled shout and the sound of a scuffle told us that he had received a check. On the next flight we met two more men, who, more hurried and less self-possessed, endeavoured to push past ; but the sergeant barred the way.

'Why, bless me !' exclaimed the latter, 'it's Moakey ; and isn't that Tom Harris ?'

'It's all right, sergeant,' said Moakey plaintively, striving to escape from the officer's grip. 'We've come to the wrong house, that's all.'

The sergeant smiled indulgently. 'I know,' he replied. 'But you're always coming to the wrong house, Moakey ; and now you're just coming along with me to the right house.'

He slipped his hand inside his captive's coat, and adroitly fished out a large, folding jemmy ; whereupon the discomforted burglar abandoned all further protest.

On our return to the first floor, we found Mr Barton sulkily awaiting us, handcuffed to one of the constables, and watched by Polton with pensive disapproval.

'I needn't trouble you tonight, Doctor,' said the sergeant, as he marshalled his little troop of captors and captives. 'You'll hear from us in the morning. Good night, sir.'

The melancholy procession moved off down the stairs, and we retired into our chambers with Anstey to smoke a last pipe.

'A capable man, that Barton,' observed Thorndyke – 'ready, plausible, and ingenious, but spoilt by prolonged contact with fools. I wonder if the police will perceive the significance of this little affair.'

'They will be more acute than I am if they do,' said I.

'Naturally,' interposed Anstey, who loved to 'cheek' his revered senior, 'because there isn't any. It's only Thorndyke's bounce. He is really in a deuce of a fog himself.'

However this may have been, the police were a good deal puzzled by the incident, for, on the following morning, we received a visit from no less a person than Superintendent Miller, of Scotland Yard.

'This is a queer business,' said he, coming to the point at once – 'this burglary, I mean. Why should they want to crack your place, right here in the Temple, too ? You've got nothing of value here, have you ? No "hard stuff ", as they call it, for instance ?'

'Not so much as a silver teaspoon,' replied Thorndyke, who had a conscientious objection to plate of all kinds.

'It's odd,' said the superintendent, 'deuced odd. When we got your note, we thought these anarchist idiots had mixed you up with the case – you saw the papers, I suppose – and wanted to go through your rooms for some reason. We thought we had our hands on the gang, instead of which we find a party of common crooks that we're sick of the sight of. I tell you, sir, it's annoying when you think you've hooked a salmon, to bring up a blooming eel.'

'It must be a great disappointment,' Thorndyke agreed, suppressing a smile.

'It is,' said the detective. 'Not but what we're glad enough to get these beggars, especially Halkett, or Barton, as he calls himself – a mighty slippery customer is Halkett, and mischievous, too – but we're not wanting any disappointments just now. There was that big jewel job in Piccadilly, Taplin and Horne's ; I don't mind telling you that we've not got the ghost of a clue. Then there's this anarchist affair. We're all in the dark there, too.'

'But what about the cipher ?' asked Thorndyke.

'Oh, hang the cipher !' exclaimed the detective irritably. 'This Professor Poppelbaum may be a very learned man, but he doesn't help *us* much. He says the document is in Hebrew, and he has translated it into Double Dutch. Just listen to this !' He dragged out of his pocket a bundle of papers, and, dabbing down a photograph of the document before Thorndyke, commenced to read the Professor's report.

' " The document is written in the characters of the well-known inscription of Mesha, King of Moab." (Who the devil's he ? Never heard of him. Well known, indeed !) "The language is Hebrew, and the words are separated by groups of letters, which are meaningless, and obviously introduced to mislead and confuse the reader. The words themselves are not strictly consecutive, but, by the interpolation of certain other words, a series of intelligible sentences is obtained, the meaning of which is not very clear, but is no doubt allegorical. The method of decipherment is shown in the accompanying tables, and the full rendering suggested on the enclosed sheet. It is to be noted that the writer of this document was apparently quite unacquainted with the Hebrew language, as appears from the absence of any grammatical construction." That's the Professor's report, Doctor, and here are the tables showing how he worked it out. It makes my head spin to look at 'em.'

He handed to Thorndyke a bundle of ruled sheets, which my colleague examined attentively for a while, and then passed on to me.

'This is very systematic and thorough,' said he. 'But now let us see the final result at which he arrives.'

'It may be all very systematic,' growled the superintendent, sorting out his papers, 'but I tell you, sir, it's all BOSH !' The latter word he jerked out viciously, as he slapped down on the table the final product of the Professor's labours. 'There,' he continued, 'that's what he calls the "full rendering", and I reckon it'll make your hair curl. It might be a message from Bedlam.'

Analysis of the cipher with transliteration into modern square Hebrew characters with a translation into English. N.B. The cipher reads from right to left.

	Space	Word	Space	Word	Space	Word
Moabite	ץ٦	ᴡჄჂᲔᲔჃ	ᲔᲦ	٩٤ο	٩Ⴔ	ᲦᲧჄᲔ
Hebrew		בְּדִים		עִיר		אוֹי
Translation		LIES		CITY		WOE
Moabite	ᘯʲ	ᲮᲧႳ	ᲮᲧᲧ	٩٩x	ᴴᲢ	ᲮᲧᲧ
Hebrew		קוֹל		טֶרֶף		גֵּוֹל
Translation		NOISE		PREY		ROBBERY
Moabite	ᴡ٩	ᲧᲧᲧᲔ	٩ᴵᴸ	ᴡᴏᲦ	ᲧᴏᲠ	ᵡᲧᴡ
Hebrew		אוֹפַן		רַעַשׁ		שׁוֹט
Translation		WHEEL		RATTLING		WHIP
Moabite	ᲧᲱ	ᲧᲧᲱ	ᲔᲧ	ᲮᲧᲧᲧᲧᲧ	ᲧᲔx	ᲶᲧᲶ
Hebrew		יוֹם		מֶרְכָּבָה		סוּס
Translation		DAY		CHARIOT		HORSE

The Professor's Analysis

Thorndyke took up the first sheet, and as he compared the constructed renderings with the literal translation, the ghost of a smile stole across his usually immovable countenance.

'The meaning is certainly a little obscure,' he observed, 'though the reconstruction is highly ingenious ; and, moreover, I think the Professor is probably right. That is to say, the words which he has supplied are probably the omitted parts of the passages from which the words of the cryptogram were taken. What do you think, Jervis ?'

He handed me the two papers, of which one gave the actual words of the cryptogram, and the other a suggested reconstruction, with omitted words supplied. The first read :

Woe	city	lies	robbery	prey
noise	whip	rattling	wheel	horse
chariot	day	darkness	gloominess	
cloud	darkness	morning	mountain	
people	strong	fire	them	flame

Turning to the second paper, I read out the suggested rendering :

' "Woe *to the bloody* city ! *It is full of* lies *and* robbery ; *the* prey *departeth not. The* noise *of a* whip, *and the noise of the* rattling *of the* wheels, *and of the prancing* horses, *and of the jumping* chariots.

' "*A* day *of* darkness *and of* gloominess, *a day of* clouds, *and of thick* darkness, *as the* morning *spread upon the* mountains, *a great* people *and a* strong.

' "*A* fire *devoureth before* them, *and behind them a* flame *burneth*." '

Here the first sheet ended, and, as I laid it down, Thorndyke looked at me inquiringly.

'There is a good deal of reconstruction in proportion to the original matter,' I objected. 'The Professor has "supplied" more than three-quarters of the final rendering.'

'Exactly,' burst in the superintendent ; 'it's all Professor and no cryptogram.'

'Still, I think the reading is correct,' said Thorndyke. 'As far as it goes, that is.'

'Good Lord !' exclaimed the dismayed detective. 'Do you mean to tell me, sir, that that balderdash is the real meaning of the thing ?'

'I don't say that,' replied Thorndyke. 'I say it is correct as far as it goes ; but I doubt its being the solution of the cryptogram.'

'Have you been studying that photograph that I gave you ?' demanded Miller, with sudden eagerness.

'I have looked at it,' said Thorndyke evasively, 'but I should like to examine the original if you have it with you.'

'I have,' said the detective. 'Professor Poppelbaum sent it back with the solution. You can have a look at it, though I can't leave it with you without special authority.'

He drew the document from his pocket-book and handed it to Thorndyke, who took it over to the window and scrutinized it closely. From the window he drifted into the adjacent office, closing the door after him ; and presently the sound of a faint explosion told me that he had lighted the gas-fire.

'Of course,' said Miller, taking up the translation again, 'this gibberish is the sort of stuff you might expect from a parcel of crack-brained anarchists ; but it doesn't seem to mean anything.'

'Not to us,' I agreed ; 'but the phrases may have some prearranged significance. And then there are the letters between the words. It is possible that they may really form a cipher.'

'I suggested that to the Professor,' said Miller, 'but he wouldn't hear of it. He is sure they are only dummies.'

'I think he is probably mistaken, and so, I fancy, does my colleague. But we shall hear what he has to say presently.'

'Oh, I know what he will say,' growled Miller. 'He will put the thing under the microscope, and tell us who made the paper, and what the ink is composed of, and then we shall be just where we were.' The Superintendent was evidently deeply depressed.

We sat for some time pondering in silence on the vague sentences of the Professor's translation, until, at length, Thorndyke reappeared, holding the document in his hand. He laid it quietly on the table by the officer, and then inquired :

'Is this an official consultation ?'

'Certainly,' replied Miller. 'I was authorized to consult you respecting the translation, but nothing was said about the original. Still, if you want it for further study, I will get it for you.'

'No, thank you,' said Thorndyke. 'I have finished with it. My theory turned out to be correct.'

'Your theory ?' exclaimed the superintendent, eagerly. 'Do you mean to say - ?'

'And, as you are consulting me officially, I may as well give you this.'

He held out a sheet of paper, which the detective took from him and began to read.

'What is this ?' he asked, looking up at Thorndyke with a puzzled frown. 'Where did it come from ?'

'It is the solution of the cryptogram,' replied Thorndyke.

The detective re-read the contents of the paper, and, with the frown of perplexity deepening, once more gazed at my colleague.

'This is a joke, sir ; you are fooling me,' he said sulkily.

'Nothing of the kind,' answered Thorndyke. 'That is the genuine solution.'

'But it's impossible !' exclaimed Miller. 'Just look at it, Dr Jervis.'

I took the paper from his hand, and, as I glanced at it, I had no difficulty in understanding his surprise. It bore a short inscription in printed Roman capitals, thus :

THE PICKERDILLEY STUF IS UP THE CHIMBLY 416 WARDOUR STREET 2ND FLOUR BACK
IT WAS HID BECOS OF OLD MOAKEYS JOOD MOAKEY IS A BLITER

'Then that fellow wasn't an anarchist at all ?' I exclaimed.

'No,' said Miller. 'He was one of Moakey's gang. We suspected Moakey of being mixed up with that job, but we couldn't fix it on him. By Jove !' he added, slapping his thigh, 'if this is right, and I can lay my hands on the loot ! Can you lend me a bag, Doctor ? I'm off to Wardour Street this very moment.'

We furnished him with an empty suitcase, and, from the window, watched him making for Mitre Court at a smart double.

'I wonder if he will find the booty,' said Thorndyke. 'It depends on whether the hiding-place was known to more than one of the gang. Well, it has been a quaint case, and instructive, too. I suspect our friend Barton and the evasive Schonberg were the collaborators who produced that curiosity of literature.'

'May I ask how you deciphered the thing ?' I said. 'It didn't appear to take long.'

'It didn't. It was merely a matter of testing a hypothesis ; and you ought not to have to ask that question,' he added, with mock severity, 'seeing that you had what turns out to have been all the necessary facts, two days ago. But I will prepare a document and demonstrate to you tomorrow morning.'

'So Miller was successful in his quest,' said Thorndyke, as we smoked our morning pipes after breakfast. 'The "entire swag", as he calls it, was "up the chimbly", undisturbed.'

He handed me a note which had been left, with the empty suitcase, by a messenger, shortly before, and I was about to read it when an agitated knock was heard at our door. The visitor, whom I admitted, was a rather haggard and dishevelled elderly gentleman, who, as he entered, peered inquisitively through his concave spectacles from one of us to the other.

'Allow me to introduce myself, gentlemen,' said he. 'I am Professor Poppelbaum.'

Thorndyke bowed and offered a chair.

'I called yesterday afternoon,' our visitor continued, 'at Scotland Yard, where I heard of your remarkable decipherment and of the convincing proof of its correctness. Thereupon I borrowed the cryptogram, and have spent the entire night studying it, but I cannot connect your solution with any of the characters. I wonder if you would do me the great favour of enlightening me as to your method of decipherment, and so save me further sleepless nights ? You may rely on my discretion.'

'Have you the document with you ?' asked Thorndyke.

The Professor produced it from his pocket-book, and passed it to my colleague.

'You observe, Professor,' said the latter, 'that this is a laid paper, and has no water-mark ?'

'Yes, I noticed that.'

'And that the writing is in indelible Chinese ink ?'

'Yes, yes,' said the savant impatiently ; 'but it is the inscription that interests me, not the paper and ink.'

'Precisely,' said Thorndyke. 'Now, it was the ink that interested me when I caught a glimpse of the document three days ago. "Why," I asked myself, "should anyone use this troublesome medium" – for this appears to be stick ink – "when good writing ink is to be had ?" What advantages has Chinese ink over writing ink ? It has several advantages as a drawing ink, but for writing purposes it has only one : it is quite unaffected by wet. The obvious inference, then, was that this document was, for some reason, likely to be exposed to wet. But this inference instantly suggested another, which I was yesterday able to put to the test – thus.'

He filled a tumbler with water, and, rolling up the document, dropped it in. Immediately there began to appear on it a new set of characters of a curious grey colour. In a few seconds Thorndyke lifted out the wet paper, and held it up to the light, and now there was plainly visible an inscription in transparent lettering, like a very distinct water-mark. It was in printed Roman capitals, written across the other writing, and read :

'The Pickerdilley stuf is up the chimbly 416 Wardour Street 2nd flour back it was hid becos of old Moakeys jood Moakey is a bliter.'

The Professor regarded the inscription with profound disfavour.

'How do you suppose this was done ?' he asked gloomily.

'I will show you,' said Thorndyke. 'I have prepared a piece of paper to demonstrate the process to Dr Jervis. It is exceedingly simple.'

He fetched from the office a small plate of glass, and a photographic dish in which a piece of thin notepaper was soaking in water.

'This paper,' said Thorndyke, lifting it out and laying it on the glass, 'has been soaking all night, and is now quite pulpy.'

He spread a dry sheet of paper over the wet one, and on the former wrote heavily with a hard pencil, 'Moakey is a bliter.' On lifting the upper sheet, the writing was seen to be transferred in a deep grey to the wet paper, and when the latter was held up to the light the inscription stood out clear and transparent as if written with oil.

'When this dries,' said Thorndyke, 'the writing will completely disappear, but it will reappear whenever the paper is again wetted.'

The Professor nodded.

'Very ingenious,' said he '– a sort of artificial palimpsest, in fact. But I do not understand how that illiterate man could have written in the difficult Moabite script.'

'He did not,' said Thorndyke. 'The "cryptogram" was probably written by one of the leaders of the gang, who, no doubt, supplied copies to the other members to use instead of blank paper for secret communications. The object of the Moabite writing was evidently to divert attention from the paper itself, in case the communication fell into the wrong hands, and I must say it seems to have answered its purpose very well.'

The Professor started, stung by the sudden recollection of his labours.

'Yes,' he snorted ; 'but I am a scholar, sir, not a policeman. Every man to his trade.'

He snatched up his hat, and with a curt 'Good morning', flung out of the room in dudgeon.

Thorndyke laughed softly.

'Poor Professor !' he murmured. 'Our playful friend Barton has much to answer for.'

Emile Gaboriau

THE LITTLE OLD MAN OF BATIGNOLLES:
A Chapter of a Detective's Memoirs

J. B. Casimir Godeuil

SOME YEARS AGO a man dressed in black, and apparently in the prime of life, presented himself at the office of the popular Parisian newspaper, *Le Petit Journal,* bringing with him a manuscript of such exquisite penmanship that even Brard, the prince of caligraphic artists, would have deemed it worthy of his talent. 'I will call again in a fortnight,' said the stranger, 'to know what you think of my work.'

The manuscript, like many and many of its predecessors, was at once stored away in a box labelled, 'MS to be read,' without the editor, the reader, or any of the staff evincing the least curiosity concerning its contents. Time passed by, and its author failed to return ; but at last the reader was in duty bound compelled to glance through the box's contents, and one day, strange to relate, he burst into the office with a beaming face. 'I have just read something most extraordinary,' said he ; 'the manuscript which that strange-looking fellow in black left with us, and without joking it is really a clever performance.' Now the readers attached to publishing firms or newspaper offices are not as a rule enthusiastic beings : rather the reverse, for they spend their lives wading through pages and pages of trash, and penning the laconic mention, 'Declined with thanks' on the margin of amateur copy. Thus when the reader of the *Petit Journal* expressed such a high opinion of the manuscript in question a general expression of surprise escaped the various regular contributors who were present. But with unabated fervour he cut all controversy short by throwing the manuscript on the table, and exclaiming : 'You doubt me, gentlemen ? Well read it yourselves.'

This sufficed to kindle curiosity. One of the writers on the paper immediately put the MS in his pocket, and when by the end of the week it had made the round of the staff, there was but one opinion : 'The *Petit Journal* must publish it.'

At this point, however, an unforeseen difficulty arose. The manuscript bore no author's name. The man in black had merely left it with a card, on which was inscribed, 'J. B. Casimir Godeuil,' without any address. What was to be done ? Was the MS to be published anonymously ? That was scarcely practicable at an epoch when the French press laws required each printed line to be signed by a responsible person. Besides was it certain that M J. B. Casimir Godeuil was the author ? Might he not have presented the manuscript on a friend's behalf ? To decide this point the only course was to find him, and inquiries were forthwith instituted in all directions, but unfortunately without result. No one had seemingly ever heard of such a being as J. B. Casimir Godeuil.

Then it was, that all Paris was placarded with gigantic bills asking for information concerning M Godeuil's whereabouts. The walls of Lyons, Marseilles, and other large cities were similarly posted, and during a whole week folks asked themselves 'Who can this man Godeuil be ?' Several opined that he was some prodigal son, whose return to the parental roof was anxiously hoped for ; others suggested that he must be the lost heir to some princely fortune ; whilst others again surmised that he might be a dishonest cashier, who had absconded with the contents of his employer's strong box. But, in the meanwhile, the manager of the *Petit Journal* had attained his object. Scarcely were the first bills posted when M J. B. Casimir Godeuil hastened in person to the office of the paper and made all necessary arrangements for the publication of his narrative, *The Little Old Man of Batignolles,* which constituted, he said, the first part of his memoirs. He, moreover, promised to bring other fragments of his autobiography, but in this respect he failed to keep his word, and all subsequent efforts to find him again proved unsuccessful. The following narrative (complete in itself), is therefore his only published work, but with the view of throwing some light on the author's character and object we have decided to print the subjoined preface, written by himself, and which was to have served for the whole series of his memoirs.

PREFACE

A prisoner had just been brought before an investigating magistrate, and despite his denials, his stratagems and an alleged alibi it had been shown that he was guilty both of forgery and theft. Conquered by the evidence I had collected against him, he confessed his crimes, exclaiming : 'Ah ! If I had only known the true power of the police and how difficult it is to escape its search, I should have remained an honest man.'

These words inspired me with the idea of writing my memoirs. Was it not advisable that every one should be made acquainted with the true

state of affairs ? Would not my revelations have a beneficial effect ?
Might I not strip crime of the poetry of romance and shew it as it really
is : cowardly and ignoble, abject and repulsive ? Would it not be useful
to prove that the most wretched beings in the world, are the madmen
who declare war against society ? And that is what I propose doing. I will
prove that everyone has an immediate, positive, mathematical interest in
remaining honest – I will show that, with our social organisation, with
the railroad and the electric telegraph, impunity is virtually impossible.
Punishment may be deferred, but it always comes at last. And profiting
by what I write, many misguided beings may reflect before allowing
themselves to slide along the road of crime. Many, whom the faint
murmurings of conscience would have failed to influence, may be
arrested in their course by the voice of fear.

Need I speak of the nature of these memoirs ? They will describe the
struggles, efforts, defeats, and victories of the few devoted men to whom
the security of the Parisians is virtually entrusted. To cope with all the
criminals of a city, which, with its suburbs, numbers more than three
millions of inhabitants, there are but two hundred detectives at the
disposal of the Préfecture of Police. It is to them that I dedicate this
narrative.

1

When I was completing my studies, in hopes of one day becoming a
medical man – it was in the good old times when I was but three and
twenty – I lived in the Rue Monsieur-le-Prince, almost at the corner of
the Rue Racine. For thirty francs a month, service included, I rented a
furnished room, which would cost more than three times as much nowadays, a room of such vast proportions that I was really able to stretch out
my arms when putting on my coat, without having to open the window.
I rose early and I went home late ; for in the morning I had my hospital
to 'walk,' and at night-time the Café Leroy possessed a seductive attraction which I was powerless to resist. Thus, it happened, that with one
exception, the other dwellers in the house – mostly quiet people,
living either by trade or on their incomes – were scarcely known to me,
even by sight. The person I have excepted from the others was a man of
medium height, with a clean-shaven face, and commonplace features,
whom every one always deferentially called 'Monsieur' Méchinet.
The doorkeeper treated him with the most profound respect, and invariably took off his cap whenever he perceived him. M Méchinet lived

on the same floor as myself ; in fact his door was just opposite mine, and on several occasions we had encountered each other on the landing. As a matter of course, we bowed to one another, whenever this happened, but for some time our acquaintance was confined to these rudimentary tokens of civility. One night, however, M Méchinet knocked at my door to ask me to oblige him with a few lucifers ; another night I borrowed some tobacco from him, and one morning we happened to leave the house at the same time and walked together down the street exchanging the usual commonplace remarks about the weather. Such was the commencement of our connection.

Although I was neither inquisitive nor suspicious – a man is seldom so at three and twenty – I nevertheless liked to know what sort of people I had to deal with, and without prying into my neighbour's life I naturally asked myself : 'Who is he ? What is his profession ?' I knew that he was married, and, to all appearances, worshipped by his wife, a plump little body with fair hair and a smiling face ; and yet it seemed to me that he was a man of most irregular habits, for he would frequently leave the house before daybreak, and I often heard him come home during the small hours of the morning, after being out all night. Moreover, every now and then he would absent himself for weeks at a time – and I could not understand how pretty little Madame Méchinet could put up with such strange behaviour, and indeed show herself so loving towards a husband of such a roaming disposition. In my perplexity I bethought myself of the doorkeeper, who, under ordinary circumstances, was as garrulous as a magpie, and who, I conjectured, would readily give me the information I desired. But I made a great mistake ; for scarcely had I mentioned the name of Méchinet to him, than he sent me about my business in fine style, fiercely rolling his eyes and indignantly declaring that he was not in the habit of 'spying' on the tenants of the house. This unwonted reception on the doorkeeper's part so fanned my curiosity, that dismissing all restraint I began to watch my neighbour in earnest.

I soon made certain discoveries which seemed to me of a most ominous character. One day I saw him come home dressed in the latest fashion, with the ribbon of the Legion of Honour displayed in his button-hole, and a couple of mornings later I met him on the stairs wearing a dirty blouse and a ragged cap, which gave him a most villainous appearance. And this was not everything, for one afternoon, just as he was going out, I perceived his wife take leave of him on the landing and kiss him with passionate fondness, exclaiming : 'Take care, my dear, be prudent, think of your little wife at home.' 'Be prudent,' indeed ! Why was he to be prudent ? What did this all mean ? Was the wife the husband's accomplice in all these strange goings on ? After this incident I was fairly stupefied, but there was even yet more to come.

One night I was in bed, asleep and dreaming. Fancy had carried me back to the Café Leroy, which I had left a few hours previously, and I was apparently absorbed in watching a most interesting game of billiards. The ivory balls sped right and left over the green baize, now striking the bands, and now cannoning with wonderful precision and effect. One thing surprised me, that whenever they came into contact there was a loud report, and at last, indeed, there was such a constant succession of cannons and clashes that I fairly started and woke up. The problem was instantaneously explained to me. What I had taken for the clashing of the billiard balls was a loud and repeated rat-tat-tat outside my room. I immediately sprang out of bed to ascertain what was the matter, and, to my surprise, as soon as I had opened the door, who should rush in but my mysterious neighbour, Méchinet, with his clothes in tatters, his shirt-front torn apart, but a wisp of his necktie left him, his head bare, and, to complete the picture, his face besmeared with blood. 'Good heavens !' cried I, in affright, 'what has happened ?'

'Speak lower ! you might be heard,' rejoined my neighbour with an imperious wave of the hand. 'This wound of mine in the face may be nothing after all, but it smarts terribly, and I thought you might be able to dress it, as you are a medical student.'

Without another word I made him sit down, and examined the wound he spoke of. As he had surmised, it was not serious, although it bled profusely. In point of fact, the skin of his left cheek was grazed from ear to mouth, and at different points the flesh was bare. As soon as I had washed the cheek and dressed it, M Méchinet warmly tendered me his acknowledgments. 'Well, I've escaped without much harm after all,' said he. 'Many thanks, M Godeuil, I'm greatly obliged to you. Pray don't mention this . . . little accident . . . to any one. Forgive me for disturbing you, and now, goodnight !'

Goodnight, indeed ! As if I could sleep in peace after such an adventure. My mind was haunted with all manner of strange ideas. It was plain enough now that this man Méchinet must be a highway robber or a burglar, possibly a cut-throat, and, at all events, a villain of the deepest dye. However, he quietly called on me the next day, thanked me over again, and, to my surprise, wound up by inviting me to dinner. Such courteous behaviour was scarcely in keeping with the character I had assigned to him, and more puzzled than ever I decided to accept his invitation, hoping that it might lead to some explanation of the mystery. I was, indeed, all eyes and ears on entering my neighbour's lodgings ;

but, despite the most minute scrutiny and patient attention, I neither saw nor heard anything at all of a nature to enlighten me.

Still, it happened that after this dinner our acquaintance considerably improved. M Méchinet seemed anxious to cultivate my friendship. Every now and then he would invite me to take 'pot luck' with himself and his wife, and nearly every afternoon, during 'the hour of absinthe,' he would join me at the Café Leroy, where we habitually indulged in a game of dominoes pending dinner-time. One afternoon, in the month of July, between five and six o'clock, while we were thus engaged at the café, an ill-clad, suspicious-looking individual hurried in and, approaching my neighbour, whispered something, which I failed to master, in his ear. M Méchinet immediately sprang to his feet with a pale face. 'I'm coming!' said he. 'Run and tell them I'm coming ;' whereupon the messenger started off as fast as his legs could carry him. Then, turning to me and holding out his hand, my neighbour remarked : 'Please excuse me, M Godeuil, but duty before everything, you know ; I must leave now, but we will resume our game tomorrow.'

All aglow with curiosity, and particularly struck by his air of excitement, I could not conceal the vexation his abrupt departure caused me ; and still actuated by anxiety to penetrate the seeming mystery, I made so bold as to say that I felt sorry I was not to accompany him. 'Eh ?' he retorted ; 'well, after all, why not ? *Will* you come ? It may be interesting ?' I was too delighted and impatient to waste time in exchanging superfluous words, so that my only answer was to put on my hat and follow him out of the café.

2

In accompanying M Méchinet, I was certainly far from thinking that such a simple act would have a most decisive influence on my own after-life. 'Well, now, I shall know what this all means,' I murmured to myself, as puffed up with puerile satisfaction I trotted down the Rue Racine in my neighbour's wake. I use the word 'trotted' advisedly, for in truth I had great difficulty in keeping pace with my companion, who rushed on, pushing the passers-by out of his way with a strange air of authority, and making such rapid strides that one might have imagined his fortune depended on his legs.

Just as we reached the Place de l'Odéon, an empty cab drove by. 'Eh, cabman, stop !' cried M Méchinet, and opening one of the doors he bade me get into the vehicle. 'Drive as fast as you can to 39 Rue de Lécluse, at

Batignolles,' he added, speaking to the Jehu, and then with a bound he reached my side. The distance made the driver swear, but cutting his thin horse with a vigorous stroke of the whip he turned him in the right direction, and we rolled off, down towards the Seine.

'Ah ! so we are going to Batignolles,' said I, in my most winning manner – that is, with courtly deference and just an interrogative touch in my tone. But, to my disappointment, M Méchinet did not answer me, and indeed, I fancy that he did not hear my remark.

A strange change had come over his demeanour. He was not precisely excited, but his pursed lips and knitted brows showed that he was greatly preoccupied. His glance, lost in space, seemed to indicate that he was studying some mysterious, intricate problem. He had drawn a snuff-box from his pocket, and incessantly drew forth enormous pinches, which, after rolling between his forefinger and his thumb, he carried to his nose – without inhaling them, however. This was one of his little private manias which I had previously observed, and which greatly amused me. The worthy man held snuff in horror, and yet he was always provided with a huge, meretriciously adorned snuff-box, such as players use when enacting a farce upon the stage. If anything unforeseen happened to him, were it either agreeable or afflictive, he invariably drew this monster snuff-box from his pocket, and pretended to regale himself with a vast number of pinches. Later on, I learnt that the subterfuge formed part of a system he had invented with the view of concealing his impressions and diverting the attention of folks around him.

In the meanwhile, we were rolling on. The cab climbed the precipitous Rue de Clichy, crossed the outer boulevard, turned into the Rue de Lécluse, and drew up a short distance from the number that had been given to the driver. It was materially impossible to go any further, for the street was crammed with a compact crowd. In front of No. 39, two or three hundred persons were standing with extended necks, gaping mouths, and inquisitive eyes. Their curiosity was so keen that they utterly disregarded the authoritative injunctions of half a dozen sergents de ville who, as they passed to and fro, kept on repeating : 'Move on ! move on !'

Alighting from the vehicle, we approached the house, elbowing our way through the crowd, and we were but a few steps from the door of No. 39, when one of the sergents de ville roughly bade us draw back. My companion took in the man's measure from head to foot at a single glance, and drawing himself up to his full height, exclaimed :

'Don't you know me ? I am Méchinet, and this young man (pointing to myself) is with me.'

'Oh, pray excuse me, sir,' stammered the sergent de ville, saluting us with military precision. 'I did not recognise you – I was not aware – but please walk in.'

We crossed the threshold. In the hall a stalwart, middle-aged woman, with a face as red as a poppy, was perorating and gesticulating in the midst of a group of tenants belonging to the house. She was evidently the concierge or doorkeeper.

'Where is it ?' roughly asked M Méchinet, cutting her recital short.

'On the third floor, sir,' she replied ; 'on the third floor – the door on the right hand. Oh Lord ! what a misfortune ! In a house like ours ! And such a worthy man, too !'

I did not hear any more, for M Méchinet had already sprung towards the staircase, up which I followed him, climbing four stairs at a time, and with my heart palpitating as if I were about to lose my breath. On the third landing, the door on the right hand side was open. We went in, crossed an ante-room, a dining-room, and a parlour, and finally reached a bed-chamber of ample size. Were I to live a thousand years, I should never forget the sight that met my eyes. At this moment even, I can still picture in my mind every particular of the scene.

Two men were leaning against the mantelpiece in front of the door. One of them, whose frock-coat was begirded with a tricolour sash, was a commissary of police ; the other, an investigating magistrate. A young man, plainly the latter's clerk, was seated writing at a table on the left hand side ; while on the floor in the centre of the room, lay a lifeless body – the body of a little, white-haired, old man, who was stretched on his back, with extended arms, in the midst of a pool of black, coagulated blood.

In my terror, I remained rooted on the threshold – so overcome, indeed, that to avoid falling I had to lean for support against the framework of the door. And yet, like every man of my profession, I was already familiar with death. I was accustomed to all the sickening sights which are every-day occurrences in an hospital or a medical school, but then, this was the first time that I found myself face to face with crime. For it was evident that an atrocious crime had been committed.

Less impressed than myself, my neighbour entered the room with a firm step.

'Ah, it's you, Méchinet,' said the commissary of police. 'I am sorry I sent for you.'

'And why, pray ?' asked my neighbour.

'Because we shan't need to appeal to your skill. We know the culprit, I have given the necessary orders, and he must be arrested by now.'

Singularly enough, it looked as if this news sadly disappointed
M Méchinet. He drew out his snuff-box, pretended to take two or three
pinches, and exclaimed : 'Ah, you know the culprit !'

It was the investigating magistrate who replied : 'Yes, know him
certainly and positively,' said he. 'When the crime was accomplished the
murderer fled, believing that his victim had ceased to live. But Providence was watching. . . . The poor old man still breathed. Summoning
all his energy he dipped a finger in the blood that was flowing from his
wound, and there on the floor he traced his murderer's name, thus
handing him over to human justice. . . . However, look for yourself.'

On hearing this I immediately glanced at the floor, on one of the oak
boards of which the letters MONIS were traced in blood, in rough but
legible fashion. 'Well ?' asked M Méchinet, laconically.

'Well,' replied the commissary of police ; 'those letters form the first
two syllables of the name of Monistrol, which is that of the murdered
man's nephew - a nephew of whom he was very fond.'

'The d——l,' ejaculated my neighbour.

'I don't fancy,' resumed the investigating magistrate ; 'I don't fancy
that the scoundrel will attempt to deny his guilt. Those five letters are
terrible proof against him. And besides, he is the only man who could
benefit by such a cowardly crime. He is the sole heir of this poor old
fellow, who leaves, I am told, considerable wealth behind him.
Moreover, the murder was committed last night, and the only person
who visited the victim was his nephew Monistrol, who, according to the
concierge, arrived at nine o'clock, and did not leave till nearly midnight.'

'It's clear, then,' replied M Méchinet, 'as clear as daylight. That fellow
Monistrol is a perfect fool.' And, shrugging his shoulders, he asked :
'Did he steal anything - did he force open any article of furniture to
mislead one as to the motive of the crime ?'

'Up to the present,' replied the commissary, 'we have not noticed
anything out of order. As you say, the scoundrel is not particularly
ingenious. As soon as he is arrested, he will no doubt confess.' Thereupon he drew M Méchinet to the window, and spoke to him in a low
voice ; while the magistrate turned to give some orders to his clerk.

3

So far as M Méchinet was concerned, my curiosity was satisfied. I had
wished to know my enigmatical neighbour's profession, and now I knew
it. He was simply a detective. Thus, all the incidents of his seemingly

erratic life were explained – his frequent absence from home, his tardy return at night-time, his frequent change of costume, his sudden disappearances, his wife's fears and complicity, and even the wound I had dressed. But all this was of little moment now. I was far less interested in M Méchinet than in the spectacle offered to my view. I had gradually recovered both my firmness and the faculty of reflecting ; and I examined everything around me with eager curiosity. Standing beside the door, my glance took in the whole room. When scenes of murder are portrayed in illustrated periodicals they are usually invested with an exaggerated aspect of disorder. But such was far from being the case in the present instance. Everything testified to the victim's easy circumstances and habits of order and relative parsimony. Everything was in its place. The bed and the window curtains were faultlessly draped ; and the woodwork of the furniture was bright with polish – proof of daily care. It appeared evident that the conjectures of the commissary and the magistrate were correct, and that the old man had been murdered the night before, just as he was going to retire to rest. In proof of this the bed was turned down, and a night-shirt and a night-cap were spread out open on the counterpane. On the little table at the head of the bed I perceived a glass of sugared water, a box of lucifers, and an evening newspaper – the *Patrie*. On the corner of the mantelshelf shone a weighty copper candlestick, but the candle which had lighted the crime had burnt away. The murderer had plainly fled without blowing it out, and the top of the candlestick, from which hung a few fragments of wax, like pendant icicles, was greatly soiled and blackened.

I noticed all these circumstances well nigh at the first glance. My eyes seemed to play the part of a photographic lens, and the scene of the murder fixed itself on my mind as on a prepared sheet of glass, with such precision, accuracy, and effect, that even to-day I could draw from memory the bedroom occupied by the Little Old Man of Batignolles, without forgetting any single object it contained – without omitting even the green-sealed cork, which I still seem to see, lying on the ground underneath the chair of the magistrate's clerk. I was not previously aware that I possessed this power of observation – this master faculty, so suddenly revealed to me, and on the spot I was too greatly excited to be able to analyse my sensations and impressions.

Curiously enough, I was possessed of an unique, irresistible desire. I felt impelled, despite myself, towards the corpse extended in the middle of the room. At first I battled with my impulse, but it was stronger than all my other feelings ; and, yielding to it at last, I approached the body. Had my presence been noticed ? I do not think so. At all events, no attention was paid to me. M Méchinet and the commissary were still talking beside the window ; and the clerk was reading the minutes of the proceedings in an undertone to the magistrate. Everything, therefore, favoured my design, and besides, I was seized, as it were, with a kind of fever which made me insensible to what was going on. Under this influence, I was well nigh unconscious of the functionaries' presence, and, acting as if I were alone and free to do whatever I liked, I knelt down beside the corpse, to examine it closely and at my ease. Indeed, far from reflecting that the magistrate or the commissary might indignantly ask : 'What are you about ?' I acted as composedly as if I were about to discharge some pre-assigned duty.

The unfortunate old man seemed to be from seventy to seventy-five years of age. He was short and very thin, but certainly very hale for his age, and constitutionally fitted to become well nigh a centenarian. He still possessed a fair crop of curly hair of a yellowish white tinge, and his face was covered with grey bristles, as if he had not shaved for five or six days. They had sprung forth, however, since his demise, and it is indeed curious to note how rapidly, under certain circumstances, the beard grows immediately after death. I was not surprised by this, for I had observed many similar cases among the 'subjects' provided for the examination of us students in the hospital dissecting hall. What *did* surprise me was the expression of the old man's face. It was calm and, I might almost say, smiling. His lips were parted as if he had been on the point of making some friendly remark. Death must have overtaken him most suddenly and promptly, for his face to retain this good-natured look. Such was the first thought that presented itself to my mind. Ay, but then, how could one reconcile these conflicting circumstances – sudden death, and the tracing of those five letters M O N I S on the floor ? To trace these letters with his own blood would require a great effort on the part of a dying man. Only the hope of vengeance could lend the requisite energy for such a task. And how enraged this poor old fellow must have been to feel the grip of death upon him before he was able to finish writing his murderer's name !

Enraged ? But no, for the face of the corpse seemed positively to smile at me, and this was all the more singular as the victim had been struck at the throat with a steel weapon, which had penetrated right through his neck. This weapon must have been a dagger, or perhaps one of those formidable double-edged Catalan knives, which are pointed as finely as a needle. In all my life I had never been a prey to such strange sensations. My temples beat with extraordinary violence, and I could feel my heart swelling and almost bursting with intensity of dilation.

What was I about to discover ?

Still under the influence of the same mysterious, irresistible impulse which annihilated my will, I took hold of the victim's frozen, rigid hands to examine them. The right hand was quite clean, unstained ; but such was not the case with the left one, the forefinger of which was red with blood ! What ! had the old man traced that accusatory inscription with his left hand ? Was it probable ? Was it likely ? No, a thousand times no ! But then . . . A score of conflicting thoughts battled in my mind, and, seized as it were with vertigo, with haggard eyes and hair on end, as pale certainly as the corpse extended on the floor, I sprung to my feet, giving vent to a terrible cry : 'Great God !'

My shriek must have resounded through the house. With one bound the magistrate and Méchinet, the commissary and the clerk were by my side. 'What is the matter ?' they asked, with eager excitement; 'What is the matter ?'

I tried to answer, but emotion well nigh paralysed my tongue. All I could do was to point at the dead man's hands, and stammer : 'There, see there !'

M Méchinet immediately knelt down beside the corpse. He observed the same particulars as myself, and evidently shared my opinion, for, quickly rising to his feet again, he exclaimed : 'After all, it was not the old man who traced those letters.' And then, as the magistrate and the commissary stared at him with gaping mouths, he showed them that the victim's left hand alone was stained with blood.

'And to think I didn't notice !' mourned the commissary, looking very much distressed.

'Ah, it's often like that,' retorted M Méchinet, frantically pretending to inhale repeated pinches of snuff. 'The things that stare us in the face are frequently those that most easily escape our view. . . . However, the situation is now quite changed. As it is evident that the old man did not write those letters, they must have been traced by the man who killed him.'

'Quite so,' observed the commissary in an approving tone.

'Well,' continued my neighbour, 'it is plain enough that a murderer is not foolish enough to denounce himself by writing his own name beside his victim's corpse. We shall all agree on that point, and so you may draw your own conclusions.'

The investigating magistrate looked thoughtful. 'Yes,' he muttered ; 'it's clear enough. We were deceived by appearances. . . . Monistrol is not guilty. But then, who can be the culprit ? It will be your business to find him, M Méchinet.'

The magistrate paused, for a police agent of subaltern rank was at that moment entering the room. 'Your orders are executed, sir,' said the new comer, addressing himself to the commissary ; 'Monistrol has been arrested, and he is now under lock and key at the Dépôt. He has confessed everything.'

4

The news created all the greater sensation as, by reason of my discovery, it was altogether unexpected. The magistrate and the commissary looked absolutely stupefied, and, for myself, I was overwhelmed. What, whilst we were busily seeking, by a mathematical course of reasoning, to establish Monistrol's innocence, he, on his side, had formally confessed his guilt ! Was it possible ? M Méchinet was the first to recover from this hard blow. He excitedly carried his fingers from his snuff-box to his nose at least a dozen times, and then, turning to the agent, roughly remarked : 'You've either been misled or else you are misleading us. There's no other alternative.'

'I swear to you, Monsieur Méchinet -' began the man.

'Don't swear, pray ; but hold your tongue. Either you misunderstood what Monistrol said, or else you've flattered yourself with the hope of astonishing us by the news that the whole affair is explained.'

The police agent, who had hitherto been most respectful in his demeanour towards the detective, now evinced signs of revolt. 'Excuse me,' he said, 'but I'm neither a fool nor a liar, and I know what I say,'

The discussion seemed so likely to turn into a dispute that the magistrate thought it advisable to intervene. 'Calm yourself, M Méchinet,' said he, 'and wait for information before pronouncing judgment.' And turning towards the agent, he added, 'Now, my good fellow, just tell us what you know, and explain what you have already said.'

Finding himself thus supported, the agent drew himself up, gave my neighbour a glance of withering irony, and then, with an air of no little self-conceit, began : 'You gentlemen instructed Inspector Goulard, my colleague, Poltin, and myself to arrest a party named Monistrol, a dealer in imitation jewellery, residing at No. 75 Rue Vivienne, and charged with the murder of his uncle here, at Batignolles.'

'Quite correct,' remarked the commissary, with an approving nod.

'Well, then,' continued the agent, 'we took a cab and drove to the Rue Vivienne. Monistrol was in a little room at the rear of his shop, and he was about to sit down to dinner with his wife – a woman of wonderful beauty, between five-and-twenty and thirty years of age. On perceiving us all three in a row, the husband at once asked us what we wanted, whereupon Inspector Goulard drew the warrant out of his pocket, and replied : "In the name of the law I arrest you." '

As the agent proceeded with his narrative, M Méchinet turned and twisted with nervous impatience. 'Can't you come to the point ?' he suddenly asked.

But the agent took no notice of the interruption. 'I have arrested a good many fellows in my time,' said he, with unabated composure ; 'but I never saw any one experience such a shock as this man Monistrol. "You must be joking," he said at last, "or else you make a mistake." "No," said Goulard ; "we don't make mistakes." "Well then, why do you arrest me ?" Goulard shrugged his shoulders. "Don't behave like a child," he said. "Come, what about your uncle ? His body has been found, you know, and there are convincing proofs against you." Ah, the scamp. What a blow it was for him ! He staggered and let himself fall on to a chair stammering some unintelligible reply, half the words of which remained in his throat. On seeing this, Goulard caught him by the collar of his coat, and said : "Take my advice : the best thing you can do is to confess." Thereupon he looked at us in an idiotic manner, and replied : 'Well, yes, I confess everything." '

'Well done, Goulard !' quoth the commissary, approvingly.

The agent triumphed. 'We were bent on getting the business over as soon as possible,' he said. 'We were instructed not to create a disturbance, and yet a lot of idlers had already collected in front of the shop. So Goulard caught hold of the prisoner by the arm, and said: "Let's be off ; they are waiting for us at the Prefecture." Monistrol drew himself up as well as he could on his quaking legs, and, summoning all his courage, answered : "Yes, let us start." We thought the business finished after that, but we had reckoned without the wife. Up till then she had remained in her armchair as still as if she had fainted, and without saying a word. Indeed, she scarcely seemed to understand what was going on. But when she saw that we were really going to carry her husband off, she sprang forward like a lioness, and threw herself before the door. "You sha'n't pass," she cried. 'Pon my word she really looked superb. But Goulard has had to deal with many similar cases. "Come, come, my little woman," said he, "don't get angry. It wouldn't do any good." But instead of moving she clung to the framework of the door, vowing that her husband was innocent, and declaring that if he were taken to prison she would follow him. At one moment she threatened us, and called us all

sorts of names, and then she began to beg and pray in her softest voice.
But when she perceived that nothing would prevent us from doing our
duty, she let go of the door and threw her arms round her husband's neck.
"Oh my poor, dear husband !" she gasped ; "is it possible that you can be
charged with such a crime ? Tell these men that you are innocent."

'Her grief was so great that we all felt compassion for her, but
Monistrol, to our surprise, was ruffian enough to push the poor little
woman back, so violently indeed that she fell all of a heap in a corner of
the room behind the shop. . . . Fortunately, that was the end of it. The
woman had fainted, and we profited of the circumstance to pack the
husband into the cab, which was waiting for us outside. He could scarcely stand, much less walk, and so we had literally to carry him into the
vehicle. His dog – a snarling, black mongrel – wanted to jump in with us,
and we had all the pains in the world to get rid of the beast. On the way
Goulard tried to revive the prisoner and induce him to talk, but we
couldn't get him to say a word. It was only on reaching the Préfecture
that he seemed to recover his wits. When he had been properly stowed
away in one of the secret cells, he flung himself on his bed, repeating,
"What have I done ! Good God ! What have I done ?" On hearing this
Goulard approached him, and for the second time, asked : "So you own
that you are guilty ?" Monistrol nodded his head affirmatively, and then
said, in a gasping voice, "Pray leave me alone." We did so, after placing
a superintendent outside the cell, in front of the grating, so as to be ready
in case the prisoner tried to play any tricks with his own life. Goulard and
Poltin remained at the Préfecture, and I came on here to report the
arrest.'

'All that is very precise,' muttered the commissary ; 'very precise
indeed.'

Such was also the magistrate's opinion, for he murmured, 'How can
any one doubt Monistrol's guilt after that ?'

As for myself, I was astonished but not convinced, and I was about to
open my mouth to raise an objection when M Méchinet forestalled me.
'All that's very well,' said he, 'only if we admit that Monistrol is the
murderer, we also have to admit that he wrote his own name there on the
floor, and to my mind that's rather too strong to be believed !'

'Pooh !' rejoined the commissary, 'as the prisoner confesses, what is
the use of troubling about a circumstance which will no doubt be explained in the course of the investigation ?'

However, the detective's remark had rekindled the magistrate's perplexity. 'I shall go to the Préfecture at once,' he said, 'and question
Monistrol this very night.' Then, after requesting the commissary to

stay and accomplish the remaining formalities, pending the arrival of the medical men who had been summoned for the post-mortem examination, he took his departure, followed by his clerk and the agent who had come to announce Monistrol's arrest.

'I only hope those doctors won't keep me waiting too long,' growled the commissary, who was thinking of his dinner ; and he then began to discharge his duties by sealing up sundry drawers and cupboards which contained articles of value.

Neither Méchinet nor myself answered him. My neighbour and I were standing in front of each other, evidently absorbed in the same train of thought. 'After all,' murmured the detective, 'after all, perhaps it *was* the old man who traced those letters.'

'With his left hand, then,' said I. 'Is it likely ? And besides, the poor fellow must have died instantaneously.'

'Are you sure of that ?'

'Well, judging by his wound, I would swear to it. But the doctors will soon be here, and they will tell you whether I'm right or wrong. Of course I am but a student, and they will be able to speak with more authority than myself.'

M Méchinet was worrying his nose with spurious pinches of snuff in frantic style. 'Perhaps,' said he ; 'perhaps there *is* a mystery underneath all this. It is a point to be examined. We must start the inquiry afresh. And after all, why not ? Well, let us begin by questioning the doorkeeper.' With these words he hurried out on to the landing, and leaning over the bannister of the stairs, exclaimed, 'Eh ! doorkeeper, doorkeeper, just come up here, please.'

5

Pending the doorkeeper's appearance, M Méchinet devoted his time to a rapid but sagacious examination of the scene of the crime. The outer door of the apartment particularly engaged his attention. The lock was intact and the key turned in either sense without the slightest difficulty. It was therefore scarcely likely that a stranger had forced his way into the old man's rooms by means of a picklock or a false key. Whilst the detective was thus occupied I returned into the bedroom to pick up the green-sealed bottle cork which I had noticed lying on the floor. I was prompted to do this by the new instinct so suddenly born within me. On the side of the sealing-wax a circular, winding hole, plainly produced by the tip of a corkscrew, was apparent, whilst at the other end, ruddy with the stain of wine, I noticed to my surprise a deep perforation, such as might be caused by the blade of a sharp, finely-pointed weapon. Instinctively suspecting that this discovery might have its importance, I showed the cork to M Méchinet, who on perceiving it could not repress an exclamation of delight. 'Ah !' said he, 'at last we are on the scent. That cork was evidently left here by the murderer. He had pricked his weapon into it – either to prevent the point from wounding him whilst he carried it in his pocket, or to keep it sharp and prevent it from breaking. So the weapon was plainly a dagger with a fixed handle, and not one of those knives that shut up. With this cork I will undertake to find the murderer, no matter who he may be.'

The commissary of police was finishing the sealing-up of the cupboards in the bedroom, and M Méchinet and I were still talking together in the parlour, when a sound of heavy breathing interrupted us. At the same moment, the portly, stalwart crone whom I had noticed in the hall perorating for the benefit of the tenants, appeared upon the threshold. Her face was ruddier than ever. 'What do you desire, sir ?' she asked, looking at M Méchinet.

'Please sit down,' he replied.

'But I have people waiting for me downstairs, sir.'

'They can wait. Just sit down.'

M Méchinet's authoritative tone evidently impressed the old woman, and without more ado she obeyed him. 'I require certain information,' he began, fixing his piercing grey eyes on hers, 'and I am going to question you. In your interest I advise you to answer me frankly. As you are the doorkeeper of the house you can tell me the name of this unfortunate old man who has been murdered.'

'His name was Pigoreau, my good sir, but he was generally called Anténor, which was a name he formerly took in his business, as being better suited to it.'

'Had he lived long in this house ?'

'For more than eight years, sir.'

'Where did he live before then ?'

'In the Rue de Richelieu, where he had his shop, for he had been a hairdresser, and it was in that calling that he made his fortune.'

'So he was rich, then ?'

'Well, I've heard his niece say that he wouldn't let his throat be cut for a million francs.'

The investigating magistrate was probably fully informed on this point, for during his sojourn in the house he had gone carefully through all the old man's papers.

'Now,' resumed M Méchinet, 'what kind of man was this M Pigoreau *alias* Anténor.'

'Oh, the best man in the world, my good sir,' replied the doorkeeper. 'He was a bit eccentric and obstinate, but he wasn't proud. And when he chose, he could be so funny ! One might have spent nights and nights listening to him when he was in the humour to talk, for he knew so many stories. Just fancy, he had been a hairdresser, and, as he often said, he had curled the hair of all the most beautiful women in Paris.'

'How did he live ?'

'Like other people – like a man living on his income, but not inclined to be prodigal.'

'Can't you give me any particulars ?'

'To be sure I can, sir, for it was I who cleaned his rooms and waited on him. Ah ! he didn't give me much trouble, for he did a great deal himself. He was always sweeping and dusting and polishing. That was his hobby ! Every day, at twelve o'clock, I used to bring him up a cup of chocolate and a roll ; and on the top of them he would drink off a big glass of water at one gulp. That was his breakfast. Then he dressed himself, and that took him till two o'clock, for he was very particular about his appearance, and arrayed himself every day just as if he were going to be married. When he was dressed he went out, and strolled about Paris till six o'clock, when he used to go and dine at a table d'hôte, kept by Mlles. Gomet in the Rue de la Paix. After dinner he usually went to the café Guerbois, took his cup of coffee, and played his game at cards with some friends he used to meet there. He generally came home at about eleven o'clock. He had only one fault, poor dear man : he was dreadfully fond of the fair sex, and I often used to say to him, "Come, Monsieur Anténor, aren't you ashamed to run after women at your age ?" But then we are none of us perfect, and, after all, his behaviour wasn't surprising on the part of a man who had been a fashionable hairdresser, and had met with so many favours in his time.'

An obsequious smile curved the portly crone's thick lips as she spoke on this point, but M Méchinet remained as grave as ever. 'Did M Pigoreau receive many visitors ?' he asked.

'Very few, sir. The person who came most frequently was his nephew, M Monistrol, whom he used to invite to dine with him every Sunday at the restaurant of "Père Lathuile ?" '

'And on what terms were they – the uncle and the nephew ?'

'Oh, they were as friendly as two fingers of the same hand.'

'And didn't they ever have any disputes together ?'

'Never ! . . . Excepting that they always used to disagree about

Madame Clara.'

'Who is this Madame Clara ?'

'Why, M Monistrol's wife, to be sure, and a superb creature she is, too ! But with all his love for the sex, M Anténor couldn't put up with her. He used to tell his nephew that he loved his wife too much, that she led him by the nose, and deceived him just whenever she chose. He pretended that she didn't love her husband, that she had tastes above her position, and that she would end one day by doing something foolish. In fact, Madame Clara and M Anténor had quite a quarrel last year. She wanted the old man to lend M Monistrol a large sum, so that he might buy the "goodwill" of a jeweller's shop in the Palais Royal ; but he refused to do so, and said he didn't care what was done with his fortune when he was dead, but that in the meantime, having earned his money himself, he meant to keep it and spend it as he chose.'

I thought that M Méchinet would insist on this point, which seemed to me of high importance, but to my surprise, and despite all the signs I made him, he did not do so. 'How was the crime discovered ?' was his next question.

'Why, it was discovered by me, my good sir !' replied the doorkeeper. 'Ah ! it was frightful ! Just fancy, at noon today I came upstairs as usual with M Anténor's chocolate. As I waited on him, I had a key of his rooms. I opened the door, came in, and, Good Heavens ! what a sight I saw !' So saying, the buxom dame gave vent to a succession of unearthly whines and groans.

'Your grief shows that you have a kind heart,' observed M Méchinet gravely. 'Only, as I am pressed for time, I must ask you to master it. Come, what did you think when you saw the old man lying there murdered ?'

'Why, to be sure, I told everyone that his rascally nephew had killed him to get hold of his fortune !'

'How is it you were so certain on the point ? For it is a grave matter to charge a man with such a crime – it's sending him to the scaffold, mind.'

'But who else could it be, sir ? M Monistrol came to see his uncle yesterday evening, and when he went away it was almost midnight. I thought it strange that he didn't speak to me, even when he came or when he left, for he generally wishes me good-day and goodbye. However, after he went away last night, and until I discovered everything this morning, I'm quite sure that no one else came to see M Anténor.'

This evidence fairly stupefied me. I was young then and wanting in experience, and therefore thought it really superfluous to continue the investigation. But, on the other hand, M Méchinet could boast of very extensive experience indeed, and he moreover possessed the art of coaxing the whole truth out of a witness, no matter however unwilling. 'So,' said he to the doorkeeper, 'you are quite certain that Monistrol came here last night ?'

'Quite certain, sir.'

'Then you saw him, and recognised him ?'

'Ah, allow me ! I didn't look him in the face, for he passed by very fast, as if he wished to hide himself, the scoundrel ! And besides, the stairs are badly lighted.'

I sprung from my chair on hearing this answer, which struck me as being of very great weight indeed, and, advancing towards the doorkeeper, I exclaimed, 'If that is the case how can you dare to pretend that you recognised M Monistrol ?'

The portly dame looked at me from head to foot, and, with an ironical smile, replied, 'If I didn't see his face, at least I saw his dog, who was with him. I always treat the animal kindly, and so he came into my room, and I was just going to give him a leg of mutton bone, when his master whistled to him from upstairs.'

I looked at M Méchinet to know what he thought of this answer, but his expression told no tales. He simply asked, 'What kind of a dog is M Monistrol's ?'

'He's a watch dog, sir - quite black, with just one white spot on the top of the head. M Monistrol calls him Pluto. He's generally very savage with strangers, but then he knows me well, for he has always been in the habit of coming here with his master, and besides, I've always been very kind to him.'

M Méchinet now rose from his chair. 'That will do,' said he to the doorkeeper ; 'you may retire. Thank you for your information.' And as soon as the woman had bustled out of the room, he turned to me exclaiming, 'I really think that the nephew must be the guilty party.'

While the doorkeeper's interrogatory was progressing, the two medical men who had been instructed to perform a post-mortem examination of the old fellow's body, had arrived and set about their task in the bedroom. I was particularly anxious to know what would be the result of their report - the more so as, despite my own conclusions, I feared they might possibly disagree. They were certainly of very dissimilar appearance and character ; for, while one of them was short and fat, with a round and jovial face, the other was lank and lean, with a grave and pompous expression of countenance. You could not look at them, indeed, without at once thinking of Molière's immortal creations, 'Doctor Tant Pis' and 'Doctor Tant Mieux.' But, at times, extremes meet, and at least on this occasion this unmatched pair not merely met in being but in ideas and opinions as well. They both took absolutely the same view of the case, and I was delighted, as an amateur detective, and flattered, as a medical student, to find that their view exactly coincided with mine. Indeed, their report resolved itself into this : 'The death of M Pigoreau was instantaneous. He expired directly the knife or dagger penetrated his neck, and consequently he could not possibly have traced those five letters MONIS, inscribed on the oak floor beside his body.'

Thus I had not been mistaken, and I turned with satisfaction towards M Méchinet to hear what he would have to say now. 'Well, if the old man did not write those letters,' he remarked at last, 'who could have written them ? Not Monistrol, I would take my oath to that. It would be altogether too incredible.'

I myself made no rejoinder, but the commissary of police, who was delighted to be able to go away to his dinner after such a long and tiring task, overheard the words, and could not resist the pleasure of taunting the detective for his perplexity and obstinacy, which, to his mind, were all the more ridiculous as Monistrol had confessed the crime.

'Ridiculous ?' ejaculated M Méchinet ; 'well, yes, perhaps I am *only* a fool ! However, the future will decide that point.' And then, abruptly turning to me, he added : 'Come, M Godeuil, let us go together to the Préfecture of Police.'

6

We had neither of us dined, but this puzzling affair so absorbed our minds that we did not even think of feeling hungry. On reaching the street we walked as far as the outer boulevard where we engaged another cab to take us to the Préfecture. While the vehicle rolled on down the Rue de Clichy and along the Chaussée d'Antin, crossing the grand boulevards, already all ablaze with light, and cutting through numerous narrow thoroughfares in the direction of the Rue de Rivoli and the Quays, M Méchinet's fingers did not stop travelling from his empty snuff-box to his nose, and vice versa - so great indeed was his preoccupation. Over and over again, moreover, I heard him grumble between his teeth, 'I must find out the truth ; I must, I will.'

All of a sudden he drew from his pocket the green-sealed cork which I had handed to him, and turned it over and over like a young monkey, who, in possession of a nut for the first time, asks himself how he is to get at the kernel. 'And yet,' he murmured, 'and yet that's a piece of evidence.

That green sealing-wax must be made to tell us something.'

Comfortably ensconced in my corner, I listened to him without saying a word. My situation was certainly very singular, and yet I did not for one moment think of its peculiarity. My mind was entirely absorbed in this affair, the diverse contradictory elements of which I tried to classify in my brain, turning to one after the other in hopes that it would give me the key of the mystery which, to my idea, assuredly existed.

When our vehicle drew up on the Quai des Orfèvres all around was silent and deserted – not a sound, not a passer-by. The few shops of the neighbourhood were all closed, with but one solitary exception – a little tavern and eating-house, situated almost at the corner of the famous Rue de Jérusalem, so long associated with the repression of crime, and the name of which, synonymous, so to say, with the word 'police', suffices to chill the blood of the most hardened rogues. Against the red curtains of the tavern windows, which shone out in the dark night with a fiery glare, I noted the shadows of numerous customers – subordinate officials of the Préfecture, who had profited of a spare moment to come out and refresh themselves, and detectives, who, after a long day's arduous tramp and toil, were bent on restoring tired nature with a crust and a glass of wine. As we walked by, M Méchinet just gave a glance inside, more from habit than curiosity (for, like myself, he was in no mood to loiter), and then turned swiftly into the Rue de Jérusalem.

'Do you think they will let you see Monistrol ?' I asked him, breaking once more into a trot so as to keep up with his rapid stride.

'Certainly they will,' he answered. 'Am I not entrusted with following up the affair ? According to the phases of the investigation, I may require to see the prisoner at any hour of the day or night.' And then turning under the dark-arched entrance of the Préfecture, he added, 'Come, come, we have no time to lose.'

I did not require encouragement. A strange, vague curiosity filled my mind as I followed in his wake. This was the first time in my life that I crossed the threshold of the Préfecture de Police, against which I had hitherto been quite as prejudiced as any other Parisian. Those who study social questions may well ask how it happens that the French police are so generally hated and despised. Even the ordinary street policemen, yclept the *sergent de ville*, is an object of aversion ; and the detective, the *mouchard*, is loathed as intensely as if he were some monstrous horror, in lieu of generally being a most useful servant of society. The deep-rooted prejudices that prevail among the Parisians in reference to the police are of distant origin, and are no doubt due to many causes ; but the fault mainly rests with the successive governments which, turning the force from its original mission as a guarantee of public security, transformed it into a political instrument, utilising its services for the execution of the most arbitrary measures, and frequently placing it under the control of low-minded, immoral men. The unpopularity of Voyer d'Argenson duly fell on the 'exempt' of the ancien régime ; and besides, the hateful Bastille and the odious lettre de cachet would alone have sufficed to make the police an object of aversion and terror in those times.

Under the Empire and the Restoration the service could not possibly hope for rehabilitation, for was it not under the control of the arch-traitor Fouché, as arrant a scoundrel as any of the criminals his subor-dinates were employed to track ? And in the days of Vidocq, moreover, when the maxim 'set a thief to catch a thief' was put into practice, and when the 'security' of the Parisians was entrusted to a band of knaves, all respect for the police became quite out of the question. Even when the force was thoroughly reorganised, the stain of former times clung to it persistently, and a new form of unpopularity awaited it when the Third Napoleon made the Préfecture the headquarters of his system of government. The ferocity displayed by many sergents de ville in days of popular turmoil, the hateful practices of the political mouchards, the invention of spurious plots and riots, 'got up' to terrify the provinces and justify acts of repression – all combined to throw odium on the force. It should be mentioned, however, that the Parisian in his aversion for the police often acts without discernment. He takes all the sergents de ville or gardiens de la paix to be of one and the same class and character, forgetting that it is mainly the Central Brigade that is employed on political duty.

This Central Brigade, indeed, does not perform ordinary strict ser-vice, but is always at the préfect's disposal to be dispatched to any part of the capital where occasion may require. To the 'Centrale' is assigned the sad privilege of charging the crowd, ill-treating inoffensive passers-by, and overturning women and children on days of popular effervescence. But the other brigades, to which are entrusted the protection of property and the safety of citizens, are composed of men of a very different stamp – men who behave reluctantly and with moderation when necessity compels them to assist the 'Centrale' in the performance of some politi-cal task ; men whose main object and desire is to prevent the perpetration of crime and to bring evil-doers to book. But then, lucklessly for them, they wear the same uniform as their colleagues of the 'Centrale', and the Parisian confounds the whole force in his blind aversion. He blunders in the same way respecting the detectives – forgetting that there is the criminal service and the political service, and that the two are utterly distinct. To him, the mouchard is invariably an unprincipled, eaves-dropping knave, who earns his living by prying into other people's secrets and denouncing them to his employers. He habitually pictures the detective as a man who slinks along the boulevard trying to overhear what the promenaders are talking about, or who lingers half asleep in the corner of a café bent on listening to the conversation of the customers. The mouchard, to his idea, is invariably the man who questions your doorkeeper, or concierge, concerning your antecedents, your trade or profession, your income, and your mode of living, and who, if your opinions are not perfectly orthodox, marks a cross against your name, signifying that you are to be watched and 'run in' as soon as an opportunity for political repression presents itself.

The Parisian does not realise, and yet he certainly should know it, that there are other detectives of a very different stamp – men like the great Monsieur Lecoq and the eminent Monsieur Méchinet, who in their whole career never do one day's political service, but, on the contrary, spend their lives constantly tracking crime and unravelling fraud – risking incredible dangers, often wounded, and at times even killed in the performance of their duty, and yet always ready and willing to undertake any task, however perilous, to ensure the safety of society and bring offenders to book. That these men, who truly constitute the 'strong arm of the law', and thanks to whose energy and enterprise Parisian crime is so swiftly and certainly punished, should be confounded with the obnoxious, political *mouchard,* is an act of utter ingratitude and injustice ; but then Paris, although priding itself on its common sense, is unfortunately too impulsive, too prejudiced, and too apt to draw sweeping conclusions, to perceive the difference – vast as it may be.

As I followed M Méchinet that night into the headquarters of the criminal service, the main 'points' of this long but I think not useless digression flashed through my mind in a twentieth part of the time it has taken me to jot them down. I realised the folly of the prejudices I had shared with so many others, and as my neighbour walked on in front of me he seemed to grow in height, importance, and dignity. Here, then, was one of those men who devote themselves to the most arduous profession that can exist, and who, for the dangers they brave, and the services they render, only reap contumely and contempt. For what is their modest stipend ? It barely suffices for their every-day wants, and does not permit of laying money by, so that a scanty pension, only acquired after long, long years of toil and peril, becomes their sole resource, in their old age. I was so immersed in thought of this character, as my neighbour and I entered the Préfecture, that I forgot to look where

I was walking, but a sudden stumble against a projecting angle of the pavement at last brought me back to reality. 'So, here is the secret of Paris !' I muttered, glancing at the damp blank walls of the passage we had entered, 'Ah, if those stones could only talk, what stories they would have to tell.'

At this moment, we reached a little room where a couple of men sat playing cards, whilst three or four others lounged on a camp bedstead, smoking their pipes. M Méchinet went inside, and I waited on the threshold. He and one of the cardplayers exchanged a few words, which did not reach me, and then he came out again, and once more bade me follow him. After crossing a courtyard and hurrying down another passage, we found ourselves in front of a formidable iron gate, with massive close-fitting bars, weighty bolts, and a huge lock. At a word from M Méchinet a keeper opened this gate, and then, leaving on our right hand a spacious guard-room, where a number of sergents de ville and gardes de Paris were assembled, we climbed a very precipitous flight of stairs. On the landing above, at the entry of a narrow passage lined with a number of little doors, we found a tall, fat, jovial-featured individual, who in no wise resembled the gaoler usually read of in novels. 'Hallo !' exclaimed this smiling colossus. 'Why it's Monsieur Méchinet !' And with a self-satisfied chuckle he added, 'To say the truth I half expected you ; come, I bet you want to see the fellow who has been arrested for murdering the little old man of Batignolles ?'

'Quite so. Is there anything new, pray ?'

'No, not that I know of.'

'But the investigating magistrate must have been here ?'

'Oh, yes ; in fact he only left a few minutes ago.'

'Ah ! did you hear him say anything ?'

'Well, he only remained two or three minutes with the prisoner, and he looked delighted when he left the cell. He met the governor at the bottom of the stairs, and I heard him say, "That fellow's account is as good as settled. He didn't even venture to deny his guilt." '

On hearing this, M Méchinet almost bounded from the floor, but the gaoler seemingly failed to notice his surprise, calmly resuming, 'I wasn't particularly astonished when I heard that, for directly the fellow was brought to me, I said to myself, "Here's a chap who won't know how to plan a defence." '

'And what is he doing now, pray ?'

'Well, he's lamenting – sobbing and crying as if he were a baby in long clothes. I was instructed to watch him, so as to prevent him from committing suicide, and as a matter of course, I perform my duty ; but, between you and I, watching is quite useless, I've taken his measure properly enough. He's only crying because he's afraid of the guillotine. He's one of those chaps who are more anxious about their own skins, than about other persons'.'

'Well, let's go and see him,' interrupted M Méchinet. 'And above everything pray don't make a noise.'

Thereupon, we all three turned round and walked on tiptoe to a door hard by. At the height of a man's head, a barred aperture had been cut in the stout oak panelling, so that the interior of the cell, badly lighted by a single gas burner, could be viewed from the passage. The gaoler gave a glance inside. M Méchinet did the same, and then my turn followed. On a narrow iron bedstead, covered with a grey blanket with yellow stripes, I could perceive a man extended on his stomach, with his head buried in his hands. He was weeping, and his sobs were plainly audible. At times he quivered from head to foot with a kind of convulsive spasm ; but otherwise he did not move.

'You may open the door now,' said M Méchinet to the keeper, after a moment's pause.

The man obeyed, and we all three walked into the cell. On hearing the key grate in the lock, the prisoner had raised himself to a sitting position, and now, with drooping arms and legs, and with his head leaning on his chest, he looked at us as if either stupefied or idiotic. He was from five to eight and thirty years of age, rather above the medium height, with a broad chest, and a short apoplectic neck. He was not a handsome man ; far from it, for he had been grievously disfigured by the smallpox, and, besides, his retreating forehead and long nose gave him altogether a simple, sheepish look. However, his blue eyes were very soft and winning, and his teeth were remarkably white and well set.

'What ? Monsieur Monistrol ! began my neighbour on entering the cell. 'What ! you are worrying yourself like that ?' And he paused as if expecting a reply. But finding the unfortunate man speechless, he determined to tackle him in a different fashion. 'Come, come,' he accordingly resumed. 'I agree that the situation isn't very lively ; and yet, if I were in your place, I should like to prove that I'm a man. I should try to curb my grief, and set about proving my innocence.'

'But I am not innocent,' answered the prisoner, in a savage tone.

This time equivocation was out of place. There was apparently no longer any room left for doubt, for it was from Monistrol's own lips that we obtained this terrible confession. And yet M Méchinet seemed scarcely satisfied. 'What !' asked he, 'was it really *you ?*'

'Yes, it was I,' interrupted the prisoner, springing to his feet with bloodshot eyes, and foaming mouth, as if he were seized with a sudden attack of madness. 'It was I - I alone. How many more times must I repeat it ? Why only a little while ago, a judge came here and I confessed everything to him, and even signed my confession. What more do you want ? Oh, I know what's in store for me, and pray don't fancy that I'm afraid ! Having killed, I must be killed in my turn as well ; so chop off my head, and the sooner you do it, the better !'

Although, at first, somewhat disconcerted by this violent outburst, M Méchinet promptly recovered himself. 'Come, come,' said he. 'Wait a minute pray. People are not guillotined like that. First of all, they must be proved to be guilty. And then, justice takes due account of certain disorders of the mind, of certain sufferings and impulses - fatalities if you like - and it was indeed for that reason, that "extenuating circum-stances" were invented.'

Monistrol's only reply was a long, low groan of mental agony.

'Now answer me,' resumed M Méchinet. 'Did you really hate your uncle so much as all that ?'

'Oh, no,' promptly answered the prisoner.

'Well, then, why did you kill him ?'

'I wanted his fortune,' replied Monistrol in a panting voice. 'My business was going to rack and ruin. You may make enquiries on that point. I needed money ; and although my uncle was very rich, he wouldn't assist me.'

'I understand,' rejoined M Méchinet. 'And you hoped that you would escape detection ?'

'Yes, I hoped so.'

At this point, I began to understand why my neighbour was conduct-ing the interrogatory in this desultory fashion, which at first had so surprised me, and I guessed what kind of trap he was preparing for the prisoner. Indeed, the very next moment he curtly asked, 'By the way, where did you buy the revolver you shot your uncle with ?'

I looked eagerly and anxiously at Monistrol, but he did not evince the least surprise. 'Oh, I had it by me for some years,' he replied.

'And what did you do with it, pray, after committing the crime ?'

'I threw it away . . . on the outer boulevard.'

'Very good. I will have a search made, and no doubt we shall be able to find the person who must have picked it up.'

While M Méchinet spoke in this fashion - deliberately lying in order to arrive at the truth - his features retained an expression of imperturb-able gravity. 'What I can't understand,' added he, after a moment's pause, 'is that you should have taken your dog with you.'

'What ! my dog !' ejaculated the prisoner, with an air of genuine surprise.

'Ay, your dog . . . Pluto . . . the doorkeeper recognised him.'

Monistrol clenched his fists, and his lips parted as if he were about to make some savage rejoinder, but at the same moment a new thought evidently darted through his mind, and he flung himself once more on his bed, exclaiming, in a tone of resolution, 'That's enough torture ; come, leave me to myself. At all events, I sha'n't answer any more.'

As he was plainly bent on keeping his word, M Méchinet refrained from insisting, and we left the cell together. We went silently downstairs, and crossed the passages and courtyards of the Préfecture, without exchanging a remark. But when we reached the quay, I could control my thoughts no longer. 'Well, what do you think now ?' I asked, catching my neighbour by the arm. 'You heard what that unfortunate fellow said. He pretends to be guilty, and yet he doesn't even know how his uncle was killed. That question about the revolver was a stroke of genius on your part. How readily he fell into the trap ! After that, it's plain enough that he's innocent ; for, otherwise, he would have told us that he did the deed with a dagger, and not with a revolver, as you pretended.'

'Perhaps so,' answered the detective, and then, with a sceptical air, he added, 'After all, who knows ? I've met with so many actors in my time. But, at all events, that's enough for today. Let us go home. You must come and eat a mouthful at my place. Tomorrow, when it's daylight, we'll continue our inquiry.'

7

It was ten o'clock at night when M Méchinet, still followed by myself, rung at the door of his lodgings. 'I never carry a key,' he said to me, 'for in our cursed trade no one knows what may happen. There are so many scoundrels who owe me a grudge, and besides, if I am not always prudent as concerns myself, I must be so for my wife.'

My neighbour's explanation was superfluous, for I fully realised the dangers to which he must be exposed. And moreover, when I was previously watching him with the view of penetrating the secret of his seemingly mysterious life, I had already noticed that he rung at his door in a peculiar manner, evidently preconcerted between his wife and himself.

The bell was answered by pretty Madame Méchinet in person. With feline agility and grace, she flung her arms round her husband's neck, gave him a pair of passionate kisses, and gaily exclaimed, 'Ah, so here you are at last ! I don't know why, but I almost felt uneasy. . . .' But all of a sudden she paused, her bright smile died away, her brow lowered, and, loosening her hold around her husband's neck, she drew several paces back. The fact is, that she had just caught sight of me, standing close by, on the threshold. That Monsieur Méchinet and myself should return together at the same time – and so late at night – seemed to her a most suspicious circumstance. 'What ! have you only just left the café ?' she asked, speaking as much to me as to her husband. 'You have been there up till ten o'clock at night ? Really, that's too bad ! . . .'

I turned to my neighbour for his reply. An indulgent smile flickered on his lips, and his attitude was that of a man who, confident in his wife's trustfulness, knows that he need only say one word to quiet her ruffled mind. 'Don't be angry with us, Caroline,' he exclaimed, thus associating me with his own cause. 'We left the café hours ago, and we haven't been wasting our time. The fact is, I was fetched away on business – for a murder committed at Batignolles.'

On hearing this, Madame Méchinet glanced suspiciously at both of us, and then, seemingly convinced that she was not being deceived, she curtly ejaculated, 'Ah !'

The exclamation was brief enough, and yet it was full of meaning. It was evidently addressed to her husband, and signified, 'So you have confided in that young man ? You have made him acquainted with your profession, and you have revealed our secrets to him ?' At least, that is how I understood the word, and my neighbour plainly construed its meaning in the same style, for he impetuously answered, 'Well, yes, M Godeuil has been with me this evening. And pray, where's the harm ? If I have to fear the scoundrels whom I've handed up to justice, what need I fear from honest folks ? Do you think, my dear, that I hide myself – that I am ashamed of my profession ?'

'You misunderstood me, dear,' objected Madame Méchinet.

But her husband did not even hear her. He had already sprung on to his favourite hobby, and, once astride, he was not easily persuaded to dismount. 'Now, really,' said he, 'you have most singular ideas, my love. What ! Here am I, a sentinel at the advanced posts of civilisation. I sacrifice my peace of mind, and risk all my life to ensure the safety of society, and yet you think I ought to blush for my profession ! It would be altogether too comical. You may tell me that there are a lot of foolish prejudices abroad respecting the police. No doubt there are, but what do I care for them ? Oh ! I know that there are a number of susceptible folks who pretend to look down on us. But, *sacrébleu*, I should like to see their faces, if my colleagues and myself were only to go on strike for a single day, leaving Paris at the mercy of the legion of scoundrels whom we keep in respect.'

Madame Méchinet was no doubt accustomed to outbursts of this kind, for she did not answer a word ; and indeed she acted wisely, for as soon as my neighbour perceived that there was no prospect of his being contradicted, he calmed down with surprising promptness. 'Well, that'll do,' said he ; 'just now we have a more pressing matter to deal with. We have neither of us dined, we are dying of hunger, and we should be glad to know if you have anything to give us to eat.'

Plainly enough, Madame Méchinet often had to cope with similar emergencies, for, with a pleasant smile, she readily answered, 'You shall be served in five minutes.' And in fact, a moment later we were seated at table before a succulent joint of cold beef ; while my neighbour's wife filled our glasses with one of those bright-coloured, refreshing wines, for which Macon enjoys renown. While M Méchinet plied knife and fork with amazing earnestness, I glanced round the cosy little room, and stole a look at plump, pleasant-faced Madame Caroline, so attentive and so full of spirits – asking myself if this were really the abode of one of those 'ferocious' detectives, so erroneously portrayed by ignorant novelists. However, the first requirements of hunger were soon appeased, and M Méchinet then began to relate our expedition to his wife. He spoke with great precision, entering into the most minute particulars ; and, seated beside him, she listened with an air of shrewd sagacity, interrupting him every now and then to ask for explanations on some obscure point, but without expressing any opinion of her own. However, I divined that her own views were to come, for, plainly enough, I was in presence of one of those homely Egerias, who are not merely accustomed to be consulted, but are also wont to give advice – and to see that advice followed. In fact, as soon as M Méchinet had finished his narrative, she drew herself up, and exclaimed, 'You have made one very great blunder, and, to my mind, an irreparable one.'

'And what is that, pray ?'

'Why, on leaving Batignolles, you ought not to have gone to the Préfecture.'

'But Monistrol –'

'Ah ! yes, I know ; you wanted to question him. But what was the use of it ?'

'Well, my examination enlightened me –'

'Not at all. Instead of going to headquarters you should have hurried to the Rue Vivienne, have seen the wife and questioned her. You would have surprised her while she was still under the effects of the emotion which her husband's arrest must necessarily have caused her ; and if she was an accomplice in the crime, as must be supposed, you might, with a little skill, have easily made her confess.'

On hearing this I almost sprung from my chair with surprise. 'What ?' cried I. 'Do you really think that Monistrol is guilty, madame ?'

She hesitated for a moment and then replied, 'Yes, I fancy so.' On hearing that, I wished to urge my own views of the case, but she prevented me from doing so by swiftly resuming : 'One thing I'm certain of - positively certain - the idea of that murder came from Monistrol's wife. Of every twenty crimes that men commit, fifteen are certainly planned or inspired by women. Just ask my husband if that is not the case. And besides, you ought to have been enlightened by the statements which the doorkeeper at Batignolles made. Who is this Madame Monistrol ? You were told that she is very beautiful, very coquettish and ambitious, hankering after wealth, and wont to lead her husband by the nose. Now what was her position prior to the crime ? Was it not needy, straightened, and precarious ? She was greatly vexed, no doubt ; she suffered acutely at not being able to satisfy her tastes for expense ; and we find proof of that in the fact that she asked her husband's uncle to lend them a large sum. The old man refused to do so, and all her hopes were crushed. She must have hated him after that ; and no doubt she often said to herself, "If that old miser only died, we should be in comfortable circumstances." But the old man still lived on ; he was hale and hearty yet, and his fortune seemed a long way off. She no doubt asked herself, "Is he going to live a hundred years ? Why, at this rate, when he dies we shall have no teeth left, and besides, who can tell, perhaps he means to bury us." That was undoubtedly her starting point. With such ideas in her head she was led by a natural gradation to think of committing a crime. And when she had determined in her own mind that, as the old man would not take himself off in the ordinary course of nature, he must be got rid of by foul means, she no doubt began to weigh on her husband, inspiring him with the idea of murder, and seeking to silence his qualms of conscience, till at last, when all was ripe, she virtually put the knife in his hand. Threatened with bankruptcy, maddened by his wife's lamentations, the unfortunate fellow started off, and murdered his uncle in a foolish, blundering manner no doubt, and without even thinking of the consequences that might overtake himself.'

'All that is logical enough,' opined M Méchinet, when his wife, who had worked herself into a state of considerable excitement whilst speaking at length brought her address to a close.

Logical - yes, no doubt it was ; but then, what became of the various particulars we had noted ? I could not forget my own observations at Batignolles ; and so, turning to Madame Méchinet, I asked her, 'Then you think that Monistrol was fool enough to denounce himself by writing his own name in blood on the floor ?'

'Fool enough ?' she answered, with a slight shrug of the shoulders. 'But come now, was it such an act of folly after all ? I myself don't think so ; for it is this very circumstance that constitutes your greatest argument in favour of his innocence.'

This reasoning was so specious that I was for a moment disconcerted. 'But he confesses his guilt,' I urged, as soon as I recovered myself.

'Well, that's an excellent system to induce the police to establish his innocence.'

'Oh, madame !'

'Why, you yourself are proof of that, Monsieur Godeuil.'

'But the unfortunate fellow doesn't even know *how* his uncle was murdered.'

'Excuse me, suppose he only *pretended* that he didn't know it - that would be a very different thing.'

My discussion with Madame Méchinet was becoming heated, and no doubt it would have lasted some time longer, if at this point her husband had thought fit to intervene. 'Come, come, Caroline,' said he, 'you are really too romantic tonight.' And, speaking to me, he added, 'I will knock at your door tomorrow morning, and we will go together to see Madame Monistrol. For the present, goodnight. I'm quite tired and half asleep already.'

He was a happy man, my neighbour, to be able to sleep in blissful forgetfulness of the problem waiting to be solved. No doubt he had only acquired this faculty of isolating his mind from his daily labours after long years of practice and experience. He had had to deal with so many crimes before, he had had to investigate such strange, mysterious cases, and almost invariably with satisfactory results, that he probably considered it futile to rack his mind, at night-time, about such an affair as this ; knowing well enough that when he awoke refreshed on the morrow, he would be able to weigh and estimate all the accumulated items of evidence with a clear head. But then, I was very differently situated ; I stood on the threshold of *terra incognita,* too absorbed and perplexed for my thoughts to allow me a moment's rest. Thus I did not close my eyes all night. A mysterious voice seemed to rise from the innermost recesses of my being and murmur, 'Monistrol is innocent !' I pictured to myself the

unfortunate fellow's sufferings as he lay on his camp bedstead at the
Dépôt ; and at the thought that his agony was perhaps undeserved my
heart softened with compassion. But then, in the midst of these phases of
pity, the same question invariably returned to my mind, rekindling all
my perplexity, 'If Monistrol were really innocent, why had he pleaded
guilty ?'

8

What lacked me in those days - as I subsequently had a hundred occasions of observing - was experience, professional practice, and exact
knowledge of the means of investigation at the disposal of the police. I
vaguely realised that this inquiry had been conducted in a far too
haphazard, superficial manner ; but I should have been greatly embarrassed had I been called upon to point out the mistakes that had been
made, or to say what ought to have been done. And yet at the same time I
took, as I have already said, a passionate interest in Monistrol. It indeed
seemed to me as if his cause were mine ; and, after all, the feeling was but
a natural one, for was not my own reputation for acumen at stake ? The
first doubt concerning his guilt had been occasioned by an observation I
myself had made, and it seemed to me as if I were now bound to prove his
innocence.

But then my discussion with Madame Méchinet, and the latter's
romantic and yet not illogical theories, had so disconcerted me that I did
not know what fact to select for the foundation of my defence. At each
circumstance I turned to I was met by Madame Caroline's objections,
and I wandered restlessly from one to the other without knowing at
which to pause. As always happens when the mind is applied during too
long a time to the solution of a problem, my ideas at last became as
entangled as a skein in a child's hands. I could distinguish nothing
clearly, and was only conscious of chaos.

It was nine o'clock in the morning, and I was still busy torturing my
brain, when M Méchinet, mindful of the promise he had made the night
before, entered my room to inform me that it was time to start. 'Come,
come,' said he ; 'let us be off.'

I sprang to my feet at once, and followed him out of the room. We
hastily went downstairs, and on reaching the street I noticed that my
worthy neighbour was rather more carefully dressed than usual. He had
succeeded in giving himself that well-to-do, easily-pleased air which
Parisian shopkeepers delight to find among their customers ; and he was,

moreover, radiant with all the gaiety of a man who knows that he is marching to certain victory. 'Well ?' he asked, as we walked down the Rue Racine, side by side ; 'well, what do you think of my wife ? The big guns at the Préfecture consider me to be a shrewd fellow, and yet you see I consult her ; and I may add that I have often done so with profit. After all, where's the harm ? Wasn't Molière in the habit of consulting his servant ? Caroline certainly has one little failing, as perhaps you may have noticed. To her mind, there are no stupid crimes, and so she invests every scamp with most diabolical powers of invention. However, my failing is just of the opposite kind. While she is always hunting after romance, I am rather too much inclined to look merely at positive facts. But, by combining our two systems – taking a little of the one, and a little of the other – it generally happens that we ultimately arrive at the truth.'

'What !' cried I, interrupting M Méchinet ; 'do you think that you have penetrated this Monistrol mystery ?'

He stopped short, drew his huge snuff-box from his pocket, took three or four imaginary pinches, according to his wont, and then, in a tone of mingled reserve and satisfaction, replied, 'Well, at least I possess the means of penetrating it.'

'Oh !' stammered I, wondering what this means might be, and yet deterred from further questioning by my companion's air of discretion.

But my mind was soon busy with a new train of thought. Crossing the Seine by the Pont des Arts, and traversing the courtyard of the Louvre, we had made for our destination by way of the Rue Croix des Petits Champs and the Bank of France. The streets were all alive with traffic ; merchants and clerks were hurrying in and out of the bank ; the neighbouring shops displayed a variety of costly wares. Signs of luxurious prosperity were indeed apparent on every side, and as I noted them I could not help remembering that surroundings often have a decisive influence on character. What indeed was Clara Monistrol, according to Mme Méchinet's theory ? An ambitious, coquettish woman, fond of display, hankering after wealth, and envious of other folks' good fortune. Even if the evil grain had not pre-existed in her mind, might not the seeds of covetousness have been sown by life in such a centre ?

The Rue Vivienne is no fit abode for poverty or struggling circumstances. From one end to another you can hear the jingle of specie and the rustle of flimsies. Here are the Boulevards – all life, splendour, and display ; here at mid-distance is the Bourse – the Giant Temple of Mammon – crowded each afternoon with the devotees of fortune ; here, at each step you take, are the offices of money-changers, stockbrokers, and bill-discounters ; and even when wealth does not assert itself in the shape of bullion, notes, and shares, it is present in a thousand other forms. Here is some shop-window crowded with precious works of art ; here are tantalising toilettes and bewitching bonnets ; and here, at the photograph stores, are portraits upon portraits of wonderfully-adorned actresses, and elegant belles of society – all appealing to the mind of a covetous woman, eager for wealth and anxious to be admired. And note that the Bank of France, with its cellars full of millions, is but a stone's throw off ; and that the Palais Royal, with its galleries scintillating with diamonds, stands at the top of the street.

What a neighbourhood for such a woman as Madame Monistrol ! If the portrait sketched by the doorkeeper of Batignolles were faithful to reality, and if Mme Méchinet's deductions were correct, must not Clara Monistrol have endured unspeakable torture, living, in her comparative poverty, in the midst of this Eldorado ? Must she not have been perpetually tantalised, tempted, goaded on by the every-day spectacle of all this wealth – all these pricely wares, of all these costly adornments ? She had looked no doubt with hungry eyes on many a coveted object, and the thought that there was only that little old man at Batignolles between her present envy and the attainment of her desires, had returned and returned, with increasing force, until at last she was persuaded to instigate this crime. Looking at the case in this light, and leaving my previous observations on one side, it really seemed to assume a very different aspect.

But I was unable to carry my deductions further, for, at this point, worthy M Méchinet interrupted my reverie. We had just reached the Rue Vivienne, and stood at the corner of the National Library. 'Now, follow me,' said my neighbour ; 'keep your eyes and ears open, but don't speak unless we remain alone ; and, no matter what happens, be careful not to express any surprise.'

He did well to warn me, for otherwise I should not have failed to manifest my astonishment at the course he took a moment later. Abruptly crossing the street, he walked straight into an umbrella shop – one of those fashionable establishments where only the most costly articles are sold. As stiff and as grave as an Englishman, he made the mistress of the shop show him, in turn, well nigh every umbrella she had in stock. But nothing seemed to please him ; he rejected even the most perfect articles, always having some objection ready to meet the praises which the shopkeeper lavished on her goods. At last, he asked her if she could not undertake to make him an umbrella on a pattern he would furnish. 'It would be the simplest thing in the world,' she answered ; and thereupon M Méchinet promised that he would return on the morrow with the pattern in question. The woman conducted us back to the door with many marks of deference – for, in Paris, the more fastidious a customer shows himself, the more he rises in a dealer's esteem – and the next moment we stood on the pavement outside, myself with admiration glowing on my face, and M Méchinet with a radiant air of self-satisfaction.

The fact is, that he had good reason to be satisfied, for the half-hour spent in that shop had by no means been thrown away. Whilst examining all the umbrellas that were shown to him, he had skilfully contrived to pump the shopwoman of all she knew about the Monistrols, both man and wife. After all, it was a comparatively easy matter, for the murder of the little old man of Batignolles, and the arrest of the dealer in imitation jewellery had caused a perfect sensation throughout the neighbourhood of the Rue Vivienne, and formed the one great topic of current gossip.

'There !' exclaimed M Méchinet, as we proceeded slowly along the street. 'There, that's how we obtain trustworthy information ! If I presented myself in my real character, folks would assume a pompous air, launch forth grandiloquent phrases about vice and virtue, and then goodbye to plain, simple, unvarnished truth !'

My neighbour enacted the same little comedy in seven or eight other shops of various kinds along the street ; and in one establishment, where the dealer and his wife at first showed themselves somewhat reserved and taciturn, he contrived to loosen their tongues by expending a 'napoleon' on a little purchase. To my amusement we spent a couple of hours or so in this fashion, and then M Méchinet opined that further inquiries would be superfluous, for we now knew enough to gauge the current of public opinion. In point of fact, we were very fairly acquainted with what the tradesfolk of the neighbourhood thought of M and Madame Monistrol, who had resided in the Rue Vivienne ever since their marriage, some four years previously.

There was but one opinion concerning the husband. He was, according to general report, a very good-natured, worthy man – obliging, honest, industrious, and fairly intelligent. It was scarcely his fault, we were told, if his business had not prospered. Fortune does not always smile on those who are most deserving of her favours. Monistrol, it appeared, had acted unwisely in taking a shop which seemed fated to bankruptcy, for, within a period of fifteen years, four dealers of different trades had failed in it. The jeweller was greatly attached to his wife – every one knew it, and repeated it ; but he had not unduly paraded his affection, or shown himself extravagantly uxorious and jealous. None of the people whom M Méchinet questioned believed in Monistrol's guilt.

In fact, they invariably remarked : 'The police must have made a mistake, and will soon find it out.'

In reference to Madame Monistrol, opinions were on one point divided. Some of the neighbours considered that her tastes were of too elegant a character for her position, whilst others opined that in a shop like her husband's, it was imperative that the mistress should be fashionably attired. However, it was only on this question that our informants differed. They united in declaring that Madame Monistrol was greatly attached to her husband. Her virtue, they said, was unimpeachable. No one had ever heard of her flirting or carrying her coquetry beyond the bounds of personal adornment ; and one individual naïvely remarked that her conduct in this respect was most meritorious, for she was remarkably beautiful, and had any number of admirers. But she had always remained deaf to their pleadings, and her reputation as a faithful wife was absolutely immaculate.

This information plainly worried M Méchinet. 'It's wonderful,' said he to me. 'No slander, no back-biting, no queer little stories of misconduct ! I begin to think that my wife must have been mistaken. According to her idea, Madame Monistrol ought to have been one of those brazen beauties who rule the household, and who are fonder of displaying their own charms than their husband's merchandise, one of those women, indeed, whose husbands are either blind fools or else shameful accomplices. And yet I find nothing of all that. The very most that people say, is, that she is rather fond of dress, but, then, that's the case with well nigh every pretty woman in the world ; and because she has a few elegant whims and a little taste we've no right to brand her with infamy.'

I made no reply to these remarks. To tell the truth, I was quite as disconcerted as the detective. What a difference between the fairly eulogious statements made by the neighbours and the disparaging assertions of the doorkeeper at Batignolles ! However, perhaps the discrepancy might be explained ; for, as it occurred to my mind just then, people in different circumstances take different views of things. And moreover, opinions vary with localities. What seems altogether scandalous and disgraceful in the Rue de Lécluse is justifiable, seemly, and even requisite in the Rue Vivienne. The staid and quiet quarter of Batignolles, and the ostentatious easy-going district of the Bourse can scarcely be expected to share the same notions of morality.

However, we had already spent too much time in prosecuting our inquiry to think of pausing to discuss our impressions and conjectures. 'Now,' said M Méchinet, 'before we tackle the enemy let's have a look at his quarters.' And familiar with the practice of carrying on these delicate investigations in the midst of the traffic and bustle of Paris, he drew me under an arched gateway situated just in front of Monistrol's shop.

It was a modest-looking shop indeed, almost a beggarly one, when compared with the fashionable establishments around. The weather-stained front, for instance, sadly required a coat of paint. Above the windows one could read the name of 'MONISTROL', formerly traced in gilt letters, but now blackened and dingy, whilst across the panes of glass, on either side of the door, ran the inscription, 'GOLD AND IMITATION.' Among the articles displayed to view there were, however, but few of standard ore. The imitation goods formed nineteentwentieths of the stock. Steel-gilt chains, jet ornaments, diadems to which rhine-stones and strass lent a fugitive, subdued brilliancy, imitation coral necklets, with brooches, rings, studs, and sleeve links set with false stones of every hue, were displayed in considerable profusion, but their spurious character was altogether too evident for the passing window thief to be deceived.

'Well, let's go in,' said I to M Méchinet, after making a brief survey of the shop.

But the detective was less impatient than myself, or rather he was more expert in restraining his impatience, for catching me by the arm, he exclaimed, 'One moment please. Before entering, I should just like to have a glimpse of Madame Monistrol.'

However, although we remained for another twenty minutes at our post of observation under the archway, the shop remained deserted. There were no signs whatever of the beautiful Madame Clara, and indeed, we did not even perceive a shop boy or a shop girl behind the counter. 'Well, well, that's enough waiting,' opined my companion at last. 'Come on, Monsieur Godeuil, let us chance it.'

9

To reach Monistrol's shop we had only to cross the street, a feat we performed in four strides. On hearing us open the door a slatternly looking little servant girl, of fifteen or sixteen years of age, with a dirty face and ill-combed hair, came out of a room in the rear of the shop. 'What do the gentlemen require ?' asked she.

'Is Madame Monistrol indoors ?'

'Yes, sir, she's in the room there, and I'll run and tell her you want her, for, you see -'

But M Méchinet did not allow the maid to finish. He roughly pushed her aside, and exclaimed : 'That'll do ; as she's there, I'll go and speak to her.' And the next moment he walked straight into the room at the rear of the shop.

I followed close behind him on the tiptoe of curiosity and expectation, feeling as it were a kind of presentiment that this visit would result in an explanation of the mystery. I required some little energy to preserve an appearance of calmness, for to tell the truth, my mind was terribly excited, and I could hear my temples throb, and my heart beat pit-a-pat, with most unwonted violence.

The apartment in the rear of the shop was a dreary looking chamber, which apparently did joint duty, as dining-room, drawing-room and bedroom. It was in a state of considerable disorder, and its appointments were such as are common to the abodes of people in straightened circumstances who wish to appear rich. At the further end stood a bedstead partially concealed by pretentiously draped curtains of blue damask. The pillow cases were fringed round with lace and embroidered with huge initial letters, and the rug at the foot of the bed was a flowery imitation of the Aubusson style. In striking contrast with this attempted display of magnificence, appeared the table in the centre of the room. Its greasy oil cloth covering was bestrewn with the remnants of what could not have been a particularly appetising breakfast, served in crockery of the commonest kind.

Reclining beside this table in a capacious arm chair, I perceived a young woman, with fair hair and blue eyes, who held between her fingers a legal document on stamped paper. This then was the beautiful Madame Monistrol. Her charms had certainly not been exaggerated. She was slightly above the average height, but admirably proportioned, as with my professional knowledge of anatomy I easily perceived, despite her somewhat recumbent position. Her nose would have done honour to a Grecian beauty, and her lips – although somewhat deficient in colour, a circumstance no doubt due to emotion – offered the graceful curves of Cupid's bow. Her ears were particularly tiny and well shaped, and her bowed neck, on which lingered the wavy curls of her back hair, seemed as white and as smooth as polished alabaster. Her feet could not be seen from where I stood ; but no doubt they were as exquisitely modelled as her hands, which, with their fair white skin, their network of pale blue veins, and their tapering fingers tipped with glistening pink nails, would have fairly sent an artist into raptures.

It would be futile to conceal it. I was at first fairly dazzled by this woman's amazing beauty, and, reversing all Madame Méchinet's theories concerning her culpability, I decided in my own mind, that it was quite impossible such a lovely creature could have instigated the heinous crime of the Rue de Lécluse. But this impression only lasted for a moment, so contradictory and so versatile indeed were my ideas at that prefatory epoch of my career as a detective. It was her dress that made me change my mind. She was in deep mourning, wearing a robe of black crape, cut slightly low at the neck. Now black is admirably adapted to set off fair complexions, and naturally enough this toilette greatly enhanced Madame Clara's charms. But on reflection, it seemed to me that a person labouring under deep grief, a prey in fact to harrowing sorrow, would scarcely have had the requisite presence of mind to array herself in this preposessing style ; and I could not help asking myself if Madame Monistrol were not, after all, an actress who had deliberately assumed the costume of the part she meant to play.

On perceiving us enter the room, she sprang to her feet like a frightened doe, and asked in a tearful voice : 'What do you desire, gentlemen ?'

From the gleam in M Méchinet's eyes I could judge that he had mentally made the same remarks as myself. 'Madame,' he answered, sternly, 'I am sent here by the judicial authorities. I am an agent of the detective police.'

At this announcement she sunk back into her armchair, sobbing, and to all appearance overcome ; but suddenly, inflamed as it were with nervous enthusiasm, with bright eyes and quivering lips, she rose once more to her feet, exclaiming in impassioned tones : 'Do you come to arrest me, then ? Ah ! I could bless you for it. Come, I am ready. Lead me away! Let me join the honest man whom you arrested last night! Whatever may be his fate I wish to share it. He is as guiltless as I am myself ; but no matter, if he is fated to be the victim of a judicial error, it will be a last joy for me to die beside him !'

She was interrupted by a prolonged growl, coming from one of the corners of the room. I looked up and perceived a black dog, who showed his teeth and glared at us as if he meant mischief. 'Down, Pluto, down !' exclaimed Madame Monistrol. 'Come, go to bed and keep quiet. These gentlemen don't mean me any harm.'

At first the animal seemed disinclined to obey his mistress's command, but at last, without once averting his glaring gaze, he slowly backed under the bedstead, where in the shadow I could still distinguish his bright eyes fixed upon us.

'You are right in saying that we don't mean you any harm, madame,' remarked M Méchinet. 'We have not come to arrest you.' He no doubt trusted that this intelligence would draw from her some expression of feeling indicative of her hopes or fears ; but he was mistaken, for she did not seem to heed it.

'This morning,' she resumed, glancing at the paper in her hand, 'I received this summons, which orders me to be at the office of an investigating magistrate at the Palace of Justice, at three o'clock this afternoon. What can be wanted of me, good heavens ! what can be wanted of me ?'

'Why, information, madame,' promptly answered M Méchinet. 'Information that may enlighten justice, and, as I hope, prove your husband's innocence. Pray don't look on me as an enemy. Indeed, so far as my professional character allows, I sincerely sympathise with you in your misfortune. My only object, my only ambition is to arrive at the truth.' So saying my neighbour drew forth his snuff-box and took a score or so of imaginary pinches. 'You will therefore understand, madame,' he resumed, in a solemn tone which I had never heard him employ before ; 'you will understand how important may prove your answers to the questions I shall have the honour of asking you. And so may I beg you to answer me frankly ?'

For fully half a minute Madame Clara fixed her big blue eyes on my neighbour and gazed at him through her tears. 'Question me, monsieur,' she said at last.

For the third time I must repeat it; I was altogether without experience, and yet the manner in which M Méchinet had initiated this interrogatory caused me intense dissatisfaction. It seemed to me that he betrayed all his perplexity and wandered on in haphazard fashion, instead of marching straight towards a predetermined object. Ah ! how my tongue itched ! How I should have liked to intervene. If I had only dared. . . . But then, of course, I was no one ; I had no *locus standi*, and was merely there on sufferance. However, during the last few minutes, my worthy neighbour had greatly fallen in my estimation. I forgot the clever manner in which he had questioned Monistrol the night before ; and it seemed to me that if he were well up in the routine of his profession, he was, at all events, quite deficient in that analytical, investigative genius, without which a man cannot hope to become a great detective. Indeed, it really seemed to me that I was his superior in the latter respect, despite my comparative youth and imperfect knowledge of men and things ; and hence I suffered all the more acutely at having to stand still and listen to what I considered his blunders, without any right to intervene and repair them.

My worthy neighbour was, of course, blissfully ignorant of what was passing in my mind. Seating himself on a chair in front of Madame Monistrol, he began as follows : 'As no doubt you are aware, madame, it was after nine o'clock on the night before last that Monsieur Pigoreau, or Anténor, as some people called him – in one word, your husband's uncle – was murdered at Batignolles.'

'Alas ! yes ; so I have been told,' answered Madame Clara.

'Now can you tell me,' continued the detective, 'where Monsieur Monistrol was between nine o'clock and midnight ?'

'Ah, Lord !' groaned the jeweller's wife, clasping her hands with anguish. 'What a fatality !'

M Méchinet paid no heed to the exclamation. 'Excuse me,' he resumed ; 'you must be able to tell us where your husband was on the evening before last ?'

It was some little time before Madame Monistrol was able to reply, for sobs were rising in her throat and seemed to choke her utterance. At last, mastering her grief, she murmured : 'On the day before yesterday my husband spent the evening away from home.'

'Do you know where he was ?'

'Ah, yes, I can tell you that. One of our work-people, living at Montrouge, was engaged on a set of false pearls, and had failed to deliver them as promised. We were afraid that the person who had ordered them of us would leave them on our hands, which would have been very annoying, for we are far from rich, and business is bad enough already. So, while we were at dinner that evening, my husband said to me : "I think I had better go to Montrouge and see if those pearls are not ready yet." And sure enough, after dinner – rather before nine o'clock – he went out, and I accompanied him as far as the corner of the Rue de Richelieu, where I saw him take the omnibus myself.'

I began to breathe again. My original idea had been the right one, and Monistrol *was* innocent ; for surely his wife's reply meant an unimpeachable alibi. M Méchinet no doubt had the same thought, for he continued in a softer tone. 'If that is the case, your workman could state that M Monistrol was with him somewhere about eleven o'clock ?'

'Ah ! unfortunately no.'

'No ? And why not pray ?'

'Because he was not at home. My husband did not see him.'

'That is a great misfortune. But still the doorkeeper of the house must have known of M Monistrol's visit.'

'No, monsieur. In fact there is no doorkeeper in the house where our workman lives.'

This might be the truth. Similar things have been heard of before ;

and yet the judicial authorities would undoubtedly consider the circumstance as a most suspicious one, indeed as an additional indication of the prisoner's guilt. At all events, with such glaring absence of proof, the plea of an alibi became quite untenable. Was it this, then, that had impelled Monistrol to plead guilty ? Had he realised that this improbable story of a journey to Montrouge, to a workman who was not at home, and who lived in a house where there was no doorkeeper, would only cause both judge and jury to shrug their shoulders with contempt ? Perhaps he had. He had very likely said to himself, 'I am the victim of a fatal combination of circumstances. My statements would be set down as a parcel of lies, concocted in the vain hope of saving myself from the guillotine. I should be doubly branded with infamy ; and so it is best that I should accept my fate and bow my head to the last stroke of that ill luck which has so persistently followed me through life.'

Whilst I was pursuing this train of thought, M Méchinet had resumed his interrogation. 'At what time did your husband come home ?' he asked.

'At sometime after midnight.'

'Didn't you think he had been a long while gone?'

'Oh yes ! Indeed, I spoke to him about it, but he said he had come back on foot, and loitered on his way. If I recollect rightly, he had rested in a café and drunk a glass of beer.'

'And pray what did he look like when he came home ?'

'Well, he looked annoyed, but that was only natural.'

'What clothes was he wearing ?'

'The same as when he was arrested.'

'And you didn't notice anything extraordinary about his manner or appearance.'

'No, nothing.'

10

Standing, at a few paces behind M Méchinet, I was able to watch Madame Monistrol's features at leisure, and take due note of her slightest change of expression. She seemed to be overcome with deep grief, and big tears streamed down her pale cheeks. And yet at certain moments I fancied I could detect something like a suppressed gleam of joy in the depths of her big, blue eyes. 'Is she guilty then ?' I asked myself. This was not the first time that the idea had occurred to me, and now, as I stood there watching the jeweller's wife, it returned and returned with such obstinate persistency, that at last I could control myself no longer. Forgetful of M Méchinet's recommendations, oblivious of the fact that I had no right to interfere in the proceedings, I took a few steps forward, and roughly asked : 'But you, madame, where were you on that fatal evening, while your husband was uselessly journeying to Montrouge, to see his workman ?'

She raised her blue eyes to mine, gave me a long look of surprise, and then softly answered : 'I was here, monsieur, as witnesses can prove to you.'

'Witnesses !'

'Yes, monsieur. It was so very warm that evening, that I felt I should like an ice. As it worried me to take it alone, I sent my servant to invite two of my neighbours, Madame Dorstrich, the bootmaker's wife, next door, and Madame Rivaille, who keeps the glove shop over the way. They both accepted my invitation, and remained here with me till half-past eleven o'clock. You may question them, and they will tell you that such was the case. In the midst of all these cruel trials, this accidental circumstance is really a favour from on high.'

Was the circumstance of such a purely accidental character as Madame Monistrol pretended ? This is what we asked each other, M Méchinet and myself, by means of a rapid questioning glance. When chance acts so appropriately, it may well have been assisted. At least, this is what I thought, and the swift gleam that shot from my neighbour's eyes in my direction seemed to imply that his opinion was the same. However, this was scarcely the moment for an exchange of observations, which would assuredly have proved suspicious to Madame Monistrol.

'You have never been suspected, madame,' declared M Méchinet, with rare effrontery. 'The worst that was supposed was that your husband might perhaps have said something to you before committing this crime.'

'Ah ! monsieur !' ejaculated Madame Monistrol. 'Ah ! if you only knew us !'

'One moment, pray. We have been told that your husband's business was not a prosperous one, that he was in needy circumstances.'

'Yes, lately, it is true ; trade has not been very bright.'

'Now your husband must have been very worried and anxious on account of his precarious position. He must have particularly suffered on thinking of you, his wife, to whom he was so attached. For your sake, more than for himself, your husband must have longed to attain a position of ease and fortune.'

'Ah ! monsieur, I can only repeat it, he is innocent.'

M Méchinet assumed a pensive air, and pretended to fill his nose with snuff ; but suddenly raising his head again he exclaimed : 'Then, *sacré-bleu*, how do you explain his confession ? For an innocent man to plead guilty as soon as the crime he stands accused of is mentioned to him is most singular, madame – singular, and indeed, astounding.'

A fleeting blush coloured Madame Méchinet's cheeks, and for the first time, since the beginning of the interrogation, her glance wavered. Was this to be interpreted as a sign of guilt ? 'I suppose,' she answered in a low voice, which a fresh fit of sobbing rendered almost inaudible ; 'I suppose that my poor husband was so frightened and stupefied at finding himself accused of such a frightful cime, that he fairly lost his head.'

M Méchinet shrugged his shoulders. 'At the very most,' said he, 'the idea of passing delirium might be entertained ; but after a long night's reflection, M Monistrol has this very morning persisted in his original avowals.'

Was this true ? Had my worthy neighbour been to the Préfecture before calling me, or had he deemed it useful to make this statement without authority ? At all events, the news had a crushing effect on Madame Monistrol. She turned ashy white, and I really thought that she was going to faint. We were both looking at her intently, and it seemed as if she could not bear our gaze, for suddenly she hid her face in her hands and murmured, 'O Lord, O Lord, my poor husband has gone mad.'

Such was certainly not *my* opinion. In fact, I had very different views. I was becoming more and more convinced that this scene, so far as Madame Clara was concerned, was merely so much pure comedy. Her great despair was to my mind so much affectation, and I asked myself if she were not in some fashion or other the cause of her husband's singular attitude, and if she were not also acquainted with the true culprit. Whilst I was thinking, however, M Méchinet continued to talk. He endeavoured to console Madame Monistrol by a few set phrases which could not possibly compromise him, and then gave her to understand that she might silence a great many suspicions by allowing him to make a minute perquisition throughout the establishment. She accepted the suggestion with unfeigned alacrity and pleasure. 'Everything is at your disposal, gentlemen,' said she. 'Examine everything. I shall really feel obliged by your doing so ; and besides it won't take you very long, for we only rent the shop, this room, our servant's room on the top floor, and a little cellar. Here are the keys of everything !'

To my very great astonishment, M Méchinet expressed his readiness to make a search at once ; and forthwith he began ferreting round the room, examining everything with the greatest attention. What could be his object? I wondered. Surely he must have some secret motive; for was it likely that such a perquisition – so readily authorised – would lead to any important discovery ? After exploring the shop and the room with as much care as if he had expected to light upon the missing link in our chain of evidence, he turned to Madame Monistrol and remarked ? 'Well, there's only the cellar left for us to look at now.'

'I'll show you the way, monsieur,' she answered ; and, taking a candlestick and a box of lucifers from off the mantelpiece, she conducted us out of the room into a courtyard behind.

We descended a score of slippery stone steps by the light of the flickering candle, and halted in front of an old door covered with cobwebs and mildew. 'Here's the cellar,' observed Madame Monistrol, unfastening the padlock ; and the next moment pushing back the door, she led the way inside. It was a damp, ill-kept vault, and its contents were in keeping with the Monistrols' needy circumstances. In one corner was a little barrel of beer, and just in front a cask of wine, more or less securely perched on a few logs of wood. Taps were affixed both to the beer barrel and the wine cask, showing that they were both on draught. On the right hand side were three or four dozen bottles of wine, probably of a superior kind, ranged on lathes ; and in a third corner an equal number of empty bottles could be perceived. I was now beginning to realise M Méchinet's object. He scarcely glanced at the casks, but taking the candle from Madame Monistrol, he scrutinised the full and the empty bottles with equal attention. I carefully followed his inspection, and like himself I noted that not one of these bottles was sealed with green wax. Thus the inference was, that the cork discovered on the floor in the bedroom at Batignolles, and in which the murderer had evidently imbedded his dagger's point, had not come from Monistrol's cellar. As M Méchinet was almost as prepossessed as myself in favour of the jeweller's innocence, this result ought to have delighted him ; but whatever may have been his secret feelings, he thought fit to assume a look of intense disappointment and remarked, 'Well, I find nothing – nothing at all ; so I think we may go upstairs again.'

I walked the first on this occasion, and thus reached the room in the rear of the shop before the others. Scarcely had I opened the door when Pluto, the black dog with the glaring eyes and ferocious growl, sprang from his resting place under the bed in such a threatening manner that I instinctively retreated a few paces back.

'He seems to be an unpleasant customer that dog of yours,' said M Méchinet to Madame Monistrol.

'No, no,' she answered with a wave of the hand, which calmed Pluto as if by magic. 'He's a good fellow, but then, you know, he's a watch dog.

We jewellers have so many thieves to fear ; and so we have trained him to keep a sharp look out.'

The animal was quiet enough now that his mistress was beside him ; and, wishing to coax him into a more friendly disposition, I called him by his name : 'Here, Pluto, here !'

'Oh, it's quite useless for you to call him,' carelessly remarked Madame Monistrol. 'He won't obey you.'

'Indeed ! Why not ?'

'Why, like all dogs of his breed, he's very faithful. He only knows his master and me.'

Many people would have considered such an answer to be altogether insignificant, and yet to me it was as a ray of light shed on the mystery we were investigating. Without pausing to reflect, yielding to the first impulse that entered my head, I eagerly asked : 'And pray, madame, where was this faithful dog on the night of the crime ?'

So great was Madame Monistrol's emotion and surprise at being asked this question, point blank, that she started back and almost let her candlestick fall from her hand. 'I don't know,' she stammered ; 'I don't recollect –'

'Perhaps he followed your husband,' I resumed.

'Yes – now I think of it. I fancy he did.'

'So you have trained him to follow vehicles then ; for you told us that you saw your husband get on the 'bus.'

She made no rejoinder, and I was about to continue when M Méchinet forestalled me. Far from seeking to profit by Madame Monistrol's confusion, he did everything he could to set her mind at ease, and after advising her in her own interest to comply with the summons she had received from the investigating magistrate, he bade her good morning, and led me away.

'Have you lost your head?' he asked, when we had walked a few yards down the street.

Lost my head, indeed! Such a remark was fairly an insult. 'You are really too hard on me, M Méchinet,' said I, 'Few people in their senses could have done more than I have just accomplished. For if I haven't solved the problem, at all events I've shown how it may be solved. Monistrol's dog will lead us to the truth.'

This outburst made my worthy neighbour smile. 'You are right,' said he in a paternal tone ; 'I quite understood your question about the dog. Only I fear you put it too abruptly. If Madame Monistrol has divined your suspicions, you may be sure that the animal will be dead, or have disappeared before the day is over.'

11

Yes, I had certainly been most imprudent. There could be no doubt of that. But on the other hand, I had discovered the weak point in the enemy's armour, the flaw which would enable us to penetrate a most artful system of defence. My worthy neighbour was fairly bowled over. Here was he, a celebrity so to say in his profession, possessed of vast experience, and said to be most shrewd. Now, what result had he arrived at during this long interrogation ? Just none at all.' He had wandered through and through the maze without finding the smallest outlet, whilst I, a mere apprentice, had discovered the right road at my very first venture. Another man might have shown himself jealous of my success, but M Méchinet was not given to envious thoughts. His only desire was to utilise my discovery to the very best advantage ; and accordingly we decided to hold council at a neighbouring restaurant, one of the best places for a *déjeuner à la fouchette* in this part of Paris.

Without neglecting to ply our knives and forks, for our morning's labours had whetted our appetites to the right degree, we began by establishing the exact position of the problem, so as to arrive more readily at the required solution. To our minds, Monistrol's innocence was a moral certainty ; and we thought we could guess why he had pleaded guilty. However, for the time being, this was a question of secondary importance. As regards Madame Monistrol we were equally certain that she had not left her neighbourhood on the night of the crime ; for it was no doubt perfectly true that she had merely accompanied her husband as far as the omnibus in the Rue de Richelieu, and that she had then returned home and spent the whole evening, as she said, in the company of two of her acquaintances. But although it might be proved that she could not possibly have taken any material part in the perpetration of the crime, there remained the charge of moral complicity, in respect of which a logical sequence of deductions seemed to prove her guilt. To our minds she had been fully acquainted with the crime - even if she had not indeed advised and prepared it - and consequently she knew the murderer.

Now, who could the murderer be ? Must he not be some man whom Pluto, the black dog, was accustomed to obey quite as readily as he obeyed his master and mistress ? For we had unimpeachable evidence that the dog had accompanied the assassin to Batignolles. It is true that, before Madame Monistrol was formally questioned on the subject of the dog, she had casually stated that he only obeyed his master and herself ; but her subsequent embarrassment pointed to a very different conclusion. Plainly enough Pluto was in the habit of obeying some third person, with whose name we were so far unacquainted. This person must, however, be a very frequent visitor to the Monistrols' shop, for we ourselves had seen how the dog was in the habit of receiving strangers. And yet, although a frequent visitor, he could scarcely be a friend (at least so far as Monsieur Monistrol was concerned), for the crime at Batignolles had been perpetrated in such a manner as to make the jeweller's guilt seem certain. The murderer must therefore be one of M Monistrol's bitter enemies, for hatred alone could have inspired such fiendish cunning. But on the other hand he must be a very dear indeed to *Madame* Monistrol ; for, although she knew his name, as was morally proven, she refrained from denouncing him, preferring to abandon her husband to the cruel fate he did not deserve.

This course of reasoning could have but one conclusion : Madame Monistrol must have a favoured lover, and that lover must be the murderer of Batignolles. Her neighbours of the Rue Vivienne had no doubt given her a certificate of virtue, but in the circumstances their assurances were insufficient. Women who enjoy the very highest reputations often carry on some shameful secret intrigue for years and years, and are honoured as models of faithfulness and virtue, whereas, if their sin were known, they would be turned from with horror and loathing. Some faithless women possess extraordinary powers of deception, and go to the grave without having been once detected. When started on the road to error, their minds prove fertile in all the resources of hypocrisy and cunning, and although the hundred eyes of Argus may be on them, their secret remains safe. Now, might not Madame Monistrol be one of these women – who are not merely expert in deceiving their husbands, but in deceiving the world as well ?

We discussed this question at length, M Méchinet and I, and our deductions were so fully in keeping with our original theory, that we could not fail to accept them. On the one hand this system proved Monistrol's innocence, even if it did not explain his plea of guilty ; and on the other, it was in keeping with a great deal of what Madame Méchinet had said at supper the night before. Clara Monistrol had certainly instigated the crime, but in lieu of entrusting its perpetration to her husband, she had confided it to her lover, hoping to enjoy this ill-gotten wealth in his company, after the unfortunate jeweller had perished on the scaffold, a victim of judicial error, like Lesurques in the famous case of the Lyons mail. But then, accepting these premises, who could this lover of hers be, and how could we discover him ?

After torturing my mind for some time, I at length ventured to expound a plan. 'It seems to me,' said I to M Méchinet, 'that the murderer can be easily found out. He and Madame Monistrol must have agreed not to see each other for some little time after the crime. The most elementary rules of prudence must have impelled them to take that course. The man will no doubt remain quiet enough. He must know that a false move would cost him his head, and so he will not dare to show himself in the Rue Vivienne ; but, on the other hand, the woman will probably become impatient. She will be anxious to see her accomplice, and, fancying that she has diverted all suspicion from herself, she will not hesitate to go and meet him somewhere. I would therefore suggest that you should employ one of your colleagues to dog her steps, to follow her wherever she may go ; and, if this is only done, properly, why, we shall have caught the murderer before another forty-eight hours are over our heads.'

M Méchinet was grumbling unintelligibly between his teeth, and dipping his fingers into his empty snuff-box with all his wonted persistency. At first he gave me no answer, but suddenly leaning forward he exclaimed : 'That won't do, my dear fellow. We mustn't let the bird slip through our fingers. We must rather strike the iron while it's hot. No doubt you possess the genius requisite for the profession – in fact, I'm sure you do ; but you are wanting in experience and practice. However, fortunately I'm here. Now, listen to me. A single phrase put you on the right track, and yet you don't follow up your advantage.'

'I don't understand you.'

'Don't understand me ? But that dog, we must turn him to account.'

'How so ?'

'Well, wait and you shall see. In an hour's time or so, Madame Monistrol will leave her shop, for she has to be at the Palais de Justice by three o'clock ; and the little servant girl will remain behind alone. That will be the time for action, and you will see how I shall settle the whole business.'

I did everything I could to induce M Méchinet to explain himself properly ; but in spite of all my prayers and exhortations he refused to say another word on the subject. He carried me off to the nearest café, and compelled me to play him a game at dominoes, which, as a matter of course, I lost ; for my mind was too preoccupied to allow me to engage successfully in such a frivolous pastime, whereas M Méchinet possessed the happy gift of being able to dismiss business from his thoughts at a moment's notice. Two o'clock was striking when at last he pushed back the dominoes and exclaimed : 'To work ! to work.'

We paid the score and left the café, and a moment later we were standing once more under the arched gateway in front of Monistrol's shop. We had only waited there a few minutes when we saw the door open and the jeweller's wife appear upon the threshold. She wore the same black dress as during the morning, and a long crape veil hung from her bonnet, giving her the appearance of a widow. 'She's a clever wench,' grumbled M Méchinet between his teeth; 'she means to excite the magistrate's compassion and sympathy.'

Whilst he was speaking she walked swiftly down the street, and soon disappeared from view in the direction of the Palais Royal. However, M Méchinet decided to wait another five minutes under the archway, and then catching me by the arm he led me towards the shop. As he had opined, the little servant girl was quite alone. She was sitting behind the counter, munching a piece of sugar she had purloined from her mistress. As soon as we entered she recognised us, and rose to her feet with a flushed face and rather frightened air. Before she could open her mouth, however, M Méchinet roughly asked her : 'Where is Madame Monistrol ?'

'She has gone out, monsieur.'

'Gone out ! That can't be. You must be deceiving me. She must be in the room there, behind the shop.'

'Oh, no, monsieur ; she has really gone out, and if you don't believe me, you may look yourself.'

M Méchinet struck his forehead, as if he were grievously disappointed. 'What a pity, what a pity !' he repeated. 'How disappointed poor Madame Monistrol will be !' And as the girl gazed at him, with gaping mouth and astonished eyes, he continued : 'But perhaps you might be able to tell me what I want to know, my good girl. I have only come back because I have lost the address of the person your mistress asked me to visit.'

'What person, monsieur ?'

'Ah ! you know him. Monsieur . . . Confound it ! Why, I've even forgotten his name now ! Monsieur . . . Monsieur . . . But surely you'll recollect him. He's the person that your dog Pluto obeys so readily.'

'Ah yes, monsieur ! I know who you mean ; it's Monsieur Victor.'

'Yes, that's it, to a T. Monsieur Victor ! I mustn't forget again. By the way, what does he do, this Monsieur Victor ?'

'He's a working jeweller, monsieur. He was a great friend of Monsieur Monistrol's, and they used to work together before M Monistrol set up in business. That's why M Victor can do anything he likes with Pluto.'

'Ah ! Then, if that's the case, perhaps you can tell me where this

Monsieur Victor lives ?'

'Certainly I can, monsieur ; he lives at No. 23 Rue du Roi Doré, in the Marais.'

The poor girl was seemingly delighted to be able to furnish all this information ; but it was not without a pang that I heard her answer in this trusting manner, unconsciously betraying the secret which her mistress must hold as dear as life itself. M Méchinet's was a more hardened nature, however ; and far from being touched by this involuntary treachery, he grimly indulged in a stroke of sarcasm. 'Thanks,' said he, as he turned to leave the shop. 'Thanks ; you have just rendered your mistress a very great service indeed, and she will be exceedingly pleased with you.' Then, with a chuckle, he opened the door, and we walked out into the street.

12

My first impulse was to hurry off to the Rue du Roi Doré, and apprehend this fellow Victor, who, plainly enough was the real murderer ; but M Méchinet damped my enthusiasm with the remark : 'And the law ! Don't you know that we are powerless to act, so long as we are without a warrant ? We must first of all, go to the Palais de Justice, and interview the investigating magistrate.'

'But suppose we meet Madame Monistrol there ?' I asked. 'If she sees us, she will certainly warn her accomplice.'

'Perhaps so,' retorted M Méchinet, with undisguised bitterness ; 'perhaps so. The culprit may escape, simply because we have to go through so many irksome formalities. Still, I might perchance parry the blow. However, let us make haste. Come, stretch out your legs.'

Anxiety and hope of success lent unparalleled speed to both of us, and a quarter of an hour afterwards we were scrambling up the staircase of the Palais de Justice. The offices occupied by the investigating magistrates communicate with a long gallery, where several attendants are invariably stationed to answer all inquiries. 'Can you tell me,' asked M Méchinet, in a breathless voice ; 'can you tell me if the magistrate who has to deal with the murder of the little old man of Batignolles is in his office ?'

'Yes, he is,' answered one of the attendants ; 'but he has a witness with him just now – a young woman dressed in black.'

'That must be Madame Monistrol,' whispered the detective in my ear ; and then, turning again to the attendant, he added aloud : 'You know who I am, so just give me a pen and a slip of paper, that I may write a word to the magistrate. Take it to him, and bring me back the answer.'

The attendant started off, dragging his shoes along the dusty floor of the gallery, and soon returned to say that the magistrate was waiting for us in an adjoining room. To receive M Méchinet, he had, indeed, left Madame Monistrol in his own office with his clerk, and had borrowed the use of one of his colleagues' rooms.

'What is the matter ?' he asked, in a tone which allowed me to estimate the immense difference between an investigating magistrate and a humble detective.

In a clear, brief manner, M Méchinet related what we had accomplished, what he had learnt, and what we hoped for. But the magistrate scarcely seemed inclined to share our views. 'All that is very interesting,' said he ; 'but Monistrol confesses.' And, with an obstinacy that well nigh maddened me, he kept on repeating : 'He confesses, he confesses.' However, after another series of protracted explanations, he at last consented to sign a warrant authorising my neighbour to apprehend Madame Monistrol's presumed lover – M Victor.

As soon as the detective was in possession of this indispensable document, he hurriedly bowed to the magistrate, and bounded out of the room, along the passage, and down the stairs. It was as much as I could do to keep up with him, and, in less than a quarter of an hour, we covered the whole distance, from the Palace of Justice to the Rue du Roi Doré – one of those narrow, unkempt streets in the heart of the Marais, where each tenement is a busy hive of industry, and whence *articles de Paris,* in all varieties, go forth to the entire world.

On reaching the corner of the street, M Méchinet paused to draw breath. 'Now,' said he, 'attention !' And, with an air of complete composure, he entered the narrow alley of the house bearing the number 23. 'M Victor, if you please ?' he asked of the doorkeeper.

'On the fourth floor, monsieur – the door on the right hand as you reach the landing.'

'Is he at home ?'

'Oh, yes ; he must be at work.'

M Méchinet took a step in the direction of the staircase, and then abruptly pausing, turned round again, faced the doorkeeper, and exclaimed : 'I must treat my old friend, Victor, to a good bottle of wine. What wine shop does he usually go to near here ?'

'To the one over the way.'

We reached the shop in six strides, and with the air of an *habitué*, M Méchinet immediately ordered : 'A bottle of wine, please – something good. That wine of yours with the green seal !'

I must confess that this idea had not occurred to me, and yet it was simple enough. As soon as the bottle was brought, my companion produced the green-sealed cork which I had found in the bedroom at Batignolles, and we immediately perceived that the wax was identical in shade and appearance with that on the cork of the cork that had just been served to us. Thus our moral certitude was reinforced by a material proof. As M Méchinet had no intention of regaling M Victor with the bottle of wine he had ordered, we proceeded to imbibe its contents, and then recrossed the street and climbed the stairs of 'No. 23.'

M Méchinet gave a sharp rat-tat at Victor's door, and a voice with a pleasant ring immediately responded, 'Come in.' The key was outside, and accordingly we opened the door. At a table, placed before the window of the room we entered, sat a man wearing a black blouse, and engaged in setting a stone in a gold ring. He was a fellow of thirty or thereabouts, tall and thin, with a pale face and black hair. He was scarcely handsome, but his features were fairly regular, and his eyes were not without expression.

He seemed in no wise disconcerted by our visit. 'What do you desire, gentlemen ?' he asked politely, at the same time turning round on his stool.

'In the name of the law, I arrest you !' exclaimed M Méchinot, springing forward and catching the workman by the arm.

Victor turned livid, but he did not lower his eyes. 'Don't play the fool,' he exclaimed, in an insolent tone. 'What have I done ?'

M Méchinet shrugged his shoulders. 'Come, no child's play, please,' said he ; 'your account is settled. You were seen when you left the Rue de Lécluse at Batignolles, and in my pocket I've got the cork in which you planted your dagger so as to prevent the point from breaking.'

These words proved a crushing blow for the murderer, who, taken utterly by surprise, fell back against his table, stammering, 'I am innocent, I am innocent !'

'You can say that to the magistrate,' retorted M Méchinet ; 'but I'm very much afraid that he won't believe you. Why, your accomplice, the woman Monistrol, has confessed everything.'

'That's impossible !' replied Victor, springing up as if he had been touched by an electric battery. 'She knew nothing about it.'

'Oh ! so then you planned the little game by yourself, eh ? All right. That confession will do to begin with.'

And turning towards me, with the air of a man who knows what he is about, M Méchinet added : 'Please just search the drawers, M Godeuil.

In one or another of them you will probably find this fine fellow's dagger, and I'm sure you'll light on his mistress's portrait and her love letters.'

Victor clenched his teeth with rage, and a gleam of fury shot from his dark eyes ; but he no doubt realised that all resistance would be futile against a man of M Méchinet's muscular build, endowed with such a pair of iron wrists.

In a chest of drawers in one corner of the room I speedily found the dagger, the portrait, and the love letters, just as my companion had opined ; and a quarter of an hour afterwards Victor had been securely stowed away in a cab between M Méchinet and myself, and was rolling in the direction of the Préfecture de Police. The simplicity of the scene had well nigh stupefied me. 'And so,' I mused, 'that's how a murderer is arrested. What, is it no more difficult than that to secure the person of a man whose crime is punishable with death ?' But in later years I learnt at my own cost and peril that there are other criminals of a far more dangerous stamp.

As for Victor, as soon as he found himself in a cell at the Dépôt, he gave himself up as lost, and made a most minute confession of his crime. He told us that, being one of Monistrol's friends, he had been acquainted with old M Pigoreau for several years. His main object in murdering him had been to designate Monistrol for the punishment of the law, and for this reason he had dressed himself like the jeweller, and had taken Pluto to Batignolles. As soon as the poor old man had ceased to live, he had seized him by the hand, dipped one of his fingers in the blood that flowed from the fatal wound, and traced on the floor those five letters, M O N I S - the discovery of which had so nearly resulted in a deplorable judicial error. 'Ah! it was cleverly combined,' he added, with cynical effrontery ; 'if I had only succeeded, I would have killed two birds with one stone. On the one hand, I got rid of that fool Monistrol, whom I hated, and I enriched the woman I loved. No doubt I might have persuaded her to live with me, after her husband had gone either to the scaffold or the galleys. But now - '

'Ah ! my fine fellow !' retorted M Méchinet ; 'unfortunately for you, you lost your head at the last moment. But then, no one is perfect. When you traced those letters in blood on the floor, you made a terrible mistake, for you wrote them with one of the fingers of the old man's left hand.'

Victor sprung to his feet in astonishment. 'You don't mean to say that put you on my track ?' he asked.

'Yes, I do.'

With the gesture of a man whose genius is misjudged, Victor raised his arms to the ceiling. 'Ah !' said he ; 'it's no use being an artist – no use remaining true to nature !' And, with a glance of mingled pity and contempt, he added : 'Don't you know that old M Pigoreau was *Left -Handed* ?'

He spoke the truth, as subsequent inquiries enabled me to ascertain. So thus, it was a mistake – a blunder perpetrated by myself – which, after all, had led us to the truth. The discovery, on which I had so particularly prided myself, was, in reality, none at all. And it was strange, indeed, that none of us had ever ventured to surmise that the little old man of Batignolles might have been in the habit of writing with his left hand. It is true that such cases are not very frequent – still they exist ; but neither the magistrate nor the commissary, neither M Méchinet nor his wife, had for one moment met my so-called discovery with such an objection – so true it is that the simplest things often escape our minds. However, the lesson was not lost to me, for I profited by it, with good result, on a subsequent occasion of my afterlife as a detective.

On the morrow, Monistrol was released from prison. The investigating magistrate reproached him in stringent terms, for having led justice astray ; but he met all exhortations and reproaches with the same answer : 'I love my wife. . . I wished to sacrifice myself for her. . . I thought that she was guilty.'

He would say no more, but his conduct implied that he must have had some very serious grounds to believe in his wife's guilt. What could they have been ? I decided, in my own mind, that Madame Clara must have previously tried to tempt her husband to commit this crime ; but, although weak-minded, beyond a doubt, and passionately attached to her, he had nevertheless had the courage to resist her entreaties. Finding that her efforts were useless, she had, no doubt, turned to her lover, who proved to be of a more pliable character – especially when he was offered such a prize as wealth and undisputed possession of the woman he loved ; for the latter contingency would, no doubt, have followed, had Monistrol been sent to the scaffold or the galleys.

It was in this manner that I explained the affair to myself. I could swear that Madame Monistrol was the instigator of the crime. And yet she escaped punishment. Juries do not content themselves with moral proof ; and the discovery of her letters and her portrait in Victor's room, was not accounted sufficient evidence against her, when she appeared at the assizes by her lover's side. She was, moreover, defended by one of the most famous advocates of the Paris bar ; and then, her tears, which flowed at will, no doubt, touched the hearts of her judges with compassion. Her charms, like those of Phyrné, might also have inspired them with a yet more tender sentiment. To be brief, she was acquitted ; whilst Victor, in whose favour the jury saddled their verdict with an admission of 'extenuating circumstances', was sentenced to hard labour for life.

After giving such proof of his conjugal attachment, it is scarcely surprising that weak-minded M Monistrol should have taken his wife back to his home, if not entirely to his heart, when, after securing the benefit of a doubt, she was ordered to be set at liberty. As a matter of course, old M Pigoreau's fortune was handed over to the jeweller, but, with Madame Monistrol's extravagant tastes, it could not be expected to last long. Nowadays, the Monistrols keep an ill-famed drinking den on the Cours de Vincennes, nigh the Place du Trone, and when the barrière bullies, who are their principal customers, are in good humour, they pay mocking court to the wife, now a corpulent woman, with a bloated face and a husky voice, and sadly addicted to brandy and absinthe. Her charms have fled long since, like old Antenor's money ; and she and her weakminded husband, whom she often beats in her fits of drunkenness, are swiftly descending the slope of degradation and misery.

                                                    J. B. CASIMIR GODEUIL

Dulcie Gray

THE SCARLET BUTTERFLY

SHE WAS DEAD, and I looked down at her contorted body in amazement. I'd known her so long, and her death had wiped out in one stroke, all my youth. She had been strangled with a purple scarf, which was still wound round her neck. Her eyes appeared to be starting out of her head, and on her dark hair, now streaked with grey, there perched, inappropriately, a butterfly brooch made of scarlet feathers.'

'Well ?' asked the superintendent, impatiently.

'Terrible,' I replied, brokenly. 'Quite terrible !'

'Yes, sir. Quite so, sir, but you haven't answered my question.'

I looked at him, bewildered. 'I'm sorry,' I replied. 'I don't think I heard you.'

'I asked why you were here this particular weekend.'

'Because Lydia invited me,' I answered simply.

'Have you any idea why ?'

'She's been getting threatening letters, and I suppose she thought I might help her.'

'Help her ? In what way ?'

'She didn't want to go to the police, so she sent for me.'

'Why ?'

'She didn't like the police.' I couldn't stop myself from sounding slightly smug.

'And she liked you ?' The superintendent's voice was sarcastic.

I stared at him angrily. 'Have you any reason to believe she didn't ?' I demanded. There was no reply. 'In fact,' I continued, 'I'm probably here because I was instrumental in helping the police with a case in Scotland two years ago, when I was on holiday, and I suppose Lydia remembered it.'

'Ah, yes. The girl who was murdered in Arbroath. Sheila McNairn, wasn't it ?'

'Exactly. Sheila McNairn.' I looked at the policeman with new respect. It seemed to amuse him.

'A tricky case, that, sir,' he said. 'How was it that you came to be implicated ?'

I didn't enjoy the use of the word 'implicated', but I tried not to show my annoyance, and said, 'I happened to notice the girl from my hotel window. She used to pass it on her way to school. She was outstandingly pretty, and when I was told what had happened to her, I felt a compulsion to do all I could to help.'

'You arrived here precisely when, sir ?'

'You'd better ask Saunders, the chauffeur,' I said. 'He met me at Melbury station this evening. The five-ten train from Paddington.'

'And you left your office in London precisely when, sir ?'

'Yesterday evening. At five-thirty.'

'You didn't go in today ?'

'No.'

'Why not ?'

'I'm my own master, more or less, and I sometimes skip Fridays, I'm afraid.'

'Not very often, I'm told.'

'Eh ?'

'Your secretary.' The policeman smiled vaguely.

'Fiona !' So he'd been on to the office already – a fast worker, evidently.

'How long had Mrs Harwood been receiving the threatening letters, sir ?'

'She started getting them two or three months ago, I believe.'

'Did she tell you about them immediately ?'

'Pretty soon, I understand. I stay down here fairly often, as my secretary has doubtless told you. Lydia and I had been good friends for years. We nearly married once . . . oh, about twenty-five years ago, now, but Mr Harwood beat me to the post.'

I can still remember the shock of that rejection. Lydia and I had even announced the wedding day, when she came to my flat, and, as cool as you please, told me that she had decided to marry Bobby instead. 'He has the right background, you see,' she'd said, and I hated her for it. 'And I suppose I've come to see that it must count in marriage. Don't take it too hard, Verney. I've loved you very dearly, but we disagree about so much, that it's been scaring me lately.'

'But Bobby Harwood !' I objected. 'Bobby Harwood !'

'Don't underestimate him, Verney,' she'd said. 'He's not clever like you, or ambitious like you, but he's good and kind, and I adore him. Sorry, Verney darling. I really am. Please forgive me.'

But I couldn't.

The marriage had been idyllic. I had prospered, too – beyond my wildest dreams – becoming not only very rich, but being knighted for my pains. But I'd never married, and I hadn't seen Lydia again until after Bobby had been killed in a car crash. I'd written to say how sorry I was, and she had replied warmly, and from then on, when she needed an extra man at one of her weekend parties, she'd invited me to stay.

She'd first mentioned the letters in June. Now it was late August. She'd telephoned me. 'They're horrid, Verney,' she'd said. 'They threaten death.'

'Good God ! do they say why ?' I'd asked.

'No, they don't, and I can't think why. Can you ? I mean who would actually want to kill me ? It's a pretty extreme act.'

'Tell me everything you know, my dear. Everything.' And she did, unravelling the whole twisted skein from end to end.

And so, after much discussion, we had fixed up this particular weekend party, if you could describe it as a party. Besides myself she'd invited Clara, her elder daughter, who hated her for breaking up an early romance – one that she'd never got over – Vincent, her stepson, who was a vicious playboy, and who would inherit her house and money after her death, through her father's will. Finally there was Colonel Lethbridge – Eddie to his few friends – to whom Lydia had written some foolishly passionate letters when she was lonely after Bobby's death, and for which he was mildly blackmailing her. The plan was that I was to be there with all of them, to try and make out which, if any of them, could conceivably be the writer, and then I was to deal with the situation in any way I saw fit. The trouble was that we hadn't been able to fix up the party until now, and she had been growing more and more frightened in the meantime. She utterly refused to tell the police, as Clara and Vincent were part of the family.

'Your movements, sir,' murmured the superintendent implacably.

'What ?'

'Today. How did you spend today ?'

'What has that got to do with anything ?' I asked. 'You can hardly suspect me ! I wasn't here when it happened.'

There was a knock on the door, and a sergeant came in. 'The van's here now, sir. OK ?'

'Go ahead,' replied the superintendent. He turned to me. 'They're taking the body to the mortuary now, sir.' I felt sick. 'Perhaps you'll come down to the study with me. It has been turned over to the police for questioning.'

'When did you get here ?' I asked, and added waspishly, 'Precisely ?'

'The body was found at six, and we were on the scene about a quarter of an hour later.'

'Has the doctor a theory as to when exactly she was killed ?'

'Since it's a very hot day, it's difficult to pin it down ; heat delays *rigor mortis.* It could have been any time between two-thirty and six.'

'It was good of you to let me see her,' I said.

'Not at all.' He stroked his chin and looked at me speculatively.

We left Lydia's bedroom, and began walking down the stairs. As we reached the bottom he said, 'Did she often wear ornaments in her hair ?'

'Never !' I was emphatic.

'Was she especially fond of butterflies ?'

'Not that I know of.'

'And you, sir ?'

'Me ?'

'Yes. Do you have an affinity with butterflies ?'

'None,' I said. 'Should I ?'

'If she never wore hair ornaments, that butterfly might have something to tell us, don't you agree ? If, for instance, it was put there by the murderer, it must have been put there for a reason.'

'She hadn't been wearing it all day, then ?'

'You should know, sir.'

'Why me ?'

'You came down to these parts yesterday, sir. We have every reason to know that you spent the night here, and a man answering your description, caught the three o'clock train from Melbury to Sundbury ; the only stop, as I'm sure you are aware, that the five-ten from Paddington makes.'

'Are you accusing me of anything in particular ?' I asked furiously. We were not in the study now, and he motioned me to sit.

'No, sir, of course not, sir. I would merely be glad of an explanation of some sort.'

'Any time,' I answered haughtily.

'Sheila McNairn,' he murmured.

'Well ?'

'How old was she ?'

'Ten, poor child.'

'Fair or dark ?'

'Dark.'

'You claim you never met her, sir ?'

'I do.'

'When she was found strangled, I understand that she was clutching a locket in the shape of a heart. A blue heart.'

'Yes.'

'And today Mrs Harwood had a scarlet butterfly pinned in her hair. Strange, don't you think?'

'I don't think I quite get the point,' I said.

'She never wore hair ornaments, you told me, yet she was wearing one today. Let us assume for the moment that it was put there by the murderer, what would it signify, would you suppose, sir?'

'I've no idea.'

'Sin, perhaps, sir?'

'Sin?'

'As scarlet as sin? Jezebel? A scarlet woman who once turned you down, and you never forgave her?'

'Certainly not!'

'And butterflies are often thought of as frivolous. Worthless creatures – beautiful but useless – only fit to live for a day.'

'All this sounds very fanciful,' I said scornfully.

'Does it, sir? Perhaps the murderer is a fanciful sort of man.'

'Or a fanciful woman,' I replied vaguely.

'Woman, sir?'

'Clara, for instance?' He didn't answer, and I sat back in my chair for a few moments, then said, 'Who pointed you in my direction?'

'Sir?'

'I mean, why should it have occurred to you to think of me in connection with the murder at all? Ostensibly I reached here at seven o'clock – one hour after you had been called. Yet only a short time after seeing Mrs Harwood, you had checked on all my movements since yesterday, and seem to dismiss all the others who were present in the house from the case. Why?'

'We always check on the movements of everyone concerned, sir, and it so happens that everyone else has a perfect alibi. They were all together all afternoon; so, unless they were all implicated, which on the face of it seems unlikely, they are all in the clear.'

'Interesting. Another thing that I find interesting is Lydia was a creature of habit, and everyone who knew her, knew it. She always rested from two until four every afternoon, and at half-past four she always made tea. When she didn't appear at half-past four, why did no one apparently find it unusual? Indeed, why did no one go up to her bedroom until six o'clock?'

'I don't know, sir.'

'I should check, if I were you.'

'I will.'

'It just might be that someone needed time.'

'For what ?'

'I came here last night at Lydia's instigation. She was scared that the murderer might carry out his threat during the night, so I slept on the sofa in her room. I spent most of the morning in her wardrobe, by the way, and damned uncomfortable it was. I couldn't emerge until the daily had tidied the bedroom. Lydia smuggled food to me in the cupboard, and she found me a razor. After lunch, I managed to get out of the house, but I missed the two o'clock, and caught the three o'clock train. We both thought Lydia would be safe until my return. I also thought that my presence had been undetected, but someone knew that I was there. Someone, indeed, knew the whole plan, and told you about me. What's more, someone managed to get into her room during the afternoon, and strangle her, although she was frightened of everyone left in the house. How ? And as you so pertinently ask, why the butterfly ?'

'Are you suggesting you've been framed, sir ?'

'Something like that,' I agreed.

'By whom, sir ?' He sounded sceptical.

'Precisely,' I said again, unpleasantly.

The superintendent rose to his feet. 'I think we've wasted enough time, sir,' he said. 'If you wouldn't mind coming down to the station.'

'Not so fast. Not so fast,' I protested. 'Tell me, did the doctor think there had been a struggle ?'

'Yes.'

'So the extra time may have been needed to remove the traces of the struggle. Perhaps a button got pulled off a jacket, or a collar was torn, or a face was scratched. Perhaps a garment had to be disposed of. One moment. . . .'

'Sir ?'

'How stupid of me ! Why was the purple scarf round Lydia's neck when I saw her ? The doctor must have removed it when he examined her.'

'Well ?'

'I suppose you'd already been informed that it was one that I gave her last Christmas ?'

'We are aware of that fact, sir, yes.'

And now, suddenly, everything fell into place, and I knew who had murdered Lydia ! As a child I'd possessed a toy called a kaleidoscope. It was a sort of telescope, filled with coloured beads. You put it to your eye, and found a marvellous and intricate pattern. You turned it, and immediately all the glass pieces shifted, and another equally intricate pattern was formed. The same pieces of glass, in the same little telescope, yet when looked at one way they gave an entirely different design from the one they formed when looked at another way. And so it was with the case on hand. I suddenly realized that Lydia's death hadn't been the prime object ; that in fact it was only an elaborate trap to catch and ruin me. I was the prey, and Lydia was dead because she had been the only love of my life.

I put an imaginary kaleidoscope to my eye, and there she lay, with Vincent standing over her, pulling the scarf tightly round her throat. He needed money, and Lydia's death would provide it for him. He had no wish to be caught, of course, so when the police came, he threw the blame on me.

I turned the toy, and the picture shifted. Now it was the Colonel, and he too was pulling on that infernal purple scarf. He too needed money, and he too was prepared to implicate me. Lydia had refused to pay any more blackmail, and had threatened to expose him into the bargain.

I twisted it for the last time, and there she was. Clara. The real killer. She was winding the scarf round her mother's neck, and Lydia was struggling wildly. But Clara was too strong for her, and when she was dead, Clara took the scarlet feather butterfly out of her pocket, and fixed it in her mother's hair.

My mind reeled back to a day last summer, when Clara had telephoned me in that voice so like her mother's, that even after all those years of loving, I still couldn't tell them apart, and she'd invited herself out to dinner with me. She had sounded so desperate that I had agreed to take her to a favourite restaurant of mine and Lydia's. She had been strained and slightly hysterical all through the meal, and had persisted in discussing my feelings about her mother throughout the entire evening. She had drunk far too much, and when it was time to go, I'd had to see her back, not only to her home, but to her bedroom. She'd tried to get me to make love to her, and when I had refused as gently as I could, she had pleaded : 'Why, Verney ? Why won't you ? Am I so much less attractive than my mother ?'

'Yes,' I had replied. 'You're a million light years apart.' I had drunk too much, too.

She had nearly struck me, then she had cried as if her heart would break, and then at last she had let me go. Neither of us had ever referred to the incident again, and latterly she had seemed so ordinary and cheerful when she was with me, that I had all but forgotten about it.

But Clara hadn't.

It was she, I now realized, who had telephoned me to make the arrangements for my stay last night. She would have been able to persuade her mother that I alone could be trusted to protect her ; and so of course it was she who had been able to tell the police that I had been in the house. It was she, I now remembered, who had refused to come to Lydia's until this particular weekend ; although she had toyed with the idea of murder, she couldn't perhaps bring herself to act until now. I was sure that further questions would reveal her as the instigator of the idea that all the house guests spent the entire afternoon together, so providing a neat collective alibi, and immunity (especially valuable to Lethbridge) from over-zealous questioning from the police.

The superintendent was right. The butterfly had been the real pointer to the identity of the killer. Clara had wanted revenge ; on her mother, and on me. What need had Vincent - decadent, greedy, but cold-hearted, Vincent - to demonstrate by means of a scarlet ornament, his feelings for his step-mother ? Or Lethbridge, whose reaction to Lydia's infatuation had been to seize the chance of blackmail ? But Clara, over-emotional, always too clever by half, had perhaps seen in the feathered brooch an echo of the blue heart in the McNairn case - an echo which had carried to the superintendent's ear - as well as an opportunity to besmirch her mother in death by this jealous frivolity, and 'sinfulness'.

'Before you take me to the station,' I said, 'search Clara's room. Either there or in the dustbin, or even in the incinerator, I can't help feeling that your forensic experts will find clues which will help you to solve this case correctly. I have only one advantage over you. I know positively that I didn't commit the crime. I also happen to know, and know well, the characters of the people concerned.'

There was a noise outside the room, and there Clara stood, framed in the doorway. Her eyes blazed hatred at me. 'You're a sod, Verney - you always were. But you're too late, Superintendent. I had a plan for every eventuality. For this one, I had cyanide.'

With these last defiant words, she pitched forward at my feet.

E. W. Hornung

OUT OF PARADISE

IF I MUST tell more tales of Raffles, I can but go back to our earliest days together, and fill in the blanks left by discretion in existing annals. In so doing I may indeed fill some small part of an infinitely greater blank, across which you may conceive me to have stretched my canvas for a first frank portrait of my friend. The whole truth cannot harm him now. I shall paint in every wart. Raffles was a villain, when all is written ; it is no service to his memory to glaze the fact ; yet I have done so myself before today. I have omitted whole heinous episodes. I have dwelt unduly on the redeeming side. And this I may do again, blinded even as I write by the gallant glamour that made my villain more to me than any hero. But at least there shall be no more reservations, and as an earnest I shall make no further secret of the greatest wrong that even Raffles ever did me.

I pick my words with care and pain, loyal as I still would be to my friend, and yet remembering as I must those Ides of March when he led me blindfold into temptation and crime. That was an ugly office, if you will. It was a moral bagatelle to the treacherous trick he was to play me a few weeks later. The second offence, on the other hand, was to prove the less serious of the two against society, and might in itself have been published to the world years ago. There have been private reasons for my reticence. The affair was not only too intimately mine, and too discreditable to Raffles ; one other was involved in it, one dearer to me than Raffles himself, one whose name shall not even now be sullied by association with ours.

Suffice it that I had been engaged to her before that mad March deed. True, her people called it 'an understanding', and frowned even upon that, as well they might. But their authority was not direct ; we bowed to it as an act of politic grace ; between us, all was well but my unworthiness. That may be gauged when I confess that this was how the matter stood on the night I gave a worthless cheque for my losses at baccarat, and afterwards turned to Raffles in my need. Even after that I saw her sometimes. But I let her guess that there was more upon my soul than she must ever share, and at last I had written to end it all. I remember that week so well ! It was the close of such a May as we have never had since, and I was too miserable even to follow the heavy scoring in the papers ! Raffles was the only man who could get a wicket up at Lord's, and I never once went to see him play. Against Yorkshire, however, he helped himself to a hundred runs as well ; and that brought Raffles round to me, on his way home to the Albany.

'We must dine and celebrate the rare event,' said he. 'A century takes it out of one at my time of life ; and you, Bunny, you look quite as much in need of your end of a worthy bottle. Suppose we make it the Café Royal, and eight sharp ? I'll be there first to fix up the table and the wine.'

And at the Café Royal I incontinently told him of the trouble I was in. It was the first he had ever heard of my affair, and I told him all, though not before our bottle had been succeeded by a pint of the same exemplary brand. Raffles heard me out with grave attention. His sympathy was the more grateful for the tactful brevity with which it was indicated rather than expressed. He only wished that I had told him of this complication in the beginning ; as I had not, he agreed with me that the only course was a candid and complete renunciation. It was not as though my divinity had a penny of her own, or I could earn an honest one. I had explained to Raffles that she was an orphan, who spent most of her time with an aristocratic aunt in the country, and the remainder under the repressive roof of a pompous politician in Palace Gardens. The aunt had, I believed, still a sneaking softness for me, but her illustrious brother had set his face against me from the first.

'Hector Carruthers !' murmured Raffles, repeating the detested name with his clear, cold eye on mine. 'I suppose you haven't seen much of him ?'

'Not a thing for ages,' I replied. 'I was at the house two or three days last year, but they've neither asked me since nor been at home to me when I've called. The old beast seems a judge of men.'

And I laughed bitterly in my glass.

'Nice house ?' said Raffles, glancing at himself in his silver cigarette-case.

'Top shelf,' said I. 'You know the houses in Palace Gardens, don't you ?'

'Not so well as I should like to know them, Bunny.'

'Well, it's about the most palatial of the lot. The old ruffian is as rich as Croesus. It's a country place in town.'

'What about the window fastenings ?' asked Raffles, casually.

I recoiled from the open cigarette-case that he proffered as he spoke.

Our eyes met ; and in his there was that starry twinkle of mirth and mischief, that sunny beam of audacious devilment, which had been my undoing two months before, which was to undo me as often as he chose until the chapter's end. Yet for once I withstood its glamour ; for once I turned aside that luminous glance with front of steel. There was no need for Raffles to voice his plans. I read them all between the strong lines of his smiling, eager face. And I pushed back my chair in the equal eagerness of my own resolve.

'Not if I know it !' said I. 'A house I've dined in – a house I've seen *her* in – a house where *she* stays by the month together ! Don't put it into words, Raffles, or I'll get up and go.'

'You mustn't do that before the coffee and liqueur,' said Raffles, laughing. 'Have a small Sullivan first : it's the royal road to a cigar. And now let me observe that your scruples would do you honour if old Carruthers still lived in the house in question.'

'Do you mean to say he doesn't ?'

Raffles struck a match, and handed it first to me. 'I mean to say, my dear Bunny, that Palace Gardens knows the very name no more. You began by telling me you had heard nothing of these people all this year. That's quite enough to account for our little misunderstanding. I was thinking of the house, and you were thinking of the people in the house.'

'But who are they, Raffles ? Who has taken the house, if old Carruthers has moved, and how do you know that it is still worth a visit ?'

'In answer to your first question – Lord Lochmaben,' replied Raffles, blowing bracelets of smoke towards the ceiling. 'You look as though you had never heard of him ; but as the cricket and racing are the only part of your paper that you condescend to read, you can't be expected to keep track of all the peers created in your time. Your other question is not worth answering. How do you suppose that I know these things ? It's my business to get to know them, and that's all there is to it. As a matter of fact, Lady Lochmaben has just as good diamonds as Mrs Carruthers ever had ; and the chances are that she keeps them where Mrs Carruthers kept hers, if you could enlighten me on that point.'

As it happened, I could, since I knew from his niece that it was one on which Mr Carruthers had been a faddist in his time. He had made quite a study of the cracksman's craft, in a resolve to circumvent it with his own. I remembered myself how the ground-floor windows were elaborately bolted and shuttered, and how the doors of all the rooms opening upon the square inner hall were fitted with extra Yale locks, at an unlikely height, not to be discovered by one within the room. It had been the butler's business to turn and to collect all these keys before retiring for the night. But the key of the safe in the study was supposed to be in the jealous keeping of the master of the house himself. That safe was in its turn so ingeniously hidden that I never should have found it for myself. I well remember how one who showed it to me (in the innocence of her heart) laughed as she assured me that even her little trinkets were solemnly locked up in it every night. It had been let into the wall behind one end of the bookcase, expressly to preserve the barbaric splendour of Mrs Carruthers ; without a doubt these Lochmabens would use it for the same purpose ; and in the altered circumstances I had no hesitation in giving Raffles all the information he desired. I even drew a rough plan of the ground floor on the back of my menu-card.

'It was rather clever of you to notice the kind of locks on the inner doors,' he remarked as he put it in his pocket. 'I suppose you don't remember if it was a Yale on the front door as well ?'

'It was not,' I was able to answer quite promptly. 'I happen to know because I once had the key when – when we went to a theatre together.'

'Thank you, old chap,' said Raffles, sympathetically. 'That's all I shall want from you, Bunny, my boy. There's no night like tonight !'

It was one of his sayings when bent upon his worst. I looked at him aghast. Our cigars were just in blast, yet already he was signalling for his bill. It was impossible to remonstrate with him until we were both outside in the street.

'I'm coming with you,' said I, running my arm through his.

'Nonsense, Bunny !'

'Why is it nonsense ? I know every inch of the ground, and since the house has changed hands I have no compunction. Besides, "I have been there" in the other sense as well : once a thief, you know ! In for a penny, in for a pound !'

It was ever my mood when the blood was up. But my old friend failed to appreciate the characteristic as he usually did. We crossed Regent Street in silence. I had to catch his sleeve to keep a hand in his inhospitable arm.

'I really think you had better stay away,' said Raffles, as we reached the other kerb. 'I've no use for you this time.'

'Yet I thought I had been useful up to now ?'

'That may be, Bunny, but I tell you frankly I don't want you tonight.'

'Yet I know the ground, and you don't ! I tell you what,' said I : 'I'll just come to show you the ropes, and I won't take a pennyweight of the swag.'

Such was the teasing fashion in which he invariably prevailed upon me ; it was delightful to note how it caused him to yield in his turn. But

Raffles had the grace to give in with a laugh, whereas I too often lost my temper with my point.

'You little rabbit !' he chuckled. 'You shall have your share, whether you come or not ; but, seriously, don't you think you might remember the girl ?'

'What's the use ?' I groaned. 'You agree there is nothing for it but to give her up. I am glad to say I saw that for myself before I asked you, and wrote to tell her so on Sunday. Now it's Wednesday, and she hasn't answered by line or sign. It's waiting for one word from her that's driving me mad.'

'Perhaps you wrote to Palace Gardens ?'

'No, I sent it to the country. There's been time for an answer, wherever she may be.'

We had reached the Albany, and halted with one accord at the Piccadilly portico, red cigar to red cigar.

'You wouldn't like to go and see if the answer's in your rooms ?' he asked.

'No. What's the good ? Where's the point in giving her up if I'm going to straighten out when it's too late ? It *is* too late, I *have* given her up, and I *am* coming with you !'

The hand that bowled the most puzzling ball in England (once it found its length) descended on my shoulder with surprising promptitude.

'Very well, Bunny ! That's finished ; but your blood be on your own pate if evil comes of it. Meanwhile we can't do better than turn in here till you've finished your cigar as it deserves, and topped up with such a cup of tea as you must learn to like if you hope to get on in your new profession. And when the hours are small enough, Bunny, my boy, I don't mind admitting I shall be very glad to have you with me.'

I have a vivid memory of the interim in his rooms. I think it must have been the first and last of its kind that I was called upon to sustain with so much knowledge of what lay before me. I passed the time with one restless eye upon the clock, and the other on the Tantalus which Raffles ruthlessly declined to unlock. He admitted it was like waiting with one's pads on ; and in my slender experience of the game of which he was a world's master, that was an ordeal not to be endured without a general quaking of the inner man. I was, on the other hand, all right when I got to the metaphorical wicket ; and half the surprises that Raffles sprung on me were doubtless due to his early recognition of the fact.

On this occasion I fell swiftly and hopelessly out of love with the prospect I had so gratuitously embraced. It was not only my repugnance to enter the house in that way, which grew upon my better judgment as the artificial enthusiasm of the evening evaporated from my veins. Strong as that repugnance became, I had an even stronger feeling that we were embarking on an important enterprise far too much upon the spur of the moment. The latter qualm I had the temerity to confess to Raffles ; not have I often loved him more than when he freely admitted it to be the most natural feeling in the world. He assured me, however, that he had had my Lady Lochmaben and her jewels in his mind for several months ; he had sat behind them at first nights, and long ago determined what to take or to reject ; in fine, he had only been waiting for those topographical details which it had been my chance privilege to supply. I now learnt that he had numerous houses in a similar state upon his list ; something or other was wanting in each case in order to complete his plans. In that of the Bond Street jeweller it was a trusty accomplice ; in the present instance, a more intimate knowledge of the house. And lastly, this was a Wednesday night, when the tired legislator gets early to his bed.

How I wish I could make the whole world see and hear him, and smell the smoke of his beloved Sullivan, as he took me into these the secrets of his infamous trade ! Neither look nor language would betray his infamy. As a mere talker, I shall never listen to the like of Raffles on this side of the sod ; and his talk was seldom garnished by an oath, never in my remembrance by the unclean word. Then, he looked like a man who had dressed to dine out, not like one who had long since dined ; for his curly hair, though longer than another's, was never untidy in its length ; and these were the days when it was still as black as ink. Nor were there many lines as yet upon the smooth and mobile face ; and its frame was still that dear den of disorder and good taste, with the carved bookcase, the dresser and chests of still older oaks, and the Wattses and Rossettis hung anyhow on the walls.

It must have been one o'clock before we drove in a hansom as far as Kensington Church, instead of getting down at the gates of our private road to ruin. Constitutionally shy of the direct approach, Raffles was further deterred by a ball in full swing at the Empress Rooms, whence potential witnesses were pouring between dances into the cool deserted street. Instead he led me a little way up Church Street, and so through the narrow passage into Palace Gardens. He knew the house as well as I did. We made our first survey from the other side of the road. And the house was not quite in darkness ; there was a dim light over the door, a brighter one in the stables, which stood still further back from the road.

'That's a bit of a bore,' said Raffles. 'The ladies have been out somewhere - trust them to spoil the show ! They would get to bed before the stable folk, but insomnia is the curse of their sex and our profession. Somebody's not home yet ; that will be the son of the house ; but he's a beauty, who may not come home at all.'

'Another Alick Carruthers,' I murmured, recalling the one I liked least of all the household as I remembered it.

'They might be brothers,' rejoined Raffles, who knew all the loose fish about town. 'Well, I'm not sure that I shall want you after all, Bunny.'

'Why not ?'

'If the front door's only on the latch, and you're right about the lock, I shall walk in as though I were the son of the house myself.'

And he jingled the skeleton bunch that he carried on a chain as honest men carry their latchkeys.

'You forget the inner doors and the safe.'

'True. You might be useful to me there. But I still don't like leading you in where it isn't absolutely necessary, Bunny.'

'Then let me lead you,' I answered, and forthwith marched across the broad, secluded road, with the great houses standing back on either side in their ample gardens, as though the one opposite belonged to me. I thought Raffles had stayed behind, for I never heard him at my heels, yet there he was when I turned round at the gate.

'I must teach you the step,' he whispered, shaking his head. 'You shouldn't use your heel at all. Here's a grass border for you : walk it as you would the plank ! Gravel makes a noise, and flowerbeds tell a tale. Wait – I must carry you across this.'

It was the sweep of the drive, and in the dim light from above the door, the soft gravel, ploughed into ridges by the night's wheels, threatened an alarm at every step. Yet Raffles, with me in his arms, crossed the zone of peril softly as the pard.

'Shoes in your pocket – that's the beauty of pumps !' he whispered on the step ; his light bunch tickled faintly ; a couple of keys he stooped and tried, with the touch of a humane dentist ; the third let us into the porch. And as we stood together on the mat, as he was gradually closing the door, a clock within chimed a half-hour in fashion so thrillingly familiar to me that I caught Raffles by the arm. My half-hours of happiness had flown to just such chimes ! I looked wildly about me in the dim light. Hatstand and oak settee belonged equally to my past. And Raffles was smiling in my face as he held the door wide for my escape.

'You told me a lie !' I gasped in whispers.

'I did nothing of the sort,' he replied. 'The furniture's the furniture of Hector Carruthers, but the house is the house of Lord Lochmaben. Look here !'

He had stooped and was smoothing out the discarded envelope of a telegram. 'Lord Lochmaben,' I read in pencil by the dim light ; and the case was plain to me on the spot. My friends had let their house furnished, as anybody but Raffles would have explained in the beginning.

'All right,' I said. 'Shut the door.'

And he not only shut it without a sound, but shot a bolt that might have been sheathed in rubber.

In another minute we were at work upon the study door, I with the tiny lantern and the bottle of rock-oil, he with the brace and the largest bit. The Yale lock he had given up at a glance. It was placed high up in the door, feet above the handle, and the chain of holes with which Raffles had soon surrounded it were bored on a level with his eyes. Yet the clock in the hall chimed again, and two ringing strokes resounded through the silent house, before we gained admittance to the room.

Raffles's next care was to muffle the bell on the shuttered window (with a silk handkerchief from the hat-stand), and to prepare an emergency exit by opening first the shutters and then the window itself. Luckily it was a still night, and very little wind came in to embarrass us. He then began operations on the safe, revealed by me behind its folding screen of books, while I stood sentry on the threshold. I may have stood there for a dozen minutes, listening to the loud hall clock and to the gentle dentistry of Raffles in the mouth of the safe behind me, when a third sound thrilled my every nerve. It was the equally cautious opening of a door in the gallery overhead.

I moistened my lips to whisper a word of warning to Raffles. But his ears had been as quick as mine, and something longer. His lantern darkened as I turned my head ; next moment I felt his breath upon the back of my neck. It was now too late even for a whisper, and quite out of the question to close the mutilated door. There we could only stand, I on the threshold, Raffles at my elbow, while one carrying a candle crept down the stairs.

The study door was at right angles to the lowest flight, and just to the right of one alighting in the hall. It was thus impossible for us to see who it was until the person was close abreast of us ; but by the rustle of the gown we knew that it was one of the ladies, and dressed just as she had come from theatre to ball. Insensibly I drew back as the candle swam into our field of vision : it had not traversed many inches when a hand was clapped firmly but silently across my mouth.

I could forgive Raffles for that, at any rate ! In another breath I should have cried aloud : for the girl with the candle, the girl in her ball-dress at dead of night, the girl with the letter for the post, was the last girl on

God's wide earth whom I should have chosen thus to encounter – a midnight intruder in the very house where I had been reluctantly received on her account !

I forgot Raffles. I forgot the new and unforgivable grudge I had against him now. I forgot his very hand across my mouth, even before he paid me the compliment of removing it. There was the only girl in all my world : I had eyes and brains for no one and for nothing else. She had neither seen nor heard us, had turned neither to the right hand nor the left. But a small oak table stood on the opposite side of the hall ; it was to this table that she went. On it was one of those boxes in which one puts one's letters for the post ; and she stooped to read by her candle the times at which this box was cleared.

The loud clock ticked and ticked. She was standing at her full height now, her candle on the table, her letter in both hands, and in her downcast face a sweet and pitiful perplexity that drew the tears to my eyes. Through a film I saw her open the envelope so lately sealed, and read her letter once more, as though she would have altered it a little at the last. It was too late for that ; but of a sudden she plucked a rose from her bosom, and was pressing it in with her letter when I groaned aloud.

How could I help it ? The letter was for me : of that I was as sure as though I had been looking over her shoulder. She was as true as tempered steel ; there were not two of us to whom she wrote and sent roses at dead of night. It was her one chance of writing to me. None would know that she had written. And she cared enough to soften the reproaches I had richly earned with a red rose warm from her own warm heart. And there, there was I, a common thief, who had broken in to steal ! Yet I was unaware that I had uttered a sound until she looked up, startled, and the hands behind me pinned me where I stood.

I think she must have seen us, even in the dim light of the solitary candle. Yet not a sound escaped her as she peered courageously in our direction ; neither did one of us move ; but the hall clock went on and on, every tick like the beat of a drum to bring the house about our ears, until a minute must have passed as in some breathless dream. And then came the awakening – with such a knocking and a ringing at the front door as brought all three of us to our senses on the spot.

'The son of the house !' whispered Raffles in my ear, as he dragged me back to the window he had left open for our escape. But as he leaped out first a sharp cry stopped me at the sill. 'Get back ! Get back ! We're trapped !' he cried ; and in the single second that I stood there, I saw him fell one officer to the ground, and dart across the lawn with another at his heels. A third came running up to the window. What could I do but

double back into the house ? And there in the hall I met my lost love face
to face.

Till that moment she had not recognised me. I ran to catch her as she
all but fell. And my touch repelled her into life, so that she shook me off,
and stood gasping : 'You, of all men ! You, of all men !' until I could bear
it no more, but broke again for the study window. 'Not that way – not
that way !' she cried, in an agony at that. Her hands were upon me now.
'In there, in there,' she whispered, pointing and pulling me to a mere
cupboard under the stairs, where hats and coats were hung ; and it was
she who shut the door on me with a sob.

Doors were already opening overhead, voices calling, voices answering, the alarm running like wildfire from room to room. Soft feet pattered in the gallery and down the stairs about my very ears. I do not know
what made me put on my own shoes as I heard them, but I think that I
was ready and even longing to walk out and give myself up. I need not
say what and who it was that alone restrained me. I heard her name. I
heard them crying to her as though she had fainted. I recognised the
detested voice of my *bête noire,* Alick Carruthers, thick as might be
expected of the dissipated dog, yet daring to stutter out her name. And
then I heard, without catching, her low reply ; it was in answer to the
somewhat stern questioning of quite another voice ; and from what
followed, I knew that she had never fainted at all.

'Upstairs, miss, did he ? Are you sure ?'

I did not hear her answer. I conceive her as simply pointing up the
stairs. In any case, about my very ears once more there now followed
such a patter and tramp of bare and booted feet as renewed in me a base
fear for my own skin. But voices and feet passed over my head, went up
and up, higher and higher ; and I was wondering whether or not to make
a dash for it, when one light pair came running down again, and in very
despair I marked out to meet my preserver, looking as little as I could
like the abject thing I felt.

'Be quick !' she cried in a harsh whisper, and pointed peremptorily to
the porch.

But I stood stubbornly before her, my heart hardened by her hardness, and perversely indifferent to all else. And as I stood I saw the
letter she had written, in the hand with which she pointed, crushed into
a ball.

'Quickly !' She stamped her foot. 'Quickly – *if you ever cared* !'

This in a whisper, without bitterness, without contempt, but with a
sudden wild entreaty that breathed upon the dying embers of my poor
manhood. I drew myself together for the last time in her sight. I turned,

and left her as she wished – for her sake, not for mine. And as I went I heard her tearing her letter into little pieces, and the little pieces falling on the floor.

Then I remembered Raffles, and could have killed him for what he had done. Doubtless by this time he was safe and snug in the Albany : what did my fate matter to him ? Never mind ; this should be the end between him and me as well ; it was the end of everything, this dark night's work ! I would go and tell him so. I would jump into a cab and drive there and then to his accursed rooms. But first I must escape from the trap in which he had been so ready to leave me. And on the very steps I drew back in despair. They were searching the shrubberies between the drive and the road ; a policeman's lantern kept flashing in and out among the laurels, while a young man in evening clothes directed him from the gravel sweep. It was this young man whom I must dodge, but at my first step in the gravel he wheeled round, and it was Raffles himself.

'Hulloa !' he cried. 'So you've come up to join the dance as well ! Had a look inside, have you ? You'll be better employed in helping to draw the cover in front here. It's all right, officer – only another gentleman from the Empress Rooms.'

And we made a brave show of assisting in the futile search, until the arrival of more police, and a broad hint from an irritable sergeant, gave us an excellent excuse for going off arm in arm. But it was Raffles who had thrust his arm through mine. I shook him off as we left the scene of shame behind.

'My dear Bunny !' he exclaimed. 'Do you know what brought me back ?'

I answered savagely that I neither knew nor cared.

'I had the very devil of a squeak for it,' he went on. 'I did the hurdles over two or three garden walls, but so did the flyer who was on my tracks, and he drove me back into the straight and down to High Street like any lamp-lighter. If he had only had the breath to sing out it would have been all up with me then ; as it was I pulled off my overcoat the moment I was round the corner, and took a ticket for it at the Empress Rooms.'

'I suppose you had one for the dance that was going on,' I growled. Nor would it have been a coincidence for Raffles to have had a ticket for that or any other entertainment of the London season.

'I never asked what the dance was,' he returned. 'I merely took the opportunity of revising my toilet, and getting rid of that rather distinctive overcoat, which I shall call for now. They're not too particular at such stages of such proceedings, but I've not doubt I should have seen someone I knew if I had gone right in ; I might even have had a turn, if only I had been less uneasy about you, Bunny.'

'It was like you to come back and help me out,' said I. 'But to lie to me, and to inveigle me with your lies into that house of all houses – that was not like you, Raffles – and I never shall forgive it or you !'

Raffles took my arm again. We were near the High Street gates of Palace Gardens, and I was too miserable to resist an advance which I meant never to give him an opportunity to repeat.

'Come, come, Bunny, there wasn't much inveigling about it,' said he. 'I did my level best to leave you behind, but you wouldn't listen to me.'

'If you had told me the truth I should have listened fast enough,' I retorted. 'But what's the use of talking ? You can boast of your own adventures after you bolted. You don't care what happened to me.'

'I cared so much that I came back to see.'

'You might have spared yourself the trouble ! The wrong had been done. Raffles – Raffles – don't you know who she was ?'

It was my hand that gripped his arm once more.

'I guessed,' he answered, gravely enough even for me.

'It was she who saved me, not you,' I said. 'And that is the bitterest part of all !'

Yet I told him that part with a strange sad pride in her whom I had lost, through him, for ever. As I ended, we turned into High Street ; in the prevailing stillness, the faint strains of the band reached us from the Empress Rooms ; and I hailed a crawling hansom as Raffles turned that way.

'Bunny,' said he, 'it's no use saying I'm sorry. Sorrow adds insult in a case like this – if ever there was or will be such another ! Only believe me, Bunny, when I swear to you that I had not the smallest shadow of a suspicion that *she* was in the house.'

And in my heart of hearts I did believe him ; but I could not bring myself to say the words.

'You told me yourself that you had written to her in the country,' he pursued.

'And that letter !' I rejoined, in a fresh wave of bitterness : 'that letter she had written at dead of night, and stolen down to post, it was the one I had been waiting for all these days ! I should have got it tomorrow. Now I shall never get it, never hear from her again, nor have another chance in this world or in the next. I don't say it was all your fault. You no more knew that she was there than I did. But you told me a deliberate lie about her people, and that I never shall forgive.'

I spoke as vehemently as I could under my breath. The hansom was waiting at the kerb.

'I can say no more than I have said,' returned Raffles with a shrug. 'Lie or no lie, I didn't tell it to bring you with me, but to get you to give me certain information without feeling a beast about it. But, as a matter of fact, it was no lie about old Hector Carruthers and Lord Lochmaben, and anybody but you would have guessed the truth.'

'What is the truth ?'

'I as good as told you, Bunny, again and again.'

'Then tell me now.'

'If you read your paper there would be no need ; but if you want to know, old Carruthers headed the list of the Birthday Honours, and Lord Lochmaben is the title of his choice.'

And this miserable quibble was not a lie ! My lip curled, I turned my back without a word, and drove home to my Mount Street flat in a new fury of savage scorn. Not a lie, indeed ! It was one that is half a truth, the meanest lie of all, and the very last to which I could have dreamt that Raffles would stoop. So far there had been a degree of honour between us, if only of the kind understood to obtain between thief and thief. Now all that was at an end. Raffles had cheated me. Raffles had completed the ruin of my life. I was done with Raffles, as she who shall not be named was done with me.

And yet, even while I blamed him most bitterly, and utterly abominated his deceitful deed, I could not but admit in my heart that the result was out of all proportion to the intent : he had never dreamt of doing me this injury, or indeed any injury at all. Intrinsically the deceit had been quite venial, the reason for it obviously the reason that Raffles had given me. It was quite true that he had spoken of this Lochmaben peerage as a new creation, and of the heir to it in a fashion only applicable to Alick Carruthers. He had given me hints, which I had been too dense to take, and he had certainly made more than one attempt to deter me from accompanying him on this fatal emprise ; had he been more explicit, I might have made it my business to deter him. I could not say in my heart that Raffles had failed to satisfy such honour as I might reasonably expect to subsist between us. Yet it seems to me to require a superhuman sanity always and unerringly to separate cause from effect, achievement from intent. And I, for one, was never quite able to do so in this case.

I could not be accused of neglecting my newspaper during the next few wretched days. I read every word that I could find about the attempted jewel robbery in Palace Gardens, and the reports afforded me my sole comfort. In the first place, it was only an attempted robbery ; nothing had been taken after all. And then - and then - the one member of the household who had come nearest to a personal encounter with either of us was unable to furnish any description of the man – had even expressed a doubt as to any likelihood of identification in the event of an arrest !

I will not say with what mingled feelings I read and dwelt on that announcement. It kept a certain faint glow alive within me until the morning that brought me back the only presents I had ever made her. They were but books ; jewellery had been tabooed by the authorities. And the books came back without a word, though the parcel was directed in her hand.

I had made up my mind not to go near Raffles again, but in my heart I already regretted my resolve. I had forfeited love, I had sacrificed honour, and now I must deliberately alienate myself from the one being whose society might yet be some recompense for all that I had lost. The situation was aggravated by the state of my exchequer. I expected an ultimatum from my banker by every post. Yet this influence was nothing to the other. It was Raffles I loved. It was not the dark life we led together, still less its base rewards ; it was the man himself, his gaiety, his humour, his dazzling audacity, his incomparable courage and resource. And a very horror of turning to him again in mere need or greed set the seal on my first angry resolution. But the anger was soon gone out of me, and when at length Raffles bridged the gap by coming to me, I rose to greet him almost with a shout.

He came as though nothing had happened ; and, indeed, not very many days had passed, though they might have been months to me. Yet I fancied the gaze that watched me through our smoke a trifle less sunny than it had been before. And it was a relief to me when he came out with few preliminaries to the inevitable point.

'Did you ever hear from her, Bunny ?' he asked.

'In a way,' I answered. 'We won't talk about it, if you don't mind, Raffles.'

'That sort of way !' he exclaimed. He seemed both surprised and disappointed.

'Yes,' I said, 'that sort of way. It's finished. What did you expect ?'

'I don't know,' said Raffles. 'I only thought that the girl who went so far to get a fellow out of a tight place might go a little further to keep him from getting into another.'

'I don't see why she should,' said I, honestly enough, yet with the irritation of a less just feeling deep down in my inmost consciousness.

'Yet you did hear from her ?' he persisted.

'She sent me back my poor presents, without a word,' I said, 'if you call that hearing.'

I could not bring myself to own to Raffles that I had given her only books. He asked if I was sure that she had sent them back herself ; and that was his last question. My answer was enough for him. And to this day I cannot say whether it was more in relief than in regret that he laid a hand upon my shoulder.

'So you are out of Paradise after all !' said Raffles. 'I was not sure, or I should have come round before. Well, Bunny, if they don't want you there, there's a little Inferno in the Albany where you'll be as welcome as ever !'

And still, with all the magic mischief of his smile, there was that touch of sadness which I was yet to read aright.

Dorothy L. Sayers

THE CAVE OF ALI BABA

IN THE FRONT ROOM of a grim and narrow house in Lambeth, a man sat eating kippers and glancing through the *Morning Post*. He was smallish and spare, with brown hair rather too regularly waved and a strong, brown beard, cut to a point. His double-breasted suit of navy-blue and his socks, tie and handkerchief, all scrupulously matched, were a trifle more point-device than the best taste approves, and his boots were slightly too bright a brown. He did not look a gentleman, not even a gentleman's gentleman, yet there was something about his appearance which suggested that he was accustomed to the manner of life in good families. The breakfast-table, which he had set with his own hands, was arrayed with the attention to detail which is exacted of good-class servants. His action, as he walked over to a little side-table and carved himself a plate of ham, was the action of a superior butler ; yet he was not old enough to be a retired butler ; a footman, perhaps, who had come into a legacy.

He finished the ham with good appetite, and, as he sipped his coffee, read through attentively a paragraph which he had already noticed and put aside for consideration.

LORD PETER WIMSEY'S WILL
BEQUEST TO VALET
£10,000 TO CHARITIES

The will of Lord Peter Wimsey, who was killed last December while shooting big game in Tanganyika, was proved yesterday at £500,000. A sum of £10,000 was left to various charities, including [here followed a list of bequests]. To his valet, Mervyn Bunter, was left an annuity of £500 and the lease of the testator's flat in Piccadilly. [Then followed a number of personal bequests.] The remainder of the estate, including the valuable collection of books and pictures at 110A Piccadilly, was left to the testator's mother, the Dowager Duchess of Denver.

Lord Peter Wimsey was thirty-seven at the time of his death. He was the younger brother of the present Duke of Denver, who is the wealthiest peer in the United Kingdom. Lord Peter was distinguished as a criminologist and took an active part in the solution of several famous mysteries. He was a well-known book-collector and man-about-town.

The man gave a sigh of relief.

'No doubt about that,' he said aloud. 'People don't give their money away if they're going to come back again. The blighter's dead and buried right enough. I'm free.'

He finished his coffee, cleared the table and washed up the crockery, took his bowler hat from the hall-stand, and went out.

A bus took him to Bermondsey. He alighted, and plunged into a network of gloomy streets, arriving after a quarter of an hour's walk at a seedy-looking public house in a low quarter. He entered and called for a double whisky.

The house had only just opened, but a number of customers, who had apparently been waiting on the doorstep for this desirable event, were already clustered about the bar. The man who might have been a footman reached for his glass, and in doing so jostled the elbow of a flash person in a check suit and regrettable tie.

'Here !' expostulated the flash person, 'what d'yer mean by it. We don't want your sort here. Get out !'

He emphasised his remarks with a few highly coloured words, and a violent push in the chest.

'Bar's free to everybody, isn't it ?' said the other, returning the shove with interest.

'Now then !' said the barmaid, 'none o' that. The gentleman didn't do it intentional, Mr Jukes.'

'Didn't he ?' said Mr Jukes. 'Well, I *did*.'

'And you ought to be ashamed of yourself' retorted the young lady, with a toss of the head. 'I'll have no quarrelling in my bar - not this time in the morning.'

'It was quite an accident,' said the man from Lambeth. 'I'm not one to make a disturbance, having always been used to the best houses. But if any gentleman *wants* to make trouble - '

'All right, all right,' said Mr Jukes, more pacifically. 'I'm not too keen to give you a new face. Not but what any alteration wouldn't be for the better. Mind your manners another time, that's all. What'll you have ?'

'No, no,' protested the other, 'this one must be on me. Sorry I pushed you. I didn't mean it. But I didn't like to be taken up so short.'

'Say no more about it,' said Mr Jukes generously. 'I'm standing this. Another double whisky, miss, and one of the usual. Come over here where there isn't so much of a crowd, or you'll be getting yourself into trouble again.'

He led the way to a small table in the corner of the room.

'That's all right,' said Mr Jukes. 'Very nicely done. I don't think there's any danger here, but you can't be too careful. Now, what about it, Rogers ? Have you made up your mind to come in with us ?'

'Yes,' said Rogers, with a glance over his shoulder, 'yes, I have. That is, mind you, if everything seems all right. I'm not looking for trouble, and I don't want to get let in for any dangerous games. I don't mind giving you information, but it's understood as I take no active part in whatever goes on. Is that straight ?'

'You wouldn't be allowed to take an active part if you wanted to,' said Mr Jukes. 'Why, you poor fish, Number One wouldn't have anybody but experts on his jobs. All you have to do is to let us know where the stuff is and how to get it. The Society does the rest. It's some organisation, I can tell you. You won't even know who's doing it, or how it's done. You won't know anbody, and nobody will know you - except Number One, of course. He knows everybody.'

'And you,' said Rogers.

'And me, of course. But I shall be transferred to another district. We shan't meet again after today, except at the general meeting, and then we shall all be masked.'

'Go on !' said Rogers incredulously.

'Fact. You'll be taken to Number One - he'll see you, but you won't see him. Then, if he thinks you're any good, you'll be put on the roll, and after that you'll be told where to make your reports to. There is a divisional meeting called once a fortnight, and every three months there's a general meeting and a share-out. Each member is called up by number and has his whack handed over to him. That's all.'

'Well, but suppose two members are put on the same job together ?'

'If it's a daylight job, they'll be so disguised their mothers wouldn't know 'em. But it's mostly night work.'

'I see. But, look here - what's to prevent somebody following me home and giving me away to the police ?'

'Nothing, of course. Only I wouldn't advise him to try it, that's all. The last man who had that bright idea was fished out of the river down Rotherhithe way before he had time to get his precious report in. Number One knows everybody, you see.'

'Oh ! - and who is this Number One ?'

'There's lots of people would give a good bit to know that.'

'Does nobody know ?'

'Nobody. He's a fair marvel, is Number One. He's a gentleman, I can tell you that, and a pretty high-up one, from his ways. *And* he's got eyes all round his head. *And* he's got an arm as long as from here to Australia. *But* nobody knows anything about him, unless it's Number Two, and I'm not even sure about her.'

'There are women in it, then ?'

'You can bet your boots there are. You can't do a job without 'em nowadays. But that needn't worry you. The women are safe enough. They don't want to come to a sticky end, no more than you and me.' .

'But, look here, Jukes - how about the money ? It's a big risk to take. Is it worth it ?'

'Worth it ?' Jukes leant across the little marble-topped table and whispered.

'Coo !' gasped Rogers. 'And how much of that would I get now ?'

'You'd share and share alike with the rest, whether you'd been in that particular job or not. There's fifty members, and you'd get one-fiftieth, same as Number One and same as me.'

'Really ? No kidding ?'

'See that wet, see that dry !' Jukes laughed. 'Say, can you beat it ? There's never been anything like it. It's the biggest thing ever known. He's a great man, is Number One.'

'And do you pull off many jobs ?'

'Many ? Listen. You remember the Carruthers necklace, and the Gorleston Bank robbery ? And the Faversham burglary ? And the big Rubens that disappeared from the National Gallery ? And the Frensham pearls ? All done by the Society. And never one of them cleared up.'

Rogers licked his lips.

'But now, look here,' he said cautiously. 'Supposing I was a spy, as you might say, and supposing I was to go straight off and tell the police about what you've been saying ?'

'Ah !' said Jukes, 'suppose you did, eh ? Well, supposing something nasty didn't happen to you on the way there - which I wouldn't answer for, mind - '

'Do you mean to say you've got me watched ?'

'You can bet your sweet life we have. Yes. Well, *supposing* nothing happened on the way there, and you was to bring the slops to this pub, looking for yours truly - '

'Yes ?'

'You wouldn't find me, that's all. I should have gone to Number Five.'

'Who's Number Five ?'

'Ah ! I don't know. But he's the man that makes you a new face while you wait. Plastic surgery, they call it. And new finger-prints. New everything. We go in for up-to-date methods in our show.'

Rogers whistled.

'Well, how about it ?' asked Jukes, eyeing his acquaintance over the rim of his tumbler.

'Look here – you've told me a lot of things. Shall I be safe if I say "No ?"'

'Oh, yes – if you behave yourself and don't make trouble for us.'

'H'm, I see. And if I say "Yes" ?'

'Then you'll be a rich man in less than no time, with money in your pocket to live like a gentleman. And nothing to do for it, except to tell us what you know about the houses you've been to when you were in service. It's money for jam if you'll act straight by the Society.'

Rogers was silent, thinking it over.

'I'll do it !' he said at last.

'Good for you. Miss ! The same again, please. Here's to it, Rogers ! I knew you were one of the right sort the minute I set eyes on you. Here's to money for jam, and take care of Number One ! Talking of Number One, you'd better come round and see him tonight. No time like the present.'

'Right you are. Where'll I come to ? Here ?'

'Nix. No more of this little pub for us. It's a pity, because it's nice and comfortable, but it can't be helped. Now, what you've got to do is this. At ten o'clock tonight exactly you walk north across Lambeth Bridge' (Rogers winced at this intimation that his abode was known), 'and you'll see a yellow taxi standing there, with the driver doing something to his engine. You'll say to him, "Is your bus fit to go ?" and he'll say, "Depends where you want to go to." And you'll say, "Take me to Number One, London." There's a shop called that, by the way, but he won't take you there. You won't know where he *is* taking you, because the taxi-windows will be covered up, but you musn't mind that. It's the rule for the first visit. Afterwards, when you're regularly one of us, you'll be told the name of the place. And when you get there, do as you're told and speak the truth, because if you don't, Number One will deal with you. See ?'

'I see.'

'Are you game ? You're not afraid ?'

'Of course I'm not afraid.'

'Good man ! Well, we'd better be moving now. And I'll say goodbye, because we shan't see each other again. Goodbye - and good luck !'

'Goodbye.'

They passed through the swing-doors, and out into the mean and dirty street.

The two years subsequent to the enrolment of the ex-footman Rogers in a crook society were marked by a number of startling and successful raids on the houses of distinguished people. There was the theft of the great diamond tiara from the Dowager Duchess of Denver ; the burglary at the flat formerly occupied by the late Lord Peter Wimsey, resulting in the disappearance of £7000 worth of silver and gold plate ; the burglary at the country mansion of Theodore Wintrop, the millionaire - which, incidentally, exposed the thriving gentleman as a confirmed society blackmailer and caused a reverberating scandal in Mayfair ; and the snatching of the famous eight-string necklace of pearls from the neck of the Marchioness of Dinglewood during the singing of the Jewel Song in *Faust* at Covent Garden. It is true that the pearls turned out to be imitation, the original string having been pawned to the Marquis, but the *coup* was nevertheless a sensational one.

On a Saturday afternoon in January, Rogers was sitting in his room in Lambeth, when a slight noise at the front door caught his ear. He sprang up almost before it had ceased, dashed through the small hallway, and flung the door open. The street was deserted. Nevertheless, as he turned back to the sitting-room, he saw an envelope lying on the hat-stand. It was addressed briefly to 'Number Twenty-one.' Accustomed by this time to the somewhat dramatic methods used by the Society to deliver its correspondence, he merely shrugged his shoulders, and opened the note.

It was written in cipher, and when transcribed, ran thus :

Number Twenty-one - An Extraordinary General Meeting will be held tonight at the house of Number One at 11.30. You will be absent at your peril. The word is FINALITY.

Rogers stood for a little time considering this. Then he made his way to a room at the back of the house, in which there was a tall safe, built into the wall. He manipulated the combination and walked into the safe, which ran back for some distance, forming, indeed, a small strong-room. He pulled out a drawer marked 'Correspondence,' and added the paper he had just received to the contents.

After a few moments he emerged, reset the lock to a new combination, and returned to the sitting-room.

'Finality,' he said. 'Yes – I think so.' He stretched out his hand to the telephone – then appeared to alter his mind.

He went upstairs to an attic, and thence climbed into a loft close under the roof. Crawling among the rafters, he made his way into the farthest corner ; then carefully pressed a knob on the timberwork. A concealed trapdoor swung open. He crept through it, and found himself in the corresponding loft of the next house. A soft cooing noise greeted him as he entered. Under the skylight stood three cages, each containing a carrier pigeon.

He glanced cautiously out of the skylight, which looked out upon a high blank wall at the back of some factory or other. There was nobody in the dim little courtyard, and no window within sight. He drew in his head again, and, taking a small fragment of thin paper from his pocket-book, wrote a few letters and numbers upon it. Going to the nearest cage, he took out the pigeon and attached the message to its wing. Then he carefully set the bird on the window-ledge. It hesitated a moment, shifted its pink feet a few times, lifted its wings, and was gone. He saw it tower up into the already darkening sky over the factory roof and vanish into the distance.

He glanced at his watch and returned downstairs. An hour later he released the second pigeon, and in another hour the third. Then he sat down to wait.

At half-past nine he went up to the attic again. It was dark, but a few frosty stars were shining, and a cold air blew through the open window. Something pale gleamed faintly on the floor. He picked it up – it was warm and feathery. The answer had come.

He ruffled the soft plumes and found the paper. Before reading it, he fed the pigeon and put it into one of the cages. As he was about to fasten the door, he checked himself.

'If anything happens to me,' he said, 'there's no need for you to starve to death, my child.'

He pushed the window a little wider open and went downstairs again. The paper in his hand bore only the two letters, 'OK'. It seemed to have been written hurriedly, for there was a long smear of ink on the upper left-hand corner. He noted this with a smile, put the paper in the fire, and, going out into the kitchen, prepared and ate a hearty meal of eggs and corned beef from a new tin. He ate it without bread, though there was a loaf on the shelf near at hand, and washed it down with water from the tap, which he let run for some time before venturing to drink it. Even then he carefully wiped the tap, both inside and outside, before drinking.

When he had finished, he took a revolver from a locked drawer, inspecting the mechanism with attention to see that it was in working order, and loaded it with new cartridges from an unbroken packet. Then he sat down to wait again.

At a quarter before eleven, he rose and went out into the street. He walked briskly, keeping well away from the wall, till he came out into a well-lighted thoroughfare. Here he took a bus, securing the corner seat next to the conductor, from which he could see everybody who got on and off. A succession of buses eventually brought him to a respectable residential quarter of Hampstead. Here he alighted and, still keeping well away from the walls, made his way up to the Heath.

The night was moonless, but not altogether black, and, as he crossed a deserted part of the Heath, he observed one or two other dark forms closing in upon him from various directions. He paused in the shelter of a large tree, and adjusted to his face a black velvet mask, which covered him from brow to chin. At its base the number 21 was clearly embroidered in white thread.

At length a slight dip in the ground disclosed one of those agreeable villas which stand, somewhat isolated, among the rural surroundings of the Heath. One of the windows was lighted. As he made his way to the door, other dark figures, masked like himself, pressed forward and surrounded him. He counted six of them.

The foremost man knocked on the door of the solitary house. After a moment it was opened slightly. The man advanced his head to the opening ; there was a murmur, and the door opened wide. The man stepped in, and the door was shut.

When three of the men had entered, Rogers found himself to be the next in turn. He knocked, three times loudly, then twice faintly. The door opened to the extent of two or three inches, and an ear was presented to the chink. Rogers whispered 'Finality.' The ear was withdrawn, the door opened, and he passed in.

Without any further word of greeting, Number Twenty-one passed into a small room on the left, which was furnished like an office, with a desk, a safe, and a couple of chairs. At the desk sat a massive man in evening dress, with a ledger before him. The new arrival shut the door carefully after him ; it clicked to, on a spring lock. Advancing to the desk, he announced, 'Number Twenty-one, sir,' and stood respectfully waiting. The big man looked up, showing the number 1 startlingly white on his velvet mask. His eyes, of a curious hard blue, scanned Rogers attentively. At a sign from him, Rogers removed his mask. Having verified his identity with care, the President said, 'Very well, Number Twenty-one,' and made an entry in the ledger. The voice was hard and metallic like his eyes. The close scrutiny from behind the immovable black mask seemed to make Rogers uneasy ; he shifted his feet, and his eyes fell. Number One made a sign of dismissal, and Rogers, with a faint sigh as though of relief, replaced his mask and left the room. As he came out, the next comer passed in in his place.

The room in which the Society met was a large one, made by knocking the two largest of the first-floor rooms into one. It was furnished in the standardised taste of twentieth-centurey suburbia and brilliantly lighted. A gramophone in one corner blared out a jazz tune, to which about ten couples of masked men and women were dancing, some in evening dress and others in tweeds and jumpers.

In one corner of the room was an American bar. Rogers went up and asked the masked man in charge for a double whisky. He consumed it slowly, leaning on the bar. The room filled. Presently somebody moved across to the gramophone and stopped it. He looked round. Number One had appeared on the threshold. A tall woman in black stood beside him. The mask, embroidered with a white 2, covered hair and face completely ; only her fine bearing and her white arms and bosom and the dark eyes shining through the eye-slits proclaimed her a woman of power and physical attraction.

'Ladies and gentlemen.' Number One was standing at the upper end of the room. The woman sat beside him ; her eyes were cast down and betrayed nothing, but her hands were clenched on the arms of the chair and her whole figure seemed tensely aware.

'Ladies and gentlemen. Our numbers are two short tonight.' The masks moved ; eyes were turned, seeking and counting. 'I need not inform you of the disastrous failure of our plan for securing the plans of the Court-Windlesham helicopter. Our courageous and devoted comrades, Number Fifteen and Number Forty-eight, were betrayed and taken by the police.'

An uneasy murmur arose among the company.

'It may have occurred to some of you that even the well-known steadfastness of these comrades might give way under examination. There is no cause for alarm. The usual orders have been issued, and I have this evening received the report that their tongues have been effectively silenced. You will, I am sure, be glad to know that these two brave men have been spared the ordeal of so great a temptation to dishonour, and that they will not be called upon to face a public trial and the rigours of a long imprisonment.'

A hiss of intaken breath moved across the assembled members like the wind over a barley-field.

'Their dependents will be discreetly compensated in the usual manner. I call upon Numbers Twelve and Thirty-four to undertake this agreeable task. They will attend me in my office for their instructions after the meeting. Will the numbers I have named kindly signify that they are able and willing to perform this duty ?'

Two hands were raised in salute. The President continued, looking at his watch :

'Ladies and gentlemen, please take your partners for the next dance.'

The gramophone struck up again. Rogers turned to a girl near him in a red dress. She nodded, and they slipped into the movement of a fox-trot. The couples gyrated solemnly and in silence. Their shadows were flung against the blinds as they turned and stepped to and fro.

'What has happened ?' breathed the girl in a whisper, scarcely moving her lips. 'I'm frightened, aren't you ? I feel as if something awful is going to happen.'

'It does take one a bit short, the President's way of doing things,' agreed Rogers, 'but it's safer like that.'

'Those poor men - '

A dancer, turning and following on their heels, touched Rogers on the shoulder.

'No talking, please,' he said. His eyes gleamed sternly ; he twirled his partner into the middle of the crowd and was gone. The girl shuddered.

The gramophone stopped. There was a burst of clapping. The dancers again clustered before the President's seat.

'Ladies and gentlemen. You may wonder why this extraordinary meeting has been called. The reason is a serious one. The failure of our recent attempt was no accident. The police were not on the premises that night by chance. We have a traitor among us.'

Partners who had been standing close together fell distrustfully apart. Each member seemed to shrink, as a snail shrinks from the touch of a finger.

'You will remember the disappointing outcome of the Dinglewood affair,' went on the President, in his harsh voice. 'You may recall other smaller matters which have not turned out satisfactorily. All these troubles have been traced to their origin. I am happy to say that our minds can now be easy. The offender has been discovered and will be removed. There will be no more mistakes. The misguided member who introduced the traitor to our Society will be placed in a position where his lack of caution will have no further ill-effects. There is no cause for alarm.'

Every eye roved about the company, searching for the traitor and his unfortunate sponsor. Somewhere beneath the black masks a face must have turned white ; somewhere under the stifling velvet there must have been a brow sweating, not with the heat of the dance. But the masks hid everything.

'Ladies and gentlemen, please take your partners for the next dance.'

The gramophone struck into an old half-forgotten tune : 'There ain't nobody loves me.' The girl in red was claimed by a tall man in evening dress. A hand laid on Rogers arm made him start. A small, plump woman in a green jumper slipped a cold hand into his. The dance went on.

When it stopped, amid the usual applause, everyone stood, detached, stiffened in expectation. The President's voice was raised again.

'Ladies and gentlemen, please behave naturally. This is a dance, not a public meeting.'

Rogers led his partner to a chair and fetched her an ice. As he stooped over her, he noticed the hurried rise and fall of her bosom.

'Ladies and gentlemen.' The endless interval was over. 'You will no doubt wish to be immediately relieved from suspense. I will name the persons involved. Number Thirty-seven !'

A man sprang up with a fearful cry.

'Silence !'

The wretch choked and gasped.

'I never – I swear I never – I'm innocent.'

'Silence. You have failed in discretion. You will be dealt with. If you have anything to say in defence of your folly, I will hear it later. Sit down.'

Number Thirty-seven sank down upon a chair. He pushed his handkerchief under the mask to wipe his face. Two tall men closed in upon him. The rest fell back, feeling the recoil of humanity from one striken by mortal disease.

The gramophone struck up.

'Ladies and gentleman, I will now name the traitor. Number Twenty-one, stand forward.'

Rogers stepped forward. The concentrated fear and loathing of forty-eight pairs of eyes burned upon him. The miserable Jukes set up a fresh wail.

'Oh, my God ! Oh, my God !'

'Silence ! Number Twenty-one, take off your mask.'

The traitor pulled the thick covering from his face. The intense hatred of the eyes devoured him.

'Number Thirty-seven, this man was introduced here by you, under the name of Joseph Rogers, formerly second footman in the service of the Duke of Denver, dismissed for pilfering. Did you take steps to verify that statement ?'

'I did – I did ! As God's my witness, it was all straight. I had him identified by two of the servants. I made enquiries. The tale was straight – I'll swear it was.'

The President consulted a paper before him, then he looked at his watch again.

'Ladies and gentlemen, please take your partners. . . .'

Number Twenty-one, his arms twisted behind him and bound, and his wrists handcuffed, stood motionless, while the dance of doom circled about him. The clapping, as it ended, sounded like the clapping of the men and women who sat, thirsty-lipped beneath the guillotine.

'Number Twenty-one, your name has been given as Joseph Rogers, footman, dismissed for theft. Is that your real name ?'

'No.'

'What is your name ?'

'Peter Death Bredon Wimsey.'

'We thought you were dead.'

'Naturally. You were intended to think so.'

'What has become of the genuine Joseph Rogers ?'

'He died abroad. I took his place. I may say that no real blame attaches to your people for not having realised who I was. I not only took Rogers's place ; I *was* Rogers. Even when I was alone, I walked like Rogers, I sat like Rogers, I read Rogers's books and wore Rogers's clothes. In the end, I almost thought Rogers's thoughts. The only way to keep up a successful impersonation is never to relax.'

'I see. The robbery of your own flat was arranged ?'

'Obviously.'

'The robbery of the Dowager Duchess, your mother, was connived at by you ?'

'It was. It was a very ugly tiara – no real loss to anybody with decent taste. May I smoke, by the way ?'

'You may not. Ladies and gentlemen. . . .'

The dance was like the mechanical jigging of puppets. Limbs jerked, feet faltered. The prisoner watched with an air of critical detachment.

'Numbers Fifteen, Twenty-two, and Forty-nine. You have watched the prisoner. Has he made any attempts to communicate with anybody ?'

'None.' Number Twenty-two was the spokesman. 'His letters and parcels have been opened, his telephone tapped, and his movements followed. His water-pipes have been under observation for morse signals.'

'You are sure of what you say ?'

'Absolutely.'

'Prisoner, have you been alone in this adventure ? Speak the truth, or things will be made somewhat more unpleasant for you than they might otherwise be.'

'I have been alone. I have taken no unnecessary risks.'

'It may be so. It will, however, be as well that steps should be taken to silence the man at Scotland Yard – what is his name ? – Parker. Also the prisoner's manservant, Mervyn Bunter, and possibly also his mother and sister. The brother is a stupid oaf, and not, I think, likely to have been taken into the prisoner's confidence. A precautionary watch will, I think, meet the necessities of his case.'

The prisoner appeared, for the first time, to be moved.

'Sir, I assure you that my mother and sister know nothing which could possibly bring danger on the Society.'

'You should have thought of their situation earlier. Ladies and gentlemen, please take –'

'No – no !' Flesh and blood could endure the mockery no longer. 'No ! Finish with him. Get it over. Break up the meeting. It's dangerous. The police –'

'Silence !'

The President glanced round at the crowd. It had a dangerous look about it. He gave way.

'Very well. Take the prisoner away and silence him. He will receive Number 4 treatment. And be sure you explain it to him carefully first.'

'Ah !'

The eyes expressed a wolfish satisfaction. Strong hands gripped Wimsey's arms.

'One moment – for God's sake let me die decently.'

'You should have thought this over earlier. Take him away. Ladies and gentlemen, be satisfied – he will not die quickly.'

'Stop ! Wait !' cried Wimsey desperately. 'I have something to say. I don't ask for life – only for a quick death. I – I have something to sell.'

'To sell ?'

'Yes.'

'We make no bargains with traitors.'

'No – but listen ! Do you think I have not thought of this ? I am not so mad. I have left a letter.'

'Ah ! now it is coming. A letter. To whom ?'

'To the police. If I do not return tomorrow –'

'Well ?'

'The letter will be opened.'

'Sir,' broke in Number Fifteen. 'This is bluff. The prisoner has not sent any letter. He has been strictly watched for many months.'

'Ah ! but listen. 'I left the letter before I came to Lambeth.'

'Then it can contain no information of value.'

'Oh, but it does.'

'What ?'

'The combination of my safe.'

'Indeed ? Has this man's safe been searched ?'

'Yes, sir.'

'What did it contain ?'

'No information of importance, sir. An outline of our organisation – the name of this house – nothing that cannot be altered and covered before morning.'

Wimsey smiled.

'Did you investigate the inner compartment of the safe ?'

There was a pause.

'You hear what he says,' snapped the President sharply. 'Did you find this inner compartment ?'

'There was no inner compartment, sir. He is trying to bluff.'

'I hate to contradict you,' said Wimsey, with an effort at his ordinary pleasant tone, 'but I really think you must have overlooked the inner compartment.'

'Well,' said the President, 'and what do you say is in this inner compartment, if it does exist ?'

'The names of every member of this Society, with their addresses, photographs, and finger-prints.'

'What ?'

The eyes round him now were ugly with fear. Wimsey kept his face steadily turned towards the President.

'How do you say you have contrived to get this information ?'

'Well, I have been doing a little detective work on my own, you know.'

'But you have been watched.'

'True. The finger-prints of my watchers adorn the first page of the collection.'

'This statement can be proved ?'

'Certainly. I will prove it. The name of Number Fifty, for example –'

'Stop !'

A fierce muttering arose. The President silenced it with a gesture.

'If you mention names here, you will certainly have no hope of mercy.

There is a fifth treatment – kept specially for people who mention names. Bring the prisoner to my office. Keep the dance going.'

The President took an automatic from his hip-pocket and faced his tightly fettered prisoner across the desk.

'Now speak !' he said.

'I should put that thing away, if I were you,' said Wimsey contemptuously. 'It would be a much pleasanter form of death than treatment Number 5, and I might be tempted to ask for it.'

'Ingenious,' said the President, 'but a little too ingenious. Now, be quick ; tell me what you know.'

'Will you spare me if I tell you ?'

'I make no promises. Be quick.'

Wimsey shrugged his bound and aching shoulders.

'Certainly. I will tell you what I know. Stop me when you have heard enough.'

He leaned forward and spoke low. Overhead the noise of the gramophone and the shuffling of feet bore witness that the dance was going on. Stray passers-by crossing the Heath noted that the people in lonely house were making a night of it again.

'Well,' said Wimsey, 'am I to go on ?'

From beneath the mask the President's voice sounded as though he were grimly smiling.

'My lord,' he said, 'your story fills me with regret that you are not, in fact, a member of our Society. Wit, courage and industry are valuable to an association like ours. I fear I cannot persuade you ? No – I supposed not.'

He touched a bell on his desk.

'Ask the members kindly to proceed to the supper-room,' he said to the mask who entered.

The 'supper-room' was on the ground floor, shuttered and curtained. Down its centre ran a long, bare table, with chairs set about it.

'A Barmecide feast, I see,' said Wimsey pleasantly. It was the first time he had seen this room. At the far end, a trapdoor in the floor gaped ominously.

The President took the head of the table.

'Ladies and gentlemen,' he began, as usual – and the foolish courtesy had never sounded so sinister – 'I will not conceal from you the seriousness of the situation. The prisoner has recited to me more than twenty names and addresses which were thought to be unknown, except to their owners and to me. There has been great carelessness' – his voice rang harshly – 'which will have to be looked into. Fingerprints have been obtained – he has shown me the photographs of some of them. How our investigators came to overlook the inner door of this safe is a matter which calls for enquiry.'

'Don't blame them,' put in Wimsey. 'It was meant to be overlooked, you know. I made it like that on purpose.'

The President went on, without seeming to notice the interruption.

'The prisoner informs me that the book with the names and addresses is to be found in this inner compartment, together with certain letters and papers stolen from the houses of members, and numerous objects bearing authentic fingerprints. I believe him to be telling the truth. He offers the combination of the safe in exchange for a quick death. I think the offer should be accepted. What is your opinion, ladies and gentlemen ?'

'The combination is known already,' said Number Twenty-two.

'Imbecile ! This man has told us, and has proved to me, that he is Lord Peter Wimsey. Do you think he will have forgotten to alter the combination ? And then there is the secret of the inner door. If he disappears tonight and the police enter his house –'

'I say,' said a woman's rich voice, 'that the promise should be given and the information used – and quickly. Time is getting short.'

A murmur of agreement went round the table.

'You hear,' said the President, addressing Wimsey. 'The Society offers you the privilege of a quick death in return for the combination of the safe and the secret of the inner door.'

'I have your word for it ?'

'You have.'

'Thank you. And my mother and sister ?'

'If you in your turn will give us your word – you are a man of honour – that these women know nothing that could harm us, they shall be spared.'

'Thank you, sir. You may rest assured, upon my honour, that they know nothing. I should not think of burdening any woman with such dangerous secrets – particularly those who are dear to me.'

'Very well. It is agreed – yes ?'

The murmur of assent was given, though with less readiness than before.

'Then I am willing to give you the information you want. The word of the combination is UNRELIABILITY.'

'And the inner door ?'

'In anticipation of the visit of the police, the inner door – which might have presented difficulties – is open.'

'Good ! You understand that if the police interfere with our messenger –'

'That would not help me, would it ?'

'It is a risk,' said the President thoughtfully, 'but a risk which I think we must take. Carry the prisoner down to the cellar. He can amuse himself by contemplating apparatus Number 5. In the meantime, Numbers Twelve and Forty-six –'

'No, no !'

A sullen mutter of dissent arose and swelled threateningly.

'No,' said a tall man with a voice like treacle. 'No – why should any members be put in possession of this evidence ? We have found one traitor among us tonight, and more than one fool. How are we to know that Numbers Twelve and Forty-six are not fools and traitors also ?'

The two men turned savagely upon the speaker, but a girl's voice struck into the discussion, high and agitated.

'Hear, hear ! That's right, I say. How about us ? We ain't going to have our names read by somebody we don't know nothing about. I've had enough of this. They might sell the 'ole lot of us to the narks.'

'I agree,' said another member. 'Nobody ought to be trusted, nobody at all.'

The President shrugged his shoulders.

'Then, what, ladies and gentlemen, do you suggest ?'

There was a pause. Then the same girl shrilled out again :

'I say Mr President oughter go himself. He's the only one as knows all the names. It won't be no cop to him. Why should we take all the risk and trouble and him sit at home and collar the money ? Let him go himself, that's what I say.'

A long rustle of approbation went round the table.

'I second that motion,' said a stout man who wore a bunch of gold seals at his fob. Wimsey smiled as he looked at the seals ; it was that trifling vanity which had led him directly to the name and address of the stout man, and he felt a certain affection for the trinkets on that account.

The President looked round.

'It is the wish of the meeting, then, that I should go ?' he said, in an ominous voice.

Forty-five hands were raised in approbation. Only the woman known as Number Two remained motionless and silent, her strong white hands clenched on the arm of the chair.

The President rolled his eyes slowly round the threatening ring till they rested upon her.

'Am I to take it that this vote is unanimous ?' he enquired.

The woman raised her head.

'Don't go,' she gasped faintly.

'You hear,' said the President, in a faintly derisive tone. 'This lady says, don't go.'

'I submit that what Number Two says is neither here nor there,' said the man with the treacly voice. 'Our own ladies might not like us to be going, if they were in madame's privileged position.' His voice was an insult.

'Hear, hear !' cried another man. 'This is a democratic society, this is. We don't want no privileged classes.'

'Very well,' said the President. 'You hear, Number Two. The feeling of the meeting is against you. Have you any reasons to put forward in favour of your opinion ?'

'A hundred. The President is the head and soul of our Society, if anything should happen to him – where should we be ? You' – she swept the company magnificently with her eyes – 'you have all blundered. We have your carelessness to thank for all this. Do you think we should be safe for five minutes if the President were not here to repair our follies ?'

'Something in that,' said a man who had not hitherto spoken.

'Pardon my suggesting,' said Wimsey maliciously, 'that as the lady appears to be in a position peculiarly favourable for the reception of the President's confidences, the contents of my modest volume will probably be no news to her. Why should not Number Two go herself ?'

'Because I say she must not,' said the President sternly, checking the quick reply that rose to his companion's lips. 'If it is the will of the meeting, I will go. Give me the key of the house.'

One of the men extracted it from Wimsey's jacket-pocket and handed it over.

'Is the house watched ?' he demanded of Wimsey.

'No.'

'That is the truth ?'

'It is the truth.'

The President turned at the door.

'If I have not returned in two hours' time,' he said, 'act for the best to save yourselves, and do what you like with the prisoner. Number Two will give orders in my absence.'

He left the room. Number Two rose from her seat with a gesture of command.

'Ladies and gentlemen. Supper is now considered over. Start the dancing again.'

Down in the cellar the time passed slowly, in the contemplation of apparatus Number 5. The miserable Jukes, alternately wailing and raving, at length shrieked himself into exhaustion. The four members guarding the prisoners whispered together from time to time.

'An hour and a half since the President left,' said one.

Wimsey glanced up. Then he returned to his examination of the room. There were many curious things in it, which he wanted to memorise.

Presently the trapdoor was flung open. 'Bring him up !' cried a voice. Wimsey rose immediately, and his face was rather pale.

The members of the gang were again seated round the table. Number Two occupied the President's chair, and her eyes fastened on Wimsey's face with a tigerish fury, but when she spoke it was with a self-control which roused his admiration.

'The President has been two hours gone,' she said. 'What has happened to him ? Traitor twice over - what has happened to him ?'

'How should I know ?' said Wimsey. 'Perhaps he has looked after Number One and gone while the going was good !'

She sprang up with a little cry of rage, and came close to him.

'Beast ! Liar !' she said, and struck him on the mouth. 'You know he would never do that. He is faithful to his friends. What have you done with him ? Speak - or I will make you speak. You two, there - bring the irons. He *shall* speak !'

'I can only form a guess, madame,' replied Wimsey, 'and I shall not guess any the better for being stimulated with hot irons, like Pantaloon at the circus. Calm yourself, and I will tell you what I think. I think - indeed, I greatly fear - that Monsieur le Président in his hurry to examine the interesting exhibits in my safe may, quite inadvertently, no doubt, have let the door of the inner compartment close behind him. In which case -'

He raised his eyebrows, his shoulders being too sore for shrugging, and gazed at her with a limpid and innocent regret.

'What do you mean ?'

Wimsey glanced round the circle.

'I think,' he said, 'I had better begin from the beginning by explaining to you the mechanism of my safe. It is rather a nice safe,' he added plaintively. 'I invented the idea myself - not the principle of its working, of course ; that is a matter for scientists - but just the idea of the thing.

'The combination I gave you is perfectly correct as far as it goes. It is a three-alphabet, thirteen-letter lock by Bunn & Fishett - a very good one of its kind. It opens the outer door, leading into the ordinary strong-room, where I keep my cash and my Froth-Blower's cuff-links and all that. But there is an inner compartment with two doors, which open in a quite different manner. The outermost of these two inner doors is merely a thin steel skin, painted to look like the back of the safe and fitting closely, so as not to betray any join. It lies in the same plane as the wall of the room, you understand, so that if you were to measure the outside and the inside of the safe you would discover no discrepancy. It opens outwards with an ordinary key, and, as I truly assured the President, it was left open when I quitted my flat.'

'Do you think,' said the woman sneeringly, 'that the President is so simple as to be caught in a so obvious trap ? He will have wedged open that inner door undoubtedly.'

'Undoubtedly, madame. But the sole purpose of that outer inner door, if I may so express myself, is to appear to be the only inner door. But hidden behind the hinge of that door is another door, a sliding panel, set so closely in the thickness of the wall that you would hardly see it unless you knew it was there. This door was also left open. Our revered Number One had nothing to do but to walk straight through into the inner compartment of the safe, which, by the way, is built into the chimney of the old basement kitchen, which runs up the house at that point. I hope I make myself clear ?'

'Yes, yes - get on. Make your story short.'

Wimsey bowed, and, speaking with even greater deliberation than ever, resumed :

'Now, this interesting list of the Society's activities, which I have had the honour of compiling, is written in a very large book - bigger, even, than Monsieur le Président's ledger which he uses downstairs. (I trust, by the way, madame, that you have borne in mind the necessity of putting that ledger in a safe place. Apart from risk of investigation by some officious policeman, it would be inadvisable that any junior member of the Society should get hold of it. The feeling of the meeting would, I fancy, be opposed to such an occurrence).'

'It is secure,' she answered hastily. '*Mon dieu !* get on with your story.'

'Thank you - you have relieved my mind. Very good. This big book lies on a steel shelf at the back of the inner compartment. Just a moment. I have not described this inner compartment to you. It is six feet high, three feet wide and three feet deep. One can stand up in it quite comfortably, unless one is very tall. It suits me nicely - as you may see. I am no more than five feet eight and a half. The President has the advantage of me in height ; he might be a little cramped, but there would be room for him to squat if he grew tired of standing. By the way, I don't know if you know it, but you have tied me up rather tightly.'

'I would have you tied till your bones were locked together. Beat him, you ! He is trying to gain time.'

'If you beat me,' said Wimsey, 'I'm damned if I'll speak at all. Control yourself, madame ; it does not do to move hastily when your king is in check.'

'Get on !' she cried again, stamping with rage.

'Where was I ? Ah ! the inner compartment. As I say, it is a little snug – the more so that it is not ventilated in any way. Did I mention that the book lay on a steel shelf ?'

'You did.'

'Yes. The shelf steel is balanced on a very delicate concealed spring. When the weight of the book – a heavy one, as I said – is lifted, the shelf rises almost imperceptibly. In rising it makes an electrical contact. Imagine to yourself, madame ; our revered President steps in – propping the false door open behind him – he sees the book – quickly he snatches it up. To make sure that it is the right one, he opens it – he studies the pages. He looks about for the other objects I have mentioned, which bear the marks of finger-prints. And silently, but very, very quickly – you can imagine it, can you not ? – the secret panel, released by the rising of the shelf, leaps across like a panther behind him. Rather a trite simile, but apt, don't you think ?'

'My God ! Oh, my God !' Her hand went up as though to tear the choking mask from her face. 'You – you devil – devil ! What is the word that opens the inner door ? Quick ! I will have it torn out of you – the word !'

'It is not a hard word to remember, madame – though it has been forgotten before now. Do you recollect, when you were a child, being told the tale of "Ali Baba and the Forty Thieves" ? When I had the door made, my mind reverted, with rather a pretty touch of sentimentality, in my opinion, to the happy hours of my childhood. The words that open the door are – "Open Sesame". '

'Ah ! How long can a man live in this devil's trap of yours ?'

'Oh,' said Wimsey cheerfully, 'I should think he might hold out a few hours if he kept cool and didn't use up the available oxygen by shouting and hammering. If we went there at once, I dare say we should find him fairly all right.'

'I shall go myself. Take this man and – do your worst with him. Don't finish him till I come back. I want to see him die !'

'One moment,' said Wimsey, unmoved by this amiable wish. 'I think you had better take me with you.'

'Why – why ?'

'Because, you see, I'm the only person who can open the door.'

'But you have given me the word. Was that a lie?'

'No – the word's all right. But, you see, it's one of these new-style electric doors. In fact, it's really the very latest thing in doors. I'm rather proud of it. It opens to the words "Open Sesame" all right – *but to my voice only.*'

'Your voice? I will choke your voice with my own hands. What do you mean – your voice only?'

'Just what I say. Don't clutch my throat like that, or you may alter my voice so that the door won't recognise it. That's better. It's apt to be rather pernickety about voices. It got stuck up for a week once, when I had a cold and could only implore it in a hoarse whisper. Even in the ordinary way, I sometimes have to try several times before I hit on the exact right intonation.'

She turned and appealed to a short, thick-set man standing beside her.

'Is this true? Is it possible?'

'Perfectly, ma'am, I'm afraid,' said the man civilly. From his voice, Wimsey took him to be a superior workman of some kind – probably an engineer.

'Is it an electrical device? Do you understand it?'

'Yes, ma'am. It will have a microphone arrangement somewhere, which converts the sound into a series of vibrations controlling an electric needle. When the needle has traced the correct pattern, the circuit is completed and the door opens. The same thing can be done by light vibrations equally easily.'

'Couldn't you open it with tools?'

'In time, yes, ma'am. But only by smashing the mechanism, which is probably well protected.'

'You may take that for granted,' interjected Wimsey reassuringly.

She put her hands to her head.

'I'm afraid we're done for,' said the engineer, with a kind of respect in his tone for a good job of work.

'No – wait! Somebody must know – the workmen who made this thing?'

'In Germany,' said Wimsey briefly.

'Or – yes, yes, I have it – a gramophone. This – this – *he* – shall be made to say the word for us. Quick – how can it be done?'

'Not possible, ma'am. Where should we get the apparatus at half-past three on a Sunday morning? The poor gentleman would be dead long before –'

There was a silence, during which the sounds of the awakening day came through the shuttered windows. A motor-horn sounded distantly.

'I give in,' she said. 'We must let him go. Take the ropes off him. You will free him, won't you ?' she went on, turning piteously to Wimsey. 'Devil as you are, you are not such a devil as that ! You will go straight back and save him ?'

'Let him go, nothing !' broke in one of the men. 'He doesn't go to peach to the police, my lady, don't you think it. The President's done in, that's all, and we'd all better make tracks while we can. It's all up, boys. Chuck this fellow down the cellar and fasten him in, so he can't make a row and wake the place up. I'm going to destroy the ledgers. You can see it done if you don't trust me. And you, Thirty, you know where the switch is. Give us a quarter of an hour to clear, and then you can blow the place to glory.'

'No ! You can't go – you can't leave him to die – your President – your leader – my – I won't let it happen. Set this devil free. Help me, one of you, with the ropes –'

'None of that, now,' said the man who had spoken before. He caught her by the wrists, and she twisted, shrieking, in his arms, biting and struggling to get free.

'Think, think,' said the man with the treacly voice. 'It's getting on to morning. It'll be light in an hour or two. The police may be here any minute.'

'The police !' She seemed to control herself by a violent effort. 'Yes, yes, you are right. We must not imperil the safety of all for the sake of one man. *He* himself would not wish it. That is so. We will put this carrion in the cellar where it cannot harm us, and depart, every one to his own place, while there is time.'

'And the other prisoner ?'

'He ? Poor fool – he can do no harm. He knows nothing. Let him go,' she answered contemptuously.

In a few minutes' time, Wimsey found himself bundled un-ceremoniously into the depths of the cellar. He was a little puzzled. That they should refuse to let him go, even at the price of Number One's life, he could understand. He had taken the risk with his eyes open. But that they should leave him as a witness against them seemed incredible.

The men who had taken him down strapped his ankles together and departed, switching the lights out as they went.

'Hi ! *Kamerad* !' said Wimsey. 'It's a bit lonely sitting here. You might leave the light on.'

'It's all right, my friend,' was the reply. 'You will not be in the dark long. They have set the time-fuse.'

The other man laughed with rich enjoyment, and they went out together. So that was it. He was to be blown up with the house. In that case the President would certainly be dead before he was extricated. This worried Wimsey ; he would rather have been able to bring the big crook to justice. After all, Scotland Yard had been waiting six years to break up this gang.

He waited, straining his ears. It seemed to him that he heard footsteps over his head. The gang had all crept out by this time. . . .

There was certainly a creak. The trapdoor had opened ; he felt, rather than heard, somebody creeping into the cellar.

'Hush !' said a voice in his ear. Soft hands passed over his face, and went fumbling about his body. There came the cold touch of steel on his wrists. The ropes slackened and dropped off. A key clicked in the handcuffs. The strap about his ankles was unbuckled.

'Quick ! quick ! they have set the time-switch. The house is mined. Follow me as fast as you can. I stole back – I said I had left my jewellery. It was true. I left it on purpose. *He* must be saved – only you can do it. Make haste !'

Wimsey, staggering with pain, as the blood rushed back into his bound and numbed arms, crawled after her into the room above. A moment, and she had flung back the shutters and thrown the window open.

'Now go ! Release him ! You promise ?'

'I promise. And I warn you, madame, that this house is surrounded. When my safe-door closed it gave a signal which sent my servant to Scotland Yard. Your friends are all taken –'

'Ah ! But you go – never mind me – quick ! The time is almost up.'

'Come away from this !'

He caught her by the arm, and they went running and stumbling across the little garden. An electric torch shone suddenly in the bushes.

'That you, Parker ?' cried Wimsey. 'Get your fellows away. Quick ! the house is going up in a minute.'

The garden seemed suddenly full of shouting, hurrying men. Wimsey, floundering in the darkness, was brought up violently against the wall. He made a leap at the coping, caught it, and hoisted himself up. His hands groped for the woman ; he swung her up beside him. They jumped ; every one was jumping ; the woman caught her foot and fell with a gasping cry. Wimsey tried to stop himself, tripped over a stone, and came down headlong. Then, with a flash and a roar, the night went up in fire.

Wimsey picked himself painfully out from among the debris of the garden wall. A faint moaning near him proclaimed that his companion was still alive. A lantern was turned suddenly upon them.

'Here you are !' said a cheerful voice. 'Are you all right, old thing ? Good lord ! what a hairy monster !'

'All right,' said Wimsey. 'Only a bit winded. Is the lady safe ? H'm – arm broken apparently – otherwise sound. What's happened ?'

'About half a dozen of 'em got blown up ; the rest we've bagged.' Wimsey became aware of a circle of dark forms in the wintry dawn. 'Good Lord, what a day ! What a comeback for a public character ! You old stinker – to let us go on for two years thinking you were dead ! I bought a bit of black for an arm-band. I did, really. Did anybody know, besides Bunter ?'

'Only my mother and sister. I put it in a secret trust – you know, the thing you send to executors and people. We shall have an awful time with the lawyers, I'm afraid, proving I'm me. Hullo ! Is that friend Sugg ?'

'Yes, my lord,' said Inspector Sugg, grinning and nearly weeping with excitement. 'Damned glad to see your lordship again. Fine piece of work, your lordship. They're all wanting to shake hands with you, sir.'

'Oh, Lord ! I wish I could get washed and shaved first. Awfully glad to see you all again, after two years' exile in Lambeth. Been a good little show, hasn't it ?'

'Is he safe ?'

Wimsey started at the agonised cry.

'Good Lord !' he cried. 'I forgot the gentleman in the safe. Here, fetch a car, quickly. I've got the great big top Moriarty of the whole bunch quietly asphyxiating at home. Here – hop in, and put the lady in too. I promised we'd get back and save him – though' (he finished the sentence in Parker's ear) 'there may be murder charges too, and I wouldn't give much for his chance at the Old Bailey. Whack her up. He can't last much longer shut up there. He's the bloke you've been wanting, the man at the back of the Morrison case and the Hope Wilmington case, and hundreds of others.'

The cold morning had turned the streets grey when they drew up before the door of the house in Lambeth. Wimsey took the woman by the arm and helped her out. The mask was off now, and showed her face, haggard and desperate, and white with fear and pain.

BOOK TWO

Margaret Cole

SUPERINTENDENT WILSON'S HOLIDAY

IT IS ALWAYS a difficult job to persuade Wilson to take a holi-day; for, as he is fond of saying, his work is his recreation, and he is apt to feel lost without it. On the occasion of which I am writing, however, I was adamant; for he was really badly run down after a succession of gruelling cases, and I was afraid that, unless he gave himself a rest, even his physique would give way. In my double capacity therefore, of friend and medical adviser, I brought strong pressure to bear. I not only ordered him posi-tively to take an absolute rest, but proposed a joint walking tour, during which I made up my mind to ensure that neither cases nor adventures should come his way. Finally, as old Plato used to say, 'with great difficulty he agreed'; and that was how it was that a bright June afternoon found us walking together along the low sand-hills which border, but do not protect, the coast of Norfolk a few miles north of Yarmouth.

It was the third day of our tour. On the first we had been content with running to Norwich in my Morris-Oxford, and refreshing our memories of the old city. The next day we had poked about among the Broads, and ended up at Yarmouth, where we decided to leave the car behind and walk in a leisurely fashion right round the coast to King's Lynn, zigzagging inland to look at an old church or village as we felt inclined.

This afternoon we were walking through a region sparsely populated enough. It was a part where the sea was still steadily eating away the land, and in the memory of man whole villages had vanished. Already we had inspected the ruins of an old church, still lying strewn about the beach, where, we were told, the parson still preached one sermon yearly in order to maintain his right to the stipend. That left behind, we were walking along a very low range of sand-cliffs. One solitary house was in sight, perched on the very edge, and some miles ahead we could see the big black and white bulk of a lighthouse, and behind it a tall church tower.

'Upon my word, Michael,' said Wilson, 'I've got a thirst. A drink, or even a cup of tea, would come in mighty handy.' He took out the map. 'There doesn't appear to be a village nearer than that lighthouse, and that's a good three miles. There's a small place called Happisburgh just behind it, where that church tower is.'

I, too, looked at the map. 'There seem to be a few houses half a mile or so inland,' I said. 'We might get something at one of them.'

'Better push on,' said Wilson. 'There's sure to be a pub in the village. And the only house in our immediate neighbourhood doesn't look at all hospitable.' He pointed to the lonely building on the edge of the cliff ahead.

Most certainly it did not. We had come a good deal nearer while we were talking and could now see that it was no longer a house at all, but only its skeleton. More than half of it had slid right down off the edge on to the beach below; and the remainder stood desolate – roof and windows gone, with heaps of broken brickwork lying as they had fallen. The door was boarded up; but an intruder could have readily walked in through broken wall or window.

'That looks a little more promising,' I said, pointing to a bell-tent which had just come into view round the corner of the deserted house. 'If there are campers there, they will at any rate tell us the lie of the land.'

'There's quite a village of them beyond,' said Wilson. 'It looks to me like a boy scouts' camp, or something of the sort. Now's our chance, Michael, of giving one of them an opportunity for his daily good deed. The Good Samaritan up to date, you know.'

'I don't see a soul about,' I answered.

By this time, we had come abreast of the ruined cottage, and within twenty yards or so of the solitary tent. The scouts' camp, if it was so, still lay a good half mile ahead on the opposite side of a track which ran down to the beach through a gap in the cliffs. It looked very white and trim, with the sun upon it, whereas the tent nearer to us, even in the bright sunshine, still looked dirty and somehow forlorn. We passed the ruin and went towards it. Not a soul appeared. The tent flap was waving idly about in the light wind; and, as we came up to it, we saw the remains of a fire before it, scattered broadcast by the wind, and a number of cooking utensils and other miscellaneous objects lying about.

'Slovenly people, these campers,' said Wilson. 'Apparently there's no one here; but we may as well make sure.' So saying, he strode up to the tent opening and looked in. A minute later he withdrew his head. 'You have a look too,' he said.

The inside of the tent was in wild disorder. In two places the canvas had come away from the ground, and the wind had been blowing freely through the interior. Bedclothes and a few garments were flung about here and there in confusion. Moreover, it looked as if the rain had got in; for many of the things were wet and sodden, though the tent itself appeared quite dry. There was, however, on the farther side a long tear in the canvas, and through this a shaft of sunlight was streaming in.

'Well, Michael, any deductions?' my companion asked, as I turned away.

'Only that any sensible camper would have sewn up that hole, pegged the tent down, and put out his bedclothes in the sun to dry.'

'True, O sage. And, from the fact that these campers didn't, what do you conclude?'

'It looks as if they weren't here last night.'

'Because it hasn't rained since yesterday, you mean?'

'Yes,' I answered. 'Those things must have got wet at least eighteen hours ago. No one could have slept in them in that state.'

'True,' said Wilson, 'and equally, nobody would have left them in that state if he had been here since the weather turned fine. Ergo, these campers left here before last night, and presum-

ably in a hurry, since they didn't even stop to straighten things up.
or close the tent-flap. Queer campers, Michael. Now, why were
they in such a devil of a hurry? It's not natural.' He stood
pondering.

'Hanged if I know. Perhaps they were catching a train.'

Wilson strode round the little encampment. Suddenly he
stopped. 'Hullo!' he said. 'You see that bucket.'

'Yes; what about it?'

'Only that there isn't any water in it.'

'Why should there be?'

'My dear Michael, it rained heavily last night. A regular downpour. If that bucket had been standing there then, it wouldn't
have been dry now.'

'You mean it shows they were here after it turned fine. Perhaps
they went away in a hurry just after the rain stopped.'

'At midnight? To catch a train? Hardly.'

'Somebody else may have been here and put the bucket there
since.'

'Perhaps,' said Wilson. He seemed to be hardly listening. Instead, he was poking about among the scattered remains of the
fire. 'Eh? What's this?'

'Come off it,' I said. 'I've not brought you here to practise detecting why a pair of campers didn't wash up the dinner things.
It's none of our business, thank heaven!'

'No,' said Wilson, hesitatingly, and with a faint note of interrogation in his voice. 'But this is interesting, all the same.' He
held out for my inspection what looked like the charred fragment
of a penny note-book.

I took it from him. 'Why,' I exclaimed, 'it's a bit of the butt-
end of somebody's cheque-book.'

'It is; and somebody has been kind enough to leave the number
of the cheques all ready for identification.'

'I suppose a man may burn the butt-end of his cheque-book if
he likes.'

'But he doesn't usually burn the butt-ends of several different
cheque-books over a camp-fire during his holidays.' Raking among
the ashes, he had disinterred what were clearly the ends of two

other cheque-books. In both, the numbering of the cheques was intact.

'You know, Michael,' Wilson went on, 'this is really extraordinarily odd.'

'Damn it, man, come away before you find any more mare's nests.'

Wilson chuckled. 'Mare's nests? Is this a mare's nest? That's exactly what I'm wondering, my dear fellow. It might be a singularly appropriate name. Let's have another look in here.' This time he dived right into the tent. Peering in, I saw him carefully turning over the various objects which lay strewn about it. Presently he gave a long whistle. 'Look here,' he said.

I looked. He was holding up a sheet on which, unmistakably, there was a long stain of blood. That it was blood I had no doubt. But it looked, not as if someone had bled upon the sheet, but as if some sharp, bloodstained implement had been wiped clean upon it. There were little tears in the midst of the stain, as if the sharp edge had cut into the fabric. 'What do you make of that?' Wilson asked. I told him. 'Right first time,' he observed. 'Is my medical adviser still of opinion that these campers' affairs are none of our business?'

I could no longer deny it. 'If they are,' I said, 'let me report it to the local police, while you clear out before you get involved. You've got to rest.'

'My dear Michael, I ask you. You bring me to this desolate spot, and walk me straight into the middle of a mystery. To begin with, I'm human; and secondly, this is evidently the hand of fate. Never flout Providence, Michael; she knows better even than my doctor what is good for me.'

I shrugged my shoulders helplessly. 'May it be a mare's nest,' I said, 'and may you quickly find the eggs.'

'I've just found something; but it's not an egg.' He held up his hand, and in it was a long, sharp steel blade, still unrusted.

'The weapon,' I gasped.

Wilson laughed. 'So doubting Thomas believes at last,' he said. 'Precisely – the weapon. All we require now is the corpse.'

'It doesn't follow there is a corpse,' I objected. 'Even if you strike a man with a knife, you don't always kill him.'

'A profoundly surgical observation, doctor. But we may as well see if there is a corpse all the same. At any rate, there seems to be – or to have been – a fair amount of blood about.' He went to the back of the tent and showed me on a patch of sand a large dark stain which had soaked deeply into the ground. 'The man who lost all that blood, Michael, didn't dash off at top speed to catch a train. Let's have another look round.'

He dived into the tent, and reappeared, carrying a Norfolk coat, a pair of gray flannel trousers, and an exceedingly dirty shirt. These he proceeded carefully to examine.

'Well,' I said at last, 'what are the conclusions?'

'They are fairly obvious. The shirt is marked "H.P." Inside the pocket of the coat is a tailor's label, which announces it as the property of Alec Courage, Esq., St Mary's Mansions, s w i. It is a large coat, obviously made for a fat, but fairly short man. The trousers, on the other hand, were made for a thin man, and bear no mark. Either they belong to "H.P.", the owner of the shirt, who, by the way, may also be identifiable by his laundry mark, or they are the property of some third person unknown. We will give "H.P.", for the present, the benefit of the doubt. We have thus the traces of two men, one fat and one thin, and we have good reason for believing that we know the name of one and the initials of the other. Beyond that, there are a few obvious indications. The large man is a heavy smoker, and in the habit of carrying tobacco loose in the pocket. The small man keeps a car or motor-cycle – for there are numerous petrol and grease stains on his trousers, and they are of very varying age. He has the habit of keeping his hands in his trousers pockets, and he has something wrong with his left leg. There are other inferences; but for the present they seem unimportant. It is to be observed that there are no papers of any sort in either the coat or the trousers.'

'I think I follow you so far,' I said. 'What next?'

'We will now,' said Wilson, 'look a little farther afield. And the first thing we observe strikes me as distinctly interesting. May I call your attention to the footprints, Michael?'

I looked closely at the trodden sand before the tent and tried to follow what I knew of Wilson's methods. 'I can see signs,' I said, 'of four distinct pairs of feet – or at least I think so.'

'Good,' said Wilson.

'First, there is a large blank impression – with no nails or studmarks or anything. Secondly, there is a rather smaller impression, in which the sole is blank, but the heel is round with a star-shaped figure in the middle. Thirdly, there is a very small pair of marks that might almost have been made by a woman. They are noticeable because of the barred impressions of the soles. And lastly, there is a pair with very large hobnails, or something of the sort. Am I right?'

'Quite right,' Wilson answered. 'And it can hardly have escaped you that pairs one and two are regularly on top of the others – or that, in fact, the large blank impression is your own crepe-rubber, while the star and the circle belong to me.' He held up his foot for my inspection.

'Oh,' I said rather ruefully. 'Then that leaves only the other two. And as we have signed our presence so plainly, and there are no other marks, it seems pretty plain that nobody except these two men has been here till we came.'

Wilson nodded. 'Yes,' he said; 'that is, since the rain, which would have washed away any previous impressions. But it also follows that these two men have been here since the rain.'

'But what about the wet camping clothes?'

'My dear Michael, that was the bucket, not the rain. Someone upset the bucket over them, and then set it upright again. And that was done since the rain, or the bucket would not have been empty. No, what we have proved is that these two men *were* here after the rain, and that they left in a hurry.'

Drawing out a piece of paper and a pencil, Wilson made a sketch. 'Let us call the small prints "A," ' he said, and the big hobnails "B." Now, here we have "B" prints first coming towards the tent up from the road that leads inland from the beach. Then we have again "B's" prints going in the direction of that ruined cottage, and then returning. You see, he has trodden on one of his own steps just here, and that proves which way he went first. Lastly, on the opposite side, we have again "B's" prints going away inland, towards that road that comes up from the beach.' He cast about for a minute or two. 'No,' he said, 'I can find no other prints at all. "A" has left none except just in front of the tent, and "B" only some more just by the tent and these other two lines. It looks, then, as if they were both here at the same time. We have, however, tracks of "B" going away, but not of "A." Puzzle: where is "A"?'

'He's not here, at all events.'

'True. Now, suppose we try following "B's" tracks. Towards the cottage first, I think. Study the footprints carefully, and don't walk in them. They are, to say the least, suggestive.'

They suggested nothing to me, but I followed obediently. The steps led to a gap in the broken wall. Wilson, who was leading, looked in, and immediately uttered an exclamation.

In the half-room to which the gap in the wall led stood the remains of a deal table. The two walls nearest the sea had collapsed, and one leg of the table was actually standing upon air, protruding over the edge of the cliff. And on the table lay a cap, a walking-stick and a macintosh. The stick lay a little apart, and under it, as under a paperweight, was a letter. Wilson silently picked it up. It was stuck down, stamped and addressed to George Chalmers, Esq., St Mary's Mansions, s w 1.

Wilson held it irresolutely in his hand for a moment. Then he produced a pocket-knife and slowly and carefully worked the blade under the flap. In a few seconds he had the letter open, leaving the envelope to all appearance intact. 'I think, in the circumstances, we will take the liberty,' he said. A minute later, he handed me the letter.

'Dear George,' it ran, 'Very sorry to leave you in the lurch, and all that. But you'll find out soon enough why I'd better not live any longer. Forgive me, if you can. Yours, Hugh.'

'Suicide!' I said. 'But how . . .?'

Wilson, meanwhile, was leaning over the edge of the cliff, gazing down at something below. 'Well?' I asked. 'The exhibits are complete,' he answered; 'item, one body.'

I climbed beside him and gazed down. Below us a clump of jejune bushes was growing precariously on the face of the cliff.

And among them lay the body of a man, huddled up awkwardly, as it had fallen from the room in which we stood. 'I must get down to him,' I said.

It was an unpleasant scramble; but I managed it. In a minute or so, I stood beside the body. There was no doubt about the cause of death. The man's throat was slit from ear to ear. 'His throat's been cut,' I shouted up to Wilson. A minute later he stood beside me, and we gazed down together at the dead man. He was small and fair-haired, not more than thirty years old, with a face almost childishly pretty, but now frozen in a strange look of horror. And he had been dead many hours. There was no doubt of that.

Wilson spoke my thought. 'Does a suicide look like that, Michael?' he asked, gravely.

I bent down again, and studied the wound. 'This is no suicide,' I said. 'The man's been murdered.'

'Precisely,' said Wilson. 'Men do not commit suicide by first cutting their throats, and then jumping off a fifty foot cliff into a bush. Do you mean more than that?'

'Yes, I do. That wound is not self-inflicted. The man was seized from behind, and held roughly by someone who then slit his throat. . . . But . . . what does that letter mean? He said he was committing suicide.'

'Or his murderer said it for him,' Wilson answered. 'But look! What's that?'

In the bush, close by the dead man, lay an open razor, stained with blood. 'The weapon,' I said.

Wilson smiled grimly. 'You said that before,' he said. 'Two bloodstained weapons are surely an undue allowance for one throat.'

'I'm out of my depth,' said I.

Wilson by now was bending down and making a search of the body. The murdered man was dressed in a silver grey lounge suit; and from this he quickly extracted a bundle of papers and letters. Among them were two envelopes addressed to 'Hugh Parsons, Esq.,' at an address in Hampstead. The letters and papers seemed to be purely personal, and, after a cursory examination, Wilson thrust them back into the dead man's pocket. '*Prima facie*,' he said, 'this appears to be the body of Hugh Parsons, whom we can identify with the "H.P." of the shirt we found in the tent and the "Hugh" of the letter.'

'But I don't understand,' I said. 'This man has been murdered; but he has left a letter announcing his suicide. What's the explanation?'

'On the face of it, there is one obvious answer. Parsons has been murdered, and his murderer has tried to make it look like suicide.'

'But the letter?'

'If we are right, then the letter is a forgery. We can't tell for certain, at present; but I think we may safely accept the hypothesis of murder. To begin with – we found sufficient reason to suspect a murderous attempt *before* we had even encountered the body or the suggestion of suicide.'

'As a suggested suicide,' I observed, 'it doesn't seem very successful. It didn't deceive you at all.'

'Nor could it have deceived anyone for five minutes,' Wilson said. 'Let's go over the points. First, we have a plain set of footprints leading to and from the cliff. They are not the dead man's. Secondly, there are no footprints of the dead man leading here, though he clearly came, or was brought, here after the rain; for his body is quite dry, though the ground under him is still damp. Thirdly, we have the traces up at the tent simply shouting "Murder." And, fourthly, we have two bloodstained weapons instead of one. No murderer could possibly have thought this arrangement made a plausible suicide. Yet he left it like that. Why?'

'Perhaps he staged the suicide, and then was surprised before he had time to remove either his own footprints or the traces up at the tent.'

'That is possible; but I don't think it is correct. For we know he wasn't actually surprised. There are no other footprints. Of course, he might have got panic and done a bunk. But he didn't. The steps leading inland from the tent are those of a man walking slowly.'

'Then what is the explanation?'

'Part of it, I think, is clear. The murder was done just by the tent. Then the murderer carried the body here and staged this absurd suicide. If you remember the tracks, " B's " stride was shorter, and the impressions of his feet were much deeper when he was coming this way than on his return. That suggests that he was carrying a heavy burden – to wit, the body. What I don't understand is why he didn't clear the traces away. As he left things, he was bound to be seen through. And then, again, you say the wound was obviously not self-inflicted.'

'He may not have had medical knowledge enough to know that,' I said.

'He must have had enough to know that two weapons were not likely,' Wilson said. 'And that just deepens the mystery. The thing's so well done in some respects, and so badly in others. Now, why?'

'I'm damned if I know,' said I. 'Do you?'

'I can think of at any rate one possible explanation,' Wilson said, puckering his brow. 'But I'm not at all sure that it will work. Anyway, our immediate job, I suppose, is to tell the local police what we've found.'

It was not, however, quite our next job. For at this moment a voice – a fresh, young voice – hailed us from above. 'Hullo!' it said. 'Something wrong here. Bill!' Looking up, we saw two boy scouts staring down at us as we stood beside the body.

'Something very much wrong,' said Wilson. 'Do either of you boys know this man?'

With extraordinary agility, the two boys clambered down beside us. 'It's one of the blokes from that tent up there,' he said.

'There were two of them, weren't there?' Wilson inquired.

'Three. Leastways, two of them was campin' out 'ere, and there was a friend of theirs stayin' at the Bear and Cross.'

'Where's that?'

''Bout a mile inland, up the track. 'E 'ad a car wiv 'im, and used to drive it down 'ere.'

'When did you last see any of them?'

'Mr Chalmers – 'e's the chap with the car – ain't seen him for two or three days. But I seen the other two night before last.

Quarrellin', they was. Oo! D'yer think t'other chap done this
one in?'

'Somebody's done him in,' said Wilson. 'Now, mind, nothing
up here or at the tent must be touched till the police come. But
I've a job for you chaps. I want you to hunt all down this bit of
cliff and see if you can find anything that might throw more light
on this affair. And, Michael, I've a job for you too. I'm going to
stay here till help comes. But I want you to buzz off and find the
nearest telephone, and get straight on to the police station at
Norwich. Tell them I'm here, and they're to send an inspector
and some men out in a car at once. See? And then go to the Bear
and Cross, and see if this Mr Chalmers is still about, or what's
become of him. And find out anything you can about those two
fellows down at the tent. When that's done, come back here, and,
if you value your life, don't forget to bring a couple of bottles of
beer and some sandwiches.'

By the time we had clambered up to the ruined cottage, several
more boy scouts had appeared on the scene. Wilson at once took
command, and set them to hunt the entire neighbourhood for
clues. One was assigned to me as guide to the Bear and Cross,
where, it appeared, the nearest telephone was to be found. As I
left the scene of the crime, I saw Wilson neatly covering the tell-
tale footsteps with a blanket taken from the tent.

At the Bear and Cross, I found no difficulty in carrying out
Wilson's suggestions. In the presence of a gaping landlord, to
whom I had given the barest minimum of information, I rang up
the police station at Norwich, and was lucky enough to get through
at once. A recital of the main facts sufficed to secure a promise
that an inspector should be despatched at once to the scene of the
crime, and, as soon as I mentioned Wilson's name, there was no
mistaking the alacrity with which the local police took up the case.
But I did not want to waste time; and as soon as I could, I rang
off, and turned my attention to the landlord.

He seemed a typical country innkeeper enough – an ex-soldier
by the look of him, and indeed I soon found he had been a
sergeant in a regular regiment before the war and had seen plenty
of service in France. His great desire was to question me; but I

speedily made it plain that I meant to get more information than I gave, and before long I had him talking.

The two campers in the tent – Hugh Parsons and Alec Courage – had been there for about ten days, and had had their letters sent to the inn. The previous week-end, a friend of theirs, named George Chalmers, had come down with his car, and had put up at the inn. He had stayed only a few days, and had returned to town on Tuesday, leaving the other two behind. The two campers had been before his coming regular visitors at the inn; and during the week-end they had been there more than ever, and Chalmers had several times taken them out in his car – a Morris-Oxford. Three days ago, on Tuesday afternoon, Chalmers had received a telegram, and on receipt of it had announced that he must go back to town at once. The other two had been with him when it came, and they had stayed to take a farewell drink together and to see him off. The last the landlord had seen of them was their going off arm in arm, and a little unsteadily (for it had been a wet leave-taking) along the track towards the sea. He had been rather surprised to see nothing of them for the past three days; for previously they had been frequent and thirsty visitors at the inn. But it was quite possible that, now their friend was no longer there, they had transferred their attention to the Swan at Happisburgh. It was only a couple of miles or so from their camp.

At my suggestion the landlord rang up the Swan, and found that his surmise was correct. The two men had spent the greater part of Wednesday there, drinking and playing billiards and strumming on the piano – for the day had been wet. They had also walked over together on Thursday afternoon, and stayed for a drink and a game. The Swan, however, had seen nothing of them since then, and it was now late on Friday afternoon. There were, I ascertained, no other licensed premises within several miles. This seemed to bear out the conclusion already formed that the murder had taken place some time on Thursday night.

'What sort of man was Courage?' I asked. The landlord's view was that he was a bit of a sport – an athlete, too, by his talk; shortish, but very strongly and sturdily built, with curly dark hair and a small moustache – about thirty years of age.

'We found a queer-looking long knife down at the tent,' I said; 'a very thin, sharp blade about eight inches long, with a white bone handle. Do you know it?'

'Why,' said the landlord, staring. 'I shouldn't wonder if it was my ham and beef knife. I lost it on Tuesday after those chaps were here. You don't mean it was –'

'It may have been the weapon,' I said. 'Anyway, it's at the tent now. One of them must have picked it up. Could they have got at it easily?'

'It was kept in a drawer in the parlour, where they were all sitting. And, now you mention it, I remember Mr Courage went back in there after Mr Chalmers had driven off. He may have taken it then.'

'When did you see it last?'

'When I put it back in the drawer after lunch on Tuesday. When I wanted it on Wednesday morning it wasn't there.'

'Any of them could have taken it?'

'It must 'a' been Mr Courage, when he went back into the parlour.'

That was the sum of the information I gleaned; but, as I made my way back to the scene of the tragedy, accompanied by the boy scout bearing a plentiful supply of Bass and sandwiches, I felt well enough pleased with it. It all seemed to fit in; and especially the theft of the knife from the inn seemed to prove that the crime had been premeditated for at least two days before its actual execution. Parsons was dead, and Courage was presumably his murderer. Else why had the man vanished off the face of the earth? Courage, too, was proved to have had ample opportunity for stealing the knife. Things certainly looked black for Mr Alec Courage.

I found Wilson the centre of an excited group of boy scouts, among whom was a man, dressed as a scoutmaster, whom I had not seen before. Wilson hailed me cheerily, and, seizing a bottle of Bass from my companion, took a long pull. 'That's better,' he said.

I told my news, which seemed to please him, while he hungrily ate a sandwich. 'We've some news too,' he said, 'and it's rather curious. To begin with, Mr Evanson here knows a bit about our two friends.'

The scoutmaster proceeded to explain. He and Courage had been at school together; but they had not met for years until their accidental encounter a few days before. Indeed, Mr Evanson gave it clearly to be understood that, in his view, Courage was a good deal of a bad hat. Meeting, however, by chance on the beach, they had renewed their old acquaintance and exchanged experiences. Courage had introduced Parsons to him, and explained that they were partners in a firm of outside brokers in the City. Evanson had gathered that their business was highly speculative; indeed, they had spoken of it in the spirit of gamblers who enjoyed playing for high stakes. He had met Chalmers once at the Bear and Cross, and gathered that he was the senior partner in the concern.

On the tragedy itself Evanson could throw no direct light. He said he had last spoken with the two friends on Thursday afternoon, when they were going down to the sea for a bathe. They had told him of Chalmers's return to town, and had announced that they were staying on at least for another week. They had seemed in the best of spirits and on excellent terms with each other.

That was the end of Evanson's direct evidence. But he produced one of his boys, who had been in the neighbourhood of the tent later on Thurday evening. The boy said that he had heard high voices, as of two men quarrelling, proceeding from the tent, and had caught some words about 'a tight place' and 'letting a pal down.' The boy had not thought much of it at the time, and had, in fact, forgotten all about it till the discovery of the tragedy brought the incident back to his mind.

Evanson's story seemed to me quite straightforward. He gave of Courage a most unflattering portrait, which showed that he thought him quite the sort of man who might be guilty of a serious crime. Of Parsons he seemed to know little, but to regard him as in all probability a harmless 'pigeon' who had fallen into Courage's skilful hands. But I, at any rate, was disposed to discount a good deal of Mr Evanson's testimony; for it was obvious that he was more than a bit of a prig.

'Come over here, Michael,' said Wilson; 'there's something I want to look at again.'

'Anything fresh since I went away?' I asked, as soon as we were alone.

'Yes and no,' was the answer. 'You know those footprints of "B" leading inland from the tent?' I nodded. 'Well, there's an odd thing about them. You remember I said that Mr "B's" stride was shorter and his footmarks deeper on the way to the ruined cottage than back?' Again I nodded acquiescence. 'Well, those steps leading inland from the tent are the same as those leading to the cottage – short and deep.'

'I don't quite see what you mean,' I said.

'I concluded from the first lot of footsteps that "B" had been carrying a heavy burden going to the cottage, but not on his return. That squared with our finding the body on the cliffs below the cottage. But how does it square with our finding the same sort of footsteps – deep, and close together – leading from the tent in the opposite direction?'

'It doesn't seem to square at all,' I said. 'Where do the other footsteps lead, by the way?'

'They go to the road leading to the inn; and there they stop. The road surface is too hard to leave an impression.'

'Then you simply don't know where "B" went after he reached the road?'

'That's where those boy scouts come in. I set them to search, and one of them says he's found some of "B's" footsteps again a bit farther up the road, leading off into a disused path that apparently runs along parallel to the cliffs. I've had no chance to follow it yet; but the boy says the tracks are quite plain. Hullo, that must be the police!'

A car was running swiftly down the road that led from the Bear and Cross to the sea. In it were two policemen and a man in plain clothes. Wilson went to meet the car, and it came to a stop about a hundred yards from the tent. I hung in the background while the plain clothes man deferentially saluted Wilson. They remained a minute or two in conversation, and then came over towards me. 'This is Inspector Davey,' said Wilson. 'My friend, Dr Prendergast.'

In a few minutes Wilson had given the local inspector a full account of what we had so far discovered. 'We'll leave you to look round here,' he said then, 'while we follow up these footsteps.' But we were not destined to follow them just yet; for, as we turned to leave the inspector, a second car appeared, coming at full speed along the road from the Bear and Cross. 'Hullo, who's this?' said the inspector.

The second car – a new Morris-Oxford – came to a stop beside the police car, and its sole occupant, a tall, broad man of forty or so, came hastily towards us. 'What the devil's all this?' he said. 'My name's Chalmers. They told me up at the pub there was something wrong.'

The inspector glanced at Wilson. 'You are Mr George Chalmers,' said the latter.

'Yes. Is it true that Parsons is dead?' The big man seemed greatly agitated.

'He was a friend of yours?' Wilson asked.

'My partner – he and Mr Courage, who was staying here with him. I've just run down from town to see them, and they told me at the inn . . .'

'What did they tell you?'

'That Parsons was dead, and Courage had disappeared. Is that true? What has happened?'

'Mr Parsons left this letter for you, Mr Chalmers,' said Wilson, handing over the note which we had found at the ruined cottage. 'We took the liberty of opening it.'

Chalmers took the note, and read it with puckered brows. 'I don't understand,' he said. 'The landlord said Parsons had been murdered. But this means suicide. Though why –'

'You do not know of any reason why Mr Parsons should have taken his life?'

'The thing's preposterous. Now, if it had been Courage, I might have understood. This is the devil of a business. I say, I suppose anything I tell you won't go any further – I mean, unless it has to, you know.'

'I think,' said Wilson, 'you had better tell us frankly all you know, Mr Chalmers.'

'It's a beastly business,' said Chalmers, 'and I don't under-

stand it at all. You realise, Parsons and Courage were my partners
– we're stockbrokers, you know. Ten days ago, the two of them
came away here on a holiday together, leaving me to run the show
in town while they were away. Last Friday, my bank manager
asked me to come round and see him. I went, and he produced
a cheque, drawn to bearer for a very large sum on the firm's account, and asked me if it was all right. It was signed with
Courage's name and mine. I told him at once the damned thing
was a forgery and I'd never signed any such cheque. It was a
damned good forgery, mind you; and I could hardly tell the
signature from my own. Well, to cut a long story short, we went
into the accounts, and we found that during the past week several
other bearer cheques had been paid out, all purporting to be signed
by Courage and me – and all forgeries, so far as my signature was
concerned at any rate. Of course, I was in the devil of a stew –
I may tell you the cheques were big enough to cause our firm
serious embarrassment. We rang up the police at once and put
the matter in their hands, and then I went back to the office, collected the cheque-books in which the counterfoils were, and buzzed
off down here with them to see Courage. Of course, I assumed
his signature had been forged as well as mine.

'Well, over the week-end, we had a tremendous confab about
it. Courage said he'd never signed the cheques, and couldn't give
any explanation. But we knew the cheque-books had been locked
up in a safe to which only we three had the keys. Finally, Courage
and Parsons fell out about it, and accused each other of forging
the cheques. I trusted them both, and told them it was all nonsense, and at length they made it up and shook hands. I stayed
down here till Tuesday, keeping in telephonic communication with
London all the time. Then, on Tuesday, I got a wire from the
office, asking me to go up to town at once over some important
business. And now comes the beastly part of the affair. I had to
go to Courage's desk for some papers this morning, and there I
found, in his blotting book, some unmistakable transfers of a series
of attempts at my signature. Of course, that put the lid on it.
I simply buzzed down here at once; and I don't mind telling you
I meant to cut my losses and advise Courage to make himself

scarce. We've been close friends, and I'd sooner lose all I have than have to put him in the dock over it. You can say that's compounding a felony if you like. Anyway, it's what I meant to do. I got to the Bear and Cross a few minutes ago, and there the landlord told me Parsons was dead and Courage vanished. Of course, I was dumbfounded. Forgery's one thing; but murder's another. I came right on here to tell you all I know. But, of course, if it's suicide . . . though why on earth . . .' His voice tailed away.

' It was not suicide, Mr Chalmers,' said Wilson. ' It was murder. The suicide was merely a clumsy pretence. The murderer burned, or endeavoured to burn, the butt-ends of the cheque-books, and then made off.' And in a few words he told Chalmers the state of the affair.

Chalmers seemed more and more downcast. ' I'd never have believed it,' he said at the close.

' Well, what's your conclusion now?' Wilson asked.

' I've no wish to draw conclusions. Unfortunately, they seem too obvious.'

'You mean that Courage killed Parsons and fled. But why should he kill Parsons?'

' I suppose Parsons must have found out that he had forged the cheques. He killed him in order to shut his mouth, and then got panic and ran away.'

' Parsons, you think, was entirely innocent?'

' Lord bless you, yes. Hugh Parsons had nothing to do with this. No, it was Courage who forged the cheques, sorry as I am to say it.'

' Well, Mr Chalmers, will you kindly go with the inspector here and identify Parsons, and give him any help you can?' Wilson drew the inspector aside and communed with him a moment. ' Now, Michael,' he said. ' *A nos moutons.*' We waited until Inspector Davey and Chalmers had disappeared into the ruined cottage, and then set off up the road. 'About here is where the boy found the footprints,' said Wilson. 'Yes, here they are. He's a sharp lad.'

The footprints were rather faint; but there was no doubt that they had been made by the same boots as the 'B' prints by the tent. There were only two or three of them visible, for the track was loose sand, and so overgrown that the rain had only penetrated at one or two points. But it was quite clear that they were leading away from the tent along a sunken lane which ran parallel to the shore and about a hundred yards from it, and was screened from view by a thick covering of bushes on either side. We walked along the track for a little distance. I could see no further marks; but Wilson's more experienced eyes seemed to be satisfied that he was still on the trail. Eventually, after about five minutes' walking, the lane came out on a wider track leading on one side up to the main road inland, and on the other still keeping roughly parallel to the shore.

'Hullo!' said Wilson. 'There's been a car here. You notice the tracks. And just here it stood for some time. You can see the oil ran down and made a little pool. Dunlop tyres, with a notice-able patch on the left back wheel. That may come in useful. The tracks run both ways – up to the road, and in the other direction – a double track each way. Left turn, I think.' He led the way along the track, away from the main road.

For some distance we followed the track, which, though wider here, was still sunken. Marks were few and far between; but Wilson seemed sure that we were still following the trail of the car. After about a mile the track bent round in the direction of the shore, and within five minutes brought us out, through another gap in the low cliffs, right on the beach, and within a few yards of the ruined church we had already visited earlier in the day. No tyre marks were visible on the beach; either the wind had obliterated them all from the loose sand, or, if the car had de-scended below high-water mark, the tide had been up and washed them away. But Wilson strode unhesitatingly towards the ruin, which stood well above high-water mark, temporarily protected by a range of low artificial sand-hills planted with juniper. There he paused and stared meditatively at the bushes.

'What on earth do you expect to find here?' I asked.

'Who knows,' he returned. 'One can but look.'

'But for what?'

'For what one may find. Look here, for instance.' I looked, but could see nothing but the sandy soil between the ruins. 'Trampled ground,' Wilson interpreted. 'And recently trampled. But someone's obliterated all clear marks. Anyway, we might as well experiment there as anywhere. Prod with your stick.' So saying, he began prodding with his own, thrusting it in as deep as it would go into the sand at one place after another. I followed his example. In some places the stick, with a little coaxing, went right down. In others, it was speedily stopped by something hard below the surface. 'Never mind the hard stuff,' said Wilson. 'That's masonry from the church. Try for something soft but resistant.' A minute or so later he gave an exclamation. 'This feels like something, Michael,' he said. 'Come and help me clear away the sand.'

With sticks and hands we cleared away the loose sand as best we could. Less than a foot down, my hand caught hold of something hard but yielding. Together we scraped for a moment and brought to light a human boot. Another followed, and within a few minutes we had exposed to view the entire body of a man, buried a foot deep below the drifting sand. He was a young man, short but stout and strongly built, with a crisp black moustache, and to all appearances not long dead. And the manner of death was evident. Round his neck a cord had been tightly knotted, and the stained and swollen flesh plainly showed the marks.

I had been too occupied first in scraping away the sand and then in making a brief inspection of the body to give vent to my curiosity till now. But when I had assured myself how the man had died, I turned to Wilson. 'What in God's name does this mean?' I cried. 'Was this what you were looking for?'

'Permit me to introduce you to the suspected murderer, Mr Courage,' he said.

'Courage!' I exclaimed. 'Then who . . .' But a sharp exclamation from Wilson cut short my sentence. He had turned the body over, and now from beneath it he drew – a big gold cigar case, which gleamed brightly in the evening sun. He pressed the catch and the case flew open. Within were two fat cigars, and with them a scrap of paper – a tearing from a newspaper. Wilson read it and passed it to me. It was an extract from the city page of the *Financial Times*, describing the dramatic slump in the shares of the Anglo-Asiatic Corporation.

'From yesterday's paper,' said Wilson. '*Yesterday*'s, mark you.'

'Why not?' I asked.

'The *Financial Times* is hardly likely to be on sale at Happisburgh,' he answered. 'This grave was made last night, or at all events the man died then. How did a bit of yesterday's *Financial Times* get into his grave?'

'It may have come by post,' I hazarded.

'We can probably find out whether he received any newspapers by post. The question is whether this is his cigar case or someone else's. If it's someone else's, we're in luck.'

'But how did it get into the grave?'

'Do you ever dig, Michael? If you do, and don't take precautions to secure your loose property, as likely as not you'll drop some of it, and cover it over before you find out your loss. If the murderer has been kind enough to drop his cigar case for us, I say we're in luck. And I'm inclined to think he has. Judging from Mr Courage's coat which we inspected at the tent, he was a pipe, and not a cigar smoker.'

'But how do you know this is Courage?'

For answer, Wilson bent down and felt in the dead man's pockets. They were entirely empty. 'I don't,' he said at last. 'But I'll bet you anything you like it is. You see, I've been looking for him.'

'You suspected – this?' I asked.

'Certainly. It was plain from the first that we were meant to see through the pretence of suicide – plain that the murderer had meant us to see through it. But, once we did see through it, all the surface indications pointed to Courage as the murderer. Clearly that would not do. If Courage had been the murderer, either he would not have wanted us to see through the suicide, or he would have arranged that, when we did see through it, the clues should not point to him. Ergo, Courage was not the murderer. Then where was Courage, and why had he disappeared? One possible explanation was that he had taken fright and run away, even though he was innocent of the murder. But a far more plausible theory was that he had been murdered too.

'That theory was confirmed by a study of the footprints. We concluded, on good evidence, that the murderer had been carrying a heavy burden on his way from the tent to the ruined cottage. We found we were right. He had been carrying Parsons. But we had equally good evidence that he was carrying a burden in the second set of footprints leading to the car; for they too were deep, and showed a shortened stride. The inference was clear. The murderer had also been carrying a body towards the car. But that body could not be Parsons. Who was it? Obviously Courage himself.'

I listened to this convincing deduction with increasing amazement. At this point I broke in. 'But his boots, man! Look at his boots!' For the boots on the feet of the body before us were identical with the 'B' tracks we had found at the tent.

'I have looked at his boots,' said Wilson. 'That is the final link in the argument. We found three sets of 'B' footprints, did we not? One set led up from the shore to the tent, a second from the tent to the ruined cottage and back again, and the third from the tent to the path we have just followed.' I nodded. 'Very well,' said Wilson. 'Now observe that the left boot on the body has two nails missing. If you go back to the tent, you'll find that of our 'B' footprints, set number one has those two nails missing; sets numbers two and three have not. This man's boots have two nails missing. Otherwise, the tracks are the same. Now, do you see?'

'You never told me that,' I said reproachfully.

'You looked at them just as much as I did,' said the provoking fellow. 'Can you now tell me what they mean?'

'Mr "B" was two men,' I said, rather sulkily. 'And only one of them is Courage.'

'Precisely. Two men with almost identical boots – but fortunately not quite identical. Does that suggest anything to you?'

'Only a very odd coincidence, I'm afraid. And, of course, the fact that we have to look for a new murderer.'

'Yes,' said Wilson. 'Perhaps we'd better start.'

Wilson left me to watch by the body while he went back to the tent to inform the police and summon assistance. But hardly had he left me when the scoutmaster, Evanson, appeared, scrambling down the cliff by a narrow path. I did not quite know what to do; for Wilson had said that he was particularly anxious, for the present, to keep the finding of the second body a secret. But I did not see how I could keep the newcomer away. I went towards him in the hope of heading him off.

'What were you two doing here?' he asked. 'I happened to notice you from the path above and I thought I'd come down and see if you had found anything fresh. Have you?'

'I'm afraid,' I said, 'I'm hardly at liberty . . .'

Evanson laughed. 'Official secrets, eh? I'm sure I've no desire to pry. But, while I am here, I want to have a look at these ruins. Any objection?'

'Well,' I said, 'if you don't mind . . .'

At this moment his hat, lifted by a gust of wind, went flying along the beach. He followed it, and, with some dismay, I watched the chase end within a few feet of the shallow hole in which the body lay. I ran after him.

'My God! What's this?' I heard him say. 'Courage!'

I came up, panting, 'Well, Mr Evanson, since you have seen this, I must ask you not to say a word about it to anybody. It is most important that no one should –'

'But Courage! I thought Courage was the murderer.'

'If he was, Nemesis has soon overtaken him.'

'How did you find him? Who –?'

I was scarcely able to answer; for suddenly, on the firm sand, I had noticed the print of the scoutmaster's feet. They were, to say the least, extraordinarily like the 'B' footprints we had seen at the tent, and tracked to the lonely grave in the sand. And they were a perfect impression, without a nail missing. 'We tracked him here,' I said.

Evanson clearly noticed something odd in my manner, for he looked at me strangely. I did my best not to show my excitement; and I flattered myself that, after my first start of astonishment, I managed pretty well. Evanson went on plying me with questions, direct and indirect; and I did my best to make answers that sounded innocent, and at the same time gave nothing away. The man was not to know I suspected him if I could help it. But it was wearing work; and I was mightily relieved when the police car came running down the track and the local inspector leapt out beside us.

'Thank you, doctor, for keeping watch for us. I see Mr Evanson is here. Does he recognise the body?'

'It is Courage,' said Evanson. 'But I thought . . .'

'Lord bless you, sir, we all thought. In a case like this, one's apt to think a lot of the wrong things before thinking of the right one. And now, you won't mind leaving me to manage this little affair myself. The superintendent says he would like to see you at the inn, doctor.'

I had been hesitating whether or not to tell the inspector of my discovery. But it seemed best to keep it for Wilson's ear. 'Are you coming back towards the tent?' I asked the scoutmaster.

Evanson shook his head. 'No, I'm going a bit farther along the shore,' he answered. I wondered if Wilson would blame me for letting him go; but on the whole that seemed preferable to giving my knowledge away. I left him, and set off at a smart pace towards the inn.

There, the sound of voices attracted me to the sitting-room. I found Wilson there with George Chalmers. Eagerly I asked Wilson to let me speak to him for a moment alone. He came out at once, and I told him what I had found, and expressed my fear that Evanson might even now be making his escape. To my chagrin, I found that my news was no news to him. 'Yes,' he said, 'I noticed Evanson's boots when we were talking to him by the ruined cottage. But I don't think he'll run away, all the same.' He smiled.

'Not now he knows the other body has been found?'

'I think we'll chance it,' said Wilson, leaving me to wonder whether he had really something up his sleeve, or whether in this case he was not quite up to the mark. Sadly disappointed, and more than a little perplexed, I followed him back into the room where Chalmers was still sitting.

'I've just been getting Mr Chalmers to give me all the particulars about this man Courage,' he said. 'For purposes of offering a reward for his apprehension, you know.' I took the hint. Chalmers was to know nothing yet of the discovery of Courage's body.

'Now, Mr Chalmers,' Wilson went on. 'You say Courage and Parsons quarrelled badly over the week-end, but had made it up before you left.'

'Yes.'

'Since you went away, have you either heard from, or communicated with, either of them?'

'No.'

'Is there any way you can think of in which either could have got to know what you have since discovered about Courage?'

'Impossible. I only found it out myself this morning.'

'But it is possible Mr Parsons may have found out somehow for himself?'

'Yes, that's possible. But I don't see how.'

'Then how do you explain what happened?'

'I don't like having to explain it at all. But I fear the facts speak for themselves.'

At this point Wilson's tone suddenly changed. 'Was your firm in Anglo-Asiatics, Mr Chalmers?' he said sharply.

Chalmers gave a violent start, and seemed unable to make up his mind what to answer. 'I don't see what bearing –' he began.

'I only asked,' said Wilson sweetly, 'because I noticed you cut out that bit about it from Wednesday's *Financial Times*.'

'What the devil d'you mean?'

'Well, you did, didn't you?'

'Certainly not,' Chalmers snapped.

'You see,' said Wilson, 'I thought you had, because we found the cutting in your cigar case. This is yours, isn't it?' He passed the heavy gold case across the table.

Chalmers stared down at it as if the opulent little object were a snake. 'Yes,' he said, 'that's mine. I must have left it behind here on Tuesday.'

'Oh, no, I think not, Mr Chalmers. The landlord here saw you take it out, and light a cigar just as you started the car. And he is sure you put it back in your pocket.'

'He's mistaken. I must have left it behind at the tent, or it couldn't have been found there.'

'It wasn't found at the tent, Mr Chalmers. It was found on the sands beside the old ruined church at Eccles. Does that refresh your memory?'

This time there was no mistaking Chalmers' consternation. His hand shook so violently that he knocked the cigar case to the floor with a clatter.

'What! Oh, I – I walked that way on Tuesday. I must have dropped it then.'

'With a cutting from Wednesday's *Financial Times* inside?'

'Somebody must have found the case, and put the cutting in, and dropped it later.'

'It was not dropped. It was buried.'

'I – can only say I have not had it since last Tuesday.'

Wilson changed the subject. 'On Tuesday, you drove back to London in your car?'

'Yes.'

'Where has the car been since then?'

'In my garage, except when I was using it in town.'

'It has not been out of your possession?'

'N – no.'

'Then, if your car was down here yesterday, we can take it that you were here to. Is that so?'

'It was not here yesterday. I was in London all day.'

'Supposing I tell you that you and your car were seen to turn off the main road and stop at a point where two tracks join on the way between here and Eccles, and that subsequently your car was driven down to a point near the church at Eccles, and near where the cigar case was found?'

Chalmers's alarm seemed to increase with every word that Wilson spoke. 'It's not true,' he said wildly. 'I tell you I've not been here since Tuesday.'

'Are you aware that your car has a highly distinctive patch on the left back tyre, Mr Chalmers?'

Chalmers had apparently made up his mind by now what to say. 'Look here,' he said, 'this is a ridiculous misunderstanding. You're quite right. I did drive that way. But it was on Tuesday.'

'Come, come, Mr Chalmers. The marks could not possibly have survived the rain. Will you tell me where you were on Thursday, if you were not here?'

Chalmers sprang up. 'That's enough,' he said furiously. 'I thought third degree methods were confined to the American police. I tell you I have not been near the place since Tuesday last, when I left Parsons and Courage alive and well!'

'And what makes you think Mr Courage is not alive now?' Wilson asked sharply. Chalmers saw his slip and made a sudden movement for the door. Opening it, he stepped straight into the arms of a large Norfolk policeman.

'George Chalmers,' said Wilson, signing to the policeman, 'I arrest you for the murder of Hugh Parsons and Alec Courage. And I warn you that anything you say may be used in evidence against you.'

A minute later, when the policeman, assisted by another, had led Chalmers away, I turned to Wilson.

'But what about Evanson's boots?' I cried.

'My dear Michael, what about them? They had the same arrangement of nails – it's a common one – but they were at least a size and a half too small.'

'Then it was I after all who discovered the mare's nest.'

'I'm afraid it was, Michael,' said Wilson gently. 'We all do at times.'

'I'll get my own back on you when you have that nervous breakdown,' said I. But Wilson only laughed.

Of course, Wilson's work did not end with the arrest of Chalmers. We might be as morally certain as we liked that he had murdered both his partners, but proof was another matter. Wilson himself admitted that it was Chalmers's own suspicious manner at the interview just described which had decided him to risk an immediate arrest, rather than give the man the chance of destroying incriminating evidence. And it was as well that he did so; for in Chalmers's rooms at the flat which he shared with Courage in St Mary's Mansions were found not only the copy of the *Financial Times* from which the incriminating cutting had been torn, but also a pair of boots, the twin of those on the dead man's feet, except that they had all their nails intact. They were half a size smaller than Chalmers's own footgear, and were still partly covered with Norfolk sand. Thirdly, in the desk, at the back, there turned up a scrap of paper covered with attempts at Courage's signature.

Armed with this last piece of evidence, Wilson interviewed the bank, with the result that the forged bearer cheques were submitted to further expert examination; and it was discovered that, of the two signatures which they bore – those of Courage and Chalmers – the former was really the forgery, though it had been executed so cleverly that no suspicion of it had been entertained by the bank. Chalmers had deliberately so written his own signature that it would be easily recognized as a forgery, whereas he had been at pains to make the imitation of his partner's signature as plausible as possible. This conclusion was borne out by a piece of paper found where it had blown behind the desk in his study. On this he had actually tried out both signatures. This discovery led to a close investigation of Chalmers's affairs, from which it eventually transpired that, having got the firm into serious difficulties through unwarrantable speculation, Chalmers had converted the sums represented by these cheques into bearer securities, which he had retained in preparation for the inevitable collapse.

At this point Courage's solicitor, who had also been his personal friend, disclosed a statement made by the dead man just before leaving for his holiday. In this Courage explained that he had detected a certain amount of irregularity and had eventually connected it with Chalmers. Receiving no satisfactory explanation from the latter, he had taken with him to Norfolk certain of the papers and cheque-books of the firm, with the object of discussing the position fully with Parsons, and deciding on a line of action. (These were the cheque-books whose butt-ends we found at the tent, Chalmers having burnt just enough of them to create additional suspicion and bolster up his own story.)

Even with this evidence the Crown had a hard struggle to get its conviction. Chalmers and his lawyers fought to the very last gasp, blackened Courage's character – which, indeed, was none of the best – and poured scorn on the story reconstructed by Wilson; namely, that Chalmers, having failed to secure his partners' complicity in his frauds, had decided to murder them both, and then, knowing that suspicion would almost certainly be directed to himself, had staged the clumsy pretence of suicide, which was, of course, intended to lead straight to Courage as the murderer. Even supposing the police did not see through the pretence, Courage's disappearance, together with Chalmers's statements about the forged cheques, would have amply sufficed to throw suspicion on him, and prevent any search for another criminal. What finally clinched the case against Chalmers was, curiously enough, his own alibi for the fatal night, which he had prepared with care and which very nearly saved him. Eventually, however, the police proved it to be a palpable fraud; the defence collapsed, and Chalmers was hanged.

'The Happisburgh murderer,' Wilson said to me one day when

the case was over, 'illustrates one important point in the science of crime. Chalmers had brains. No one could have planned murder much better than he planned it; but he was a clumsy executant. At every point, he lacked technique. Thus, he failed to make the suicide plausible enough. It was so barefaced a fake that it was obviously meant to be seen through. But, if that was so, one naturally distrusted the obvious explanation of the murder to which it pointed when one saw through it. Then again, he dropped his cigar case, and he failed to obliterate the traces of his car. If he had merely carried Courage's body a short distance and buried it in the sand, and then really carefully obliterated the traces, I very much doubt if we should ever have found it, and then the odds are he would have got off scot-free. No, Michael, a really good criminal needs two things – brains and technique. Chalmers had plenty of brains; but, as an executant, the fellow was a bungler. The combination of brains and technique is fortunately rare – or we policemen should never catch our hares. Which would be a great pity.'

I agreed. It was wonderful how well Wilson was looking. Our little holiday in Norfolk had quite set him up.

Edgar Wallace

THE TREASURE HUNT

THERE IS A tradition in criminal circles that even the humblest of detective officers is a man of wealth and substance, and that his secret hoard was secured by thieving, bribery, and blackmail. It is the gossip of the fields, the quarries, the tailor's shop, the laundry, and the bakehouse of fifty county prisons and three convict establishments, that all highly placed detectives have by nefarious means laid up for themselves sufficient earthly treasures to make work a hobby and their official pittance the most inconsiderable portion of their incomes.

Since Mr J. G. Reeder had for over twenty years dealt exclusively with bank robbers and forgers, who are the aristocrats and capitalists of the underworld, legend credited him with country houses and immense secret reserves. Not that he would have a great deal of money in the bank. It was admitted that he was too clever to risk discovery by the authorities. No, it was hidden somewhere: it was the pet dream of hundreds of unlawful men that they would some day discover the hoard and live happily ever after. The one satisfactory aspect of his affluence (they all agreed) was that, being an old man – he was over fifty – he couldn't take his money with him, for gold melts at a certain temperature and gilt-edged stock is seldom printed on asbestos paper.

The Director of Public Prosecutions was lunching one Saturday at his club with a judge of the King's Bench – Saturday being one of the two days in the week when a judge gets properly fed. And the conversation drifted to a certain Mr J. G. Reeder, the chief of the Director's sleuths.

'He's capable,' he confessed reluctantly, 'but I hate his hat. It is the sort that So-and-so used to wear,' he mentioned by name

an eminent politician; 'and I loathe his black frock-coat, people
who see him coming into the office think he's a coroner's officer,
but he's capable. His side-whiskers are an abomination, and I
have a feeling that, if I talked rough to him, he would burst into
tears – a gentle soul. Almost too gentle for my kind of work.
He apologizes to the messenger every time he rings for him!'

The judge, who knew something about humanity, answered
with a frosty smile.

'He sounds rather like a potential murderer to me,' he said
cynically.

Here, in his extravagance, he did Mr J. G. Reeder an injustice, for Mr Reeder was incapable of breaking the law –
quite. At the same time there were many people who formed
an altogether wrong conception of J. G.'s harmlessness as an
individual. And one of these was a certain Lew Kohl, who
mixed bank-note printing with elementary burglary.

Threatened men live long, a trite saying but, like most things
trite, true. In a score of cases, when Mr J. G. Reeder had
descended from the witness stand, he had met the baleful eye
of the man in the dock and had listened with mild interest to
divers promises as to what would happen to him in the near
or the remote future. For he was a great authority on forged
bank-notes and he had sent many men to penal servitude.

Mr Reeder, that inoffensive man, had seen prisoners foaming
at the mouth in their rage, he had seen them white and livid, he
had heard their howling execrations and he had met these men
after their release from prison and had found them amiable souls
half ashamed and half amused at their nearly forgotten outbursts
and horrific threats.

But when, in the early part of 1914, Lew Kohl was sentenced
for ten years, he neither screamed his imprecations nor registered
a vow to tear Mr Reeder's heart, lungs, and important organs
from his frail body.

Lew just smiled and his eyes caught the detective's for the space
of a second – the forger's eyes were pale blue and speculative, and
they held neither hate nor fury. Instead, they said in so many
words:

'At the first opportunity I will kill you.'

Mr Reeder read the message and sighed heavily, for he disliked fuss of all kinds, and resented, in so far as he could resent anything, the injustice of being made personally responsible for the performance of a public duty.

Many years had passed, and considerable changes had occurred in Mr Reeder's fortune. He had transferred from the specialized occupation of detecting the makers of forged bank-notes to the more general practice of the Public Prosecutor's bureau, but he never forgot Lew's smile.

The work in Whitehall was not heavy and it was very interesting. To Mr Reeder came most of the anonymous letters which the Director received in shoals. In the main they were self-explanatory, and it required no particular intelligence to discover their motive. Jealousy, malice, plain mischief-making, and occasionally a sordid desire to benefit financially by the information which was conveyed, were behind the majority. But occasionally:

Sir James is going to marry his cousin, and it's not three months since his poor wife fell overboard from the Channel steamer crossing to Calais. There's something very fishy about this business. Miss Margaret doesn't like him, for she knows he's after her money. Why was I sent away to London that night? He doesn't like driving in the dark, either. It's strange that he wanted to drive that night when it was raining like blazes.

This Particular letter was signed 'A Friend'. Justice has many such friends.

'Sir James' was Sir James Tithermite, who had been a director of some new public department during the war and had received a baronetcy for his services.

'Look it up,' said the Director when he saw the letter. 'I seem to remember that Lady Tithermite was drowned at sea.'

'On the nineteenth of December last year,' said Mr Reeder solemnly. 'She and Sir James were going to Monte Carlo, breaking their journey in Paris. Sir James, who has a house near Maidstone, drove to Dover, garaging the car at the Lord Wilson Hotel. The night was stormy and the ship had a rough crossing –

they were half-way across when Sir James came to the purser and said that he had missed his wife. Her baggage was in the cabin, her passport, rail ticket, and hat, but the lady was not found, indeed was never seen again.'

The Director nodded.

'I see, you've read up the case.'

'I remember it,' said Mr Reeder. 'The case is a favourite speculation of mine. Unfortunately, I see evil in everything and I have often thought how easy – but I fear that I take a warped view of life. It is a horrible handicap to possess a criminal mind.'

The Director looked at him suspiciously. He was never quite sure whether Mr Reeder was serious. At that moment his sobriety was beyond challenge.

'A discharged chauffeur wrote that letter, of course,' he began.

'Thomas Dayford, of 179 Barrack Street, Maidstone,' concluded Mr Reeder. 'He is at present in the employ of the Kent Motor-Bus Company, and has three children, two of whom are twins and bonny little rascals.'

The Chief laughed helplessly.

'I'll take it that you *know*'! he said. 'See what there is behind the letter. Sir James is a big fellow in Kent, a Justice of the Peace, and he has powerful political influences. There is nothing in this letter, of course. Go warily, Reeder – if any kick comes back to this office, it goes on to you – intensified!'

Mr Reeder's idea of walking warily was peculiarly his own. He travelled down to Maidstone the next morning, and, finding a bus that passed the lodge gates of Elfreda Manor, he journeyed comfortably and economically, his umbrella between his knees. He passed through the lodge gates, up a long and winding avenue of poplars, and presently came within sight of the grey manor house.

In a deep chair on the lawn he saw a girl sitting, a book on her knees, and evidently she saw him, for she rose as he crossed the lawn and came towards him eagerly.

'I'm Miss Margaret Letherby – are you from –?' She mentioned the name of a well-known firm of lawyers, and her face fell when Mr Reeder regretfully disclaimed connection with those legal lights.

She was as pretty as a perfect complexion and a round, not too intellectual, face could, in combination, make her.

' I thought – do you wish to see Sir James? He is in the library. If you ring, one of the maids will take you to him.'

Had Mr Reeder been the sort of man who could be puzzled by anything, he would have been puzzled by the suggestion that any girl with money of her own should marry a man much older than herself against her own wishes. There was little mystery in the matter now. Miss Margaret would have married any strong-willed man who insisted.

' Even me,' said Mr Reeder to himself, with a certain melancholy pleasure.

There was no need to ring the bell. A tall, broad man in a golfing suit stood in the doorway. His fair hair was long and hung over his forehead in a thick flat strand; a heavy tawny moustache hid his mouth and swept down over a chin that was long and powerful.

' Well?' he asked aggressively.

' I'm from the Public Prosecutor's office,' murmured Mr Reeder. ' I have had an anonymous letter.'

His pale eyes did not leave the face of the other man.

' Come in,' said Sir James gruffly.

As he closed the door he glanced quickly first to the girl and then to the poplar avenue.

' I'm expecting a fool of a lawyer,' he said, as he flung open the door of what was evidently the library.

His voice was steady; not by a flicker of eyelash had he betrayed the slightest degree of anxiety when Reeder had told his mission.

' Well – what about this anonymous letter? You don't take much notice of that kind of trash, do you?'

Mr Reeder deposited his umbrella and flat-crowned hat on a chair before he took a document from his pocket and handed it to the baronet, who frowned as he read. Was it Mr Reeder's vivid imagination, or did the hard light in the eyes of Sir James soften as he read?

'This is a cock-and-bull story of somebody having seen my wife's jewellery on sale in Paris,' he said. 'There is nothing in it. I can account for every one of my poor wife's trinkets. I brought back the jewel-case after that awful night. I don't recognize the handwriting: who is the lying scoundrel who wrote this?'

Mr Reeder had never before been called a lying scoundrel, but he accepted the experience with admirable meekness.

'I thought it untrue,' he said, shaking his head. 'I followed the details of the case very thoroughly. You left here in the afternoon –'

'At night,' said the other, brusquely. He was not inclined to discuss the matter, but Mr Reeder's appealing look was irresistible. 'It is only eighty minutes' run to Dover. We got to the pier at eleven o'clock, about the same time as the boat train, and we went on board at once. I got my cabin key from the purser and put her ladyship and her baggage inside.'

'Her ladyship was a good sailor?'

'Yes, a very good sailor; she was remarkably well that night. I left her in the cabin dozing, and went for a stroll on the deck –'

'Raining very heavily and a strong sea running,' nodded Reeder, as though in agreement with something the other man had said.

'Yes – I'm a pretty good sailor – anyway, that story about my poor wife's jewels is utter nonsense. You can tell the Director that, with my compliments.'

He opened the door for his visitor, and Mr Reeder was some time replacing the letter and gathering his belongings.

'You have a beautiful place here, Sir James – a lovely place. An extensive estate?'

'Three thousand acres.' This time he did not attempt to disguise his impatience. 'Good afternoon.'

Mr Reeder went slowly down the drive, his remarkable memory at work.

He missed the bus which he could easily have caught, and pursued an apparently aimless way along the winding road which marched with the boundaries of the baronet's property. A walk of a quarter of a mile brought him to a lane shooting off at right angles from the main road, and marking, he guessed, the southern boundary. At the corner stood an old stone lodge, on the inside of a forbidding iron gate. The lodge was in a pitiable state of neglect and disrepair. Tiles had been dislodged from the roof, the windows were grimy or broken, and the little garden was overrun with docks and thistles. Beyond the gate was a narrow, weed-covered drive that trailed out of sight into a distant plantation.

Hearing the clang of a letter-box closing, he turned to see a postman mounting his bicycle.

'What place is this?' asked Mr Reeder, arresting the postman's departure.

'South Lodge – Sir James Tithermite's property. It's never used now. Hasn't been used for years – I don't know why: it's a short cut if they happen to be coming this way.'

Mr Reeder walked with him towards the village, and he was a skilful pumper of wells, however dry; and the postman was not dry by any means.

'Yes, poor lady! She was very frail – one of those sort of invalids that last out many a healthy man.'

Mr Reeder put a question at random and scored most unexpectedly.

'Yes, her ladyship was a bad sailor. I know because every time she went abroad she used to get a bottle of that stuff people take for sea-sickness. I've delivered many a bottle till Raikes the chemist stocked it – "Pickers' Travellers' Friend", that's what it was called. Mr Raikes was only saying to me the other day that he'd got half a dozen bottles on hand, and he didn't know what to do with them. Nobody in Climbury ever goes to sea.'

Mr Reeder went on to the village and idled his precious time in most unlikely places. At the chemist's, at the blacksmith's shop, at the modest building-yard. He caught the last bus back to Maidstone, and by great good luck the last train to London.

And, in his vague way, he answered the Director's query the next day with:

'Yes, I saw Sir James: a very interesting man.'

This was on the Friday. All day Saturday he was busy. The Sabbath brought him a new interest.

On this bright Sunday morning, Mr Reeder, attired in a flowered dressing-gown, his feet encased in black velvet slippers, stood at the window of his house in Brockley Road and surveyed the deserted thoroughfare. The bell of a local church, which was accounted high, had rung for early Mass, and there was nothing living in sight except a black cat that lay asleep in a patch of sunlight on the top step of the house opposite. The hour was seven-thirty, and Mr Reeder had been at his desk since six, working by artificial light, the month being October, towards the close.

From the half-moon of the window he regarded a section of the Lewisham High Road and as much of Tanners Hill as can be seen before it dips past the railway bridge into sheer Deptford.

Returning to his table, he opened a carton of the cheapest cigarettes and, lighting one, puffed in an amateurish fashion. He smoked cigarettes rather like a woman who detests them but feels that it is the correct thing to do.

'Dear me,' said Mr Reeder feebly.

He was back at the window, and he had seen a man turn out of Lewisham High Road. He had crossed the road and was coming straight to Daffodil House – which frolicsome name appeared on the door-posts of Mr Reeder's residence, A tall, straight man, with a sombre brown face, he came to the front gate, passed through and beyond the watcher's range of vision.

'Dear me!' said Mr Reeder, as he heard the tinkle of a bell.

A few minutes later his housekeeper tapped on the door.

'Will you see Mr Kohl, sir?' she asked. Mr J. G. Reeder nodded.

Lew Kohl walked into the room to find a middle-aged man in a flamboyant dressing-gown sitting at his desk, a pair of pince-nez set crookedly on his nose.

'Good morning, Kohl.'

Lew Kohl looked at the man who had sent him to seven and a half years of hell, and the corner of his thin lips curled.

''Morning, Mr Reeder.' His eyes flashed across the almost bare surface of the writing-desk on which Reeder's hands were lightly clasped. 'You didn't expect to see me, I guess?'

'Not so early,' said Reeder in his hushed voice, 'but I should have remembered that early rising is one of the good habits which are inculcated by penal servitude.'

He said this in the manner of one bestowing praise for good conduct.

'I suppose you've got a pretty good idea of why I have come, eh? I'm a bad forgetter, Reeder, and a man in Dartmoor has time to think.'

The older man lifted his sandy eyebrows, the steel-rimmed glasses on his nose slipped farther askew.

'That phrase seems familiar,' he said, and the eyebrows lowered in a frown. 'Now let me think – it was in a melodrama, of course, but was it *Souls in Harness* or *The Marriage Vow*?'

He appeared genuinely anxious for assistance in solving this problem.

'This is going to be a different kind of play,' said the long-faced Lew through his teeth. 'I'm going to get you, Reeder – you can go along and tell your boss, the Public Prosecutor. But I'll get you sweet! There will be no evidence to swing me. And I'll get that nice little stocking of yours, Reeder!'

The legend of Reeder's fortune was accepted even by so intelligent a man as Kohl.

'You'll get my stocking! Dear me, I shall have to go bare-footed,' said Mr Reeder, with a faint show of humour.

'You know what I mean – think that over. Some hour and day you'll go out, and all Scotland Yard won't catch me for the killing! I've thought it out –'

'One has time to think in Dartmoor,' murmured Mr J. G. Reeder encouragingly. 'You're becoming one of the world's thinkers, Kohl. Do you know Rodin's masterpiece – a beautiful statue throbbing with life –'

'That's all.' Lew Kohl rose, the smile still trembling at the corner of his mouth. 'Maybe you'll turn this over in your mind, and in a day or two you won't be feeling so gay.'

Reeder's face was pathetic in its sadness. His untidy sandy-grey hair seemed to be standing on end; the large ears, that stood out at right angles to his face, gave the illusion of quivering movement.

Lew Kohl's hand was on the door-knob.

'*Womp!*'

It was the sound of a dull weight striking a board; something winged past his cheek, before his eyes a deep hole showed in the wall, and his face was stung by flying grains of plaster. He spun round with a whine of rage.

Mr Reeder had a long-barrelled Browning in his hand, with a barrel-shaped silencer over the muzzle, and he was staring at the weapon open-mouthed.

'Now how on earth did that happen?' he asked in wonder.

Lew Kohl stood trembling with rage and fear, his face yellow-white.

'You – you swine!' he breathed. 'You tried to shoot me!'

Mr Reeder stared at him over his glasses.

'Good gracious – you think that? Still thinking of killing me, Kohl?'

Kohl tried to speak but found no words, and, flinging open the door, he strode down the stairs and through the front entrance. His foot was on the first step when something came hurtling past him and crashed to fragments at his feet. It was a large stone vase that had decorated the window-sill of Mr Reeder's bedroom. Leaping over the debris of stone and flower-mould, he glared up into the surprised face of Mr J. G. Reeder.

'I'll get you!' he spluttered.

'I hope you're not hurt?' asked the man at the window in a tone of concern. 'These things happen. Some day and some hour –'

As Lew Kohl strode down the street, the detective was still talking.

Mr Stan Bride was at his morning ablutions when his friend and sometime prison associate came into the little room that overlooked Fitzroy Square.

Stan Bride, who bore no resemblance to anything virginal, being a stout and stumpy man with a huge red face and many chins, stopped in the act of drying himself and gazed over the edge of the towel.

'What's the matter with you?' he asked sharply. 'You look as

if you'd been chased by a busy. What did you go out so early
for?'

Lew told him, and the jovial countenance of his room-mate
grew longer and longer.

'You poor fish!' he hissed. 'To go after Reeder with that stuff!
Don't you think he was waiting for you? Do you suppose he
didn't know the very moment you left the Moor?'

'I've scared him, anyway,' said the other, and Mr Bride
laughed.

'Good scout!' he sneered. 'Scare that old person!' (He did not
say 'person'.) 'If he's as white as you, he *is* scared! But he's not.
Of course he shot past you – if he'd wanted to shoot you, you'd
have been stiff by now. But he didn't. Thinker, eh – he's given
you somep'n' to think about.'

'Where that gun came from I don't –'

There was a knock at the door and the two men exchanged
glances.

'Who's there?' asked Bride, and a familiar voice answered.

'It's that busy from the Yard,' whispered Bride, and opened
the door.

The 'busy' was Sergeant Allford, CID, an affable and portly
man and a detective of some promise.

''Morning, boys – not been to church, Stan?'

Stan grinned politely.

'How's trade, Lew?'

'Not so bad.' The forger was alert, suspicious.

'Come to see you about a gun – got an idea you're carrying
one, Lew – Colt automatic R 7/94318. That's not right, Lew –
guns don't belong to this country.'

'I've got no gun,' said Lew sullenly.

Bride had suddenly become an old man, for he also was a
convict on licence, and the discovery might send him back to
serve his unfinished sentence.

'Will you come a little walk to the station, or will you let me
go over you?'

'Go over me,' said Lew, and put out his arms stiffly whilst the
detective rubbed him down.

'I'll have a look round,' said the detective, and his 'look round' was very thorough.

'Must have been mistaken,' said Sergeant Allford. And then, suddenly: 'Was that what you chucked into the river as you were walking along the Embankment?'

Lew started. It was the first intimation he had received that he had been 'tailed' that morning.

Bride waited till the detective was visible from the window crossing Fitzroy Square; then he turned in a fury on his companion.

'Clever, ain't you! That old hound knew you had a gun – knew the number. And if Allford had found it you'd have been " dragged " and me too!'

'I threw it in the river,' said Lew sulkily.

'Brains – not many but some!' said Bride, breathing heavily. 'You cut out Reeder – he's hell and poison, and if you don't know it you're deaf! Scared him? You big stiff! He'd cut your throat and write a hymn about it.'

'I didn't know they were tailing me,' growled Kohl; 'but I'll get him! And his money, too.'

'Get him from another lodging,' said Bride curtly. 'A crook I don't mind, being one; a murderer I don't mind, but a talking jackass makes me sick. Get his stuff if you can – I'll bet it's all invested in real estate, and you can't lift houses – but don't talk about it. I like you, Lew, up to a point; you're miles before the point and out of sight. I don't like Reeder – I don't like snakes, but I keep away from the zoo.'

So Lew Kohl went into new diggings on the top floor of an Italian's house in Dean Street, and here he had leisure and inclination to brood upon his grievances and to plan afresh the destruction of his enemy. And new plans were needed, for the schemes which had seemed so watertight in the quietude of a Devonshire cell showed daylight through many crevices.

Lew's homicidal urge had undergone considerable modification. He had been experimented upon by a very clever psychologist – though he never regarded Mr Reeder in this light, and, indeed, had the vaguest idea as to what the word meant. But there were other ways of hurting Reeder, and his mind fell constantly back to the drama of discovering this peccant detective's hidden treasure.

It was nearly a week later that Mr Reeder invited himself into the Director's private sanctum, and that great official listened spellbound while his subordinate offered his outrageous theory about Sir James Tithermite and his dead wife. When Mr Reeder had finished, the Director pushed back his chair from the table.

'My dear man,' he said, a little irritably, 'I can't possibly give a warrant on the strength of your surmises – not even a search warrant. The story is so fantastic, so incredible, that it would be more at home in the pages of a sensational story than in a Public Prosecutor's report.'

'It was a wild night, and yet Lady Tithermite was not ill,' suggested the detective gently. 'That is a fact to remember, sir.'

The Director shook his head.

'I can't do it – not on the evidence,' he said. 'I should raise a storm that'd swing me into Whitehall. Can't you do anything – unofficially?'

Mr Reeder shook his head.

'My presence in the neighbourhood has been remarked,' he said primly. 'I think it would be impossible to – er – cover up my traces. And yet I have located the place, and could tell you within a few inches –'

Again the Director shook his head.

'No, Reeder,' he said quietly, 'the whole thing is sheer deduction on your part. Oh, yes, I know you have a criminal mind – I think you have told me that before. And that is a good reason why I should not issue a warrant. You're simply crediting this unfortunate man with your ingenuity. Nothing doing!'

Mr Reeder sighed and went back to his bureau, not entirely despondent, for there had intruded a new element into his investigations.

Mr Reeder had been to Maidstone several times during the week, and he had not gone alone; though seemingly unconscious

of the fact that he had developed a shadow, for he had seen
Lew Kohl on several occasions, and had spent an uncomfortable
few minutes wondering whether his experiments had failed.

On the second occasion an idea had developed in the detective's
mind, and if he were a laughing man he would have chuckled
aloud when he slipped out of Maidstone station one evening and,
in the act of hiring a cab, had seen Lew Kohl negotiating for
another.

Mr Bride was engaged in the tedious but necessary practice
of so cutting a pack of cards that the ace of diamonds remained
at the bottom, when his former co-lodger burst in upon him, and
there was a light of triumph in Lew's cold eyes which brought
Mr Bride's heart to his boots.

'I've got him!' said Lew.

Bride put aside the cards and stood up.

'Got who?' he asked coldly. 'And if it's killing, you needn't
answer, but get out!'

'There's no killing.'

Lew sat down squarely at the table, his hands in his pockets,
a real smile on his face.

'I've been trailing Reeder for a week, and that fellow wants
some trailing!'

'Well?' asked the other, when he paused dramatically.

'I've found his stocking!'

Bride scratched his chin, and was half convinced.

'You never have?'

Lew nodded.

'He's been going to Maidstone a lot lately, and driving to a
little village about five miles out. There I always lost him. But
the other night, when he came back to the station to catch the
last train, he slipped into the waiting-room and I found a place
where I could watch him. What do you think he did?'

Mr Bride hazarded no suggestion.

'He opened his bag,' said Lew impressively, 'and took out a
wad of notes as thick as that! He'd been drawing on his bank!
I trailed him up to London. There's a restaurant on the station
and he went in to get a cup of coffee, with me keeping well out

of his sight. As he came out of the restaurant he took out his handkerchief and wiped his mouth. He didn't see the little book that dropped, but I did. I was scared sick that somebody else would see it, or that he'd wait long enough to find it himself. But he went out of the station and I got that book before you could say "knife". Look!'

It was a well-worn little notebook, covered with faded red morocco. Bride put out his hand to take it.

'Wait a bit,' said Lew. 'Are you in this with me fifty-fifty, because I want some help?'

Bride hesitated.

'If it's just plain thieving, I'm with you,' he said.

'Plain thieving – and sweet,' said Lew exultantly, and pushed the book across the table.

For the greater part of the night they sat together talking in low tones, discussing impartially the methodical book-keeping of Mr J. G. Reeder and his exceeding dishonesty.

The Monday night was wet. A storm blew up from the south-west, and the air was filled with falling leaves as Lew and his companion footed the five miles which separated them from the village. Neither carried any impedimenta that was visible, yet under Lew's waterproof coat was a kit of tools of singular ingenuity, and Mr Bride's coat pockets were weighted down with the sections of a powerful jemmy.

They met nobody in their walk, and the church bell was striking eleven when Lew gripped the bars of the South Lodge gates, pulled himself up to the top and dropped lightly on the other side. He was followed by Mr Bride, who, in spite of his bulk, was a singularly agile man. The ruined lodge showed in the darkness, and they passed through the creaking gates to the door and Lew flashed his lantern upon the keyhole before he began manipulation with the implements which he had taken from his kit.

The door was opened in ten minutes and a few seconds later they stood in a low-roofed little room, the principal feature of which was a deep, grateless fireplace. Lew took off his mackintosh and stretched it over the window before he spread the light in his lamp, and, kneeling down, brushed the debris from the hearth, examining the joints of the big stone carefully.

'This work's been botched,' he said. 'Anybody could see that.'

He put the claw of the jemmy into a crack and levered up the stone, and it moved slightly. Stopping only to dig a deeper crevice with a chisel and hammer, he thrust the claw of the jemmy farther down. The stone came up above the edge of the floor and Bride slipped the chisel underneath.

'Now together,' grunted Lew.

They got their fingers beneath the hearth-stone and with one heave hinged it up. Lew picked up the lamp, and, kneeling down, flashed a light into the dark cavity. And then:

'Oh, my God' he shrieked.

A second later two terrified men rushed from the house into the drive. And a miracle had happened, for the gates were open and a dark figure stood squarely before them.

'Put up your hands, Kohl!' said a voice and, hateful as it was to Lew Kohl, he could have fallen on the neck of Mr Reeder.

At twelve o'clock that night Sir James Tithermite was discussing matters with his bride-to-be: the stupidity of her lawyer, who wished to safeguard her fortune, and his own cleverness and foresight in securing complete freedom of action for the girl who was to be his wife.

'These blackguards think of nothing but their fees,' he began, when his footman came in unannounced, and behind him the Chief Constable of the county and a man he remembered seeing before.

'Sir James Tithermite?' said the Chief Constable unnecessarily, for he knew Sir James very well.

'Yes, Colonel, what is it?' asked the baronet, his face twitching.

'I am taking you into custody on a charge of wilfully murdering your wife, Eleanor Mary Tithermite.'

'The whole thing turned upon the question as to whether Lady Tithermite was a good or a bad sailor,' explained J. G. Reeder to his chief. 'If she were a bad sailor, it was unlikely that she would be on the ship, even for five minutes, without calling for the stewardess. The stewardess did not see her ladyship, nor did anybody on board, for the simple reason that she was not on board! She was murdered within the grounds of the manor; her body was buried beneath the hearth-stone of the old lodge, and Sir James continued his journey by car to Dover, handing over his packages to a porter and telling him to take them to his cabin before he returned to put the car into the hotel garage. He had timed his arrival so that he passed on board with a crowd of passengers from the boat train, and nobody knew whether he was alone or whether he was accompanied, and, for the matter of that, nobody cared. The purser gave him his key, and he put the baggage, including his wife's hat, into the cabin, paid the porter and dismissed him. Officially, Lady Tithermite was on board, for he surrendered her ticket to the collector and received her landing voucher. And then he discovered she had disappeared. The ship was searched, but, of course, the unfortunate lady was not found. As I remarked before –'

'You have a criminal mind,' said the Director good-humouredly. 'Go on, Reeder.'

'Having this queer and objectionable trait, I saw how very simple a matter it was to give the illusion that the lady was on board, and I decided that, if the murder was committed, it must have been within a few miles of the house. And then the local builder told me that he had given Sir James a little lesson in the art of mixing mortar. And the local blacksmith told me that the gate had been damaged, presumably by Sir James's car – I had seen the broken rods and all I wanted to know was when the repairs were effected. That she was beneath the hearth in the lodge I was certain. Without a search warrant it was impossible to prove or disprove my theory, and I myself could not conduct a private investigation without risking the reputation of our department – if I may say " our ",' he said apologetically.

The Director was thoughtful.

'Of course, you induced this man Kohl to dig up the hearth by pretending you had money buried there. I presume you revealed that fact in your notebook? But why on earth did he imagine that you had a hidden treasure?'

Mr Reeder smiled sadly.

'The criminal mind is a peculiar thing,' he said, with a sigh.
'It harbours illusions and fairy stories. Fortunately, I understand
that mind. As I have often said –'

Agatha Christie

SING A SONG OF SIXPENCE

SIR EDWARD PALLISER, KC, lived at No. 9 Queen Anne's Close. Queen Anne's Close is a *cul de sac*. In the very heart of Westminster it manages to have a peaceful old-world atmosphere far removed from the turmoil of the twentieth century. It suited Sir Edward Palliser admirably.

Sir Edward had been one of the most eminent criminal barristers of his day and now that he no longer practised at the Bar he had amused himself by amassing a very fine criminological library. He was also the author of a volume of Reminiscences of Eminent Criminals.

On this particular evening Sir Edward was sitting in front of his library fire sipping some very excellent black coffee, and shaking his head over a volume of Lombroso. Such ingenious theories and so completely out of date.

The door opened almost noiselessly and his well-trained manservant approached over the thick pile carpet, and murmured discreetly:

'A young lady wishes to see you, sir.'

'A young lady?'

Sir Edward was surprised. Here was something quite out of the usual course of events. Then he reflected that it might be his niece, Ethel – but no, in that case Armour would have said so.

He inquired cautiously.

'The lady did not give her name?'

'No sir, but she said she was quite sure you would wish to see her.'

'Show her in,' said Sir Edward Palliser. He felt pleasurably intrigued.

A tall, dark girl of close on thirty, wearing a black coat and skirt, well cut, and a little black hat, came to Sir Edward with outstretched hand and a look of eager recognition on her face. Armour withdrew, closing the door noiselessly behind him.

'Sir Edward – you do know me, don't you? I'm Magdalen Vaughan.'

'Why, of course.' He pressed the outstretched hand warmly.

He remembered her perfectly now. That trip home from America on the *Siluric*! This charming child – for she had been little more than a child. He had made love to her, he remembered, in a discreet elderly man-of-the-world fashion. She had been so adorably young – so eager – so full of admiration and hero worship – just made to captivate the heart of a man nearing sixty. The remembrance brought additional warmth into the pressure of his hand.

'This is most delightful of you. Sit down, won't you.' He arranged an arm-chair for her, talking easily and evenly, wondering all the time why she had come. When at last he brought the easy flow of small talk to an end, there was a silence.

Her hand closed and unclosed on the arm of the chair, she moistened her lips. Suddenly she spoke – abruptly.

'Sir Edward – I want you to help me.'

He was surprised and murmured mechanically:

'Yes?'

She went on, speaking more intensely:

'You said that if ever I needed help – that if there was anything in the world you could do for me – you would do it.'

Yes, he *had* said that. It was the sort of thing one did say – particularly at the moment of parting. He could recall the break in his voice – the way he had raised her hand to his lips.

'*If there is ever anything I can do – remember, I mean it . . .*'

Yes, one said that sort of thing. . . . But very, very rarely did one have to fulfil one's words! And certainly not after – how many? – nine or ten years. He flashed a quick glance at her – she was still a very good-looking girl, but she had lost what had been to him her charm – that look of dewy untouched youth. It was a more interesting face now, perhaps – a younger man might have thought so – but Sir Edward was far from feeling the tide of warmth and emotion that had been his at the end of that Atlantic voyage.

His face became legal and cautious. He said in a rather brisk way:

'Certainly, my dear young lady, I shall be delighted to do anything in my power – though I doubt if I can be very helpful to any one in these days.'

If he was preparing his way of retreat she did not notice it. She was of the type that can only see one thing at a time and what she was seeing at this moment was her own need. She took Sir Edward's willingness to help for granted.

'We are in terrible trouble, Sir Edward.'

'*We?* You are married?'

'No – I meant my brother and I. Oh! and William and Emily too, for that matter. But I must explain. I have – I had an aunt – Miss Crabtree. You may have read about her in the papers? It was horrible. She was killed – murdered.'

'Ah!' A flash of interest lit up Sir Edward's face. 'About a month ago, wasn't it?'

The girl nodded.

'Rather less than that – three weeks.'

'Yes. I remember. She was hit on the head in her own house. They didn't get the fellow who did it.'

Again Magdalen Vaughan nodded.

'They didn't get the man – I don't believe they ever will get the man. You see – there mightn't be any man to get.'

'What?'

'Yes – it's awful. Nothing's come out about it in the papers. But that's what the police think. They *know* nobody came to the house that night.'

'You mean –?'

'That it's one of us four. It *must* be. They don't know which – and *we* don't know which. . . . *We don't know.* And we sit there every day looking at each other surreptitiously and wondering.

Oh! if only it could have been someone from outside – but I
don't see how it can . . .'

Sir Edward stared at her, his interest arising.

'You mean that the members of the family are under suspicion?'

'Yes, that's what I mean. The police haven't said so, of course.
They've been quite polite and nice. But they've ransacked the
house, they've questioned us all, and Martha again and again. . . .
And because they don't know which, they're holding their hand.
I'm so frightened – so horribly frightened. . . .'

'My dear child. Come now, surely you are exaggerating.'

'I'm not. It's one of us four – it must be.'

'Who are the four to whom you refer?'

Magdalen sat up straight and spoke more composedly.

'There's myself and Matthew. Aunt Lily was our great aunt.
She was my grandmother's sister. We've lived with her ever
since we were fourteen (we're twins, you know). Then there was
William Crabtree. He was her nephew – her brother's child. He
lived there too, with his wife, Emily.'

'She supported them?'

'More or less. He has a little money of his own, but he's not
strong and has to live at home. He's a quiet, dreamy sort of man.
I'm sure it would have been impossible for him to have – oh! it's
awful of me to think of it even!'

'I am still very far from understanding the position. Perhaps
you would not mind running over the facts – if it does not distress
you too much.'

'Oh! no – I want to tell you. And it's all quite clear in my
mind still – horribly clear. We'd had tea, you understand, and
we'd all gone off to do things of our own. I to do some dress-
making, Matthew to type an article – he does a little journalism;
William to do his stamps. Emily hadn't been down to tea. She'd
taken a headache powder and was lying down. So there we were,
all of us, busy and occupied. And when Martha went in to lay
supper at half-past seven, there Aunt Lily was – dead. Her head –
oh! it's horrible – all crushed in.'

'The weapon was found, I think?'

'Yes. It was a heavy paper-weight that always lay on the table by the door. The police tested it for fingerprints, but there were none. It had been wiped clean.'

'And your first surmise?'

'We thought of course it was a burglar. There were two or three drawers of the bureau pulled out, as though a thief had been looking for something. Of course we thought it was a burglar! And then the police came – and they said she had been dead at least an hour, and asked Martha who had been to the house, and Martha said nobody. And all the windows were fastened on the inside, and there seemed no signs of anything having been tampered with. And then they began to ask us questions. . . .'

She stopped. Her breast heaved. Her eyes, frightened and imploring, sought Sir Edward's in search of reassurance.

'For instance, who benefited by your aunt's death?'

'That's simple. We all benefit equally. She left her money to be divided in equal shares among the four of us.'

'And what was the value of her estate?'

'The lawyer told us it will come to about eighty thousand pounds after the death duties are paid.'

Sir Edward opened his eyes in some slight surprise.

'That is quite a considerable sum. You knew, I suppose, the total of your aunt's fortune?'

Magdalen shook her head.

'No – it came quite as a surprise to us. Aunt Lily was always terribly careful about money. She kept just the one servant and always talked a lot about economy.'

Sir Edward nodded thoughtfully. Magdalen leaned forward a little in her chair.

'You will help me – you will?'

Her words came to Sir Edward as an unpleasant shock just at the moment when he was becoming interested in her story for its own sake.

'My dear young lady – what can I possibly do? If you want good legal advice, I can give you the name –'

She interrupted him.

'Oh! I don't want that sort of thing! I want you to help me personally – as a friend.'

'That's very charming of you, but –'

'I want you to come to our house. I want you to ask questions. I want you to see and judge for yourself.'

'But my dear young –'

'Remember, you promised. Anywhere – any time – you said, if I wanted help . . .'

Her eyes, pleading yet confident, looked into his. He felt ashamed and strangely touched. That terrific sincerity of hers, that absolute belief in an idle promise, ten years old, as a sacred binding thing. How many men had not said those self-same words – a *cliché* almost! – and how few of them had ever been called upon to make good.

He said rather weakly: 'I'm sure there are many people who could advise you better than I could.'

'I've got lots of friends – naturally.' (He was amused by the naïve self-assurance of that.) 'But you see, none of them are clever. Not like you. You're used to questioning people. And with all your experience you must *know*.'

'Know what?'

'Whether they're innocent or guilty.'

He smiled rather grimly to himself. He flattered himself that on the whole he usually *had* known! Though, on many occasions, his private opinion had not been that of the jury.

Magdalen pushed back her hat from her forehead with a nervous gesture, looked round the room, and said:

'How quiet it is here. Don't you sometimes long for some noise?'

The *cul de sac*! All unwittingly her words, spoken at random, touched him on the raw. A *cul de sac*. Yes, but there was always a way out – the way you had come – the way back into the world. . . . Something impetuous and youthful stirred in him. Her simple trust appealed to the best side of his nature – and the condition of her problem appealed to something else – the innate criminologist in him. He wanted to see these people of whom she spoke. He wanted to form his own judgment.

He said: 'If you are really convinced I can be of any use. . . . Mind, I guarantee nothing.'

He expected her to be overwhelmed with delight, but she took it very calmly.

' I knew you would do it. I've always thought of you as a real friend. Will you come back with me now?'

' No. I think if I pay you a visit tomorrow it will be more satisfactory. Will you give me the name and address of Miss Crabtree's lawyer? I may want to ask him a few questions.'

She wrote it down and handed it to him. Then she got up and said rather shyly:

' I – I'm really most awfully grateful. Good-bye.'

' And your own address?'

' How stupid of me. 18 Palatine Walk, Chelsea.'

It was three o'clock on the following afternoon when Sir Edward Palliser approached 18 Palatine Walk with a sober, measured tread. In the interval he had found out several things. He had paid a visit that morning to Scotland Yard, where the Assistant Commissioner was an old friend of his, and he had also had an interview with the late Miss Crabtree's lawyer. As a result he had a clearer vision of the circumstances. Miss Crabtree's arrangements in regard to money had been somewhat peculiar. She never made use of a cheque-book. Instead she was in the habit of writing to her lawyer and asking him to have a certain sum in five-pound notes waiting for her. It was nearly always the same sum. Three hundred pounds four times a year. She came to fetch it herself in a four-wheeler which she regarded as the only safe means of conveyance. At other times she never left the house.

At Scotland Yard Sir Edward learned that the question of finance had been gone into very carefully. Miss Crabtree had been almost due for her next instalment of money. Presumably the previous three hundred had been spent – or almost spent. But this was exactly the point that had not been easy to ascertain. By checking the household expenditure, it was soon evident that Miss Crabtree's expenditure per quarter fell a good deal short of the three hundred. On the other hand she was in the habit of sending five-pound notes away to needy friends or relatives. Whether there had been much or little money in the house at the time of her death was a debatable point. None had been found.

It was this particular point which Sir Edward was revolving in his mind as he approached Palatine Walk.

The door of the house (which was a non-basement one) was opened to him by a small elderly woman with an alert gaze. He was shown into a big double room on the left of the small hallway and there Magdalen came to him. More clearly than before, he saw the traces of nervous strain in her face.

'You told me to ask questions, and I have come to do so,' said Sir Edward, smiling as he shook hands. 'First of all I want to know who last saw your aunt and exactly what time that was?'

'It was after tea – five o'clock. Martha was the last person with her. She had been paying the books that afternoon, and brought Aunt Lily the change and the accounts.'

'You trust Martha?'

'Oh, absolutely. She was with Aunt Lily for – oh! thirty years, I suppose. She's honest as the day.'

Sir Edward nodded.

'Another question. Why did your cousin, Mrs Crabtree, take a headache powder?'

'Well, because she had a headache.'

'Naturally, but was there any particular reason why she *should* have a headache?'

'Well, yes, in a way. There was rather a scene at lunch. Emily is very excitable and highly strung. She and Aunt Lily used to have rows sometimes.'

'And they had one at lunch?'

'Yes. Aunt Lily was rather trying about little things. It all started out of nothing – and then they were at it hammer and tongs – with Emily saying all sorts of things she couldn't possibly have meant – that she'd leave the house and never come back – that she was grudged every mouthful she ate – oh! all sorts of silly things. And Aunt Lily said the sooner she and her husband packed their boxes and went the better. But it all meant nothing, really.'

'Because Mr and Mrs Crabtree couldn't afford to pack up and go?'

'Oh, not only that. William was fond of Aunt Emily. He really was.'

'It wasn't a day of quarrels by any chance?'

Magdalen's colour heightened.

'You mean me? The fuss about my wanting to be a mannequin?'

'Your aunt wouldn't agree?'

'No.'

'Why did you want to be a mannequin, Miss Magdalen? Does the life strike you as a very attractive one?'

'No, but anything would be better than going on living here.'

'Yes, then. But now you will have a comfortable income, won't you?'

'Oh! yes, it's quite different *now*.'

She made the admission with the utmost simplicity.

He smiled but pursued the subject no further. Instead he said: 'And your brother? Did he have a quarrel too?'

'Matthew? Oh, no.'

'Then no one can say he had a motive for wishing his aunt out of the way?'

He was quick to seize on the momentary dismay that showed in her face.

'I forgot,' he said casually. 'He owed a good deal of money, didn't he?'

'Yes; poor old Matthew.'

'Still, that will be all right now.'

'Yes –' She sighed. 'It *is* a relief.'

And still she saw nothing! He changed the subject hastily.

'Your cousins and your brother are at home?'

'Yes; I told them you were coming. They are all so anxious to help. Oh, Sir Edward – I feel, somehow, that you are going to find out that everything is all right – that none of us had anything to do with it – that, after all, it *was* an outsider.'

'I can't do miracles. I may be able to find out the truth, but I can't make the truth be what you want it to be..'

'Can't you? I feel that you could do anything – anything.'

She left the room. He thought, disturbed, 'What did she mean by that? Does she want me to suggest a line of defence? For whom?'

His meditations were interrupted by the entrance of a man about fifty years of age. He had a naturally powerful frame, but stooped slightly. His clothes were untidy and his hair carelessly brushed. He looked good-natured but vague.

'Sir Edward Palliser? Oh, how do you do? Magdalen sent me along. It's very good of you, I'm sure, to wish to help us. Though I don't think anything will ever be really discovered. I mean, they won't catch the fellow.'

'You think it was a burglar then – someone from outside?'

'Well, it must have been. It couldn't be one of the family. These fellows are very clever nowadays, they climb like cats and they get in and out as they like.'

'Where were you, Mr Crabtree, when the tragedy occurred?'

'I was busy with my stamps – in my little sitting-room upstairs.'

'You didn't hear anything?'

'No – but then I never do hear anything when I'm absorbed. Very foolish of me, but there it is.'

'Is the sitting-room you refer to over this room?'

'No, it's at the back.'

Again the door opened. A small fair woman entered. Her hands were twitching nervously. She looked fretful and excited.

'William, why didn't you wait for me? I said "wait".'

'Sorry, my dear, I forgot. Sir Edward Palliser – my wife.'

'How do you do, Mrs Crabtree? I hope you don't mind my coming here to ask a few questions. I know how anxious you must all be to have things cleared up.'

'Naturally. But I can't tell you anything – can I, William? I was asleep – on my bed – I only woke up when Martha screamed.'

Her hands continued to twitch.

'Where is your room, Mrs Crabtree?'

'It's over this. But I didn't hear anything – how could I? I was asleep.'

He could get nothing out of her but that. She knew nothing – she had heard nothing – she had been asleep. She reiterated it with the obstinacy of a frightened woman. Yet Sir Edward knew very well that it might easily be – probably was the bare truth.

He excused himself at last – said he would like to put a few questions to Martha. William Crabtree volunteered to take him to the kitchen. In the hall, Sir Edward nearly collided with a tall dark young man who was striding towards the front door.

'Mr Matthew Vaughan?'

'Yes – but look here, I can't wait. I've got an appointment.'

'Matthew!' It was his sister's voice from the stairs. 'Oh! Matthew, you promised –'

'I know, sis. But I can't. Got to meet a fellow. And, anyway, what's the good of talking about the damned thing over and over again. We have enough of that with the police. I'm fed up with the whole show.'

The front door banged. Mr Matthew Vaughan had made his exit.

Sir Edward was introduced into the kitchen. Martha was ironing. She paused, iron in hand. Sir Edward shut the door behind him.

'Miss Vaughan has asked me to help her,' he said. 'I hope you won't object to my asking you a few questions.'

She looked at him, then shook her head.

'None of them did it, sir. I know what you're thinking, but it isn't so. As nice a set of ladies and gentlemen as you could wish to see.'

'I've no doubt of it. But their niceness isn't what we call evidence, you know.'

'Perhaps not sir. The law's a funny thing. But there is evidence – as you call it, sir. None of them could have done it without *my* knowing.'

'But surely –'

'I know what I'm talking about, sir. There, listen to that –'

'That' was a creaking sound above their heads.

'The stairs, sir. Every time any one goes up or down, the stairs creak something awful. It doesn't matter how quiet you go. Mrs Crabtree, she was lying on her bed, and Mr Crabtree was fiddling about with them wretched stamps of his, and Miss Magdalen she was up above again working her machine, and if any one of those three had come down the stairs I should have known it. And they didn't!'

She spoke with a positive assurance which impressed the barrister. He thought: 'A good witness. She'd carry weight.'

'You mightn't have noticed.'

'Yes, I would. I'd have noticed without noticing, so to speak. Like you notice when a door shuts and somebody goes out.'

Sir Edward shifted his ground.

'That is three of them accounted for, but there is a fourth. Was Mr Matthew Vaughan upstairs also?'

'No, but he was in the little room downstairs. Next door. And he was typewriting. You can hear it plain in here. His machine never stopped for a moment. Not for a moment, sir. I can swear to it. A nasty irritating tap-tapping noise it is, too.'

Sir Edward paused a minute.

'It was you who found her, wasn't it?'

'Yes, sir, it was. Lying there with blood on her poor hair. And no one hearing a sound on account of the tap-tapping of Mr Matthew's typewriter.'

'I understand you are positive that no one came to the house?'

'How could they, sir, without my knowing? The bell rings in here. And there's only the one door.'

He looked at her straight in the face.

'You were attached to Miss Crabtree?'

A warm glow – genuine – unmistakable – came into her face.

'Yes, indeed, I was, sir. But for Miss Crabtree – well, I'm getting on and I don't mind speaking of it now. I got into trouble, sir, when I was a girl, and Miss Crabtree stood by me – took me back into her service, she did, when it was all over. I'd have died for her – I would indeed.'

Sir Edward knew sincerity when he heard it. Martha was sincere.

'As far as you know, no one came to the door – ?'

'No one could have come.'

'I said as far as you know. But if Miss Crabtree had been expecting some one – if she opened the door to that some one herself . . .'

'Oh!' Martha seemed taken aback.

'That's possible, I suppose?' Sir Edward urged.

'It's possible – yes – but it isn't very likely. I mean . . .'

She was clearly taken aback. She couldn't deny and yet she wanted to do so. Why? Because she knew that the truth lay elsewhere. Was that it? The four people in the house – one of them guilty? Did Martha want to shield that guilty party? *Had* the stairs creaked? Had someone come stealthily down and did Martha know who that someone was?

She herself was honest – Sir Edward was convinced of that. He pressed his point, watching her.

'Miss Crabtree might have done that, I suppose? The window of that room faces the street. She might have seen whoever it was she was waiting for from the window and gone out into the hall and let him – or her – in. She might even have wished that no one should see the person.'

Martha looked troubled. She said at last reluctantly:

'Yes, you may be right, sir. I never thought of that. That she was expecting a gentleman – yes, it well might be.'

It was as though she began to perceive advantages in the idea.

'You were the last person to see her, were you not?'

'Yes, sir. After I'd cleared away the tea. I took the receipted books to her and the change from the money she'd given me.'

'Had she given the money to you in five-pound notes?'

'A five-pound note, sir,' said Martha in a shocked voice. 'The books never came up as high as five pounds. I'm very careful.'

'Where did she keep her money?'

'I don't rightly know, sir. I should say that she carried it about with her – in her black velvet bag. But of course she may have kept it in one of the drawers in her bedroom that were locked. She was very fond of locking up things, though prone to lose her keys.'

Sir Edward nodded.

'You don't know how much money she had – in five-pound notes, I mean?'

'No, sir, I couldn't say what the exact amount was.'

'And she said nothing to you that could lead you to believe that she was expecting anybody?'

'No, sir.'

'You're quite sure? What exactly did she say?'

'Well,' Martha considered, 'She said the butcher was nothing more than a rogue and a cheat, and she said I'd had in a quarter of a pound of tea more than I ought, and she said Mrs Crabtree was full of nonsense for not liking to eat margarine, and she didn't like one of the sixpences I'd brought her back – one of the new ones with oak leaves on it – she said it was bad, and I had a lot of trouble to convince her. And she said – oh, that the fishmonger had sent haddocks instead of whitings, and had I told him about it, and I said I had – and, really, I think that's all, sir.'

Martha's speech had made the deceased lady loom clear to Sir Edward as a detailed description would never have done. He said casually:

'Rather a difficult mistress to please, eh?'

'A bit fussy, but there, poor dear, she didn't often get out, and staying cooped up she had to have something to amuse herself like. She was pernicketty but kind-hearted – never a beggar sent away from the door without something. Fussy she may have been, but a real charitable lady.'

'I am glad, Martha, that she leaves one person to regret her.'

The old servant caught her breath.

'You mean – oh, but they were all fond of her – really – underneath. They all had words with her now and again, but it didn't mean anything.'

Sir Edward lifted his head. There was a creak above.

'That's Miss Magdalen coming down.'

'How do you know?' he shot at her.

The old woman flushed. 'I know her step,' she muttered.

Sir Edward left the kitchen rapidly. Martha had been right. Magdalen had just reached the bottom stair. She looked at him hopefully.

'Not very far on as yet,' said Sir Edward, answering her look, and added, 'You don't happen to know what letters your aunt received on the day of her death?'

'They are all together. The police have been through them, of course.'

She led the way to the big double drawing-room, and unlocking a drawer took out a large black velvet bag with an old-fashioned silver clasp.

'This is aunt's bag. Everything is in here just as it was on the day of her death. I've kept it like that.'

Sir Edward thanked her and proceeded to turn out the contents of the bag on the table. It was, he fancied, a fair specimen of an eccentric elderly lady's hand-bag.

There was some odd silver change, two ginger nuts, three newspaper cuttings about Joanna Southcott's box, a trashy printed poem about the unemployed, an *Old Moore's Almanack,* a large piece of camphor, some spectacles and three letters. A spidery one from someone called 'Cousin Lucy,' a bill for mending a watch, and an appeal from a charitable institution.

Sir Edward went through everything very carefully, then repacked the bag and handed it to Magdalen with a sigh.

'Thank you, Miss Magdalen. I'm afraid there isn't much there.'

He rose, observed that from the window you commanded a good view of the front door steps, then took Magdalen's hand in his.

'You are going?'

'Yes.'

'But it's – it's going to be all right?'

'Nobody connected with the law ever commits himself to a rash statement like that,' said Sir Edward solemnly, and made his escape.

He walked along the street lost in thought. The puzzle was there under his hand – and he had not solved it. It needed something – some little thing. Just to point the way.

A hand fell on his shoulder and he started. It was Matthew Vaughan, somewhat out of breath.

'I've been chasing you, Sir Edward. I want to apologise. For my rotten manners half an hour ago, But I've not got the best temper in the world, I'm afraid. It's awfully good of you to bother about this business. Please ask me whatever you like. If there's anything I can do to help –'

Suddenly Sir Edward stiffened. His glance was fixed – not on

Matthew – but across the street. Somewhat bewildered, Matthew repeated:

'If there's anything I can do to help –'

'You have already done it, my dear young man,' said Sir Edward. 'By stopping me at this particular spot and so fixing my attention on something I might otherwise have missed.'

He pointed across the street to a small restaurant opposite.

'*The Four and Twenty Blackbirds?*' asked Matthew in a puzzled voice.

'Exactly.'

'It's an odd name – but you get quite decent food there, I believe.'

'I shall not take the risk of experimenting,' said Sir Edward. 'Being further from my nursery days than you are, my young friend, I probably remember my nursery rhymes better. There is a classic that runs thus, if I remember rightly: *Sing a song of sixpence, a pocket full of rye, Four and twenty blackbirds, baked in a pie* – and so on. The rest of it does not concern us.'

He wheeled round sharply.

'Where are you going?' asked Matthew Vaughan.

'Back to your house, my friend.'

They walked there in silence, Matthew Vaughan shooting puzzled glances at his companion. Sir Edward entered, strode to a drawer, lifted out a velvet bag and opened it. He looked at Matthew and the young man reluctantly left the room.

Sir Edward tumbled out the silver change on the table. Then he nodded. His memory had not been at fault.

He got up and rang the bell, slipping something into the palm of his hand as he did so.

Martha answered the bell.

'You told me, Martha, if I remember rightly, that you had a slight altercation with your late mistress over one of the new sixpences.'

'Yes, sir.'

'Ah! but the curious thing is, Martha, that among this loose change, *there is no new sixpence*. There are two sixpences, but they are both old ones.'

She stared at him in a puzzled fashion.

'You see what that means? *Some one did come to the house that evening – some one to whom your mistress gave sixpence.* . . . I think she gave it him in exchange for this . . .'

With a swift movement, he shot his hand forward, holding out the doggerel verse about unemployment.

One glance at her face was enough.

'The game is up, Martha – you see, I know. You may as well tell me everything.'

She sank down on a chair – the tears raced down her face.

'It's true – it's true – the bell didn't ring properly – I wasn't sure, and then I thought I'd better go and see. I got to the door just as he struck her down. The roll of five-pound notes was on the table in front of her – it was the sight of them as made him do it – that and thinking she was alone in the house as she'd let him in. I couldn't scream. I was too paralysed and then he turned – and I saw it was my boy. . . .

'Oh, he's been a bad one always. I gave him all the money I could. He's been in gaol twice. He must have come around to see me, and then Miss Crabtree, seeing as I didn't answer the door, went to answer it herself, and he was taken aback and pulled out one of those unemployment leaflets, and the mistress being kind of charitable, told him to come in and got out a sixpence. And all the time that roll of notes was lying on the table where it had been when I was giving her the change. And the devil got into my Ben and he got behind her and struck her down.'

'And then?' asked Sir Edward.

'Oh, sir, what could I do? My own flesh and blood. His father was a bad one, and Ben takes after him – but he was my own son. I hustled him out, and I went back to the kitchen and I went to lay for supper at the usual time. Do you think it was very wicked of me, sir? I tried to tell you no lies when you was asking me questions.'

Sir Edward rose.

'My poor woman,' he said with feeling in his voice. 'I am very sorry for you. All the same, the law will have to take its course, you know.'

'He's fled the country, sir. I don't know where he is.'

'There's a chance, then, that he may escape the gallows, but don't build upon it. Will you send Miss Magdalen to me.'

'Oh, Sir Edward. How wonderful of you – how wonderful you are,' said Magdalen when he had finished his brief recital. 'You've saved us all. How can I ever thank you?'

Sir Edward smiled down at her and patted her hand gently. He was very much the great man. Little Magdalen had been very charming on the *Siluric*. That bloom of seventeen – wonderful! She had completely lost it now, of course.

'Next time you need a friend –' he said.

'I'll come straight to you.'

'No, no,' cried Sir Edward in alarm. 'That's just what I don't want you to do. Go to a younger man.'

He extricated himself with dexterity from the grateful household and hailing a taxi sank into it with a sigh of relief.

Even the charm of a dewy seventeen seemed doubtful.

It could not really compare with a really well-stocked library on criminology.

The taxi turned into Queen Anne's Close.

His *cul-de-sac*.

H. R. F. Keating

INSPECTOR GHOTE AND THE MIRACLE BABY

WHAT HAS SANTA Claus got in store for me, Inspector Ghote said to himself, bleakly echoing the current cheerful Bombay newspaper advertisements, as he waited to enter the office of Deputy Superintendent Naik that morning of December 25th.

Whatever the DSP had lined up for him, Ghote knew it was going to be nasty. Ever since he had recently declined to turn up for 'voluntary' hockey, DSP Naik had viewed him with sad-eyed disapproval. But what exact form would his displeasure take?

Almost certainly it would have something to do with the big Navy Week parade that afternoon, the chief preoccupation at the moment of most of the ever-excitable and drama-loving Bombay-ites. Probably he would be ordered out into the crowds watching the Fire Power demonstration in the bay, ordered to come back with a beltful of pickpocketing arrests.

'Come,' the DSP's voice barked out.

Ghote went in and stood squaring his bony shoulders in front of the papers-strewn desk.

'Ah, Ghote, yes. Tulsi Pipe Road for you. Up at the north end. Going to be big trouble there. Rioting. Intercommunity outrages even.'

Ghote's heart sank even deeper than he had expected. Tulsi Pipe Road was a two-kilometres-long thoroughfare that shot straight up from the racecourse into the heart of a densely crowded mill district where badly paid Hindus, Muslims in hundreds and Goans by the thousand, all lived in prickling closeness, either in great areas of tumbledown hutments or in high tottering chawls, floor upon floor of massed humanity. Trouble between the religious communities there meant hell, no less.

'Yes, DSP?' he said, striving not to sound appalled.

'We are having a virgin birth business, Inspector.'

'Virgin birth, DSP sahib?'

'Come, man, you must have come across such cases.'

'I am sorry, DSP' Ghote said, feeling obliged to be true to hard-won scientific principles. 'I am unable to believe in virgin birth.'

The DSP's round face suffused with instant wrath.

'Of course I am not asking you to believe in virgin birth, man! It is not you who are to believe: it is all those Christians in the Goan community who are believing it about a baby born two days ago. It is the time of year, of course. These affairs are always coming at Christmas. I have dealt with half a dozen in my day.'

'Yes, DSP,' Ghote said, contriving to hit on the right note of awe.

'Yes. And there is only one way to deal with it. Get hold of the girl and find out the name of the man. Do that pretty damn quick and the whole affair drops away to nothing, like monsoon water down a drain.'

'Yes, DSP.'

'Well, what are you waiting for man? Hop it!'

'Name and address of the girl in question, DSP sahib.'

The DSP's face darkened once more. He padded furiously over the jumble of papers on his desk top. And at last he found the chit he wanted.

'There you are, man. And also you will find there the name of the Head Constable who first reported the matter. See him straightaway. You have got a good man there, active, quick on his feet, sharp. If he could not make that girl talk, you will be having a first-class damn job, Inspector.'

Ghote located Head Constable Mudholkar one hour later at the local chowkey where he was stationed. The Head Constable confirmed at once the blossoming dislike for a sharp bully that Ghote had been harbouring ever since DSP Naik had praised the fellow. And, what was worse, the chap turned out to be very like the DSP in looks as well. He had the same round type of face, the same puffy-looking lips, even a similar soft blur of moustache. But the

Head Constable's appearance was nevertheless a travesty of the DSP's. His face was, simply, slewed.

To Ghote's prejudiced eyes, at the first moment of their encounter, the man's features seemed grotesquely distorted, as if in some distant time some god had taken one of the Head Constable's ancestors and had wrenched his whole head sideways between two omnipotent god-hands.

But, as the fellow supplied him with the details of the affair, Ghote forced himself to regard him with an open mind, and he then had to admit that the facial twist which had seemed so pronounced was in fact no more than a drooping corner of the mouth and of one ear being oddly longer than the other.

Ghote had to admit, too, that the chap was efficient. He had all the circumstances of the affair at his fingertips. The girl, named D'Mello, now in a hospital for her own safety, had been rigorously questioned both before and after the birth, but she had steadfastly denied that she had ever been with any man. She was indeed not the sort, the sole daughter of a Goan railway waiter on the Madras Express, a quiet girl, well brought up though her parents were poor enough; she attended Mass regularly with her mother, and the whole family kept themselves to themselves.

'But with those Christians you can never tell,' Head Constable Mudholkar concluded.

Ghote felt inwardly inclined to agree. Fervid religion had always made him shrink inwardly, whether it was a Hindu holy man spending twenty years silent and standing upright or whether it was the Catholics, always caressing lifeless statues in their churches till glass protection had to be installed, and even then they still stroked the thick panes. Either manifestation rendered him uneasy.

That was the real reason, he now acknowledged to himself, why he did not want to go and see Miss D'Mello in the hospital where she would be surrounded by nuns amid all the trappings of an alien religion, surrounded with all the panoply of a newly found goddess.

Yet go and see the girl he must.

But first he permitted himself to do every other thing that

might possibly be necessary to the case. He visited Mrs D'Mello,
and by dint of patient wheedling, and a little forced toughness,
confirmed from her the names of the only two men that Head
Constable Mudholkar – who certainly proved to know inside-out
the particular chawl where the D'Mellos lived – had suggested as
possible fathers. They were both young men – a Goan, Charlie
Lobo, and a Sikh, Kuldip Singh.

The Lobo family lived one floor below the D'Mellos. But that
one flight of dirt-spattered stairs, bringing them just that much
nearer the courtyard tap that served the whole crazily leaning
chawl, represented a whole layer higher in social status. And Mrs
Lobo, a huge, tightly fat woman in a brightly flowered western-
style dress, had decided views about the unexpected fame that had
come to the people upstairs.

'Has my Charlie been going with that girl?' she repeated after
Ghote had managed to put the question, suitably wrapped up, to
the boy. 'No, he has not. Charlie, tell the man you hate and
despise trash like that.'

'Oh, Mum,' said Charlie, a teenage wisp of a figure suffocating
in a necktie beside his balloon-hard mother.

'Tell the man, Charlie.'

And obediently Charlie muttered something that satisfied his
passion-filled parent. Ghote put a few more questions for form's
sake, but he realized that only by getting hold of the boy on his
own was he going to get any worthwhile answers. Yet it turned
out that he did not have to employ any cunning. Charlie proved
to have a strain of sharp slyness of his own, and hardly had Ghote
climbed the stairs to the floor above the D'Mellos where Kuldip
Singh lived when he heard a whispered call from the shadow-
filled darkness below.

'Mum's got her head over the stove,' Charlie said. 'She don't
know I slipped out.'

'There is something you have to tell me?' Ghote said, acting
the indulgent uncle. 'You are in trouble – that's it, isn't it?'

'My only trouble is Mum,' the boy replied. 'Listen, mister,
I had to tell you. I love Miss D'Mello – yes, I love her. She's
the most wonderful girl ever was.'

'And you want to marry her, and because you went too far before –'

'No, no, no. She's far and away too good for me. Mister, I've never even said "Good morning" to her in the two years we've lived here. But I love her, mister, and I'm not going to have Mum make me say different.'

Watching him slip cunningly back home, Ghote made his mental notes and then turned to tackle Kuldip Singh, his last comparatively easy task before the looming interview at the nun-ridden hospital he knew he must have.

Kuldip Singh, as Ghote had heard from Head Constable Mudholkar, was different from his neighbours. He lived in this teeming area from choice not necessity. Officialy a student, he spent all his time in a series of antisocial activities – protesting, writing manifestoes, drinking. He seemed an ideal candidate for the unknown and elusive father.

Ghote's suspicions were at once heightened when the young Sikh opened his door. The boy, though old enough to have a beard, lacked this status symbol. Equally he had discarded the obligatory turban of his religion. But all the Sikh bounce was there, as Ghote discovered when he identified himself.

'Policewallah, is it? Then I want nothing at all to do with you. Me and the police are enemies, bhai. Natural enemies.'

'Irrespective of such considerations,' Ghote said stiffly, 'it is my duty to put to you certain questions concerning one Miss D'Mello.'

The young Sikh burst into a roar of laughter.

'The miracle girl, is it?' he said. 'Plenty of trouble for policemen there, I promise you. Top-level rioting coming from that business. The fellow who fathered that baby did us a lot of good.'

Ghote plugged away a good while longer – the hospital nuns awaited – but for all his efforts he learned no more than he had in that first brief exchange. And in the end he still had to go and meet his doom.

Just what he had expected at the hospital he never quite formulated to himself. What he did find was certainly almost the exact opposite of his fears. A calm reigned. White-habited nuns, mostly Indian but with a few Europeans, flitted silently to and fro or talked quietly to the patients whom Ghote glimpsed lying on beds in long wards. Above them swung frail but bright paper chains in honour of the feast day, and these were all the excitement there was.

The small separate ward in which Miss D'Mello lay in a broad bed all alone was no different. Except that the girl was isolated, she seemed to be treated in just the same way as the other new mothers in the big maternity ward that Ghote had been led through on his way in. In the face of such matter-of-factness he felt hollowly cheated.

Suddenly, too, to his own utter surprise he found, looking down at the big calm-after-storm eyes of the Goan girl, that he wanted the story she was about to tell him to be true. Part of him knew that, if it were so, or if it was widely believed to be so, appalling disorders could result from the feverish religious excitement that was bound to mount day by day. But another part of him now simply wanted a miracle to have happened.

He began, quietly and almost diffidently, to put his questions. Miss D'Mello would hardly answer at all, but such syllables as she did whisper were of blank inability to name anyone as the father of her child. After a while Ghote brought himself, with a distinct effort of will, to change his tactics. He banged out the hard line. Miss D'Mello went quietly and totally mute.

Then Ghote slipped in, with adroit suddenness, the name of Charlie Lobo. He got only a small puzzled frown.

Then, in an effort to make sure that her silence was not a silence of fear, he presented, with equal suddenness, the name of Kuldip Singh. If the care-for-nothing young Sikh had forced this timid creature, this might be the way to get an admission. But instead there came something approaching a laugh.

'That Kuldip is a funny fellow,' the girl said, with an out-of-place and unexpected offhandedness.

Ghote almost gave up. But at that moment a nun nurse appeared carrying in her arms a small, long, white-wrapped, minutely crying bundle – the baby.

While she handed the hungry scrap to its mother Ghote stood and watched. Perhaps holding the child she would –?

He looked down at the scene on the broad bed, awaiting his moment again. The girl fiercely held the tiny agitated thing to her breast and in a moment or two quiet came, the tiny head applied to the life-giving nipple. How human the child looked already, Ghote thought. How much a man at two days old. The round skull, almost bald, as it might become again toward the end of its span. The frown on the forehead that would last a lifetime, the tiny, perfectly formed, plainly asymmetrical ears –

And then Ghote knew that there had not been any miracle. It was as he had surmised, but with different circumstances. Miss D'Mello was indeed too frightened to talk. No wonder, when the local bully, Head Constable Mudholkar with his slewed head and its one ear so characteristically longer than the other, was the man who had forced himself on her.

A deep smothering of disappointment floated down on Ghote. So it had been nothing miraculous after all. Just a sad case, to be cleared up painfully. He stared down at the bed.

The tiny boy suckled energetically. And with a topsy-turvy welling up of rose-pink pleasure, Ghote saw that there had after all been a miracle. The daily, hourly, every-minute miracle of a new life, of a new flicker of hope in the tired world.

William Wilkie Collins

THE BITER BIT

[*Extracted from the Correspondence of the London Police*]
FROM CHIEF INSPECTOR THEAKSTONE, OF THE
DETECTIVE POLICE, TO SERGEANT BULMER OF THE
SAME FORCE

LONDON, *4 July, 18—*.

SERGEANT BULMER, – This is to inform you that you are
wanted to assist in looking up a case of importance, which will
require all the attention of an experienced member of the force.
The matter of the robbery on which you are now engaged, you
will please to shift over to the young man who brings you this
letter. You will tell him all the circumstances of the case, just as
they stand; you will put him up to the progress you have made (if
any) towards detecting the person or persons by whom the money
has been stolen; and you will leave him to make the best he can
of the matter now in your hands. He is to have the whole responsibility of the case, and the whole credit of his success, if he brings
it to a proper issue.

So much for the orders that I am desired to communicate to
you.

A word in your ear, next, about this new man who is to take
your place. His name is Matthew Sharpin; and he is to have the
chance given him of dashing into our office at a jump – supposing
he turns out strong enough to take it. You will naturally ask me
how he comes by this privilege. I can only tell you that he has
some uncommonly strong interest to back him in certain high
quarters which you and I had better not mention except under
our breaths. He has been a lawyer's clerk; and he is wonderfully

conceited in his opinion of himself, as well as mean and under-
hand to look at. According to his own account, he leaves his old
trade, and joins ours, of his own free will and preference. You will
no more believe that than I do. My notion is, that he has managed
to ferret out some private information in connection with the
affairs of one of his master's clients, which makes him rather an
awkward customer to keep in the office for the future, and which,
at the same time, gives him hold enough over his employer to
make it dangerous to drive him into a corner by turning him
away. I think the giving him this unheard-of chance among us, is,
in plain words, pretty much like giving him hush-money to keep
him quiet. However that may be, Mr Matthew Sharpin is to have
the case now in your hands; and if he succeeds with it, he pokes
his ugly nose into our office, as sure as fate. I put you up to this,
Sergeant, so that you may not stand in your own light by giving
the new man any cause to complain of you at headquarters, and
remain yours,

Francis Theakstone

FROM MR MATTHEW SHARPIN TO CHIEF INSPECTOR
THEAKSTONE

LONDON, 5 July, 18—.

DEAR SIR,—Having now been favoured with the necessary instructions from Sergeant Bulmer, I beg to remind you of certain
directions which I have received, relating to the report of my
future proceedings which I am to prepare for examination at
headquarters.

The object of my writing, and of your examining what I have
written, before you send it in to the higher authorities, is, I am
informed, to give me, as an untried hand, the benefit of your
advice, in case I want it (which I venture to think I shall not) at
any stage of my proceedings. As the extraordinary circumstances
of the case on which I am now engaged, make it impossible for
me to absent myself from the place where the robbery was committed, until I have made some progress towards discovering the
thief, I am necessarily precluded from consulting you personally.
Hence the necessity of my writing down the various details, which

might, perhaps, be better communicated by word of mouth. This, if I am not mistaken, is the position in which we are now placed. I state my own impressions on the subject, in writing, in order that we may clearly understand each other at the outset; and have the honour to remain, your obedient servant,

Matthew Sharpin

FROM CHIEF INSPECTOR THEAKSTONE TO MR MATTHEW SHARPIN

LONDON, 5 *July*, 18—.

SIR,—You have begun by wasting time, ink, and paper. We both of us perfectly well knew the position we stood in towards each other, when I sent you with my letter to Sergeant Bulmer. There was not the least need to repeat it in writing. Be so good as to employ your pen, in future, on the business actually in hand.

You have now three separate matters on which to write to me. First, you have to draw up a statement of your instructions received from Sergeant Bulmer, in order to show us that nothing has escaped your memory, and that you are thoroughly acquainted with all the circumstances of the case which has been entrusted to you. Secondly, you are to inform me what it is you propose to do. Thirdly, you are to report every inch of your progress (if you make any) from day to day, and, if need be, from hour to hour as well. This is *your* duty. As to what *my* duty may be, when I want you to remind me of it, I will write and tell you so. In the meantime, I remain, yours,

Francis Theakstone

FROM MR MATTHEW SHARPIN TO CHIEF INSPECTOR THEAKSTONE

LONDON, 6 *July*, 18—.

SIR, – You are rather an elderly person, and, as such, naturally inclined to be a little jealous of men like me, who are in the prime of their lives and their faculties. Under these circumstances, it is my duty to be considerate towards you, and not to bear too hardly on your small failings. I decline, therefore, altogether, to take offence at the tone of your letter; I give you the full benefit of the natural generosity of my nature; I sponge the very existence of your surly communication out of my memory – in short, Chief Inspector Theakstone, I forgive you, and proceed to business.

My first duty is to draw up a full statement of the instructions I have received from Sergeant Bulmer. Here they are at your service, according to my version of them.

At number 13 Rutherford Street, Soho, there is a stationer's shop. It is kept by one Mr Yatman. He is a married man, but has no family. Besides Mr and Mrs Yatman, the other inmates in the house are a young single man named Jay, who lodges in the front room on the second floor – a shopman, who sleeps in one of the attics, – and a servant-of-all-work, whose bed is in the back-kitchen. Once a week a charwoman comes for a few hours in the morning only, to help this servant. These are all the persons who, on ordinary occasions, have means of access to the interior of the house, placed, as a matter of course, at their disposal.

Mr Yatman has been in business for many years, carrying on his affairs prosperously enough to realize a handsome independence for a person in his position. Unfortunately for himself, he endeavoured to increase the amount of his property by speculating. He ventured boldly in his investments, luck went against him, and rather less than two years ago he found himself a poor man again. All that was saved out of the wreck of his property was the sum of two hundred pounds.

Although Mr Yatman did his best to meet his altered circumstances, by giving up many of the luxuries and comforts to which he and his wife had been accustomed, he found it impossible to retrench so far as to allow of putting by any money from the income produced by his shop. The business has been declining of late years – the cheap advertising stationers having done it injury with the public. Consequently, up to the last week the only surplus property possessed by Mr Yatman consisted of the two hundred pounds which had been recovered from the wreck of his fortune. This sum was placed as a deposit in a joint-stock bank of the highest possible character.

Eight days ago, Mr Yatman and his lodger, Mr Jay, held a

conversation on the subject of the commercial difficulties which are hampering trade in all directions at the present time. Mr Jay (who lives by supplying the newspapers with short paragraphs relating to accidents, offences, and brief records of remarkable occurrences in general – who is, in short, what they call a penny-a-liner) told his landlord that he had been in the city that day, and had heard unfavourable rumours on the subject of the joint-stock banks. The rumours to which he alluded had already reached the ears of Mr Yatman from other quarters; and the confirmation of them by his lodger had such an effect on his mind – predisposed as it was to alarm by the experience of his former losses – that he resolved to go at once to the bank and withdraw his deposit.

It was then getting on towards the end of the afternoon; and he arrived just in time to receive his money before the bank closed.

He received the deposit in bank-notes of the following amounts; – one fifty-pound note, three twenty-pound notes, six ten-pound notes, and six-five pound notes. His object in drawing the money in this form was to have it ready to lay out immediately in trifling loans, on good security, among the small tradespeople of his district, some of whom are sorely pressed for the very means of existence at the present time. Investments of this kind seemed to Mr Yatman to be the most safe and the most profitable on which he could now venture.

He brought the money back in an envelope placed in his breast-pocket; and asked his shopman, on getting home, to look for a small flat tin cash-box, which had not been used for years, and which, as Mr Yatman remembered it, was exactly of the right size to hold the bank-notes. For some time the cash-box was searched for in vain. Mr Yatman called to his wife to know if she had any idea where it was. The question was overheard by the servant-of-all-work, who was taking up the tea-tray at the time, and by Mr Jay, who was coming downstairs on his way out to the theatre. Ultimately the cash-box was found by the shopman. Mr Yatman placed the bank-notes in it, secured them by a padlock, and put the box in his coat-pocket. It stuck out of the coat pocket a very little, but enough to be seen. Mr Yatman remained at home, upstairs, all the evening. No visitors called. At eleven o'clock he went to bed, and put the cash-box along with his clothes, on a chair by the bedside.

When he and his wife woke the next morning, the box was gone. Payment of the notes was immediately stopped at the Bank of England; but no news of the money has been heard of since that time.

So far, the circumstances of the case are perfectly clear. They point unmistakably to the conclusion that the robbery must have been committed by some person living in the house. Suspicion falls, therefore, upon the servant-of-all-work, upon the shopman, and upon Mr Jay. The two first knew that the cash-box was being inquired for by their master, but did not know what it was he wanted to put into it. They would assume, of course that it was money. They both had opportunities (the servant, when she took away the tea – and the shopman, when he came, after shutting up, to give the keys of the till to his master) of seeing the cash-box in Mr Yatman's pocket, and of inferring naturally, from its position there, that he intended to take it into his bedroom with him at night.

Mr Jay, on the other hand, had been told, during the afternoon's conversation on the subject of joint-stock banks, that his landlord had a deposit of two hundred pounds in one of them. He also knew that Mr Yatman left him with the intention of drawing that money out; and he heard the inquiry for the cash-box, afterwards, when he was coming downstairs. He must, therefore, have inferred that the money was in the house, and that the cash-box was the receptacle intended to contain it. That he could have had any idea, however, of the place in which Mr Yatman intended to keep it for the night, is impossible, seeing that he went out before the box was found, and did not return till his landlord was in bed. Consequently, if he committed the robbery, he must have gone into the bedroom purely on speculation.

Speaking of the bedroom reminds me of the necessity of noticing the situation of it in the house, and the means that exist of gaining easy access to it any hour of the night.

The room in question is the back-room on the first-floor. In consequence of Mrs Yatman's constitutional nervousness on the subject of fire (which makes her apprehend being burnt alive in her room, in case of accident, by the hampering of the lock if the key is turned in it) her husband has never been accustomed to lock the bedroom door. Both he and his wife are, by their own admission, heavy sleepers. Consequently the risk to be run by any evil-disposed persons wishing to plunder the bedroom, was of the most trifling kind. They could enter the room by merely turning the handle of the door; and if they moved with ordinary caution, there was no fear of their waking the sleepers inside. This fact is of importance. It strengthens our conviction that the money must have been taken by one of the inmates of the house, because it tends to show that the robbery, in this case, might have been committed by persons not possessed of the superior vigilance and cunning of the experienced thief.

Such are the circumstances, as they were related to Sergeant Bulmer, when he was first called in to discover the guilty parties, and, if possible, to recover the lost bank-notes. The strictest inquiry which he could institute, failed of producing the smallest fragment of evidence against any of the persons on whom suspicion naturally fell. Their language and behaviour, on being informed of the robbery, was perfectly consistent with the language and behaviour of innocent people. Sergeant Bulmer felt from the first that this was a case for private inquiry and secret observation. He began by recommending Mr and Mrs Yatman to affect a feeling of perfect confidence in the innocence of the persons living under their roof; and he then opened the campaign by employing himself in following the goings and comings, and in discovering the friends, the habits, and the secrets of the maid-of-all-work.

Three days and nights of exertion on his own part, and on that of others who were competent to assist his investigations, were enough to satisfy him that there was no sound cause for suspicion against the girl.

He next practised the same precaution in relation to the shopman. There was more difficulty and uncertainty in privately clearing up this person's character without his knowledge, but the obstacles were at last smoothed away with tolerable success; and though there is not the same amount of certainty, in this case, which there was in that of the girl, there is still fair reason for supposing that the shopman has had nothing to do with the robbery of the cash-box.

As a necessary consequence of these proceedings, the range of suspicion now becomes limited to the lodger, Mr Jay.

When I presented your letter of introduction to Sergeant Bulmer, he had already made some inquiries on the subject of this young man. The result, so far, has not been at all favourable. Mr Jay's habits are irregular; he frequents public houses, and seems to be familiarly acquainted with a great many dissolute characters; he is in debt to most of the tradespeople whom he employs; he has not paid his rent to Mr Yatman for the last month; yesterday evening he came home excited by liquor, and last week he was seen talking to a prize-fighter. In short, though Mr Jay does call himself a journalist, in virtue of his penny-a-line contributions to the newspapers, he is a young man of low tastes, vulgar manners, and bad habits. Nothing has yet been discovered in relation to him, which resounds to his credit in the smallest degree.

I have now reported, down to the very last details, all the particulars communicated to me by Sergeant Bulmer. I believe you will not find an omission anywhere; and I think you will admit, though you are prejudiced against me, that a clearer statement of facts was never laid before you than the statement I have now made. My next duty is to tell you what I propose to do, now that the case is confided to my hands.

In the first place, it is clearly my business to take up the case at the point where Sergeant Bulmer has left it. On his authority, I am justified in assuming that I have no need to trouble myself about the maid-of-all-work and the shopman. Their characters are now to be considered as cleared up. What remains to be privately investigated is the question of the guilt or innocence of Mr Jay. Before we give up the notes for lost, we must make sure, if we can, that he knows nothing about them.

This is the plan that I have adopted, with the full approval of Mr and Mrs Yatman, for discovering whether Mr Jay is or is not the person who has stolen the cash-box:

I propose, today, to present myself at the house in the character of a young man who is looking for lodgings. The back room on the second-floor will be shown to me as the room to let; and I shall establish myself there tonight, as a person from the country who has come to London to look for a situation in a respectable shop or office.

By this means I shall be living next to the room occupied by Mr Jay. The partition between us is mere lath and plaster. I shall make a small hole in it, near the cornice, through which I can see what Mr Jay does in his room, and hear every word that is said when any friend happens to call on him. Whenever he is at home, I shall be at my post of observation. Whenever he goes out, I shall be after him. By employing these means of watching him, I believe I may look forward to the discovery of his secret – if he knows anything about the lost bank-notes – as to a dead certainty.

What you may think of my plan of observation I cannot undertake to say. It appears to me to unite the invaluable merits of boldness and simplicity. Fortified by this conviction, I close the present communication with feelings of the most sanguine description in regard to the future, and remain your obedient servant,

Matthew Sharpin.

FROM THE SAME TO THE SAME

7 July.

SIR, – As you have not honoured me with any answer to my last communication, I assume that, in spite of your prejudices against me, it has produced the favourable impression on your mind which I ventured to anticipate. Gratified beyond measure by the token of approval which your eloquent silence conveys to me, I proceed to report the progress that has been made in the course of the last twenty-four hours.

I am now comfortably established next door to Mr Jay; and I am delighted to say that I have two holes in the partition, instead of one. My natural sense of humour has led me into the pardonable extravagance of giving them appropriate names. One I call my peep-hole, and the other my pipe-hole. The name of the first explains itself, the name of the second refers to a small tin pipe, or tube, inserted in the hole, and twisted so that the mouth of it comes close to my ear, while I am standing at my post of observation. Thus, while I am looking at Mr Jay through my peep-hole, I can hear every word that may be spoken in his room through my pipe-hole.

Perfect candour – a virtue which I have possessed from my childhood – compels me to acknowledge, before I go any further, that the ingenious notion of adding a pipe-hole to my proposed peep-hole originated with Mrs Yatman. This lady – a most intelligent and accomplished person, simple, and yet distinguished, in her manners – has entered into all my little plans with an enthusiasm and intelligence which I cannot too highly praise. Mr Yatman is so cast down by his loss, that he is quite incapable of affording me any assistance. Mrs Yatman, who is evidently most tenderly attached to him, feels her husband's sad condition of mind even more acutely than she feels the loss of the money; and is mainly stimulated to exertion by her desire to assist in raising him from the miserable state of prostration into which he has now fallen.

'The money, Mr Sharpin,' she said to me yesterday evening, with tears in her eyes, 'the money may be regained by rigid economy and strict attention to business. It is my husband's wretched state of mind that makes me so anxious for the discovery of the thief. I may be wrong, but I felt hopeful of success as soon as you entered the house; and I believe, if the wretch who has robbed us is to be found, you are the man to discover him. I accepted this gratifying compliment in the spirit in which it was offered – firmly believing that I shall be found, sooner or later, to have thoroughly deserved it.

Let me now return to business; that is to say, to my peep-hole and my pipe-hole.

I have enjoyed some hours of calm observation of Mr Jay. Though rarely at home, as I understand from Mrs Yatman, on ordinary occasions, he has been indoors the whole of this day. That is suspicious, to begin with. I have to report, further that he rose at a late hour this morning (always a bad sign in a young man), and that he lost a great deal of time, after he was up, in yawning and complaining to himself of headache. Like other debauched characters, he ate little or nothing for breakfast. His next proceeding was to smoke a pipe – a dirty clay pipe, which a gentleman would have been ashamed to put between his lips. When he had done smoking, he took out pen, ink, and paper, and sat down to write with a groan – whether of remorse for having taken the bank-notes, or of disgust at the task before him, I am unable to say. After writing a few lines (too far away from my peep-hole to give me a chance of reading over his shoulder), he leaned back in his chair, and amused himself by humming the tunes of certain popular songs. Whether these do, or do not, represent secret signals by which he communicates with his accomplices remains to be seen. After he had amused himself for some time by humming, he got up and began to walk about the room, occasionally stopping to add a sentence to the paper on his desk. Before long, he went to a locked cupboard and opened it. I strained my eyes eagerly, in expectation of making a discovery. I saw him take something carefully out of the cupboard – he turned round – and it was only a pint bottle of brandy! Having drunk some of the liquor, this extremely indolent reprobate lay down on his bed again, and in five minutes was fast asleep.

After hearing him snoring for at least two hours, I was recalled to my peep-hole by a knock at his door. He jumped up and opened it with suspicious activity.

A very small boy, with a very dirty face, walked in, said, 'Please, sir, they're waiting for you,' sat down on a chair, with his legs a long way from the ground, and instantly fell asleep! Mr Jay swore an oath, tied a wet towel round his head, and going back to his paper, began to cover it with writing as fast as his fingers could move the pen. Occasionally getting up to dip the towel in water and tie it on again, he continued at this employment for nearly three hours; then folded up the leaves of writing, woke the boy, and gave them to him, with this remarkable expression: 'Now then, young sleepy-head, quick – march! If you see the governor, tell him to have the money ready when I call for it.' The boy grinned, and disappeared. I was sorely tempted to

follow 'sleepy-head,' but, on reflection, considered it safest still
to keep my eye on the proceedings of Mr Jay.

In half an hour's time, he put on his hat and walked out. Of
course, I put on my hat and walked out also. As I went down
stairs, I passed Mrs Yatman going up. The lady has been kind
enough to undertake, by previous arrangement between us, to
search Mr Jay's room, while he is out of the way, and while I am
necessarily engaged in the pleasing duty of following him where-
ever he goes. On the occasion to which I now refer, he walked
straight to the nearest tavern, and ordered a couple of mutton
chops for his dinner. I placed myself in the next box to him, and
ordered a couple of mutton chops for my dinner. Before I had
been in the room a minute, a young man of highly suspicious
manners and appearance, sitting at a table opposite, took his glass
of porter in his hand and joined Mr Jay. I pretended to be reading
the newspaper, and listened, as in duty bound, with all my might.

'Jack has been here inquiring after you,' says the young man.

'Did he leave any message?' asks Mr Jay.

'Yes,' says the other. 'He told me, if I met with you, to say
that he wished very particularly to see you tonight; and that he
would give you a look in, at Rutherford Street, at seven o'clock.'

'All right,' says Mr Jay. 'I'll get back in time to see him.'

Upon this, the suspicious-looking young man finished his
porter, and saying that he was rather in a hurry, took leave of his
friend (perhaps I should not be wrong if I said his accomplice)
and left the room.

At twenty-five minutes and a half past six – in these serious
cases it is important to be particular about time – Mr Jay finished
his chops and paid his bill. At twenty-six minutes and three-
quarters I finished my chops and paid mine. In ten minutes more
I was inside the house in Rutherford Street, and was received by
Mrs Yatman in the passage. That charming woman's face
exhibited an expression of melancholy and disappointment which
it quite grieved me to see.

'I am afraid, Ma'am,' says I, 'that you have not hit on any
little criminating discovery in the lodger's room?'

She shook her head and sighed. It was a soft, languid, fluttering sigh; – and, upon my life, it quite upset me. For the moment I forgot business, and burned with envy of Mr Yatman.

'Don't despair, Ma'am,' I said, with an insinuating mildness which seemed to touch her. 'I have heard a mysterious conversation – I know of a guilty appointment –and I expect great things from my peep-hole and my pipe-hole to-night. Pray, don't be alarmed, but I think we are on the brink of a discovery.'

Here my enthusiastic devotion to business got the better of my tender feelings. I looked – winked – nodded – left her.

When I got back to my observatory, I found Mr Jay digesting his mutton chops in an arm-chair, with his pipe in his mouth. On his table were two tumblers, a jug of water, and the pint bottle of brandy. It was then close upon seven o'clock. As the hour struck, the person described as 'Jack' walked in.

He looked agitated – I am happy to say he looked violently agitated. The cheerful glow of anticipated success diffused itself (to use a strong expression) all over me, from head to foot. With breathless interest I looked through my peep-hole, and saw the visitor – the 'Jack' of this delightful case – sit down, facing me, at the opposite side of the table to Mr Jay. Making allowance for the difference in expression which their countenances just now happened to exhibit, these two abandoned villains were so much alike in other respects as to lead at once to the conclusion that they were brothers. Jack was the cleaner man and the better dressed of the two. I admit that, at the outset. It is, perhaps, one of my failings to push justice and impartiality to their utmost limits. I am no Pharisee; and where vice has its redeeming point, I say, let vice have its due – yes, yes, by all manner of means, let vice have its due.

'What's the matter now, Jack?' says Mr Jay.

'Can't you see it in my face?' says Jack. 'My dear fellow, delays are dangerous. Let us have done with suspense, and risk it the day after tomorrow.'

'So soon as that?' cried Mr Jay, looking very much astonished. 'Well, I'm ready, if you are. But, I say, Jack, is Somebody Else ready too? Are you quite sure of that?'

He smiled as he spoke – a frightful smile – and laid a very

strong emphasis on those two words, 'Somebody Else.' There is evidently a third ruffian, a nameless desperado, concerned in the business.

'Meet us tomorrow,' says Jack, 'and judge for yourself. Be in the Regent's Park at eleven in the morning, and look out for us at the turning that leads to the Avenue Road.'

'I'll be there,' says Mr Jay. 'Have a drop of brandy and water? What are you getting up for? You're not going already?'

'Yes, I am,' says Jack. 'The fact is, I'm so excited and agitated that I can't sit still anywhere for five minutes together. Ridiculous as it may appear to you, I'm in a perpetual state of nervous flutter. I can't, for the life of me, help fearing that we shall be found out. I fancy that every man who looks twice at me in the street is a spy –'

At those words, I thought my legs would have given way under me. Nothing but strength of mind kept me at my peep-hole – nothing else, I give you my word of honour.

'Stuff and nonsense!' cried Mr Jay, with all the effrontery of a veteran in crime. 'We have kept the secret up to this time, and we will manage cleverly to the end. Have a drop of brandy and water, and you will feel as certain about it as I do.'

Jack steadily refused the brandy and water, and steadily persisted in taking his leave.

'I must try if I can't walk it off,' he said. 'Remember tomorrow morning – eleven o'clock, Avenue Road side of the Regent's Park.'

With those words he went out. His hardened relative laughed desperately, and resumed the dirty clay pipe.

I sat down on the side of my bed, actually quivering with excitement.

It is clear to me that no attempt has yet been made to change the stolen bank-notes; and I may add that Sergeant Bulmer was of that opinion also, when he left the case in my hands. What is the natural conclusion to draw from the conversation which I have just set down? Evidently, that the confederates meet tomorrow to take their respective shares in the stolen money, and to decide on the safest means of getting the notes changed the day after. Mr Jay is, beyond a doubt, the leading criminal in this business, and he will probably run the chief risk – that of changing the fifty-pound note. I shall, therefore, still make it my business to follow him – attending at the Regent's Park, tomorrow, and doing my best to hear what is said there. If another appointment is made for the day after, I shall, of course, go to it. In the meantime, I shall want the immediate assistance of two competent persons (supposing the rascals separate after their meeting) to follow the two minor criminals. It is only fair to add, that, if the rogues all retire together, I shall probably keep my subordinates in reserve. Being naturally ambitious, I desire, if possible, to have the whole credit of discovering this robbery to myself.

8 July.

I have to acknowledge, with thanks, the speedy arrival of my two subordinates – men of very average abilities, I am afraid; but, fortunately, I shall always be on the spot to direct them.

My first business this morning was, necessarily, to prevent mistakes by accounting to Mr and Mrs Yatman for the presence of two strangers on the scene. Mr Yatman (between ourselves, a poor feeble man) only shook his head and groaned. Mrs Yatman (that superior woman) favoured me with a charming look of intelligence.

'Oh, Mr Sharpin!' she said, 'I am so sorry to see those two men! Your sending for their assistance looks as if you were beginning to be doubtful of success.'

I privately winked at her (she is very good in allowing me to do so without taking offence), and told her, in my facetious way, that she laboured under a slight mistake.

'It is because I am sure of success, Ma'am, that I send for them. I am determined to recover the money, not for my own sake only, but for Mr Yatman's sake – and for yours.'

I laid a considerable amount of stress on those last three words. She said, 'Oh, Mr Sharpin!' again – and blushed of a heavenly red – and looked down at her work. I could go to the world's end with that woman, if Mr Yatman would only die.

I sent off the two subordinates to wait, until I wanted them, at

the Avenue Road gate of the Regent's Park. Half an hour
afterwards I was following in the same direction myself, at the
heels of Mr Jay.

The two confederates were punctual to the appointed time, I
blush to record it, but it is nevertheless necessary to state, that
the third rogue – the nameless desperado of my report, or if you
prefer it, the mysterious 'Somebody Else' of the conversation
between the two brothers – is a Woman! and, what is worse, a
young woman! and what is more lamentable still, a nice-looking
woman! I have long resisted a growing conviction, that, wherever
there is mischief in this world, an individual of the fair sex is inevitably certain to be mixed up in it. After the experience of this
morning, I can struggle against that sad conclusion no longer.
– I give up the sex – excepting Mrs Yatman, I give up the
sex.

The man named 'Jack' offered the woman his arm. Mr Jay
placed himself on the other side of her. The three then walked
away slowly among the trees. I followed them at a respectful
distance. My two subordinates, at a respectful distance also,
followed me.

It was, I deeply regret to say, impossible to get near enough
to them to overhear their conversation, without running too great
a risk of being discovered. I could only infer from their gestures
and actions that they were all three talking with extraordinary
earnestness on some subject which deeply interested them. After
having been engaged in this way a full quarter of an hour, they
suddenly turned round to retrace their steps. My presence of mind
did not forsake me in this emergency. I signed to the two sub-
ordinated to walk on carelessly and pass them, while I myself
slipped dexterously behind a tree. As they came by me, I heard
'Jack' address these words to Mr Jay:

'Let us say half-past ten tomorrow morning. And mind you
come in a cab. We had better not risk taking one in this
neighbourhood.'

Mr Jay made some brief reply, which I could not overhear.
They walked back to the place at which they had met, shaking
hands there with an audacious cordiality which it quite sickened

me to see. They then separated. I followed Mr Jay. My subordinates paid the same delicate attention to the other two.

Instead of taking me back to Rutherford Street, Mr Jay led me to the Strand. He stopped at a dingy, disreputable-looking house, which, according to the inscription over the door, was a newspaper office, but which, in my judgment, had all the external appearance of a place devoted to the reception of stolen goods.

After remaining inside for a few minutes, he came out whistling, with his finger and thumb in his waistcoat pocket. A less discreet man than myself would have arrested him on the spot. I remembered the necessity of catching the two confederates, and the importance of not interfering with the appointment that had been made for the next morning. Such coolness as this, under trying circumstances, is rarely to be found, I should imagine, in a young beginner, whose reputation as a detective policeman is still to make.

From the house of suspicious appearance, Mr Jay betook himself to a cigar-divan, and read the magazines over a cheroot. I sat at a table near him, and read the magazines likewise over a cheroot. From the divan he strolled to the tavern and had his chops. I strolled to the tavern and had my chops. When he had done, he went back to his lodging. When I had done, I went back to mine. He was overcome with drowsiness early in the evening, and went to bed. As soon as I heard him snoring, I was overcome with drowsiness, and went to bed also.

Early in the morning my two subordinates came to make their report.

They had seen the man named 'Jack' leave the woman near the gate of an apparently respectable villa-residence, not far from the Regent's Park. Left to himself, he took a turning to the right, which led to a sort of suburban street, principally inhabited by shopkeepers. He stopped at the private door of one of the houses, and let himself in with his own key – looking about him as he opened the door, and staring suspiciously at my men as they lounged along on the opposite side of the way. These were all the particulars which the subordinates had to communicate. I kept them in my room to attend on me, if needful, and mounted to my peep-hole to have a look at Mr Jay.

He was occupied in dressing himself, and was taking extra-ordinary pains to destroy all traces of the natural slovenliness of his appearance. This was precisely what I expected. A vagabond like Mr Jay knows the importance of giving himself a respectable look when he is going to run the risk of changing a stolen bank-note. At five minutes past ten o'clock, he had given the last brush to his shabby hat and the last scouring with bread-crumbs to his dirty gloves. At ten minutes past ten he was in the street, on his way to the nearest cab-stand, and I and my subordinates were close on his heels.

He took a cab, and we took a cab. I had not overheard them appoint a place of meeting, when following them in the Park on the previous day; but I soon found that we were proceeding in the old direction of the Avenue Road gate.

The cab in which Mr Jay was riding turned into the Park slowly. We stopped outside, to avoid exciting suspicion. I got out to follow the cab on foot. Just as I did so, I saw it stop, and detected the two confederates approaching it from among the trees. They got in, and the cab was turned about directly. I ran back to my own cab, and told the driver to let them pass him, and then to follow as before.

The man obeyed my directions, but so clumsily as to excite their suspicions. We had been driving after them about three minutes (returning along the road by which we had advanced) when I looked out of the window to see how far they might be ahead of us. As I did this, I saw two hats popped out of the windows of their cab, and two faces looking back at me. I sank into my place in a cold sweat; the expression is coarse, but no other form of words can describe my condition at that trying moment.

'We are found out!' I said faintly to my two subordinates. They stared at me in astonishment. My feelings changed instantly from the depth of despair to the height of indignation.

'It is the cabman's fault. Get out, one of you,' I said, with dignity – 'get out and punch his head.'

Instead of following my directions (I should wish this act of disobedience to be reported at head-quarters) they both looked out of the window. Before I could pull them back, they both sat down again. Before I could express my just indignation, they both grinned, and said to me, 'Please to look out, sir!'

I did look out. The thieves' cab had stopped.

Where?

At a church door!!!

What effect this discovery might have had upon the ordinary run of men, I don't know. Being of a strong religious turn myself, it filled me with horror. I have often read of the unprincipled cunning of criminal persons; but I never before heard of three thieves attempting to double on their pursuers by entering a church! The sacrilegious audacity of that proceeding is, I should think, unparalleled in the annals of crime.

I checked my grinning subordinates by a frown. It was easy to see what was passing in their superficial minds. If I had not been able to look below the surface, I might, on observing two nicely-dressed men and one nicely-dressed woman enter a church before eleven in the morning on a weekday, have come to the same hasty conclusion at which my inferiors had evidently arrived. As it was, appearances had no power to impose on *me*. I got out, and, followed by one of my men, entered the church. The other man I sent round to watch the vestry door. You may catch a weasel asleep – but not your humble servant, Matthew Sharpin!

We stole up the gallery stairs, diverged to the organ loft and peered through the curtains in front. There they were all three, sitting in a pew below – yes, incredible as it may appear, sitting in a pew below!

Before I could determine what to do, a clergyman made his appearance in full canonicals, from the vestry door, followed by a clerk. My brain whirled, and my eyesight grew dim. Dark remembrances of robberies committed in vestries floated through my mind. I trembled for the excellent man in full canonicals – I even trembled for the clerk.

The clergyman placed himself inside the altar rails. The three desperadoes approached him. He opened his book, and began to read. What? – you will ask.

I answer, without the slightest hesitation, the first lines of the Marriage Service.

My subordinate had the audacity to look at me, and then to stuff his pocket-handkerchief into his mouth. I scorned to pay any attention to him. After I had discovered that the man 'Jack' was the bridegroom, and that the man Jay acted the part of father, and gave away the bride, I left the church, followed by my man, and joined the other subordinate outside the vestry door. Some people in my position would now have felt rather crestfallen, and would have begun to think that they had made a very foolish mistake. Not the faintest misgiving of any kind troubled me. I did not feel in the slightest degree depreciated in my own estimation. And even now, after a lapse of three hours, my mind remains, I am happy to say, in the same calm and hopeful condition.

As soon as I and my subordinates were assembled together outside the church, I intimated my intention of still following the other cab, in spite of what had occurred. My reason for deciding on this course will appear presently. The two subordinates were astonished at my resolution. One of them had the impertinence to say to me:

'If you please, sir, who is it that we are after? A man who has stolen money, or a man who has stolen a wife?'

The other low person encouraged him by laughing. Both have deserved an official reprimand; and both, I sincerely trust, will be sure to get it.

When the marriage ceremony was over, the three got into their cab; and once more our vehicle (neatly hidden round the corner of the church, so that they could not suspect it to be near them) started to follow theirs.

We traced them to the terminus of the South-Western Railway. The newly-married couple took tickets for Richmond – paying their fare with a half-sovereign, and so depriving me of the pleasure of arresting them, which I should certainly have done, if they had offered a bank-note. They parted from Mr Jay, saying, 'Remember the address, – 14 Babylon Terrace. You dine with us tomorrow week.' Mr Jay accepted the invitation, and added, jocosely, that he was going home at once to get off his clean clothes, and to be comfortable and dirty again for the rest of the day. I have to report that I saw him home safely, and that he is comfortable and dirty again (to use his own disgraceful language) at the present moment.

Here the affair rests, having by this time reached what I may call its first stage.

I know very well what persons of hasty judgment will be inclined to say of my proceedings thus far. They will assert that I have been deceiving myself all through, in the most absurd way; they will declare that the suspicious conversations which I have reported, referred solely to the difficulties and dangers of successfully carrying out a runaway match; and they will appeal to the scene in the church, as offering undeniable proof of the correctness of their assertions. So let it be. I dispute nothing up to this point. But I ask a question, out of the depths of my own sagacity as a man of the world, which the bitterest of my enemies will not, I think, find it particularly easy to answer.

Granted the fact of the marriage, what proof does it afford me of the innocence of the three persons concerned in that clandestine transaction? It gives me none. On the contrary, it strengthens my suspicions against Mr Jay and his confederates, because it suggests a distinct motive for their stealing the money. A gentleman who is going to spend his honeymoon at Richmond wants money; and a gentleman who is in debt to all his tradespeople wants money. Is this an unjustifiable imputation of bad motives? In the name of outraged morality, I deny it. These men have combined together, and have stolen a woman. Why should they not combine together, and steal a cash-box? I take my stand on the logic of rigid virtue; and I defy all the sophistry of vice to move me an inch out of my position.

Speaking of virtue, I may add that I have put this view of the case to Mr and Mrs Yatman. That accomplished and charming woman found it difficult, at first, to follow the close chain of my reasoning. I am free to confess that she shook her head, and shed tears, and joined her husband in premature lamentation over the loss of the two hundred pounds. But a little careful explanation on my part, and a little attentive listening on hers, ultimately changed her opinion. She now agrees with me, that there is nothing in this unexpected circumstance of the clandestine marriage which absolutely tends to divert suspicion from Mr Jay, or Mr 'Jack,' or the runaway lady. 'Audacious hussy' was the term my fair friend used in speaking of her, but let that pass. It is more to the purpose to record that Mrs Yatman has not lost confidence in me and that Mr Yatman promises to follow her example, and do his best to look hopefully for future results.

I have now, in the new turn that circumstances have taken, to await advice from your office. I pause for fresh orders with all the composure of a man who has got two strings to his bow. When I traced the three confederates from the church door to the railway terminus, I had two motives for doing so. First, I followed them as a matter of official business, believing them still to have been guilty of the robbery. Secondly, I followed them as a matter of private speculation, with a view of discovering the place of refuge to which the runaway couple intended to retreat, and of making my information a marketable commodity to offer to the young lady's family and friends. Thus, whatever happens, I may congratulate myself beforehand on not having wasted my time. If the office approves of my conduct, I have my plan ready for further proceedings. If the office blames me, I shall take myself off, with my marketable information, to the genteel villa-residence in the neighbourhood of the Regent's Park. Anyway, the affair puts money into my pocket, and does credit to my penetration as an uncommonly sharp man.

I have only one word more to add, and it is this: If any individual ventures to assert that Mr Jay and his confederates are innocent of all share in the stealing of the cash-box, I, in return, defy that individual – though he may even be Chief Inspector Theakstone himself – to tell me who has committed the robbery at Rutherford Street, Soho.

I have the honour to be,

Your very obedient servant,

Matthew Sharpin.

FROM CHIEF INSPECTOR THEAKSTONE TO SERGEANT
BULMER

BIRMINGHAM, 9 *July*

Sergeant Bulmer, – That empty-headed puppy, Mr Matthew
Sharpin, has made a mess of the case at Rutherford Street, exactly
as I expected he would. Business keeps me in this town; so I write
to you to set the matter straight. I enclose, with this, the pages of
feeble scribble-scrabble which the creature, Sharpin, calls a report.
Look them over; and when you have made your way through all
the gabble, I think you will agree with me that the conceited booby
has looked for the thief in every direction but the right one. You
can lay your hand on the guilty person in five minutes, now. Settle
the case at once; forward your report to me at this place; and tell
Mr Sharpin that he is suspended till further notice.

Yours,

Francis Theakstone.

FROM SERGEANT BULMER TO CHIEF INSPECTOR
THEAKSTONE

LONDON, *10 July*

Inspector Theakstone, – Your letter and enclosure came safe to
hand. Wise men, they say, may always learn something, even from
a fool. By the time I had got through Sharpin's maundering report
of his own folly, I saw my way clear enough to the end of the
Rutherford Street case, just as you thought I should. In half an
hour's time I was at the house. The first person I saw there was
Mr Sharpin himself.

'Have you come to help me?' says he.

'Not exactly,' says I. 'I've come to tell you that you are
suspended till further notice.'

'Very good,' says he, not taken down, by so much as a single
peg, in his own estimation. 'I thought you would be jealous of
me. It's very natural; and I don't blame you. Walk in, pray, and
make yourself at home. I'm off to do a little detective business on
my own account, in the neighbourhood of the Regent's Park.
Ta-ta, sergeant, ta-ta!'

With those words he took himself out of the way – which was exactly what I wanted him to do.

As soon as the maid-servant had shut the door, I told her to inform her master that I wanted to say a word to him in private. She showed me into the parlour behind the shop; and there was Mr Yatman, all alone, reading the newspaper.

'About this matter of the robbery, sir,' says I.

He cut me short, peevishly enough – being naturally a poor, weak, womanish sort of man. 'Yes, yes, I know,' says he. 'You have come to tell me that your wonderfully clever man, who has bored holes in my second-floor partition, has made a mistake, and is off the scent of the scoundrel who has stolen my money.'

'Yes, sir,' says I. 'That *is* one of the things I came to tell you. But I have got something else to say, besides that.'

'Can you tell me who the thief is?' says he, more pettish than ever.

'Yes, sir,' says I, 'I think I can.'

He put down the newspaper, and began to look rather anxious and frightened.

'Not my shopman?' says he. 'I hope, for the man's own sake, it's not my shopman.'

'Guess again, sir,' says I.

'That idle slut, the maid?' says he.

'She is idle, sir,' says I, 'and she is also a slut; my first inquiries about her proved as much as that. But she's not the thief.'

'Then in the name of heaven, who is?' says he.

'Will you please to prepare yourself for a very disagreeable surprise, sir?' says I. 'And in case you lose your temper, will you excuse my remarking that I am the stronger man of the two, and that, if you allow yourself to lay hands on me, I may unintentionally hurt you, in pure self-defence?'

He turned as pale as ashes, and pushed his chair two or three feet away from me.

'You have asked me to tell you, sir, who has taken your money,' I went on. 'If you insist on my giving you an answer –'

'I do insist,' he said, faintly. 'Who has taken it?'

'Your wife has taken it,' I said very quietly, and very positively at the same time.

He jumped out of the chair as if I had put a knife into him, and struck his fist on the table, so heavily that the wood cracked again.

'Steady, sir,' says I. 'Flying into a passion won't help you to the truth.'

'It's a lie!' says he, with another smack of his fist on the table –'a base, vile, infamous lie! How dare you –'

He stopped, and fell back into the chair again, looked about him in a bewildered way, and ended by bursting out crying.

'When your better sense comes back to you, sir,' says I, 'I am sure you will be gentleman enough to make an apology for the language you have just used. In the meantime, please to listen, if you can, to a word of explanation. Mr Sharpin has sent in a report to our inspector, of the most irregular and ridiculous kind; setting down, not only all his own foolish doings and sayings, but the doings and sayings of Mrs Yatman as well. In most cases, such a document would have been fit for the waste-paper basket; but, in this particular case, it so happens that Mr Sharpin's budget of nonsense leads to a certain conclusion, which the simpleton of a writer has been quite innocent of suspecting from the beginning to the end. Of that conclusion I am so sure, that I will forfeit my place, if it does not turn out that Mrs Yatman has been practising upon the folly and conceit of this young man, and that she has tried to shield herself from discovery by purposely encouraging him to suspect the wrong persons. I tell you that confidently; and I will even go further. I will undertake to give a decided opinion as to why Mrs Yatman took the money, and what she has done with it, or with a part of it. Nobody can look at that lady, sir, without being struck by the great taste and beauty of her dress –'

As I said those last words, the poor man seemed to find his powers of speech again. He cut me short directly, as haughtily as if he had been a duke instead of a stationer.

'Try some other means of justifying your vile calumny against my wife,' says he. 'Her milliner's bill for the past year, is on my file of receipted accounts at this moment.'

'Excuse me, sir,' says I, 'but that proves nothing. Milliners, I must tell you, have a certain rascally custom which comes within the daily experience of our office. A married lady who wishes it, can keep two accounts at her dressmaker's; one is the account which her husband sees and pays; the other is the private account, which contains all the extravagant items, and which the wife pays secretly, by instalments, whenever she can. According to our usual experience, these instalments are mostly squeezed out of the housekeeping money. In your case, I suspect no instalments have been paid; proceedings have been threatened; Mrs Yatman, knowing your altered circumstances, has felt herself driven into a corner; and she has paid her private account out of your cashbox.'

'I won't believe it,' says he. 'Every word you speak is an abominable insult to me and to my wife.'

'Are you man enough, sir,' says I, taking him up short, in order to save time and words, 'to get that receipted bill you spoke of just now off the file, and come with me at once to the milliner's shop where Mrs Yatman deals?'

He turned red in the face at that, got the bill directly, and put on his hat. I took out of my pocket-book the list containing the numbers of the lost notes, and we left the house together immediately.

Arrived at the milliner's (one of the expensive West-end houses, as I expected), I asked for a private interview, on important business, with the mistress of the concern. It was not the first time that she and I had met over the same delicate investigation. The moment she set eyes on me, she sent for her husband. I mentioned who Mr Yatman was, and what we wanted.

'This is strictly private?' inquires her husband. I nodded my head.

'And confidential?' says the wife. I nodded again.

'Do you see any objection, dear, to obliging the sergeant with a sight of the books?' says the husband.

'None in the world, love, if you approve of it,' says the wife.

All this while poor Mr Yatman sat looking the picture of astonishment and distress, quite out of place at our polite conference. The books were brought – and one minute's look at the pages in which Mrs Yatman's name figured was enough, and more than enough, to prove the truth of every word I had spoken.

There, in one book, was the husband's account, which Mr Yatman had settled. And there, in the other, was the private account, crossed off also; the date of settlement being the very day after the loss of the cash-box. This said private account amounted to the sum of a hundred and seventy-five pounds, odd shillings; and it extended over a period of three years. Not a single instalment had been paid on it. Under the last line was an entry to this effect: 'Written to for the third time, June 23rd.' I pointed to it, and asked the milliner if that meant 'last June.' Yes, it did mean last June; and she now deeply regretted to say that it had been accompanied by a threat of legal proceedings.

'I thought you gave good customers more than three years credit?' says I.

The milliner looks at Mr Yatman, and whispers to me – 'Not when a lady's husband gets into difficulties.'

She pointed to the account as she spoke. The entries after the time when Mr Yatman's circumstances became involved were just as extravagant, for a person in his wife's situation, as the entries for the year before that period. If the lady had economised in other things, she had certainly not economised in the matter of dress.

There was nothing left now but to examine the cash-book, for form's sake. The money had been paid in notes, the amounts and numbers of which exactly tallied with the figures set down in my list.

After that, I thought it best to get Mr Yatman out of the house immediately. He was in such a pitiable condition, that I called a cab and accompanied him home in it. At first he cried and raved like a child: but I soon quieted him – and I must add, to his credit, that he made me a most handsome apology for his language, as the cab drew up at his house door. In return, I tried to give him some advice about how to set matters right, for the future, with his wife. He paid very little attention to me, and went upstairs muttering to himself about a separation. Whether Mrs

Yatman will come cleverly out of the scrape or not, seems doubtful. I should say, myself, that she will go into screeching hysterics,
and so frighten the poor man into forgiving her. But this is no
business of ours. So far as we are concerned, the case is now at
an end; and the present report may come to a conclusion along
with it.

I remain, accordingly, yours to command,

Thomas Bulmer.

P.S. – I have to add, that, on leaving Rutherford Street, I
met Mr Matthew Sharpin coming to pack up his things.

'Only think!' says he, rubbing his hands in great spirits, 'I've
been to the genteel villa-residence; and the moment I mentioned
my business, they kicked me out directly. There were two witnesses of the assault; and it's worth a hundred pounds to me, if
it's worth a farthing.'

'I wish you joy of your luck,' says I.

'Thank you,' says he. 'When may I pay you the same compliment on finding the thief?'

'Whenever you like,' says I, 'for the thief is found.'

'Just what I expected,' says he. 'I've done all the work; and
now you cut in, and claim all the credit – Mr Jay of course?'

'No,' says I.

'Who is it then?' says he.

'Ask Mrs Yatman,' says I. 'She's waiting to tell you.'

'All right! I'd much rather hear it from that charming woman
than from you,' says he, and goes into the house in a mighty
hurry.

What do you think of that, Inspector Theakstone? Would you
like to stand in Mr Sharpin's shoes? I shouldn't, I can promise
you!

FROM CHIEF INSPECTOR THEAKSTONE TO MR
MATTHEW SHARPIN

12 July

Sir, – Sergeant Bulmer has already told you to consider yourself
suspended until further notice. I have now authority to add, that
your services as a member of the Detective Police are positively

declined. You will please to take this letter as notifying officially your dismissal from the force.

I may inform you, privately, that your rejection is not intended to cast any reflections on your character. It merely implies that you are not quite sharp enough for our purpose. If we *are* to have a new recruit among us, we should infinitely prefer Mrs Yatman.

> Your obedient servant,
> Francis Theakstone.

NOTE ON THE PRECEDING CORRESPONDENCE, ADDED BY MR THEAKSTONE

The Inspector is not in a position to append any explanations of importance to the last of the letters. It has been discovered that Mr Matthew Sharpin left the house in Rutherford Street five minutes after his interview outside of it with Sergeant Bulmer – his manner expressing the liveliest emotions of terror and astonishment, and his left cheek displaying a bright patch of red, which might have been the result of a slap on the face from a female hand. He was also heard, by the shopman at Rutherford Street, to use a very shocking expression in reference to Mrs Yatman; and was seen to clench his fist vindictively, as he ran round the corner of the street. Nothing more has been heard of him; and it is conjectured that he has left London with the intention of offering his valuable services to the provincial police.

On the interesting domestic subject of Mr and Mrs Yatman still less is known. It has, however, been positively ascertained that the medical attendant of the family was sent for in a great hurry, on the day when Mr Yatman returned from the milliner's shop. The neighbouring chemist received, soon afterwards, a prescription of a soothing nature to make up for Mrs Yatman. The day after, Mr Yatman purchased some smelling-salts at the shop, and afterwards appeared at the circulating library to ask for a novel, descriptive of high life, that would amuse an invalid lady. It has been inferred from these circumstances, that he has not thought it desirable to carry out his threat of separating himself from his wife – at least in the present (presumed) condition of that lady's sensitive nervous system.

Edmund Crispin

WE KNOW YOU'RE
BUSY WRITING . . .

(i)

'After all, it's only us,' they said.

I must introduce myself.

None of this is going to be read, even, let alone printed. Ever.

Nevertheless, there is habit – the habit of putting words together in the most effective order you can think of. There is self-respect, too. That, and habit, make me try to tell this as if it were in fact going to be read.

Which God forbid.

I am forty-seven, unmarried, living alone, a minor crime-fiction writer, earning, on average, rather less than a thousand pounds a year.

I live in Devon.

I live in a small cottage which is isolated, in the sense that there is no one nearer than a quarter of a mile.

I am not, however, at a loss for company.

For one thing, I have a telephone.

I am a hypochondriac, well into the coronary belt. Also, I go in fear of accidents, with broken bones. The telephone is thus a necessity. I can afford only one, so its siting is a matter of great discretion. In the end, it is in the hall, just at the foot of the steep stairs. It is on a shelf only two feet from the floor, so that if I have to crawl to it, it will still be within reach.

If I have my coronary *up*stairs, too bad.

The telephone is for me to use in an emergency. Other people, however, regard it differently.

Take, for example, my Bank Manager.

'Torhaven 153,' I say.

'Hello? Bradley, is that Mr Bradley?'

'Bradley speaking.'

'This is Wimpole, Wimpole. Mr Bradley, I have to talk to you.'

'Speaking.'

'Now, it's like this, Mr Bradley. How soon can we expect some further payments in, Mr Bradley? Payments out, yes, we have plenty of those, but payments in . . .'

'I'm doing everything I can, Mr Wimpole.'

'Everything, yes, everything, but payments in, what is going to be coming in during the next month, Mr Bradley?'

'Quite a lot, I hope.'

'Yes, you hope, Mr Bradley, you hope, you hope. But what am I going to say to my Regional Office, Mr Bradley, how am I going to represent the matter to them, to it? You have this accommodation with us, this matter of five hundred pounds . . .'

'Had it for years, Mr Wimpole.'

'Yes, Mr Bradley, and that is exactly the trouble. You must reduce it, Mr Bradley, reduce it, I say,' this lunatic bawls at me.

I can no more reduce my overdraft than I can fly.

I am adequately industrious. I aim to write two thousand words a day, which would support me in the event that I were ever able to complete them. But if you live alone you are not, contrary to popular supposition, in a state of unbroken placidity.

Quite the contrary.

I have tried night-work, a consuming yawn to every tap on the typewriter, I have tried early morning work.

And here H. L. Mencken comes in, suggesting that bad writing is due to bad digestion.

My own digestion is bad at any time, particularly bad during milkmen's hours, and I have never found that I could do much in the dawn. This is a weakness, and I admit it. But apparently it has to be. Work, for me, is thus office hours, nine till five.

I have told everyone about this, begging them, if it isn't a matter of emergency, to get in touch with me in the *evenings*. Office hours, I tell them, same as everyone else. You wouldn't telephone a solicitor about nothing in particular during his office hours, would you? Well, so why ring me?

I am typing a sentence which starts *His crushed hand, paining him less now, nevertheless gave him a sense of.*

I know what is going to happen after ' of ': *the appalling frailty of the human body.*

Or rather, I did know, and it wasn't that. It might have been that (feeble though it is) but for the fact that then the door-bell rang. (I hope that it might have been something better.)

The door-bell rang. It was a Mrs Prance morning, but she hadn't yet arrived, so I answered the door myself, clattering down from the upstairs room where I work. It was the meter-reader. The meter being outside the door, I was at a loss to know why I had to sanction its being scrutinised.

'A sense of the dreadful agonies,' I said to the meter-reader, ' of which the human body is capable.'

'Wonderful weather for the time of year.'

' I'll leave you, if you don't mind. I'm a bit busy.'

' Suit yourself,' he said, offended.

Then Mrs Prance came.

Mrs Prance comes three mornings a week. She is slow, and deaf, but she is all I can hope to get, short of winning the Pools.

She answers the door, but is afraid of the telephone, and consequently never answers that, though I've done my utmost to train her to it.

She is very anxious that I should know precisely what she is doing in my tatty little cottage, and approve of it.

' Mr Bradley?'

' Yes, Mrs Prance?'

' It's the Hi-Glow.'

' What about it, Mrs Prance?'

'Pardon?'

'I said, what about it?'

'We did ought to change.'

'Yes, well, let's change, by all means.'

'Pardon?'

'I said, "Yes".'

'Doesn't bring the wood up, not the way it ought to.'

'You're the best judge, Mrs Prance.'

'Pardon?'

'I'm sorry, Mrs Prance, but I'm working now. We'll talk about it some other time.'

'Toffee-nosed,' says Mrs Prance.

Gave him a sense of – a sense of – a sense of burr-burr, burr-burr, burr-burr.

Mrs Prance shouts that it's the telephone.

I stumble downstairs and pick the thing up.

'Darling.'

'Oh, hello, Chris.'

'How are you, darling?'

'A sense of the gross cruelty which filled all history.'

'What, darling? What was that you said?'

'Sorry. I was just trying to keep a glass of water balanced on my head.'

A tinkle of laughter.

'You're a poppet. Listen, I've had a wonderful idea. It's a party. Here in my flat. Today week. You will come, Edward, won't you?'

'Yes, of course, I will, Chris, but may I just remind you about something?'

'What's that, darling?'

'You said you wouldn't ring me up during working hours.'

A short silence then:

'Oh, but *just this once*. It's going to be such a lovely party, darling. You don't mind *just this once*.'

'Chris, are you having a coffee break?'

'Yes, darling, and Oh, God, don't I need it!'

'Well, I'm *not* having a coffee break.'

A rather longer silence; then:

'You don't love me any more.'

'It's just that I'm trying to get a story written. There's a deadline for it.'

'If you don't want to come to the party, all you've got to do is say so.'

'I do want to come to the party, but I also want to get on with earning my living. Seriously, Chris, as it's a week ahead, couldn't you have waited till this evening to ring me?'

A sob.

'I think you're beastly. I think you're utterly, utterly *horrible*.'

'Chris.'

'And I never want to *see* you again.'

A sense of treachery, I typed, sedulously. *The agony still flamed up his arm, but it was now –*

The door-bell rang.

– it was now less than – more than –

'It's the laundry, Mr Bradley,' Mrs Prance shouted up the stairs at me.

'Coming, Mrs Prance.'

I went out on to the small landing. Mrs Prance's great moon-face peered up at me from below.

'Coming Thursday next week,' she shouted at me, 'because of Good Friday.'

'Yes, Mrs Prance, but what has that got to do with *me*? I mean, you'll be here on Wednesday as usual, won't you, to change the sheets?'

'Pardon?'

'Thank you for telling me, Mrs Prance.'

One way and another, it was a remarkable Tuesday morning: seven telephone calls, none of them in the least important, eleven people at the door and Mrs Prance anxious that no scintilla of her efforts should lack my personal verbal approval. I had sat down in front of my typewriter at nine-thirty. By twelve noon, I had achieved the following:

His crushed hand, paining him less now, nevertheless gave him a sense of treachery, the appalling frailty of the human body, but it was now less than it had been, more than indifferent to him since, after, because though the pain could be shrugged off the betrayal was a

I make no pretence to be a quick writer, but that really was a very bad morning indeed.

(ii)

Afternoon started better. With some garlic sausage and bread inside me, I ran to another seven paragraphs, unimpeded.

As he clawed his way out, hatred seized him, I tapped out, enthusiastically embarking on the eighth. *No such emotion had ever before –*

The door-bell rang.

– had ever before disturbed his quiet existence. It was as if –

The door-bell rang again, lengthily, someone leaning on it.

– as if a beast had taken charge, a beast inordinate, insatiable.

The door-bell was now ringing for many seconds at a time, uninterruptedly.

Was this a survival factor, or would it blur his mind? He scarcely knew. One thing was abundantly clear, namely that he was going to have to answer the bloody door-bell.

He did so.

On the doorstep, their car standing in the lane beyond, were a couple in early middle age, who could be seen at a glance to be fresh out from The Duke.

The Duke of Devonshire is my local. When I first moved to this quiet part of Devon I had nothing against The Duke: it was a small village pub serving small village drinks, with an occasional commercialized pork pie or sausage-roll. But then it changed hands. A Postgate admirer took over. Hams, game patties, quail eggs and other such fanciful foods were introduced to a noise of trumpets; esurient lunatics began rolling up in every sort of car, gobble-mad for exotic ploughman's lunches and suavely served

lobster creams, their throats parched for the vinegar of 1964 clarets
or the ullage of the abominable home-brewed beer; and there was
no longer any peace for anyone.

In particular, there was no longer any peace for me. 'Let's go
and see old Ted,' people said to one another as they were shooed
out of the bar at closing time. 'He lives near here.'

'Charles,' said this man on the doorstep, extending his hand.

The woman with him tittered. She had fluffy hair, and lips so
pale that they stood out disconcertingly, like scars, against her
blotched complexion. 'It's Ted, lovey,' she said.

'Ted, of course it's Ted. Known him for years. How are you,
Charley boy?'

'*Ted*, angel.'

I recognised them both, slightly, from one or two parties. They
were presumably a married couple, but not married for long, if
offensive nonsenses like 'Angel' were to be believed.

'We're not interrupting anything,' she said.

Interested by this statement of fact, I found spouting up in
my pharynx the reply, 'Yes, you sodding well are.' But this had
to be choked back; bourgeois education forbids such replies, other
than euphemistically.

'Come on in,' I said.

They came on in.

I took them into the downstairs living-room, which lack of money
has left a ghost of its original intention. There are two armchairs,
a chesterfield, a coffee-table, a corner cupboard for drinks; but
all, despite Hi-Glow, dull and tattered on the plain carpet.

I got them settled on the chesterfield.

'Coffee?' I suggested.

But this seemed not to be what was wanted.

'You haven't got a drink, old boy?' the man said.

'*Stanislas*,' the girl said.

'Yes, of course. Whisky? Gin? Sherry?'

'Oh, Stanislas darling, you are *awful*,' said this female. 'Fancy
asking.'

I had no recollection of the name of either of them, but surely Stanislas couldn't be right. 'Stanislas?' I asked.

'It's private,' she said, taking one of his hands in one of hers, and wringing it. 'You don't mind? It's sort of a joke. It's private between us.'

'I see. Well, what would you like to drink?'

He chose whisky, she gin and Italian.

'If you'll excuse me I'll have to go upstairs for a minute,' I said, after serving them.

One thing was abundantly clear: Giorgio's map had been wrong, and as a consequence –

'Ooh-hooh!'

I went out on to the landing.

'Yes?'

'We're lonely.'

'Down in just a minute.'

'You're doing that nasty writing.'

'No, just checking something.'

'We heard the typewriter. Do come down, Charles, Edward I mean, we've got something terribly, terribly important to tell you.'

'Coming straight away,' I said, my mind full of Giorgio's map.

I refilled their glasses.

'You're Diana,' I said to her.

'Daphne,' she squeaked.

'Yes, of course, Daphne. Drink all right?'

She took a great swallow of it, and so was unable to speak for fear of vomiting. Stanislas roused himself to fill the conversational gap.

'How's the old writing, then?'

'Going along well.'

'Mad Martians, eh? Don't read that sort of thing myself, I'm afraid, too busy with biography and history. Has Daphne told you?'

'No. Told me what?'

'About Us, old boy, about Us.'

This was the first indication I'd had that they *weren't* a married couple. Fond locutions survive courtship by God knows how many years, fossilising to automatic gabble, and so are no guide to actual relationships. But in 'Us', the capital letter, audible anyway, flag-wags something new.

'Ah-ha!' I said.

With an effort, Stanislas leaned forward. 'Daphne's husband is a beast,' he said, enunciating distinctly.

'Giorgio's map,' I said. 'Defective.'

'A mere brute. So she's going to throw in her lot with me.' Satisfied, he fell back on to the cushions. 'Darling,' he said.

As a consequence, we were two miles south-west of our expected position. 'So what is the expected position?' I asked.

'We're eloping,' Daphne said.

'This very day. Darling.'

'Angel.'

'Yes, this very day,' said Stanislas, ostentatiously sucking up the last drops from the bottom of his glass. 'This very day as ever is. We've planned it,' he confided.

The plan had gone wrong, had gone rotten. Giorgio had failed.

'Had gone rotten,' I said, hoping I might just possibly remember the phrase when this pair of lunatics had taken themselves off.

'Rotten is the word for that bastard,' said Stanislas. Suddenly his eyes filled with alcoholic tears. 'What Daphne has suffered, no one will ever know,' he gulped. 'There's even been . . . beating.' Daphne lowered her lids demurely, in tacit confirmation. 'So we're off and away together,' said Stanislas, recovering slightly. 'A new life. Abroad. A new humane relationship.'

But was his failure final? Wasn't there still a chance?

'If you'll excuse me,' I said, 'I shall have to go upstairs again.'

But this attempt aborted. Daphne seized me so violently by the wrist, as I was on the move, that I had difficulty in not falling over sideways.

'You're with us, aren't you? she breathed.

'Oh, yes, of course.'

'My husband would come after us, if he knew.'

'A good thing he doesn't know, then.'

'But he'll guess. He'll guess it's Stanislas.'

'I suppose so.'

'You don't mind us being here, Charles, do you? We have to
wait till dark.'

'Well, actually, there is a bit of work I ought to be getting on
with.'

'I'm sorry, Ted,' she said, smoothing her skirt. 'We've been
inconsiderate. We must go.' She went on picking at her hem-line,
but there was no tensing of the leg muscles, preliminary to rising,
so I refilled her glass. 'No, don't go,' I said, the British middle
class confronting its finest hour. 'Tell me more about it.'

'Stanislas.'

'H'm, h'm.'

'Wake *up*, sweetie-pie. Tell Charles all about it.'

Stanislas got himself approximately upright. 'All about what?'

'About Us, angel.'

*But the devil of it was, if Giorgio's map was wrong, our chances
had receded to nil.*

'To nil,' I said, 'Nil.'

'Not nil at all, old boy,' Stanislas said. 'And as a matter of fact,
if you don't mind my saying so, I rather resent that "nil". We
may not be special, like writer blokes like you, but we aren't "nil",
Daphne and me. We're human, and so forth. Cut us and we
bleed, and that. I'm no great cop, I'll grant you that, but Daphne
– Daphne –'

'A splendid girl,' I said.

'Yes, you say that now, but what would you have said five
minutes ago? Eh? Eh?'

'The same thing, of course.'

'You think you're rather marvellous, don't you? You think
you've . . . got it made. Well, let me tell you one thing, Mr so-
called Bradley: you may think you're very clever, with all this
writing of westerns and so on, but I can tell you, there are more
important things in life than westerns. I don't suppose you'll
understand about it, but there's Love. Daphne and I, we love
one another. You can jeer, and you do jeer. All I can tell you is,

you're wrong as can be. Daphne and I, we're going off together, and to hell with people who . . . jeer.'

'Have another drink.'

'Well, thanks, I don't mind if I do.'

They stayed for four whole hours.

Somewhere in the middle they made a pretence of drinking tea. Some time after that they expressed concern at the length of time they had stayed – without, however, giving any sign of leaving. I gathered, as Giorgio and his map faded inexorably from my mind, that their elopement plans were dependent on darkness: this, rather than the charm of my company, was what they were waiting for. Meanwhile, with my deadline irrevocably lost, I listened to their soul-searching – he unjustifiably divorced, she tied to a brutish lout who unfortunately wielded influence over a large range of local and national affairs, and would pursue her to the ends of the earth unless precautions were taken to foil him.

I heard a good deal about these precautions, registering them without, at the time, realizing how useful they were going to be.

'Charles, Edward.'

'Yes?'

'We've been bastards.'

'Of course not.'

'We haven't been letting you get on with your work.'

'Too late now.'

'Not really too late,' lachrymosely. 'You go and write, and we'll just sit here, and do no harm to a soul.'

'I've rather forgotten what I was saying, and in any case I've missed the last post.'

'Oh, Charles, Charles, you shame us. We abase ourselves.'

'No need for that.'

'*Naturally* we abase ourselves. We've drunk your liquor, we've sat on your . . . your sofa, we've stopped you working. Sweetie-pie, isn't that true? Haven't we stopped him working?'

'If you say so, sweetie-pie.'

'I most certainly do say so. And it's a disgrace.'

'So we're disgraced, Poppet. *Bad*,' she said histrionically. 'But are we so bad? I mean, he's self-employed, he's got all the time in the world, he can work just whenever he likes. Not like you and me. He's got it *made*.'

'Oh, God,' I mumbled.

'Well, that's true,' Stanislas said, with difficulty. 'And it's a nice quiet life.'

'Quiet, that's it.'

'Don't have to do anything if you don't want to. Ah, come the day.'

'He's looking cross.'

'What's that? Old Charles looking cross? Angel, you're mistaken. Don't you believe it. Not cross, Charles, are you?'

'We *have* stayed rather long, darling. Darling, are you awake? I say, we *have* stayed rather long.'

'H'm.'

'But it's special. Edward, it's special. You do see that, don't you? Special. Because of Stanislas and me.'

I said, 'All I know is that I —'

'Just this once,' she said. 'You'll forgive us just this once? After all, you *are* a free agent. And after all, it's only us.'

I stared at them.

I looked at him, nine-tenths asleep. I looked at her, half asleep. I thought what a life they were going to have if they eloped together.

But 'It's only us' had triggered something off.

I remembered that on just that one day, not an extraordinary one, there had been Mrs Prance, the meter-reader, Chris (twice: she had telephoned a second time during working hours to apologize for telephoning the first time during working hours), the laundry-man, the grocer (no Chiver Peas this week), my tax accountant, a woman collecting for the Church, a Frenchman wanting to know if he was on the right road to The Duke.

I remembered that a frippet had come from the National Insurance, or whatever the hell it's called now, to ask what I was doing about Mrs Prance, and if not, why not. I remembered a long, inconclusive telephone call from someone's secretary at the

BBC – the someone, despite his anxiety to be in touch with me, having vanished without notice into the BBC Club. I remembered that undergraduates at the University of Essex were wanting me to give them a talk, and were going to be so good as to pay second-class rail fare, though no fee.

I remembered that my whole morning's work had been a single, botched, incomplete paragraph, and that my afternoon's work, before this further interruption, had been little more than two hundred words.

I remembered that I had missed the post.

I remembered that I had missed the post before, for much the same reasons, and that publishers are unenthusiastic about writers who keep failing to meet deadlines.

I remembered that I was very short of money, and that sitting giving drink to almost total strangers for four hours on end wasn't the best way of improving the situation.

I remembered.

I saw red.

A red mist swam before his eyes, doing the butterfly stroke.

I picked up the poker from the fireplace, and went round behind them.

Did they – I sometimes ask myself – wonder what I could possibly be doing, edging round the back of the chesterfield with a great lump of iron in my hand?

They were probably too far gone to wonder.

In any case, they weren't left wondering for long.

(iii)
Eighteen months have passed.

At the end of the first week a Detective Constable came to see me. His name was Ellis. He was thin to the point of emaciation, and seemed, despite his youth, permanently depressed. He was in plain clothes.

He told me that their names were Daphne Fiddler and Clarence Oates.

'Now, sir, we've looked into this matter, and we understand

that you didn't know this lady and gentleman at all well.'

'I'd just met them once or twice.'

'They came here, though, that Tuesday afternoon.'

'Yes, but they'd been booted out of the pub. People often come here because they've been booted out of the pub.'

Lounging on the chesterfield, ignoring its blotches, Ellis said, 'They were looking for a drink, eh?'

'Yes, they did seem to be doing that.'

'I'm not disturbing your work, sir, I hope.'

'Yes, you are, Officer, as a matter of fact. So did they.'

'If you wouldn't mind, sir, don't call me "Officer". I am one, technically. But as a mode of address it's pointless.'

'Sorry.'

'I'll have to disturb your work a little bit more still, sir, I'm afraid. Now, if I may ask, did this – this *pair* say anything to you about their plans?'

'Did they say anything to anyone else?'

'Yes, Mr Bradley, to about half the population of South Devon.'

'Well, I can tell you what they said to me. They said they were going to get a boat from Torquay to Jersey, and then a plane from Jersey to Guernsey, and then a Hovercraft from Guernsey to France. They were going to go over to France on day passes, but they were going to carry their passports with them, and cash sewn into the linings of their clothes. Then they were going on from France to some other country, where they could get jobs without a *permis de sejour*.'

'Some countries, there's loopholes big as camel's gates,' said Ellis biblically.

I said, 'They'll make a mess of it, you know.'

'Hash-slinging for her,' said Ellis despondently, 'and driving a taxi for him. What was the last you saw of them?'

'They drove off.'

'Yes, but when?'

'Oh, after dark. Perhaps seven. What happened to them after that?'

'The Falls.'

'Sorry?'

'The *Falls*. Their car was found abandoned there.'

'Oh.'

'No luggage in it.'

'Oh.'

'So presumably they got on the Torquay bus.'

'You can't find out?'

Ellis wriggled on the cushions. 'Driver's an idiot. Doesn't see or hear *anything*.'

'I was out at the Falls myself.'

'Pardon?'

'I say, I was out at the Falls myself. I followed them on foot – though of course, I didn't *know* I was doing that.'

'Did you see their car there?' Ellis asked.

'I saw several cars, but they all look alike nowadays. And they all had their lights off. You don't go around peering into cars at the Falls which have their lights off.'

'And then, sir?'

'I just walked back. It's a fairly normal walk for me in the evenings, after I've eaten. I mean, it's a walk I quite often take.'

(And I had, in fact, walked back by the lanes as usual, resisting the temptation to skulk across fields. Good for me to have dumped the car unnoticed near the bus-stop, and good for me to have remembered about the luggage before I set out.)

'Good for me,' I said.

'Pardon?'

'Good for me to be able to do that walk, still.'

Ellis unfolded himself, getting up from the chesterfield. Good for me that he hadn't got a kit with him to test the blotches.

'It's just a routine inquiry, Mr Bradley,' he said faintly, his vitality seemingly at a low ebb. 'Mrs Fiddler's husband, Mr Oates's wife, they felt they should inquire. Missing Persons, you see. But just between ourselves,' he added, his voice livening momentarily, 'they neither of 'em care a button. It's obvious what's happened, and they neither of 'em care a button. Least said, Mr Bradley, soonest mended.'

He went.

I should feel guilty; but in fact, I feel purged.

Catharsis.

Am I purged of pity? I hope not. I feel pity for Daphne and Stanislas, at the same time as irritation at their unconscionable folly.

Purged of fear?

Well, in an odd sort of way, yes.

Things have got worse for me. The strain of reducing my over-draft by £250 has left me with Mrs Prance only two days a week, and rather more importantly, I now have to count the tins of baked beans and the loaves I shall use for toasting.

But I feel better.

The interruptions are no less than before. Wimpole, Chris, my tax accountant all help to fill my working hours, in the same old way.

But now I feel almost indulgent towards them. Towards everyone, even Mrs Prance.

For one thing, I garden a lot.

I get a fair number of flowers, but this is more luck than judgment. Vegetables are my chief thing.

And this autumn the cabbages have done particularly well. Harvest cabbages, they stand up straight and conical, their dark green outer leaves folded close, moisture-globed, protecting firm, crisp hearts.

For harvest cabbages you can't beat nicely rotted organic fertilizer.

Can I ever bring myself to cut my harvest cabbages and eat them?

At the *moment* I don't want to eat my harvest cabbages. But I dare say in the end I shall.

After all, it's only them.

Arnold Bennett

MURDER!

I

MANY GREAT ONES of the earth have justified murder as a social act, defensible, and even laudable in certain instances. There is something to be said for murder, though perhaps not much. All of us, or nearly all of us, have at one time or another had the desire and the impulse to commit murder. At any rate, murder is not an uncommon affair. On an average, two people are murdered every week in England, and probably about two hundred every week in the United States. And forty per cent of the murderers are not brought to justice. These figures take no account of the undoubtedly numerous cases where murder has been done but never suspected. Murders and murderesses walk safely abroad among us, and it may happen to us to shake hands with them. A disturbing thought! But such is life, and such is homicide.

II

Two men, named respectively Lomax Harder and John Franting, were walking side by side one autumn afternoon, on the Marine Parade of the seaside resort and port of Quangate (English Channel). Both were well-dressed and had the air of moderate wealth, and both were about thirty-five years of age. At this point the resemblances between them ceased. Lomax Harder had refined features, an enormous forehead, fair hair, and a delicate, almost apologetic manner. John Franting was low-browed, heavy chinned, scowling, defiant, indeed what is called a tough customer. Lomax Harder corresponded in appearance with the popular notion of a poet – save that he was carefully barbered. He was in fact a poet, and not unknown in the tiny, trifling, mad world where poetry is a matter of first-rate interest. John Franting corresponded in appearance with the popular notion of a gambler, an amateur boxer, and, in spare time, a deluder of women. Popular notions sometimes fit the truth.

Lomax Harder, somewhat nervously buttoning his overcoat, said in a quiet but firm and insistent tone:

'Haven't you got anything to say?'

John Franting stopped suddenly in front of a shop whose façade bore the sign: 'Gontle. Gunsmith.'

'Not in words,' answered Franting. 'I'm going in here.'

And he brusquely entered the small, shabby shop.

Lomax Harder hesitated half a second, and then followed his companion.

The shopman was a middle-aged gentleman wearing a black velvet coat.

'Good afternoon,' he greeted Franting, with an expression and in a tone of urbane condescension which seemed to indicate that Franting was a wise as well as a fortunate man in that he knew of the excellence of Gontle's and had the wit to come into Gontle's.

For the name of Gontle was favourably and respectfully known wherever triggers are pressed. Not only along the whole length of the Channel coast, but throughout England, was Gontle's renowned. Sportsmen would travel to Quangate from the far north, and even from London, to buy guns. To say: 'I bought it at Gontle's,' or 'Old Gontle recommended it,' was sufficient to silence any dispute concerning the merits of a fire-arm. Experts bowed the head before the unique reputation of Gontle. As for old Gontle, he was extremely and pardonably conceited. His conviction that no other gunsmith in the wide world could compare with him was absolute. He sold guns and rifles with the gesture of a monarch conferring an honour. He never argued; he stated; and the customer who contradicted him was as likely as not to be courteously and icily informed by Gontle of the geographical situation of the shop-door. Such shops exist in the English provinces, and nobody knows how they have achieved their renown. They could exist nowhere else.

''d afternoon,' said Franting gruffly, and paused.

'What can I do for you?' asked Mr Gontle, as if saying: 'Now don't be afraid. This shop is tremendous, and I am tremendous; but I shall not eat you.'

'I want a revolver,' Franting snapped.

'Ah! A revolver!' commented Mr Gontle, as if saying: 'A gun or a rifle, yes! But a revolver – an arm without individuality, manufactured wholesale! . . . However, I suppose I must deign to accommodate you.'

'I presume you know something about revolvers?' asked Mr Gontle, as he began to produce the weapons.

'A little.'

'Do you know the Webley Mark III?'

'Can't say that I do.'

'Ah! It is the best for all common purposes.' And Mr Gontle's glance said: 'Have the goodness not to tell me it isn't.'

Franting examined the Webley Mark III.

'You see,' said Mr Gontle. 'The point about it is that until the breach is properly closed it cannot be fired. So that it can't blow open and maim or kill the would-be murderer.' Mr Gontle smiled archly at one of his oldest jokes.

'What about suicides?' Franting grimly demanded.

'Ah!'

'You might show me just how to load it,' said Franting.

Mr Gontle, having found ammunition, complied with this reasonable request.

'The barrel's a bit scratched,' said Franting.

Mr Gontle inspected the scratch with pain. He would have denied the scratch, but could not.

'Here's another one,' said he, 'since you're so particular.' He simply had to put customers in their place.

'You might load it,' said Franting.

Mr Gontle loaded the second revolver.

'I'd like to try it,' said Franting.

'Certainly,' said Mr Gontle, and led Franting out of the shop by the back, and down to a cellar where revolvers could be experimented with.

Lomax Harder was now alone in the shop. He hesitated a long

time and then picked up the revolver rejected by Franting, fingered it, put it down, and picked it up again. The back-door of the shop opened suddenly, and, startled, Harder dropped the revolver into his overcoat pocket: a thoughtless, quite unpremeditated act. He dared not remove the revolver. The revolver was as fast in his pocket as though the pocket had been sewn up.

'And cartridges?' asked Mr Gontle of Franting.

'Oh,' said Franting, 'I've only had one shot. Five'll be more than enough for the present. What does it weigh?'

'Let me see. Four inch barrel? Yes. One pound four ounces.'

Franting paid for the revolver, receiving thirteen shillings in change from a five-pound note, and strode out of the shop, weapon in hand. He was gone before Lomax Harder decided upon a course of action.

'And for you, sir?' said Mr Gontle, addressing the poet.

Harder suddenly comprehended that Mr Gontle had mistaken him for a separate customer, who had happened to enter the shop a moment after the first one. Harder and Franting had said not a word to one another during the purchase, and Harder well knew that in the most exclusive shops it is the custom utterly to ignore a second customer until the first one has been dealt with.

'I want to see some foils.' Harder spoke stammeringly the only words that came into his head.

'Foils!' exclaimed Mr Gontle, shocked, as if to say: 'Is it conceivable that you should imagine that I, Gontle, gunsmith, sell such things as foils?'

After a little talk Harder apologized and departed – a thief.

'I'll call later and pay the fellow,' said Harder to his restive conscience. 'No. I can't do that. I'll send him some anonymous postal orders.'

He crossed the Parade and saw Franting, a small left-handed figure all alone far below on the deserted sands, pointing the revolver. He thought that his ear caught the sound of a discharge, but the distance was too great for him to be sure. He continued to watch, and at length Franting walked westward diagonally across the beach.

'He's going back to the Bellevue,' thought Harder, the Bellevue being the hotel from which he had met Franting coming out half an hour earlier. He strolled slowly towards the white hotel. But Franting, who had evidently come up the face of the cliff in the penny lift, was before him. Harder, standing outside, saw Franting seated in the lounge. Then Franting rose and vanished down a long passage at the rear of the lounge. Harder entered the hotel rather guiltily. There was no hall-porter at the door, and not a soul in the lounge or in sight of the lounge. Harder went down the long passage.

III

At the end of the passage Lomax Harder found himself in a billiard-room – an apartment built partly of brick and partly of wood on a sort of courtyard behind the main structure of the hotel. The roof, of iron and grimy glass, rose to a point in the middle. On two sides the high walls of the hotel obscured the light. Dusk was already closing in. A small fire burned feebly in the grate. A large radiator under the window was steel-cold, for though summer was finished, winter had not officially begun in the small economically-run hotel: so that the room was chilly; nevertheless, in deference to the English passion for fresh air and discomfort, the window was wide open.

Franting, in his overcoat, and an unlit cigarette between his lips, stood lowering with his back to the bit of fire. At sight of Harder he lifted his chin in a dangerous challenge.

'So you're still following me about,' he said resentfully to Harder.

'Yes,' said the latter, with his curious gentle primness of manner. 'I came down here specially to talk to you. I should have said all I had to say earlier, only you happened to be going out of the hotel just as I was coming in. You didn't seem to want to talk in the street; but there's some talking has to be done. I've a few things I must tell you.' Harder appeared to be perfectly calm, and he felt perfectly calm. He advanced from the door towards the billiard-table.

Franting raised his hand, displaying his square-ended, brutal fingers in the twilight.

'Now listen to me,' he said with cold, measured ferocity. 'You can't tell me anything I don't know. If there's some talking to be done I'll do it myself, and when I've finished you can get out. I know that my wife has taken a ticket for Copenhagen by the steamer from Harwich, and that she's been seeing to her passport, and packing. And of course I know that you have interests in Copenhagen and spend about half your precious time there. I'm not worrying to connect the two things. All that's got nothing to do with me. Emily has always seen a great deal of you, and I know that the last week or two she's been seeing you more than ever. Not that I mind that. I know that she objects to my treatment of her and my conduct generally. That's all right, but it's a matter that only concerns her and me. I mean that it's no concern of yours, for instance, or anybody else's. If she objects enough she can try and divorce me. I doubt if she'd succeed, but you can never be sure – with these new laws. Anyhow she's my wife till she does divorce me, and so she has the usual duties and responsibilities towards me – even though I was the worst husband in the world. That's how I look at it, in my old-fashioned way. I've just had a letter from her – she knew I was here, and I expect that explains how you knew I was here.'

'It does,' said Lomax Harder quietly.

Franting pulled a letter out of his inner pocket and unfolded it.

'Yes,' he said, glancing at it, and read some sentences aloud: 'I have absolutely decided to leave you, and I won't hide from you that I know you know who is doing what he can to help me. I can't live with you any longer. You may be very fond of me, as you say, but I find your way of showing your fondness too humiliating and painful. I've said this to you before, and now I'm saying it for the last time." And so on and so on.'

Franting tore the letter in two, dropped one half on the floor, twisted the other half into a spill, turned to the fire, and lit his cigarette.

'That's what I think of her letter,' he proceeded, the cigarette between his teeth. 'You're helping her, are you? Very well. I don't say you're in love with her, or she with you. I'll make no wild statements. But if you aren't in love with her I wonder why you're taking all this trouble over her. Do you go about the world helping ladies who say they're unhappy just for the pure sake of helping? Never mind. Emily isn't going to leave me. Get that into your head. I shan't let her leave me. She has money, and I haven't. I've been living on her, and it would be infernally awkward for me if she left me for good. That's a reason for keeping her, isn't it? But you may believe me or not – it isn't my reason. She's right enough when she says I'm very fond of her. That's a reason for keeping her too. But it isn't my reason. My reason is that a wife's a wife, and she can't break her word just because everything isn't lovely in the garden. I've heard it said I'm unmoral. I'm not all unmoral. And I feel particularly strongly about what's called the marriage tie.' He drew the revolver from his overcoat pocket, and held it up to view. 'You see this thing. You saw me buy it. Now you needn't be afraid. I'm not threatening you; and it's no part of my game to shoot you. I've nothing to do with your goings-on. What I have to do with is the goings-on of my wife. If she deserts me – for you or for anybody or for nobody – I shall follow her, whether it's to Copenhagen or Bangkok or the North Pole, and I shall kill her – with just this very revolver that you saw me buy. And now you can get out.'

Franting replaced the revolver, and began to consume the cigarette with fierce and larger puffs.

Lomax Harder looked at the grim, set, brutal, scowling bitter face, and knew that Franting meant what he had said. Nothing would stop him from carrying out his threat. The fellow was not an argufier; he could not reason; but he had unmistakable grit and would never recoil from the fear of consequences. If Emily left him, Emily was a dead woman; nothing in the end could protect her from the execution of her husband's menace. On the other hand, nothing would persuade her to remain with her husband. She had decided to go, and she would go. And indeed the mere thought of this lady to whom he, Harder, was utterly devoted, staying with her husband and continuing to suffer the tortures and humiliations which she had been suffering for years – this thought revolted him. He could not think it.

He stepped forward along the side of the billiard-table, and

simultaneously Franting stepped forward to meet him. Lomax
Harder snatched the revolver which was in his pocket, aimed, and
pulled the trigger.

Franting collapsed, with the upper half of his body somehow
balanced on the edge of the billiard-table. He was dead. The sound
of the report echoed in Harder's ear like the sound of a violin
string loudly twanged by a finger. He saw a little reddish hole in
Franting's bronzed right temple.

'Well,' he thought, 'somebody had to die. And it's better him
than Emily.' He felt that he had performed a righteous act. Also
he felt a little sorry for Franting.

Then he was afraid. He was afraid for himself, because he
wanted not to die, especially on the scaffold; but also for Emily
Franting who would be friendless and helpless without him; he
could not bear to think of her alone in the world – the central
point of a terrific scandal. He must get away instantly. . . .

Not down the corridor back into the hotel-lounge! No! That
would be fatal! The window. He glanced at the corpse. It was
more odd, curious, than affrighting. He had made the corpse.
Strange! He could not unmake it. He had accomplished the ir-
revocable. Impressive! He saw Franting's cigarette glowing on
the linoleum in the deepening dusk, and picked it up and threw
it into the fender.

Lace curtains hung across the whole width of the window.
He drew one aside, and looked forth. The light was much stronger
in the courtyard than within the room. He put his gloves on. He
gave a last look at the corpse, straddled the window-sill, and was
on the brick pavement of the courtyard. He saw that the curtain
had fallen back into the perpendicular.

He gazed around. Nobody! Not a light in any window! He
saw a green wooden gate, pushed it; it yielded; then a sort of
entry-passage. . . . In a moment, after two half-turns, he was on
the Marine Parade again. He was a fugitive. Should he fly to the
right, to the left? Then he had an inspiration. An idea of genius
for baffling pursuers. He would go into the hotel by the main-
entrance. He went slowly and deliberately into the portico, where
a middle-aged hall-porter was standing in the gloom.

'Good evening, sir.'

'Good evening. Have you got any rooms?'

'I think so, sir. The housekeeper is out, but she'll be back in a moment – if you'd like a seat. The manager's away in London.'

The hall-porter suddenly illuminated the lounge, and Lomax Harder, blinking, entered and sat down.

'I might have a cocktail while I'm waiting,' the murderer suggested with a bright and friendly smile. 'A Bronx.'

'Certainly, sir. The page is off duty. He sees to orders in the lounge, but I'll attend to you myself.'

'What a hotel!' thought the murderer, solitary in the chilly lounge, and gave a glance down the long passage. 'Is the whole place run by the hall-porter? But of course it's the dead season.'

Was it conceivable that nobody had heard the sound of the shot?

Harder had a strong impulse to run away. But no! To do so would be highly dangerous. He restrained himself.

'How much?' he asked of the hall-porter, who had arrived with surprising quickness, tray in hand and glass on tray.

'A shilling, sir.'

The murderer gave him eighteenpence, and drank off the cocktail.

'Thank you very much, sir.' The hall-porter took the glass.

'See here!' said the murderer. 'I'll look in again. I've got one or two little errands to do.'

And he went, slowly, into the obscurity of the Marine Parade.

IV

Lomax Harder leant over the left arm of the sea-wall of the man-made port of Quangate. Not another soul was there. Night had fallen. The lighthouse at the extremity of the right arm was oc-culting. The lights – some red, some green, many white – of ships at sea passed in both directions in endless processions. Waves plashed gently against the vast masonry of the wall. The wind, blowing steadily from the north-west, was not cold. Harder, looking about – though he knew he was absolutely alone, took his revolver from his overcoat pocket and stealthily dropped it into the sea. Then he turned round and gazed across the small harbour at the mysterious amphitheatre of the lighted town, and heard public clocks and religious clocks striking the hour.

He was a murderer, but why should he not successfully escape detection? Other murderers had done so. He had all his wits. He was not excited. He was not morbid. His perspective of things was not askew. The hall-porter had not seen his first entrance into the hotel, nor his exit after the crime. Nobody had seen them. He had left nothing behind in the billiard-room. No finger marks on the window-sill. (The putting-on of his gloves was in itself a clear demonstration that he had fully kept his presence of mind.) No footmarks on the hard, dry pavement of the court-yard.

Of course there was the possibility that some person unseen had seen him getting out of the window. Slight: but still a possibility! And there was also the possibility that someone who knew Franting by sight had noted him walking by Franting's side in the streets. If such a person informed the police and gave a description of him, inquiries might be made. . . . No! Nothing in it. His appearance offered nothing remarkable to the eye of a casual observer – except his forehead, of which he was rather proud, but which was hidden by his hat.

It was generally believed that criminals always did something silly. But so far he had done nothing silly, and he was convinced that, in regard to the crime, he never would do anything silly. He had none of the desire, supposed to be common among mur-derers, to revisit the scene of the crime or to look upon the corpse once more. Although he regretted the necessity for his act, he felt no slightest twinge of conscience. Somebody had to die, and surely it was better that a brute should die than the heavenly, enchanting, martyrized creature whom his act had rescued for ever from the brute! He was aware within himself of an ecstasy of devotion to Emily Franting – now a widow and free. She was a unique woman. Strange that a woman of such gifts should have come under the sway of so obvious a scoundrel as Franting. But she was very young at the time, and such freaks of sex had hap-pened before and would happen again; they were a widespread phenomenon in the history of the relations of men and women. He would have killed a hundred men if a hundred men had threatened her felicity. His heart was pure; he wanted nothing from Emily in exchange for what he had done in her defence. He was passionate in her defence. When he reflected upon the coarseness and cruelty of the gesture by which Franting had used Emily's letter to light his cigarette, Harder's cheeks grew hot with burning resentment.

A clock struck the quarter. Harder walked quickly to the harbour front, where was a taxi-rank, and drove to the station. . . . A sudden apprehension! The crime might have been discovered! Police might already be watching for suspicious-looking travellers! Absurd! Still, the apprehension remained despite its absurdity. The taxi-driver looked at him queerly. No! Imagination! He hesitated on the threshold of the station, then walked boldly in, and showed his return ticket to the ticket-inspector. No sign of a policeman. He got into the Pullman car, where five other passengers were sitting. The train started.

V

He nearly missed the boat-train at Liverpool Street because according to its custom the Quangate flyer arrived twenty minutes late at Victoria. And at Victoria the foolish part of him, as distinguished from the common-sense part, suffered another spasm of fear. Would detectives, instructed by telegraph, be waiting for the train? No! An absurd idea! The boat-train from Liverpool Street was crowded with travellers, and the platform crowded with senders-off. He gathered from scraps of talk overheard that an international conference was about to take place at Copenhagen. And he had known nothing of it – not seen a word of it in the papers! Excusable perhaps; graver matters had held his attention.

Useless to look for Emily in the vast bustle of the compartments! She had her through ticket (which she had taken herself, in order to avoid possible complications), and she happened to be the only woman in the world who was never late and never in a hurry. She was certain to be in the train. But was she in the train? Something sinister might have come to pass. For instance, a tele-

phone message to the flat that her husband had been found dead
with a bullet in his brain.

The swift two-hour journey to Harwich was terrible for Lomax
Harder. He remembered that he had left the unburnt part of the
letter lying under the billiard-table. Forgetful! Silly! One of the
silly things that criminals did! And on Parkeston Quay the confusion was enormous. He did not walk, he was swept, on to the
great shaking steamer whose dark funnels rose amid wisps of
steam into the starry sky. One advantage: detectives would have
no chance in that multitudinous scene, unless indeed they held up
the ship.

The ship roared a warning, and slid away from the quay, groped
down the tortuous channel to the harbour mouth, and was in the
North Sea; and England dwindled to naught but a string of lights.
He searched every deck from stem to stern, and could not find
Emily. She had not caught the train, or, if she had caught the
train, she had not boarded the steamer because he had failed to
appear. His misery was intense. Everything was going wrong.
And on the arrival at Esbjerg would not detectives be lying in
wait for the Copenhagen train? . . .

Then he descried her, and she him. She too had been searching.
Only chance had kept them apart. Her joy at finding him was
ecstatic; tears came into his eyes at sight of it. He was everything
to her, absolutely everything. He clasped her right hand in both
his hands and gazed at her in the dim, diffused light blended of
stars, moon and electricity. No woman was ever like her: mature,
innocent, wise, trustful, honest. And the touching beauty of her
appealing, sad, happy face, and the pride of her carriage! A
unique jewel – snatched from the brutal grasp of that fellow –
who had ripped her solemn letter in two and used it as a spill for
his cigarette! She related her movements; and he his. Then she
said:

'Well?'

'I didn't go,' he answered. 'Thought it best not to. I'm
convinced it wouldn't have been any use.'

He had not intended to tell her this lie. Yet when it came to the
point, what else could he say? He told one lie instead of twenty.

He was deceiving her, but for her sake. Even if the worst occurred, she was for ever safe from that brutal grasp. And he had
saved her. As for the conceivable complications of the future, he
refused to front them; he could live in the marvellous present. He
felt suddenly the amazing beauty of the night at sea, and beneath
all his other sensations was the obscure sensation of a weight at
his heart.

'I expect you were right,' she angelically acquiesced.

VI

The Superintendent of Police (Quangate was the county town of
the western half of the county), and a detective-sergeant were in
the billiard-room of the Bellevue. Both wore mufti. The powerful
green-shaded lamps usual in billiard-rooms shone down ruthlessly
on the green table, and on the reclining body of John Franting,
which had not moved and had not been moved.

A charwoman was just leaving these officers when a stout
gentleman, who had successfully beguiled a policeman guarding
the other end of the long corridor, squeezed past her, greeted the
two officers, and shut the door.

The Superintendent, a thin man, with lips to match, and a
moustache, stared hard at the arrival.

'I am staying with my friend Dr Furnival,' said the arrival
cheerfully. 'You telephoned for him, and as he had to go out
to one of those cases in which nature will not wait, I offered to
come in his place. I've met you before, Superintendent, at
Scotland Yard.'

'Dr Austin Bond!' exclaimed the Superintendent.

'He,' said the other.

They shook hands, Dr Bond genially, the Superintendent half-
consequential, half-deferential, as one who had his dignity to think
about; also as one who resented an intrusion, but dared not show
resentment.

The detective-sergeant recoiled at the dazzling name of the
great amateur detective, a genius who had solved the famous
mysteries of 'The Yellow Hat,' 'The Three Towns,' 'The Three
Feathers,' 'The Gold Spoon,' etc., etc., etc., whose devilish perspi-

cacity had again and again made professional detectives both look and feel foolish, and whose notorious friendship with the loftiest heads of Scotland Yard compelled all police forces to treat him very politely indeed.

'Yes,' said Dr Austin Bond, after detailed examination. 'Been shot about ninety minutes, poor fellow! Who found him?'

'That woman who's just gone out. Some servant here. Came in to look after the fire.'

'How long since?'

'Oh! About an hour ago.'

'Found the bullet? I see it hit the brass on that cue-rack there.'

The detective-sergeant glanced at the Superintendent, who, however, resolutely remained unastonished.

'Here's the bullet,' said the Superintendent.

'Ah!' commented Dr Austin Bond, glinting through his spectacles at the bullet as it lay in the Superintendent's hand. 'Decimal 38, I see. Flattened. It would be.'

'Sergeant,' said the Superintendent. 'You can get help and have the body moved, now Dr Bond has made his examination. Eh, Doctor?'

'Certainly,' answered Dr Bond, at the fireplace. 'He was smoking a cigarette, I see.'

'Either he or his murderer.'

'You've got a clue?'

'Oh yes,' the Superintendent answered, not without pride. 'Look here. Your torch, sergeant.'

The detective-sergeant produced a pocket electric-lamp, and the Superintendent turned to the window-sill.

'I've got a stronger one than that,' said Dr Austin Bond, producing another torch.

The Superintendent displayed finger-prints on the window-frame, footmarks on the sill, and a few strands of inferior blue cloth. Dr Austin Bond next produced a magnifying glass, and inspected the evidence at very short range.

'The murderer must have been a tall man — you can judge that from the angle of fire; he wore a blue suit, which he tore slightly on this splintered wood of the window-frame; one of his boots

had a hole in the middle of the sole, and he'd only three fingers
on his left hand. He must have come in by the window and gone
out by the window, because the hall-porter is sure that nobody
except the dead man entered the lounge by any door within an
hour of the time when the murder must have been committed.'
The Superintendent proudly gave many more details, and ended
by saying that he had already given instructions to circulate a
description.

'Curious,' said Dr Austin Bond, 'that a man like John Franting
should let anyone enter the room by the window! Especially a
shabby-looking man!'

'You knew the deceased personally then?'

'No! But I know he was John Franting.'

'How, Doctor?'

'Luck.'

'Sergeant,' said the Superintendent, piqued. 'Tell the constable
to fetch the hall-porter.'

Dr Austin Bond walked to and fro, peering everywhere, and
picked up a piece of paper that had lodged against the step of the
platform which ran round two sides of the room for the raising of
the spectators' benches. He glanced at the paper casually, and
dropped it again.

'My man,' the Superintendent addressed the hall-porter. 'How
can you be sure that nobody came in here this afternoon?'

'Because I was in my cubicle all the time, sir.'

The hall-porter was lying. But he had to think of his own
welfare. On the previous day he had been reprimanded for quitting
his post against the rule. Taking advantage of the absence of the
manager, he had sinned once again, and he lived in fear of dismissal if found out.

'With a full view of the lounge?'

'Yes, sir.'

'Might have been in there beforehand,' Dr Austin Bond
suggested.

'No,' said the Superintendent. 'The charwoman came in twice.
Once just before Franting came in. She saw the fire wanted making up and she went for some coal, and then returned later with

some coal. But the look of Franting frightened her, and she went
back with her coal.'

'Yes,' said the hall-porter. 'I saw that.'

Another lie.

At a sign from the Superintendent he withdrew.

'I should like to have a word with that charwoman,' said Dr
Austin Bond.

The Superintendent hesitated. Why should the great amateur
meddle with what did not concern him? Nobody had asked his
help. But the Superintendent thought of the amateur's relations
with Scotland Yard, and sent for the charwoman.

'Did you clean the window here to-day?' Dr Austin Bond
interrogated her.

'Yes, please, sir.'

'Show me your left hand.' The slattern obeyed. 'How did you
lose your little finger?'

'In a mangle accident, sir.'

'Just come to the window, will you, and put your hands on it.
But take off your left boot first.'

The slatten began to weep.

'It's quite all right, my good creature.' Dr Austin Bond reassured her. 'Your skirt is torn at the hem, isn't it?'

When the slattern was released from her ordeal and had gone,
carrying one boot in her grimy hand, Dr Austin Bond said genially
to the Superintendent:

'Just a fluke. I happened to notice she'd only three fingers on
her left hand when she passed me in the corridor. Sorry I've
destroyed your evidence. But I felt sure almost from the first
that the murderer hadn't either entered or decamped by the
window.'

'How?'

'Because I think he's still here in the room.'

The two police officers gazed about them as if exploring
the room for the murderer.

'I think he's there.'

Dr Austin Bond pointed to the corpse.

'And where did he hide the revolver after he'd killed himself?'

demanded the thin-lipped Superintendent icily, when he had somewhat recovered his aplomb.

'I'd thought of that, too,' said Dr Austin Bond, beaming. 'It is always a very wise course to leave a dead body absolutely untouched until a professional man has seen it. But *looking* at the body can do no harm. You see the left-hand pocket of the overcoat. Notice how it bulges. Something unusual in it. Something that has the shape of a – Just feel inside it, will you?'

The Superintendent, obeying, drew a revolver from the overcoat pocket of the dead man.

'Ah! Yes!' said Dr Austin Bond. 'A Webley Mark III. Quite new. You might take out the ammunition.' The Superintendent dismantled the weapon. 'Yes, yes! Three chambers empty. Wonder how he used the other two! Now, where's that bullet? You see? He fired. His arm dropped, and the revolver happened to fall into the pocket.'

'Fired with his left hand, did he?' asked the Superintendent, foolishly ironic.

'Certainly. A dozen years ago Franting was perhaps the finest amateur light-weight boxer in England. And one reason for it was that he bewildered his opponents by being left-handed. His lefts were much more fatal than his rights. I saw him box several times.'

Whereupon Dr Austin Bond strolled to the step of the platform near the door and picked up the fragment of very thin paper that was lying there.

'This,' said he, 'must have blown from the hearth to here by the draught from the window when the door was opened. It's part of a letter. You can see the burnt remains of the other part in the corner of the fender. He probably lighted the cigarette with it. Out of bravado! His last bravado! Read this.'

The Superintendent read:

'. . . repeat that I realize how fond you are of me, but you have killed my affection for you, and I shall leave our home tomorrow. This is absolutely final. E.'

Dr Austin Bond, having for the nth time satisfactorily demonstrated in his own unique, rapid way, that police-officers were a set of numskulls, bade the Superintendent a most courteous good evening, nodded amicably to the detective-sergeant, and left in triumph.

VII

'I must get some mourning and go back to the flat,' said Emily Franting.

She was sitting one morning in the lobby of the Palads Hotel, Copenhagen. Lomax Harder had just called on her with an English newspaper containing an account of the inquest at which the jury had returned a verdict of suicide upon the body of her late husband. Her eyes filled with tears.

'Time will put her right,' thought Lomax Harder, tenderly watching her. 'I was bound to do what I did. And I can keep a secret for ever.'

G. K. Chesterton

THE EYE OF APOLLO

THAT SINGULAR SMOKY sparkle, at once a confusion and a transparency, which is the strange secret of the Thames, was changing more and more from its grey to its glittering extreme as the sun climbed to the zenith over Westminster, and the two men crossed Westminster Bridge. One man was very tall and the other very short; they might even have been fantastically compared to the arrogant clock-tower of Parliament and the humbler humped shoulders of the Abbey, for the short man was in clerical dress. The official description of the tall man was M. Hercule Flambeau, private detective, and he was going to his new offices in a new pile of flats facing the Abbey entrance. The official description of the short man was the Rev. J. Brown, attached to St Francis Xavier's Church, Camberwell, and he was coming from a Camberwell death-bed to see the new offices of his friend.

The building was American in its sky-scraping altitude, and American also in the oiled elaboration of its machinery of telephones and lifts. But it was barely finished and still understaffed: only three tenants had moved in; the office just above Flambeau was occupied, as also was the office just below him; the two floors above that and the three floors below were entirely bare. But the first glance at the new tower of flats caught something much more arresting. Save for a few relics of scaffolding; the one glaring object was erected outside the office just above Flambeau's. It was an enormous gilt effigy of the human eye, surrounded with rays of gold, and taking up as much room as two or three office windows.

'What on earth is that?' asked Father Brown, and stood still.

'Oh, a new religion,' said Flambeau, laughing; 'one of those new religions that forgive your sins by saying you never had any.

Rather like Christian Science, I should think. The fact is that a
fellow calling himself Kalon (I don't know what his name is, except that it can't be that) has taken the flat just above me. I have
two lady typewriters underneath me, and this enthusiastic old
humbug on top. He calls himself the New Priest of Apollo, and he
worships the sun.'

'Let him look out,' said Father Brown. 'The sun was the
cruellest of all the gods. But what does that monstrous eye mean?'

'As I understand it, it is a theory of theirs,' answered Flambeau,
'that a man can endure anything if his mind is quite steady. Their
two great symbols are the sun and the open eye; for they say
that if a man were really healthy he could stare at the sun.'

'If a man were really healthy,' said Father Brown, 'he would
not bother to stare at it.'

'Well, that's all I can tell you about the new religion,' went on
Flambeau carelessly. 'It claims, of course, that it can cure all
physical diseases.'

'Can it cure the one spiritual disease?' asked Father Brown,
with a serious curiosity.

'And what is the one spiritual disease?' asked Flambeau,
smiling.

'Oh, thinking one is quite well,' said his friend.

Flambeau was more interested in the quiet little office below
him than in the flamboyant temple above. He was a lucid
Southerner, incapable of conceiving himself as anything but a
Catholic or an atheist; and new religions of a bright and pallid
sort were not much in his line. But humanity was always in his
line, especially when it was good-looking; moreover, the ladies
downstairs were characters in their way. The office was kept by
two sisters, both slight and dark, one of them tall and striking.
She had a dark, eager and aquiline profile, and was one of those
women whom one always thinks of in profile, as of the clean-cut
edge of some weapon. She seemed to cleave her way through life.
She had eyes of startling brilliancy, but it was the brilliancy of
steel rather than of diamonds; and her straight, slim figure was
a shade too stiff for its grace. Her younger sister was like her
shortened shadow, a little greyer, paler, and more insignificant.

They both wore a business-like black, with little masculine cuffs and collars. There are thousands of such curt, strenuous ladies in the offices of London, but the interest of these lay rather in their real than their apparent position.

For Pauline Stacey, the elder, was actually the heiress of a crest and half a county, as well as great wealth; she had been brought up in castles and gardens, before a frigid fierceness (peculiar to the modern woman) had driven her to what she considered a harsher and a higher existence. She had not, indeed, surrendered her money; in that there would have been a romantic or monkish abandon quite alien to her masterful utilitarianism. She held her wealth, she would say, for use upon practical social objects. Part of it she had put into her business, the nucleus of a model type-writing emporium; part of it was distributed in various leagues and causes for the advancement of such work among women. How far Joan, her sister and partner, shared this slightly prosaic ideal-ism no one could be very sure. But she followed her leader with a dog-like affection which was somehow more attractive – with its touch of tragedy – than the hard, high spirits of the elder. For Pauline Stacey had nothing to say to tragedy; she was understood to deny its existence.

Her rigid rapidity and cold impatience had amused Flambeau very much on the first occasion of his entering the flats. He had lingered outside the lift in the entrance-hall waiting for the lift-boy, who generally conducts strangers to the various floors. But this bright-eyed falcon of a girl had openly refused to endure such official delay. She said sharply that she knew all about the lift, and was not dependent on boys – or on men either. Though her flat was only three floors above, she managed in the few seconds of ascent to give Flambeau a great many of her fundamental views in an off-hand manner; they were to the general effect that she was a modern working woman and loved modern working ma-chinery. Her bright black eyes blazed with abstract anger against those who rebuke mechanic science and ask for the return of romance. Everyone, she said, ought to be able to manage ma-chines, just as she could manage the lift. She seemed almost to resent the fact of Flambeau opening the lift-door for her; and that gentleman went up to his own apartments smiling with somewhat mingled feelings at the memory of such spit-fire self-dependence.

She certainly had a temper, of a snappy, practical sort; the gestures of her thin, elegant hands were abrupt or even destructive. Once Flambeau entered her office on some typewriting business, and found she had just flung a pair of spectacles belonging to her sister into the middle of the floor and stamped on them. She was already in the rapids of an ethical tirade about the 'sickly medical notions' and the morbid admission of weakness implied in such an apparatus. She dared her sister to bring such artificial, unhealthy rubbish into the place again. She asked if she was expected to wear wooden legs or false hair or glass eyes; and as she spoke her eyes sparkled like the terrible crystal.

Flambeau, quite bewildered with this fanaticism, could not refrain from asking Miss Pauline (with direct French logic) why a pair of spectacles was a more morbid sign of weakness than a lift, and why, if science might help us in the one effort, it might not help us in the other.

'That is *so* different,' said Pauline Stacey loftily. 'Batteries and motors and all those things are marks of the force of man – yes, Mr Flambeau, and the force of women, too! We shall take our turn at these great engines that devour distance and defy time. That is high and splendid – that is really science. But these nasty props and plasters the doctors sell – why, they are just badges of poltroonery. Doctors stick on legs and arms as if we were born cripples and sick slaves. But I was free-born, Mr Flambeau! People only think they need these things because they have been trained in fear instead of being trained in power and courage, just as the silly nurses tell children not to stare at the sun, and so they can't do it without blinking. But why among the stars should there be one star I may not see? The sun is not my master, and I will open my eyes and stare at him whenever I choose.'

'Your eyes,' said Flambeau, with a foreign bow, 'will dazzle the sun.' He took pleasure in complimenting this strange stiff beauty, partly because it threw her a little off her balance. But as he went upstairs to his floor he drew a deep breath and whistled, saying to himself: 'So she has got into the hands of that conjurer upstairs with his golden eye.' For, little as he knew or cared about the new religion of Kalon, he had heard of his special notion about sun-gazing.

He soon discovered that the spiritual bond between the floors above and below him was close and increasing. The man who called himself Kalon was a magnificent creature, worthy, in a physical sense, to be the pontiff of Apollo. He was nearly as tall even as Flambeau, and very much better looking, with a golden beard, strong blue eyes, and a mane flung back like a lion's. In structure he was the blond beast of Nietzsche, but all this animal beauty was heightened, brightened and softened by genuine intellect and spirituality. If he looked like one of the great Saxon kings he looked like one of the kings that were also saints. And this despite the cockney incongruity of his surroundings; the fact that he had an office half-way up a building in Victoria Street; that the clerk (a commonplace youth in cuffs and collars) sat in the outer room, between him and the corridor; that his name was on a brass plate, and the gilt emblem of his creed hung above his street, like the advertisement of an occulist. All this vulgarity could not take away from the man called Kalon the vivid oppression and inspiration that came from his soul and body. When all was said, a man in the presence of this quack did feel in the presence of a great man. Even in the loose jacket-suit of linen that he wore as a workshop dress in his office he was a fascinating and formidable figure; and when robed in the white vestments and crowned with the golden circlet, in which he daily saluted the sun, he really looked so splendid that the laughter of the street people sometimes died suddenly on their lips. For three times in the day the new sun-worshipper went out on his little balcony, in the face of all Westminster, to say some litany to his shining lord: once at day-break, once at sunset, and once at the shock of noon. And it was while the shock of noon still shook faintly from the towers of Parliament and parish church that Father Brown, the friend of Flambeau, first looked up and saw the white priest of Apollo.

Flambeau had seen quite enough of these daily salutations of Phœbus, and plunged into the porch of the tall building without even looking for his clerical friend to follow. But Father Brown, whether from a professional interest in ritual or a strong individual interest in tomfoolery, stopped and stared up at the balcony of the sun-worshipper, just as he might have stopped and stared up at a Punch and Judy. Kalon the Prophet was already erect, with argent garments and uplifted hands, and the sound of his strangely penetrating voice could be heard all the way down the busy street uttering his solar litany. He was already in the middle of it; his eyes were fixed upon the flaming disc. It is doubtful if he saw anything or anyone on this earth; it is substantially certain that he did not see a stunted, round-faced priest who, in the crowd below, looked up at him with blinking eyes. That was perhaps the most startling difference between even these two far divided men. Father Brown could not look at anything without blinking; but the priest of Apollo could look on the blaze at noon without a quiver of the eyelid.

'O sun,' cried the prophet, 'O star that art too great to be allowed among the stars! O fountain that flowest quietly in that secret spot that is called space. White father of all white unwearied things, white flames and white flowers and white peaks. Father, who art more innocent than all thy most innocent and quiet children; primal purity, into the peace of which –'

A rush and crash like the reversed rush of a rocket was cloven with a strident and incessant yelling. Five people rushed into the gate of the mansions as three people rushed out, and for an instant they all deafened each other. The sense of some utterly abrupt horror seemed for a moment to fill half the street with bad news – bad news that was all the worse because no one knew what it was. Two figures remained still after the crash of commotion: the fair priest of Apollo on the balcony above, and the ugly priest of Christ below him.

At last the tall figure and titanic energy of Flambeau appeared in the doorway of the mansions and dominated the little mob. Talking at the top of his voice like a fog-horn, he told somebody or anybody to go for a surgeon; and as he turned back into the dark and thronged entrance his friend Father Brown slipped in insignificantly after him. Even as he ducked and dived through the crowd he could still hear the magnificent melody and monotony of the solar priest still calling on the happy god who is the friend of fountains and flowers.

Father Brown found Flambeau and some six other people standing round the enclosed space into which the lift commonly descended. But the lift had not descended. Something else had descended; something that ought to have come by a lift.

For the last four minutes Flambeau had looked down on it; had seen the brained and bleeding figure of that beautiful woman who denied the existence of tragedy. He had never had the slightest doubt that it was Pauline Stacey; and, though he had sent for a doctor, he had not the slightest doubt that she was dead.

He could not remember for certain whether he had liked her or disliked her; there was so much both to like and dislike. But she had been a person to him, and the unbearable pathos of details and habit stabbed him with all the small daggers of bereavement. He remembered her pretty face and priggish speeches with a sudden secret vividness which is all the bitterness of death. In an instant, like a bolt from the blue, like a thunderbolt from nowhere, that beautiful and defiant body had been dashed down the open well of the lift to death at the bottom. Was it suicide? With so insolent an optimist it seemed impossible. Was it murder? But who was there in those hardly inhabited flats to murder anybody? In a rush of raucous words, which he meant to be strong and suddenly found weak, he asked where was that fellow Kalon. A voice, habitually heavy, quiet and full, assured him that Kalon for the last fifteen minutes had been away up on his balcony worshipping his god. When Flambeau heard the voice, and felt the hand of Father Brown, he turned his swarthy face and said abruptly:

'Then, if he has been up there all the time, who can have done it?'

'Perhaps,' said the other, 'we might go upstairs and find out. We have half an hour before the police will move.'

Leaving the body of the slain heiress in charge of the surgeons,

Flambeau dashed up the stairs to the typewriting office, found it utterly empty, and dashed up to his own. Having entered that, he returned with a new and white face to his friend.

'Her sister,' he said, with an unpleasant seriousness, 'her sister seems to have gone out for a walk.'

Father Brown nodded. 'Or, she may have gone up to the office of that sun man,' he said. 'If I were you I should just verify that, and then let us talk it over in your office. No,' he added suddenly, as if remembering something; 'shall I ever get over that stupidity of mine? Of course, in their office downstairs.'

Flambeau stared; but he followed the little father downstairs to the empty flat of the Staceys, where that impenetrable pastor took a large red-leather chair in the very entrance, from which he could see the stairs and landings, and waited. He did not wait very long. In about four minutes three figures descended the stairs, alike only in their solemnity. The first was Joan Stacey, the sister of the dead woman – evidently she *had* been upstairs in the temporary temple of Apollo; the second was the priest of Apollo himself, his litany finished, sweeping down the empty stairs in utter magnificence – something in his white robes, beard and parted hair had the look of Doré's Christ leaving the Pretorium; the third was Flambeau, black browed and somewhat bewildered.

Miss Joan Stacey, dark, with a drawn face and hair prematurely touched with grey, walked straight to her own desk and set out her papers with a practical flap. The mere action rallied everyone else to sanity. If Miss Joan Stacey was a criminal, she was a cool one. Father Brown regarded her for some time with an odd little smile, and then, without taking his eyes off her, addressed himself to somebody else.

'Prophet,' he said, presumably addressing Kalon, 'I wish you would tell me a lot about your religion.'

'I shall be proud to do it,' said Kalon, inclining his still crowned head, 'but I am not sure that I understand.'

'Why, it's like this,' said Father Brown, in his frankly doubtful way. 'We are taught that if a man has really bad first principles, that must be partly his fault. But, for all that, we can make some difference between a man who insults his quite clear conscience more or less crowded with sophistries. Now, do you really think that murder is wrong at all?'

'Is this an accusation?' asked Kalon very quietly.

'No,' answered Brown, equally gently, 'it is the speech for the defence.'

In the long and startled stillness of the room the prophet of Apollo slowly rose, and really it was like the rising of the sun. He filled that room with his light and life in such a manner that a man felt he could as easily have filled Salisbury Plain. His robed form seemed to hang the whole room with classic draperies; his epic gesture seemed to extend it into grander perspectives, till the little black figure of the modern cleric seemed to be a fault and an intrusion, a round, black blot upon some splendour of Hellas.

'We meet at last, Caiaphas,' said the prophet. 'Your church and mine are the only realities on this earth. I adore the sun, and you the darkening of the sun; you are the priest of the dying, and I of the living God. Your present work of suspicion and slander is worthy of your coat and creed. All your church is but a black police; you are only spies and detectives seeking to tear from men confessions of guilt, whether by treachery or torture. You would convict men of crime, I would convict them of innocence. You would convince them of sin, I would convince them of virtue.

'Reader of the books of evil, one more word before I blow away your baseless nightmares for ever. Not even faintly could you understand how little I care whether you can convict me or no. The things you call disgrace and horrible hanging are to me no more than an ogre in a child's toybook to a man once grown up. You said you were offering the speech for the defence. I care so little for the cloudland of this life that I will offer you the speech for the prosecution. There is but one thing that can be said against me in this matter, and I will say it myself. The woman that is dead was my love and my bride; not after such manner as your tin chapels call lawful, but by a law purer and sterner than you will ever understand. She and I walked another

world from yours, and trod places of crystal while you were
plodding through tunnels and corridors of brick. Well, I know
that policemen, theological and otherwise, always fancy that
where there has been love there must soon be hatred; so there
you have the first point made for the prosecution. But the second
point is stronger; I do not grudge it you. Not only is it true that
Pauline loved me, but it is also true that this very morning, before
she died, she wrote at that table a will leaving me and my new
church half a million. Come, where are the handcuffs? Do you
suppose I care what foolish things you do with me? Penal servitude will only be like waiting for her at a wayside station. The
gallows will only be going to her in a headlong car.'

He spoke with the brain-shaking authority of an orator, and
Flambeau and Joan Stacey stared at him in an amazed admiration. Father Brown's face seemed to express nothing but extreme
distress; he looked at the ground with one wrinkle of pain across
his forehead. The prophet of the sun leaned easily against the
mantelpiece and resumed:

'In a few words I have put before you the whole case against
me – the only possible case against me. In fewer words still I will
blow it to pieces, so that not a trace of it remains. As to whether
I have committed this crime, the truth is in one sentence: I
could not have committed this crime. Pauline Stacey fell from
this floor to the ground at five minutes past twelve. A hundred
people will go into the witness-box and say that I was standing
out upon the balcony of my own rooms above from just before
the stroke of noon to a quarter-past – the usual period of my
public prayers. My clerk (a respectable youth from Clapham,
with no sort of connection with me) will swear that he sat in my
outer office all the morning, and that no communication passed
through. He will swear that I arrived a full ten minutes before
the hour, fifteen minutes before any whisper of the accident, and
that I did not leave the office or the balcony all that time. No
one ever had so complete an alibi: I could subpœna half Westminster. I think you had better put the handcuffs away again.
The case is at an end.

'But last of all, that no breath of this idiotic suspicion remain in the air, I will tell you all you want to know. I believe I do know how my unhappy friend came by her death. You can, if you choose, blame me for it, or my faith and philosophy at least; but you certainly cannot lock me up. It is well known to all students of the higher truths that certain adepts and *illuminati* have in history attained the power of levitation – that is, of being self-sustained upon the empty air. It is but a part of that general conquest of matter which is the main element in our occult wisdom. Poor Pauline was of an impulsive and ambitious temper. I think, to tell the truth, she thought herself somewhat deeper in the mysteries than she was; and she has often said to me, as we went down in the lift together, that if one's will were strong enough, one could float down as harmlessly as a feather. I solemnly believe that in some ecstasy of noble thoughts she attempted the miracle. Her will, or faith, must have failed her at the crucial instant, and the lower law of matter had its horrible revenge. There is the whole story, gentlemen, very sad and, as you think, very presumptuous and wicked, but certainly not criminal or in any way connected with me. In the shorthand of the police-courts, you had better call it suicide. I shall always call it heroic failure for the advance of science and the slow scaling of heaven.'

It was the first time Flambeau had ever seen Father Brown vanquished. He still sat looking at the ground, with a painful and corrugated brow, as if in shame. It is impossible to avoid the feeling which the prophet's winged words had fanned, that here was a sullen, professional suspector of men overwhelmed by a prouder and purer spirit of natural liberty and health. At last he said, blinking as if in bodily distress: 'Well, if that is so, sir, you need do no more than take the testamentary paper you spoke of and go. I wonder where the poor lady left it.'

'It will be over there on her desk by the door, I think,' said Kalon, with that massive innocence of manner that seemed to acquit him wholly. 'She told me specially she would write it this morning, and I actually saw her writing as I went up in the lift to my own room.'

'Was her door open then?' asked the priest, with his eye on a corner of the matting.

'Yes,' said Kalon calmly.

'Ah! it has been open ever since,' said the other, and resumed his silent study of the mat.

'There is a paper over here,' said the grim Miss Joan, in a somewhat singular voice. She had passed over to her sister's desk by the doorway, and was holding a sheet of blue foolscap in her hand. There was a sour smile on her face that seemed unfit for such a scene or occasion, and Flambeau looked at her with a darkening brow.

Kalon the prophet stood away from the paper with that royal unconsciousness that had carried him through. But Flambeau took it out of the lady's hand and read it with the utmost amazement. It did, indeed, begin in the formal manner of a will, but after the words 'I give and bequeath all of which I die possessed' the writing abruptly stopped with a set of scratches, and there was no trace of the name of any legatee. Flambeau, in wonder, handed this to his friend, who glanced at it and silently gave it to the priest of the sun.

An instant afterwards that pontiff, in his splendid sweeping draperies, had crossed the room in two great strides, and was towering over Joan Stacey, his blue eyes standing from his head.

'What monkey tricks have you been playing here?' he cried. 'That's not all Pauline wrote.'

They were startled to hear him speak in quite a new voice, with a Yankee shrillness in it; all his grandeur and good English had fallen from him like a cloak.

'That is the only thing on her desk,' said Joan, and confronted him steadily with the same smile of evil favour.

Of a sudden the man broke out into blasphemies and cataracts of incredulous words. There was something shocking about the dropping of his mask; it was like a man's real face falling off.

'See here!' he cried in broad American, when he was breathless with cursing; 'I may be an adventurer, but I guess you're a murderess. Yes, gentlemen, here's your death explained, and without any levitation. The poor girl is writing a will in my favour; her cursed sister comes in, struggles for the pen, drags her to the well, and throws her down before she can finish it. Sakes! I reckon we want the handcuffs after all.'

'As you have truly remarked,' replied Joan, with ugly calm, 'your clerk is a very respectable young man, who knows the nature of an oath; and he will swear in any court that I was up in your office arranging some typewriting work for five minutes before and five minutes after my sister fell. Mr Flambeau will say he found me there.'

There was a silence.

'Why, then,' cried Flambeau, 'Pauline was alone when she fell, and it was suicide!'

'She was alone when she fell,' said Father Brown, 'but it was not suicide.'

'Then how did she die?' asked Flambeau impatiently.

'She was murdered.'

'But she was all alone,' objected the detective.

'She was murdered when she was all alone,' answered the priest.

All the rest stared at him, but he remained sitting in the same old dejected attitude, with a wrinkle in his round forehead and an appearance of impersonal shame and sorrow; his voice was colourless and sad.

'What I want to know,' cried Kalon, with an oath, 'is when the police are coming for this bloody and wicked sister. She's killed her flesh and blood; she's robbed me of half a million that was just as sacredly mine as –'

'Come, come, prophet,' interrupted Flambeau, with a kind of sneer; 'remember that all this world is a cloudbank.'

The hierophant of the sun-god made an effort to climb back on to his pedestal. 'It is not the mere money,' he cried, 'though that would equip the cause throughout the world. It is also my beloved one's wishes. To Pauline all this was holy. In Pauline's eyes –'

Father Brown suddenly sprang erect, so that his chair fell over flat behind him. He was deathly pale, yet he seemed fired with a hope; his eyes shone.

' That's it! ' he cried in a clear voice. ' That's the way to begin.
In Pauline's eyes –'

The tall prophet retreated before the tiny priest in an almost
mad disorder. 'What do you mean? How dare you?' he cried
repeatedly.

' In Pauline's eyes,' repeated the priest, his own shining more
and more. 'Go on – in God's name, go on. The foulest crime the
fiends ever prompted feels lighter after confession; and I implore
you to confess. Go on, go on – in Pauline's eyes –'

' Let me go, you devil! ' thundered Kalon, struggling like a
giant in bonds. 'Who are you, you cursed spy, to weave your
spider's webs round me, and peep and peer? Let me go.'

' Shall I stop him?' asked Flambeau, bounding towards the
exit, for Kalon had already thrown the door wide open.

' No; let him pass,' said Father Brown, with a strange deep
sigh that seemed to come from the depths of the universe. ' Let
Cain pass by, for he belongs to God.'

There was a long-drawn silence in the room when he had left
it, which was to Flambeau's fierce wits one long agony of interrogation. Miss Joan Stacey very coolly tidied the papers on her
desk.

' Father,' said Flambeau at last, ' it is my duty, not my curiosity
only – it is my duty to find out if I can, who committed the
crime.'

' Which crime?' asked Father Brown.

' The one we are dealing with, of course,' replied his impatient
friend.

' We are dealing with two crimes,' said Brown; 'crimes of a
very different weight – and by very different criminals.'

Miss Joan Stacey, having collected and put away her papers,
proceeded to lock up her drawer. Father Brown went on, noticing
her as little as she noticed him.

' The two crimes,' he observed, ' were committed against the
same weakness of the same person, in a struggle for her money.
The author of the larger crime found himself thwarted by the
smaller crime; the author of the smaller crime got the
money.'

'Oh, don't go on like a lecturer,' groaned Flambeau; 'put it in a few words.'

'I can put it in one word,' answered his friend.

Miss Joan Stacey skewered her business-like black hat on to her head with a business-like black frown before a little mirror, and, as the conversation proceeded, took her handbag and umbrella in an unhurried style, and left the room.

'The truth is in one word, and a short one.' said Father Brown. 'Pauline Stacey was blind.'

'Blind!' repeated Flambeau, and rose slowly to his whole huge stature.

'She was subject to it by blood,' Brown proceeded. 'Her sister would have started eyeglasses if Pauline would have let her; but it was her special philosophy or fad that one must not encourage such diseases by yielding to them. She would not admit the cloud; or she tried to dispel it by will. So her eyes got worse and worse with straining; but the worst strain was to come. It came with this precious prophet, or whatever he calls himself, who taught her to stare at the hot sun with the naked eye. It was called accepting Apollo. Oh, if these new pagans would only be old pagans, they would be a little wiser! The old pagans knew that mere naked Nature-worship has a cruel side. They knew that the eye of Apollo can blast and blind.'

There was a pause, and the priest went on in a gentle and even broken voice: 'Whether or no that devil deliberately made her blind, there is no doubt that he deliberately killed her through her blindness. The very simplicity of the crime is sickening. You know he and she went up and down in those lifts without official help; you know also how smoothly and silently the lifts slide. Kalon brought the lift to the girl's landing, and saw her, through the open door, writing in her slow, sightless way the will she had promised him. He called out to her cheerily that he had the lift ready for her, and she was to come out when she was ready. Then he pressed a button and shot soundlessly up to his own floor, walked through his own office, out on to his own balcony, and was safely praying before the crowded street when the poor girl, having finished her work, ran gaily out to where her lover and lift were to receive her, and stepped –'

'Don't!' cried Flambeau.

'He ought to have got half a million by pressing that button,' continued the little father in the colourless voice in which he talked of such horrors; 'but that went smash. It went smash because there happened to be another person who also wanted the money, and who also knew the secret about poor Pauline's sight. There was one thing about that will that I think nobody noticed: although it was unfinished and without a signature, the other Miss Stacey and some servant of hers had already signed it as witnesses. Joan had signed first, saying Pauline could finish it later, with a typical feminine contempt for legal forms. Therefore, Joan wanted her sister to sign the will without real witnesses. Why? I thought of the blindness, and felt sure she had wanted Pauline to sign in solitude because she had wanted her not to sign at all.

'People like the Staceys always use fountain pens; but this was specially natural to Pauline. By habit and her strong will and her memory she could still write almost as well as if she saw; but she could not tell when her pen needed dipping. Therefore, her fountain pens were carefully filled by her sister – all except this fountain pen. This was carefully *not* filled by her sister; the remains of the ink held out for a few lines and then failed altogether. And the prophet lost five hundred thousand pounds and committed one of the most brutal and brilliant murders in human history for nothing.'

Flambeau went to the open door and heard the official police ascending the stairs. He turned and said: 'You must have followed everything devilish close to have traced the crime to Kalon in ten minutes.'

Father Brown gave a sort of start.

'Oh! to him,' he said. 'No; I had to follow rather close to find out about Miss Joan and the fountain pen. But I knew Kalon was the criminal before I came into the front door.'

'You must be joking!' cried Flambeau.

'I'm quite serious,' answered the priest. 'I tell you I knew he had done it, even before I knew what he had done.'

'But why?'

'These pagan stoics,' said Brown reflectively, 'always fail by their strength. There came a crash and a scream down the street, and the priest of Apollo did not start or look round. I did not know what it was; but I knew that he was expecting it.'

Michael Innes

A MATTER OF GOBLINS

'YOU'RE SURE IT'S uninhabited?' Sir John Appleby peered ahead rather apprehensively as the car moved slowly over the uneven track. 'There isn't a resident squire? The Pooles are one of those families that have entirely evaporated from the English scene?'

'How inquiring you turn when we have a small job of trespass on hand.' Lady Appleby pressed firmly on the accelerator. 'I don't know why even an eminent policeman need be so law-abiding. As for the Pooles, I believe there are plenty of them.'

'But not here? Look out for that cow.'

'Not here. I don't know that Water Poole ought to be called uninhabited. That, to my mind, suggests ruins and generations of emptiness. But I understand that it's certainly unoccupied and beginning to tumble to pieces. You'll see for yourself.'

'You mean we're to go *in*?'

'Of course. That's always the real fun. There'll be a window.'

Appleby groaned. 'Judith my dear, I forsee it all. Indeed, it has happened again and again. We break in. We cover ourselves with dust and cobweb. We twist our ankles in rotting floorboards. And then the man comes.'

'Nonsense.'

'We hear him approaching with a sinister limp. He is simply some cottager told off to keep an eye on the place. But we are petrified. You are even more terror-struck than I am. Your bravado deserts you. Out of compassion for your pitiable condition, I consent to our hiding in a cupboard. And there the man finds us.'

'I never heard such rot. Such a thing has never happened to us. Or only once.'

'I rattle my small change loudly in my pocket and assume an air of jaunty patronage. The good old man –'

'The what?'

'That's what he is. The good old man fails to hear the half-crowns. He is unaware of my manner, which I myself distinguish with piercing clarity as indistinguishable from that of numerous petty criminals of my acquaintance. But he does recognize both your accent and your clothes as virtually identical with those of the late squire's dear old mother –'

'I think you're abominable.'

'And so – in a humiliating sort of way – all is well, and we are shown round and offered a lot of inaccurate antiquarian information. As we leave, I give the good old man five shillings. He touches his hat respectfully – to you.'

'Then that's all right.' Judith Appleby slowed down to avoid another cow. 'It looks to me as if there has been a car along here already today.'

'I'd say there have been several.' Appleby picked up a map. 'And that's odd, for this certainly leads to the manor house and no further. And it's curious, by the way, that a place of some apparent consequence should never have run to a better approach.'

'It may have been less primitive at one time. And, of course, they always had the river.' Judith pointed to a line of poplars in the middle distance. 'It's quite navigable from here to where it joins the Thames, and probably some of their heavy stuff used to come and go by water. But one of the fascinating things about Water Poole, I gather, is just its remarkable isolation. There's really nothing for miles. . . . And there it is.'

They had swung round a clump of beech trees still in their freshest green, and now the venerable Elizabethan house was directly in front of them. Involuntarily, they both exclaimed in dismay. Water Poole was a larger place than they had expected, and much more nearly ruinous. Approaching from this aspect, one might have supposed some labour of demolition to be in progress – had one not become aware at the same time of absolute solitude and silence.

The ground-plan of the building appeared to be the familiar Tudor H. And one of the end pavilions – it must in fact have constituted a stack of handsome rooms – had come down in a mass of rubble which spread far across the derelict open court-yard before them. Already the tumbled stone and plaster was in part overgrown with hemlock and thistle. And high up, in-congruously reminiscent of bomb damage in a London square, they could see a single slice of an augustly panelled apartment, with swallows nesting under the narrow strip of ceiling that re-mained to it. Elsewhere the long grey façade, which for centuries had faced this empty landscape with a mellow confidence, was flaked and cracked and crumbling round gaping windows and below a broken balustrade. It had been a noble dwelling – and now its whole appearance was so forlorn and disgraced that Appleby had the feeling of having committed an unseemly in-trusion. Even the hum of the car seemed an impertinence. The same impression must have come to Judith, for she slipped out of gear and switched off the engine. They glided forward silently into the embracing silence of the place. It was like a physical medium receiving them and covering them, as if they had been swimmers plunging without a ripple into a deep still lake.

'Somebody told me it was occupied during the war – shared by two families.' Unconsciously Judith had lowered her voice, as one might do in the presence of some meditating sage. 'But it looks far too ruinous for that.'

'There's plenty of it, and matters mayn't be so bad on the other side.'

'But they've plainly let it go. Nobody is hoping ever to bring it to life again.' Judith stopped the car and they got out. 'It's enormous. And that's made it too stiff a commitment for what-ever Pooles remain.'

Appleby nodded. 'Certainly it's on the large side. Indeed, it's more like one of the show-places put up by Elizabeth's great courtiers than a run-of-the-mill manor house. Who are these Pooles?'

'An old family, I believe, taking their name from this part of the shire, and giving it to the house when they built it. They met disaster in the Civil War; a father and two sons all killed at Naseby. Now, I imagine, they are impoverished, and quite insignificant as well. Shall we go ahead?' Judith, as she asked this question, was already in vigorous forward motion.

'There will be no harm in walking round the gardens.' Appleby put forward this proposition not very hopefully. 'But undoubtedly it lays us open to misconception.'

'We might be taken for thieves?' Judith was amused. 'I don't see much that we could make away with.'

'There's probably thousands of pounds' worth of lead on the roof.' Appleby stopped suddenly. 'I wonder if somebody *has* been after that? The ground suggests a good deal of recent coming and going. Or perhaps people help themselves to loads of that rubble. It could be useful in all sorts of ways. We'll go round the house and down to the river.'

For some seconds they walked on without speaking. Even in the clear light and gentle warmth of this early morning in June there was something insistently depressing about Water Poole in its last long agony. They climbed by insecure and treacherous steps to a mouldering terrace fast disappearing under a lush growth of summer weeds. They passed between the side of the house and a large formal garden which was now mere wilderness. And presently they came to the river frontage. 'Why,' Judith exclaimed, 'it *is* better — ever so much better. It's almost cheerful.'

'I don't know that I'd go as far as that. But at least they've cut the grass. Odd, perhaps – but meritorious.'

On this side too the house was elevated behind a terrace, and between the terrace and the river lay a broad expanse of turf. This was not in good condition, but it had certainly been recently mown with some care. Judith looked at it in perplexity. 'I suppose it's a gallant attempt to make a decent show. But who's to see it? No one would bring a sail up here, and its decidedly remote for canoes or punts. . . . The fabric's better, too.'

Appleby turned. The house as viewed from this angle was plainly in disastrous disrepair, but it bore no suggestion of falling to pieces. The terrace here was in tolerable order, the windows were either glazed or decently shuttered, and under a massive portico a stout oak door appeared firmly shut. Rather to his wife's surprise, Appleby led the way across the grass and climbed a broad flight of steps that rose to the house between battered statues. 'Weeded,' he said. 'And they don't tilt disconcertingly when you tread on them.' He stooped. 'Patched up, after a fashion.' He reached the terrace, walked to the oak door and tried it. 'Locked.' And this time, to Judith's positive astonishment, he gave it an impatient rattle. 'Shades of Dr Johnson's father.'

'Dr Johnson's father, John?'

'Don't you remember? Every night old Michael Johnson went out and locked with great care the front door of a building which no longer had any back to it. Young Sam was afraid he was going off his head. Well, Water Poole has a back rather like that. So if we *do* want to go inside there's no particular difficulty. We just go round to the other side again.'

'Then here goes – and I believe you're quite as curious as I am.'

'It's the place that's curious – not me.' For a moment Appleby turned to glance again at the river. It was no more than a stream, but he judged it to hold promise of excellent trout. 'And as for that lawn –' He broke off, and they returned to the back of the house in silence.

On this side the terrace half-obscured a basement floor of cellars and offices, and into these they walked without hindrance. For a time they wandered among flagged chambers and passages, either vaulted or with plaster ceilings most of which now lay on the floors. Here and there were vast fire-places, cumbersome stone troughs, gloomy larders and pantries with massive slate shelves on a scale suggesting a morgue. Nothing movable was to be seen – except in one obscure recess a heap of brushwood disposed into a rough bed, with signs of a small fire nearby, as if a tramp of the more pronouncedly melancholic sort had recently chosen this congenial spot for temporary residence. It was clear that in modern times the house when occupied must have achieved more practicable domestic arrangements on the next floor. And to this the Applebys presently climbed. So far, it had all been most depressing, and Judith's whole exploration appeared to hold every promise of ending in mere dismalness. Appleby endeavoured to enliven the proceedings by affecting to hear the threatening approach of the man. His wife however was not amused.

But upstairs it was different. The great hall was a stately place, with high mullioned windows looking towards the river, a fine linen-fold panelling which must have been older than the house itself, and an elaborately ribbed plaster vaulting with pendants. These last had mostly broken off, and the effect was oddly like one of those caves or grottos in which eighteenth-century gentlemen amused themselves by shooting down the stalactites. But to an eye failing to travel so high as this the impression was less of decay than of suspended animation. Here was the very heart of the house, and it still faintly beat. It seemed only to be awaiting some prompting occasion to pulse more strongly, until the place felt the quickening flood in all its enchanted limbs, and stirred and breathed again.

Judith paced the length of the hall from screen to dais, and there stood quite still, as if she were listening. When she came back her expression had changed. 'It's queer,' she said. 'There's something.'

'Something?'

'Don't you feel it?' She smiled at him, faintly puzzled. 'But of course you don't. It's not your line.'

'If you mean ghosts and what not, I didn't know it was your line either.'

'Not quite ghosts. Unless – yes – a throng of ghosts. I have a feeling of time shutting up, telescoping. Our time and theirs. So that they were here – and have all gone away – only today or yesterday.'

Appleby was examining on the great carved screen a fine series of panels exhibiting the motive of an arch in perspective. 'My dear girl, who are "they"?'

'I don't know.' She laughed at her own absurdity. 'Gentlemen adventurers bound for the Spanish Main. Cavaliers riding away to join Prince Rupert or the King. If we had been just a little earlier we might have seen them. They forded the river, I think, and rode away at dawn.'

'You ought to have gone in for historical novels, not for sculpture. But – talking of that – look at the chimney-piece. It's rather good, in a florid way.'

They studied it for some minutes: an affair of Hermes-figures dolphins and cupids, surmounted by an ornate heraldic carving. 'It's odd about names,' Judith said. 'They don't go in for a pool, but a pole.' She pointed to this element in the elaborate coat of arms that crowned the structure. 'But what's that piece of carving lower down? I'd say it's been added later.'

'It's another pole – chopped in two by a sword. What's called an emblem, rather than heraldry proper. And there's a motto. No – it's simply a date. Can you see?'

'Yes.' There was clear sunlight in the hall, and Judith had no difficulty. What she read was:

y^e *14 June*

16$\frac{1}{4}$5

Appleby thought for a moment. 'Naseby, in fact. The Pooles were in no doubt about that battle's being the end of them.'

'And this is the tenth.'

'The tenth?' He was at a loss.

'Of June. Four days to the anniversary. No wonder –' She broke off. 'John, there's somebody coming. There really is, this time.'

Appleby listened. There could be no doubt about the advancing footsteps. 'Then we go through with it, as usual. Unless, of course, it's not the man, but a ghost. One of Prince Rupert's friends, say, who forgot some weapon – or some piece of finery – and has come back for it.'

'What nonsense we talk. But there *is* something queer.'

'I rather agree.'

They looked at each other for a moment in whimsical alarm, before turning expectantly to the far end of the hall, from which the sound came. In a dark doorway beyond the dais they glimpsed what for an instant might have been identified as a gleam of armour. And then they saw that it was human hair. Advancing upon them was a silver-haired clergyman. He was carrying in his arms a square wooden box; he walked gingerly to a window embrasure and set down his burden then he turned to inspect the Applebys over the top of small and uncertainly poised steel-rimmed spectacles. 'Good morning,' he said politely. 'So you are before me, after all.'

Appleby took a hand from his trousers pocket – it was clear that no five shillings would be called for – and contrived a polite bow. 'Good morning, sir. But I don't think –'

'How quickly these things get about nowadays. I am most surprised. But, of course, your Society is always on the *qui-vive* – decidedly on the *qui-vive.*'

'I'm really afraid I don't know what Society you are talking about.'

'Come, come – frankness, my dear sir, frankness.' The old clergyman shook his head disapprovingly, so that his silver locks shimmered in the thin clear sunlight which flooded the hall. 'The lady and yourself indubitably come from the Society for Psychical Research.'

'You are wholly mistaken. If I come from anywhere, it's from the Metropolitan Police. But my visit here is entirely private – and, I'm afraid, unauthorized. My wife' – and Appleby looked at Judith with some shade of malice – 'is keenly interested in old houses.'

'We must get to work.' The old clergyman appeared to make very little of Appleby's remarks. 'But first let me introduce myself. My name is Buttery – Horace Buttery – and I have been the incumbent of this parish for many years.'

'How do you do.' Appleby presented Mr Buttery to Judith with appropriate formality. 'I wonder if you will tell us what it is that you suppose to have got about?'

'I'm bound to say that I had come to regard it as a vanishing legend. For good or ill, these old stories are dying out. Mr Buttery advanced to the chimney-piece and peered up at the carving. 'The date is about right, you must agree.'

'The date is certainly about right.' It was Judith who replied, and Appleby realized with misgiving that she was determined to probe the intentions or persuasions of the old parson before them. 'Today is the tenth of June.'

'Quite so.' Mr Buttery, much gratified, nodded so vigorously that his spectacles appeared likely to fly from his nose. 'But I have heard very little talk of it, you know, of recent years. Only now and then, and from the older cottagers. The younger people – and it is they, mark you, who are often out late at night, human nature being what it is – the younger people never report anything. Perhaps because they don't expect anything – eh?' Mr Buttery glanced at Judith with an air of great acuteness. 'But then, of course, I'm bound to say I didn't expect anything myself. It was entirely a surprise. My mind, naturally, was entirely on the gamekeeper.'

'I beg your pardon?' Judith was puzzled.

'No matter, no matter.' Mr Buttery might have been supposed momentarily confused. 'The point is that I have seen it with my own eyes. And so I feel bound to get to work.' He turned back to his wooden box. 'As you do too. Well, our purposes are not the same, but there need be no conflict – no conflict at all. A great deal in our present ills, if you ask me, proceeds from this disastrous notion of a necessary conflict between religion and science. I have a very cogent sermon on the subject, and I find that there is unfailing interest in it, year by year. I am not without the thought, indeed, of printing it and sending a copy to the Bishop. Between you and me, it might do him good. But here we are, here we are.' Mr Buttery was now rummaging in his box. 'Bell, book, candle – surely I didn't forget the candle? No – here it is.'

Judith advanced and peered into the box. 'You are proposing some sort of exorcism?'

'Precisely. Not that I consider the manifestation as serious.' Again Mr Buttery glanced up with an air of great acuteness— which had, somehow, the comical effect of exhibiting him as a very innocent man. 'I am not at all sure that a single White Paternoster might not very adequately meet the case. Still, one ought to be on the safe side. My reading inclines me to the view that we are dealing with goblins. A really populous affair like this is commonly a matter of goblins. I have little doubt that we shall get the better of them.'

'Do I understand' – Appleby in his turn had come forward –' that you yourself have lately seen at Water Poole a considerable concourse of what you took to be disembodied spirits?'

'My dear sir, you are perfectly justified from your scientific point of view in beginning your inquiry in this purely objective fashion. But I am persuaded that you know very well what I saw here last night.'

'Can you put a name to it?'

'Of course I can. It was the Naseby Ball.'

'Exactly – the Naseby Ball. And – as you can imagine – we are extremely interested.' Appleby gave Judith a swift glance which might have been an injunction to accept without more ado the rôle of psychical researcher. 'It would be invaluable if you were good enough to give us a full account of your experience.'

'By all means.' Mr Buttery picked up his bell, gave it what appeared to be an experimental tinkle, and then adressed himself courteously to meet this request. 'The historical background of the legend is no doubt familiar to you. In the summer of 1645 Lady Elizabeth Poole – she was a daughter of the Earl of Warmington – gave a magnificent entertainment here at Water Poole. On any sober calculation, of course, it was no time for anything of the sort, and the ball was clearly intended as a gesture in the grand manner. The Pooles prized nothing more highly than their reputation for being both resourceful and gay – and indeed they are said to be so still. But it took this great aristocratic lady, perhaps, to light that particular beacon against the darkness that was then closing in on the King's party.' Mr Buttery paused. 'One admires it, does one not?'

'And remembers it.' Judith glanced down the hall as if attempting to picture the scene. 'And that is the point, I imagine? Lady Elizabeth's entertainment became legendary?'

'So it would appear. On the stroke of midnight, the story goes, a messenger arrived from Prince Rupert. He announced that Sir Thomas Fairfax was marching with the New Model army upon

Northampton, and that in a few days a critical battle must be joined. The ball ended instantly with a loyal toast, there was a bustle of martial preparation, and at day-break the gentlemen rode away.' Again Mr Buttery paused. 'How vividly one sees it: the candles growing pale in the dawn, the women ashen under their paint and jewels, the men all assurance and arrogance and inflexibly maintained courtesy, but with thoughts only for their horses and weapons and accoutrements. Among those who departed were Richard Poole and his two sons. As you no doubt know, none of them came back.'

'And the family never recovered?'

Mr Buttery nodded his venerable head. 'It is perhaps true to say that the family never completely recovered – although Pooles lived on, the unquestioned masters of this place, into the present century. In the Kaiser's war the old history repeated itself after a fashion, for a father and two sons were killed, and the estate became impossibly burdened with debt. No Poole has lived here regularly since then. During the last war, when remote places were at a premium, Water Poole was let out and partially occupied for a time. But now it scarcely appears that it can ever be lived in again, and I am sorry to say that the shooting and fishing have been leased to some very unpleasant people – commercial folk, no doubt – from London. The present owner of the house is almost unknown to me. He is a young man in his early thirties – a Richard, as most of the lords of the manor have been christened – and I believe he has gone on the stage.'

'I wonder what Lady Elizabeth Poole would make of that? To think of one of her descendants become a common player would probably make her turn in her grave.' Judith looked at Mr Buttery with sudden indiscreet mischief. 'But perhaps it's that sort of thing that Lady Elizabeth is by way of doing – turning in her grave, or even rising from it on stated occasions to dance a pavane or a saraband?'

Mr Buttery shook his head. 'No, no, my dear madam. That is an error – I am bound to say a grave error.' He picked up his bell again and tinkled it, as if here was something in itself calling for the rite in which he proposed to engage. 'We must not suppose that the souls of virtuous persons, or their bodies either, engage in any such pranks. We are not in any sense confronted with true apparitions. Goblins are the explanation. I have not the slightest doubt of it.'

'It is a most interesting supposition.' Appleby interposed this with gravity. 'But just *what* do they explain? You haven't yet told us that. We have only gathered, so far, that last night you witnessed something remarkable. How did it happen? Were you called out to it?'

'Not precisely.' For the third time Mr Buttery tinkled his bell, but on this occasion what appeared to prompt the action was mild discomfiture. 'The fact is that, round about midnight, I was on the river. For purposes of meditation, and on a fine summer night, it may confidently be recommended.'

'Particularly when there is no moon?'

'Oh, most decidedly so. There is a great deal of distraction in a handsome moon.'

'I see.' Appleby felt constrained to conclude that – astonishing as the fact must seem – this reverend old parson's nocturnal occasions were not unconnected with possessing himself of other people's trout. Perhaps Mr Buttery was an instance of the shocking poverty of the rural clergy prompting to a life of crime. Perhaps he simply derived entertainment from outwitting, with arts leant in boyhood, those unpleasant commercial people from London. 'And being on the river, sir, you saw this spectral ball?'

'I did indeed.'

'I believe you said that the occurrence of something of the sort is a traditional belief among some of the older people in these parts. Perhaps you had been thinking of it yourself?'

'Decidedly not. My walk from the rectory to the river is by a path from which there is some view of the back of the house, and I could just dimly distinguish its outline against the sky. I recall simply reflecting how lonely and deserted it seemed.'

'There were no lights?'

'None. Anything of the sort would have attracted my attention and interest at once. For the astonishing spectacle which I saw later I was utterly unprepared. It came upon me, indeed, with the suddenness of a *coup de théâtre*.' Mr Buttery paused upon this phrase with some satisfaction. 'I was dropping quietly – I may say very quietly – down the stream in my dinghy. My thoughts were occupied with – um – entirely other matters. In fact I was meditating'– Mr Buttery, who seemed to feel that verisimilitude and conviction called here for more specific statement, visibly paused for inspiration – 'I was meditating upon the mutability of human affairs.'

'A very proper subject for reflection, sir. And then?'

'I came round the little bend that brings Water Poole into view. It was all lit up.'

'All?'

'Certainly this hall and its adjacent apartments. And there were lights on the terrace and – I think – the lawn. I was extremely startled.'

'Naturally. And what was your first thought?'

Mr Buttery considered. 'It must appear very absurd now – but undoubtedly it was of my own situation. I was struck by the impropriety and – er – inexplicability of my dropping down, at that hour, upon some private occasion. And then I realized that there could *be* no private occasion. For Water Poole, as you have yourselves seen, is an empty shell. Indeed, there could be no natural explanation whatever. And as soon as I had made this reflection, I noticed the peculiar character of the light. It was *not* that of a normally illuminated mansion.'

'Have you ever seen this particular mansion lit up before?'

'Certainly – although it is now long ago. As you may notice, there is an old electrical installation of sorts. But the light last night was utterly different,'

Appleby had walked to a window and was looking out thoughtfully over the lawn and the stream beyond. 'Can you describe it?' he asked.

'A low, soft, golden light. The effect was strikingly beautiful.'

'I see. And you have reason to believe that goblins command that sort of thing?' Appleby put this question with gravity. 'I am myself inclined to think of goblins as restricted to glow-worms. But glow-worms would scarcely be equal to the job.'

'Decidedly not. Glow-worms could not possibly illuminate a large party of ladies and gentlemen.'

'And that was what you saw?'

'That was what I appeared to see. And I need scarcely remark that their costume was Caroline. It would not be correct to say that the effect was as of a canvas by Van Dyck – since, you see, from my point of view, it was all in miniature and in open air. But if you may suppose Van Dyck to have painted something in the manner of Watteau's *fêtes champêtres* you have the impression exactly.' Mr Buttery smiled ingenuously over this triumph of precision. 'I may perhaps be permitted to mention that I possess a great love of the visual arts.'

'No doubt.' Appleby was looking at the old clergyman in some perplexity. 'Did you think to study this particular example at closer quarters?'

'I must confess that I did not. There they were – Caroline ladies and gentlemen strolling on the terrace and across the lawn. Behind them – here in this hall – I had an impression of dancing, and strains of music were definitely detectable. My mental state was peculiar. I recollected the circumstances of Lady Elizabeth's ball but not, oddly enough, the legend of its periodical re-enactment. As is so frequently the case during an actual encounter with supernatural appearances, no thought of the supernatural formed itself clearly in my head. I accused myself of inebriety.'

'It is a thought that might come to anyone. But I am sure there was no justification for it.'

'Reflection shows me that there was not. It is true that I had ventured upon a glass of burgundy at dinner, followed by a little madeira. But I hardly consider –'

'Plainly it is not a supposition with which you need distress yourself.' Appleby contrived a stern glance at Judith, who was displaying some signs of amusement at this exhibition of her husband's professional manner. 'Did you think of anything else?'

'Certainly. I thought of those two Oxford ladies – learned and sensible women, they appear to have been – who believed themselves to have had an adventure with time at Versailles. You no doubt recall their story. They saw Marie Antoinette. It seemed possible that I had met a similar kink in the centuries and was back with the real Lady Elizabeth Poole.'

'I believe there's decidedly something in that.' It was Judith who interposed, and she spoke with decision. 'It goes with what I felt myself when I entered this hall. It goes with what I *still* feel.' She gave her husband a glance of some defiance. 'Time has been squashed up like a concertina, and it's only just expanding again to the dimensions familiar to us. I fancy that - ever so faintly - I can hear that music now. I fancy I can hear those people: the sound of their voices and the rustle of their silks. And I *know* I can smell them.'

'Smell them?' Appleby was positively startled by this primitive assertion.

'Yes, John. The powdered hair. The scents - *their* scents. And their mere seventeenth-century humanity too. Mr Buttery caught them and we just missed them. I'm sure of it.'

'I think Mr Buttery was not without a feeling that they might catch him.' Appleby offered this rather drily. 'Isn't it so, sir?'

For a moment Mr Buttery looked quite startled. And then he blandly smiled. 'I must confess to having been under that uneasiness. I should hate to be caught. By goblins, that is to say. Not unnaturally, they are particularly malevolently disposed to persons of my cloth.' He produced a box of matches and lit his candle. 'But I fancy that we can get decidedly on top of them now.'

Mr Buttery was evidently about to open his campaign. Whether the manner of his announcing this constituted an invitation to participate was obscure, and Appleby appeared to feel that it was rather a tactful withdrawal that was indicated. The proper deportment for spectators during a ceremony of exorcism is not easy to hit upon impromptu, and his decision was perhaps occasioned merely by this. Judith, whose natural bent was for trying anything once, followed him from the hall with some reluctance. 'Do you think he's telling the truth?' she presently asked.

'Part of it, at least - or part of it as he believes it to be. Presumably he simply turned his dinghy round and stole away. And now with daylight and the paraphernalia collected in that box he's nerved himself to come back again. Or at least that's the obvious picture. And I can't think he's making up that queer vision. Certainly you didn't seem to think he was.'

Judith frowned. 'I believe – I don't know why – that all these people were here.'

'Did I say you ought to have become a historical novelist? Perhaps you ought to have become a detective. Would you care to be one now?'

'Assisting Scotland Yard?' She glanced at him cautiously, for it was not always easy to tell when John was being serious. 'I don't mind having a go.'

'Then just keep an eye on our reverend friend while I make another cast round the place.'

Judith was puzzled. 'Does the old gentleman really need keeping an eye on?'

'I don't quite know. He may be nothing more than an endearing clerical eccentric, much beloved by all the parish. But I have my doubts.'

'Very well. I expect he'll relish a bit of an audience.' And Judith slipped back into the hall.

Water Poole would take some time to explore systematically, and Appleby contented himself for the moment with a prowl through some of the neighbouring rooms. The place was none of his business. He had been decidedly aware of this as Judith had driven him up to it, and he told himself that nothing had happened since to alter this basic fact. Even a policeman should be ready to admit that not everything enigmatical is necessarily nefarious. Even if Mr Buttery was a poacher, it was not a matter of which an Assistant Commissioner from Scotland Yard need take any very active notice. Nor ought he to concern himself with investigating an elaborate joke; to do so, indeed, was only to invite annoyance or ridicule. But yet . . .

He had paused in a large and gloomy chamber which had been converted at some period to the uses of a library. There were handsome shelves for many thousands of books, but they now harboured nothing but dust. Dust was thick on them, and thick on the floor. The sight was melancholy – but for Appleby it was finally and definitively informative. He stirred the dust with his toe. It was the first thick dust upon which he had come. One can't, in a hurry, do anything much with an enormous empty library. So it had been left out. It had been left out of the joke. But the hall and one or two rooms around it had been dusted. They had been needed for the fun.

The joke . . . the fun. Appleby prowled on, dissatisfied. There was one very simple and very obvious explanation of Mr Buttery's vision. Water Poole had been used for a fancy-dress ball. Or better perhaps, for a sort of theatrical party or green-room rag. The owner, young Richard Poole, was an actor. It seemed very probable that the old legend connected with his house had prompted him to organize what he conceived to be an appropriate entertainment there for his friends. This was at least a more tenable theory than Mr Buttery's of a kink in time.

As for goblins – Appleby thought – they don't drop cigarette ash. They don't leave candle-wax on mantelpieces. They don't – he had moved once more into the open air – presumably leave a lawn something the worse for wear. When Judith had imagined herself to be obscurely sensing presences in the house, she had merely been letting these and other prosaic evidences of the late party filter unnoticed into her imagination. A perfectly commonplace if rather elaborate joke. . . .

But goblins disappear at dawn, and nobody sees them go. The cock crows, whereupon they fade and vanish. And some thing very like this had happened. Any sort of large party creates a good deal of litter; but the litter left by this party was so inconsiderable that a trained eye was required to perceive it. There had been a deliberate care taken to obliterate all traces of whatever proceedings had been going forward. The probability appeared to be that, but for the curious nocturnal habits of the local rector, nobody except the actual participants would have had any knowledge of the affair.

This was queer. It suggested that perhaps Richard Poole bore no responsibility in the matter. It was a joke unobtrusively perpetrated, followed by a careful – and astonishingly rapid – tidy-up. Why? Appleby shook his head as he found himself confronted with this tiresome little, yet perpetually fascinating, key-word of his profession. *Why?* There must be a reason. Probably it was a harmless reason. Perhaps it was a quite stupid and uninteresting reason, and any beguilement an explanation seemed to promise was no more than an effect of the romantic associations of this lonely and mouldering house. Still, explanation must be possible. There was a reason if it could be found.

He had strolled down to the river again. It must, after all be termed something more than a stream – for although narrow, it was quite deep and decidedly navigable. One could bring up a motor-boat – say one of those substantially powered house-boat affairs that were now so popular on the Thames itself. . . . It struck him that he had seen no boat-house. Yet this was something which Water Poole must surely possess. The absence of anything of the sort intrigued him. He began to poke about.

There was certainly no boat-house on the bank – but the reason, when after some minutes' search he found it, was interesting. An arm of the river – it was in fact a cut, but of evident antiquity and perhaps indeed as old as the mansion itself – passed clean under one wing of the house. Each end was secured by an iron grille which extended perhaps a couple of feet below the level of the water. That by which the cut emerged had quite clearly been undisturbed for generations. But at the entrance the state of affairs was different. The grille was rusty and bore every appearance of disuse – yet as Appleby peered at it he had his doubts. It was secured by an enormous padlock, plainly manufactured in early Victorian times – and on this too the rust was thick. Appleby however found it of considerable interest, and performed some complicated gymnastic manœuvres in order to get a hand on it. When he rose and walked away he was softly whistling a melancholy little stave of his own composition. Judith would have marked the sign. His spirits were rising.

And then he found the motor cars. They had not exactly been concealed; they were simply parked on the farther side of an outbuilding which only one rather pertinaciously interested in Water Poole would have been likely to visit. Both were large cars, but one was a good deal more resplendent than the other. Perhaps it would presently be necessary to examine them with some care, but for the moment Appleby contented himself with feeling the radiators. That of the resplendent car was quite cold. The other was warm.

He turned and walked back thoughtfully in the direction of the house. He had almost reached it when he heard the sound of an engine behind him. He glanced back over his shoulder. An open car with a single occupant was approaching. He had just time to distinguish the figure as that of a young man when the car turned off the track and vanished round the outbuildings which Appleby had just left. He heard the engine stop. The suddenly restored silence brought him a curious sense of impending drama. The situation upon which he and Judith had stumbled had so far presented rather a meagre cast. It was possible, he thought, that the principal characters were now beginning to drop in.

Perhaps he should go back and welcome this particular accession. He hesitated, and then his eye fell upon one part of Water Poole which he had not yet explored. It was the totally ruined part, where something like a whole wing had come down. If, as seemed very probable, one of the new arrivals was the owner or some other accredited person, he himself had perhaps only a few minutes left for further investigation before receiving a stiff request to make himself scarce. This persuaded him to press forward, even at the expense of an uncomfortably dusty scramble. In a moment he was climbing over the mountain of rubble with which this part of the forecourt was filled.

As he progressed, he saw that even more of the house than he supposed had been gashed open when the end pavilion fell. A staircase, intact to the second storey and there breaking off in air, had the appearance of a hazardous fire-escape; below it was a tumble of stone, brick and splintered beams. Appleby surveyed this, stopped for a moment, and then quickened his forward scramble. An onlooker would have seen him vanish among the débris – and might have reflected that he remained invisible for rather a long time.

The principal characters were beginning to drop in. The phrase reiterated itself rather grimly in Appleby's mind as he made his way back to the great hall. It was perhaps because he was walking in marked abstraction that, turning a corner of the building, he bumped straight into somebody approaching from the opposite direction. It was a lady. Fortunately she was substantially – indeed powerfully – built, and took the shock well. Appleby steadied her and apologized. 'I am extremely sorry. It was careless of me. One doesn't expect much traffic just here.'

'Pardon *me*.' The lady spoke with an accent that was unmistakably transatlantic. She was alarmed – but this by no means prevented her from being alarming. She was formidable – it might have been ventured almost professionally formidable, as if her everyday business was that of dominating large public meetings. And now she gave Appleby and Appleby's clothes a rapidly appraising glance. 'Would you,' she asked, 'be the owner of this wonderful spot?'

'No, madam. I am not the owner.' Appleby's glance was certainly not less searching than the American lady's. 'May I ask if you have just arrived here?'

'Just arrived?' It was discernible that the lady regarded this question as needing care. She eyed Appleby for a moment as if she were an accomplished chairman debating how to deal with a troublesome questioner in the body of the hall. 'I guess so. Isn't it just the most romantic house you could imagine?'

'It has considerable picturesque appeal, no doubt.'

The lady appeared to find this disconcerting. It was as if the body of the hall had produced something really awkward. 'Why – I'd say it's just out of this world.'

'I fear not.'

This was evidently more disconcerting still – the more so as Appleby's tone might fairly have been described as sombre. The lady looked at him in some alarm. 'And you say you're not the owner? If that isn't too bad.'

'Possibly so. My name is Appleby – Sir John Appleby.' He looked at the lady steadily. 'I am an Assistant Commissioner of the Metropolitan Police.'

The lady gave what in a less massively built person would have been a jump. 'Does that mean –?'

'It means Scotland Yard.' Appleby remarked with interest that at this information the lady turned quite pale. 'May I ask your name?'

'Jones.' The lady made this announcement with large conviction. 'Miss Jones.'

'And the name of this house?'

'Say?' The formidable Miss Jones was confused.

'Do you know it, or don't you?'

'Why, it's –' Miss Jones lamentably hesitated. 'Of course I don't.'

'Then, madam, why and how did you come here?' And Appleby paused. 'Perhaps you simply saw the house from the highroad and decided to turn aside and have a look?'

'Just that.' Miss Jones, as if thus reminded that her business was with the visual scene, tilted her head and gave Water Poole a glance of unrestrained if somewhat hurried approval. 'If it isn't a sweet spot. Would it belong to a lord?' She transferred her gaze briskly to a wrist-watch and gave an exclamation of dismay. She might once more have been the busy committee-woman with a fresh engagement pressing. 'But I must be getting along.'

'I am afraid not. It is unfortunately essential that you should remain. You will be kind enough to accompany me into the house and answer certain further questions.'

'Accompany a strange man into a lonely and deserted house!' Miss Jones's tone spoke of the largest moral outrage. 'I shall do nothing –'

'Here is my authority.' Appleby fished in a pocket, produced what was in fact a driving-licence, and with shameless resource held it momentarily before Miss Jones's startled gaze. 'This way, madam, if you please.'

'I call this outrageous.' Miss Jones delivered herself of her protest with energy. But she walked, nevertheless, in the direction which Appleby politely indicated.

Mr Buttery had either concluded or broken off his contest with the goblins. He and Judith were standing on one side of the fireplace, as if they had formed for the moment a defensive alliance.

On the other side was the young man whom Appleby had lately seen drive up to the house; it was apparent that he had been in the hall for only a couple of minutes, and that the entrance of Appleby and Miss Jones was a complicating factor in a situation of which he was trying to take the measure. It was to Appleby that he addressed himself now. 'Really, sir, I don't get the hang of this at all. Mr Buttery I'm more or less prepared to see – although I can't make head or tail of his talk at the moment. I have gathered before that he has rather a fondness for the place. But why you and these ladies –'

'We owe you a great many apologies.' Appleby was entirely bland. 'May I take it that you are Mr Poole, and that my wife has made herself known to you? And may I now introduce you to Miss Jones, a lady who has performed the astonishing feat of noticing Water Poole from the highroad? We are all quite frankly trespassers, and of course we must take ourselves off. I have no doubt that you find our intrusion most vexatious.'

'I don't know that I want to say that.' Richard Poole was willing to be mollified. 'Of course one doesn't very much welcome trippers. But it would be churlish to cut up rough at the appearance of people with an informed interest in the place. Particularly' – and he glanced sharply at Miss Jones – 'if they are American visitors.'

'Miss Jones is certainly from the United States. She isn't, by the way, already known to you?'

'Known to me?' The owner of Water Poole was startled. 'Certainly not.'

'And you, madam?' Appleby turned and looked attentively at Miss Jones. 'Do you know Mr Poole here by sight – or perhaps by name?'

There was a moment's silence while Miss Jones subjected this question to her customary wary analysis. 'I'm quite sure I never got acquainted with Mr Poole before. I don't know many folk in this country.'

'That gets something clear.' Appleby indicated Mr Buttery. 'And you don't know this gentleman either?'

'One moment.' Richard Poole had stepped forward – slightly

impatient, slightly perplexed. 'Is there really a question of getting things clear? I am, after all, the owner of this place, and I'm not aware of anything of the sort.'

'I have no desire, I assure you, to express any impertinent curiosity.' Appleby's mildness continued to be notable. 'But it is true, you know, that Mr Buttery has had a most perplexing experience here.'

'To be sure he has.' Poole's tone was politely amused. 'Goblins and fairies at midnight – and as a consequence of his encounter with them he has been trying out some sort of exorcism. It isn't one of my own interests, I'm afraid. But I don't in the least object to his going right ahead.'

'You just can't have been listening, Mr Poole, if you propose to treat the matter in that off-hand fashion.' Judith now took a hand in the conversation. 'What Mr Buttery saw was a whole ball – call it the Naseby Ball.'

'Then I think he was uncommonly lucky.' Poole glanced whimsically at the venerable clergyman, clearly determined not to budge from his airy attitude. 'It's a spectacle that seems commonly to be reserved for the very old. And also, I must add, for the simplest classes of society. Gaffer Odgers of Poole Parva is the last ancient I heard of as having been favoured in that way.'

'You have never witnessed this legendary manifestation yourself?' Appleby had strolled to a window and now turned to study the young man in a full light.

'Of course not.'

'Nor taken any part in – well, occasioning it?'

'No. I'm not a medium, or anything of that sort.'

'You have never come and kept watch, even, at the appropriate season?'

'Good lord, no.' Poole was again determinedly amused. 'I tell you I don't take any interest in spooks.'

'Nor very much in Water Poole?' Appleby paused. 'May I ask when you were here last?'

The young man hesitated. 'Can that really be any business of yours? But the answer, if it interests you, is about eighteen months ago.'

'Why are you here to-day?'

This time Poole flushed. 'Dash it all, sir, this is a bit too much.'

'On the contrary, it's not nearly enough.' Quite suddenly Appleby was no less grim than he had been with Miss Jones a little earlier. 'Mr Buttery is an educated man in a responsible position. He gives a most circumstantial account of very odd goings-on here last night. And this morning you, sir, turn up for the first time in eighteen months. Do you ask me to believe that this is purely coincidental?'

'I don't ask you to believe anything. I simply tell you to clear –' Richard Poole's glance fell on Judith and he checked himself. 'I must ask you to be good enough to withdraw from my house and land at once.'

'Possibly our introductions haven't gone far enough. Appleby produced a pocket-book. 'May I give you my card?'

There was a moment's silence while Poole took the slip of pasteboard and glanced at it. His flush died away and his manner became uncertain. 'I don't know what to say about this. I must have a minute to think.'

'By all means. And I feel bound to emphasize, Mr Poole, that – however it may be with *your* arrival here – mine is a matter of pure chance.'

'I don't think I want to say anything.'

'As you please. But I think you have a story to tell, and that you had better tell it.' Appleby paused and looked at the young man gravely. 'There is one circumstance, of which you may or may not be aware, which makes this queer business upon which my wife and I have stumbled extremely serious.'

Poole frowned. 'You speak in riddles, so far as I'm concerned. I don't know what you're talking about.'

'That may be so. At present, I don't intend to divulge the circumstance to which I refer. But I solemnly assure you that it is something which makes all concealment on your part dangerous and in all probability impossible.'

The young man was impressed. 'I still don't know that I ought to say anything – without a solicitor and so-forth. It occurs to me that I have been breaking the law. I hadn't thought of it that way

– and indeed the idea's fantastic. Still, I may have been trying to get money by false pretences.' He looked at Appleby with a sudden odd naïvety. 'It's devilish awkward.'

'It does sound as if it might be a shade uncomfortable.' Appleby was mildly sardonic. 'But I still advise you to speak out, Mr Poole.'

'Very well. I will. You won't believe a word of my story, I expect. But you shall have it.' Richard Poole glanced about him. 'I don't mind your wife – or, for that matter, Mr Buttery. But I really don't see that this Miss – er – Jones –'

'Sure.' Miss Jones took this broad hint with alacrity. 'Mr Poole's affairs are no business of mine. If you'll pardon me, I'll be getting along.'

Appleby shook his head. 'I'm afraid I can't allow you to do that.' He turned to Poole. 'Do you think Miss Jones has simply strayed in on the party? There isn't likely to be any place for her in your story?'

Poole stared. 'I can't think –' He stopped. 'Unless –'

'Perhaps we had better take things in order.' Appleby glanced around the empty hall. 'It's a pity there's nothing to sit down on except Mr Buttery's box.'

'Dear me! I have been most remiss.' Mr Buttery pushed forward the box, and then found himself in some embarrassment as to which lady should have the offer of it.

'You'd better sit on it yourself.' Miss Jones eyed the clergyman searchingly. 'How old are you?'

'How old, madam?' Mr Buttery was so surprised by this outrageous question that he did in fact sit down without more ado. 'Sixty-eight.'

'You look ten years older. I suppose you drink. A pale-faced drinker, too. Do you know about your expectation of life? Remind me to let you have some statistics.' Miss Jones paused in this astonishing homily. 'It ought to be more generally known –'

'That's it.' Richard Poole was regarding the lady with a sort of horrified recognition. 'She has a place in my story after all.'

Appleby nodded. 'I hardly supposed otherwise. But please begin.'

'It's going to sound very queer.' Richard Poole put his hands in his trouser-pockets and paced nervously across the hall. 'Perhaps you know that I'm an actor by profession? In other words, my regular concern is with illusion – with creating and sustaining one or another pleasurable illusion. And that is what, together with a group of friends, I set myself to do here last night. My motive was entirely benevolent and disinterested.'

Miss Jones gave a sardonic laugh. 'What you call a charity matinée with an all-star cast?'

'We were none of us stars and it wasn't a matinée. The curtain had to go up at night – and any old night wouldn't do. It had to be a *dark* night. If too much had appeared – if the illusion had failed, you see – well, it would have been just too bad. As it was, only a very remarkable combination of circumstances made it possible.'

Appleby nodded. 'Do I understand you to believe, Mr Poole, that this benevolent illusion did in fact pass off successfully?'

'I certainly supposed so. The only snag was its turning out that I might be suspected of having a motive that I'd never thought of. Quite suddenly, and out of the blue, I was presented with a totally unexpected moral issue. I failed to cope with it. It's before me still.'

'I wonder.' Miss Jones, although she had the appearance of one who feels it desirable to keep her own counsel, allowed herself this enigmatical interjection with some emphasis. 'But go on.'

'If you'll keep quiet, madam, that's just what I mean to do ... I suppose we all have American cousins. I suppose even *you* are somebody's cousin. And *my* cousin turned out to be Hiram Poole. It's queer to think of a Poole being called Hiram – but there he was, complete with family tree. The genealogy was all quite accurate, and he actually had the thing hung up in his suite at Murray's. Hiram is a very modest man. In fact he is quite pathologically shy and unassuming – which is an essential factor in my story. But he is excessively rich, and it wouldn't occur to him not to put up in the best hotel in town. I found him there when

I responded to his letter. I can't say that I was summoned, since what he sent me might best be described as a mere diffident hint of his existence.

'It is essential that you should appreciate my lively feeling from the first that Hiram is an agreeable figure of considerable pathos. His money is of his own making, I gather, and has come from the manufacture of some nameless but certainly humble object of domestic utility. Might it be wash-tubs? Perhaps they are out of date. I just don't know.

'It turned out that he had never been in Europe before, although making the trip had been a life's dream with him. He had nerved himself to it now only because it was his last chance. Hiram is a dying man. He told me in a fashion that was entirely matter-of-fact that his doctors had given him only a few months to live. Well, that has increased the effect of pathos, I need hardly say. But it isn't what has made poor old Hiram so attractive to me. He is thoroughly romantic, and this trip has been for him a purely romantic pilgrimage. That to me, is appealing in itself. But he combines with it an elusive and wholly engaging sense of humour. Deep down in him there's gaiety. I think that's it.'

'Isn't that a quality your family prides itself in?' Appleby had remembered Mr Buttery's description of the Pooles 'That and resourcefulness?'

'Hiram would like that comment – because the great point about him is his family piety. It isn't of course snobbish. Having identifiable ancestors in the thirteenth century would never occur to him as an occasion for giving himself airs. With him it's rather something for a large wonder. And I soon saw that he had been hoping for some deep draught of it before he said goodbye.

'In the last few weeks Hiram and I have done a good many showplaces together. Have you ever been to the Tower of London? It's perfectly horrible – the dungeon and torture chamber of England – but Hiram loved it. He told me about Pooles of whom I'd never heard who had come to a violent end there. We had an ecstatic day at Hampton Court. All that sort of thing. And now you must see, clearly enough where all this is leading to.'

'To Water Poole.' It was Judith who replied. 'You offered
to get up a sort of historical pageant for him.'

'It was more than that. He has, as you can guess, a very strong
feeling for Water Poole. But he hadn't ventured down here. He
hadn't, I mean, made as much as a private trip to peep at the
place. The notion of peeping would somehow offend his sense
of delicacy. He was waiting for something. It was quite a while
before I realized what it was.

'I did know that he had brought over from America with him
a big County History published early in the present century, and
the part dealing with Water Poole he had grangerized – I believe
that's the word – with all sorts of additional cuttings and engrav-
ings. But his information wasn't very up to date – as presently
appeared.

'I had asked him to lunch at my flat – I live just off Piccadilly
– to meet one or two people who I thought would please him. It
was a reasonable success, and he lingered with me after the others
had gone. He had quite a lot to say in praise of the few old things
I possess and keep lying about there; but nevertheless there was
some undercurrent of disappointment that I didn't at first catch
hold of. But in the end Hiram brought out a remark that was entirely revealing. " This is certainly a pleasant apartment, Richard,"
he said. " But, all the same, you must find it wonderful when you
can get away from London to Water Poole." '

'As you can see, there would have been only one honest reply
to make. But for a moment I hesitated – it seemed so wicked to
disillusion the old chap – and after that I was lost.'

There was a moment's silence, broken by Judith. 'And then you
set about the business of what you call creating and sustaining a
pleasurable illusion? You allowed it to be supposed that Water
Poole is a going concern?'

'Just that. I won't tell you how, in half an hour's talk, I was
hopelessly edged into it. Such a lamentable piece of weakness
doesn't make comfortable remembering. The crucial point was
that I found Hiram to set tremendous store by the notion that
I lived here. He called it keeping the flag flying, sticking to our

guns, and that sort of thing. You see, he may have spent his life giving better and brighter wash-tubs to a great democracy, but at heart Hiram is an aristocrat. What made my position the more uncomfortable was the fact that there is nothing second-rate or silly about Hiram's ideas. He would take no pleasure, for instance, in the contemplation of grand relations simply leading a fashionable life. But he liked his picture of the head of the family with his back to the ancestral wall, and holding out against the degeneracy of the modern world.

'Well, here I was in a false position, and there was only one factor which might possibly save me from disgrace. Hiram's English visit was drawing to an end. And he was so shy – so reluctant to move in any sort of strange society – that he was quite unlikely to hear anything of the true situation here at Water Poole unless I told him myself. But of course there was a snag.' Richard Poole paused, and then appealed to Appleby 'You can see what it was?'

'It was hardly decent not to invite him here.'

'Exactly. When Hiram took his leave of me after that luncheon party it was impossible for me not to say something to that effect. To avoid it would have been utterly indecent. Of course I can see now things that I could have said. I might have declared that some theatrical tour was carrying me off to Brazil next morning. But no ingenuity of that sort came into my head. I did the only conceivably proper thing, and said that I hoped within the next few days to have some suggestion for his coming down to the old place. I could see that he was overjoyed. And as he went away he did, in his diffident fashion, say something quite positive. He would rather his visit didn't take the form of an active social engagement. His health was as I knew it to be, and his remaining vitality was sufficient for spectatorship rather than intercourse. That gave me my idea.'

'Was it quite a new venture?' Appleby asked the question curiously. 'Or are you in the habit of organizing elaborate hoaxes?'

'I've never done anything of the sort before – and as a matter

of fact it took some time to come to me. At first my only notion
was of some procedure amounting to a confession with the addition
of anything I could think of to soften the blow. I'd have Hiram
down, show him the place as it is, and say how much I hoped
to get back one day. What prevented me from doing this was
a scruple.'

'I'd call it the honest course to have pursued.'

'It would have been a sort of begging.' Richard Poole spoke
with sudden heat. 'Don't you see? Hiram is a tremendously
wealthy man. Showing him Water Poole in its decay would simply
be asking him to put his hand in his pocket. I found I couldn't
do it.'

'I don't believe him!' Once more the force of her emotions
constrained Miss Jones to intervene. 'And I shan't believe another
word he says. It is perfectly obvious that Mr Poole contrived
some disgraceful mercenary plot against his relative – his distant
relative – and that now he is perverting the whole matter.'

'Didn't I say I'd meet with incredulity?' The owner of Water
Poole appealed this time to Judith. 'But that is the simple fact.
I had reached a position at which it became a point of honour to
exhibit this house as a going concern, standing in no need of the
wash-tub millions. I had a good idea, by the way, to what purposes
Hiram was proposing that those millions should in fact be devoted,
for he had spoken to me, very briefly, of his philanthropic interests and – as he called them – testamentary dispositions. But
that's by the way. Here I was, thinking up some means of pleasing
Hiram and getting myself out of a ridiculous scrape.

'Nothing at first came to me, and I let the matter rest for longer
than I intended. Then I got a note from Hiram, telling me when
he was due to sail for New York. He said nothing about Water
Poole, of course, but in the circumstances this intimation of his
departure could not be other than an implicit reproach. I was
rather desperate. And then I noticed the date on which he was
sailing.

'It was, as a matter of fact, today's date – and at that I had my
inspiration. I became a demon – perhaps Mr Buttery would say a
goblin – of energy, and by that same evening I had got together

a sort of committee of my closest friends. What had come to me was that, just at this time of the year, we could manage a sort of lightning revivification of Water Poole without raising any awkward curiosity in the neighbourhood. Anything observed, and anything talked about, would be put down at once to the lingering superstition that attaches to the place.

'Hiram, needless to say, knew the story of the first Naseby Ball, and I was sure that the notion of some species of commemoration would appeal to him. But I had an additional reason for making my party a costume affair. It was a matter of what you might call the psychology of successful illusion.

'My friends and myself were going to create the appearance of a house-party here at Water Poole, in such a way that Hiram could be asked to drop in on it and get the impression of that going concern. But in reality we should be actors putting on a show in a decayed theatre with crumbling scenery and unreliable props. For example, the whole business of lighting was going to be uncommonly tricky – probably there would have to be nothing but candles – and the project only looked remotely feasible because of that crucial fact of Hiram's temperament: his diffidence, and his unwillingness to treat himself to more than one entranced glimpse of the ancestral home. Even so, the project was technically daunting, and I soon saw that our only chance was this: *that our illusion should be of an illusion.* If we were all confessedly engaged in creating a fiction, then the basic fiction – or the action within the fiction, so to speak – might be something we could get away with.'

'Your plan was undoubtedly a very clever one.' Appleby glanced at Richard Poole with what might have been reluctant admiration. 'Did it occur to you that if your cousin detected the fraud it would be very much more painful for him than a frank statement of the truth?'

'It certainly did – which is why I determined not to fail. And I don't think I *did* fail.' Poole turned a thoughtful eye on Miss Jones. 'At least, that's what I've been imagining.'

'It all went like clockwork?'

'Yes. We moved in with several vans just after dark. The *décor* had been planned in minute detail beforehand, and there wasn't a hitch. When my cousin Hiram arrived, driving his own car, I was on the look-out for him, and got him straight round to the presentable side of the house. It was clear almost at once – an actor has a sense of these things – that we were successfully putting our show across. Mr Poole of Water Poole was giving one of his accustomed house-parties, and his guests, with others invited in for the evening, were indulging in a historically appropriate costume ball. My only fear was that Hiram, in his unassuming way, would ask if he might quietly make a tour of the whole house. He knows its history well; and there must be various rooms – some of them perhaps now in ruins – with associations of great interest to him. But of course Hiram would never have dreamed of giving even that amount of trouble. He stayed just over an hour, moving about quietly with me among the guests, accepting a few introductions, drinking a glass of champagne, and so on. And then he took his leave. The whole thing, which had been so terrifying in the prospect, proved astoundingly easy. Long before dawn – the early June dawn – we had folded our tents like the Arabs and silently stolen away.'

'But that wasn't, in fact, all?' A sombre expression had returned to Appleby's face. 'And it would have been better if it had been?'

'Precisely.' Poole hesitated. 'When Hiram left me it was plain that he was very much moved. Our imposture had been only too effective. It had been one of the deepest experiences of his life.'

'That must have been rather uncomfortable for you.'

'It was. He apologized for not stopping longer. He confessed that it had been a strain, and that he didn't think he had better take any more. And then he brought out the astounding thing. "Richard," he said, "there's something I must tell you – in strict confidence."'

'We were standing beside his car. I felt instantly uneasy – partly because of an odd feeling that we were being overheard, and partly from sheer foreboding. I muttered something about respecting any confidence he cared to make.

'"I've made a mistake," he said. "To leave money out of the family – a family like *our* family – is utterly wrong. This night

has been a revelation to me. You stand by the old ways, Richard –
and I know enough about the economic difficulties of this country
to know that it must be against tremendous odds." I could see his
glance going back to the dark bulk of the house. " It's magnificent,
Richard. I can't tell you. I can't begin to speak. But you shall be
my sole heir. God bless you. And good-bye." And with that Hiram
climbed into his car and drove away. And now you have the whole
story. Of course he will have to be told. I see that now. I've been
a frightful ass, and I'm back pretty well where I started.'

There was a long silence. Richard Poole produced a silk handkerchief and mopped his forehead. Mr Buttery, as if he were
some aged anthropoid of an imitative bent, promptly did the
same. Appleby took a turn round the hall, and on coming back
addressed its owner quietly. 'And where do you suppose Hiram
Poole to be now?'

'On board the *Queen Mary*, steaming for New York. He was to
drive straight to London, change, and catch the boat train.'

'He was to change? Did he come here in fancy dress?'

'Yes. He had realized that it was the unnoticeable thing to do.'

'A black Caroline costume with a gold-embroidered cloak?'

'Yes.' Richard Poole's eyes widened. 'But I don't see –'

'Your cousin is grey-haired, with a small scar on his chin?'

'Yes.'

'Then I am very sorry to say that he is not on board the *Queen
Mary*. His dead body is lying at the bottom of the ruined staircase
in this house.'

Miss Jones had fainted, been resuscitated, and at last accommodated on Mr Buttery's box. Judith had driven off rapidly in
her car. Richard Poole had identified his cousin's body and was
now back in the hall, looking pale and troubled. ' It's unbelieve-
able,' he said.

' That is what you felt your tale was going to be.' Appleby spoke
very seriously. ' Hiram Poole has died, so to speak, at the end of
a decidedly tall story put up by yourself. There are various possibilities. Some of them can't be explored until we have a medical
report. Others suggest themselves at once.'

'Such as?' The young man looked at him dully.

'You no doubt see for yourself that it would be easy to set your proceedings in a very damaging light. You are a poor man. You have admitted what it would be impossible long to conceal: that you brought this rich American cousin down to Water Poole and submitted him to a gross imposture. Your own story is that he was prompted by this fraud to declare his intention of making you his heir. It may very well be so. But one can conceive of other turns that the affair may have taken. It might be suggested that you were aware that you had already been constituted, at least in some degree, your cousin's heir. It might be suggested that last night he penetrated to the nature of the charade in which you had involved him.'

'Stop!' Richard Poole's face was bloodless. 'You have no right to confront me with these insinuations. It is utterly irregular.'

'My dear sir, I have no official standing in this matter at all. I am speaking to you as a private citizen; and at the same time I am giving you, for your own benefit, an experienced view of certain lines of speculation which the officers who will investigate this business may be prompted to follow.'

'I see. Very well. Go on.'

'It is conceivable that Hiram Poole drove away more or less as you have claimed – but that he had his doubts. Suspicion grew on him; eventually he turned his car and came back to Water Poole; and what he found in the dawn was a derelict house, and his hopeful young heir pottering round clearing up a bit of litter. He wasn't very pleased, and there may even have been a quarrel. So much for one hypothesis. We needn't follow it further at the moment.'

'It sounds damnably convincing.' Richard Poole managed rather a harsh laugh.

'It has, as it happens, one weakness. It leaves something out. I think you claim to know certain particulars of Hiram's existing testamentary dispositions? He had been proposing to leave his fortune to philanthropic organizations?'

'Yes – and to one such organization in particular. The bulk of his estate was to go to a body advocating temperance reform.

I remember thinking it odd in him. It didn't really cohere with
the kind of feelings and attitudes that Hiram revealed when he
was over here. But there it was. Prohibition all over again: it
was something like that, I gathered, that his money was to go to
the support of.'

'Capital!'

Appleby turned in astonishment, to see Mr Buttery emphati-
cally nodding his venerable head. 'You approve of such an
endeavour?'

'Certainly.' Mr Buttery was quite excited. 'I declare Mr Poole's
cousin to have been most enlightened. The attempt to prohibit by
law all use of alcoholic beverages is one which interests me very
much. I think I can say that I approve of it. I regret that it has
never made more headway on this side of the Atlantic.'

'Sir, let me say that you do honour to your calling.' Miss Jones
had risen from the box, advanced upon the clergyman, and was
now shaking him vigorously by the hand. She turned to Appleby
and Richard Poole. 'Thousands will take fresh heart when they
hear of the noble declaration of this truly reverend old man!'

'Thank you, madam, thank you.' Mr Buttery – perhaps recalling that he had been termed a pale-faced drinker – appeared
a little embarrassed by this unexpected effusion.

And Appleby was looking at him in surprise. 'What about that
burgundy and madeira? Would you propose, sir, that in framing
their !egislation our prohibitionists should insert a clause exempt-
ing the clergy?' He turned to Miss Jones. 'I'm not quite certain
that you and Mr Buttery are going to be at one in this matter,
after all. But, for the moment, we have another sort of concern
with it. May I take it, madam, that it would not be incorrect to
assert that the urging of temperance reform constitutes your profession? Mr Poole, I think, has already had an inkling of it.'

'It has certainly been hovering in my head for some time.'
Poole swung round to survey the American lady, and as he did so
he produced a strained smile. 'The rival charity – that's what
you are!'

Appleby nodded. 'Exactly. Water Poole or water wagon – it
might be expressed like that. Which was cousin Hiram's fortune

going to the support of? . . . And now perhaps Miss Jones will speak.'

'I am *not* Miss Jones.' The American lady had advanced to the middle of the hall, and her announcement was made with a very sufficient sense of drama. 'Let there be no more subterfuge. I am not Miss Jones. I am Miss Brown.'

'Not, surely'– Richard Poole, despite his awkward situation, was prompted to a freak of humour –' not, surely, *the* Miss Brown?'

'I guess so.' Miss Brown's was a wholly modest acknowledgement. 'I am Louisa Brown, Vice-President of the Daughters of Abstinence.'

'It sounds like William Blake.' Poole might have been slightly dazed. 'Are they something in America?'

'Certainly. They constitute one of our leading temperance bodies, and the one to which the late Hiram Poole has bequeathed almost his entire fortune. And I have been acting as a Guardian.'

'Why should Hiram require a Guardian? I never heard such nonsense.'

'It's a precaution we are accustomed to take with potential major benefactors. Particularly when they go overseas.' Miss Brown spoke with confidence. 'Temptations are manifold. Haven't we just heard that Mr Hiram Poole was seduced, in this very house, into drinking a glass of champagne? Disgusting! Revolting!'

This view of the hospitality of Water Poole appeared to strike the owner of the mansion as decidedly offensive. 'As a self-appointed bodyguard, madam, you have been thoroughly inefficient. Hiram is dead, and when you get back to your own country I sincerely trust that all the other Daughters will give you a thoroughly bad time.'

'You haven't got the picture quite right.' Appleby intervened drily. 'It wasn't Miss Brown's business to keep your cousin alive. Her guardianship consisted in ensuring that, if he died, it wasn't with the wrong sort of last will and testament immediately behind him. It is a consideration in which there is food for thought. But we still haven't had Miss Brown's story. Will you please proceed?'

'I certainly will.' Miss Brown put her hands behind her back and eyed the three men before her as if they had been a large assembly of recalcitrant brewers or vintners. 'It was well known to me that Mr Hiram Poole had these unwholesome interests in family history and a feudal past. So when upon his arrival in England he made the acquaintance of Mr Poole – *this* Mr Poole – I realized that the utmost vigilance would be required of me. As a matter of routine, I got to know all about Water Poole. I got to know all about Mr Richard Poole's feelings for it – or lack of feelings for it.'

Richard Poole exploded. 'The woman's crazy!'

'For instance, I have in my file – it struck me as worth paying for – a letter from Mr Richard offering to sell this house for the purpose of what is called an approved school. He also had a project for turning the place over to a syndicate to run as a scientific pig farm.'

'Crazy?' Appleby looked rather grimly at the owner of Water Poole. 'I'd be inclined to say myself that there's method in her madness.'

'Madness in her method, if you ask me.' Poole was gloomy. 'But go on, madam – go on.'

'Murray's is an excellent hotel, and the servants don't gossip. But it was a different matter with the firm from whom Mr Hiram hired a car, and I was soon in a position to know most of his movements a day or so in advance. That's how it came about that, when he set out for Water Poole in his fancy dress last night, I was on the road in my own car a hundred yards behind.'

Appleby was looking at Miss Brown in admiration. 'That was very efficient, I'm bound to say. And just what did you know about what was going forward?'

'I knew that Mr Richard had been dashing round the firms that provide stage furniture, and that he had been holding long meetings with large numbers of his theatrical friends. I think I may say that I had the greater part of the picture already in my head. When we got down here, of course, I let Mr Hiram get a good lead, and then I parked my own car and explored the ground.

I guess I hadn't got hold of the fancy-dress aspect of the affair, and the significance of that puzzled me a good deal. But the rest was clear enough. I saw that the moment to expose Mr Richard Poole had arrived.'

'You were probably right.' Appleby contributed this soberly. 'And how did you propose to set about it?'

'I thought at first of simply walking in upon the feast and denouncing it – denouncing the imposture and denouncing the champagne. Then it occurred to me that I might, as a consequence, put myself in considerable personal danger. I might be thrown in the river and drowned, and the Daughters of Abstinence would never so much as know what had become of me.'

'Bless me!' Richard Poole stared. 'The woman might believe herself to be on the banks of the Niger, not of the –'

'Mr Richard and his friends were flown with wine.' Miss Brown interrupted brusquely. 'The expression is that of the great English poet Milton, justly celebrated for confining himself at the supper-table to a few olives and a glass of water. Any insolence, any outrage might be expected of them. I therefore skulked.'

'I bet you did.' Richard Poole breathed heavily.

'I was almost at Mr Richard's elbow when Mr Hiram made the shameful speech.'

'The shameful speech?' For a moment Appleby was at sea.

'About making this dishonest and intemperate young man his heir. Then Mr Hiram drove off, and I hurried to my own car and followed. But he had a good lead and was driving very fast. It was many miles before I overtook him and signalled him to stop. He took no notice. I therefore passed him and edged him almost into the ditch. One sees it done on the movies. He stopped, but I found it very hard to open communication with him. I have an idea that he took me for a person of disreputable character.'

'You must remember it was in the dark.' Richard Poole produced this with obscure but massive irony. 'And then?'

'It took what must have been hours – but at length I did contrive to explain to him the imposture to which he had been subjected. He refused to believe it. Finally I persuaded him to drive back to Water Poole. When we arrived, the place was already in darkness. I got out a torch and led him on a tour of inspection. It was then that he began to behave very queerly.'

'What do you mean?' Poole's voice held real anxiety. 'Was he very angry – or upset?'

'He wouldn't speak. We went over almost the whole place with the aid of a torch he had brought from his car. And he wouldn't speak a word to me. I thought it most discourteous. There was one particularly striking instance. We had glanced into a small pantry – one from which a staircase runs down to some of the cellars – and it simply reeked of spirits. No doubt it was your disgusting champagne and so on. I drew Mr Hiram's attention to it as evidence of the depraved society into which his acquaintance with you had brought him. He simply stared at me without uttering a syllable. And then, when we had emerged again into the open air, we parted.'

'Parted?' Appleby was surprised. 'In what circumstances?' Miss Brown hesitated. 'He told me to go away.'

Richard Poole laughed again – less harshly this time. 'Hiram, you know, had very good taste. When he did speak, he said the sensible thing. He asked you to clear out. And you did?'

'I did.' Miss Brown flushed. 'I considered that my good offices had been scorned, and that I had been personally insulted. I got into my car and drove away.'

'Leaving Hiram alone at Water Poole?'

'I guess so. Unless you were still here yourself, Mr Poole.'

Appleby looked up sharply. 'Have you any reason, Miss Brown, to suppose anything of the sort?'

Miss Brown hesitated. 'I can't swear to Mr Poole here. But I did have a hunch that there was somebody lurking around.'

'I see. Now, when you left Water Poole, however much you may have felt personally insulted, you must have supposed your work there to be done. Mr Richard Poole was wholly discredited. May I ask you why, in these circumstances, you returned here this morning?'

'Because I was uneasy. Mr Hiram Poole was an old man, whom I knew to be in poor health. And I had left him here in the small hours, after subjecting him to painful disillusion. I returned in order to make quite sure that nothing had happened to him.'

'Well – it had.' Appleby uttered this shortly and then took one of his brief walks to a window. 'In the ruined part of this house there is a staircase that mounts through two storeys and then goes on to end nowhere. From that hazardous eminence, some time in the small hours, Mr Hiram Poole was precipitated. And there are still a good many possibilities. For example, we don't know – at least *I* don't know – what was in the dead man's mind. How did he take the revelation which it is agreed was made to him? Miss Brown, the only person to be in his company after the truth was revealed, quite failed to get any change out of him. That, at least, is her story. Suppose it to be true. . . . Do you hear a car? It will be my wife with a doctor.'

'I am not in the habit of prevarication.'

'Very well. Your story is gospel, so far as it goes. But there may have been – indeed, if it *is* gospel, there must have been – a further and distinct act in the drama. Mr Richard Poole *may* have been lurking around – or he may have returned after you left, encountered his cousin, and become involved in some altercation with fatal consequences. In the circumstances it is a possible picture.' Appleby paused. 'I mentioned the chance of Mr Richard's being *already,* in some degree, Hiram Poole's heir – and knowing it. On that, the actual truth must, of course, eventually become available. For what my own opinion is worth, it is slightly improbable. But one fact is admitted. As matters stood last night, and still stand now, the Daughters of Abstinence are very large beneficiaries under Hiram Poole's will. And this bring us back to Miss Brown. Her story may *not* be gospel. It may be quite untrue.'

'I am not in the –'

'No doubt, madam. But there are tight corners in which the most inflexibly truthful persons find themselves a little inclined to stretch a point. Suppose that this investigation of the true state of Water Poole brought both Hiram Poole and yourself to the top of that staircase. He had been silent. You became vehement in your denunciation of Mr Richard. And then Hiram Poole did something which surprised you very much, but which in fact was thoroughly consonant with human nature. He cried a plague on both your houses.'

'He did what?' Miss Brown was both startled and at a loss.

'He declared that Richard should not have a penny of his. And then he said precisely the same thing about the Daughters of Abstinence.'

'He would never do such a thing.'

'I repeat that I think it extremely likely that he would. Your organization had set a spy on him, and subjected him to an acute humiliation of which you, madam, cannot have the faintest imaginative understanding. So here is another sober possibility. Up there, at the top of that crazy staircase, this old man told you that your organization would be struck out of his will tomorrow.'

Miss Brown was silent – and suddenly old and spectral. Richard Poole looked at her not unkindly and then turned to Appleby. 'I must say you have considerable skill in making it uncomfortable for everybody in turn. Is there more to come? What about Mr Buttery?'

And Appleby nodded. 'I'm coming to Mr Buttery now.'

'To me?' Over his steel-rimmed spectacles the clergyman looked at Appleby in naïve alarm. 'I fear all this has been incomprehensible to me, and that I am unlikely to be able to assist. Here and there – on the goblin side of the thing – I am fairly clear. But all this of wills eludes me. Mr Poole, it seems, has told one story; this lady who keeps on changing her name has told another; and I suppose you, sir, must choose between them.'

Appleby shook his head. 'That may be unnecessary. I have myself ventured some alternative hypotheses which are no doubt mutually exclusive. But the stories of Mr Poole and Miss Brown do not in themselves contradict each other. Both may have told as much of the truth as they know. And now it is up to you to tell the rest.'

Mr Buttery considered this injunction for a moment in silence. Then, disconcertingly, his venerable features assumed an expression of the deepest cunning. 'I suppose,' he asked, 'that what is called motive is of great importance in a matter of this sort?'

'Undoubtedly.'

'You were asking, for instance, *why* this lady returned to Water Poole when she did. Stress is put upon things like that?'

'Certainly it is.'

'Awkward. Troublesome. Vexatious.' And Mr Buttery shook his head. 'If I myself had what might be termed a *respectable* motive –'

'Folk-lore.' Appleby was brisk. 'Your own further investigations of Water Poole last night, sir, were prompted entirely by your interest in folk-lore. You were after the goblins, and nothing but the goblins. And now perhaps you can go ahead.'

'I don't quite follow this.' Richard Poole was curious 'Am I to understand that Mr Buttery –'

'Mr Buttery is a great law-breaker.' Appleby announced this without any appearance of censure. 'A little quiet poaching warms the cockles of his heart. But lately he has taken larger flight. He found, I think, a very tempting cellar, to be entered unobtrusively by a cut from the river. Perhaps he found some suitable implements and utensils as well. Anyway, he has been having great fun distilling illicit spirits. Hence the smell remarked by Miss Brown. And hence Mr Buttery's own enthusiasm for Total Prohibition. He feels that if that came in he might go into business in a large way. But these are irrelevant matters –'

'Really irrelevant?' Mr Buttery was sharply hopeful.

'At least there is a very good chance of it. Last night, sir, you watched the goblins in some alarm until they packed up. And then you came to investigate. They are said, after all, to do terrible things in dairies. Perhaps they might have been behaving equally mischievously in your distillery.'

'I certainly waited in my dinghy until all was dark and silent again.' Mr Buttery now spoke with much placidity. 'It was a tedious vigil. I was not however greatly surprised. For goblins, as you know, have a great reputation for keeping it up till dawn. Gradually their lights went out, and I was conscious of intermittent rumblings. Parties of them were returning to the nether world.'

'Or our vans were driving away.' Richard Poole was looking at the clergyman in some perplexity, as if finding it hard to gauge just how deep his eccentricity went.

'When at length I ventured to land they had all vanished – as our national poet puts it, following darkness like a dream. Or all, that is, except the Goblin King.'

'The Goblin King?' Miss Brown, whose spirits appeared to be a little revived, interrupted. 'Do Goblins have that?'

'Certainly – and he is rather a fine personage. It is a mistake, you know, to suppose that goblins are dwarfs, or in any sense little people. I was not at all surprised to find that the Goblin King was a most distinguished figure, magnificently attired in black and gold.'

'Cousin Hiram!'

'With him he had an obscure familiar. I caught only glimpses, you know. As I remarked earlier, it is very dangerous for the clergy to get involved with goblins. So the utmost circumspection was necessary. The Goblin King had some species of lantern. I had to be very careful to keep out of its beam; and it was only from the oblique light coming from it that I could distinguish him at all. The familiar puzzled me. Could it have been Hecate? I am more inclined to suppose a minor Teutonic divinity. Possibly the Sow Goddess.' Mr Buttery looked ingenuously at Miss Brown. 'Would that appear to you to be a tenable hypothesis?'

'I think you are a very wicked old man.' Miss Brown's response, if not strictly relevant, was spirited.

'Presently however the familiar was banished. This was the only occasion upon which I actually heard the Goblin King speak. "Go away," he said. I was much struck by his tone of authority. Without more ado, the Sow Goddess – I am sure she was that – took her departure.'

Richard Poole looked wickedly at Miss Brown. 'With more rumbling?'

'I should rather say with a purr. I am inclined to suppose some species of chariot. The Goblin King then withdrew to the house. In fact, he withdrew to this hall, and sat for a long time there in the window, quite still and silent. He appeared lost in sombre thought. When at last he stirred, it was because the dawn was breaking. He then began once more to explore the house. I felt that I had seen enough, and I slipped out to recover my dinghy. I was half-way across the lawn when I heard the laughter.'

'The laughter?' Richard Poole was startled.

'It came from high in air, and I knew at once that it was supernatural. Very cautiously I skirted the house – and suddenly I saw the Goblin King again, silhouetted against the dawn. He had climbed the ruined stair – climbed right to the top – and now he was looking down on all that part of Water Poole that is mere ruin. And he was laughing. I have never heard such laughter. It was, I say, supernatural – and yet all the gaiety and all the fun of the world we know seemed to be in it. I was astounded. I was strangely moved. Once more it pealed out – and then, quite abruptly, ceased. And the Goblin King had vanished.'

There was a long silence. At last Richard Poole spoke softly. 'He had vanished?'

'Yes – following darkness. Following darkness like a dream. That was all.'

The silence renewed itself, until broken by Appleby. 'Yes,' he said. 'That – I am very glad indeed to say – was all.'

And Appleby and Judith drove away. He waited until they were on the highroad and then asked a question. 'The doctor is quite sure?'

'Quite sure. It will be confirmed at the post-mortem. Hiram Poole was dead before he reached the ground. He died of the heart-failure that had threatened him for a long time.'

'That's one way of putting it. Another is to say that he died of laughter. It was appropriate enough, for the whole affair was comedy. Once or twice it looked like crime – but it proved to be comedy in the end. One can't consider that Richard Poole was very culpable, and he told the truth as he knew it. So did that tiresome but perfectly honest temperance crusader. . . . But of course there was more to it than that.'

'More to Hiram Poole's death?' Judith nodded over the wheel. 'Decidedly.'

'One can't doubt that young Richard's deception was something the discovery of which was very painful to him. Imagine him, sick and chill and tired, being haled around that derelict shrine – for it was that to him – in the small hours.'

'And by a Daughter of Abstinence, at that.'

'Quite. It must have been sheer nightmare. And any common man would simply have felt himself abominably cheated and betrayed.'

'Any common man would have suspected the very obvious mercenary motive.'

'Hiram had his dark hour, I don't doubt, hunched there in a window of the hall. But he rose to the thing.'

'He rose to it.'

'That Pooles are still resourceful and gay. Hiram saw it like that, and his own laughter attested it. I take off my hat to him.'

Baroness Orczy

THE WOMAN
IN THE BIG HAT

LADY MOLLY ALWAYS had the idea that if the finger of fate had pointed to Mathis' in Regent Street, rather than to Lyons', as the most advisable place for us to have a cup of tea that afternoon, Mr Culledon would be alive at the present moment.

My dear lady is quite sure – and needless to say that I share her belief in herself – that she would have anticipated the murderer's intentions, and thus prevented one of the most cruel and callous of crimes which were ever perpetrated in the heart of London.

She and I had been to a matinée of *Trilby*, and were having tea at Lyons', which is exactly opposite Mathis' Vienna café in Regent Street. From where we sat we commanded a view of the street and of the café, which had been very crowded during the last hour.

We had lingered over our toasted muffin until past six, when our attention was drawn to the unusual commotion which had arisen both outside and in the brilliantly lighted place over the road.

We saw two men run out of the doorway, and return a minute or two later in company with a policeman. You know what is the inevitable result of such a proceeding in London. Within three minutes a crowd had collected outside Mathis'. Two or three more constables had already assembled, and had some difficulty in keeping the entrance clear of intruders.

But already my dear lady, keen as a pointer on the scent, had hastily paid her bill, and, without waiting to see if I followed her or not, had quickly crossed the road, and the next moment her graceful form was lost in the crowd.

I went after her, impelled by curiosity, and presently caught sight of her in close conversation with one of our own men. I have always thought that Lady Molly must have eyes at the back of her head, otherwise how could she have known that I stood behind her now? Anyway, she beckoned to me, and together we entered Mathis', much to the astonishment and anger of the less fortunate crowd.

The usually gay little place was indeed sadly transformed. In one corner the waitresses, in dainty caps and aprons, had put their heads together, and were eagerly whispering to one another whilst casting furtive looks at the small group assembled in front of one of those pretty alcoves, which, as you know, line the walls all round the big tea room at Mathis'.

Here two of our men were busy with pencil and notebook, whilst one fair-haired waitress, dissolved in tears, was apparently giving them a great deal of irrelevant and confused information.

Chief Inspector Saunders had, I understood, been already sent for; the constables, confronted with this extraordinary tragedy, were casting anxious glances towards the main entrance, whilst putting the conventional questions to the young waitress.

And in the alcove itself, raised from the floor of the room by a couple of carpeted steps, the cause of all this commotion, all this anxiety, and all these tears, sat huddled up on a chair, with arms lying straight across the marble-topped table, on which the usual paraphernalia of afternoon tea still lay scattered about. The upper part of the body, limp, backboneless, and awry, half propped up against the wall, half falling back upon the outstretched arms, told quite plainly its weird tale of death.

Before my dear lady and I had time to ask any questions, Saunders arrived in a taxicab. He was accompanied by the medical officer, Dr Townson, who at once busied himself with the dead man, whilst Saunders went up quickly to Lady Molly.

'The chief suggested sending for you,' he said quickly; 'he was phoning you when I left. There's a woman in this case, and we shall rely on you a good deal.'

'What has happened?' asked my dear lady, whose fine eyes were glowing with excitement at the mere suggestion of work.

'I have only a few stray particulars,' replied Saunders, 'but the chief witness is that yellow-haired girl over there. We'll find out what we can from her directly Dr Townson has given us his opinion.'

The medical officer, who had been kneeling beside the dead man, now rose and turned to Saunders. His face was very grave.

'The whole matter is simple enough, so far as I am concerned,' he said. 'The man has been killed by a terrific dose of morphia – administered, no doubt, in this cup of chocolate,' he added, pointing to a cup in which there still lingered the cold dregs of the thick beverage.

'But when did this occur?' asked Saunders, turning to the waitress.

'I can't say,' she replied, speaking with obvious nervousness. 'The gentleman came in very early with a lady, somewhere about four. They made straight for this alcove. The place was just beginning to fill, and the music had begun.'

'And where is the lady now?'

'She went off almost directly. She had ordered tea for herself and a cup of chocolate for the gentleman, also muffins and cakes. About five minutes afterwards, as I went past their table, I heard her say to him, "I am afraid I must go now, or Jay's will be closed, but I'll be back in less than half an hour. You'll wait for me, won't you?"'

'Did the gentleman seem all right then?'

'Oh, yes,' said the waitress. 'He had just begun to sip his chocolate, and merely said "S'long" as she gathered up her gloves and muff and then went out of the shop.'

'And she has not returned since?'

'No.'

'When did you first notice there was anything wrong with this gentleman?' asked Lady Molly.

'Well,' said the girl with some hesitation, 'I looked at him once or twice as I went up and down, for he certainly seemed to have fallen all of a heap. Of course, I thought that he had gone to sleep, and I spoke to the manageress about him, but she thought that I ought to leave him alone for a bit. Then we got very busy, and I paid no more attention to him, until about six o'clock, when most afternoon tea customers had gone, and we were beginning to get

the tables ready for dinners. Then I certainly did think there was
something wrong with the man. I called to the manageress, and
we sent for the police.'

'And the lady who was with him at first, what was she like?
Would you know her again?' queried Saunders.

'I don't know,' replied the girl; 'you see, I have to attend to
such crowds of people of an afternoon, I can't notice each one.
And she had on one of those enormous mushroom hats; no one
could have seen her face – not more than her chin – unless they
looked right under the hat.'

'Would you know the hat again?' asked Lady Molly.

'Yes – I think I should,' said the waitress. 'It was black velvet
and had a lot of plumes. It was enormous,' she added, with a
sigh of admiration and of longing for the monumental headgear.

During the girl's narrative one of the constables had searched
the dead man's pockets. Among other items, he had found several
letters addressed to Mark Culledon, Esq., some with an address
in Lombard Street, others with one in Fitzjohn's Avenue,
Hampstead. The initials M.C., which appeared both in the hat
and on the silver mount of a letter-case belonging to the unfortunate gentleman, proved his identity beyond a doubt.

A house in Fitzjohn's Avenue does not, somehow suggest a
bachelor establishment. Even whilst Saunders and the other men
were looking through the belongings of the deceased, Lady Molly
had already thought of his family – children, perhaps a wife, a
mother – who could tell?

What awful news to bring to an unsuspecting, happy family,
who might even now be expecting the return of father, husband,
or son, at the very moment when he lay murdered in a public
place, the victim of some hideous plot or feminine revenge!

As our amiable friends in Paris would say, it jumped to the
eyes that there was a woman in the case – a woman who had worn
a gargantuan hat for the obvious purpose of remaining unidenti-
fiable when the question of the unfortunate victim's companion
that afternoon came up for solution. And all these facts to put
before an expectant wife or an anxious mother!

As, no doubt, you have already foreseen, Lady Molly took the difficult task on her own kind shoulders. She and I drove together to Lorbury House, Fitzjohn's Avenue, and on asking of the manservant who opened the door if his mistress were at home, we were told that Lady Irene Culledon was in the drawing-room.

Mine is not a story of sentiment, so I am not going to dwell on that interview, which was one of the most painful moments I recollect having lived through.

Lady Irene was young – not five-and-twenty, I should say – petite and frail-looking, but with a quiet dignity of manner which was most impressive. She was Irish, as you know, the daughter of the Earl of Athyville, and, it seems, had married Mr Mark Culledon in the teeth of strenuous opposition on the part of her family, which was as penniless as it was aristocratic, whilst Mr Culledon had great prospects and a splendid business, but possessed neither ancestors nor high connections. She had only been married six months, poor little soul, and from all accounts must have idolized her husband.

Lady Molly broke the news to her with infinite tact, but there it was! It was a terrific blow – wasn't it? – to deal to a young wife – now a widow; and there was so little that a stranger could say in these circumstances. Even my dear lady's gentle voice, her persuasive eloquence, her kindly words, sounded empty and conventional in the face of such appalling grief.

Of course, everyone expected that the inquest would reveal something of the murdered man's inner life – would, in fact, allow the over-eager public to get a peep into Mr Mark Culledon's secret orchard, wherein walked a lady who wore abnormally large velvet hats, and who nourished in her heart one of those terrible grudges against a man which can only find satisfaction in crime.

Equally, of course, the inquest revealed nothing that the public did not already know. The young widow was extremely reticent on the subject of her late husband's life, and the servants had all been fresh arrivals when the young couple, just home from their honeymoon, organized their new household at Lorbury House.

There was an old aunt of the deceased – a Mrs Steinberg – who lived with the Culledons, but who at the present moment was very ill. Someone in the house – one of the younger servants, probably – very foolishly had told her every detail of the awful tragedy. With positively amazing strength, the invalid thereupon insisted on making a sworn statement, which she desired should be placed before the coroner's jury. She wished to bear solemn testimony to the integrity of her late nephew, Mark Culledon, in case the personality of the mysterious woman in the big hat suggested to evilly disposed minds any thoughts of scandal.

'Mark Culledon was the one nephew whom I loved,' she stated with solemn emphasis. 'I have shown my love for him by bequeathing to him the large fortune which I inherited from the late Mr Steinberg. Mark was the soul of honour, or I should have cut him out of my will as I did my other nephews and nieces. I was brought up in a Scotch home, and I hate all this modern fastness and smartness, which are only other words for what I call profligacy.'

Needless to say, the old lady's statement, solemn though it was, was of no use whatever for the elucidation of the mystery which surrounded the death of Mr Mark Culledon. But as Mrs Steinberg had talked of 'other nephews', whom she had cut out of her will in favour of the murdered man, the police directed inquiries in those various quarters.

Mr Mark Culledon certainly had several brothers and sisters, also cousins, who at different times – usually for some peccadillo or other – seemed to have incurred the wrath of the strait-laced old lady. But there did not appear to have been any ill-feeling in the family owing to this. Mrs Steinberg was sole mistress of her fortune. She might just as well have bequeathed it in toto to some hospital as to one particular nephew whom she favoured, and the various relations were glad, on the whole, that the money was going to remain in the family rather than be cast abroad.

The mystery surrounding the woman in the big hat deepened as the days went by. As you know, the longer the period of time which elapses between a crime and the identification of the criminal, the greater chance the latter has of remaining at large.

In spite of strenuous efforts and close questionings of every one of the employees at Mathis', no one could give a very accurate description of the lady who had tea with the deceased on that fateful afternoon.

The first glimmer of light on the mysterious occurrence was thrown, about three weeks later, by a young woman named Katherine Harris, who had been parlourmaid at Lorbury House when first Mr and Lady Irene Culledon returned from their honeymoon.

I must tell you that Mrs Steinberg had died a few days after the inquest. The excitement had been too much for her enfeebled heart. Just before her death she had deposited £250 with her banker, which sum was to be paid over to any person giving information which would lead to the apprehension and conviction of the murderer of Mr Mark Culledon.

This offer had stimulated everyone's zeal, and, I presume, had aroused Katherine Harris to a realization of what had all the while been her obvious duty.

Lady Molly saw her in the chief's private office, and had much ado to disentangle the threads of the girl's confused narrative. But the main point of Harris's story was that a foreign lady had once called at Lorbury House, about a week after the master and mistress had returned from their honeymoon. Lady Irene was out at the time, and Mr Culledon saw the lady in his smoking-room.

'She was a very handsome lady,' explained Harris,' 'and was beautifully dressed.'

'Did she wear a large hat?' asked the chief.

'I don't remember if it was particularly large,' replied the girl.

'But you remember what the lady was like?' suggested Lady Molly.

'Yes, pretty well. She was very, very tall, and very good-looking.'

'Would you know her again if you saw her?' rejoined my dear lady.

'Oh, yes; I think so,' was Katherine Harris's reply.

Unfortunately, beyond this assurance the girl could say nothing very definite. The foreign lady seems to have been closeted with Mr Culledon for about an hour, at the end of which time Lady Irene came home.

The butler being out that afternoon it was Harris who let her mistress in, and as the latter asked no questions, the girl did not volunteer the information that her master had a visitor. She went back to the servants' hall, but five minutes later the smoking-room bell rang, and she had to run up again. The foreign lady was then in the hall alone, and obviously waiting to be shown out. This Harris did, after which Mr Culledon came out of his room, and, in the girl's own graphic words, 'he went on dreadful'.

'I didn't know I 'ad done anything so very wrong,' she explained, 'but the master seemed quite furious, and said I wasn't a proper parlour-maid, or I'd have known that visitors must not be shown in straight away like that. I ought to have said that I didn't know if Mr Culledon was in; that I would go and see. Oh, he did go on at me!' continued Katherine Harris, volubly. 'And I suppose he complained to the mistress, for she give me notice the next day.'

'And you have never seen the foreign lady since?' concluded Lady Molly.

'No; she never come while I was there.'

'By the way, how did you know she was foreign? Did she speak like a foreigner?'

'Oh, no,' replied the girl. 'She did not say much – only asked for Mr Culledon – but she looked French like.'

This unanswerable bit of logic concluded Katherine's statement. She was very anxious to know whether, if the foreign lady was hanged for murder, she herself would get the £250.

On Molly's assurance that she certainly would, she departed in apparent content.

'Well! we are no nearer than we were before,' said the chief, with an impatient sigh, when the door had closed behind Katherine Harris.

'Don't you think so?' rejoined Lady Molly, blandly.

'Do you consider that what we have heard just now has helped us to discover who was the woman in the big hat?' retorted the chief, somewhat testily.

'Perhaps not,' replied my dear lady, with her sweet smile; 'but it may help us to discover who murdered Mr Culledon.'

With which enigmatical statement she effectually silenced the chief, and finally walked out of his office, followed by her faithful Mary.

Following Katherine Harris's indications, a description of the lady who was wanted in connection with the murder of Mr Culledon was very widely circulated, and within two days of the interview with the ex-parlour-maid another very momentous one took place in the same office.

Lady Molly was at work with the chief over some reports, whilst I was taking shorthand notes at a side desk, when a card was brought in by one of the men, and the next moment, without waiting either for permission to enter or to be more formally announced, a magnificent apparition literally sailed into the dust-covered little back office, filling it with an atmosphere of Parma violets and Russia leather.

I don't think that I had ever seen a more beautiful woman in my life. Tall, with a splendid figure and perfect carriage, she vaguely reminded me of the portraits one sees of the late Empress of Austria. This lady was, moreover, dressed to perfection, and wore a large hat adorned with a quantity of plumes.

The chief had instinctively risen to greet her, whilst Lady Molly, still and placid was eyeing her with a quizzical smile.

'You know who I am, sir,' began the visitor as soon as she had sunk gracefully into a chair; 'my name is on that card. My appearance, I understand, tallies exactly with that of a woman who is supposed to have murdered Mark Culledon.'

She said this so calmly, with such perfect self-possession, that I literally gasped. The chief, too, seemed to have been metaphorically lifted off his feet. He tried to mutter a reply.

'Oh, don't trouble yourself, sir!' she interrupted him, with a smile. 'My landlady, my servant, my friends have all read the description of the woman who murdered Mr Culledon. For the past twenty-four hours I have been watched by your police, therefore I come to you of my own accord, before they came to arrest me in my flat. I am not too soon, am I?' she asked, with that same cool indifference which was so startling, considering the subject of her conversation.

She spoke English with a scarcely perceptible foreign accent, but I quite understood what Katherine Harris had meant when she said that the lady looked 'French like'. She certainly did not look English, and when I caught sight of her name on the card, which the chief had handed to Lady Molly, I put her down at once as Viennese. Miss Elizabeth Lowenthal had all the charm, the grace, the elegance, which one associates with Austrian women more than with those of any other nation.

No wonder the chief found it difficult to tell her that, as a matter of fact, the police were about to apply for a warrant that very morning for her arrest on a charge of wilful murder.

'I know – I know,' she said, seeming to divine his thoughts; 'but let me tell you at once, sir, that I did not murder Mark Culledon. He treated me shamefully, and I would willingly have made a scandal just to spite him; he had become so respectable and strait-laced. But between scandal and murder there is a wide gulf. Don't you think so, madam?' she added, turning for the first time towards Lady Molly.

'Undoubtedly,' replied my dear lady, with the same quizzical smile.

'A wide gulf which, no doubt, Miss Elizabeth Lowenthal will best be able to demonstrate to the magistrate tomorrow,' rejoined the chief, with official sternness of manner.

I thought that, for the space of a few seconds, the lady lost her self-assurance at this obvious suggestion – the bloom on her cheeks seemed to vanish, and two hard lines appeared between her fine eyes. But, frightened or not, she quickly recovered herself, and said quietly:

'Now, my dear sir, let us understand one another. I came here for that express purpose. I take it that you don't want your police to look ridiculous any more than I want a scandal. I don't want detectives to hang about round my flat, questioning my neighbours and my servants. They would soon find out that I did not murder

Mark Culledon, of course; but the atmosphere of the police would hang round me, and I – I prefer Parma violets,' she added, raising a daintily perfumed handkerchief to her nose.

'Then you have come to make a statement?' asked the chief.

'Yes,' she replied; 'I'll tell you all I know. Mr Culledon was engaged to marry me; then he met the daughter of an earl, and thought he would like her better as a wife than a simple Miss Lowenthal. I suppose I should be considered an undesirable match for a young man who has a highly respectable and snobbish aunt, who would leave him all her money only on the condition that he made a suitable marriage. I have a voice, and I came over to England two years ago to study English, so that I might sing in oratorio at the Albert Hall. I met Mark on the Calais-Dover boat, when he was returning from a holiday abroad. He fell in love with me, and presently he asked me to be his wife. After some demur, I accepted him; we became engaged, but he told me that our engagement must remain a secret, for he had an old aunt from whom he had great expectations, and who might not approve of his marrying a foreign girl, who was without connections and a professional singer. From that moment I mistrusted him, nor was I very astonished when gradually his affection for me seemed to cool. Soon after he informed me quite callously that he had changed his mind, and was going to marry some swell English lady. I didn't care much, but I wanted to punish him by making a scandal, you understand. I went to his house just to worry him, and finally I decided to bring an action for breach of promise against him. It would have upset him, I know; no doubt his aunt would have cut him out of her will. That is all I wanted, but I did not care enough about him to murder him.'

Somehow her tale carried conviction. We were all of us obviously impressed. The chief alone looked visibly disturbed, and I could read what was going on in his mind.

'As you say, Miss Lowenthal,' he rejoined, 'the police would have found all this out within the next few hours. Once your connection with the murdered man was known to us, the record of your past and his becomes an easy one to peruse. No doubt, too,' he added insinuatingly, 'our men would soon have been placed in possession of the one undisputable proof of your complete innocence with regard to that fateful afternoon spent at Mathis' café.'

'What is that?' she queried blandly.

'An alibi.'

'You mean, where I was during the time that Mark was being murdered in a tea shop?'

'Yes,' said the chief.

'I was out for a walk,' she replied quietly.

'Shopping, perhaps?'

'No.'

'You met someone who would remember the circumstance – or your servants could say at what time you came in?'

'No,' she repeated dryly; 'I met no one, for I took a brisk walk on Primrose Hill. My two servants could only say that I went out at three o'clock that afternoon and returned after five.'

There was silence in the little office for a moment or two. I could hear the scraping of the pen with which the chief was idly scribbling geometrical figures on his blotting pad.

Lady Molly was quite still. Her large, luminous eyes were fixed on the beautiful woman who had just told us her strange story, with its unaccountable sequel, its mystery which had deepened with the last phrase which she had uttered. Miss Lowenthal, I felt sure, was conscious of her peril. I am not sufficiently a psychologist to know whether it was guilt or merely fear which was distorting the handsome features now, hardening the face and causing the lips to tremble.

Lady Molly scribbled a few words on a scrap of paper, which she then passed over to the chief. Miss Lowenthal was making visible efforts to steady her nerves.

'That is all I have to tell you,' she said, in a voice which sounded dry and harsh. 'I think I will go home now.'

But she did not rise from her chair, and seemed to hesitate as if fearful lest permission to go were not granted her.

To her obvious astonishment – and, I must add, to my own – the chief immediately rose and said, quite urbanely:

'I thank you very much for the helpful information which you have given me. Of course, we may rely on your presence in town for the next few days, may we not?'

She seemed greatly relieved, and all at once resumed her former charm of manner and elegance of attitude. The beautiful face was lit up by a smile.

The chief was bowing to her in quite a foreign fashion, and in spite of her visible reassurance she eyed him very intently. Then she went up to Lady Molly and held out her hand.

My dear lady took it without an instant's hesitation. I, who knew that it was the few words hastily scribbled by Lady Molly which had dictated the chief's conduct with regard to Miss Lowenthal, was left wondering whether the woman I loved best in all the world had been shaking hands with a murderess.

No doubt you will remember the sensation which was caused by the arrest of Miss Lowenthal, on a charge of having murdered Mr Mark Culledon, by administering morphia to him in a cup of chocolate at Mathis' cafe in Regent Street.

The beauty of the accused, her undeniable charm of manner, the hitherto blameless character of her life, all tended to make the public take violent sides either for or against her, and the usual budget of amateur correspondence, suggestions, recriminations and advice poured into the chief's office in titanic proportions.

I must say that, personally, all my sympathies went out to Miss Lowenthal. As I have said before, I am no psychologist, but I had seen her in the original interview at the office, and I could not get rid of an absolutely unreasoning certitude that the beautiful Viennese singer was innocent.

The magistrate's court was packed, as you may well imagine, on that first day of the inquiry; and, of course, sympathy with the accused went up to fever pitch when she staggered into the dock, beautiful still, despite the ravages caused by horror, anxiety, fear, in face of the deadly peril in which she stood.

The magistrate was most kind to her; her solicitor was unimpeachably assiduous; even our fellows, who had to give evidence against her, did no more than their duty, and were as lenient in their statements as possible.

Miss Lowenthal had been arrested in her flat by Danvers, accompanied by two constables. She had loudly protested her innocence all along, and did so still, pleading 'Not guilty' in a firm voice.

The great points in favour of the arrest were, firstly, the undoubted motive of disappointment and revenge against a faithless sweetheart, then the total inability to prove any kind of alibi, which, under the circumstances, certainly added to the appearance of guilt.

The question of where the fatal drug was obtained was more difficult to prove. It was stated that Mr Mark Culledon was director of several important companies, one of which carried on business as wholesale druggists.

Therefore it was argued that the accused, at different times and under some pretext or other, had obtained drugs from Mr Culledon himself. She had admitted to having visited the deceased at his office in the City, both before and after his marriage.

Miss Lowenthal listened to all this evidence against her with a hard, set face, as she did also to Katherine Harris's statement about her calling on Mr Culledon at Lorbury House, but she brightened up visibly when the various attendants at Mathis' café were placed in the box.

A very large hat belonging to the accused was shown to the witnesses, but, though the police upheld the theory that this was the headgear worn by the mysterious lady at the café on that fatal afternoon, the waitresses made distinctly contradictory statements with regard to it.

Whilst one girl swore that she recognized the very hat, another was equally positive that it was distinctly smaller than the one she recollected, and when the hat was placed on the head of Miss Lowenthal, three out of the four witnesses positively refused to identify her.

Most of these young women declared that though the accused, when wearing the big hat, looked as if she might have been the lady in question, yet there was a certain something about her which was different.

With that vagueness which is a usual and highly irritating characteristic of their class, the girls finally parried every question by refusing to swear positively either for or against the identity of Miss Lowenthal.

'There's something that's different about her somehow,' one of the waitresses asserted positively.

'What is it that's different?' asked the solicitor for the accused, pressing his point.

'I can't say,' was the perpetual, maddening reply.

Of course the poor young widow had to be dragged into the case, and here, I think, opinions and even expressions of sympathy were quite unanimous.

The whole tragedy had been inexpressibly painful to her, of course, and now it must have seemed doubly so. The scandal which had accumulated round her late husband's name must have added the poignancy of shame to that of grief. Mark Culledon had behaved as callously to the girl whom clearly he had married from interested, family motives, as he had to the one whom he had heartlessly cast aside.

Lady Irene, however, was most moderate in her statements. There was no doubt that she had known of her husband's previous entanglement with Miss Lowenthal, but apparently had not thought fit to make him accountable for the past. She did not know that Miss Lowenthal had threatened a breach of promise action against her husband.

Throughout her evidence she spoke with absolute calm and dignity, and looked indeed a strange contrast, in her closely fitting tailor-made costume of black serge and tiny black toque, to the more brilliant woman who stood in the dock.

The two great points in favour of the accused were, firstly, the vagueness of the witnesses who were called to identify her, and, secondly, the fact that she had undoubtedly begun proceedings for breach of promise against the deceased. Judging by the latter's letters to her, she would have had a splendid case against him, which fact naturally dealt a severe blow to the theory as to motive for the murder.

On the whole, the magistrate felt that there was not a sufficiency of evidence against the accused to warrant his committing her for trial; he therefore discharged her, and, amid loud applause from the public, Miss Lowenthal left the court a free woman.

Now, I know that the public did loudly, and, to my mind, very justly, blame the police for that arrest, which was denounced as being as cruel as it was unjustifiable. I felt as strongly as anybody on the subject, for I knew that the prosecution had been instituted in defiance of Lady Molly's express advice, and in distinct contradiction to the evidence which she had collected. When, therefore, the chief again asked my dear lady to renew her efforts in that mysterious case, it was small wonder that her enthusiasm did not respond to his anxiety. That she would do her duty was beyond a doubt, but she had very naturally lost her more fervent interest in the case.

The mysterious woman in the big hat was still the chief subject of leading articles in the papers, coupled with that of the ineptitude of the police who could not discover her. There were caricatures and picture post-cards in all the shop windows of a gigantic hat covering the whole figure of its wearer, only the feet and a very long and pointed chin, protruding from beneath the enormous brim. Below was the device, ‘Who is she? Ask the police?’

One day – it was the second since the discharge of Miss Lowenthal – my dear lady came into my room beaming. It was the first time I had seen her smile for more than a week, and already I had guessed what it was that had cheered her.

‘Good news, Mary,’ she said gaily. ‘At last I've got the chief to let me have a free hand. Oh, dear! What a lot of argument it takes to extricate that man from the tangled meshes of red tape!’

‘What are you going to do?’ I asked.

‘Prove that my theory is right as to who murdered Mark Culledon,’ she replied seriously, ‘and as a preliminary we'll go and ask his servants at Lorbury House a few questions.’

It was then three o'clock in the afternoon. At Lady Molly's bidding, I dressed somewhat smartly, and together we went off in a taxi to Fitzjohn's Avenue.

Lady Molly had written a few words on one of her cards, urgently requesting an interview with Lady Irene Culledon. This she handed over to the manservant who opened the door at Lorbury House. A few moments later we were sitting in the cosy boudoir. The young widow, high-bred and dignified in her tight-fitting black gown, sat opposite to us, her white hands folded demurely before her, her small head, with its very close coiffure, bent in closest attention towards Lady Molly.

'I most sincerely hope, Lady Irene,' began my dear lady, in her most gentle and persuasive voice, 'that you will look with all possible indulgence on my growing desire – shared, I may say, by all my superiors at Scotland Yard – to elucidate the mystery which still surrounds your late husband's death.'

Lady Molly paused, as if waiting for encouragement to proceed. The subject must have been extremely painful to the young widow; nevertheless she responded quite gently:

'I can understand that the police wish to do their duty in the matter; as for me, I have done all, I think, that could be expected of me. I am not made of iron, and after that day in the police court –'

She checked herself, as if afraid of having betrayed more emotion than was consistent with good breeding, and concluded more calmly:

'I cannot do any more.'

'I fully appreciate your feelings in the matter,' said Lady Molly, 'but you would not mind helping me – would you – in a passive way, if you could, by some simple means, further the cause of justice?'

'What is it you want me to do?' asked Lady Irene.

'Only to allow me to ring for two of your maids and to ask them a few questions. I promise you that they shall not be of such a nature as to cause you the slightest pain.'

For a moment I thought that the young widow hesitated, then, without a word, she rose and rang the bell.

'Which of my servants did you wish to see?' she asked, turning to my dear lady as soon as the butler entered in answer to the bell.

'Your own maid and your parlour-maid, if I may,' replied Lady Molly.

Lady Irene gave the necessary orders, and we all sat expectant and silent until, a minute or two later, two girls entered the room. One wore a cap and apron, the other, in neat black dress and dainty lace collar, was obviously the lady's maid.

'This lady,' said their mistress, addressing the two girls, 'wishes to ask you a few questions. She is a representative of the police, so you had better do your best to satisfy her with your answers.'

'Oh!' rejoined Lady Molly pleasantly – choosing not to notice the tone of acerbity with which the young widow had spoken, nor the unmistakable barrier of hostility and reserve which her words had immediately raised between the young servants and the 'representative of the police'–'what I am going to ask these two young ladies is neither very difficult nor very unpleasant. I merely want their kind help in a little comedy which will have to be played this evening, in order to test the accuracy of certain statements made by one of the waitresses at Mathis' tea shop with regard to the terrible tragedy which has darkened this house. You will do that much, will you not?' she added, speaking directly to the maids.

No one can be so winning or so persuasive as my dear lady. In a moment I saw the girls' hostility melting before the sunshine of Lady Molly's smile.

'We'll do what we can, ma'am,' said the maid.

'That's a brave, good girl!' replied my lady. 'You must know that the chief waitress at Mathis' has, this very morning, identified the woman in the big hat who, we all believe, murdered your late master. Yes!' she continued, in response to a gasp of astonishment which seemed to go round the room like a wave, 'the girl seems quite positive, both as regards the hat and the woman who wore it. But, of course, one cannot allow a human life to be sworn away without bringing every possible proof to bear on such a statement, and I am sure that everyone in this house will understand that we don't want to introduce strangers more than we can help into this sad affair, which already has been bruited abroad too much.'

She paused a moment; then, as neither Lady Irene nor the maids made any comment, she continued:

'My superiors at Scotland Yard think it their duty to try and confuse the witness as much as possible in her act of identification. They desire that a certain number of ladies wearing abnormally large hats should parade before the waitress. Among them will be, of course, the one whom the girl has already identified as being the mysterious person who had tea with Mr Culledon at Mathis' that afternoon.

'My superiors can then satisfy themselves whether the waitress is or is not so sure of her statement that she invariably picks out again and again one particular individual amongst a number of others or not.'

'Surely,' interrupted Lady Irene, dryly, 'you and your superiors do not expect my servants to help in such a farce?'

'We don't look upon such a proceeding as a farce, Lady Irene,' rejoined Lady Molly, gently. 'It is often resorted to in the interests of an accused person, and we certainly would ask the co-operation of your household.'

'I don't see what they can do.'

But the two girls did not seem unwilling. The idea appealed to them, I felt sure; it suggested an exciting episode, and gave promise of variety in their monotonous lives.

'I am sure both these young ladies possess fine big hats,' continued Lady Molly with an encouraging smile.

'I should not allow them to wear ridiculous headgear,' retorted Lady Irene, sternly.

'I have the one your ladyship wouldn't wear and threw away,' interposed the young parlour-maid. 'I put it together again with the scraps I found in the dusthole.'

There was just one instant of absolute silence, one of those magnetic moments when Fate seems to have dropped the spool on which she was spinning the threads of a life, and is just stooping in order to pick it up.

Lady Irene raised a black-bordered handkerchief to her lips, then said quietly:

'I don't know what you mean, Mary. I never wear big hats.'

'No, my lady,' here interposed the lady's maid; 'but Mary

means the one you ordered at Sanchia's and only wore the once –
the day you went to that concert.'

'Which day was that?' asked Lady Molly, blandly.

'Oh! I couldn't forget that day,' ejaculated the maid; 'her
ladyship came home from the concert – I had undressed her, and
she told me that she would never wear her big hat again – it was
too heavy. That same day Mr Culledon was murdered.'

'That hat would answer our purpose very well,' said Lady
Molly, quite calmly. 'Perhaps Mary will go and fetch it, and you
had better go and help her put it on.'

The two girls went out of the room without another word, and
there were we three women left facing one another, with that
awful secret, only half-revealed, hovering in the air like an in-
tangible spectre.

'What are you going to do, Lady Irene?' asked Lady Molly,
after a moment's pause, during which I literally could hear my
own heart beating, whilst I watched the rigid figure of the widow
in deep black crepe, her face set and white, her eyes fixed steadily
on Lady Molly.

'You can't prove it!' she said defiantly.

'I think we can,' rejoined Lady Molly, simply; 'at any rate,
I mean to try. I have two of the waitresses from Mathis' outside
in a cab, and I have already spoken to the attendant who served
you at Sanchia's, an obscure milliner in a back street near Portland
Road. We know that you were at great pains there to order a hat
of certain dimensions and to your own minute description; it was
a copy of one you had once seen Miss Lowenthal wear when you
met her at your late husband's office. We can prove that meeting,
too. Then we have your maid's testimony that you wore that
same hat once, and once only, the day, presumably, that you
went out to a concert – a statement which you will find it difficult
to substantiate – and also the day on which your husband was
murdered.'

'Bah! the public will laugh at you!' retorted Lady Irene, still
defiantly. 'You would not dare to formulate so monstrous a
charge!'

'It will not seem monstrous when justice has weighed in the

balance the facts which we can prove. Let me tell you a few of
these, the result of careful investigation. There is the fact that you
knew of Mr Culledon's entanglement with Miss Elizabeth
Lowenthal, and did your best to keep it from old Mrs Steinberg's
knowledge, realizing that any scandal round her favourite nephew
would result in the old lady cutting him – and therefore you –
out of her will. You dismissed a parlour-maid for the sole reason
that she had been present when Miss Lowenthal was shown into
Mr Culledon's study. There is the fact that Miss Steinberg had
so worded her will that, in the event of her nephew dying before
her, her fortune would devolve on you; the fact that, with
Miss Lowenthal's action for breach of promise against your husband, your last hope of keeping the scandal from the old lady's
ears had effectually vanished. You saw the fortune eluding your
grasp; you feared Mrs Steinberg would alter her will. Had you
found the means, and had you dared, would you not rather have
killed the old lady? But discovery would have been certain. The
other crime was bolder and surer. You have inherited the old lady's
millions, for she never knew of her nephew's earlier peccadilloes.

'All this we can state and prove, and the history of the hat,
bought, and worn one day only, that same memorable day, and
then thrown away.'

A loud laugh interrupted her – a laugh that froze my very
marrow.

'There is one fact you have forgotten, my lady of Scotland
Yard,' came in sharp, strident accents from the black-robed figure,
which seemed to have become strangely spectral in the fast
gathering gloom which had been enveloping the luxurious little
boudoir. 'Don't omit to mention the fact that the accused took
the law into her own hands.'

And before my dear lady and I could rush to prevent her, Lady
Irene Culledon had conveyed something – we dared not think
what – to her mouth.

'Find Danvers quickly, Mary!' said Lady Molly, calmly.
'You'll find him outside. Bring a doctor back with you.'

Even as she spoke Lady Irene, with a cry of agony, fell sense-
less in my dear lady's arms.

The doctor, I may tell you, came too late. The unfortunate woman evidently had a good knowledge of poisons. She had been determined not to fail; in case of discovery, she was ready and able to mete out justice to herself.

I don't think the public ever knew the real truth about the woman in the big hat. Interest in her went the way of all things. Yet my dear lady had been right from beginning to end. With unerring precision she had placed her dainty finger on the real motive and the real perpetrator of the crime – the ambitious woman who had married solely for money, and meant to have that money even at the cost of one of the most dastardly murders that have ever darkened the criminal annals of this country.

I asked Lady Molly what it was that first made her think of Lady Irene as the possible murderess. No one else for a moment had thought her guilty.

'The big hat,' replied my dear lady with a smile. 'Had the mysterious woman at Mathis' been tall, the waitresses would not, one and all, have been struck by the abnormal size of the hat. The wearer must have been petite, hence the reason that under a wide brim only the chin would be visible. I at once sought for a small woman. Our fellows did not think of that, because they are men.'

You see how simple it all was!

BOOK THREE

Raymond Chandler

GOLDFISH

I

I WASN'T DOING ANY WORK that day, just catching up on my
foot-dangling. A warm gusty breeze was blowing in at the office
window and the soot from the Mansion House Hotel oil-burners
across the alley was rolling across the glass top of my desk in
tiny particles, like pollen drifting over a vacant lot.

I was just thinking about going to lunch when Kathy Horne
came in.

She was a tall, seedy, sad-eyed blonde who had once been a
policewoman and had lost her job when she married a cheap little
cheque-bouncer named Johnny Horne, to reform him. She hadn't
reformed him, but she was waiting for him to come out so she
could try again. In the meantime she ran the cigar counter at the
Mansion House, and watched the grifters go by in a haze of nickel
cigar smoke. And once in a while lent one of them ten dollars to
get out of town. She was just that soft. She sat down and opened
her big shiny bag and got out a package of cigarettes and lit one
with my desk lighter. She blew a plume of smoke, wrinkled her
nose at it.

'Did you ever hear of the Leander pearls?' she asked. 'Gosh,
that blue serge shines. You must have money in the bank, the
clothes you wear.'

'No,' I said, 'to both your ideas. I never heard of the Leander
pearls and don't have any money in the bank.'

'Then you'd like to make yourself a cut of twenty-five grand
maybe.'

I lit one of her cigarettes. She got up and shut the window,
saying: 'I get enough of that hotel smell on the job.'

She sat down again, went on: 'It's nineteen years ago. They
had the guy in Leavenworth fifteen and it's four since they let him
out. A big lumberman from up north named Sol Leander bought

them for his wife – the pearls, I mean – just two of them. They cost two hundred grand.'

'It must have taken a hand truck to move them,' I said.

'I see you don't know a lot about pearls,' Kathy Horne said. 'It's not just size. Anyhow they're worth more today and the twenty-five grand reward the Reliance people put out is still good.'

'I get it,' I said. 'Somebody copped them off.'

'Now you're getting yourself some oxygen.' She dropped her cigarette into a tray and let it smoke, as ladies will. I put it out for her. 'That's what the guy was in Leavenworth for, only they never proved he got the pearls. It was a mail-car job. He got himself hidden in the car somehow and up in Wyoming he shot the clerk, cleaned out the registered mail and dropped off. He got to BC before he was nailed. But they didn't get any of the stuff – not then. All they got was him. He got life.'

'If it's going to be a long story, let's have a drink.'

'I never drink until sundown. That way you don't get to be a heel.'

'Tough on the Eskimos,' I said. 'In the summertime anyway.'

She watched me get my little flat bottle out. Then she went on:

'His name was Sype – Wally Sype. He did it alone. And he wouldn't squawk about the stuff, not a peep. Then after fifteen long years they offered him a pardon, if he would loosen up with the loot. He gave up everything but the pearls.'

'Where did he have it?' I asked. 'In his hat?'

'Listen, this isn't just a bunch of gag lines. I've got a lead to those marbles.'

I shut my mouth with my hand and looked solemn.

'He said he never had the pearls and they must have halfway believed him because they gave him the pardon. Yet the pearls were in the load, registered mail, and they were never seen again.'

My throat began to feel a little thick. I didn't say anything.

Kathy Horne went on: 'One time in Leavenworth, just one time in all those years, Wally Sype wrapped himself around a can of white shellac and got as tight as a fat lady's girdle. His cell mate was a little man called Peeler Mardo. He was doing twenty-seven months for splitting twenty dollar bills. Sype told him he had the pearls buried somewhere in Idaho.'

I leaned forward a little.

'Beginning to get to you, eh?' she said. 'Well get this. Peeler Mardo is rooming at my house and he's a coke-hound and he talks in his sleep.'

I leaned back again. 'Good grief,' I said. 'And I was practically spending the reward money.'

She stared at me coldly. Then her face softened. 'All right,' she said a little hopelessly. 'I know it sounds screwy. All those years gone by and all the smart heads that must have worked on the case, postal men and private agencies and all. And then a coke-head to turn it up. But he's a nice little runt and somehow I believe him. He knows where Sype is.'

I said: 'Did he talk all this in his sleep?'

'Of course not. But you know me. An old policewoman's got ears. Maybe I was nosy, but I guessed he was an ex-con and I worried about him using the stuff so much. He's the only roomer I've got now and I'd kind of go in by his door and listen to him talking to himself. That way I got enough to brace him. He told me the rest. He wants help to collect.'

I leaned forward again. 'Where's Sype?'

Kathy Horne smiled, and shook her head. 'That's the one thing he wouldn't tell, that and the name Sype is using now. But it's somewhere up North, in or near Olympia, Washington. Peeler saw him up there and found out about him and he says Sype didn't see *him*.'

'What's Peeler doing down here?' I asked.

'Here's where they put the Leavenworth rap on him. You know an old con always goes back to look at the piece of sidewalk he slipped on. But he doesn't have any friends here now.'

I lit another cigarette and had another little drink.

'Sype has been out four years, you say. Peeler did twenty-seven months. What's he been doing with all the time since?'

Kathy Horne widened her china blue eyes pityingly. 'Maybe you think there's only one jailhouse he could get into.'

'Okay,' I said. 'Will he talk to me? I guess he wants help to deal with the insurance people, in case there are any pearls and Sype will put them right in Peeler's hand and soon. Is that it?'

Kathy Horne sighed. 'Yes, he'll talk to you. He's aching to. He's scared about something. Will you go out now, before he gets junked up for the evening?'

'Sure – if that's what you want.'

She took a flat key out of her bag and wrote an address on my pad. She stood up slowly.

'It's a double house. My side's separate. There's a door in between, with the key on my side. That's just in case he won't come to the door.'

'Okay,' I said. I blew smoke at the ceiling and stared at her.

She went towards the door, stopped, came back. She looked down at the floor.

'I don't rate much in it,' she said. 'Maybe not anything. But if I could have a grand or two waiting for Johnny when he came out, maybe – '

'Maybe you could hold him straight,' I said. 'It's a dream, Kathy. It's all a dream. But if it isn't you cut an even third.'

She caught her breath and glared at me to keep from crying. She went towards the door, stopped and came back again.

'That isn't all,' she said. 'It's the old guy – Sype. He did fifteen years. He paid. Paid hard. Doesn't it make you feel kind of mean?'

I shook my head. 'He stole them, didn't he? He killed a man. What does he do for a living?'

'His wife has money,' Kathy Horne said. 'He just plays around with goldfish.'

'Goldfish?' I said. 'To hell with him.'

She went on out.

2

The last time I had been in the Gray Lake district I had helped a DA's man named Bernie Obis shoot a gunman named Poke Andrews. But that was higher up the hill, further away from the lake. This house was on the second level, in a loop the street made rounding a spur of the hill. It stood by itself high up, with a cracked retaining wall in front and several vacant lots behind.

Being originally a double house it had two front doors and two sets of front steps. One of the doors had a sign tacked over the grating that masked the peep window: Ring 1432.

I parked my car and went up right-angle steps, passed between two lines of pinks, went up more steps to the side with the sign. That should be the roomer's side. I rang the bell. Nobody answered it, so I went across to the other door. Nobody answered that one either.

While I was waiting a grey Dodge coupé whished around the curve and a small neat girl in blue looked up at me for a second. I didn't see who else was in the car. I didn't pay much attention. I didn't know it was important.

I took out Kathy Horne's key and let myself into a closed living-room that smelled of cedar oil. There was just enough furniture to get by, net curtains, a quiet shaft of sunlight under the drapes in front. There was a tiny breakfast room, a kitchen, a bedroom in the back that was obviously Kathy's, a bathroom, another bedroom in front that seemed to be used as a sewing-room. It was this room that had the door cut through to the other side of the house.

I unlocked it and stepped, as it were, through a mirror. Everything was backwards, except the furniture. The living-room on that side had twin beds, didn't have the look of being lived in.

I went towards the back of the house, past the second bathroom, knocked at the shut door that corresponded to Kathy's bedroom.

No answer. I tried the knob and went in. The little man on the bed was probably Peeler Mardo. I noticed his feet first, because although he had on trousers and a shirt, his feet were bare and hung over the end of the bed. They were tied there by a rope around the ankles.

They had been burned raw on the soles. There was a smell of scorched flesh in spite of the open window. Also a smell of scorched wood. An electric iron on a desk was still connected. I went over and shut it off.

I went back to Kathy Horne's kitchen and found a pint of Brooklyn Scotch in the cooler. I used some of it and breathed deeply for a little while and looked out over the vacant lots. There was a narrow cement walk behind the house and green wooden steps down to the street.

I went back to Peeler Mardo's room. The coat of a brown suit with a red pin stripe hung over a chair with the pockets turned out and what had been in them on the floor.

He was wearing the trousers of the suit, and their pockets were turned out also. Some keys and change and a handkerchief lay on the bed beside him, and a metal box like a woman's compact, from which some glistening white powder had spilled. Cocaine.

He was a little man, not more, than five feet four, with thin brown hair and large ears. His eyes had no particular colour. They were just eyes, and very wide open, and quite dead. His arms were pulled out from him and tied at the wrists by a rope that went under the bed.

I looked him over for bullet or knife wounds, didn't find any. There wasn't a mark on him except his feet. Shock or heart failure or a combination of the two must have done the trick. He was still warm. The gag in his mouth was both warm and wet.

I wiped off everything I had touched, looked out of Kathy's front window for a while before I left the house.

It was three-thirty when I walked into the lobby of the Mansion House, over to the cigar counter in the corner. I leaned on the glass and asked for Camels.

Kathy Horne flicked the pack at me, dropped the change into my outside breast pocket, and gave me her customer's smile.

'Well? You didn't take long,' she said, and looked sidewise along her eyes at a drunk who was trying to light a cigar with the old-fashioned flint and steel lighter.

'It's heavy,' I told her. 'Get set.'

She turned away quickly and flipped a pack of paper matches along the glass to the drunk. He fumbled for them, dropped both matches and cigar, scooped them angrily off the floor and went off looking back over his shoulder, as if he expected a kick.

Kathy looked past my head, her eyes cool and empty.

'I'm set,' she whispered.

'You cut a full half,' I said. 'Peeler's out. He's been bumped off – in his bed.'

Her eyes twitched. Two fingers curled on the glass near my elbow. A white line showed around her mouth. That was all.

'Listen,' I said. 'Don't say anything until I'm through. He died of shock. Somebody burned his feet with a cheap electric iron. Not yours. I looked. I'd say he died rather quickly and couldn't have said much. The gag was still in his mouth. When I went out there, frankly, I thought it was all hooey. Now I'm not so sure. If he gave up his dope, we're through, and so is Sype, unless I can find him first. Those workers didn't have any inhibitions at all. If he didn't give up, there's still time.'

Her head turned, her set eyes looked towards the revolving door
of the lobby entrance. White patches glared in her cheeks.

'What do I do?' she breathed.

I poked at a box of wrapped cigars, dropped her key into it.
Her long fingers got it out smoothly, hid it.

'When you get home you find him. You don't know a thing.
Leave the pearls out, leave me out. When they check his prints
they'll know he had a record and they'll just figure it was something caught up with him.'

I broke my cigarettes open and lit one, watched her for a
moment. She didn't move an inch.

'Can you face it down?' I asked. 'If you can't, now's the time
to speak.'

'Of course.' Her eyebrows arched. 'Do I look like a torturer?'

'You married a crook,' I said grimly.

She flushed, which was what I wanted. 'He isn't! He's just a
damn fool! Nobody thinks any the worse of me, not even the boys
down at Headquarters.'

'All right. I like it that way. It's not our murder, after all. And
if we talk now, you can say good-bye to any share in any reward –
even if one is ever paid.'

'Darn tootin',' Kathy Horne said pertly. 'Oh, the poor little
runt,' she almost sobbed.

I patted her arm, grinned as heartily as I could and left the
Mansion House.

3

The Reliance Indemnity Company had offices in the Graas Building, three small rooms that looked like nothing at all. They were a
big enough outfit to be as shabby as they liked.

The resident manager was named Lutin, a middle-aged bald-
headed man with quiet eyes, dainty fingers that caressed a dappled
cigar. He sat behind a large, well-dusted desk and stared peacefully at my chin.

'Carmady, eh? I've heard of you.' He touched my card with a
shiny little finger. 'What's on your mind?'

I rolled a cigarette around in my fingers and lowered my voice.
'Remember the Leander pearls?'

His smile was slow, a little bored. 'I'm not likely to forget them. They cost this company one hundred and fifty thousand dollars. I was a cocky young adjuster then.'

I said: 'I've got an idea. It may be all haywire. It very likely is. But I'd like to try it out. Is your twenty-five grand reward still good?'

He chuckled. 'Twenty grand, Carmady. We spent the difference ourselves. You're wasting time.'

'It's my time. Twenty it is then. How much co-operation can I get?'

'What kind of co-operation?'

'Can I have a letter identifying me to your other branches? In case I have to go out of the State. In case I need kind words from some local law.'

'Which way out of the State?'

I smiled at him. He tapped his cigar on the edge of a tray and smiled back. Neither of our smiles was honest.

'No letter,' he said. 'New York wouldn't stand for it. We have our own tie-up. But all the co-operation you can use, under the hat. And the twenty grand, if you click. Of course you won't.'

I lit my cigarette and leaned back, puffed smoke at the ceiling.

'No? Why not? You never got those marbles. They existed, didn't they?'

'Darn' right they existed. And if they still do, they belong to us. But two hundred grand doesn't get buried for twenty years – and then get dug up.'

'All right. It's still my own time.'

He knocked a little ash off his cigar and looked down his eyes at me. 'I like your front,' he said, 'even if you are crazy. But we're a large organization. Suppose I have you covered from now on. What then?'

'I lose. I'll know I'm covered. I'm too long in the game to miss that. I'll quit, give up what I know to the law, and go home.'

'Why would you do that?'

I leaned forward over the desk again. 'Because,' I said slowly, 'the guy that had the lead got bumped off today.'

'Oh – oh.' Lutin rubbed his nose.

'I didn't bump him off,' I added.

We didn't talk any more for a little while. Then Lutin said: 'You don't want any letter. You wouldn't even carry it. And after your telling me that, you know damn well I won't dare give it to you.'

I stood up, grinned, started for the door. He got up himself, very fast, ran around the desk and put his small neat hand on my arm.

'Listen, I know you're crazy, but if you do get anything bring it in through our boys. We need the advertising.'

'What the hell do you think I live on?' I growled.

'Twenty-five grand.'

'I thought it was twenty.'

'Twenty-five. And you're still crazy. Sype never had those pearls. If he had, he'd have made some kind of terms with us many years ago.'

'Okay,' I said. 'You've had plenty of time to make up your mind.'

We shook hands, grinned at each other like a couple of wise boys who know they're not kidding anybody, but won't give up trying.

It was a quarter to five when I got back to the office. I had a couple of short drinks and stuffed a pipe and sat down to interview my brains. The phone rang.

A woman's voice said: 'Carmady?' It was a small, tight, cold voice. I didn't know it.

'Yeah.'

'Better see Rush Madder. Know him?'

'No,' I lied. 'Why should I see him?'

There was sudden tinkling, icy-cold laugh on the wire. 'On account of a guy had sore feet,' the voice said.

The phone clicked. I put my end of it aside, struck a match and stared at the wall until the flame burned my fingers.

Rush Madder was a shyster in the Quorn Building. An ambulance chaser, a small time fixer, an alibi builder-upper, anything that smelled a little and paid a little more. I hadn't heard of him in connection with any big operations like burning people's feet.

4

It was getting toward quitting time on lower Spring Street. Taxis were dawdling close to the kerb, stenographers were getting an early start home, street cars were clogging up, and traffic cops were preventing people from making perfectly legal right turns.

The Quorn Building was a narrow front, the colour of dried mustard, with a large case of false teeth in the entrance. The directory held the names of painless dentists, people who teach you how to become a letter-carrier, just names, and numbers without any names. Rush Madder, Attorney-at-Law, was in Room 619.

I got out of a jolting open cage elevator, looked at a dirty spittoon on a dirty rubber mat, walked down a corridor that smelled of butts, and tried the knob below the frosted glass panel of 619. The door was locked. I knocked.

A shadow came against the glass and the door was pulled back with a squeak. I was looking at a thick-set man with a soft round chin, heavy black eyebrows, an oily complexion and a Charlie Chan moustache that made his face look fatter than it was.

He put out a couple of nicotined fingers. 'Well, well, the old dog-catcher himself. The eye that never forgets. Carmady is the name, I believe?'

I stepped inside and waited for the door to squeak shut. A bare carpetless room paved in brown linoleum, a flat desk and a rolltop at right angles to it, a big green safe that looked as fireproof as a delicatessen bag, two filing cases, three chairs, a built-in closet and washbowl in the corner by the door.

'Well, well, sit down,' Madder said. 'Glad to see you.' He fussed around behind his desk and adjusted a burst-out seat cushion, sat on it. 'Nice of you to drop around. Business?'

I sat down and put a cigarette between my teeth and looked at him. I didn't say a word. I watched him start to sweat. It started up in his hair. Then he grabbed a pencil and made marks on his blotter. Then he looked at me with a quick darting glance, down at his blotter again. He talked – to the blotter.

'Any ideas?' he asked softly.

'About what?'

He didn't look at me. 'About how we could do a little business together. Say, in stones.'

'Who was the wren?' I asked.

'Huh? What wren?' He still didn't look at me.

'The one that phoned me.'

'Did somebody phone you?'

I reached for his telephone, which was the old-fashioned

gallows type. I lifted off the receiver and started to dial the number of Police Headquarters, very slowly. I knew he would know that number about as well as he knew his hat.

He reached over and pushed the hook down. 'Now, listen,' he complained. 'You're too fast. What you calling copper for?'

I said slowly: 'They want to talk to you. On account of you know a broad that knows a man had sore feet.'

'Does it have to be that way?' His collar was too tight now. He yanked at it.

'Not from my side. But if you think I'm going to sit here and let you play with my reflexes, it does.'

Madder opened a flat tin of cigarettes and pushed one past his lips with a sound like somebody gutting a fish. His hand shook.

'All right,' he said thickly. 'All right. Don't get sore.'

'Just stop trying to count clouds with me,' I growled. 'Talk sense. If you've got a job for me, it's probably too dirty for me to touch. But I'll at least listen.'

He nodded. He was comfortable now. He knew I was bluffing. He puffed a pale swirl of smoke and watched it float up.

'That's all right,' he said evenly. 'I play dumb myself once in a while. The thing is we're wise. Carol saw you go to the house and leave it again. No law came.'

'Carol?'

'Carol Donovan. Friend of mine. She called you up.'

I nodded. 'Go ahead.'

He didn't say anything. He just sat there and looked at me owlishly.

I grinned and leaned across the desk a little and said: 'Here's what's bothering you. You don't know why I went to the house or why, having gone, I didn't yell police. That's easy. I thought it was a secret.'

'We're just kidding each other,' Madder said sourly.

'All right,' I said. 'Let's talk about pearls. Does that make it any easier?'

His eyes shone. He wanted to let himself get excited, but he didn't. He kept his voice down, said coolly:

'Carol picked him up one night, the little guy. A crazy little number, full of snow, but way back in his noodle an idea. He'd talk about pearls, about an old guy up in the northwest of Canada that swiped them a long time ago and still had them. Only he

wouldn't say who the old guy was or where he was. Foxy about
that. Holding out. I wouldn't know why.'

'He wanted to get his feet burned,' I said.

Madder's lips shook and another fine sweat showed in his hair.
'I didn't do that,' he said thickly.

'You or Carol, what's the odds? The little guy died. They can
make murder out of it. You didn't find out what you wanted to
know. That's why *I'm* here. You think I have information you
didn't get. Forget it. If I knew enough, I wouldn't be here, and
if you knew enough, you wouldn't want me here. Check?'

He grinned, very slowly, as if it hurt him. He struggled up in
his chair and dragged a deep drawer out from the side of his
desk, put a nicely moulded brown bottle up on the desk, and two
striped glasses. He whispered: 'Two way split. You and me. I'm
cutting Carol out. She's too damn rough, Carmady. I've seen hard
women, but she's the blueing on armour plate. And you'd never
think it to look at her, would you?'

'Have I seen her?'

'I guess so. She says you did.'

'Oh, the girl in the Dodge.'

He nodded, and poured two good-sized drinks, put the bottle
down and stood up. 'Water? I like it in mine.'

'No,' I said, 'but why cut me in? I don't know any more than
you mentioned. Or very little. Certainly not as much as you must
know to go that far.'

He leered across the glasses. 'I know where I can get fifty grand
for the Leander pearls, twice what you could get. I can give you
yours and still have mine. You've got the front I need to work in
the open. How about the water?'

'No water,' I said.

He went across to the built-in wash place and ran the water and
came back with his glass half full. He sat down again, grinned,
lifted it.

We drank.

5

So far I had only made four mistakes. The first was mixing in
it at all, even for Kathy Horne's sake. The second was staying

mixed after I found Peeler Mardo dead. The third was letting Rush Madder see I knew what he was talking about. The fourth, the whisky, was the worst.

It tasted funny even on the way down. Then there was that sudden moment of sharp lucidity when I knew, exactly as though I had seen it, that he had switched his drink for a harmless one cached in the closet.

I sat still for a moment, with the empty glass at my fingers' ends, gathering my strength. Madder's face began to get large and moony and vague. A fat smile jerked in and out under his Charlie Chan moustache as he watched me.

I reached back into my hip pocket and pulled out a loosely wadded handkerchief. The small safe inside it didn't seem to show. At least Madder didn't move, after his first grab under the coat.

I stood up and swayed forward drunkenly and smacked him square on the top of the head.

He gagged. He started to get up. I tapped him on the jaw. He became limp and his hand sweeping down from under his coat knocked his glass over on the desk top. I straightened it, stood silent, listening, struggling with a rising wave of nauseous stupor.

I went over to a communicating door and tried the knob. It was locked. I was staggering by now. I dragged an office chair to the entrance door and propped the back of it under the knob. I leaned against the door panting, gritting my teeth, cursing myself. I got handcuffs out and started back towards Madder.

A very pretty black-haired, grey-eyed girl stepped out of the clothes closet and poked a .32 at me.

She wore a blue suit cut with a lot of snap. An inverted saucer of a hat came down in a hard line across her forehead. Shiny black hair showed at the sides. Her eyes were slate-grey, cold, and yet light-hearted. Her face was fresh and young and delicate and as hard as a chisel.

'All right, Carmady. Lie down and sleep it off. You're through.'

I stumbled towards her waving my sap. She shook her head. When her face moved it got large before my eyes. Its outlines changed and wobbled. The gun in her hand looked like anything from a tunnel to a toothpick.

'Don't be a goof, Carmady,' she said. 'A few hours sleep for you, a few hours start for us. Don't make me shoot. I would.'

'Damn you,' I mumbled. 'I believe you would.'

'Right as rain, toots. I'm a lady that wants her own way. That's fine. Sit down.'

The floor rose up and bumped me. I sat on it as on a raft in a rough sea. I braced myself on flat hands. I could hardly feel the floor. My hands were numb. My whole body was numb.

I tried to stare her down. 'Ha-a! L-lady K-killer!' I giggled.

She threw a chilly laugh at me which I only just barely heard. Drums were beating in my head now, war drums from a far off jungle. Waves of light were moving, and dark shadows and a rustle as of a wind in tree-tops. I didn't want to lie down. I lay down.

The girl's voice came from very far off, an elfin voice.

'Two-way split, eh? He doesn't like my method, eh? Bless his big soft heart. We'll see about him.'

Vaguely as I floated off I seemed to feel a dull jar that might have been a shot. I hoped she had shot Madder, but she hadn't. She had merely helped me on my way out – with my own sap.

When I came around again it was night. Something clacked overhead with a heavy sound. Through the open window beyond the desk yellow light splashed on the high side walls of a building. The thing clacked again and the light went off. An advertising sign on the roof.

I got up off the floor like a man climbing out of thick mud. I waded over to the washbowl, splashed water on my face, felt the top of my head and winced, waded back to the door and found the light switch.

Strewn papers lay around the desk, broken pencils, envelopes, an empty brown whisky bottle, cigarette ends and ashes. The debris of hastily emptied drawers. I didn't bother going through any of it. I left the office, rode down to the street in the shuddering elevator, slid into a bar and had a brandy, then got my car and drove on home.

I changed clothes, packed a bag, had some whisky and answered the telephone. It was about nine-thirty.

Kathy Horne's voice said: 'So you're not gone yet. I hoped you wouldn't be.'

'Alone?' I asked, still thick in the voice.

'Yes, but I haven't been. The house has been full of coppers for hours. They were very nice, considering. Old grudge of some kind, they figured.'

'And the line is likely tapped now,' I growled. 'Where was I supposed to be going?'

'Well – you know. Your girl told me.'

'Little dark girl? Very cool? Name of Carol Donovan?'

'She had your card. Why, wasn't it – '

'I don't have any girl,' I said simply. 'And I bet that just very casually, without thinking at all, a name slipped past your lips – the name of a town up North. Did it?'

'Ye-es,' Kathy Horne admitted weakly.

I caught the night plane north.

It was a nice trip except that I had a sore head and a raging thirst for ice-water.

6

The Snoqualmie Hotel in Olympia was on Capitol Way, fronting on the usual square city block of park. I left by the coffee-shop door and walked down a hill to where the last, loneliest reach of Puget Sound died and decomposed against a line of disused wharves. Corded firewood filled the foreground and old men pottered about in the middle of the stacks, or sat on boxes with pipes in their mouths and signs behind their heads reading: 'Firewood and Split Kindling. Free Delivery.'

Behind them a low cliff rose and the vast pines of the north loomed against a grey-blue sky.

Two of the old men sat on boxes about twenty feet apart, ignoring each other. I drifted near one of them. He wore corduroy pants and what had been a red and black mackinaw. His felt hat showed the sweat of twenty summers. One of his hands clutched a short black pipe, and with the grimed fingers of the other he slowly, carefully, ecstatically jerked at a long curling hair that grew out of his nose.

I set a box on end, sat down, filled my own pipe, lit it, puffed a cloud of smoke. I waved a hand at the water and said: 'You'd never think that ever met the Pacific Ocean.'

He looked at me.

I said: 'Dead end – quiet, restful, like your town. I like a town like this.' He went on looking at me.

'I'll bet,' I said, 'that a man that's been around a town like this knows everybody in it and in the country near it.'

He said: 'How much you bet?'

I took a silver dollar out of my pocket. They still had a few up there. The old man looked it over, nodded, suddenly yanked the long hair out of his nose and held it up against the light.

'You'd lose,' he said.

I put the dollar down on my knee. 'Know anybody around here that keeps a lot of goldfish?' I asked.

He stared at the dollar. The other old man near by was wearing overalls and shoes without any laces. He stared at the dollar. They both spat at the same instant. The first old man turned his head and yelled at the top of his voice: 'Know anybody keeps goldfish?'

The other old man jumped up off his box and seized a big axe, set a log on end and whanged the axe down on it, splitting it evenly. He looked at the first old man triumphantly and screamed: 'I ain't neither.'

The first old man said: 'Leetle deef.' He got up slowly and went over to a shack built of old boards of uneven lengths. He went into it, banged the door.

The second old man threw his axe down pettishly, spat in the direction of the closed door and went off among the stacks of cordwood.

The door of the shack opened, the man in the mackinaw poked his head out of it.

'Sewer crabs is all,' he said, and slammed the door again.

I put my dollar in my pocket and went back up the hill. I figured it would take too long to learn their language.

Capitol Way ran north and south. A dull green street car shuttled past on the way to a place called Tumwater. In the distance I could see the government buildings. Northward the street passed two hotels and some stores and branched right and left. Right went to Tacoma and Seattle. Left went over a bridge and out on to the Olympic Peninsula.

Beyond this right and left turn the street suddenly became old and shabby, with broken asphalt paving, a Chinese restaurant, a boarded-up movie house, a pawnbroker's establishment. A sign jutting over the dirty sidewalk said: 'Smoke Shop', and in small letters underneath, as if it hoped nobody was looking, 'Pool'.

I went in past a rack of gaudy magazines and a cigar show-case that had flies inside it. There was a long wooden counter on the left, a few slot machines, a single pool table. Three kids fiddled with the slot machines and a tall thin man with a long nose and no chin played pool all by himself, with a dead cigar in his face.

I sat on a stool and a hard-eyed bald-headed man behind the counter got up from a chair, wiped his hands on a thick grey apron, showed me a gold tooth.

'A little rye,' I said. 'Know anybody that keeps goldfish?'

'Yeah,' he said. 'No.'

He poured something behind the counter and shoved a thick glass across.

'Two bits.'

I sniffed the stuff, wrinkled my nose. 'Was it the rye the "yeah" was for?'

The bald-headed man held up a large bottle with a label that said something about: 'Cream of Dixie Straight Rye Whisky Guaranteed at Least Four Months Old.'

'Okay,' I said. 'I see it just moved in.'

I poured some water in it and drank it. It tasted like a cholera culture. I put a quarter on the counter. The barman showed me a gold tooth on the other side of his face and took hold of the counter with two hard hands and pushed his chin at me.

'What was that crack?' he asked, almost gently.

'I just moved in,' I said. 'I'm looking for some goldfish for the front window. Goldfish.'

The barman said very slowly: 'Do I look like a guy would know a guy would have goldfish?' His face was a little white.

The long-nosed man who had been playing himself a round of pool racked his cue and strolled over to the counter beside me and threw a nickel on it.

'Draw me a drink before you wet yourself,' he told the barman.

The barman pried himself loose from the counter with a good deal of effort. I looked down to see if his fingers had made any dents in the wood. He drew a coke, stirred it with a swizzle-stick, dumped it on the bar top, took a deep breath and let it out through his nose, grunted and went away towards a door marked: 'Toilet'.

The long-nosed man lifted his coke and looked into the smeared mirror behind the bar. The left side of his mouth twitched briefly. A dim voice came from it, saying: 'How's Peeler?'

I pressed my thumb and forefinger together, put them to my nose, sniffed, shook my head sadly.

'Hitting it high, huh?'

'Yeah,' I said. 'I didn't catch the name.'

'Call me Sunset. I'm always movin' west. Think he'll stay clammed?'

'He'll stay clammed,' I said.

'What's your handle?'

'Dodge Willis, El Paso,' I said.

'Got a room somewhere?'

'Hotel.'

He put his glass down empty. 'Let's dangle.'

7

We went up to my room and sat down and looked at each other over a couple of glasses of Scotch and ginger ale. Sunset studied me with his close-set expressionless eyes, a little at a time, but very thoroughly in the end, adding it all up.

I sipped my drink and waited. At last he said in his lipless 'stir' voice: 'How come Peeler didn't come hisself?'

'For the same reason he didn't stay when he was here.'

'Meaning which?'

'Figure it out for yourself,' I said.

He nodded, just as though I had said something with a meaning. Then: 'What's the top price?'

'Twenty-five grand.'

'Nuts.' Sunset was emphatic, even rude.

I leaned back and lit a cigarette, puffed smoke at the open window and watched the breeze pick it up and tear it to pieces.

'Listen,' Sunset complained. 'I don't know you from last Sunday's sports section. You may be all to the silk. I just don't know.'

'Why'd you brace me?' I asked.

'You had the word, didn't you?'

This was where I took the dive. I grinned at him. 'Yeah. Goldfish was the password. The Smoke Shop was the place.'

His lack of expression told me I was right. It was one of those breaks you dream of, but don't handle right even in dreams.

'Well, what's the next angle?' Sunset inquired, sucking a piece of ice out of his glass and chewing on it.

I laughed. 'Okay, Sunset. I'm satisfied you're cagey. We could go on like this for weeks. Let's put our cards on the table. Where is the old guy?'

Sunset tightened his lips, moistened them, tightened them again. He set his glass down very slowly and his right hand hung lax on his thigh. I knew I had made a mistake, that Peeler knew where the old guy was, exactly. Therefore I should know.

Nothing in Sunset's voice showed I had made a mistake. He said crossly: 'You mean why don't I put my cards on the table and you just sit back and look 'em over. Nix.'

'Then how do you like this?' I growled. 'Peeler's dead.'

One eyebrow twitched, and one corner of his mouth. His eyes got a little blanker than before, if possible. His voice rasped lightly, like a finger on dry leather.

'How come?'

'Competition you two didn't know about.' I leaned back, smiled.

The gun made a soft metallic blur in the sunshine. I hardly saw where it came from. Then the muzzle was round and dark and empty looking at me.

'You're kidding the wrong guy,' Sunset said lifelessly. 'I ain't no soft spot for chiselers to lie on.'

I folded my arms, taking care that my right hand was outside, in view.

'I would be – if I was kidding. I'm not. Peeler played with a girl and she milked him – up to a point. He didn't tell her where to find the old fellow. So she and her top man went to see Peeler where he lived. They used a hot iron on his feet. He died of the shock.'

Sunset looked unimpressed. 'I got a lot of room in my ears yet,' he said.

'So have I,' I snarled, suddenly pretending anger. 'Just what the hell have you said that means anything – except that you know Peeler?'

He spun his gun on his trigger finger, watching it spin. 'Old man Sype's at Westport,' he said casually. 'That mean anything to you?'

'Yeah. Has he got the marbles?'

'How the hell would I know?' He steadied the gun again, dropped it to his thigh. It wasn't pointing at me now. 'Where's this competish you mentioned?'

'I hope I ditched them,' I said. 'I'm not too sure. Can I put my hands down and take a drink?'

'Yeah, go ahead. How did you cut in?'

'Peeler roomed with the wife of a friend of mine who's in stir. A straight girl, one you can trust. He let her in and she passed it to me – afterwards.'

'After the bump? How many cuts your side? My half is set.'

I took my drink, shoved the empty glass away. 'The hell it is.'

The gun lifted an inch, dropped again. 'How many altogether?' he snapped.

'Three, now Peeler's out. If we can hold off the competition.'

'The feet-toasters? No trouble about that. What they look like?'

'Man named Rush Madder, a shyster down south, fifty, fat, thin down-curving moustache, dark hair thin on top, five-nine, a hundred and eighty, not much guts. The girl, Carol Donovan, black hair, long bob, grey eyes, pretty, small features, twenty-five to eight, five-two, hundred twenty, last seen wearing blue, hard as they come. The real iron in the combination.'

Sunset nodded indifferently and put his gun away. 'We'll soften her, if she pokes her snoot in,' he said. 'I've got a heap at the house. Let's take the air Westport way and look it over. You might be able to ease in on the goldfish angle. They say he's nuts about them. I'll stay under cover. He's too stir-wise for me. I smell of the bucket.'

'Swell,' I said heartily. 'I'm an old goldfish fancier myself.'

Sunset reached for the bottle, poured two fingers of Scotch and put it down. He stood up, twitched his collar straight, then shot his chinless jaw forward as far as it would go.

'But don't make no error, bo. It's goin' to take pressure. It's goin' to mean a run out in the deep woods and some thumb twisting. Snatch stuff, likely.'

'That's okay,' I said. 'The insurance people are behind us.'

Sunset jerked down the points of his vest and rubbed the back of his thin neck. I put my hat on, locked the Scotch in the bag by the chair I'd been sitting in, went over and shut the window.

We started towards the door. Knuckles rattled on it just as I reached for the knob. I gestured Sunset back along the wall. I stared at the door for a moment and then I opened it up.

The two guns came forward almost on the same level, one small – a .32, one a big Smith and Wesson. They couldn't come into the room abreast, so the girl came in first.

'Okay, hot shot,' she said dryly. 'Ceiling zero. See if you can reach it.'

8

I backed slowly into the room. The two visitors bored in on me, either side. I tripped over my bag and fell backwards, hit the floor and rolled on my side groaning.

Sunset said casually: 'H'ist 'em, folks. Pretty now!'

Two heads jerked away from looking down at me and then I had my gun loose, down at my side. I kept on groaning.

There was a silence. I didn't hear any guns fall. The door of the room was still wide open and Sunset was flattened against the wall more or less behind it.

The girl said between her teeth: 'Cover the shamus, Rush – and shut the door. Skinny can't shoot here. Nobody can.' Then, in a whisper I barely caught, she added: 'Slam it!'

Rush Madder waddled backwards across the room keeping the Smith and Wesson pointed my way. His back was to Sunset and the thought of that made his eyes roll. I could have shot him easily enough, but it wasn't the play. Sunset stood with his feet spread and his tongue showing. Something that could have been a smile wrinkled his flat eyes.

He stared at the girl and she stared at him. Their guns stared at each other.

Rush Madder reached the door, grabbed the edge of it and gave it a hard swing. I knew exactly what was going to happen. As the door slammed the .32 was going to go off. It wouldn't be heard if it went off at the right instant. The explosion would be lost in the slamming of the door.

I reached out and took hold of Carol Donovan's ankle and jerked it hard.

The door slammed. Her gun went off and chipped the ceiling. She whirled on me kicking. Sunset said in his tight but somehow penetrating drawl: 'If this is it, this is it. Let's go!' The hammer clicked back on his Colt.

Something in his voice steadied Carol Donovan. She relaxed, let her automatic fall to her side and stepped away from me with a vicious look back.

Madder turned the key in the door and leaned against the wood, breathing noisily. His hat had tipped over one ear and the ends of two strips of adhesive showed under the brim.

Nobody moved while I had these thoughts. There was no sound of feet outside in the hall, no alarm. I got up on my knees, slid my gun out of sight, rose on my feet and went over to the window. Nobody down on the sidewalk was staring up at the upper floors of the Snoqualmie Hotel.

I sat on the broad old-fashioned sill and looked faintly embarrassed, as though the minister had said a bad word.

The girl snapped at me: 'Is this lug your partner?'

I didn't answer. Her face flushed slowly and her eyes burned. Madder put a hand out and fussed: 'Now listen, Carol, now listen here. This sort of act ain't the way – '

'Shut up!'

'Yeah,' Madder said in a clogged voice. 'Sure.'

Sunset looked the girl over lazily for the third or fourth time. His gunhand rested easily against his hip bone and his whole attitude was of complete relaxation. Having seen him pull his gun once I hoped the girl wasn't fooled.

He said slowly: 'We've heard about you two. What's your offer? I wouldn't listen even, only I can't stand a shooting rap.'

The girl said: 'There's enough in it for four.' Madder nodded his big head vigorously, almost managed a smile.

Sunset glanced at me. I nodded. 'Four it is,' he sighed. 'But that's the top. We'll go to my place and gargle. I don't like it here.'

'We must look simple,' the girl said nastily.

'Kill-simple,' Sunset drawled. 'I've met lots of them. That's why we're going to talk it over. It's not a shooting play.'

Carol Donovan slipped a suede bag from under her left arm and tucked her .32 into it. She smiled. She was pretty when she smiled.

'My ante is in,' she said quietly. 'I'll play. Where is the place?'

'Out Water Street. We'll go in a hack.'

'Lead on, sport.'

We went out of the room and down in the elevator, four friendly people walking out through a lobby full of antlers and stuffed birds and pressed wildflowers in glass frames. The taxi went out Capitol Way, past the square, past a big red apartment house that was too big for the town except when the Legislature was sitting. Along car tracks past the distant capitol buildings and the high closed gates of the governor's mansion.

Oak trees bordered the sidewalks. A few largish residences showed behind garden walls. The taxi shot past them and veered on to a road that led towards the tip of the Sound. In a short while a house showed in a narrow clearing between tall trees. Water glistened far back behind the tree trunks. The house had a roofed porch, a small lawn rotten with weeds and overgrown bushes. There was a shed at the end of a dirt driveway and an antique touring car squatted under the shed.

We got out and I paid the taxi. All four of us carefully watched it out of sight. Then Sunset said:

'My place is upstairs. There's a schoolteacher lives down below. She ain't home. Let's go up and gargle.'

We crossed the lawn to the porch and Sunset threw a door open, pointed up narrow steps.

'Ladies first. Lead on, beautiful. Nobody locks a door in this town.'

The girl gave him a cool glance and passed him to go up the stairs. I went next, then Madder, Sunset last.

The single room that made up most of the second floor was dark from the trees, had a dormer window, a wide day-bed pushed back under the slope of the roof, a table, some wicker chairs, a small radio and a round black stove in the middle of the floor.

Sunset drifted into a kitchenette and came back with a square bottle and some glasses. He poured drinks, lifted one and left the others on the table.

We helped ourselves and sat down.

Sunset put his drink down in a lump, leaned over to put his glass on the floor and came up with his Colt out.

I heard Madder's gulp in the sudden cold silence. The girl's mouth twitched as if she were going to laugh. Then she leaned forward, holding her glass on top of her bag with her left hand.

Sunset slowly drew his lips into a thin straight line. He said slowly and carefully: 'Feet-burners, huh? Burned my pal's feet, huh?'

Madder choked, started to spread his fat hands. The Colt flicked at him. He put his hands on his knees and clutched his kneecaps.

'And suckers at that,' Sunset went on tiredly. 'Burn a guy's feet to make him sing and then walk right into the parlour of one of his pals. You couldn't tie that with Christmas ribbon.'

Madder said jerkily: 'All r-right. W-what's the p-pay-off?' The girl smiled slightly but she didn't say anything.

Sunset grinned. 'Rope,' he said softly. 'A lot of rope tied in hard knots, with water on it. Then me and my pal trundle off to catch fireflies – pearls to you – and when we come back – ' he stopped, drew his left hand across the front of his throat. 'Like the idea?' he glanced at me.

'Yeah, but don't make a song about it,' I said. 'Where's the rope?'

'Bureau,' Sunset answered, and pointed with one ear at the corner.

I started in that direction, by way of the walls. Madder made a sudden thin whimpering noise and his eyes turned up in his head and he fell straight forward off the chair on his face, in a dead faint.

That jarred Sunset. He hadn't expected anything so foolish. His right hand jerked around until the Colt was pointing down at Madder's back.

The girl slipped her hand under her bag. The bag lifted an inch. The gun that was caught there in a trick clip – the gun that Sunset thought was inside the bag – spat and flamed briefly.

Sunset coughed. His Colt boomed and a piece of wood detached itself from the back of the chair Madder had been sitting in. Sunset dropped the Colt and put his chin down on his chest and tried to look at the ceiling. His long legs slid out in front of him and his heels made a rasping sound on the floor. He sat like that, limp, his chin on his chest, his eyes looking upward. Dead as a pickled walnut.

I kicked Miss Donovan's chair out from under her and she banged down on her side in a swirl of silken legs. Her hat went crooked on her head. She yelped. I stood on her hand and then

shifted suddenly and kicked her gun clear across the attic. I sent
her bag after it – with her other gun inside it. She screamed at
me.

'Get up,' I snarled.

She got up slowly, backed away from me biting her lip, savage-
eyed, suddenly a nasty-faced little brat at bay. She kept on backing until the wall stopped her. Her eyes glittered in a ghastly
face.

I glanced down at Madder, went over to a closed door. A bathroom was behind it. I reversed a key and gestured at the girl.

'In.'

She walked stiff-legged across the floor and passed in front of
me, almost touching me.

'Listen a minute, shamus – '

I pushed her through the door and slammed it and turned the
key. It was all right with me if she wanted to jump out of the
window. I had seen the windows from below.

I went across to Sunset, felt him, felt the small hard lump of
keys on a ring in his pocket, and got them out without quite
knocking him off his chair. I didn't look for anything else.

There were car keys on the ring.

I looked at Madder again, noticed that his fingers were as white
as snow. I went down the narrow dark stairs to the porch, around
to the side of the house and got into the old touring car under
the shed. One of the keys on the ring fitted its ignition lock.

The car took a beating before it started up and let me back it
down the dirt driveway to the kerb. Nothing moved in the house
that I saw or heard. The tall pines behind and beside the house
stirred their upper branches listlessly and a cold heartless sunlight sneaked through them intermittently as they moved.

I drove back to Capitol Way and downtown again as fast as I
dared, past the square and the Snoqualmie Hotel and over the
bridge towards the Pacific Ocean and Westport.

9

An hour's fast driving through thinned-out timberland, interrupted by three stops for water and punctuated by the cough of
a head gasket leak, brought me within sound of surf. The broad

white road, striped with yellow down the centre, swept around the flank of a hill, a distant cluster of buildings loomed up in front of the shine of the ocean, and the road forked. The left fork was signposted: 'Westport – 9 Miles', and didn't go towards the buildings. It crossed a rusty cantilever bridge and plunged into a region of wind-distorted apple orchards.

Twenty minutes more and I chugged into Westport, a sandy spit of land with scattered frame houses dotted over rising ground behind it. The end of the spit was a long narrow pier, and the end of the pier a cluster of sailing boats with half-lowered sails flapping against their single masts. And beyond them a buoyed channel and a long irregular line where the water creamed on a hidden sandbar.

Beyond the sandbar the Pacific rolled over to Japan. This was the last outpost of the coast, the farthest west a man could go and still be on the mainland of the United States. A swell place for an ex-convict to hide out with a couple of somebody else's pearls the size of new potatoes – if he didn't have any enemies.

I pulled up in front of a cottage that had a sign in the yard: 'Luncheons, Teas, Dinners'. A small rabbit-faced man with freckles was waving a garden rake at two black chickens. The chickens appeared to be sassing him back. He turned when the engine of Sunset's car coughed itself still.

I got out, went through a wicket gate, pointed to the sign.

'Luncheon ready?'

He threw the rake at the chickens, wiped his hands on his trousers and leered. 'The wife put that up,' he confided to me in a thin, impish voice. 'Ham and eggs is what it means.'

'Ham and eggs get along with me,' I said.

We went into the house. There were three tables covered with patterned oilcloth, some chromos on the walls, a full-rigged ship in a bottle on the mantel. I sat down. The host went away through a swing door and somebody yelled at him and a sizzling noise was heard from the kitchen. He came back and leaned over my shoulder, put some cutlery and a paper napkin on the oilcloth.

'Too early for apple brandy, ain't it?' he whispered.

I told him how wrong he was. He went away again and came back with glasses and a quart of clear amber fluid. He sat down with me and poured. A rich baritone voice in the kitchen was singing 'Chloe' over the sizzling.

We clinked glasses and drank and waited for the heat to crawl up our spines.

'Stranger, ain't you?' the little man asked.

I said I was.

'From Seattle maybe? That's a nice piece of goods you got on.'

'Seattle,' I agreed.

'We don't git many strangers,' he said, looking at my left ear. 'Ain't on the way to nowheres. Now before repeal – ' he stopped, shifted his sharp, woodpecker gaze to my other ear.

'Ah, before repeal,' I said with a large gesture, and drank knowingly.

He leaned over and breathed on my chin. 'Hell, you could load up in any fish stall on the pier. The stuff come in under catches of crabs and oysters. Hell, Westport was lousy with it. They give the kids cases of Scotch to play with. There wasn't a car in this town that slept in a garage, mister. The garages was all full to the roof of Canadian hooch. Hell, they had a coastguard cutter off the pier watchin' the boats unload one day every week. Friday. Always the same day.' He winked.

I puffed a cigarette and the sizzling noise and the baritone rendering of 'Chloe' went on in the kitchen.

'But hell, you wouldn't be in the liquor business,' he said.

'Hell, no. I'm a goldfish buyer,' I said.

'Okay,' he said sulkily.

I poured us another round of the apple brandy. 'This bottle is on me,' I said. 'And I'm taking a couple more with me.'

He brightened up. 'What did you say the name was?'

'Carmady. You think I'm kidding you about the goldfish. I'm not.'

'Hell, there ain't a livin' in them little fellers, is there?'

I held my sleeve out. 'You said it was a nice piece of goods. Sure there's a living out of the fancy brands. New brands, new types all the time. My information is there's an old guy down here somewhere that has a real collection. Maybe would sell it. Some he's bred himself.'

I poured us another round of the apple brandy. A large woman with a moustache kicked the swing door open a foot and yelled: 'Pick up the ham and eggs!'

My host scuttled across and came back with my food. I ate.

He watched me minutely. After a time he suddenly smacked his skinny leg under the table.

'Old Wallace,' he chuckled. 'Sure, you come to see old Wallace. Hell, we don't know him right well. He don't act neighbourly.'

He turned around in his chair and pointed out through the sleazy curtains at a distant hill. On the top of the hill was a yellow and white house that shone in the sun.

'Hell, that's where he lives. He's got a mess of them. Goldfish, huh? Hell, you could bend me with an eye-dropper.'

That ended my interest in the little man. I gobbled my food, paid off for it and for three quarts of apple brandy at a dollar a quart, shook hands and went back out to the touring car.

There didn't seem to be any hurry. Rush Madder would come out of his faint, and he would turn the girl loose. But they didn't know anything about Westport. Sunset hadn't mentioned the name in their presence. They didn't know it when they reached Olympia, or they would have gone there at once. And if they had listened outside my room at the hotel, they would have known I wasn't alone. They hadn't acted as if they knew that when they charged in.

I had lots of time. I drove down to the pier and looked it over. It looked tough. There were fishstalls, drinking dives, a tiny honkytonk for the fishermen, a pool-room, an arcade of slot machines and smutty peep-shows. Bait fish squirmed and darted in big wooden tanks down in the water along the piles. There were loungers and they looked like trouble for anyone that tried to interfere with them. I didn't see any law enforcement around.

I drove back up the hill to the yellow and white house. It stood very much alone, four blocks from the next nearest dwelling. There were flowers in front, a trimmed green lawn, a rock garden. A woman in a brown and white print dress was popping at aphids with a spray-gun.

I let my heap stall itself, got out and took my hat off.

'Mister Wallace live here?'

She had a handsome face, quiet, firm-looking. She nodded.

'Would you like to see him?' She had a quiet firm voice, a good accent.

It didn't sound like the voice of a train-robber's wife.

I gave her my name, said I'd been hearing about his fish down in the town. I was interested in fancy goldfish.

She put the spray gun down and went into the house. Bees buzzed around my head, large fuzzy bees that wouldn't mind the cold wind off the sea. Far off like background music the surf pounded on the sandbars. The northern sunshine seemed bleak to me, had no heat in the core of it.

The woman came out of the house and held the door open.

'He's at the top of the stairs,' she said, 'if you'd like to go up.'

I went past a couple of rustic rockers and into the house of the man who had stolen the Leander pearls.

10

Fish tanks were all around the big room, two tiers of them on braced shelves, big oblong tanks with metal frames, some with lights over them and some with lights down in them. Water grasses were festooned in careless patterns behind the algae-coated glass and the water held a ghostly greenish light and through the greenish light moved fish of all the colours of the rainbow.

There were long slim fish like golden darts and Japanese Veiltails with fantastic trailing tails, and X-ray fish as transparent as coloured glass, tiny guppies half an inch long, calico popeyes spotted like a bride's apron, and big lumbering Chinese Moors with telescope eyes, froglike faces and unnecessary fins, waddling through the green water like fat men going to lunch.

Most of the light came from a big sloping skylight. Under the skylight at a bare wooden table a tall gaunt man stood with a squirming red fish in his left hand, and in his right hand a safety razor blade backed with adhesive tape.

He looked at me from under wide grey eyebrows. His eyes were sunken, colourless, opaque. I went over beside him and looked down at the fish he was holding.

'Fungus?' I asked.

He nodded slowly. 'White fungus.' He put the fish down on the table and carefully spread its dorsal fin. The fin was ragged and split and the ragged edges had a mossy white colour.

'White fungus,' he said, 'ain't so bad. I'll trim this feller up and he'll be right as rain. What can I do for you, Mister?'

I rolled a cigarette around in my fingers and smiled at him.

'Like people,' I said. 'The fish, I mean. They get things wrong with them.'

He held the fish against the wood and trimmed off the ragged part of the fin. He spread the tail and trimmed that. The fish had stopped squirming.

'Some you can cure,' he said, 'and some you can't. You can't cure swimming-bladder disease, for instance.' He glanced up at me. 'This don't hurt him, case you think it does,' he said. 'You can shock a fish to death but you can't hurt it like a person.'

He put the razor blade down and dipped a cotton swab in some purplish liquid, painted the cut places. Then he dipped a finger in a jar of white vaseline and smeared that over. He dropped the fish in a small tank off to one side of the room. The fish swam around peacefully, quite content.

The gaunt man wiped his hands, sat down at the edge of a bench and stared at me with lifeless eyes. He had been good-looking once, a long time ago.

'You interested in fish?' he asked. His voice had the quiet careful murmur of the cell block and the exercise yard.

I shook my head. 'Not particularly. That was just an excuse. I came a long way to see you, Mister Sype.'

He moistened his lips and went on staring at me. When his voice came again it was tired and soft.

'Wallace is the name, Mister.'

I puffed a smoke ring and poked my finger through it. 'For my job it's got to be Sype.'

He leaned forward and dropped his hands between his spread bony knees, clasped them together. Big gnarled hands that had done a lot of hard work in their time. His head tipped up at me and his dead eyes were cold under the shaggy brows. But his voice stayed soft.

'Haven't seen a dick in a year. To talk to. What's your lay?'

'Guess,' I said.

His voice got still softer. 'Listen, dick. I've got a nice home here, quiet. Nobody bothers me any more. Nobody's got a right to. I got a pardon straight from the White House. I've got the fish to play with and a man gets fond of anything he takes care of. I don't owe the world a nickel. I paid up. My wife's got enough dough for us to live on. All I want is to be let alone, dick.' He

stopped talking, shook his head once. 'You can't burn me up –
not any more.'

I didn't say anything. I smiled a little and watched him.

'Nobody can touch me,' he said. 'I got a pardon straight from
the President's study. I just want to be let alone.'

I shook my head and kept on smiling at him. 'That's the one
thing you can never have – until you give in.'

'Listen,' he said softly. 'You may be new on this case. It's kind
of fresh to you. You want to make a rep for yourself. But me, I've
had almost twenty years of it, and so have a lot of other people,
some of 'em pretty smart people too. *They* know I don't have
nothing that don't belong to me. Never did have. Somebody else
got it.'

'The mail clerk,' I said. 'Sure.'

'Listen,' he said, still softly. 'I did my time. I know all the
angles. I know they ain't going to stop wondering – long as anybody's alive that remembers. I know they're going to send some
punk out once in a while to kind of stir it up. That's okay. No
hard feelings. Now what do I do to get you to go home again?'

I shook my head and stared past his shoulder at the fish drifting
in their big silent tanks. I felt tired. The quiet of the house made
ghosts in my brain, ghosts of a lot of years ago. A train pounding
through the darkness, a stickup hidden in a mail car, a gun flash,
a dead clerk on the floor, a silent drop off at some water tank, a
man who had kept a secret for nineteen years – almost kept it.

'You made one mistake,' I said slowly. 'Remember a fellow named
Peeler Mardo?'

He lifted his head. I could see him searching in his memory.
The name didn't seem to mean anything to him.

'A fellow you knew in Leavenworth,' I said. 'A little runt that
was in there for splitting twenty-dollar bills and putting phony
backs on them.'

'Yeah,' he said. 'I remember.'

'You told him you had the pearls,' I said.

I could see he didn't believe me. 'I must have been kidding
him,' he said slowly, emptily.

'Maybe. But here's the point. He didn't think so. He was up in
this country a while ago with a pal, a guy who called himself Sunset. They saw you somewhere and Peeler recognized you. He got to

thinking how he could make himself some jack. But he was a coke hound and he talked in his sleep. A girl got wise and then another girl and a shyster. Peeler got his feet burned and he's dead.'

Sype stared at me unblinkingly. The lines at the corners of his mouth deepened.

I waved my cigarette and went on: 'We don't know how much he told, but the shyster and a girl are in Olympia. Sunset's in Olympia, only he's dead. They killed him. I don't know if they know where you are or not. But they will sometime, or others like them. You can wear the cops down, if they can't find the pearls and you don't try to sell them. You can wear the insurance company down and even the postal men.'

Sype didn't move a muscle. His big knotty hands clenched between his knees didn't move. His dead eyes just stared.

'But you can't wear the chiselers down,' I said. 'They'll never lay off. There'll always be a couple or three with time enough and money enough and meanness enough to bear down. They'll find out what they want to know some way. They'll snatch your wife or take you out in the woods and give you the works. And you'll have to come through.... Now I've got a decent, square proposition.'

'Which bunch are you?' Sype asked suddenly. 'I thought you smelled of dick, but I ain't so sure now.'

'Insurance,' I said. 'Here's the deal. Twenty-five grand reward in all. Five grand to the girl that passed me the info. She got it on the square and she's entitled to that cut. Ten grand to me. I've done all the work and looked into all the guns. Ten grand to you, through me. You couldn't get a nickel direct. Is there anything in it? How does it look?'

'It looks fine,' he said gently. 'Except for one thing. I don't have no pearls, dick.'

I scowled at him. That was my wad. I didn't have any more. I straightened away from the wall and dropped a cigarette end on the wood floor, crushed it out. I turned to go.

He stood up and put a hand out. 'Wait a minute,' he said gravely, 'and I'll prove it to you.'

He went across the floor in front of me and out of the room. I stared at the fish and chewed my lip. I heard the sound of a car engine somewhere, not very close. I heard a drawer open and shut apparently in a near-by room.

Sype came back into the fish room. He had a shiny Colt .45 in his gaunt fist. It looked as long as a man's forearm.

He pointed it at me and said: 'I got pearls in this, six of them. Lead pearls. I can comb a fly's whiskers at sixty yards. You ain't no dick. Now get up and blow – and tell your red-hot friends I'm ready to shoot their teeth out any day of the week and twice on Sunday.'

I didn't move. There was a madness in the man's dead eyes. I didn't dare move.

'That's grandstand stuff,' I said slowly. 'I can prove I'm a dick. You're an ex-con and it's felony just having that rod. Put it down and talk sense.'

The car I had heard seemed to be stopping outside the house. Brakes whined on drums. Feet clattered, up a walk, up steps. Sudden sharp voices, a caught exclamation.

Sype backed across the room until he was between the table and a big twenty or thirty gallon tank. He grinned at me, the wide clear grin of a fighter at bay.

'I see your friends kind of caught up with you,' he drawled. 'Take your gat out and drop it on the floor while you still got time – and breath.'

I didn't move. I looked at the wiry hair above his eyes. I looked into his eyes. I knew if I moved – even to do what he told me – he would shoot.

Steps came up the stairs. They were clogged, shuffling steps, with a hint of struggle in them.

Three people came into the room.

11

Mrs Sype came in first, stiff-legged, her eyes glazed, her arms bent rigidly at the elbows and the hands clawing straight forward at nothing, feeling for something that wasn't there. There was a gun in her back, one of Carol Donovan's small .32's, held efficiently in Carol Donovan's small ruthless hand.

Madder came last. He was drunk, brave from the bottle, flushed and savage. He threw the Smith and Wesson down on me and leered.

Carol Donovan pushed Mrs Sype aside. The older woman

stumbled over into the corner and sank down on her knees, blank-eyed.

Sype stared at the Donovan girl. He was rattled because she was a girl and young and pretty. He hadn't been used to the type. Seeing her took the fire out of him. If men had come in he would have shot them to pieces.

The small dark white-faced girl faced him coldly, said in her tight chilled voice: 'All right, Dad. Shed the heater. Make it smooth now.'

Sype leaned down slowly, not taking his eyes off her. He put his enormous frontier Colt on the floor.

'Kick it away from you, Dad.'

Sype kicked it. The gun skidded across the bare boards, over towards the centre of the room.

'That's the way, old-timer. You hold on him, Rush, while I unrod the dick.'

The two guns swivelled and the hard grey eyes were looking at me now. Madder went a little way towards Sype and pointed his Smith and Wesson at Sype's chest.

The girl smiled, not a nice smile. 'Bright boy, eh? You sure stick your neck out all the time, don't you? Made a beef, shamus. Didn't frisk your skinny pal. He had a little map in one shoe.'

'I didn't need one,' I said smoothly, and grinned at her.

I tried to make the grin appealing, because Mrs Sype was moving her knees on the floor, and every move took her nearer to Sype's Colt.

'But you're all washed up now, you and your big smile. Hoist the mitts while I get your iron. Up, Mister.'

She was a girl, about five feet two inches tall, and weighed around a hundred and twenty. Just a girl. I was five-eleven and a half, weighted one-ninety-five. I put my hands up and hit her on the jaw.

That was crazy, but I had all I could stand of the Donovan-Madder act, the Donovan-Madder guns, the Donovan-Madder tough talk. I hit her on the jaw.

She went back a yard and her popgun went off. A slug burned my ribs. She started to fall. Slowly, like a slow-motion picture, she fell. There was something silly about it.

Mrs Sype got the Colt and shot her in the back.

Madder whirled and the instant he turned Sype rushed him.

Madder jumped back and yelled and covered Sype again. Sype stopped cold and the wide crazy grin came back on his gaunt face.

The slug from the Colt knocked the girl forward as though a door had whipped in a high wind. A flurry of blue cloth, something thumped my chest – her head. I saw her face for a moment as she bounced back, a strange face that I had never seen before.

Then she was a huddled thing on the floor at my feet, small, deadly, extinct, with redness coming out from under her, and the tall quiet woman behind her with the smoking Colt held in both hands.

Madder shot Sype twice. Sype plunged forward still grinning and hit the end of the table. The purplish liquid he had used on the sick fish sprayed up over him. Madder shot him again as he was falling.

I jerked my Luger out and shot Madder in the most painful place I could think of that wasn't likely to be fatal – the back of the knee. He went down exactly as if he had tripped over a hidden wire. I had cuffs on him before he even started to groan.

I kicked guns here and there and went over to Mrs Sype and took the big Colt out of her hands.

It was very still in the room for a little while. Eddies of smoke drifted towards the skylight, filmy grey, pale in the afternoon sun. I heard the surf booming in the distance. Then I heard a whistling sound close at hand.

It was Sype trying to say something. His wife crawled across to him, still on her knees, huddled beside him. There was blood on his lips and bubbles. He blinked hard, trying to clear his head. He smiled up at her. His whistling voice said very faintly: 'The Moors, Hattie – the Moors.'

Then his neck went loose and the smile melted off his face. His head rolled to one side on the bare floor.

Mrs Sype touched him, then got very slowly to her feet and looked at me, calm, dry-eyed.

She said in a low clear voice: 'Will you help me carry him to the bed? I don't like him here with these people.'

I said: 'Sure. What was that he said?'

'I don't know. Some nonsense about his fish, I think.'

I lifted Sype's shoulders and she took his feet and we carried him into the bedroom and put him on the bed. She folded his hands on his chest and shut his eyes. She went over and pulled the blinds down.

'That's all, thank you,' she said, not looking at me. 'The telephone is downstairs.'

She sat down in a chair beside the bed and put her head down on the coverlet near Sype's arm.

I went out of the room and shut the door.

12

Madder's leg was bleeding slowly, not dangerously. He stared at me with fear-crazed eyes while I tied a tight handkerchief above his knee. I figured he had a cut tendon and maybe a chipped kneecap. He might walk a little lame when they came to hang him.

I went downstairs and stood on the porch looking at the two cars in front, then down the hill towards the pier. Nobody could have told where the shots came from, unless he happened to be passing. Quite likely nobody had even noticed them. There was probably shooting in the woods around there a good deal.

I went back into the house and looked at the crank telephone on the living-room wall, but didn't touch it yet. Something was bothering me. I lit a cigarette and stared out of the window and a ghost voice said in my ears: 'The Moors, Hattie. The Moors.'

I went back upstairs into the fish room. Madder was groaning now, thick panting groans. What did I care about a torturer like Madder?

The girl was quite dead. None of the tanks was hit. The fish swam peacefully in their green water, slow and peaceful and easy. They didn't care about Madder either.

The tank with the black Chinese Moors in it was over in the corner, about ten gallon size. There were just four of them, big fellows, about four inches body length, coal black all over. Two of them were sucking oxygen on top of the water and two were waddling sluggishly on the bottom. They had thick deep bodies with a lot of spreading tail and high dorsal fins and their bulging telescope eyes that made them look like frogs when they were head towards you.

I watched them fumbling around in the green stuff that was growing in the tank. A couple of red pond snails were window-cleaning. The two on the bottom looked thicker and more sluggish than the two on the top. I wondered why.

There was a long-handled strainer made of woven string lying between two of the tanks. I got it and fished down in the tank, trapped one of the big Moors and lifted it out. I turned it over in the net, looked at its faintly silver belly. I saw something that looked like a suture. I felt the place. There was a hard lump under it.

I pulled the other one off the bottom. Same suture, same hard round lump. I got one of the two that had been sucking air on top. No suture, no hard round lump. It was harder to catch too.

I put it back in the tank. My business was with the other two. I like goldfish as well as the next man, but business is business and crime is crime. I took my coat off and rolled my sleeves up and picked the razor blade backed with adhesive off the table.

It was a very messy job. It took about five minutes. Then they lay in the palm of my hand, three-quarters of an inch in diameter, heavy, perfectly round, milky white and shimmering with that inner light no other jewel has. The Leander pearls.

I washed them off, wrapped them in my handkerchief, rolled down my sleeves and put my coat back on. I looked at Madder, at his little pain and fear-tortured eyes, the sweat on his face. I didn't care anything about Madder. He was a killer, a torturer.

I went out of the fish room. The bedroom door was still shut. I went down below and cranked the wall telephone.

'This is the Wallace place at Westport,' I said. 'There's been an accident. We need a doctor and we'll have to have the police. What can you do?'

The girl said: 'I'll try and get you a doctor, Mr Wallace. It may take a little time though. There's a town marshal at Westport. Will he do?'

'I suppose so,' I said and thanked her and hung up. There were points about a country telephone after all.

I lit another cigarette and sat down in one of the rustic rockers on the porch. In a little while there were steps and Mrs Sype came out of the house. She stood a moment looking off down the hills, then she sat down in the other rocker beside me. Her dry eyes looked at me steadily.

'You're a detective, I suppose,' she said slowly, diffidently.

'Yes. I represent the company that insured the Leander pearls.'

She looked off into the distance. 'I thought he would have peace here,' she said. 'That nobody would bother him any more. That this place would be a sort of sanctuary.'

'He ought not to have tried to keep the pearls.'

She turned her head, quickly this time. She looked blank now, then she looked scared.

I reached down in my pocket and got out the wadded handkerchief, opened it up on the palm of my hand. They lay there together on the white linen, two hundred grand worth of murder.

'He could have had his sanctuary,' I said. 'Nobody wanted to take it away from him. But he wasn't satisfied with that.'

She looked slowly, lingeringly at the pearls. Then her lips twitched. Her voice got hoarse.

'Poor Wally,' she said. 'So you did find them. You're pretty clever, you know. He killed dozens of fish before he learned how to do that trick.' She looked up into my face. A little wonder showed at the back of her eyes.

She said: 'I always hated the idea. Do you remember the old Bible theory of the scapegoat?'

I shook my head, no.

'The animal on which the sins of a man were laid and then it was driven off into the wilderness. The fish were his scapegoat.'

She smiled at me. I didn't smile back.

She said, still smiling faintly: 'You see, he once had the pearls, the real ones, and suffering seemed to him to make them his. But he couldn't have had any profit from them, even if he had found them again. It seems some landmark changed, while he was in prison, and he never could find the spot in Idaho where they were buried.'

An icy finger was moving slowly up and down my spine. I opened my mouth and something I supposed might be my voice said: 'Huh?'

She reached a finger out and touched one of the pearls. I was still holding them out, as if my hand was a shelf nailed to the wall.

'So he got these,' she said. 'In Seattle. They're hollow, filled with white wax. I forget what they call the process. They look very fine. Of course I never saw any really valuable pearls.'

'What did he get them for?' I croaked.

'Don't you see? They were his sin. He had to hide them in the wilderness, this wilderness. He hid them in the fish. And do you know – ' she leaned towards me again and her eyes shone. She said very slowly, very earnestly:'Sometimes I think that in the very end, just the last year or so, he actually believed they were the real pearls he was hiding. Does all this mean anything to you?'

I looked down at my pearls. My hand and the handkerchief closed over them slowly.

I said: 'I'm a plain man, Mrs Sype. I guess the scapegoat idea is a bit over my head. I'd say he was just trying to kid himself a bit – like any heavy loser.'

She smiled again. She was handsome when she smiled. Then she shrugged, quite lightly.

'Of course, you would see it that way. But me – ' she spread her hands. 'Oh, well, it doesn't matter much now. May I have them for a keepsake?'

'Have them?'

'The – the phoney pearls. Surely you don't – '

I stood up. An old Ford roadster without a top was chugging up the hill. A man in it had a big star on his vest. The chatter of the motor was like the chatter of some old angry bald-headed ape in the zoo.

Mrs Sype was standing beside me, with her hand half out, a thin, beseeching look on her face.

I grinned at her with sudden ferocity.

'Yeah, you were pretty good in there for a while,' I said. 'I damn near fell for it. And was I cold down the back, lady! But you helped. "Phoney" was a shade out of character for you. Your work with the Colt was fast and kind of ruthless. Most of all Sype's last words queered it. "The Moors, Hattie – the Moors." He wouldn't have bothered with that if the stones had been ringers. And he wasn't sappy enough to kid himself all the way.'

For a moment her face didn't change at all. Then it did. Something horrible showed in her eyes. She put her lips out and spat at me. Then she slammed into the house.

I tucked twenty-five thousand dollars into my vest pocket. Twelve thousand five hundred for me and twelve thousand five hundred for Kathy Horne. I could see her eyes when I brought her the cheque, and when she put it in the bank, to wait for Johnny to get paroled from Quentin.

The Ford had pulled up behind the other cars. The man driving spat over the side, yanked his emergency brake on, got out without using the door. He was a big fellow in shirt sleeves.

I went down the steps to meet him.

June Thomson

THE GIRL WITH THE RED-GOLD HAIR

HAVE YOU EVER HEARD a woman scream? Really scream, I mean; not the little moan of pain or half-hearted squeal of fear that most women can produce on occasions. No, I am thinking of the full-throated, uninhibited vocalizing of agony or terror that stops up the listener's blood and cuts across the brain like knives.

The first time I heard it I was five. It came from my mother's bedroom although I could not recognize it as being hers. It went on and on and nothing could shut it out. Then, suddenly, it stopped, as if someone, unable to bear it any longer, had switched it off.

Later, I was told my mother had died, although the word 'dead' meant very little to me at the time. She had gone to live with Jesus, my father told me, together with my baby sister. I imagined them, borne away to bliss, on that upward-pouring stream of agony, to find silence at last.

The second time I heard the screaming I was about ten years old. I was walking down Romford High Street with my father, although I have now forgotten the reason why we were there. Suddenly, I heard it again and there, standing on the pavement on the other side of the road, was a woman, quite immobile, her mouth open, letting out this torrent of sound. Passers-by and onlookers seemed transfixed by it. So, too, did the little group in the centre of the road – a brewer's dray, drawn up, with a man holding one of the horses by the head, their breath streaming white in the cold air, while another man bent down to examine a small bundle of what looked like old clothes lying on the ground.

'A child. . . .' my father murmured and hurried me away.

The third occasion – but that needs a little more explanation. It was 1921 and I was seventeen. I had left home and had come to London to work as an insurance clerk in an office at Clapham

Junction, with lodgings in one of the turnings off Battersea Rise.

I was considered to be 'getting on'. Not only had I made the transfer from the provinces to the main office at a time when many ex-servicemen were still unemployed, but I was studying in the evenings to become further qualified. My father predicted a promising future for me. He was proud of me but in a distanced, uninvolved way. Even since my mother's death, he had been retreating more and more into a bachelor existence. Sometimes, meeting at meal times or on the stairs, he seemed surprised by my presence. My departure for London was merely a culmination to a protracted farewell.

At the time, the thought of 'getting on' compensated to some extent for the drab reality of my life. The days were filled with the routine of the office and, when that was over, I walked through the brief, tram-rattling bustle of the Junction and climbed the hill to my room in a nondescript side street, to the asthmatic gas-fire, the curtains that didn't quite meet in the middle, the books spread out on the table that had to be cleared away when my landlady brought in my tray of supper; never quite enough to satisfy my hunger and yet not small enough to justify a complaint. Not that I would have complained. I was too diffident and lacking in self-assurance to assert myself. Besides, the landlady had her own problems. She was a war-widow with three children to bring up; little girls with grave faces and thin arms and legs like pale, brittle stalks.

So, when she brought in my supper tray, I smiled and said thank you and cleared a space for it on the table under the window, eating the meagre helpings facing the gap in the curtains.

It was through this gap that I first caught a glimpse of the girl. The street was very quiet and the sound of footsteps passing along the pavement, especially in the evenings, always made me glance up to see who it was. Perhaps I half hoped it might be someone for me, although whom I had no idea. I knew no one in London except for the other clerks in the office and, as I was young and inexperienced, they only deigned to notice me with an off-hand, professional amity that didn't extend beyond the door.

The footsteps I heard that autumn evening in 1921 were light and youthful, a brisk, purposeful tapping of heels. I knew it was a woman even before I glanced up and saw her. It was raining, I remember; not proper rain but a fine, misty, melancholy drizzle that formed a halo round the gas-lamps that were spaced out at sparse intervals along the street.

She was passing under one of them and the light caught her hair. It was red-gold, I noticed, and she was wearing a short fur jacket with a bunch of artificial violets pinned to one shoulder and the combination of red and purple was vividly rich and vibrant in that drab, grey street.

A few seconds later, she passed out of my line of vision between the curtains, although I could still hear her footsteps echoing along the pavement.

I'm not sure what it was about her that fired my imagination. I hadn't been able to discern her features and yet I assumed she was pretty. She walked with the confident, assured manner of a woman who knows she is attractive. I assumed, too, that she was going to meet her lover, for the brisk, almost joyful way in which her footsteps had rung out in the quiet evening suggested eagerness, in the same way that the fur jacket and the bunch of violets implied some festive, celebratory occasion. I imagined her turning right at the bottom of the street towards the Junction where there was a cab-rank or perhaps picking up a cruising taxi in St John's Road, before setting out on some wonderful evening in the West End which I had only glimpsed on the rare occasions I had gone there as an onlooker to the world of theatres and restaurants and night-clubs, warm, perfumed, glittering.

I envied them both their money, their success, their assurance, as finally the footsteps faded and the street became silent once more.

A few days later I heard them again and this time I was more alert to her brief passage across the gap in the curtains. She was wearing a black and white check coat that evening, with a high collar and deep cuffs of some dark, dense fabric that was probably velvet and her hair was partly hidden under a black, tight-fitting hat with a little burst of feathers over one ear, like a glossy flower. It shielded her face, too, so that I was still not able to see her features although there was a glint of her red-gold hair as she passed under the lamp. Then she was gone and once more there was only the sound of her footsteps clicking up the street which I was left to follow in my imagination.

I saw her twice more in the following week but each time it was raining; a heavier downpour than on the first occasion and she carried an umbrella of dark-red silk, tilted over her head at a jaunty angle, that glowed in that drenched and sodden drabness with the startling vividness of a carnation on a rubbish tip. I could see nothing of her face, not even her hair, only the bottom half of her black and white checked coat and her feet in high-heeled shoes with a small, bright object on the front of them, twinkling in and out as she hurried under the lamp and disappeared beyond the scope of my vision.

By this time, I was fascinated by her; you might even say besotted. I found myself waiting every evening for her to appear, sitting over my books, pretending to study but, in fact, glancing up every few seconds to the gap in the curtains. It was the same when the landlady brought in my supper. I scarcely noticed the food in front of me, eating it in snatched mouthfuls, unwilling to take my eyes from the window. It occurred to me to open the curtains wider so that, when she came, I would have a longer time in which to observe her but I didn't dare risk it. Like a child who believes it will be bad luck to tread on the cracks between the paving stones or deviate a yard from his accustomed route home, I trusted in the sympathetic magic of that narrow slot of discovery. If I left it just as it was, she would return.

But it didn't seem to work.

It was on the Tuesday of the following week that I decided to alter my routine. For three evenings in succession I hadn't seen her and the thought of spending another alone in my room, watching at the window, perhaps fruitlessly, was more than I could endure. I would go for a walk, I told myself; not to meet her, of course. That would sour the magic. But simply to stroll along Battersea Rise and back for the sake of the fresh air and for something to do although, if I had been honest with myself, I knew I was hoping for a chance to meet her face to face at last.

The decision excited me. It gave purpose and a sense of adventure to what would otherwise be another dull and lonely evening. Putting on my overcoat again, I ran down the stairs and knocked at my landlady's door.

She occupied the back kitchen which was used as a living-room by herself and the children during the day. It was a small, dark room in which they seemed to live an intense, huddled and yet almost silent life, like noiseless animals in an underground burrow.

When I went in, the three little girls were eating bread and jam at the table, their pale faces even more bleached by the white glare of the incandescent gas mantle, while their mother peeled potatoes on to a sheet of newspaper. Washing was drying on a ceiling rack over the stove, the wet clothes hanging down like bedraggled flags.

I explained, with some excitement, that I had to go out unexpectedly and could my supper be kept hot in the oven until I returned?

The landlady agreed, the little girls stared without speaking and I withdrew, feeling I had disturbed the peace and silence of their lives by my intrusion and talk of the world outside their drawn curtains.

It was a gusty evening, threatening rain, with low, dark clouds sweeping along over the rooftops, showing ragged gaps of lighter sky. As I turned right at the end of the street towards Battersea Rise, I could see the lamps along the edge of Clapham Common, blowing in and out, it seemed, as the wind threshed the branches of the trees to and fro in front of them. There were few people about and those that were hurried along, coat collars turned up, heads bent, slanted to the gale.

I walked the length of the Rise twice and then, as I returned the second time towards the Common, I saw her on the far side of the road and a little ahead of me, making her way along the pavement under the boisterous trees. There was no mistaking her for, although she was walking slowly, almost sauntering, in fact, she was wearing the fur jacket and the black hat with the cockade of feathers. She had her back to me and was going in the opposite direction to that which I had expected; not towards the Junction but along the boundary of the Common towards Clapham High Street.

I followed her keeping to the far side of the road where a terrace of large houses faced the dark, open stretch of grass and trees.

A taxi drove past and I expected her to hail it but she continued walking.

We went another hundred yards before anything else happened and then a man approached on my side of the pavement. Seeing her, he walked quickly across the road and went up to her and it was then that I understood the situation. This was the lover she had come out to meet. They would kiss under the trees and then walk away arm in arm, laughing together.

I slowed down my own pace in order to witness the encounter, feeling oddly excluded. I had watched and waited for her night after night and yet it was another man who had come to claim her.

And then something totally unexpected happened that, for a moment, I could not understand.

They met. They even stood for a few seconds talking to each other. Then the man made an angry, dismissive gesture with one arm and, turning abruptly, began to walk away, leaving her standing irresolute upon the pavement.

What had happened? Had they quarrelled in those few seconds of tête à tête? Perhaps she had rebuked him for being late and this was why he had become impatient.

I was nearly opposite her now. The man had gone, striding off down the road. The woman was alone. I hesitated, imagining her feelings of loss and disappointment, embarrassed at having witnessed this brief scene of rejection in an otherwise empty street.

To hide my confusion, I stopped and began searching hurriedly in my inside pocket, at the same time glancing up at the numbers of the houses as if looking for a particular address.

I heard her footsteps cross the road but didn't think anything of it. She was, I supposed, returning home.

'Looking for somewhere, dearie?'

At first, I didn't connect the voice with her and I glanced round, startled, expecting to find that someone else had approached me silently.

She stood in front of me, one hand gripping the edges of her fur jacket together, the glossy feathers on her hat flicking against her cheek as the wind ruffled them. It was a commonplace little face, small and tight and very pale, in which her lips and eyes, heavily made-up, looked as grotesque as a clown's.

'No...no...I was....' I stammered.

'You can come home with me if you like,' she offered. Her voice was slightly nasal with a wheedling note in it. Her mouth smiled but her eyes were watchful.

I looked up and down the street, feeling trapped. Women had smiled at me before. One or two had called out softly 'Goodnight', as they brushed against me in passing. I wasn't so naive that I didn't know what sort of women they were. But it was the first time that I had been directly accosted and I didn't know how to deal with it. Besides, I was still confused by the unexpectedness of the situation. That *she*, the girl with the red-gold hair who passed like a vision under the lamp should be the same person who was now standing in front of me with her small, caked, red mouth stretched open and the fur jacket clutched up tight to her neck, every hair of it glistening as if it were still alive, was difficult to believe.

'I – I don't know,' I began.

'Ten bob,' she said, with professional briskness.

'I haven't got ten shillings on me,' I replied, speaking the truth out of a kind of helpless desperation.

'How much have you got then?'

'I'm not sure. About seven and six, I think.'

Her mouth stopped smiling and made a little pout of impatience and, I thought, distaste. She glanced briefly up and down the street and then made up her mind.

'All right. It'll have to do, I suppose. Come on.'

She took my arm with a gesture that was determined and yet a little contemptuous, like a mother taking charge of an unwilling child and, like a child, I acquiesced, not knowing what else to do. We began to walk back towards Battersea Rise, she setting the pace, walking once more with that purposeful clicking of her heels that sounded too loud.

'How old are you?' she asked, after a few minutes' silence.

It didn't occur to me to lie.

'Nearly eighteen.'

She glanced at me sideways and laughed.

'Christ! Does your mother know you're out?'

'My mother's....'

I was about to say 'dead' and then I stopped. I didn't want to talk about her. It seemed inappropriate and disloyal.

'I live by myself,' I said instead. 'I've got digs nearby. I work in an office.'

She shrugged indifferently, putting an end to further explanation.

To my relief, we turned up another side street before we reached the road where I lived. It was similar to mine, however, with little drab, huddled houses and sparse lamps. Each time we passed beneath one, I felt a *frisson* of fear, imagining people were watching from behind the curtained windows as I had watched from mine, listening to our footsteps, marking our progress from one small island of light to the next. I felt horribly exposed.

At the end of the street, we turned right into a road of taller houses, with basements and an extra upper storey. Halfway along it, she stopped and fumbled at an area gate.

'Wait,' she told me. 'I'll go down first and put a light on else you'll break a bleeding leg.'

It was dark for the house was midway between two lamps and the gateway was further shadowed by a privet hedge that bulged over the pavement. I waited thankfully in its shelter, smelling the rank, dusty odour of the leaves and listening to her footsteps descending the steps.

Presently a light sprang up behind the frosted glass panels in a door, illuminating sooty bricks and an iron hand-rail.

It was only then that it occurred to me that I could leave. All I had to do was walk away up the street. But at the same time that the thought came into my mind, the door opened and she appeared in the lighted rectangle, beckoning to me to descend and, with the same sense of commitment I had felt when she first took my arm, I began walking down the steps towards her.

The door opened into a tiny hallway from which another door led into the basement room. It was quite large but seemed smaller because of the low ceiling and the clutter of furniture and other objects that filled it. Most of the space was taken up by a large, high bed that jutted out into the room like a raft, an effect that was increased by the pink and black patterned silk shawl, with a deep fringe, that had been pinned against the wall behind it like a tawdry sail. The same shabby finery was evident elsewhere; in the vases of paper flowers; the multiplicity of little pictures in *passepartout* frames that crowded the walls; the ostrich-feather fan that was propped up behind the ornaments on the mantleshelf in front of an oval gilt mirror from which the gold paint was flaking.

The woman was standing in front of this mirror, unpinning her hat which she threw down carelessly on one of the arm-chairs drawn up to the fireplace, revealing her hair. Now that I could see it in the full, harsh light of the gas brackets, it no longer seemed rich and unusual but cheap, twopence-coloured like everything else in the room.

And yet it wasn't all bad. After the drab, chilly discomfort of my own lodgings, the room was warm and bright. The gas fire hissed pleasantly in the hearth, giving out waves of heat that lapped against my legs. The orange curtains were closed across the window in full folds and, once I had accepted the crowded objects and no longer noticed their individual gaudiness, the general effect was one of colour, even gaiety.

The figure of the woman, too, bending down to rub her ankles in front of the fire, was slim and, with her face turned away and only the angle of her cheek visible, it was possible to imagine she might be pretty.

'Well, what do you think of it?' she asked me over her shoulder.

'The room, you mean?' I stammered, conscious that she must have seen me looking about as I entered; perhaps even read in my face my initial criticism. 'It's very nice.'

'It suits me,' she replied with an off-hand casualness that I knew wasn't meant. She was proud of it; proud of the possessions it contained and the way she had arranged them. 'Take your coat off, for God's sake,' she added impatiently. 'Look as if you're staying. Do you want a cup of tea first?'

I jibbed at the word 'first'. Now that I was down there in the intimacy of that enclosed, cluttered room, it suddenly struck me with a sickening realization what I was expected to do. I took off my overcoat slowly, folding it with exaggerated care and laying it over the back of the arm-chair before sitting down. I had, thank God, my back to the bed. I felt the heat of the fire through the cloth of my trouser legs but I didn't dare get up to move the chair back, remaining rigid, in a state of terror, my hands tightly clasped between my knees.

She had walked past me to a curtained-off alcove on the far side of the room which I saw, when I took one brief, frightened glance in her direction, was a tiny kitchen, equipped with a gas ring, a sink and a flap-table on which she was setting out cups and saucers and a teapot with a busy rattle, humming under her breath as she did so like a woman who is happily occupied and alone.

I knew suddenly with one of those flashes of intuitive insight that have nothing to do with experience that she didn't usually treat her clients in this way. It was only because I was young and embarrassed and obviously inept that she could be so relaxed and off-hand.

'You can put the seven and six on the mantelpiece,' she told me. I heard her voice behind me, slightly raised and bossy like a mother used to ordering a young son about. 'And for that it's straight, see? No funny business.'

I rose slowly, fumbling in my pocket for the coins, ranging them in neat piles at the foot of a statuette of a semi-naked woman, standing on tiptoe with her metal draperies and hair blown stiffly and elaborately backwards, exposing high, round breasts and a curved throat. I had two half crowns, a florin and the rest in coppers. I put the silver in one pile and the pennies in a little stout column by themselves.

And then, as I turned to sit down again, something happened. She was lifting the kettle off the gas ring to pour the boiling water into the teapot when some of it splashed on her hand and she gave a sharp scream of pain and surprise. Only a small scream. Nothing much at all. But, with my nerves already stretched to breaking point, it was enough to trigger off all the long-repressed terror and agony of those other occasions when I had heard the same kind of sound.

Perversely, I wanted it to go on and on, as it had before; to tear the air apart; to reach the pitch of exquisitely unendurable climax and then, when that point had been reached, to stop. Only this time, I wanted to be the one who controlled it; the one who finally cried 'Enough!' and called down silence. I could no longer bear to be the passive listener who merely endured.

I hit her several times with the statuette and each time she let out that pure, crystal stream of vocalized fear and pain that was mine as well as hers. It only stopped for both of us when she was lying on the floor between the sink and the flap-table, her feet sticking out beyond the curtain and her clown's eyes staring up with an expression of fixed surprise at the fly-paper, dotted with black specks, that hung down from the gas fitting.

It was over. The room was filled with silence. I felt oddly calm and fulfilled, as if I had climbed a mountain and, having reached the summit, was looking down over a valley, distanced and sunlit.

The mood lasted for several seconds; long enough for me to put the statuette down beside her, pick up my overcoat and make for the door. It was only as I mounted the steps and felt the iron hand-rail cold under my hand that I realized what I had done and I began to run, racing from one patch of darkness to the next between the lamps while, behind me, I heard doors opening and voices shouting.

There is not much more to tell. Eventually, I went back to my lodgings where I changed out of my blood-spattered trousers, making them up into a parcel which I dropped over Albert Bridge the following night. My landlady brought in my supper which I made a pretence of eating. She asked me about my evening out and I managed to make some answer.

No one came to arrest me, although for the first few days I waited in a state of terrified anticipation. Her death was reported in the evening newspaper that I was in the habit of buying from the one-legged news vendor at the corner of Lavender Hill and that merely stated the facts and went on to say that the police were baffled by the apparent lack of motive for there was no sign of robbery and no evidence of a quarrel leading up to the attack.

I am an old man now. I live alone. I have no family or friends and I feel it is now too late to try to explain my reasons except in this manner, at second-hand, writing it down on sheets of paper which I assume will be found among my belongings after my death. Besides, I am not sure myself that I fully understand it. I only know that whatever happened that evening was a kind of terrible fulfilment that has left me isolated on my summit of consummation, incapable of returning to the distant valley where, if women scream, other women with red-gold hair pass under street-lamps to worlds of delight and passion that I can no longer imagine or share.

L. T. Meade and Robert Eustace

MR BOVEY'S
UNEXPECTED WILL

AMONG ALL MY PATIENTS there were none who excited my sense of curiosity like Miss Florence Cusack. I never thought of her without a sense of baffled inquiry taking possession of me, and I never visited her without the hope that someday I should get to the bottom of the mystery which surrounded her.

Miss Cusack was a young and handsome woman. She possessed to all appearance superabundant health, her energies were extraordinary, and her life completely out of the common. She lived alone in a large house in Kensington Court Gardens, kept a good staff of servants, and went much into society. Her beauty, her sprightliness, her wealth, and, above all, her extraordinary life caused her to be much talked about. As one glanced at this handsome girl with her slender figure, her eyes of the darkest blue, her raven-black hair and clear complexion, it was almost impossible to believe that she was a power in the police courts, and highly respected by every detective in Scotland Yard.

I shall never forget my first visit to Miss Cusack. I had been asked by a brother doctor to see her in his absence. Strong as she was, she was subject to periodical and very acute nervous attacks. When I entered her house she came up to me eagerly.

'Pray do not ask me too many questions or look too curious, Dr Lonsdale,' she said. 'I know well that my whole condition is abnormal; but, believe me, I am forced to do what I do.'

'What is that?' I inquired.

'You see before you,' she continued, with emphasis, 'the most acute and, I believe, successful lady detective in the whole of London.'

'Why do you lead such an extraordinary life?' I asked.

· 'To me the life is fraught with the very deepest interest,' she answered. 'In any case,' and now the colour faded from her cheeks, and her eyes grew full of emotion, 'I have no choice; I am under a promise, which I must fulfil. There are times, however, when I need help – such help as you, for instance, can give me. I have never seen you before, but I like your face. If the time should ever come, will you give me your assistance?'

I asked her a few more questions, and finally agreed to do what she wished.

From that hour Miss Cusack and I became the staunchest friends. She constantly invited me to her house, introduced me to her friends, and gave me her confidence to a marvellous extent.

On my first visit I noticed in her study two enormous brazen bulldogs. They were splendidly cast, and made a striking feature in the arrangements of the room; but I did not pay them any special attention until she happened to mention that there was a story, and a strange one, in connection with them.

'But for these dogs,' she said, 'and the mystery attached to them, I should not be the woman I am, nor would my life be set apart for the performance of duties at once herculean and ghastly.'

When she said these words her face once more turned pale, and her eyes flashed with an ominous fire.

On a certain afternoon in November 1894, I received a telegram from Miss Cusack, asking me to put aside all other work and go to her at once. Handing my patients over to the care of my partner, I started for her house. I found her in her study and alone. She came up to me holding a newspaper in her hand.

'Do you see this?' she asked. As she spoke she pointed to the agony column. The following words met my eyes:

Send more sand and charcoal dust. Core and mould ready for casting.
– JOSHUA LINKLATER.

I read these curious words twice, then glanced at the eager face of the young girl.

'I have been waiting for this,' she said, in a tone of triumph.

'But what can it mean?' I said. ' "*Core and mould ready for casting*"?'

She folded up the paper, and laid it deliberately on the table.

'I thought that Joshua Linklater would say something of the kind,' she continued. 'I have been watching for a similar advertisement in all the dailies for the last three weeks. This may be of the utmost importance.'

'Will you explain?' I said.

'I may never have to explain, or, on the other hand, I may,' she answered. 'I have not really sent for you to point out this advertisement, but in connection with another matter. Now, pray, come into the next room with me.'

She led me into a prettily and luxuriously furnished boudoir on the same floor. Standing by the hearth was a slender fair-haired girl, looking very little more than a child.

'May I introduce you to my cousin, Letitia Ransom?' said Miss Cusack eagerly. 'Pray sit down, Letty,' she continued, addressing the girl with a certain asperity, 'Dr Lonsdale is the man of all others we want. Now, doctor, will you give me your very best attention, for I have an extraordinary story to relate.'

At Miss Cusack's words Miss Ransom immediately seated herself. Miss Cusack favoured her with a quick glance, and then once more turned to me.

'You are much interested in queer mental phases, are you not?' she said.

'I certainly am,' I replied.

'Well, I should like to ask your opinion with regard to such a will as this.'

Once again she unfolded a newspaper, and, pointing to a paragraph, handed it to me. I read as follows:

EXTRAORDINARY TERMS OF A MISER'S WILL

Mr Henry Bovey, who died last week at a small house at Kew, has left one of the most extraordinary wills on record. During his life his eccentricities and miserly habits were well known, but this eclipses them all, by the surprising method in which he has disposed of his property.

Mr Bovey was unmarried, and, as far as can be proved, has no near relations in the world. The small balance at his banker's is to be used for defraying fees, duties, and sundry charges, also any existing debts, but the main bulk of his securities were recently realized, and the money in sovereigns is locked in a safe in his house.

A clause in the will states that there are three claimants to this property, and that the one whose net bodily weight is nearest to the weight of these sovereigns is to become the legatee. The safe containing the property is not to be opened till the three claimants are present; the competition is then to take place, and the winner is at once to remove his fortune.

Considerable excitement has been manifested over the affair, the amount of the fortune being unknown. The date of the competition is also kept a close secret for obvious reasons.

'Well,' I said, laying the paper down, 'whoever this Mr Bovey was, there is little doubt that he must have been out of his mind. I never heard of a more crazy idea.'

'Nevertheless it is to be carried out,' replied Miss Cusack. 'Now listen, please, Dr Lonsdale. This paper is a fortnight old. It is now three weeks since the death of Mr Bovey, his will has been proved, and the time has come for the carrying out of the competition. I happen to know two of the claimants well, and intend to be present at the ceremony.'

I did not make any answer, and after a pause she continued:

'One of the gentlemen who is to be weighed against his own fortune is Edgar Wimburne. He is engaged to my cousin Letitia. If he turns out to be the successful claimant, there is nothing to prevent their marrying at once; if otherwise –' here she turned and looked full at Miss Ransom, who stood up, the colour coming and going in her cheeks – 'if otherwise, Mr Campbell Graham has to be dealt with.'

'Who is he?' I asked.

'Another claimant, a much older man than Edgar. Nay, I must tell you everything. He is a claimant in a double sense, being also a lover, and a very ardent one, of Letitia's.

'Letty must be saved,' she said, looking at me, 'and I believe I know how to do it.'

'You spoke of three claimants,' I interrupted; 'who is the third?'

'Oh, he scarcely counts, unless indeed he carries off the prize. He is William Tyndall, Mr Bovey's servant and retainer.'

'And when, may I ask, is this momentous competition to take place?' I continued.

'Tomorrow morning at half-past nine, at Mr Bovey's house. Will you come with us tomorrow, Dr Lonsdale, and be present at the weighing?'

'I certainly will,' I answered; 'it will be a novel experience.'

'Very well; can you be at this house a little before half-past eight, and we will drive straight to Kew?'

I promised to do so, and soon after took my leave. The next day I was at Miss Cusack's house in good time. I found waiting for me Miss Cusack herself, Miss Ransom, and Edgar Wimburne.

A moment or two later we all found ourselves seated in a large landau, and in less than an hour had reached our destination. We drew up at a small dilapidated-looking house, standing in a row of prim suburban villas, and found that Mr Graham, the lawyer, and the executors had already arrived.

The room into which we had been ushered was fitted up as a sort of study. The furniture was very poor and scanty, the carpet was old, and the only ornaments on the walls were a few tattered prints yellow with age.

As soon as ever we came in, Mr Southby, the lawyer, came forward and spoke.

'We are met here today,' he said, 'as you are all of course aware, to carry out the clause of Mr Bovey's last will and testament. What reasons prompted him to make these extraordinary conditions we do not know; we only know that we are bound to carry them out. In a safe in his bedroom there is, according to his own statement, a large sum of money in gold, which is to be the property of the one of these three gentlemen whose weight shall nearest approach to the weight of the gold. Messrs Hutchinson and Company have been kind enough to supply one of their latest weighing machines, which has been carefully checked, and now if you three gentlemen will kindly come with me into the next room we will begin the business at once. Perhaps you, Dr Lonsdale, as a medical man, will be kind enough to accompany us.'

Leaving Miss Cusack and Miss Ransom we then went into the old man's bedroom, where the three claimants undressed and were carefully weighed. I append their respective weight, which I noted down:

Graham	13 stone	9 lb 6 oz
Tyndall	11 stone	6 lb 3 oz
Wimburne	12 stone	11 lb

The three candidates having resumed their attire, Miss Cusack and Miss Ransom were summoned, and the lawyer, drawing out a bunch of keys, went across to a large iron safe which had been built into the wall.

We all pressed round him, everyone anxious to get the first glimpse of the old man's hoard. The lawyer turned the key, shot back the lock, and flung open the heavy doors. We found that the safe was literally packed with small canvas cags – indeed, so full was it that as the doors swung open two of the bags fell to the floor with a heavy crunching noise. Mr Southby lifted them up, and then, cutting the strings of one, opened it. It was full of bright sovereigns.

An exclamation burst from us all. If all those bags contained gold there was a fine fortune awaiting the successful candidate! The business was now begun in earnest. The lawyer rapidly extracted bag after bag, untied the string, and shot the contents with a crash into the great copper scale pan, while the attendant kept adding weights to the other side to balance it, calling out the amounts as he did so. No one spoke, but our eyes were fixed as if by some strange fascination on the pile of yellow metal that rose higher and higher each moment.

As the weight reached one hundred and fifty pounds, I heard the old servant behind me utter a smothered oath. I turned and glanced at him; he was staring at the gold with a fierce expression of disappointment and avarice. He at any rate was out of the reckoning, as at eleven stone six, or one hundred and sixty pounds, he could be nowhere near the weight of the sovereigns, there being still eight more bags to untie.

The competition, therefore, now lay between Wimburne and Graham. The latter's face bore strong marks of the agitation which consumed him: the veins stood out like cords on his forehead, and his lips trembled. It would evidently be a near thing, and the suspense was almost intolerable. The lawyer continued to deliberately add to the pile. As the last bag was shot into the scale, the attendant put four ten-pound weights into the other side. It was too much. The gold rose at once. He took one off, and then the two great pans swayed slowly up and down, finally coming to a dead stop.

'Exactly one hundred and eighty pounds, gentlemen,' he cried, and a shout went up from us all. Wimburne at twelve stone eleven, or one hundred and seventy-nine pounds, had won.

I turned and shook him by the hand.

'I congratulate you most heartily,' I cried. 'Now let us calculate the amount of your fortune.'

I took a piece of paper from my pocket and made a rough calculation. Taking £56 to the pound avoirdupois, there were at least ten thousand and eighty sovereigns in the scale before us.

'I can hardly believe it,' cried Miss Ransom.

I saw her gazing down at the gold, then she looked up into her lover's face.

'Is it true?' she said, panting as she spoke.

'Yes, it is true,' he answered. Then he dropped his voice. 'It removes all difficulties,' I heard him whisper to her.

Her eyes filled with tears, and she turned aside to conceal her emotion.

'There is no doubt whatever as to your ownership of this money, Mr Wimburne,' said the lawyer, 'and now the next thing is to ensure its safe transport to the bank.'

As soon as the amount of the gold had been made known, Graham, without bidding good-bye to anyone, abruptly left the room, and I assisted the rest of the men in shovelling the sovereigns into a stout canvas bag, which we then lifted and placed in a four-wheeled cab which had arrived for the purpose of conveying the gold to the city.

'Surely someone is going to accompany Mr Wimburne?' said Miss Cusack at this juncture. 'My dear Edgar,' she continued, 'you are not going to be so mad as to go alone?'

To my surprise, Wimburne coloured, and then gave a laugh of annoyance.

'What could possibly happen to me?' he said. 'Nobody knows that I am carrying practically my own weight in gold into the city.'

'If Mr Wimburne wishes I will go with him,' said Tyndall, now coming forward. The old man had to all appearance got over his disappointment, and spoke eagerly.

'The thing is fair and square,' he added. 'I am sorry I did not win, but I'd rather you had it, sir, than Mr Graham. Yes, that I would, and I congratulate you, sir.'

'Thank you, Tyndall,' replied Wimburne, 'and if you like to come with me I shall be very glad of your company.'

The bag of sovereigns being placed in the cab, Wimburne bade us all a hasty good-bye, told Miss Ransom that he would call to see her at Miss Cusack's house that evening, and, accompanied by Tyndall, started off. As we watched the cab turn the corner I heard Miss Ransom utter a sigh.

'I do hope it will be all right,' she said, looking at me. 'Don't you think it is a risky thing to drive with so much gold through London?'

I laughed in order to reassure her.

'Oh, no, it is perfectly safe,' I answered, 'safer perhaps than if the gold were conveyed in a more pretentious vehicle. There is nothing to announce the fact that it is bearing ten thousand and eighty sovereigns to the bank.'

A moment or two later I left the two ladies and returned to my interrupted duties. The affair of the weighing, the strange clause in the will, Miss Ransom's eager pathetic face, Wimburne's manifest anxiety, had all impressed me considerably, and I could scarcely get the affair off my mind. I hoped that the young couple would now be married quickly, and I could not help being heartily glad that Graham had lost, for I had by no means taken to his appearance.

My work occupied me during the greater part of the afternoon, and I did not get back again to my own house until about six o'clock. When I did so I was told to my utter amazement that Miss Cusack had arrived and was waiting to see me with great impatience. I went at once into my consulting room, where I found her pacing restlessly up and down.

'What is the matter?' I asked.

'Matter!' she cried; 'have you not heard? Why, it has been cried in the streets already – the money is gone, was stolen on the way to London. There was a regular highway robbery in the Richmond Road, in broad daylight too. The facts are simply these: two men in a dogcart met the cab, shot the driver, and after a desperate struggle, in which Edgar Wimburne was badly hurt, seized the gold and drove off. The thing was planned, of course – planned to a moment.'

'But what about Tyndall?' I asked.

'He was probably in the plot. All we know is that he has escaped and has not been heard of since.'

'But what a daring thing!' I cried. 'They will be caught, of course; they cannot have gone far with the money.'

'You do not understand their tricks, Dr Lonsdale; but I do,' was her quick answer, 'and I venture to guarantee that if we do not get that money back before the morning, Edgar Wimburne has seen the last of his fortune. Now, I mean to follow up this business, all night if necessary.'

I did not reply. Her dark, bright eyes were blazing with excitement, and she began to pace up and down.

'You must come with me,' she continued; 'you promised to help me if the necessity should arise.'

'And I will keep my word,' I answered.

'That is an immense relief.' She gave a deep sigh as she spoke.

'What about Miss Ransom?' I asked.

'Oh, I have left Letty at home. She is too excited to be of the slightest use.'

'One other question,' I interrupted, 'and then I am completely at your service. You mentioned that Wimburne was hurt.'

'Yes, but I believe not seriously. He has been taken to the hospital. He has already given evidence, but it amounts to very little. The robbery took place in a lonely part of the road, and just for the moment there was no one in sight.'

'Well,' I said, as she paused, 'you have some scheme in your head, have you not?'

'I have,' she answered. 'The fact is this; from the very first I feared some such catastrophe as has really taken place. I have known Mr Graham for a long time, and – distrusted him. He has passed for a man of position and means, but I believe him to be a mere adventurer. There is little doubt that all his future depended on his getting this fortune. I saw his face when the scales declared in Edgar Wimburne's favour – but there! I must ask you to accompany me to Hammersmith immediately. On the way I will tell you more.'

'We will go in my carriage,' I said. 'It happens to be at the door.'

We started directly. As we had left the more noisy streets Miss Cusack continued: 'You remember the advertisement I showed you yesterday morning?'

I nodded.

'You naturally could make no sense of it, but to me it was fraught with much meaning. This is by no means the first advertisement which has appeared under the name of Joshua Linklater. I have observed similar advertisements, and all, strange to say, in connection with founder's work, appearing at intervals in the big dailies for the last four or five months, but my attention was never specially directed to them until a circumstance occurred of which I am about to tell you.'

'What is that?' I asked.

'Three weeks ago a certain investigation took me to Hammersmith in order to trace a stolen necklace. It was necessary that I should go to a small pawnbroker's shop – the man's name was Higgins. In my queer work, Dr Lonsdale, I employ many disguises. That night, dressed quietly as a domestic servant on her evening out, I entered the pawnbroker's. I wore a thick veil and a plainly trimmed hat. I entered one of the little boxes where one stands to pawn goods, and waited for the man to appear.

'For the moment he was engaged, and looking through a small window in the door I saw to my astonishment that the pawnbroker was in earnest conversation with no less a person than Mr Campbell Graham. This was the last place I should have expected to see Mr Graham in, and I immediately used both my eyes and ears. I heard the pawnbroker address him as Linklater.

'Immediately the memory of the advertisements under that name flashed through my brain. From the attitude of the two men there was little doubt that they were discussing a matter of the utmost importance, and as Mr Graham, alias Linklater, was leaving the shop, I distinctly overheard the following words: "In all probability Bovey will die tonight. I may or may not be successful, but in order to insure against loss we must be prepared. It is not safe for me to come here often – look out for the advertisement – it will be in the agony column."

'I naturally thought such words very strange, and when I heard of Mr Bovey's death and read an account of the queer will, it seemed to me that I began to see daylight. It was also my business to look out for the advertisement, and when I saw it yesterday morning you may well imagine that my keenest suspicions were aroused. I immediately suspected foul play, but could do nothing except watch and await events. Directly I heard the details of the robbery I wired to the inspector at Hammersmith to have Higgins' house watched. You remember that Mr Wimburne left Kew in the cab at ten o'clock; the robbery must therefore have taken place some time about ten-twenty. The news reached me shortly after eleven, and my wire was sent off about eleven-fifteen. I mention these hours, as much may turn upon them. Just before I came to you I received a wire from the police station containing startling news. This was sent off about five-thirty. Here, you had better read it.'

As she spoke she took a telegram from her pocket and handed it to me. I glanced over the words it contained.

Just heard that cart was seen at Higgins's this morning. Man and assistant arrested on suspicion. House searched. No gold there. Please come down at once.

'So they have bolted with it?' I said.

'That we shall see,' was her reply

Shortly afterwards we arrived at the police station. The inspector was waiting for us, and took us at once into a private room.

'I am glad you were able to come, Miss Cusack,' he said, bowing with great respect to the handsome girl.

'Pray tell me what you have done,' she answered; 'there is not a moment to spare.'

'When I received you wire;' he said, 'I immediately placed a man on duty to watch Higgins' shop, but evidently before I did this the cart must have arrived and gone – the news with regard to the cart being seen outside Higgins' shop did not reach me till four-thirty. On receiving it I immediately arrested both Higgins and his assistant, and we searched the house from attic to cellar, but have found no gold whatever. There is little doubt that the pawnbroker received the gold, and has already removed it to another quarter.'

'Did you find a furnace in the basement?' suddenly asked Miss Cusack.

'We did,' he replied, in some astonishment; 'but why do you ask?'

To my surprise Miss Cusack took out of her pocket the advertisement which she had shown me that morning and handed it to the inspector. The man read the queer words aloud in a slow and wondering voice:

Send more sand and charcoal dust. Core and mould ready for casting – JOSHUA LINKLATER.

'I can make nothing of it, miss,' he said, glancing at Miss Cusack. 'These words seem to me to have something to do with founder's work.'

'I believe they have,' was her eager reply. 'It is also highly probable that they have something to do with the furnace in the basement of Higgins' shop.'

'I do not know what you are talking about, miss, but you have something at the back of your head which does not appear.'

'I have,' she answered, 'and in order to confirm certain suspicions I wish to search the house.'

'But the place has just been searched by us,' was the man's almost testy answer. 'It is impossible that a mass of gold should be there and be overlooked: every square inch of space has been accounted for.'

'Who is in the house now?'

'No one; the place is locked up, and one of our men is on duty.'

'What size is the furnace?'

'Unusually large,' was the inspector's answer.

Miss Cusack gave a smile which almost immediately vanished.

'We are wasting time,' she said; 'let us go there immediately.'

'I must do so, of course, if nothing else will satisfy you, miss; but I assure you – '

'Oh, don't let us waste any more time in arguing,' said Miss Cusack, her impatience now getting the better of her. 'I have a reason for what I do, and must visit the pawnbroker's immediately.'

The man hesitated no longer, but took a bunch of keys down from the wall. A blaze of light from a public-house guided us to the pawnbroker's, which bore the well-known sign, the three golden balls. These were just visible through the fog above us. The inspector nodded to the man on duty, and unlocking the door we entered a narrow passage into which the swing doors of several smaller compartments opened. The inspector struck a match, and, lighting the lantern, looked at Miss Cusack, as much as to say, 'What do you propose to do now?'

'Take me to the room where the furnace is,' said the lady.

'Come this way,' he replied.

We turned at once in the direction of the stairs which led to the basement, and entered a room on the right. At the further end was an open range which had evidently been enlarged in order to allow the consumption of a great quantity of fuel, and upon it now stood an iron vessel, shaped as a chemist's crucible. Considerable heat still radiated from it. Miss Cusack peered inside, then she slowly commenced raking out the ashes with an iron rod, examining them closely and turning them over and over. Two or three white fragments she examined with peculiar care.

'One thing at least is abundantly clear,' she said at last; 'gold has been melted here, and within a very short time; whether it was the sovereigns or not we have yet to discover.'

'But surely, Miss Cusack,' said the inspector, 'no one would be rash enough to destroy sovereigns.'

'I am thinking of Joshua Linklater's advertisement,' she said.
'"*Send more sand and charcoal dust.*" This,' she continued, once
more examining the white fragments, 'is undoubtedly sand.'

She said nothing further, but went back to the ground floor and
now commenced a systematic search on her own account.

At last we reached the top floor, where the pawnbroker and his
assistant had evidently slept. Here Miss Cusack walked at once
to the window and flung it open. She gazed out for a minute, and
then turned to face us. Her eyes looked brighter than ever, and a
certain smile played about her face.

'Well, miss,' said the police inspector, 'we have now searched
the whole house, and I hope you are satisfied.'

'I am,' she replied.

'The gold is not here, miss.'

'We will see,' she said. As she spoke she turned once more
and bent slightly out, as if to look down through the murky air
at the street below.

The inspector gave an impatient exclamation.

'If you have quite finished, miss, we must return to the station,'
he said. 'I am expecting some men from Scotland Yard to go
into this affair.'

'I do not think they will have much to do,' she answered,
'except, indeed, to arrest the criminal.' As she spoke she leant
a little further out of the window, and then withdrawing her head
said quietly, 'Yes, we may as well go back now; I have quite
finished. Things are exactly as I expected to find them; we can
take the gold away with us.'

Both the inspector and I stared at her in utter amazement.

'What do you mean, Miss Cusack?' I cried.

'What I say,' she answered, and now she gave a light laugh;
'the gold is here, close to us; we have only to take it away. Come,'
she added, 'look out, both of you. Why, you are both gazing at it.'

I glanced round in utter astonishment. My expression of face
was reproduced in that of the inspector's.

'Look,' she said, 'what do you call that?' As she spoke she
pointed to the sign that hung outside – the sign of the three balls.

'Lean out and feel that lower ball,' she said to the inspector.

He stretched out his arm, and as his fingers touched it he started
back.

'Why, it is hot,' he said; 'what in the world does it mean?'

'It means the lost gold,' replied Miss Cusack; 'it has been cast as that ball. I said that the advertisement would give me the necessary clue, and it has done so. Yes, the lost fortune is hanging outside the house. The gold was melted in the crucible downstairs and cast as this ball between twelve o'clock and four-thirty today. Remember it was after four-thirty that you arrested the pawnbroker and his assistant.'

To verify her extraordinary words was the work of a few moments. Owing to its great weight, the inspector and I had some difficulty in detaching the ball from its hook. At the same time we noticed that a very strong stay, in the shape of an iron-wire rope, had been attached to the iron frame from which the three balls hung.

'You will find, I am sure,' said Miss Cusack, 'that this ball is not of solid gold; if it were, it would not be the size of the other two balls. It has probably been cast round a centre of plaster of Paris to give it the same size as the others. This explains the advertisement with regard to the charcoal and sand. A ball of that size in pure gold would weigh nearly three hundred pounds, or twenty stone.'

'Well,' said the inspector, 'of all the curious devices that I have ever seen or heard of, this beats the lot. But what did they do with the real ball? They must have put it somewhere.'

'They burnt it in the furnace, of course,' she answered; 'these balls, as you know, are only wood covered with gold paint. Yes, it was a clever idea, worthy of the brain of Mr Graham; and it might have hung there for weeks and been seen by thousands passing daily, till Mr Higgins was released from imprisonment, as nothing whatever could be proved against him.'

Owing to Miss Cusack's testimony, Graham was arrested that night, and, finding that circumstances were dead against him, he confessed the whole. For long years he was one of a gang of coiners, but managed to pass as a gentleman of position. He knew old Bovey well, and had heard him speak of the curious will he had made. Knowing of this, he determined, at any risk, to secure the fortune, intending, when he had obtained it, to immediately leave the country. He had discovered the exact amount of the money which he would leave behind him, and had gone carefully into the weight which such a number of sovereigns would make. He knew at once that Tyndall would be out of the reckoning, and that the competition would really be between himself and Wimburne. To provide against the contingency of Wimburne's being the lucky man, he had planned the robbery; the gold was to be melted, and made into a real golden ball, which was to hang over the pawnshop until suspicion had died away.

Freeman Wills Crofts

THE MYSTERY OF THE SLEEPING-CAR EXPRESS

NO ONE WHO WAS IN ENGLAND in the autumn of 1909 can fail to remember the terrible tragedy which took place in a North-Western express between Preston and Carlisle. The affair attracted enormous attention at the time, not only because of the arresting nature of the events themselves, but even more for the absolute mystery in which they were shrouded.

Quite lately a singular chance has revealed to me the true explanation of the terrible drama, and it is at the express desire of its chief actor that I now take upon myself to make the facts known. As it is a long time since 1909, I may, perhaps, be pardoned if I first recall the events which came to light at the time.

One Thursday, then, early in November of the year in question, the 10.30 pm sleeping-car train left Euston as usual for Edinburgh, Glasgow, and the North. It was generally a heavy train, being popular with business men who liked to complete their day's work in London, sleep while travelling, and arrive at their northern destination with time for a leisurely bath and breakfast before office hours. The night in question was no exception to the rule, and two engines hauled behind them eight large sleeping-cars, two firsts, two thirds, and two vans, half of which went to Glasgow, and the remainder to Edinburgh.

It is essential to the understanding of what follows that the composition of the rear portion of the train should be remembered. At the extreme end came the Glasgow van, a long eight-wheeled, bogie vehicle, with Guard Jones in charge. Next to the van was one of the third-class coaches, and immediately in front of it came a first-class, both labelled for the same city. These coaches were fairly well filled, particularly the third-class. In front of the first-class came the last of the four Glasgow sleepers. The train was corridor throughout, and the officials could, and did, pass through it several times during the journey.

It is with the first-class coach that we are principally concerned, and it will be understood from the above that it was placed in between the sleeping-car in front and the third-class behind, the van following immediately behind the third. It had a lavatory at each end and six compartments, the last two, next the third-class, being smokers, the next three non-smoking, and the first, immediately beside the sleeping car, a 'Ladies only'. The corridors in both it and the third-class coach were on the left-hand side in the direction of travel – that is, the compartments were on the side of the double line.

The night was dark as the train drew out of Euston, for there was no moon and the sky was overcast. As was remembered and commented on afterwards, there had been an unusually long spell of dry weather, and, though it looked like rain earlier in the evening, none fell till the next day, when, about six in the morning, there was a torrential downpour.

As the detectives pointed out later, no weather could have been more unfortunate from their point of view, as, had footmarks been made during the night, the ground would have been too hard to take good impressions, while even such traces as remained would more than likely have been blurred by the rain.

The train ran to time, stopping at Rugby, Crewe and Preston. After leaving the latter station Guard Jones found he had occasion to go forward to speak to a ticket-collector in the Edinburgh portion. He accordingly left his van in the rear and passed along the corridor of the third-class carriage adjoining.

At the end of this corridor, beside the vestibule joining it to the first-class, were a lady and gentleman, evidently husband and wife, the lady endeavouring to soothe the cries of a baby she was carrying. Guard Jones addressed some civil remark to the man, who explained that their child had been taken ill, and they had brought it out of their compartment as it was disturbing the other passengers.

With an expression of sympathy, Jones unlocked the two doors across the corridor at the vestibule between the carriages, and, passing on into the first-class coach, re-closed them behind him. They were fitted with spring locks, which became fast on the door shutting.

The corridor of the first-class coach was empty, and as Jones walked down it he observed that the blinds of all the compartments were lowered, with one exception – that of the 'Ladies Only'. In this compartment, which contained three ladies, the light was fully on, and the guard noticed that two out of the three were reading.

Continuing his journey, Jones found that the two doors at the vestibule between the first-class coach and the sleeper were also locked, and he opened them and passed through, shutting them behind him. At the sleeping-car attendant's box, just inside the last of these doors, two car attendants were talking together. One was actually inside the box, the other standing in the corridor. The latter moved aside to let the guard pass, taking up his former position as, after exchanging a few words, Jones moved on.

His business with the ticket-collector finished, Guard Jones returned to his van. On this journey he found the same conditions obtaining as on the previous – the two attendants were at the rear end of the sleeping-car, the lady and gentleman with the baby in the front end of the third-class coach, the first-class corridor deserted, and both doors at each end of the latter coach locked. These details, casually remarked at the time, became afterwards of the utmost importance, adding as they did to the mystery in which the tragedy was enveloped.

About an hour before the train was due at Carlisle, while it was passing through the wild moorland country of the Westmorland highlands, the brakes were applied – at first gently, and then with considerable power. Guard Jones, who was examining parcel way-bills in the rear end of his van, supposed it to be a signal check, but as such was unusual at this place, he left his work and, walking down the van, lowered the window at the left-hand side and looked out along the train.

The line happened to be in a cutting, and the railway bank for some distance ahead was dimly illuminated by the light from the corridors of the first- and third-class coaches immediately in front of his van. As I have said, the night was dark, and, except for this bit of bank, Jones could see nothing ahead. The railway curved away to the right, so, thinking he might see better from the other side, he crossed the van and looked out of the opposite window, next the up line.

There were no signal lights in view, nor anything to suggest the cause of the slack, but as he ran his eye along the train he saw that something was amiss in the first-class coach. From the window at its rear end figures were leaning, gesticulating wildly, as if to attract attention to some grave and pressing danger. The guard at once ran through the third-class to this coach, and there he found a strange and puzzling state of affairs.

The corridor was still empty, but the centre blind of the rear compartment – that is, the first reached by the guard – had been raised. Through the glass Jones could see that the compartment contained four men. Two were leaning out of the window on the opposite side, and two were fumbling at the latch of the corridor door, as if trying to open it. Jones caught hold of the outside handle to assist, but they pointed in the direction of the adjoining compartment, and the guard, obeying their signs, moved on to the second door.

The centre blind of this compartment had also been pulled up, though here, again, the door had not been opened. As the guard peered in through the glass he saw that he was in the presence of a tragedy.

Tugging desperately at the handle of the corridor door stood a lady, her face blanched, her eyes starting from her head, and her features frozen into an expression of deadly fear and horror. As she pulled she kept glancing over her shoulder, as if some dreadful apparition lurked in the shadows behind. As Jones sprang forward to open the door his eyes followed the direction of her gaze, and he drew in his breath sharply.

At the far side of the compartment, facing the engine and huddled down in the corner, was the body of a woman. She lay limp and inert, with head tilted back at an unnatural angle into the cushions and a hand hanging helplessly down over the edge of the seat. She might have been thirty years of age, and was dressed in a reddish-brown fur coat with toque to match. But these details the guard hardly glanced at, his attention being riveted to her forehead. There, above the left eyebrow, was a sinister little hole, from which the blood had oozed down the coat and formed a tiny pool on the seat. That she was dead was obvious.

But this was not all. On the seat opposite her lay a man, and, as far as Guard Jones could see, he also was dead.

He apparently had been sitting in the corner seat, and had fallen forward so that his chest lay across the knees of the woman and his head hung down towards the floor. He was all bunched and twisted up – just a shapeless mass in a grey frieze overcoat, with dark hair at the back of what could be seen of his head. But under that head the guard caught the glint of falling drops, while a dark, ominous stain grew on the floor beneath.

Jones flung himself on the door, but it would not move. It stood fixed, an inch open, jammed in some mysterious way, imprisoning the lady with her terrible companions.

As she and the guard strove to force it open, the train came to a standstill. At once it occurred to Jones that he could now enter the compartment from the opposite side.

Shouting to reassure the now almost frantic lady, he turned back to the end compartment, intending to pass through it on to the line and so back to that containing the bodies. But here he was again baffled, for the two men had not succeeded in sliding back their door. He seized the handle to help them, and then he noticed their companions had opened the opposite door and were climbing out on to the permanent way.

It flashed through his mind that an up-train passed about this time, and, fearing an accident, he ran down the corridor to the sleeping-car, where he felt sure he would find a door that would open. That at the near end was free, and he leaped out on to the track. As he passed he shouted to one of the attendants to follow him, and to the other to remain where he was and let no one pass. Then he joined the men who had already alighted, warned them about the up-train, and the four opened the outside door of the compartment in which the tragedy had taken place.

Their first concern was to get the uninjured lady out, and here a difficult and ghastly task awaited them. The door was blocked by the bodies, and its narrowness prevented more than one man from working. Sending the car attendant to search the train for a doctor, Jones clambered up, and, after warning the lady not to look at what he was doing, he raised the man's body and propped it back in the corner seat.

The face was a strong one with clean-shaven but rather coarse features, a large nose, and a heavy jaw. In the neck, just below the right ear, was a bullet hole which, owing to the position of the head, had bled freely. As far as the guard could see, the man was dead. Not without a certain shrinking, Jones raised the feet, first of the man, and then of the woman, and placed them on the seats, thus leaving the floor clear except for its dark, creeping pool. Then, placing his handkerchief over the dead woman's face, he rolled back the end of the carpet to hide its sinister stain.

'Now, ma'am, if you please,' he said; and keeping the lady with her back to the more gruesome object on the opposite seat, he helped her to the open door, from where willing hands assisted her to the ground.

By this time the attendant had found a doctor in the third-class coach, and a brief examination enabled him to pronounce both victims dead. The blinds in the compartment having been drawn down and the outside door locked, the guard called to those passengers who had alighted to resume their seats, with a view to continuing their journey.

The fireman had meantime come back along the train to ascertain what was wrong, and to say the driver was unable completely to release the brake. An examination was therefore made, and the tell-tale disc at the end of the first-class coach was found to be turned, showing that someone in that carriage had pulled the communication chain. This, as is perhaps not generally known, allows air to pass between the train pipe and the atmosphere, thereby gently applying the brake and preventing its complete release. Further investigation showed that the slack of the chain was hanging in the end smoking-compartment, indicating that the alarm must have been operated by one of the four men who travelled there. The disc was then turned back to normal, the passengers reseated, and the train started, after a delay of about fifteen minutes.

Before reaching Carlisle, Guard Jones took the name and address of everyone travelling in the first- and third-class coaches, together with the numbers of their tickets. These coaches, as well as the van, were thoroughly searched, and it was established beyond any doubt that no one was concealed under the seats, in the lavatories, behind luggage, or, in fact, anywhere about them.

One of the sleeping-car attendants having been in the corridor in the rear of the last sleeper from the Preston stop till the completion of this search, and being positive no one except the guard had passed during that time, it was not considered necessary to take the names of the passengers in the sleeping-cars, but the numbers of their tickets were noted.

On arrival at Carlisle the matter was put into the hands of the police. The first-class carriage was shunted off, the doors being locked and sealed, and the passengers who had travelled in it were detained to make their statements. Then began a most careful and searching investigation, as a result of which several additional facts became known.

The first step taken by the authorities was to make an examination of the country surrounding the point at which the train had stopped, in the hope of finding traces of some stranger on the line. The tentative theory was that a murder had been committed and that the murderer had escaped from the train when it stopped, struck across the country, and, gaining some road, had made good his escape.

Accordingly, as soon as it was light, a special train brought a force of detectives to the place, and the railway, as well as a tract of ground on each side of it, were subjected to a prolonged and exhaustive search. But no traces were found. Nothing that a stranger might have dropped was picked up, no footsteps were seen, no marks discovered. As has already been stated, the weather was against the searchers. The drought of the previous days had left the ground hard and unyielding, so that clear impressions were scarcely to be expected, while even such as might have been made were not likely to remain after the downpour of the early morning.

Baffled at this point, the detectives turned their attention to the stations in the vicinity. There were only two within walking distance of the point of the tragedy, and at neither had any stranger been seen. Further, no trains had stopped at either of these stations; indeed, not a single train, either passenger or goods, had stopped anywhere in the neighbourhood since the sleeping-car express went through. If the murderer had left the express, it was, therefore, out of the question that he could have escaped by rail.

The investigators then turned their attention to the country roads and adjoining towns, trying to find the trail – if there was a trail – while it was hot. But here, again, no luck attended their efforts. If there were a murderer, and if he had left the train when it stopped, he had vanished into thin air. No traces of him could anywhere be discovered.

Nor were their researches in other directions much more fruitful.

The dead couple were identified as a Mr and Mrs Horatio Llewelyn, of Gordon Villa, Broad Road, Halifax. Mr Llewelyn was the junior partner of a large firm of Yorkshire ironfounders.

A man of five-and-thirty, he moved in good society and had some claim to wealth. He was of kindly though somewhat passionate disposition, and, so far as could be learnt, had not an enemy in the world. His firm was able to show that he had had business appointments in London on the Thursday and in Carlisle on the Friday, so that his travelling by the train in question was quite in accordance with his known plans.

His wife was the daughter of a neighbouring merchant, a pretty girl of some seven-and-twenty. They had been married only a little over a month, and had, in fact, only a week earlier returned from their honeymoon. Whether Mrs Llewelyn had any definite reason for accompanying her husband on the fatal journey could not be ascertained. She also, so far as was known, had no enemy, nor could any motive for the tragedy be suggested.

The extraction of the bullets proved that the same weapon had been used in each case – a revolver of small bore and modern design. But as many thousands of similar revolvers existed, this discovery led to nothing.

Miss Blair-Booth, the lady who had travelled with the Llewelyns, stated she had joined the train at Euston, and occupied one of the seats next the corridor. A couple of minutes before starting the deceased had arrived, and they sat in the two opposite corners. No other passengers had entered the compartment during the journey, nor had any of the three left it; in fact, except for the single visit of the ticket-collector shortly after leaving Euston, the door into the corridor had not been even opened.

Mr Llewelyn was very attentive to his young wife, and they had conversed for some time after starting, then, after consulting Miss Blair-Booth, he had pulled down the blinds and shaded the light, and they had settled down for the night. Miss Blair-Booth had slept at intervals, but each time she wakened she had looked round the compartment, and everything was as before. Then she was suddenly aroused from a doze by a loud explosion close by.

She sprang up, and as she did so a flash came from somewhere near her knee, and a second explosion sounded. Startled and trembling, she pulled the shade off the lamp, and then she noticed a little cloud of smoke just inside the corridor door, which had been opened about an inch, and smelled the characteristic odour of burnt powder. Swinging round, she was in time to see Mr Llewelyn dropping heavily forward across his wife's knees, and then she observed the mark on the latter's forehead and realized they had both been shot.

Terrified, she raised the blind of the corridor door which covered the handle and tried to get out to call assistance. But she could not move the door, and her horror was not diminished when she found herself locked in with what she rightly believed were two dead bodies. In despair she pulled the communication chain, but the train did not appear to stop, and she continued struggling with the door till, after what seemed to her hours, the guard appeared, and she was eventually released.

In answer to a question, she further stated that when her blind went up the corridor was empty, and she saw no one till the guard came.

The four men in the end compartment were members of one party travelling from London to Glasgow. For some time after leaving they had played cards, but, about midnight, they too, had pulled down their blinds, shaded their lamp, and composed themselves to sleep. In this case also, no person other than the ticket-collector had entered the compartment during the journey. But after leaving Preston the door had been opened. Aroused by the stop, one of the men had eaten some fruit, and having thereby soiled his fingers, had washed them in the lavatory. The door then opened as usual. This man saw no one in the corridor, nor did he notice anything out of the common.

Some time after this all four were startled by the sound of two shots. At first they thought of fog signals, then, realizing they were too far from the engine to hear such, they, like Miss Blair-Booth, unshaded their lamp, raised the blind over their corridor door, and endeavoured to leave the compartment. Like her they found themselves unable to open their door, and, like her also, they saw that there was no one in the corridor. Believing something serious had happened, they pulled the communication chain, at the same time lowering the outside window and waving from it in the hope of attracting attention. The chain came down easily as if slack, and this explained the apparent contradiction between Miss Blair-Booth's statement that she had pulled it, and the fact that the slack was found hanging in the end compartment. Evidently the lady had pulled it first, applying the brake, and the second pull had simply transferred the slack from one compartment to the next.

The two compartments in front of that of the tragedy were found to be empty when the train stopped, but in the last of the non-smoking compartments were two gentlemen, and in the 'Ladies Only', three ladies. All these had heard the shots, but so faintly above the noise of the train that the attention of none of them was specially arrested, nor had they attempted any investigation. The gentlemen had not left their compartment or pulled up their blinds between the time the train left Preston and the emergency stop, and could throw no light whatever on the matter.

The three ladies in the end compartment were a mother and two daughters, and had got in at Preston. As they were alighting at Carlisle they had not wished to sleep, so they had left their blinds up and their light unshaded. Two of them were reading, but the third was seated at the corridor side, and this lady stated positively that no one except the guard had passed while they were in the train.

She described his movements – first, towards the engine, secondly, back towards the van, and a third time, running, towards the engine after the train had stopped – so accurately in accord with the other evidence that considerable reliance was placed on her testimony. The stoppage and the guard's haste had aroused her interest, and all three ladies had immediately come out into the corridor, and had remained there till the train proceeded, and all three were satisfied that no one else had passed during that time.

An examination of the doors which had jammed so mysteriously revealed the fact that a small wooden wedge, evidently designed for the purpose, had been driven in between the floor and the bottom of the framing of the door, holding the latter rigid. It was evident therefore that the crime was premeditated, and the details had been carefully worked out beforehand. The most careful search of the carriage failed to reveal any other suspicious object or mark.

On comparing the tickets issued with those held by the passengers, a discrepancy was discovered. All were accounted for except one. A first single for Glasgow had been issued at Euston for the train in question, which had not been collected. The purchaser had therefore either not travelled at all, or had got out at some intermediate station. In either case no demand for a refund had been made.

The collector who had checked the tickets after the train left London believed, though he could not speak positively, that two men had then occupied the non-smoking compartment next to that in which the tragedy had occurred, one of whom held a Glasgow ticket, and the other a ticket for an intermediate station. He could not recollect which station nor could be describe either of the men, if indeed they were there at all.

But the ticket collector's recollection was not at fault, for the police succeeded in tracing one of these passengers, a Dr Hill, who had got out at Crewe. He was able, partially at all events, to account for the missing Glasgow ticket. It appeared that when he joined the train at Euston, a man of about five and thirty was already in the compartment. This man had fair hair, blue eyes, and a full moustache, and was dressed in dark well-cut clothes. He had no luggage, but only a waterproof and a paper-covered novel. The two travellers had got into conversation, and on the stranger learning that the doctor lived at Crewe, said he was alighting there also, and asked to be recommended to an hotel. He then explained that he had intended to go on to Glasgow and had taken a ticket to that city, but had since decided to break his journey to visit a friend in Chester next day. He asked the doctor if he thought his ticket would be available to complete the journey the following night, and if not, whether he could get a refund.

When they reached Crewe, both these travellers had alighted, and the doctor offered to show his acquaintance the entrance to the Crewe Arms, but the stranger, thanking him, declined, saying he wished to see to his luggage. Dr Hill saw him walking towards the van as he left the platform.

Upon interrogating the staff on duty at Crewe at the time, no one could recall seeing such a man at the van, nor had any inquiries about luggage been made. But as these facts did not come to light until several days after the tragedy, confirmation was hardly to be expected.

A visit to all the hotels in Crewe and Chester revealed the fact that no one in any way resembling the stranger had stayed there, nor could any trace whatever be found of him.

Such were the principal facts made known at the adjourned inquest on the bodies of Mr and Mrs Llewelyn. It was confidently believed that a solution to the mystery would speedily be found, but as day after day passed away without bringing to light any fresh information, public interest began to wane, and became directed into other channels.

But for a time controversy over the affair waxed keen. At first it was argued that it was a case of suicide, some holding that Mr Llewelyn had shot first his wife and then himself; others that both had died by the wife's hand. But this theory had only to be stated to be disproved.

Several persons hastened to point out that not only had the revolver disappeared, but on neither body was there powder blackening, and it was admitted that such a wound could not be self-inflicted without leaving marks from this source. That murder had been committed was therefore clear.

Rebutted on this point, the theorists then argued that Miss Blair-Booth was the assassin. But here again the suggestion was quickly negatived. The absence of motive, her known character and the truth of such of her statements as could be checked were against the idea. The disappearance of the revolver was also in her favour. As it was not in the compartment nor concealed about her person, she could only have rid herself of it out of the window. But the position of the bodies prevented access to the window, and, as her clothes were free from any stain of blood, it was impossible to believe she had moved these grim relics, even had she been physically able.

But the point that finally demonstrated her innocence was the wedging of the corridor door. It was obvious she could not have wedged the door on the outside and then passed through it. The belief was universal that whoever wedged the door fired the shots, and the fact that the former was wedged an inch open strengthened that view, as the motive was clearly to leave a slot through which to shoot.

Lastly, the medical evidence showed that if the Llewelyns were sitting where Miss Blair-Booth stated, and the shots were fired from where she said, the bullets would have entered the bodies from the direction they were actually found to have done.

But Miss Blair-Booth's detractors were loath to recede from the position they had taken up. They stated that of the objections to their theory only one – the wedging of the doors – was overwhelming. And they advanced an ingenious theory to meet it. They suggested that before reaching Preston Miss Blair-Booth had left the compartment, closing the door after her, that she had then wedged it, and that, on stopping at the station, she had passed out through some other compartment, re-entering her own through the outside door.

In answer to this it was pointed out that the gentleman who had eaten the fruit had opened his door *after* the Preston stop, and if Miss Blair-Booth was then shut into her compartment she could not have wedged the other door. That two people should be concerned in the wedging was unthinkable. It was therefore clear that Miss Blair-Booth was innocent, and that some other person had wedged both doors, in order to prevent his operations in the corridor being interfered with by those who would hear the shots.

It was recognized that similar arguments applied to the four men in the end compartment – the wedging of the doors cleared them also.

Defeated on these points the theorists retired from the field. No further suggestions were put forward by the public or the daily Press. Even to those behind the scenes the case seemed to become more and more difficult the longer it was pondered.

Each person known to have been present came in turn under the microscopic eye of New Scotland Yard, but each in turn had to be eliminated from suspicion, till it almost seemed proved that no murder could have been committed at all. The prevailing mystification was well summed up by the chief at the Yard in conversation with the inspector in charge of the case.

'A troublesome business, certainly,' said the great man, 'and I admit that your conclusions seem sound. But let us go over it again. There *must* be a flaw somewhere.'

'There must, sir. But I've gone over it and over it till I'm stupid, and every time I get the same result.'

'We'll try once more. We begin, then, with a murder in a railway carriage. We're sure it was a murder, of course?'

'Certain, sir. The absence of the revolver and of powder blackening and the wedging of the doors prove it.'

'Quite. The murder must therefore have been committed by some person who was either in the carriage when it was searched, or had left before that. Let us take these two possibilities in turn. And first, with regard to the searching. Was that efficiently done?'

'Absolutely, sir. I have gone into it with the guard and attendants. No one could have been overlooked.'

'Very good. Taking first, then, those who were in the carriage.

There were six compartments. In the first were the four men, and in the second Miss Blair-Booth. Are you satisfied these were innocent?'

'Perfectly, sir. The wedging of the doors eliminated them.'

'So I think. The third and fourth compartments were empty, but in the fifth there were two gentlemen. What about them?'

'Well, sir, you know who they were. Sir Gordon M'Clean, the great engineer, and Mr Silas Hemphill, the professor of Aberdeen University. Both utterly beyond suspicion.'

'But, as you know, inspector, *no one* is beyond suspicion in a case of this kind.'

'I admit it, sir, and therefore I made careful inquiries about them. But I only confirmed my opinion.'

'From inquiries I also have made I feel sure you are right. That brings us to the last compartment, the "Ladies Only". What about those three ladies?'

'The same remarks apply. Their characters are also beyond suspicion, and, as well as that, the mother is elderly and timid, and couldn't brazen out a lie. I question if the daughters could either. I made inquiries all the same, and found not the slightest ground for suspicion.'

'The corridors and lavatories were empty?'

'Yes, sir.'

'Then everyone found in the coach when the train stopped may be definitely eliminated?'

'Yes. It is quite impossible it could have been any that we have mentioned.'

'Then the murderer must have left the coach?'

'He must; and that's where the difficulty comes in.'

'I know, but let us proceed. Our problem then really becomes – *how* did he leave the coach?'

'That's so, sir, and I have never been against anything stiffer.'

The chief paused in thought, as he absently selected and lit another cigar. At last he continued:

'Well, at any rate, it is clear he did not go through the roof or the floor, or any part of the fixed framing or sides. Therefore he must have gone in the usual way – through a door. Of these, there is one at each end and six at each side. He therefore went through one of these fourteen doors. Are you agreed, inspector?'

'Certainly, sir.'

'Very good. Take the ends first. The vestibule doors were locked?'

'Yes, sir, at both ends of the coach. But I don't count that much. An ordinary carriage key opened them and the murderer would have had one.'

'Quite. Now, just go over again our reason for thinking he did not escape to the sleeper.'

'Before the train stopped, sir, Miss Bintley, one of the three in the "Ladies Only", was looking out into the corridor, and the two sleeper attendants were at the near end of their coach. After the train stopped, all three ladies were in the corridor, and one attendant was at the sleeper vestibule. All these persons swear most positively that no one but the guard passed between Preston and the searching of the carriage.'

'What about these attendants? Are they reliable?'

'Wilcox has seventeen years' service, and Jeffries six, and both bear excellent characters. Both, naturally, came under suspicion of the murder, and I made the usual investigation. But there is not a scrap of evidence against them, and I am satisfied they are all right.'

'It certainly looks as if the murderer did not escape towards the sleeper.'

'I am positive of it. You see, sir, we have the testimony of two separate lots of witnesses, the ladies and the attendants. It is out of the question that these parties would agree to deceive the police. Conceivably one or other might, but not both.'

'Yes, that seems sound. What, then, about the other end – the third-class end?'

'At that end,' replied the inspector, 'were Mr and Mrs Smith with their sick child. They were in the corridor close by the vestibule door, and no one could have passed without their knowledge. I had the child examined, and its illness was genuine. The parents are quiet persons, of exemplary character, and again quite beyond suspicion. When they said no one but the guard had passed I believed them. However, I was not satisfied with that, and I examined every person that travelled in the third-class coach, and established two things: first, that no one was in it at the time it was searched who had not travelled in it from Preston; and secondly, that no one except the Smiths had left any of the compartments during the run between Preston and the emergency stop. That proves beyond question that no one left the first-class coach for the third after the tragedy.'

'What about the guard himself?'

'The guard is also a man of good character, but he is out of it, because he was seen by several passengers as well as the Smiths running through the third-class after the brakes were applied.'

'It is clear, then, the murderer must have got out through one of the twelve side doors. Take those on the compartment side first. The first, second, fifth, and sixth compartments were occupied, therefore he could not have passed through them. That leaves the third and fourth doors. Could he have left by either of these?'

The inspector shook his head.

'No, sir,' he answered, 'that is equally out of the question. You will recollect that two of the four men in the end compartment were looking out along the train from a few seconds after the murder until the stop. It would not have been possible to open a door and climb out on to the footboard without being seen by them. Guard Jones also looked out at that side of the van and saw no one. After the stop these same two men, as well as others, were on the ground, and all agree that none of these doors were opened at any time.'

'H'm,' mused the chief, 'that also seems conclusive, and it brings us definitely to the doors on the corridor side. As the guard arrived on the scene comparatively early, the murderer must have got out while the train was running at a fair speed. He must therefore have been clinging on to the outside of the coach while the guard was in the corridor working at the sliding doors. When the train stopped all attention was concentrated on the opposite, or compartment, side, and he could easily have dropped down and made off. What do you think of that theory, inspector?'

'We went into that pretty thoroughly, sir. It was first objected that the blinds of the first and second compartments were raised too soon to give him time to get out without being seen. But I found this was not valid. At least fifteen seconds must have elapsed before Miss Blair-Booth and the men in the end compartment raised their blinds, and that would easily have allowed him to lower the window, open the door, pass out, raise the window, shut the door, and crouch down on the footboard out of sight. I estimate also that nearly thirty seconds passed before Guard Jones looked out of the van at that side. As far as time goes he could have done what you suggest. But another thing shows he didn't. It appears that when Jones ran through the third-class coach, while the train was stopping, Mr Smith, the man with the sick child, wondering what was wrong, attempted to follow him into the first-class. But the door slammed after the guard before the other could reach it, and, of course, the spring lock held it fast. Mr Smith therefore lowered the end corridor window and looked out ahead, and he states positively no one was on the footboard of the first-class. To see how far Mr Smith could be sure of this, on a dark night we ran the same carriage, lighted in the same way, over the same part of the line, and we found a figure crouching on the footboard was clearly visible from the window. It showed a dark mass against the lighted side of the cutting. When we remember that Mr Smith was specially looking out for something abnormal, I think we may accept his evidence.'

'You are right. It is convincing. And, of course, it is supported by the guard's own testimony. He also saw no one when he looked out of his van.'

'That is so, sir. And we found a crouching figure was visible from the van also, owing to the same cause – the lighted bank.'

'And the murderer could not have got out while the guard was passing through the third-class?'

'No, because the corridor blinds were raised before the guard looked out.'

The chief frowned.

'It is certainly puzzling,' he mused. There was silence for some moments, and then he spoke again.

'Could the murderer, immediately after firing the shots, have concealed himself in a lavatory and then, during the excitement of the stop, have slipped out unperceived through one of these corridor doors and, dropping on the line, moved quietly away?'

'No, sir, we went into that also. If he had hidden in a lavatory he could not have got out again. If he had gone towards the third-class the Smiths would have seen him, and the first-class corridor was under observation during the entire time from the arrival of the guard till the search. We have proved the ladies entered the corridor *immediately* the guard passed their compartment, and two of the four men in the end smoker were watching through their door till considerably after the ladies had come out.'

Again silence reigned while the chief smoked thoughtfully.

'The coroner had some theory, you say?' he said at last.

'Yes, sir. He suggested the murderer might have, immediately after firing, got out by one of the doors on the corridor side – probably the end one – and from there climbed on the outside of the coach to some place from which he could not be seen from a window, dropping to the ground when the train stopped. He suggested the roof, the buffers, or the lower step. This seemed likely at first sight, and I tried therefore the experiment. But it was no good. The roof was out of the question. It was one of those high curved roofs – not a flat clerestory – and there was no hand-hold at the edge above the doors. The buffers were equally inaccessible. From the handle and guard of the end door to that above the buffer on the corner of the coach was seven feet two inches. That is to say, a man could not reach from one to the other, and there was nothing he could hold on to while passing along the step. The lower step was not possible either. In the first place it was divided – there was only a short step beneath each door – not a continuous board like the upper one – so that no one could pass along the lower while holding on to the upper, and secondly, I couldn't imagine anyone climbing down there, and knowing that the first platform they came to would sweep him off.'

'That is to say, inspector, you have proved the murderer was in the coach at the time of the crime, that he was not in it when it was searched, and that he did not leave it in the interval. I don't know that that is a very creditable conclusion.'

'I know, sir. I regret it extremely, but that's the difficulty I have been up against from the start.'

The chief laid his hand on his subordinate's shoulder.

'It won't do,' he said kindly. 'It really won't do. You try again. Smoke over it, and I'll do the same, and come in and see me again tomorrow.'

But the conversation had really summed up the case justly. My Lady Nicotine brought no inspiration, and, as time passed without bringing to light any further facts, interest gradually waned till at last the affair took its place among the long list of unexplained crimes in the annals of New Scotland Yard.

And now I come to the singular coincidence referred to earlier whereby I, an obscure medical practitioner, came to learn the solution of this extraordinary mystery. With the case itself I had no connection, the details just given being taken from the official reports made at the time, to which I was allowed access in return for the information I brought. The affair happened in this way.

One evening just four weeks ago, as I lit my pipe after a long and tiring day, I received an urgent summons to the principal inn of the little village near which I practised. A motor-cyclist had collided with a car at a cross-roads and had been picked up terribly injured. I saw almost at a glance that nothing could be done for him, in fact, his life was a matter of a few hours. He asked coolly how it was with him, and, in accordance with my custom in such cases, I told him, inquiring was there anyone he would like sent for. He looked me straight in the eyes and replied:

'Doctor, I want to make a statement. If I tell it you will you keep it to yourself while I live and then inform the proper authorities and the public?'

'Why, yes,' I answered; 'but shall I not send for some of your friends or a clergyman?'

'No,' he said, 'I have no friends, and I have no use for parsons. You look a white man; I would rather tell you.'

I bowed and fixed him up as comfortably as possible, and he began, speaking slowly in a voice hardly above a whisper.

'I shall be brief for I feel my time is short. You remember some few years ago a Mr Horatio Llewelyn and his wife were murdered in a train on the North-Western some fifty miles south of Carlisle?'

I dimly remembered the case.

' "The sleeping-car express mystery," the papers called it?' I asked.

'That's it,' he replied. 'They never solved the mystery and they never got the murderer. But he's going to pay now. I am he.'

I was horrified at the cool, deliberate way he spoke. Then I remembered that he was fighting death to make his confession and that, whatever my feelings, it was my business to hear and record it while yet there was time. I therefore sat down and said as gently as I could:

'Whatever you tell me I shall note carefully, and at the proper time shall inform the police.'

His eyes, which had watched me anxiously, showed relief.

'Thank you. I shall hurry. My name is Hubert Black, and I live at 24, Westbury Gardens, Hove. Until ten years and two months ago I lived at Bradford, and there I made the acquaintance of what I thought was the best and most wonderful girl on God's earth – Miss Gladys Wentworth. I was poor, but she was well off. I was diffident about approaching her, but she encouraged me till at last I took my courage in both hands and proposed. She agreed to marry me, but made it a condition our engagement was to be kept secret for a few days. I was so mad about her I would have agreed to anything she wanted, so I said nothing, though I could hardly behave like a sane man from joy.

'Some time before this I had come across Llewelyn, and he had been very friendly, and had seemed to like my company. One day we met Gladys, and I introduced him. I did not know till later that he had followed up the acquaintanceship.

'A week after my acceptance there was a big dance at Halifax. I was to have met Gladys there, but at the last moment I had a wire that my mother was seriously ill, and I had to go. On my return I got a cool little note from Gladys saying she was sorry, but our engagement had been a mistake, and I must consider it at an end. I made a few inquiries, and then I learnt what had been done. Give me some stuff, doctor; I'm going down.'

I poured out some brandy and held it to his lips.

'That's better,' he said, continuing with gasps and many pauses: 'Llewelyn, I found out, had been struck by Gladys for some time. He knew I was friends with her, and so he made up to me. He wanted the introduction I was fool enough to give him, as well as the chances of meeting her he would get with me. Then he met her when he knew I was at my work, and made hay while the sun shone. Gladys spotted what he was after, but she didn't know if he was serious. Then I proposed, and she thought she would hold me for fear the bigger fish would get off. Llewelyn was wealthy, you understand. She waited till the ball, then she hooked him, and I went overboard. Nice, wasn't it?'

I did not reply, and the man went on:

'Well, after that I just went mad. I lost my head and went to Llewelyn, but he laughed in my face. I felt I wanted to knock his head off, but the butler happened by, so I couldn't go on and finish him then. I needn't try to describe the hell I went through – I couldn't, anyway. But I was blind mad, and lived only for revenge. And then I got it. I followed them till I got a chance, and then I killed them. I shot them in that train. I shot her first and then, as he woke and sprang up, I got him too.'

The man paused.

'Tell me the details', I asked; and after a time he went on in a weaker voice:

'I had worked out a plan to get them in a train, and had followed them all through their honeymoon, but I never got a chance till then. This time the circumstances fell out to suit. I was behind him at Euston and heard him book to Carlisle, so I booked to Glasgow. I got into the next compartment. There was a talkative man there, and I tried to make a sort of alibi for myself by letting him think I would get out at Crewe. I did get out, but I got in again, and travelled on in the same compartment with the blinds down. No one knew I was there. I waited till we got to the top of Shap, for I thought I could get away easier in a thinly populated country. Then, when the time came, I fixed the compartment doors with wedges, and shot them both. I left the train and got clear of the railway, crossing the country till I came on a road. I hid during the day and walked at night till after dark on the second evening I came to Carlisle. From there I went by rail quite openly. I was never suspected.'

He paused, exhausted, while the Dread Visitor hovered closer.

'Tell me,' I said, 'just a word. How did you get out of the train?'

He smiled faintly.

'Some more of your stuff,' he whispered; and when I had given him a second dose of brandy he went on feebly and with long pauses which I am not attempting to reproduce:

'I had worked the thing out beforehand. I thought if I could get out on the buffers while the train was running and before the alarm was raised, I should be safe. No one looking out of the windows could see me, and when the train stopped, as I knew it soon would, I could drop down and make off. The difficulty was to get from the corridor to the buffers. I did it like this:

'I had brought about sixteen feet of fine, brown silk cord, and the same length of thin silk rope. When I got out at Crewe I moved to the corner of the coach and stood close to it by way of getting shelter to light a cigarette. Without anyone seeing what I was up to I slipped the end of the cord through the bracket handle above the buffers. Then I strolled to the nearest door, paying out the cord, but holding on to its two ends. I pretended to fumble at the door as if it was stiff to open, but all the time I was passing the cord through the handle-guard, and knotting the ends together. If you've followed me you'll understand this gave me a loop of fine silk connecting the handles at the corner and the door. It was the colour of the carriage, and was nearly invisible. Then I took my seat again.

'When the time came to do the job, I first wedged the corridor doors. Then I opened the outside window and drew in the end of the cord loop and tied the end of the rope to it. I pulled one side of the cord loop and so got the rope pulled through the corner bracket handle and back again to the window. Its being silk made it run easily, and without marking the bracket. Then I put an end of the rope through the handle-guard, and after pulling it tight, knotted the ends together. This gave me a loop of rope tightly stretched from the door to the corner.

'I opened the door and then pulled up the window. I let the door close up against a bit of wood I had brought. The wind kept it to, and the wood prevented it from shutting.

'Then I fired. As soon as I saw that both were hit I got outside. I kicked away the wood and shut the door. Then with the rope for handrail I stepped along the footboard to the buffers. I cut both the cord and the rope and drew them after me, and shoved them in my pocket. This removed all traces.

'When the train stopped I slipped down on the ground. The people were getting out at the other side so I had only to creep along close to the coaches till I got out of their light, then I climbed up the bank and escaped.'

The man had evidently made a desperate effort to finish, for as he ceased speaking his eyes closed, and in a few minutes he fell into a state of coma which shortly preceded his death.

After communicating with the police I set myself to carry out his second injunction, and this statement is the result.

J. C. Squire

THE ALIBI

'STOP IT, TIMMY,' whispered Sir Richard, to the spaniel, who had whined.

The mere reflected the last pink flush of wintry sunset, and in the east, high above the far bed of rushes, the wisp of a moon was becoming distincter every time he looked at it. But it had rained in the afternoon when they had driven a few pheasants, and the black clouds massing on the nothern horizon looked like more rain. It was getting cold. He blew on his fingers. Damn that fellow Henderson, for wanting to spin the day out like this, and his fluffy hysterical little wife, for egging him on. Just because they had come to the duck-pond before – and she with them – chattering at the wrong moment too just when the first big lot of duck came in. She probably had a pretty bad time with her husband. He remembered last year he had had suspicions of curses and sobbing. But women's admirations took strange directions. She obviously thought Henderson a Nimrod, and the brute was a rotten bad shot. Keen enough though, in all conscience: liked killing for its own sake, probably. Why do they saddle us with such MP's – profiteers and Colonial adventurers, posing as Tories! Why on earth had he let all the servants go to the fair: cold supper! He was cold already. Again he stared from the sodden little peninsula into the water. He leaned his gun against the solitary tree and lit a cigarette, his hands carefully shadowing the match and the glow of the tip. And not even a man to look after the dog and to carry the birds. Politeness to local members of Parliament could go too far. Bad enough to have such a bumptious blackguard to stay. And that foolish little wife . . . back at the Manor . . . warm . . . reading some silly novel, or confiding some nonsense to that horrible set-faced companion of hers, with her silent movements. How on earth could Henderson let his wife saddle herself with such a death's head?

He heard a snipe but could not see it. He heard the mew of
plover, and a black stream of them flashed across the fading sky
and away into invisibility. Over there, somewhere in those low
thorns Henderson was crouching, and the width of the water
between them. The width of the water: the width of the world, he
thought. They had nothing in common at all. A small foreboding
gust of wind came over moor and marsh, and rattled the leaves
of the forlorn trees on the high ridge behind him. It carried a
sound with it, a dim sort of brazen music, faint bangs and cries.
It was the fair. Three miles away! Doubtless the servants were
enjoying themselves. He closed his eyes and saw the excited crowd
in the lambent light of the flares, roaring merry-go-rounds, cocoa-
nut shies, wheedling gipsies with games of chance – or, rather,
certainty! He opened them, and there was the darkening solitude,
the damp wilderness that had been unchanged for thousands of
years. Naked savages had seen it so, and on such dismal evenings
thought the place bewitched.

He could hear nothing of the fair now. Silence was only broken
by the ghostly noises of the swamp, twitters, rushes of wings, little
flashes of fish, all eerie now, causing the heart to tighten unreasonably, ominous, as though some evil magnitude was brooding over
the place. Richard Moorhouse pulled down his cape, drew the wet
flaps of his collar together below his damp beard, and shifted his
position on the squelching grass. Henderson was over there somewhere. Everybody knew the man was a swine, with his red face and
beastly curling moustache, his crooked eyes and crooked companions. Except his wife of course: perfectly obvious that nobody
told her about *her* precious husband's seraglio. Just the sort to go
mad out of jealousy: but she doted. Perhaps she was more cunning
than she looked: that companion, Mrs Rose, had eyes in her head;
there was no saying what women mightn't pour out to each other
when they were alone. He pulled himself together for the work in
hand, and passed his hand along the cold barrel of his gun. The
duck must surely come in now from their mysterious haunts, if
they were coming at all. If they waited much longer the clouds
would be up and across the struggling moon. The mirror of the
water was growing darker. Plover cried again. How lonely it was!
He stared hard across at Henderson's bank, but there was no form
there now, merely a dark tract that was not water. There wasn't a
sound anywhere. Henderson couldn't be there. He must have gone

away and left him alone. Perhaps he was slinking away now! Weren't those footsteps again? How his nerves were on edge tonight! He would bet that Henderson had never noticed that car that seemed to stop near them just after they had got out, and would explain all those splashes as water rats. But that's what they probably were! A sound again! He whistled, a low wailing note, and waited. Across the water from that dim shore came a reply. Henderson was there, immobile, grim, ready. The whistle roused the dog again, whom he had forgotten. 'Down you fool,' he rasped, clouting the spaniel's head.

There was a faint unmistakable whirr of wings: he held his gun ready and peered at the dusk: there was a small splash and a faint contented quacking far to the right. It was almost too late. He'd give it five minutes more, then shout for Henderson, stretch his cramped limbs and stumble the half mile back to the car.

That faint oozy sound again, far away in front of him. The spaniel whined and was angrily kicked. Damn the dog, he ought to have learned sense by now!

Wind rising. No more twilight. Only faint moonlight now. Time to go. A noise of wings and black wedges circling in against the spaces of the clouds. Bang! Bang! He fired both barrels. One splash in front. A clamour away there, a frenzied shout, 'Who are you, who are you?' a sharp shot, a scream.

Silence! A splash in the mere. Not a sound. Timmy howled. Not a sound. Yes, a splashing like hurried footsteps, faint in the distance. 'My God,' he said, in a strange voice that echoed in his ears. He tried to shout but his mouth was dry and rough and he merely croaked. He scooped up water, swallowed it and shouted. 'Henderson! Henderson!' The noise seemed to fill the whole air, but it died in the night. 'Henderson!' again he shouted, and knew there would be no reply. The trees shook. Clouds came over the moon and spots of rain fell. The mere was hardly visible now. What horror was over there? He clenched his teeth. He must go.

There was a punt below his feet, but it was full of water and useless. He left his tree and almost fell into the water-filled barrel which long ago had been a hiding-place for duck-shooters. His gun dropped and he picked it up again. He took his torch out and switched it on to guide himself along the neck of bog which led to the mainland: its arc illuminated tufted rushes, little pits of mud, stones, peaty pools, moths and pointed silver beads of rain.

Then some impulse of caution, almost like a voice crying in his ear, made him switch it off again, and he scrambled rapidly along the familiar bank in the rain, with now and then a plunge to the knees in mud and now and then a trip over a curling tree-root. At the western angle of the mere, he stopped, stared into the semi-darkness and listened again. The rain pattered heavily. No trace of a glare was visible from the east where the fair was. A tree creaked. 'Wants greasing,' he said aloud, not meaning to speak. Then, 'I'd better go on. I hope to God he's only wounded. I want company!' and laughed, without amusement, at his brutal humour. Then on in the rain, now with white marks on trunk and stone to guide him, up the slow stream, over the plank, past the willows, through the rushes, until the thorn-bushes filled the sky in front of him. It rained pitilessly now and he was soaked through. But he came to the last corner, and then, stooping, turned on his torch and step by step approached Henderson's lurking place. The spaniel flopped ahead, whimpered, and stood still. At one step nothing was visible but rain and the plants of the bog: at the next the mild rays fell full on the prone plump body of the man. He lay with his legs apart, his arms wide, his hands crisped, his head back, his mouth open. There was a dark stain on the left breast of his shooting jacket and below it – of all things on God's earth – was a dead mallard, beautiful in death through its gay colours were sobered in that light. The spaniel, obedient to his instincts, retrieved the bird and brought it to his master. Moorhouse stared at the picture like a lunatic: he trembled, his lips and teeth seemed beyond his control, he could hardly hold his gun. Then he laughed in a high voice, and 'My bird, I think,' he stammered. Then 'Don't be a fool,' he quavered: then addressing himself sternly, 'You've never lost hold over yourself before, Richard Moorhouse, and you'd better not do it now. There's this dead man and here are you. What's to be done?' With an effort he knelt and examined the body. No, never a gun shot, of course. It never sounded like it. A round bullet-hole. But no revolver in the dead man's hand, and not a sign of one on the boggy soil round about. He stood upright, and put out the torch. 'I can switch it on whenever I like,' he said, as though challenging the dead, and the elements, and some indefinable presence that mocked him. He clicked it on, stared at the body to steady himself, and was about to click it off again when he caught sight of something small and white on the bush to his left, and something at its foot. He reached for it, examined it, put it in his breeches pocket, stared at the dead again, and turned away. Then once more he turned, took the duck from the spaniel's mouth, and threw it out to the nearest clump of reeds. Once more he paused, and moved the torchlight-ray over the ground. He picked up Henderson's gun and opened it: yes, it was loaded. Darkness again. A risky game but it had better be done. He fired both triggers. The reports sounded like cannon-shots, but the sounds died, and no distant shout followed them. He ejected the cartridges at Henderson's feet, and laid the gun down again.

He had no need of the torch now, and so constant a will o' the wisp had better not be seen wavering over those sodden lands. First mark the willows. Second mark the biggish tree. Third mark the white post. Fourth mark the hummocks. He had known them all from boyhood, and knew also to a minute the quarter of an hour which would take him, rain or no rain, to pass them all and reach the copse where they had left the car. Well, footprints wouldn't be good on that boggy waste at the best of times, and with rain like this they could look as long as they liked. A good thing his clothes had been soaked in the afternoon. He had gone a quarter of his distance, now groping, now running, when, ahead of him, he heard a car start with a grinding of gears, run a little way, change up and change again and moan away in the distance towards the south. He smiled to himself acidly: 'As a magistrate, I suppose I ought to go to the police. But in the circumstances it would be better not to. I've a revolver licence, apart from anything else ... shut up, you fool, what are you talking to yourself for. ... Henderson, Henderson, Henderson, Henderson. Henderson, dead, dead, dead, dead, dead, dead, dead, dead, dead, dead, dead, dead, duck – a duck, duck-a-duck, duck-a-duck.' Wanting to yell, he set his jaws tight and closed his fists on his gun, steering his course now by a far cottage light behind pine-trees which had come into sight over a slight rise. The ground fell again and he plunged into a pool of the stream, his splash echoed by another splash. 'Pike,' he said, 'strange how they get here: but it is the spawn on the birds' legs of course.'

He reached the lightless car at last, and looked at his watch. 'It must be about midnight,' he thought: it was only seven. 'Good Lord, if it had been midnight the servants'd have been back at the

Manor again,' he thought: then cursing because he was tired and wet and must not take the car, left the car behind him and trudged off. There was a mile and a half of winding road, first bare, then thickly arched over with trees: an unpleasant walk, in rain, wind and darkness at the best of times. When nearly home he heard steps approaching and his heart thumped hard. Suppose it was a policeman with one of those damned lanterns. He picked up the spaniel and held it and his gun close up to his body on the hedgeward side. A shapeless figure drew near and passed with a labourer's good night. Something prompted him to reply in a foreign accent, thick and guttural, and he heard the man stop as though he were looking round, and then plod on. 'And leaves the world to darkness and to me' came into his head. A few hundred yards more and there was the back entrance where there was no lodge, and the old avenue of elms, and the Manor House, a huddle of shadows, and the garage. Yes, the Hendersons' car was in the next stall. He walked into the garage, turned on the light and put his hand on the bonnet, and smiled ironically: then he drew the doors to, and stole round, avoiding the gravel, to the front of the house. In one second-floor window shone a light. It was Mrs Henderson's. Moorhouse opened the front door noiselessly, and walked down the hall and got rid of his outer coverings, and turned on the light in the library. He threw a glance round the accustomed files of leather backed books.

'Looks damned ordinary,' he said. He filled a tumbler half-full of whisky and drank it neat. Then he walked up to the Georgian mirror which ran the length of the low mantelpiece and stared at his own face. It was white and drawn, the eyes bright in deep sockets, the lines from nostril to mouth cut deep, the moustache and beard dank. He watched his mouth as he spoke. 'A damned interesting position,' he said: then added, less deliberately, 'provided they don't take too long finding him. That would be trying.' Then a thought flashing across his mind, he walked out into the hall. 'Quite,' he observed, as he picked up an open note which was lying on the largest of the chests: 'To Harry and Sir Richard: I was so tired after our day's walking that I've gone to bed. I've had all I want to eat. Don't wake me. – Gladys.'

But he thought he heard her moving about upstairs. And then he thought he heard crying and the voice of a comforter. He crept upstairs, feeling like a cowardly spy, and listened. 'I wish you hadn't, oh, I wish you hadn't,' he heard in Mrs Henderson's voice; and then the determined mumbling of that woman, the companion. It was enough, he slunk downstairs again. In his own house! Biting his lip he took Mrs Henderson's note into the library, and watched it drop to ashes in the fire. He went through the library into the study where he kept rods, guns and account books, cleaned his barrels and restored the gun to the leather case which held its twin. His initials were stamped on it, 'R. M.' 'Rotten Mess. . . . Rank Madness,' he said: and then wondered why strain should make people talk rubbish aloud. Very deliberately he pressed the spring of a panel cupboard in the wall, drew from one pocket a muddy handkerchief and put it in, and then from another something wrapped in a larger handkerchief. 'Let's hope we shan't need them,' he said.

He returned to the library, stared at his shadow on the wall, poured out another whisky and sat down in a deep leather chair before the fire. At what stage ought he to get worried about Henderson's disquieting non-appearance? Over and over again he reconsidered the events of the evening and his own position. It was obvious that he must get alarmed some time, and equally obvious that he had better not be precipitant. The clock whirred and struck nine. If only those damned servants would return his mind wouldn't dwell so much on ringing up the Titbury police! There was a soft knock at the door. He sprang up, leant against the mantelpiece with his face to the door, and said, 'Come in' with visions of policemen flashing across his brain. It was Harbutt, the butler, plump, cheerful and courteous, but abnormal in a smart lounge suit. 'Oh, you, Harbutt,' remarked his master, stifling a sigh of relief, 'I thought you were all at the fair.'

'So we were, Sir Richard, but some of us 'ave come 'ome. Sick of the weather. The rest of 'em's in a cinema.'

'Is there a maid with you?'

'Yes, Sir Richard, Lucy – Simpson that is. And Banks and myself.'

'Banks hasn't gone off, I hope?'

'No, Sir Richard, 'e's down warmin' 'imself in the kitchen.'

'I may want him to drive the Daimler.'

'Nothing wrong I 'ope, Sir Richard?' He thought his master's face looked odd.

'No, I hope not, Harbutt, but Mr Henderson isn't back and

I'm worried about it. And I believe I heard Timmy outside. Mr
Henderson went off in the Chrysler by himself to the duck-pond,
and took the dog with him.'

'What, our car, sir?'

'Yes, Mrs Henderson said she might want theirs to run over
and see her mother, though in the end she went to bed instead.
He ought to have been back two hours ago. He knows the way
well enough, but it's damned dark and if he loses his way and
collapses he might get rheumatic fever.' He gave a little laugh.
'We don't want to lose our Member, do we, after taking so much
trouble to get him in?'

Harbutt gave an old servant's deferential laugh. 'No, Sir Richard.
But Banks and I will find him in no time. It's only a matter of
shouting and a lantern.'

'He may not answer if he is too far gone, you know.'

'We'll cover the ground all right, Sir Richard.'

'If you don't find him ring me up.'

'Yes, Sir Richard, and I will tell Lucy to put a kettle on.' He
bowed and closed the door. After five minutes there was the roar
and dwindling hum of a departing car.

In the morning, after that sleepless night of trampings, excited
servants, and bustling policemen, and the ultimate silence of dawn,
since rent by screams from upstairs, he received a message from
the companion saying that they must be driven over at once to
Mrs Henderson's mother at Oakhanger, her mistress being unfit
to stay in the house any longer. Moorhouse felt a strong revul-
sion against seeing them off the premises, but, with the servants
watching, he thought he had better. His solicitude, as Mrs Henderson, heavily muffled, was helped along the hall by her woman, was
thrown away. The widow of the murdered man never lifted her
head, bowed in a stillness of grief that drew murmurs of pity
from Harbutt and the chauffeur; but the stern stony face of the
maid, fiery dark eyes and tight mouth, was turned full at him as
she disclaimed his aid with a movement of her free arm. 'Thank
you,' she said, 'we can look after ourselves'; and then, with a
faint ironic smile, 'and I hope you can look after *your*self.' Of
her feelings and intentions towards himself he was uncertain, but
her almost passionate concern for her stricken mistress was evident
in every movement. Relieved to be able to stand aloof he watched

them depart from the steps, wondering at the predicaments in which human beings find themselves, at the secrets they carry about in their breasts, musing on the passions of the wronged, the desperate unscrupulousness of the frightened, the general inability of men and women to see their affairs in a due proportion, having regard to time and space, the awful tale of forgotten years, the movements of land and sea, the uncountable wars and plagues of the past, the vast and remote processions of the stars and nebulae. Yet, he reflected, as the closed car rolled off and he turned again to his room, he could hardly be expected to be immune from the general human frailty, and his own preservation and comfort, however momentary in the light of the eternities, were of some importance to him. It occurred to him then – for he was honest with himself – that he was, on the whole, a chivalrous man, though his generally ironic, even cynical, manner effectively disguised it from all except the penetrating; and that this indefensible habit of secrecy might well be useful to him.

It was after dinner, a week later. The inquest had been adjourned. He had given his evidence, a candid and straightforward account of the dead man's movements, and his own. It was, up to a point, a very simple story. Henderson had insisted on trying the pond in the evening. He had gone as far as the garage with him, but felt very tired and excused himself to his guest, who had gone on with the car and spaniel – which had found its way home later. He had returned to the house and had never moved outside it until the news that the body had been found reached him. Pressed, very courteously, for further material evidence as to the commission and motive of the crime he had said he was completely in the dark. The technical evidence ruled out suicide: the bullet was of a common type: no pistol had been found, which was not surprising with a large and muddy lake at hand. Nothing which looked like the faintest clue appeared at the inquest except that a labourer produced a vague statement about having passed a man who spoke with a foreign accent in a dark lane near the Manor. Witness could not say whether the man was carrying a gun, but could swear he was not followed by a dog: the solicitor privately apologized to Moorhouse for being compelled to ask absurd questions which might seem to hint in his direction.

'Your questions were quite proper, but I am afraid your apology is not,' Moorhouse had said with a quick smile which relieved his worried neighbour, who, once a year, was asked to shoot. The foreign accent offered the one faint gleam of hope, and the newspapers 'understood' that inquiries were being made in South Africa, where it was believed the dead man had made enemies. Mrs Henderson might still throw light on the mystery, but she was, for the moment, ill from shock. The maid, Mrs Rose, gave formal evidence: she knew nothing about Mr Henderson's affairs, having been with the family only three months. It was believed by the Press that the business associates of the 'shot MP' might be of assistance; one of them told a reporter that a year ago he had heard Henderson muttering something about 'blackmail' after receiving a cable from somewhere abroad. For the rest, there had not been a hint, except that a few of the more enterprising newspaper gossipers had thought fit to keep the name and record of Sir Richard Moorhouse before the public. 'Just in case, I suppose,' he reflected with a downward droop of the bearded lips, as he noticed casual paragraphs in which sympathy with him led by an easy transition to accounts of his pedigree, birth, and education, his brief marriage to 'a beautiful but delicate wife who died at Titford Manor', and innocent references to him as 'a great reader, with a particular penchant for criminology', 'a keen student of nature', 'a fine shot', 'a noted pedestrian', 'at one time much sought after as an amateur actor', and a 'world-traveller who might, in 1908, have met in Johannesburg (where he stayed for several months) the young prospector Henry Henderson whose path crossed his so tragically twenty years after'. Near, but not too libellously adjoining, in the latest of these paragraphs he noticed an interesting reference to the 'only peer ever hanged for murder', the mad Earl Ferrers, who murdered his servant, and went proudly to his death clad in white silk and riding in his private coach. What was to prevent anybody from wondering whether the Law wouldn't add a baronet to its gruesome bag? Nothing obviously: but he thought he had done his best so far to avert the calamity and if he had to play his last card he had to play it – or rather the next to the last, for the last of all he shrank from contemplating. Conscience spoke with an uncertain voice, or rather with several conflicting voices.

It was half-past nine. He was in the library in his dinner jacket, stretched in a chair, smoking a cigar and reading, as detachedly as he was able, a volume on 'Circumstantial Evidence'. As he read, his heart beat violently at certain cases and conclusions. The book was on his knees and he was ruminating on the extent to which the externally self-controlled among men may be tremulously emotional within, when the butler, pleased that his master should be visited by an old friend and evening companion, complacently announced Major French. French had been at school with him and lived near: but he also happened to be Chief Constable of the County.

There was a slightly feverish cordiality in French's greeting as he entered, with 'How d'ye do, Dick. You don't mind my calling at this hour, do you, and in these clothes. No, no, it's not too hot. This chair will do perfectly. Well, emm, I don't know ... perhaps ... well, yes, a small spot of whisky.'

'Almost refused my drink,' thought Moorhouse, acutely conscious of a barrier, and observing that French, slightly froglike with his round face and plump waistcoat and hips, was sitting on the edge of his chair. He brought his guest the glass of whisky, and looked him right in the eyes. 'Does he see,' he thought, as he mustered a frank and friendly expression, 'a glaze of defence and hypocrisy in my eyes also?'

'You must need it,' he said aloud, 'I expect this wretched case is giving you an awful amount of trouble. I'm damned glad you've come, it's the first normal thing that's happened here for a week.'

French took a large draught and looked round the room, challenged his host with his eyes and said:

'Look here, Moorhouse – Dick – I don't want you to be under any misapprehension. It's about this case that I've come to talk to you. There's nobody within earshot, I suppose?'

'Not unless you have a guard of police outside,' said Moorhouse. The Chief Constable winced slightly.

'I happen to have two men with me in the ordinary way, but they have no instructions to eavesdrop. I have come to you as an old friend.'

'You mean,' said Moorhouse jocularly, 'that nothing I say will be used in evidence against me!'

'There is no charge against you. I've merely come to you privately to see if you have anything to add to what you said before.'

'Are you sure you are doing the correct thing in giving me what almost sounds like a warning?'

'You can leave me to decide upon that. I have other duties too. Ethel was my cousin, after all [Moorhouse felt sick at the mention of his dead wife], and you and I have been on terms of friendship for many years.'

Words flashed across Moorhouse's brain: 'Yes, you little blighter, you were my fag, and I wangled this job for you, and you always come to me to pour out your tribulations and my whisky. Oh, you're not so bad in your way, but you are insufferably stupid.' Almost simultaneously he said:

'Look here, Ted, be frank with me, what is it that is troubling you?' French thawed at the warmth of the accustomed atmosphere, walked over and helped himself to another drink in the old way, and almost forgot his suspicion.

'I'm glad you're making it easy for me, Dick. The fact is you may be having an awkward time ahead of you. Of course you know very well that I myself should never dream that you, of all people, could have anything to do with, er ...'

'A murder, you mean. I should damn well think not.'

'You're quite right. Now, let's talk it over sensibly. You understand, I dare say, that what we're talking about is not what your old friends know, but evidence.'

'And evidence is a curious thing, of course. Fire away.'

'Well, we've been working at this case and we've got nowhere, nowhere at all.'

'And you're back at the Manor.'

'Not to put too fine a point on it, we are. You see,' French went on in his old confiding way, forgetting for the time whom he was talking about, 'we have to follow any clue that is offered to us, and ...'

'Let me tell you once and for all, Ted, that you can discuss this case as if it didn't involve me at all. Look here, I'll save you embarrassment. I'll outline the whole bloody thing myself, if you like!

French squirted from a syphon into his glass.

'I wish you would,' he said.

'Very well. Mr Henry Henderson, MP, an unpleasant man of doubtful antecedents, with an ill-treated wife ...'

'Who said she was ill-treated?'

'I did. But never mind. She at least would never be suspected by anyone. At all events this malodorous, though virile and energetic man, was staying, in his capacity as chosen of the electorate, with Sir Richard Moorhouse at Titford Manor. Is that all right?'

'Oh of course it is.'

'On a certain evening of November 1928, Mr Henderson was found dead by Sir Richard Moorhouse's duck-pond. Two dead duck accounted for the discharge of his gun barrels and he had obviously been killed by a pistol shot fired by another hand.'

'That's all right so far as it goes,' said French, looking vacantly, glass in hand, into the great fire of logs.

'Obviously, and perhaps I can skip the rest of the obvious. The question is, who did it?'

'Of course, who did it?'

'Now the first certainty is that it must have been done either by somebody who went to the duck-pond with Mr Henderson or by somebody who was following his movements, tracked him closely there, for the night was dark and the path difficult, and shot him. It is admitted by Sir Richard Moorhouse that he started for the duck-pond with Mr Henderson and a spaniel. But Sir Richard states that he only went as far as the garage, that he sent the spaniel on with Mr Henderson, and that the spaniel returned alone later in the evening. For all this there is no evidence but his own word: the servants were all out. Mrs Henderson and her companion were upstairs, as he agrees. For the moment we return to the other supposition: that some person unknown with some motive unknown for killing him had been lurking in the neighbourhood for some days.'

'Not necessarily for some days,' interjected French, the sense of evidence strong in him.

'Well, probably for some days, as the best of opportunities would probably not occur on the night of this stranger's arrival. However, it is immaterial. If we assume the stranger, we must ask ourselves whom Henderson may have injured, and who would have so strong a motive for revenge against him as to plan his deliberate murder.'

'Yes,' French muttered.

'The obvious place to look, especially after that rather sketchy statement of the man who heard a foreign accent, was South Africa.

Enemies could certainly be traced there, but – this I assume without knowledge – all those who could be identified were either dead or in jail.'

'Yes, confound it!' said French.

'The jail-birds wouldn't speak; the dead couldn't; the woman he lived with couldn't be traced.'

'How did you know that?' exclaimed French, with a sudden shrewd look in his eye.

'Oh,' replied Moorhouse, flicking off the ash of his cigarette, 'I didn't know: I merely guessed it. Persons of his kidney have always lived with women and have always deserted them. Poor creature! I bet she had a hell of a time with him. A man like that would be enough to drive a woman mad! However, the plain truth is that Africa yielded you nothing, and you came back here. And coming back here, you – I mean, of course, your colleagues – have been unable to restrain a certain amount of curiosity about myself – shared, I may say, by the newspapers – though they are diffident about saying so.'

'I wish you wouldn't talk so wildly,' said French. 'It's very uncomfortable for me, and you ought to know that I wish you well out of this.'

'I assure you,' replied Moorhouse, 'that I am not in the least wild, and you know it. You know, moreover, that, having returned to the consideration of myself, you discovered certain facts that might tend, if supported, to suggest that I went to the duck-pond with Henry Henderson, that I crept round upon him in the dark, and that I shot him, and left him, and then stole home by unfrequented ways.'

'We've got a few facts. They don't amount to much one way or the other. I never said you did it. It's ridiculous.'

'Nothing could be more ridiculous,' said Moorhouse, now pacing up and down before the fire, and shooting continual keen glances at his old fag, 'but it is not for the police to rule hypotheses out, is it? Remember what virtuous people have committed murder – professors, clergymen, retired colonels, Sunday-school teachers, suburban violinists! Why not a widower baronet, for a change? Especially as he had frequently been heard to say that the world would be much better off without swine like Henderson in it.'

'I never said you said that.'

'No, but I did, often; and you've got it all down in little note-books; and I say it again, and you can take it down again, if you like. But this of course isn't the most important thing, is it?'

'I don't quite know what you mean.'

'My dear Chief Constable, you have a perfectly sound glimmering of what I mean, though you can hardly conceive that you are right, or that I should have the audacity to mention it.'

'I don't know, all the same,' said French, obstinately, not without betraying in his expression the hope of learning something new.

'No,' said Moorhouse, with a sudden access of energy, 'I'm not telling you anything you don't know already. There's nothing to tell. I'm merely referring to your dicovering that one of my pistols is missing.'

'How the devil — '

'Naturally I was not left uninformed that your police had paid me a little call when I was well known to be off the premises. One of the pistols has gone!'

'That's the deuce of it!' said French — and Moorhouse felt a slight renewed affection for him, as it became clear that he had tried to shirk or rebut this evidence in his own mind. 'Where is it?'

'If I knew where it was,' cried Moorhouse impatiently, 'we shouldn't be having all this bother. I suppose somebody's been cleaning it, and left it somewhere.'

'But,' said French, more stiffly, 'your butler saw you showing it to the whole Henderson family only the day before.'

'What!' said Moorhouse, quietly, but in surprise, 'You mean that Harbutt said that? Harbutt? Oh, all right, it's true enough. I suppose he was quite right to tell the truth. Lies in these affairs always get found out.'

'You're right enough there,' French observed, 'we're pretty well accustomed to lies, and know the sound of them.'

'Well,' Moorhouse went on, 'you don't suppose, Ted, that I've been telling lies tonight, do you?'

'I believe every word you say,' said French, 'but it's ugly all the same. What about what Mrs Henderson was overheard to say to that companion when she was getting into the car here?'

'Whatever it was, it's news to me,' replied Moorhouse boldly. 'Who heard it?'

'My men — and your servants, I suppose.'

'What did she say?'

'Very little, but a jury might think it had great significance. It was "Oh, Sir Richard, oh, Sir Richard!"'

'That's not much from a hysterical woman, is it?'

'Possibly not, possibly it is, or a jury might think so. We have often got clues from hysteria. She might have said more if that companion of hers hadn't shut her up.'

'Yes, the dragon,' said Moorhouse, 'I suppose I ought to be obliged to her, even if she has got the stony face of a Medusa. But listen to me now. What does all this amount to?'

'How can I tell what a jury might think, or what further clues mightn't turn up? Of course, I take your word for it you're innocent; but even if there isn't enough to go on, you're not going to escape suspicion.'

'And it isn't going to leave me, eh? A pleasant prospect!'

'It isn't much. You'd be all right with a decent alibi,' said French, fencing with his eyes.

'Not always procurable,' sighed Moorhouse, 'even by the least guilty of men.'

The telephone rang in the adjoining study. 'Excuse me a moment,' said Moorhouse, 'I was expecting an answer to a message, and this is probably it.' He passed through the folding doors, left them open and spoke in the dark in full hearing of his visitor:

'Yes. . . . Is that Mrs Rose? . . . Yes. . . . I'm very sorry. . . . Oh, yes, I found it and I've got it! . . . It was rather careless, you know. . . . A man must protect himself. Can't be helped. . . . I think so. . . . In the last resort, but it has to be. . . . Good night. . . . I hope she's better.'

When he returned to the library – once more to press a drink upon the willing French – his face wore a look both anxious and determined. He paced up and down the room with quick strides, and then, facing French squarely, said quietly: 'I've been telling you lies.'

French was proud of his equilibrium as a policeman, and his plump face assumed a supercilious expression. 'So I have observed all the time,' he said.

'Very penetrating of you,' said Moorhouse, 'I suppose you imagine that I am going to say that I was there when Henderson was murdered?'

French flushed and stammered: 'I don't see why you should.
... I mean ...'

Moorhouse's mouth drooped in an acid smile. 'Never mind;
at any rate you will be relieved. Your people need hardly go
further with their conjectures. I have just been authorized to dis-
close my alibi.'

'But you said you were here,' said French.

'So I was,' replied Moorhouse. 'With Mrs Henderson.'

There was a pause.

'Oh, I see,' said French, lamely, 'you sent him out because you
were in love with his wife.'

'No,' remarked Moorhouse, shrinking from the suggestion,
'don't take it too seriously. This isn't one of those intrigues that
end in a marriage.'

French rose, helped himself abstractedly to a cigarette, and
muttered that he must be going. Then he added, half-heartedly,
'What witness had you?'

'Oh,' said Moorhouse, 'her maid was about. They are very thick
with each other.'

'I'm sorry, Dick,' said French. 'The last thing I wanted to do
was to embarrass you. But there is one thing still, you know.'

'Well?' asked Moorhouse.

'The pistol.'

'Oh, that's easy enough! Forgive me a moment, will you?'
Moorhouse went into the study, opened the cupboard, took out a
pistol in a handkerchief, carefully wiped it with the handkerchief
and brought it into the library. 'There she is!' he said jocularly.

'But why didn't you produce this before?' asked French.

'My dear boy, simply because I wanted to test your faith in
me.'

'We've got our duty to do,' mumbled French shamefacedly.

'Yes, I know you have. It was damned brutal of me. But I'm
not quite myself. You've never been suspected of a murder. 'Pon
my word I don't believe you ever will be! Sorry, old boy,' he
said.

'Oh, you're just the same as ever,' laughed French, finishing
his drink.

He showed French out, and returned to the library.

'Extraordinary,' he said to himself, 'that that woman Rose could
have been with the Hendersons for three months and that he

should never have found out that his wife knew who she was. ...
Poor devil. ... But he got what he deserved. ... It was rather
stupid of me not to guess the right one at the start, but it hardly
mattered which of his two women put him out of the world.'

Georges Simenon

THE EVIDENCE OF
THE ALTAR-BOY

A FINE COLD RAIN was falling. The night was very dark; only at the far end of the street, near the barracks from which, at half past five, there had come the sound of bugle calls and the noise of horses being taken to be watered, was there a faint light shining in someone's window – an early riser, or an invalid who had lain awake all night.

The rest of the street was asleep. It was a broad, quiet, newish street, with almost identical one- or two-storied houses such as are to be seen in the suburbs of most big provincial towns.

The whole district was new, devoid of mystery, inhabited by quite unassuming people, clerks and commercial travellers, retired men and peaceful widows.

Maigret, with his overcoat collar turned up, was huddling in the angle of a carriage gateway, that of the boys' school; he was waiting, watch in hand, and smoking his pipe.

At a quarter to six exactly, bells rang out from the parish church behind him, and he knew that, as the boy had said, it was the 'first stroke' for six o'clock Mass.

The sound of the bells was still vibrating in the damp air when he heard, or rather guessed at, the shrill clamour of an alarm clock. This lasted only a few seconds. The boy must already have stretched a hand out of his warm bed and groped in the darkness for the safety-catch that would silence the clock. A few minutes later, the attic window on the second floor lit up.

It all happened exactly as the boy had said. He must have risen noiselessly, before anyone else, in the sleeping house. Now he must be picking up his clothes, his socks, washing his face and hands and combing his hair. As for his shoes, he had declared:

'I carry them downstairs and put them on when I get to the last step, so as not to wake up my parents.'

This had happened every day, winter and summer, for nearly two years, ever since Justin had first begun to serve at Mass at the hospital.

He had asserted, furthermore: 'The hospital clock always strikes three or four minutes later than the parish church clock.'

And this had proved to be the case. The inspectors of the Flying Squad to which Maigret had been seconded for the past few months had shrugged their shoulders over these tiresome details about first bells and second bells.

Was it because Maigret had been an altar-boy himself for a long time that he had not dismissed the story with a smile?

The bells of the parish church rang first, at a quarter to six. Then Justin's alarm clock went off, in the attic where the boy slept. Then a few moments later came the shriller, more silvery sound of the hospital chapel bells, like those of a convent.

He still had his watch in his hand. The boy took barely more than four minutes to dress. Then the light went out. He must be groping his way down the stairs, anxious not to waken his parents, then sitting down on the bottom step to put on his shoes, and taking down his coat and cap from the bamboo coat-rack on the right in the passage.

The door opened. The boy closed it again without making a sound, looked up and down the street anxiously and then saw the Superintendent's burly figure coming up to him.

'I was afraid you might not be there.'

And he started walking fast. He was a thin, fair-haired little twelve-year-old with an obstinate look about him.

'You want me to do just what I usually do, don't you? I always walk fast, for one thing because I've worked out to the minute how long it takes, and for another, because in winter, when it's dark, I'm frightened. In a month it'll be getting light by this time in the morning.'

He took the first turning on the right into another quiet, somewhat shorter street, which led on to an open square planted with elms and crossed diagonally by tramlines.

And Maigret noted tiny details that reminded him of his own childhood. He noticed, for one thing, that the boy did not walk closely to the houses, probably because he was afraid of seeing someone suddenly emerge from a dark doorway. Then, that when he crossed the square he avoided the trees in the same way, because a man might have been hiding behind them.

He was a brave boy, really, since for two whole winters, in all weathers, sometimes in thick fog or in the almost total darkness of a moonless night, he had made the same journey every morning all alone.

'When we get to the middle of the Rue Sainte-Catherine you'll hear the second bell for Mass from the parish church ...'

'At what time does the first tram pass?'

'At six o'clock. I've only seen it two or three times, when I was late ... once because my alarm clock hadn't rung, another time because I'd fallen asleep again. That's why I jump out of bed as soon as it rings.'

A pale little face in the rainy night, with eyes that still retained something of the fixed stare of a sleepwalker, and a thoughtful expression with just a slight tinge of anxiety.

'I shan't go on serving at Mass. It's because you insisted that I've come today....'

They turned left down the Rue Sainte-Catherine, where, as in all the streets in this district, there was a lamp every fifty metres, each of them shedding a pool of light; and the child unconsciously quickened his pace each time he left the reassuring zone of brightness.

The noises from the barracks could still be heard in the distance. A few windows lit up. Footsteps sounded in a side street; probably a workman going to his job.

'When you got to the corner of the street, did you see nothing?'

This was the trickiest point, for the Rue Sainte-Catherine was very straight and empty, with its rectilinear pavements and its street lamps at regular intervals, leaving so little shadow between them that one could not have failed to see a couple of men quarrelling even at a hundred metres' distance.

'Perhaps I wasn't looking in front of me ... I was talking to myself, I remember ... I often do talk to myself in a whisper, when I'm going along there in the morning ... I wanted to ask mother something when I got home and I was repeating to myself what I was going to say to her ...'

'What did you want to say to her?'

'I've wanted a bike for ever such a long time ... I've already saved up three hundred francs out of my church money.'

Was it just an impression? It seemed to Maigret that the boy was keeping further away from the houses. He even stepped off the pavement, and returned to it a little further on.

'It was here. ... Look. ... There's the second bell ringing for Mass at the parish church.'

And Maigret endeavoured, in all seriousness, to enter into the world which was the child's world every morning.

'I must have looked up suddenly. ... You know, like when you're running without looking where you're going and find yourself in front of a wall. ... It was just here.'

He pointed to the line on the pavement dividing the darkness from the lamplight, where the drizzle formed a luminous haze.

'First I saw that there was a man lying down and he looked so big that I could have sworn he took up the whole width of the pavement.'

That was impossible, for the pavement was at least two and a half metres across.

'I don't know what I did exactly ... I must have jumped aside ... I didn't run away immediately, for I saw the knife stuck in his chest, with a big handle made of brown horn. I noticed it because my uncle Henri has a knife just like it and he told me it was made out of a stag's horn. I'm certain the man was dead ...'

'Why?'

'I don't know. ... He looked like a corpse.'

'Were his eyes shut?'

'I didn't notice his eyes ... I don't know. ... But I had the feeling he was dead. ... It all happened very quickly, as I told you yesterday in your office. ... They made me repeat the same thing so many times yesterday that I'm all muddled. ... Specially when I feel people don't believe me ...'

'And the other man?'

'When I looked up I saw that there was somebody a little further on, five metres away maybe, a man with very pale eyes who looked at me for a moment and then started running. It was the murderer ...'

'How do you know that?'

'Because he ran off as fast as he could.'

'In which direction?'

'Right over there ...'

'Towards the barracks?'

'Yes....'

It was a fact that Justin had been interrogated at least ten times the previous day. Before Maigret appeared in the office the detectives had even made a sort of game of it. His story had never varied in a single detail.

'And what did you do?'

'I started running too. ... It's hard to explain. ... I think it was when I saw the man running away that I got frightened. ... And then I ran as hard as I could ...'

'In the opposite direction?'

'Yes.'

'Did you not think of calling for help?'

'No ... I was too frightened ... I was specially afraid my legs might give way, for I could scarcely feel them ... I turned right-about as far as the Place du Congrès ... I took the other street, that leads to the hospital too after making a bend.'

'Let's go on.'

More bells, the shrill-toned bells of the chapel. After walking some fifty metres they reached a crossroads, on the left of which were the walls of the barracks, pierced with loopholes, and on the right a huge gateway dimly lit and surmounted by a clock-face of greenish glass.

It was three minutes to six.

'I'm a minute late. ... Yesterday I was on time in spite of it all, because I ran ...'

There was a heavy knocker on the solid oak door; the child lifted it, and the noise reverberated through the porch. A porter in slippers opened the door, let Justin go in but barred the way to Maigret, looking at him suspiciously.

'What is it?'

'Police.'

'Let's see your card?'

Hospital smells were perceptible as soon as they entered the porch. They went on through a second door into a huge court-yard surrounded by various hospital buildings. In the distance could be glimpsed the white head-dresses of nuns on their way to the chapel.

'Why didn't you say anything to the porter yesterday?'

'I don't know ... I was in a hurry to get there ...'

Maigret could understand that. The haven was not the official entrance with its crabbed, mistrustful porter, nor the unwelcoming courtyard through which stretchers were being carried in silence; it was the warm vestry near the chapel, where a nun was lighting candles on the altar.

'Are you coming in with me?'

'Yes.'

Justin looked vexed, or rather shocked, probably at the thought that this policeman, who might be an unbeliever, was going to enter into his hallowed world. And this, too, explained to Maigret why every morning the child had the courage to get up so early and overcome his fears.

The chapel had a warm and intimate atmosphere. Patients in the blue-grey hospital uniform, some with bandaged heads, some with crutches or with their arms in slings, were already sitting in the pews of the nave. Up in the gallery the nuns formed a flock of identical figures, and all their white cornets bowed simultaneously in pious worship.

'Follow me.'

They went up a few steps, passing close to the altar where candles were already burning. To the right was a vestry panelled in dark wood, where a tall gaunt priest was putting on his vestments, while a surplice edged with fine lace lay ready for the altar-boy. A nun was busy filling the holy vessels.

It was here that, on the previous day, Justin had come to a halt at last, panting and weak-kneed. It was here that he had shouted: 'A man's been killed in the Rue Sainte-Catherine!'

A small clock set in the wainscot pointed to six o'clock exactly. Bells were ringing again, sounding fainter here than outside. Justin told the nun who was helping him on with his surplice: 'This is the Police Superintendent ...'

And Maigret stood waiting while the child went in, ahead of the chaplain, the skirts of his red cassock flapping as he hurried towards the altar steps.

The vestry nun had said: 'Justin is a good little boy, who's very devout and who's never lied to us. ... Occasionally he's failed to come and serve at Mass. ... He might have pretended he'd been ill. ... Well, he never did; he always admitted frankly that he'd not had the courage to get up because it was too cold, or because he'd had a nightmare during the night and was feeling too tired . . .'

And the chaplain, after saying Mass, had gazed at the Superintendent with the clear eyes of a saint in a stained glass window: 'Why should the child have invented such a tale?'

Maigret knew, now, what had gone on in the hospital chapel on the previous morning. Justin, his teeth chattering, at the end of his tether, had been in a state of hysterics. The service could not be delayed; the vestry nun had informed the Sister Superior and had herself served at Mass in place of the child, who was meanwhile being attended to in the vestry.

Ten minutes later, the Sister Superior had thought of informing the police. She had gone out through the chapel, and everyone had realized that something was happening.

At the local police station the sergeant on duty had failed to understand.

'What's that? . . . The Sister Superior? . . . Superior to what?'

And she had told him, in the hushed tone they use in convents, that there had been a crime in the Rue Sainte-Catherine; and the police had found nothing, no victim, and, needless to say, no murderer . . .

Justin had gone to school at half past eight, just as usual, as though nothing had happened; and it was in his classroom that Inspector Besson, a strapping little fellow who looked like a boxer and who liked to act tough, had picked him up at 9.30 as soon as the Flying Squad had got the report.

Poor kid! For two whole hours, in a dreary office that reeked of tobacco fumes and the smoke from a stove that wouldn't draw, he had been interrogated not as a witness but as a suspect.

Three inspectors in turn, Besson, Thiberge and Vallin, had tried to catch him out, to make him contradict himself.

To make matters worse his mother had come too. She sat in the waiting-room, weeping and snivelling and telling everybody: 'We're decent people and we've never had anything to do with the police.'

Maigret, who had worked late the previous evening on a case of drug-smuggling, had not reached his office until eleven o'clock.

'What's happening?' he had asked when he saw the child standing there, dry-eyed but as stiffly defiant as a little fighting-cock.

'A kid who's been having us on. . . . He claims to have seen a dead body in the street and a murderer who ran away when he got near. But a tram passed along the same street four minutes later and the driver saw nothing. ... It's a quiet street, and nobody heard anything. ... And finally when the police were called, a quarter of an hour later, by some nun or other, there was absolutely nothing to be seen on the pavement, not the slightest trace of a bloodstain. ...'

'Come along into my office, boy.'

And Maigret was the first of them, that day, not to address Justin by the familiar *tu*, the first to treat him not as a fanciful or malicious urchin but as a small man.

He had listened to the boy's story simply and quietly, without interrupting or taking any notes.

'Shall you go on serving at Mass in the hospital?'

'No. I don't want to go back. I'm too frightened.'

And yet it meant a great sacrifice for him. Not only was he a devout child, deeply responsive to the poetry of that early Mass in the warm and somewhat mysterious atmosphere of the chapel; but in addition, he was paid for his services – not much, but enough to enable him to get together a little nest-egg. And he so badly wanted a bicycle which his parents could not afford to buy for him!

'I should like you to go just once more, tomorrow morning.'

'I shan't dare.'

'I'll go along with you.... I'll wait for you in front of your home. You must behave exactly as you always do.'

This was what had been happening, and Maigret, at seven in the morning, was now standing alone outside the door of the hospital, in a district which, on the previous day, he had known only from having been through it by car or in a tram.

An icy drizzle was still falling from the sky which was now paler, and it clung to the Superintendent's shoulders; he sneezed twice. A few pedestrians hurried past, their coat collars turned up and their hands in their pockets; butchers and grocers had begun taking down the shutters of their shops.

It was the quietest, most ordinary district imaginable. At a pinch one might picture a quarrel between two men, two drunks for instance, at five minutes to six on the pavement of the Rue Sainte-Catherine. One might even conceive of an assault by some ruffian on an early passer-by.

But the sequel was puzzling. According to the boy, the murderer had run off when he came near, and it was then five minutes to six. At six o'clock, however, the first tram had passed, and the driver had declared that he had seen nothing.

He might, of course, have been inattentive, or looking in the other direction. But at five minutes past six two policemen on their beat had walked along that very pavement. And they had seen nothing!

At seven or eight minutes past six a cavalry officer who lived three houses away from the spot indicated by Justin had left home, as he did every morning, to go to the barracks.

And he had seen nothing either!

Finally, at twenty-past six, the police cyclists dispatched from the local station had found no trace of the victim.

Had someone come in the meantime to remove the body in a car or van? Maigret had deliberately and calmly sought to consider every hypothesis, and this one had proved as unreliable as all the rest. At no. 42 in the same street, there was a sick woman whose husband had sat up with her all night. He had asserted categorically:

'We hear all the noises outside. I notice them all the more because my wife is in great pain, and the least noise makes her wince. The tram woke her when she'd only just dropped off ... I can give you my word no car came past before seven o'clock. The dustcart was the earliest.'

'And you heard nothing else?'

'Somebody running, at one point ...'

'Before the tram?'

'Yes, because my wife was asleep ... I was making myself some coffee on the gas-ring.'

'One person running?'

'More like two.'

'You don't know in which direction?'

'The blind was down. ... As it creaks when you lift it I didn't try to look out.'

This was the only piece of evidence in Justin's favour. There was a bridge two hundred metres further on. And the policeman on duty there had seen no car pass.

Could one assume that barely a few minutes after he'd run away the murderer had come back, picked up his victim's body and carried it off somewhere or other, without attracting attention?

Worse still, there was one piece of evidence which made people shrug their shoulders when they talked about the boy's story. The place he had indicated was just opposite no. 61. Inspector Thiberge had called at this house the day before, and Maigret, who left nothing to chance, now visited it himself.

It was a new house of pinkish brick; three steps led up to a shiny pitchpine door with a letter-box of gleaming brass.

Although it was only 7.30 in the morning, the Superintendent had been given to understand that he might call at that early hour.

A gaunt old woman with a moustache peered through a spy-hole and argued before letting him into the hall, where there was a pleasant smell of fresh coffee.

'I'll go and see if the Judge will see you.'

For the house belonged to a retired magistrate, who was reputed to have private means and who lived there alone with a house-keeper.

Some whispering went on in the front room, which should by rights have been a drawing-room. Then the old woman returned and said sourly:

'Come in. . . . Wipe your feet, please. . . . You're not in a stable.'

The room was no drawing-room; it bore no resemblance to what one usually thinks of as such. It was very large, and it was part bedroom, part study, part library and part junk-room, being cluttered with the most unexpected objects.

'Have you come to look for the corpse?' said a sneering voice that made the Superintendent jump.

Since there was a bed, he had naturally looked towards it, but it was empty. The voice came from the chimney corner, where a lean old man was huddled in the depths of an armchair, with a plaid over his legs.

'Take off your overcoat, for I adore heat and you'll not be able to stand it here.'

It was quite true. The old man, holding a pair of tongs, was doing his best to encourage the biggest possible blaze from a log fire.

'I have thought that the police had made some progress since my time and had learnt to mistrust evidence given by children. Children and girls are the most unreliable of witnesses, and when I was on the Bench . . .'

He was wearing a thick dressing-gown, and in spite of the heat of the room, he had a scarf as broad as a shawl round his neck.

'So the crime is supposed to have been committed in front of my house? And if I'm not mistaken, you are the famous Superintendent Maigret, whom they have graciously sent to our town to reorganize our Flying Squad?'

His voice grated. It was that of a spiteful, aggressive, savagely sarcastic old man.

'Well, my dear Superintendent, unless you're going to accuse me of being in league with the murderer, I am sorry to tell you, as I told your young inspector yesterday, that you're on the wrong track.

'You've probably heard that old people need very little sleep. Moreover there are people who, all their life long, sleep very little. Erasmus was one such, for instance, as was also a gentleman known as Voltaire ...'

He glanced smugly at the bookshelves where volumes were piled ceiling-high.

'This has been the case with many other people whom you're not likely to know either. ... It's the case with me, and I pride myself on not having slept more than three hours a night during the last fifteen years. ... Since for the past ten my legs have refused to carry me, and since furthermore I've no desire to visit any of the places to which they might take me, I spend my days and nights in this room which, as you can see for yourself, gives directly on to the street.

'By four in the morning I am sitting in this armchair, with all my wits about me, believe me ... I could show you the book in which I was deep yesterday morning, only it was by a Greek philosopher and I can't imagine you'd be interested.

'The fact remains that if an incident of the sort described by your over-imaginative young friend had taken place under my window, I can promise you I should have noticed it. ... My legs are weak, as I've said, but my hearing is still good.

'Moreover, I have retained enough natural curiosity to take an interest in all that happens in the street, and if it amuses you I could tell you at what time every housewife in the neighbourhood goes past my window to do her shopping.'

He was looking at Maigret with a smile of triumph.

'So you usually hear young Justin passing in front of the house?' the Superintendent asked in the meekest and gentlest of tones.

'Naturally.'

'You both hear him and see him?'

'I don't follow.'

'For most of the year, for almost two-thirds of the year, it's broad daylight at six in the morning. ... Now the child served at six o'clock Mass both summer and winter.'

'I used to see him go past.'

'Considering that this happened every day with as much regularity as the passing of the first tram, you must have been attentively aware of it ...'

'What do you mean?'

'I mean that, for instance, when a factory siren sounds every day at the same time in a certain district, when somebody passes your window with clockwork regularity, you naturally say to yourself: Hullo, it must be such and such a time.

'And if one day the siren doesn't sound, you think: Why, it's Sunday. And if the person doesn't come past you wonder: What can have happened to him? Perhaps he's ill?'

The judge was looking at Maigret with sharp, sly little eyes. He seemed to resent being taught a lesson.

'I know all that ...' he grumbled, cracking his bony finger-joints. 'I was a magistrate before you were a policeman.'

'When the altar-boy went past ...'

'I used to hear him, if that's what you're trying to make me admit.'

'And if he didn't go past?'

'I might have happened to notice it. But I might have happened not to notice it. As in the case of the factory siren you mentioned. One isn't struck every Sunday by the silence of the siren ...'

'What about yesterday?'

Could Maigret be mistaken? He had the impression that the old magistrate was scowling, that there was something sullen and savagely secretive about his expression. Old people sometimes sulk, like children; they often display the same puerile stubbornness.

'Yesterday?'

'Yes ...'

Why did he repeat the question, unless to give himself time to make a decision?

'I noticed nothing.'

'Not that he had passed?'

'No ...'

'Nor that he hadn't passed?'

'No ...'

One or the other answer was untrue, Maigret was convinced. He was anxious to continue the test, and he went on with his questions:

'Nobody ran past your windows?'

'No.'

This time the *no* was spoken frankly and the old man must have been telling the truth.

'You heard no unusual sound?'

'No' again, uttered with the same downrightness and almost with a note of triumph.

'No sound of trampling, of groaning, no sound of a body falling?'

'Nothing at all.'

'I'm much obliged to you.'

'Don't mention it.'

'Seeing that you've been a magistrate I need not of course ask you if you are willing to repeat your statement under oath?'

'Whenever you like.'

And the old man said that with a kind of delighted impatience.

'I apologize for disturbing you, Judge.'

'I wish you all success in your enquiry, Superintendent.'

The old housekeeper must have been hiding behind the door, for she was waiting on the threshold to show out the Superintendent and shut the front door behind him.

Maigret experienced a curious sensation as he re-emerged into everyday life in that quiet suburban street where housewives were beginning their shopping and children were on their way to school.

It seemed to him that he had been hoaxed, and yet he could have sworn that the judge had not withheld the truth except on one point. He had the impression, furthermore, that at a certain moment he had been about to discover something very odd, very elusive, very unexpected; that he would only have had to make a tiny effort but that he had been unable to do so.

Once again he pictured the boy, he pictured the old man; he tried to find a link between them.

Slowly he filled his pipe, standing on the kerb. Then, since he had had no breakfast, not even a cup of coffee on rising, and since his wet overcoat was clinging to his shoulders, he went to wait at the corner of the Place du Congrès for the tram that would take him home.

2

Out of the heaving mass of sheets and blankets an arm emerged, and a red face glistening with sweat appeared on the pillow; finally a sulky voice growled: 'Pass me the thermometer.'

And Madame Maigret, who was sewing by the window – she had drawn aside the net curtain so as to see in the gathering dusk – rose with a sigh and switched on the electric light.

'I thought you were asleep. It's not half an hour since you last took your temperature.'

Resignedly, for she knew from long marital experience that it was useless to cross the big fellow, she shook the thermometer to bring down the mercury and slipped the tip of it between his lips.

He asked, meanwhile: 'Has anybody come?'

'You'd know if they had, since you've not been asleep.'

He must have dozed off though, if only for a few minutes. But he was continually being roused from his torpor by that blasted jingle from down below.

They were not in their own home. Since his mission in this provincial town was to last for six months at least, and since Madame Maigret could not bear the thought of letting her husband eat in restaurants for so long a period, she had followed him, and they had rented a furnished flat in the upper part of the town.

It was too bright, with flowery wallpaper, gimcrack furniture and a bed that groaned under the Superintendent's weight. They had, at any rate, chosen a quiet street, where, as the landlady Madame Danse had told them, not a soul passed.

What she had failed to add was that, the ground floor of the house being occupied by a dairy, the whole place was pervaded by a sickly smell of cheese. Another fact which she had not revealed but which Maigret had just discovered for himself, since this was the first time he had stayed in bed in the daytime, was that the

door of the dairy was equipped not with a bell but with a strange
contraption of metal tubes which, whenever a customer came in,
clashed together with a prolonged jingling sound.

'How high?'

'38.5 ...'

'A little while ago it was 38.8.'

'And by tonight it'll be over 39.'

He was furious. He was always bad tempered when he was ill,
and he glowered resentfully at Madame Maigret, who obstinately
refused to go out when he was longing to fill himself a pipe.

It was still pouring with rain, the same fine rain that clung to
the windows and fell in mournful silence, giving one the impression of living in an aquarium. A crude glare shone down from the
electric light bulb which swung, unshaded, at the end of its cord.
And one could imagine an endless succession of streets equally
deserted, windows lighting up one after the other, people caged
in their rooms, moving about like fishes in a bowl.

'You must have another cup of tisane.'

It was probably the tenth since twelve o'clock, and then all that
lukewarm water had to be sweated away into his sheets, which
ended up as damp as compresses.

He must have caught flu or tonsillitis while waiting for the boy
in the cold early morning rain outside the school, or else afterwards while he was roaming the streets. By ten o'clock, when he
was back in his room in the Flying Squad's offices, and while
he was poking the stove with what had become almost a ritual
gesture, he had been seized with the shivers. Then he had felt
too hot. His eyelids were smarting and when he looked at himself
in the bit of mirror in the cloakroom, he had seen round staring
eyes that were glistening with fever.

Moreover his pipe no longer tasted the same, and that was a sure
sign.

'Look here, Besson: if by any chance I shouldn't come back
this afternoon, will you carry on investigating the altar-boy
problem?'

And Besson, who always thought himself cleverer than anybody
else: 'Do you really think, Chief, that there *is* such a problem,
and that a good spanking wouldn't put an end to it?'

'All the same, you must get one of your colleagues, Vallin for
instance, to keep an eye on the Rue Sainte-Catherine.'

'In case the corpse comes back to lie down in front of the judge's house?'

Maigret was too dazed by his incipient fever to follow Besson on to that ground. He had just gone on deliberately giving instructions.

'Draw up a list of all the residents in the street. It won't be a big job, because it's a short street.'

'Shall I question the kid again?'

'No ...'

And since then he had felt too hot; he was conscious of drops of sweat beading on his skin, he had a sour taste in his mouth, he kept hoping to sink into oblivion but was constantly disturbed by the ridiculous jingle of the brass tubes from the dairy.

He loathed being ill because it was humiliating and also because Madame Maigret kept a fierce watch to prevent him from smoking his pipe. If only she'd had to go out and buy something at the pharmacist's! But she was always careful to take a well-stocked medicine chest about with her.

He loathed being ill, and yet there were moments when he almost enjoyed it, moments when, closing his eyes, he felt ageless because he experienced once again the sensations of his childhood.

Then he remembered the boy Justin, whose pale face already showed such strength of character. All that morning's scenes recurred to his mind, not with the precision of everyday reality nor with the sharp outline of things seen, but with the peculiar intensity of things felt.

For instance he could have described almost in detail the attic room that he had never seen, the iron bedstead, the alarm clock on the bedside table, the boy stretching out his arm, dressing silently, the same gestures invariably repeated ...

Invariably the same gestures! It seemed to him an important and obvious truth. When you've been serving at Mass for two years at a regular time, you gestures become almost completely automatic. ... The first bell at a quarter to six. ... The alarm clock. ... The shriller sound of the chapel bells. ... Then the child would put on his shoes at the foot of the stairs, open the front door and meet the cold breath of early morning.

'You know, Madame Maigret, he's never read any detective stories.' For as long back as they could remember, possibly because it had begun as a joke, they had called one another Maigret and

Madame Maigret, and they had almost forgotten that they had Christian names like other people ...

'He doesn't read the papers either ...'

'You'd better try to sleep.'

He closed his eyes, after a longing glance at his pipe, which lay on the black marble mantelpiece.

'I questioned his mother at great length; she's a decent woman, but she's mightily in awe of the police ...'

'Go to sleep!'

He kept silence for a while. His breathing became deeper; it sounded as if he was really dozing off.

'She declares he's never seen a dead body. ... It's the sort of thing you try to keep from children.'

'Why is it important?'

'He told me the body was so big that it seemed to take up the whole pavement. ... Now that's the impression that a dead body lying on the ground makes on one.... A dead person always looks bigger than a living one.... D'you understand?'

'I can't think why you're worrying, since Besson's looking after the case.'

'Besson doesn't believe in it.'

'In what?'

'In the dead body.'

'Shall I put out the light?'

In spite of his protests, she climbed on to a chair and fastened a band of waxed paper round the bulb so as to dim its light.

'Now try to get an hour's sleep, then I'll make you another cup of tisane. You haven't been sweating enough ...'

'Don't you think if I were to have just a tiny puff at my pipe ...'

'Are you mad?'

She went into the kitchen to keep an eye on the vegetable broth, and he heard her tiptoeing back and forth. He kept picturing the same section of the Rue Saint-Catherine, with street lamps every fifty metres.

'The judge declares he heard nothing ...'

'What are you saying?'

'I bet they hate one another ...'

And her voice reached him from the far end of the kitchen:

'Who are you talking about? You see I'm busy ...'

'The judge and the altar-boy. They've never spoken to one another, but I'll take my oath they hate each other. You know, very old people, particularly old people who live by themselves, end up by becoming like children. ... Justin went past every morning, and every morning the old judge was behind his window. ... He looks like an owl.'

'I don't know what you're trying to say ...'

She stood framed in the doorway, a steaming ladle in her hand.

'Try to follow me. The judge declares that he heard nothing, and it's too serious a matter for me to suspect him of lying.'

'You see! Try to stop thinking about it.'

'Only he dared not assert that he had or had not heard Justin go past yesterday morning.'

'Perhaps he went back to sleep.'

'No. ... He daren't tell a lie, and so he's deliberately vague. And the husband at no. 42 who was sitting up with his sick wife heard somebody running in the street.'

He kept reverting to that. His thoughts, sharpened by fever, went round in a circle.

'What would have become of the corpse?' objected Madame Maigret with her womanly common sense. 'Don't think any more about it! Besson knows his job, you've often said so yourself ...'

He slumped back under the blankets, discouraged, and tried hard to go to sleep, but was inevitably haunted before long by the image of the altar-boy's face, and his pallid legs above black socks.

'There's something wrong ...'

'What did you say? Something wrong? Are you feeling worse? Shall I ring the doctor?'

Not that. He started again from scratch, obstinately; he went back to the threshold of the boys' school and crossed the Place du Congrès.

'And this is where there's something amiss.'

For one thing, because the judge had heard nothing. Unless one was going to accuse him of perjury it was hard to believe that a fight could have gone on under his window, just a few metres away, that a man had started running off towards the barracks while the boy had rushed off in the opposite direction.

'Listen, Madame Maigret ...'

'What is it now?'

'Suppose they had both started running in the same direction?'

With a sigh, Madame Maigret picked up her needlework and listened, dutifully, to her husband's monologue interspersed with wheezy gasps.

'For one thing, it's more logical ...'

'What's more logical?'

'That they should both have run in the same direction. ... Only in that case it wouldn't have been towards the barracks.'

'Could the boy have been running after the murderer?'

'No. The murderer would have run after the boy ...'

'What for, since he didn't kill him?'

'To make him hold his tongue, for instance.'

'He didn't succeed, since the child spoke ...'

'Or to prevent him from telling something, from giving some particular detail. ... Look here, Madame Maigret.'

'What is it you want?'

'I know you'll start by saying no, but it's absolutely necessary. ... Pass me my pipe and my tobacco. ... Just a few puffs. ... I've got the feeling that I'm going to understand the whole thing, that in a few minutes – if I don't lose the thread.

She went to fetch his pipe from the mantelpiece and handed it to him resignedly, sighing: 'I knew you'd think of some good excuse. ... In any case tonight I'm going to make you a poultice whether you like it or not.'

Luckily there was no telephone in the flat and one had to go down into the shop to ring up from behind the counter.

'Will you go downstairs, Madame Maigret, and call Besson for me? It's seven o'clock. He may still be at the office. Otherwise call the *Café du Centre*, where he'll be playing billiards with Thiberge.'

'Shall I ask him to come here?'

'To bring me as soon as possible a list, not of all the residents in the street but of the tenants of the houses on the left side of it, between the Place du Congrès and the Judge's house.'

'Do try to keep covered up ...'

Barely had she set foot on the staircase when he thrust both legs out of bed and rushed, barefooted, to fetch his tobacco pouch and fill himself a fresh pipe; then he lay back innocently between the sheets.

Through the flimsy floorboards he could hear a hum of voices and Madame Maigret's, speaking on the telephone. He smoked his pipe in greedy little puffs, although his throat was very sore. He could see raindrops slowly sliding down the dark panes, and this again reminded him of his childhood, of childish illnesses when his mother used to bring him caramel custard in bed.

Madame Maigret returned, panting a little, glanced round the room as if to take note of anything unusual, but did not think of the pipe.

'He'll be here in about an hour.'

'I'm going to ask you one more favour, Madame Maigret. ... Will you put on your coat ...'

She cast a suspicious glance at him.

'Will you go to young Justin's home and ask his parents to let you bring him to me. ... Be very kind to him. ... If I were to send a policeman he'd undoubtedly take fright, and he's liable enough to be prickly as it is. ... Just tell him I'd like a few minutes' chat with him.'

'And suppose his mother wants to come with him?'

'Work out your own plan, but I don't want the mother.'

Left to himself, he sank back into the hot, humid depths of the bed, the tip of his pipe emerging from the sheets and emitting a slight cloud of smoke. He closed his eyes, and he could keep picturing the corner of the Rue Sainte-Catherine; he was no longer Superintendent Maigret, he had become the altar-boy who hurried along, covering the same ground every morning at the same time and talking to himself to keep up his courage.

As he turned into the Rue Sainte-Catherine: 'Maman, I wish you'd buy me a bike ...'

For the kid had been rehearsing the scene he would play for his mother when he got back from the hospital. It would have to be more complicated; he must have thought up subtler approaches.

'You know, maman, if I had a bike, I could. ...' Or else, 'I've saved three hundred francs already. ... If you'd lend me the rest, which I promise to pay back with what I earn from the chapel, I could ...'

The corner of the Rue Sainte-Catherine ... a few seconds before the bells of the parish church rang out for the second time. And there were only a hundred and fifty metres of dark empty street to go through before reaching the safe haven of the hospital. ...

A few jumps between the pools of brightness shed by the street lamps ...

Later the child was to declare: 'I looked up and I saw ...'

That was the whole problem. The judge lived practically in the middle of the street, half way between the Place du Congrès and the corner of the barracks, and he had seen nothing and heard nothing.

The husband of the sick woman, the man from no. 42, lived closer to the Place du Congrès, on the right side of the street, and he had heard the sound of running footsteps.

Yet, five minutes later, there had been no dead or injured body on the pavement. And no car or van had passed. The policeman on duty on the bridge, the others on the beat at various spots in the neighbourhood, had seen nothing unusual such as, for instance, a man carrying another man on his back.

Maigret's temperature was certainly going up but he no longer thought of consulting the thermometer. Things were fine as they were; words evoked images, and images assumed unexpected sharpness.

It was just like when he was a sick child and his mother, bending over him, seemed to have grown so big that she took up the whole house.

There was that body lying across the pavement, looking so long because it was a dead body, with a brown-handled knife sticking out of its chest.

And a few metres away a man, a pale-eyed man who had begun running. ... Running towards the barracks, whereas Justin ran for all he was worth in the opposite direction.

'That's it!'

That's what? Maigret had made the remark out loud, as though it contained the solution of the problem, as though it had actually been the solution of the problem, and he smiled contentedly as he drew on his pipe with ecstatic little puffs.

Drunks are like that. Things suddenly appear to them self-evidently true, which they are nevertheless incapable of explaining, and which dissolve into vagueness as soon as they are examined coolly.

Something was untrue, that was it! And Maigret, in his feverish imagining, felt sure that he had put his finger on the weak point in the story.

Justin had not made it up. ... His terror, his panic on arriving at the hospital had been genuine. Neither had he made up the picture of the long body sprawling across the pavement. Moreover there was at least one person in the street who had heard running footsteps.

What had the judge with the sneering smile remarked? 'You haven't yet learned to mistrust the evidence of children?' ... or something of the sort.

However the judge was wrong. Children are incapable of inventing because one cannot construct truths out of nothing. One needs materials. Children transpose maybe, they don't invent.

And that was that! At each stage, Maigret repeated that self-congratulatory *voilà*!

There had been a body on the pavement. ... And no doubt there had been a man close by. Had he had pale eyes? Quite possibly. And somebody had run.

And the old judge, Maigret could have sworn, was not the sort of man to tell a deliberate lie.

He felt hot. He was bathed in sweat, but nonetheless he left his bed to go and fill one last pipe before Madame Maigret's return. While he was up, he took the opportunity to open the cupboard and drink a big mouthful of rum from the bottle. What did it matter if his temperature was up that night? Everything would be finished by then!

And it would be quite an achievement; a difficult case solved from a sick-bed! Madame Maigret was not likely to appreciate that, however.

The judge had not lied, and yet he must have tried to play a trick on the boy whom he hated as two children of the same age can hate one another.

Customers seemed to be getting fewer down below, for the ridiculous chimes over the door sounded less frequently. Probably the dairyman and his wife, with their daughter whose cheeks were as pink as ham, were dining together in the room at the back of the shop.

There were steps on the pavement; there were steps on the stair. Small feet were stumbling. Madame Maigret opened the door and ushered in young Justin, whose navy-blue duffel coat was glistening with rain. He smelt like a wet dog.

'Here, my boy, let me take off your coat.'

'I can take it off myself.'

Another mistrustful glance from Madame Maigret. Obviously she could not believe he was still smoking the same pipe. Who knows, perhaps she even suspected the shot of rum?

'Sit down, Justin,' said the Superintendent, pointing to a chair.

'Thanks, I'm not tired.'

'I asked you to come so that we could have a friendly chat together for a few minutes. What were you busy with?'

'My arithmetic homework.'

'Because in spite of all you've been through you've gone back to school?'

'Why shouldn't I have gone?'

The boy was proud. He was on his high horse again. Did Maigret seem to him bigger and longer than usual, now that he was lying down?

'Madame Maigret, be an angel and go and look after the vegetable broth in the kitchen, and close the door.'

When that was done he gave the boy a knowing wink.

'Pass me my tobacco pouch, which is on the mantelpiece. ... And the pipe, which must be in my overcoat pocket. ... Yes, the one that's hanging behind the door. ... Thanks, my boy. ... Were you frightened when my wife came to fetch you?'

'No.' He said that with some pride.

'Were you annoyed?'

'Because everyone keeps saying that I've made it up.'

'And you haven't, have you?'

'There was a dead man on the pavement and another who ...'

'Hush!'

'What?'

'Not so quick. ... Sit down. ...'

'I'm not tired.'

'So you've said, but I get tired of seeing you standing up. ...' He sat down on the very edge of the chair, and his feet didn't touch the ground; his legs were dangling, his bare knobbly knees protruding between the short pants and the socks.

'What sort of trick did you play on the judge?'

A swift, instinctive reaction: 'I never did anything to him.'

'You know what judge I mean?'

'The one who's always peering out of his window and who looks like an owl?'

'Just how I'd described him. . . . What happened between you?'

'In winter I didn't see him because his curtains were drawn when I went past.'

'But in summer?'

'I put out my tongue at him.'

'Why?'

'Because he kept looking at me as if he was making fun of me; he sniggered to himself as he looked at me.'

'Did you often put out your tongue at him?'

'Every time I saw him . . .'

'And what did he do?'

'He laughed in a spiteful sort of way . . . I thought it was because I served at Mass and he's an unbeliever . . .'

'Has he told a lie, then?'

'What did he say?'

'That nothing happened yesterday morning in front of his house, because he would have noticed.'

The boy stared intently at Maigret, then lowered his head.

'He was lying, wasn't he?'

'There was a body on the pavement with a knife stuck in its chest.'

'I know . . .'

'How do you know?'

'I know because it's the truth . . .' repeated Maigret gently. 'Pass me the matches . . . I've let my pipe go out.'

'Are you too hot?'

'It's nothing . . . just the flu . . .'

'Did you catch it this morning?'

'Maybe. . . . Sit down.'

He listened attentively and then called: 'Madame Maigret! Will you run downstairs? I think I heard Besson arriving and I don't want him to come up before I'm ready. . . . Will you keep him company downstairs? My friend Justin will call you . . .'

Once more, he said to his young companion: 'Sit down. . . . It's true, too, that you both ran . . .'

'I told you it was true . . .'

'And I believe you. . . . Go and make sure there's nobody behind the door and that it's properly shut.'

The children obeyed without understanding, impressed by the importance that his actions had suddenly acquired.

'Listen, Justin, you're a brave little chap.'

'Why do you say that?'

'It was true about the corpse. It was true about the man running.'

The child raised his head once again, and Maigret saw his lip quivering.

'And the judge, who didn't lie, because a judge would not dare to lie, didn't tell the whole truth...'

The room smelt of flu and rum and tobacco. A whiff of vegetable broth came in under the kitchen door, and raindrops were still falling like silver tears on the black window pane beyond which lay the empty street. Were the two now facing one another still a man and a small boy? Or two men, or two small boys?

Maigret's head felt heavy; his eyes were glistening. His pipe had a curious medical flavour that was not unpleasant, and he remembered the smells of the hospital, its chapel and its vestry.

'The judge didn't tell the whole truth because he wanted to rile you. And you didn't tell the whole truth either. ... Now I forbid you to cry. We don't want everyone to know what we've been saying to each other.... You understand, Justin?'

The boy nodded.

'If what you described hadn't happened at all, the man in no. 42 wouldn't have heard running footsteps.'

'I didn't make it up.'

'Of course not! But if it had happened just as you said, the judge would not have been able to say that he had heard nothing.... And if the murderer had run away towards the barracks, the old man would not have sworn that nobody had run past his house.'

The child sat motionless, staring down at the tips of his dangling feet.

'The judge was being honest, on the whole, in not daring to assert that you had gone past his house yesterday morning. But he might perhaps have asserted that you had not gone past. That's the truth, since you ran off in the opposite direction.... He was telling the truth, too, when he declared that no man had run past on the pavement under his window.... For the man did not go in that direction.'

'How do you know?'

He had stiffened, and was staring wide-eyed at Maigret as he must have stared on the previous night at the murderer or his victim.

'Because the man inevitably rushed off in the same direction as yourself, which explains why the husband in no. 42 heard him go past.... Because, knowing that you had seen him, that you had seen the body, that you could get him caught, he ran *after* you...'

'If you tell my mother, I...'

'Hush!... I don't wish to tell your mother or anyone else anything at all.... You see, Justin my boy, I'm going to talk to you like a man.... A murderer clever and cool enough to make a corpse disappear without trace in a few minutes would not have been foolish enough to let you escape after seeing what you had seen.'

'I don't know...'

'But I do.... It's my job to know.... The most difficult thing is not to kill a man, it's to make the body disappear afterwards, and this one disappeared magnificently.... It disappeared, even though you had seen it and seen the murderer.... In other words, the murderer's a really smart guy.... And a really smart guy, with his life at stake, would never have let you get away like that.'

'I didn't know...'

'What didn't you know?'

'I didn't know it mattered so much...'

'It doesn't matter at all now, since everything has been put right.'

'Have you arrested him?'

There was immense hope in the tone in which these words were uttered.

'He'll be arrested before long.... Sit still; stop swinging your legs...'

'I won't move.'

'For one thing, if it had all happened in front of the judge's house, that's to say in the middle of the street, you'd have been aware of it from further off, and you'd have had time to run away. ... That was the only mistake the murderer made, for all his cleverness...'

'How did you guess?'

'I didn't guess. But I was once an altar-boy myself, and I served at six o'clock Mass like you.... You wouldn't have gone a hundred metres along the street without looking in front of you.... So the corpse must have been closer, much closer, just round the corner of the street.'

'Five houses past the corner.'

'You were thinking of something else, of your bike, and you may have gone twenty metres without seeing anything.'

'How can you possibly know?'

'And when you saw, you ran towards the Place du Congrès to get to the hospital by the other street. The man ran after you...'

'I thought I should die of fright.'

'Did he grab you by the shoulder?'

'He grabbed my shoulders with both hands. I thought he was going to strangle me...'

'He asked you to say...'

The child was crying, quietly. He was pale and the tears were rolling slowly down his cheeks.

'If you tell my mother she'll blame me all my life long. She's always nagging at me.'

'He ordered you to say that it had happened further on...'

'Yes.'

'In front of the judge's house?'

'It was me that thought of the judge's house, because of putting out my tongue at him.... The man only said the other end of the street, and that he'd run off towards the barracks.'

'And so we very nearly had a perfect crime, because nobody believed you, since there was no murderer and no body, no traces of any sort, and it all seemed impossible...'

'But what about you?'

'I don't count. It just so happens that I was once an altar-boy, and that today I'm in bed with flu.... What did he promise you?'

'He told me that if I didn't say what he wanted me to, he would always be after me, wherever I went, in spite of the police, and that he would wring my neck like a chicken's.'

'And then?'

'He asked me what I wanted to have...'

'And you said a bike...?'

'How do you know?'

'I've told you, I was once an altar-boy too.'

'And you wanted a bike?'

'That, and a great many other things that I've never had.... Why did you say he had pale eyes?'

'I don't know. I didn't see his eyes. He was wearing thick glasses. But I didn't want him to be caught...'

'Because of the bike?'

'Maybe.... You're going to tell my mother, aren't you?'

'Not your mother nor anyone else. ... Aren't we pals now?. ... Look, you hand me my tobacco pouch and don't tell Madame Maigret that I've smoked three pipes since we've been here together. ... You see, grown-ups don't always tell the whole truth either. ... Which door was it in front of, Justin?'

'The yellow house next door to the delicatessen.'

'Go and fetch my wife.'

'Where is she?'

'Downstairs.... She's with Inspector Besson, the one who was so beastly to you.'

'And who's going to arrest me?'

'Open the wardrobe...'

'Right...'

'There's a pair of trousers hanging there...'

'What am I to do with it?'

'In the left hand pocket you'll find a wallet.'

'Here it is.'

'In the wallet there are some visiting-cards.'

'Do you want them?'

'Hand me one.... And also the pen that's on the table...'

With which, Maigret wrote on one of the cards that bore his name: *Supply bearer with one bicycle.*

3

'Come in, Besson.'

Madame Maigret glanced up at the dense cloud of smoke that hung round the lamp in its waxed-paper shade; then she hurried into the kitchen, because she could smell something burning there.

As for Besson, taking the chair just vacated by the boy, for whom he had only a disdainful glance, he announced:

'I've got the list you asked me to draw up. I must tell you right away...'

'That it's useless.... Who lives in no. 14?'

'One moment....' He consulted his notes. 'Let's see... no. 14. ... There's only a single tenant there.'

'I suspected as much.'

'Oh?' An uneasy glance at the boy. 'It's a foreigner, name of Frankelstein, a dealer in jewellery.'

Maigret had slipped back among his pillows; he muttered, with an air of indifference: 'A fence.'

'What did you say, Chief?'

'A fence.... Possibly the boss of a gang.'

'I don't understand.'

'That doesn't matter.... Be a good fellow, Besson, pass me the bottle of rum that's in the cupboard. Quickly, before Madame Maigret comes back. ... I bet my temperature's soaring and I'll need to have my sheets changed a couple of times tonight ... Frankelstein... Get a search warrant from the examining magistrate.... No.... At this time of night, it'll take too long, for he's sure to be out playing bridge somewhere.... Have you had dinner?... Me, I'm waiting for my vegetable broth.... There are some blank warrants in my desk – left-hand drawer. Fill one in. Search the house. You're sure to find the body, even if it means knocking down a cellar wall.'

Poor Besson stared at his Chief in some anxiety, then glanced at the boy, who was sitting waiting quietly in a corner.

'Act quickly, old man. ... If he knows that the kid's been here tonight, you won't find him in his lair. ... He's a tough guy, as you'll find out.'

He was indeed. When the police rang at his door, he tried to escape through backyards and over walls; it took them all night to catch him, which they finally did among the roof-tops. Meanwhile other policemen searched the house for hours before discovering the corpse, decomposing in a bath of quicklime.

It had obviously been a settling of accounts. A disgruntled and frustrated member of the gang had called on the boss in the small hours; Frankelstein had done him in on the doorstep, unaware that an altar-boy was at that very instant coming round the street corner.

'What does it say?' Maigret no longer had the heart to look at the thermometer himself.

'39.3 ...'

'Aren't you cheating?'

He knew that she was cheating, that his temperature was higher than that, but he didn't care; it was good, it was delicious to sink into unconsciousness, to let himself glide at a dizzy speed into a misty, yet terribly real world where an altar-boy bearing a strong resemblance to Maigret as he had once been was tearing wildly down the street, sure that he was either going to be strangled or to win a shiny new bicycle.

'What are you talking about?' asked Madame Maigret, whose plump fingers held a scalding hot poultice which she was proposing to apply to her husband's throat.

He was muttering nonsense like a feverish child, talking about the first bell and the second bell.

'I'm going to be late ...'

'Late for what?'

'For Mass.... Sister.... Sister...'

He meant the vestry-nun, the sacristine, but he could not find the word.

He fell asleep at last, with a huge compress round his neck, dreaming of Mass in his own village and of Marie Titin's inn, past which he used to run because he was afraid.

Afraid of what?...

'I got him, all the same...'

'Who?'

'The judge.'

'What judge?'

It was too complicated to explain. The judge reminded him of somebody in his village at whom he used to put out his tongue. The blacksmith? No.... It was the baker's wife's stepfather.... It didn't matter. Somebody he disliked. And it was the judge who had misled him the whole way through, in order to be revenged on the altar-boy and to annoy people.... He had said he had heard no footsteps *in front of his house*...

But he had not said that he had heard two people running off in the opposite direction...

Old people become childish. And they quarrel with children. Like children.

Mairgret was satisfied, in spite of everything. He had cheated by three whole pipes, even four.... He had a good taste of tobacco in his mouth and he could let himself drift away...

And tomorrow, since he had flu, Madame Maigret would make him some caramel custard.

J. S. Fletcher

THE JUDGE
CORROBORATES

EVER SINCE Dickinson had arrested Gamble on a charge of burglary, he, Dickinson, had carried about with him an uneasy conviction that there was something wrong. The arrest had been made very quietly, and without any fuss, as Gamble emerged from the saloon bar of the Pride of London tavern, in Maida Vale, one evening, alone. All that the passers-by had noticed – if they noticed anything at all – was that two well-dressed men went up to and exchanged a few words with a third well-dressed man, who presently turned and walked off with them, as if they were all friends. But Dickinson remembered what Gamble had said – hence his uneasiness.

'You're making a bloomer, my boy!' said Gamble. 'And no error! But – you'll find that out soon enough. In the meantime – '

In the meantime, of course, there was nothing for it but to accompany the two detectives to the nearest police-station, and be charged. The charge was that on the night of November 21 last, he, John Gamble, did feloniously break and enter the dwelling-house of Martin Philip Tyrrell, in Avenue Road, St John's Wood, and did steal from thence certain specified property. And once more Gamble had shaken his head – and laughed.

'Not me, sonny,' he answered. 'On the wrong 'bus this time! Come off it!'

The detective who had accompanied Dickinson felt curious, and looked at Gamble, who had a reputation, with something more than interest.

'What's your game?' he asked, in a quite friendly manner. 'Alibi?'

'Something of that sort, old sport!' replied Gamble. 'You won't get no conviction against yours truly this journey.' Then he turned and glanced at Dickinson, with a sneer. 'Think yourself blooming clever?' he remarked. 'Well – you ain't!'

Whatever other people might think, Dickinson knew himself to be clever – he knew, too, that he had exercised a vast amount of pains and ability in his conduct of this particular case. It had been put in his hands from the first, and he had followed it up with the patience and intelligence which had earned him high rank in the Criminal Investigation Department. On the face of it, this was a very ordinary case. Mr Tyrrell's house, a detached one standing in its own garden, had been burglariously entered on a certain dark night, and silver and jewellery stolen. The burglar had done his work quietly and well, and had got clean away without rousing any of the household. But he had left a trace – two traces – of his personality. On Mr Tyrrell's sideboard stood a decanter of whisky, and glasses, and a jug of water – the burglar had not been able to withstand the temptation to take a drink. He had helped himself – and on the sides of the glass from which he had drunk, and on the jug from which he had poured out water, he had left distinct impressions of thumbs and fingers. And Dickinson, who had an extensive and peculiar acquaintance with the higher class cracksmen of the metropolis, and who spent hours in going through finger-print records, no sooner saw those marks than he said to himself – Jack Gamble!

Jack Gamble also had a reputation. He was a smart chap, who picked up a good living by his wits. When he was not burgling or thieving, he was engaged in other shady transactions, chiefly connected with horses – sometimes he kept inside the law, and now and then he strayed over the edge. One way or another, he had often been in trouble, and at the time of his arrest outside the Pride of London he had not long been restored to liberty after a term of imprisonment. Dickinson had been keeping a patient eye upon him, and when he saw these finger-prints he felt no doubt whatever that Gamble was going to fall into his hands again. He went off and compared the prints carefully with those in the official keeping, and that done he did a little quiet and secret work in finding out what Gamble's movements had been on the night of the burglary. When he discovered that Gamble had been out most of that night, leaving his lodging at ten o'clock, and not returning until six next morning, he proceeded to act –

for Dickinson was one of the most convinced of believers in the
finger-print theory and system, and he was able, by enthusiasm,
to infect others with his faith.

Nevertheless, now that he had got him safely under lock and
key, Dickinson was upset by Gamble's cheerfulness. He kept seeing Gamble. He saw him when Gamble was before the Magistrate
– who, though apparently not quite such a firm believer in the
finger-print theory as he might have been, was sufficiently convinced by the evidence to send Gamble for trial. And Gamble,
awaiting removal to a detention prison until the next sitting at
the Central Criminal Court, nodded affably to Dickinson, who
had gone down to the cells at the police-court to take a look at
him.

'Think you're steaming ahead all right, old cock, don't yer?'
remarked Gamble. 'So don't I! You're going to get thrown clean
off the line, presently – see! And, I say! – when will the little
affair come off? What – next week? You don't happen to know
who the old bloke on the bench'll be, do yer, Mr Dickinson?'

Dickinson believed in being on good and even friendly terms
with the criminals who came under his notice; he adopted a sort
of indulgent schoolmaster attitude to them.

'Your case'll most likely come before Mr Justice Stapleton,'
he answered good-humouredly, 'and you'll have to make that alibi
you've been hinting at a pretty good one to convince him, my
lad! What're you laughing at?'

For Gamble had begun to chuckle, as if some highly humorous
notion had suddenly occurred to him. Before he could explain,
certain peremptory officials motioned him and certain other committed and remanded gentlemen to step towards the open door of
Black Maria, drawn up in the yard outside. Gamble went off, still
chuckling.

'See you later then, Mr Dickinson,' he said as he went. 'Meet
you at the CCC next week. And you won't have half a surprise,
either!'

That made Dickinson all the more uneasy – and suspicious.
Gamble had adopted a queer, half-contemptuous, defiant attitude
before the magistrate. He had not even taken the trouble to
employ a certain smart man of law who had defended him more
than once – and had once actually restored him to such friends
and relations as he happened to possess. He had listened to the

finger-print evidence and the proof of his being absent from his lodgings with sneering eyes and lips. Asked what he had got to say, he replied that he'd say what he had to say at the proper time and place – 'and not half, neither, as they'd find out.' Altogether, he had shown such certainty that Dickinson was beginning to feel afraid, and perhaps a little doubtful. But he fell back on the hard theory – *no two finger-prints are alike* – and he was dead certain that the marks left on Mr Tyrrell's glass and jug were those of Jack Gamble's fingers.

2

It was nothing but expert and circumstantial evidence against Gamble when his case came on at the Central Criminal Court before Mr Justice Stapleton and a common jury. Indeed, what was really being tried, in the opinion of at least one spectator, was not Gamble, but the finger-print theory.

The finger-prints in question were passing for an hour or two between the bench and the jury-box, the jury-box and the barristers' table; for another hour or two, experts were giving opinions, pointing out technicalities, expatiating learnedly on the theories and practice of such authorities as Bertillon, Herschel, Galton, and Henry. And Gamble sat in the dock – having been courteously accommodated with a seat in view of the probable length of the case – and listened with a half-scornful, half-bored expression.

Once more he had pleaded his innocence; once more declined to be represented by anybody but himself. But he had asked, with some eagerness, if he could give evidence on his own behalf, and call a witness, and on hearing that he could – a fact of which he was already well aware – had smiled and winked derisively at Detective-Sergeant Dickinson.

It all came to an end at last – the case for the prosecution. Every one of the experts had sworn that the marks of thumbs and fingers on Mr Tyrrell's property were, in their belief, as experts, correspondent to those stamped by the prisoner in more than one official record. Evidence had been brought forward to show that Gamble was away from his lodgings during the hours at some period of which the burglary had undoubtedly been committed.

It was, perhaps, not a very strong case; the stolen property had not been traced, nor had a single article of it been found in the prisoner's possession; nor was there any evidence to show that he had disposed of valuable goods about that time. But – though nothing of the sort was mentioned in court, in accordance with the strict principles of British justice, which takes every case on its own merits – it was generally known, even by the judge and jurymen, who are supposed to know nothing, that Gamble was an expert in these sort of things as the finger-print experts were clever in theirs, and most persons present expected to hear him found guilty, and sent to penal servitude again.

Except Dickinson. Dickinson, after giving his own evidence, had taken a seat in a corner, from whence he watched the man in the dock suspiciously and moodily.

Dickinson did not like the look of Gamble; Gamble was altogether too indifferent, too bored, too superior to his situation. He made Dickinson think of a card-player who holds all the aces – and has another card ready up his sleeve.

And when Gamble was called upon for his defence, and made his way from dock to witness-box, smiling, Dickinson felt a bit sick; he wanted to convict Gamble, and he began to have an idea that Gamble was going to put a stop to that game. Yet – how?

Gamble took the oath as piously as if he had done little else but practise religious observance all his life. Possibly he felt unusually serious at that moment. At any rate, it was with an air of great decorum that he turned to the judge, who was watching him curiously.

'As I ain't represented by counsel, my lord,' said Gamble, 'perhaps your lordship'll let me tell my tale in my own way? Sworn evidence, my lord.'

'Certainly, tell your own story after your own fashion,' answered his lordship. 'You are probably quite well aware that you can be examined by the prosecution on whatever you say?'

'Quite aware o' that, my lord,' replied Gamble, cheerfully; and smiled on the barristers in front of him. 'Any of these here gentlemen is quite welcome – or your lordship, either – to ask me any questions as seem to occur to 'em – or to you, either, my lord.' He paused, and transferred his smile to the twelve open-mouthed men in the jury-box. 'Well, my lord, and gentlemen of the jury, what I have to say to this here charge is – an alibi! I'm going to prove an alibi, and when I've finished proving it, I expect to be discharged, and no other. Finger-prints or no finger-prints, I wasn't within six miles of St John's Wood at any time of the night on which this here burglary was carried out. Why? 'Cause I was somewhere else.'

Gamble, from long experience of criminal courts, either as principal actor or interested spectator, was well aware of the importance in oratory of a dramatic pause, and he made one now, leaning over the edge of the witness-box, and glancing around him with a calm and triumphant smile. And suddenly he drew himself up, and began to check off his points on the tips of his stubby fingers.

'To start with, gentlemen,' he continued, 'the charge against me is that I broke into this house in Avenue Road, St John's Wood, on the night of November 21 last, according to the evidence, between ten o'clock – that 'ud be the evening of November 20 – and six next morning. Gentlemen, from ten o'clock in the evening of November 20 until five-thirty next morning, *I was in Wimbledon.*'

Gamble spoke the last word in a thrilling whisper, and the judge started and glanced sharply at him.

'You were – where did you say?' he asked, bending towards the prisoner.

'Wimbledon, my lord!' answered Gamble, loudly and promptly. 'Wimbledon. Where your lordship resides.'

The judge started again and frowned. It was quite true that he did live at Wimbledon, in a pretty old house on the common, and his frown meant that he was not quite sure that he was pleased to hear that Mr John Gamble had been in that select neighbourhood.

'Continue your evidence,' he said, a little sharply. 'You were saying – '

'That I was at Wimbledon that night, my lord,' replied Gamble, with a smile which sought out Dickinson in his corner. 'At Wimbledon – part of the time, anyway – and t'other part of the time on Wimbledon Common. And, gentlemen,' he went on, with a dramatic turn in the direction of the jury-box, 'why was I at Wimbledon? Gentlemen, I'm here to tell the truth, the whole truth, and nothing but the truth so – out with it. I went to Wimbledon for an unlawful purpose – which never came off.'

Gamble let this soak into the atmosphere with another dramatic pause – made suddenly. He set out again just as suddenly – with an outstretched finger pointed at the foreman of the jury, a fat man whose eyes goggled.

'Mind you,' he said. 'I'm a-going to tell the truth against myself – to clear myself of this 'ere particular charge. Now, it's quite true – I ain't going to deny it, for it 'ud be of no use to – I've been in trouble before on little matters of this sort. I got over the results of one of 'em – the last – on'y last October. And says I to myself, "I'll chuck that game – tain't no good, when all's taken into account." But about November 17 or 18 – I can't be sure to a day – a friend of mine who knew my abilities in this 'ere line, meets me one day in Long Acre, where I was looking after a bit of horse-flesh, and says he to me, confidential, "Jack, my boy," he says, "if so be as you wants a nice soft job in your line what you could work on your own without a partner," he says, "blimey if I can't put you up to the very thing!" he says. "What is it?" says I. "I ain't particular for any job; but, of course, if it's something very soft – " "You could do it standing on yer blooming head," he says. "It's this 'ere. You know I live down at Wimbledon?" "Certainly I do," says I. "Well," says he, "there's an old bloke has a very nice house on Wimbledon Common what you may be acquainted with – professional," he says. "Which I mean Mr Justice Stapleton."'

Mr Justice Stapleton, who had been obviously fidgeting for some minutes, turned a very red face on Gamble.

'I hope you're not trifling with the Court, prisoner?' he remarked acidly. 'In the circumstances you must have every indulgence, but – '

'It's all gospel truth, my lord,' answered Gamble reassuringly. 'Your lordship'll see it in a minute – can't give my evidence no other way, my lord. Well,' he continued triumphantly, and the judge leaned back with an air of patient resignation – 'well, gentlemen, that's what this here friend of mine – which I shan't give his name and address, nor call him – unless strictly necessary – said. "Mr Justice Stapleton," he says. "The old bird," he says, "is one o' them folks as doesn't draw their front blinds down o' nights, and many's the time," he says, "as I've passed the window of his dining-room, and looked in when all the lights was a-blazing, and his lordship getting his grub. And," says he, "he's a sideboard that's just creaking under gold and silver cups and plates, and that sort o' thing. I understand," he says, "as how his lordship was a bit of an athlete when he was a young 'un, and won a lot 'o pots, and then he's won more in steeple-chasing. Anyway," he says, "there's enough stuff on that side-board, Jack, to make it worth your while to pay the old chap a quiet visit – see?"

'Well, gentlemen, of course nature is nature, and when I hears this, I thinks to myself – well, it 'ud be no harm to go down to Wimbledon Common and reconnoitre, as they term it. And so, about nine o'clock in the evening of November 20 last – you'll be particular about that date, gentlemen! – I went down to Wimble-don, and I met this 'ere friend o' mine, and we took a quiet walk along by the house he spoke of – your lordship's.'

Gamble turned suddenly on the judge, and the eyes of every man in Court turned there, too. It was very evident that Mr Justice Stapleton was not so much annoyed as puzzled. He was looking at the prisoner with a queer, inquisitive, searching expression, and for an instant seemed about to speak – instead, he signed to him to proceed. And Gamble smiled and proceeded.

'Well, gentlemen, it was just as this 'ere friend o' mine – a truthful gentlemen, he is! – had said,' he continued. 'His lord-ship's house stands back a bit – not much – from the road at the side of the common. His dining-room windows front the road. And, as my friend had said, the blinds wasn't drawn – and we could see right in. Now I'll invite his lordship's particular atten-tion to what me and my friend saw. There was a full blaze of electric-light in the room; there was also an uncommonly fine fire in a big hearth. The sideboard at the back – black oak – was crammed with gold and silver plate – salvers, cups, vases, such like; it fairly shone and sparkled in the light. And in that room there were three people – a-sitting in easy-chairs in front o' the fire. Perhaps his lordship'll now take notice of how I describe 'em. One of 'em was his lordship himself, in his evening finery – no need to describe him. Another was a lady – his lordship's lady, I took her to be – she was knitting – made me think of my old mother, gentlemen, she looked that peaceful. And the third – '

Mr Justice Stapleton leaned slightly towards the witnessbox, and appeared to listen eagerly for the next words. Gamble gave him a sharp glance out of his eye-corners as he proceeded.

'The third,' he said, 'was a tall, very fine-looking old gentleman, foreigner by the look of him, with a pointed white beard and waxed moustaches, and sat between the other two at the hearth-rug, smoking a big cigar. He was in evening clothes, too, and he'd a red riband round his neck, with a sort of star or medal hanging from it. A very peaceful, nice group they was – with their cigars and their glasses.'

Mr Justice Stapleton, with an odd look at the members of the Bar, suddenly sat upright again, and plunging his hand through his robes into some inner pocket, pulled out what was evidently a pocket or memorandum book, which he laid on the desk before him. And Gamble paused – but a nod of the judicial wig motioned him to go on.

'Well, gentlemen,' he said, eyeing the fat foreman with approval, 'me and my friend we saw all this, and then we went on, quietly, and we had a drink or two, and then we went home to his house and took a bit o' supper. And when that was over: "What d'yer think o' this job, Jack?" says he. "Softish 'un, ain't it?" he says. "Leastways to a gentleman o' your ability," says he. "Might be," says I; "but I'd like to take a look round the premises when things is quiet," I says. "Just to see how things is, yer know," I says. "Well, there ain't neither dog nor cat in that house," says he. "His lordship can't abide 'em." "Cats," says I, "don't count – I've done many a bit o' business with a couple o' cats lookin' on, interested like. But dogs is different. You're sure there ain't no dogs?" "Not a dog," says he. "I knows! Horses is his lordship's 'obby – dogs he will not have!" "All right," says I. "Then we'll just sit here a bit – say till it's past midnight, and then – well, I'll just prospect a bit. Not," I says, "as I shall operate tonight, but I'll just take a little look at doors and windows." So, of course, we had a drop of something comforting on that, and we talked about one thing and another, and at half-past twelve I went back, through them bushes which is so convenient, to take a look round his lordship's house in the dark.'

Mr Justice Stapleton had opened his little book by that time, consulted some entry in it, and shut it up again. He was now leaning his chin on his hand, watching Gamble with a mingling of keenness and amusement, and he so continued to watch him while the accused went cheerfully on his way. And Gamble resumed his candid narrative with something that was very like a wink at the jury.

'Now, gentlemen,' he said, leaning still farther over the edge of the witness-box, as if to take the whole Court into his confidence more fully, 'you see that I'm being open and truthful with you, from the mere fact that I'm giving myself away! For, of course, the instant I entered his lordship's garden, I was where I oughtn't to ha' been – with intent to commit a felony. Only – I didn't intend to commit it just then – maybe not for a night or two – I only just wanted to look round. And I did look round – careful. I took a look at doors and windows – back, front, and side. I satisfied myself there wasn't no blooming dog. And, eventual, I took a carefuller look at the window of the dining-room, where all that plate was spread out on the sideboard. And while I was engaged at that, and quiet as a mouse, there was a light suddenly shone in on that room, and in walks his lordship there, a-carrying a bedroom candle. And to prove to you – and to him – that I saw him, he was wearing pink and white-striped pyjamas, and he'd a white woollen shawl tied round his throat. I ask you, gentlemen, and I asks his lordship – how could I ha' seen them little details if I hadn't been there?'

Here followed another dramatic pause, during which Gamble took a calmly disdainful look at Dickinson. Amidst a dead silence, he went on:

'And more than that, gentlemen! A second later, in comes the other old gentleman,' he said. 'Him with the pointed white beard and waxed moustache. He was in a dressing-gown – a bright red 'un, with a black cord round the middle. And he'd a candle, too, and I saw at once that both of 'em had been roused by something that I couldn't account for – for I'd certainly made no noise as I knew of, and was only looking through the window. They both talked a bit – then his lordship went out into the hall, and a second later looked in again with a big overcoat on, and a bull's eye lantern in his hand; and at that, gentlemen, I made myself scarce, and hopped it out of the garden and in amongst the trees at the other side of the road. I hadn't been there two minutes when a policeman comes along, and I heard his lordship call him from the front door – whereupon I went off across the common, and back to my friend's house. And there I stopped until the workmen's trains started running – and then I took one home to London. And – there you are! And now I asks all present – how could I ha' been in Avenue Road any time that night, when I was down at Wimbledon, miles and miles away? And I asks more

– I asks his lordship there, as a gentleman, to corroborate what I've said – for he can!'

The attention of the Court shifted itself from the prisoner to the judge. Every eye was turned on Mr Justice Stapleton as he slowly drew himself up and looked over his spectacles at Gamble, and from him to the prosecuting solicitor.

'This is certainly a very remarkable statement on the part of the prisoner,' he began. 'He puts me in a very curious situation. I am really being asked to be witness as well as judge. If this case had been tried by one of my brother judges, the prisoner would, I suppose, have raised the same defence, and called me as a witness on his behalf. Really I am somewhat at a loss – but I may as well tell you that I believe what the prisoner has just told us to be perfectly true. It is quite true that I have a prejudice – a life-long one, and possibly a very foolish one – against drawing blinds and curtains over my windows. It is also true that I have a quantity of gold and silver plate on my sideboard, and that it can be seen, I daresay, from the road outside at night, when there is a strong light in that room. I don't attach much importance – in the present matter – to these details; the prisoner might easily have gained as much knowledge at any time. But' – here his lordship picked up his little book – 'it is impossible to deny that certain events took place at my house on the night of November 20–21 exactly as the prisoner has set them out. On that night I had an old friend of mine, Monsieur Paul Lavonier, a famous French scientist, to dine and sleep there. In appearance he is precisely as the prisoner describes him – he was certainly wearing the collar and star of a much-prized decoration. It is quite true that at, or about, one o'clock in the morning I fancied I heard a sound in my garden, and that I went down to the dining-room; it is quite true that my attire was as the prisoner says. It is true, also, that M. Lavonier came down, also, in such a garment as the prisoner spoke of. It is also true that I put on an overcoat, lighted a lantern which I keep in my hall, opened the front door, and hailed a passing constable, who afterwards looked round the grounds, and found nothing suspicious. And, frankly,' continued the judge, glancing with a shrewd and humorous smile, 'I do not see how this man who undoubtedly witnessed these things at my house on Wimbledon Common on the night in question, could possibly have committed a burglary in the north of London at the same time. It

might be suggested that he left Wimbledon at once on being
baffled at my house, at or about one o'clock, and proceeded straight
to Avenue Road. But you will remember, gentlemen of the jury,
that, according to Mr Tyrrell's evidence, Mr Tyrrell himself was
up until two o'clock that morning, that he only went to bed for
two hours, as he had to catch a train at King's Cross, and that
burglary at his house certainly took place between two and four.
Now there are no trains from Wimbledon to town at that time of
night and it is extremely improbable that the prisoner could get
from one point – my house, where he certainly was about a quarter
or half-past one – to another, many miles away, before four. I
am, of course, informally corroborating the prisoner's evidence –
I really don't see that I can avoid doing so in this particular and
extraordinary situation. The case against the prisoner rests entirely
on these finger-prints – I shall make some remarks on that matter
presently.' He glanced at the prosecuting counsel. 'Do you wish
to ask this man anything?' he inquired.

'If your lordship pleases,' answered the barrister addressed,
who was plainly taken aback.

He turned to Gamble.

'Why didn't you tell all this before the magistrate?' he
demanded.

'Because I preferred to tell it here,' retorted Gamble.

'Did you know that his lordship was going to try this case?'

'Not till Dickinson told me – after I'd been committed,' said
Gamble, pointing at the detective.

'Were you intending to call his lordship as a witness then?'
asked the counsel.

'What do you think?' sneered Gamble. 'Course I was!'

'Why haven't you called that friend of yours at Wimbledon?'

'What?' exclaimed Gamble. 'To give him away for putting me
on to the job? Not likely; he's a highly respectable man, he is, as
keeps a shop down there.'

'You need not have let us know that he put you on to the job –
this respectable shopkeeper!' retorted the counsel. 'You could
have called him to prove that you spent most of that night with
him at Wimbledon, without saying why. What proof have you,
besides what you've said, that you ever were at Wimbledon?'

Gamble smiled, and suddenly thrust his fingers into his waistcoat pocket. There was evidently a hole in its lining, and, after

some fumbling and fishing, he extracted something which he held up, and then passed in the direction of the bench.

'That!' he said. 'Ticket from Wimbledon to Waterloo. They didn't take it, and I didn't give it up. Look at the date!'

There was some consultation between the Bench and the Bar, and then his lordship, taking off his spectacles, turned leisurely to the jury and began to talk about the fingerprint system. And Dickinson frowned and nudged a fellow detective, who sat by him. For he knew that Mr Justice Stapleton was a good deal of a sceptic about that system, and had more than once made caustic remarks about it and its exponents, and he expected what precisely came to pass within the next twenty minutes. For the jury returned a verdict of 'Not Guilty,' and Gamble walked out of the dock a free man once more.

And, once free, Gamble sought out Dickinson in the precincts of the Court, and openly sneered at him.

'What did I tell yer, Mr Clever?' he said, making a face at the detective. 'Didn't I say you were making a bloomer this time? Yah!'

'It's you that's the clever man, my lad!' answered Dickinson. 'You've done me – and everybody – somehow! I wouldn't mind giving you a fiver to be let into the secret.'

But Gamble only made another face, and took himself off for a much-needed drink.

3

Dickinson was as certain that Gamble had bamboozled the Court as he was certain that Gamble was the culprit in the Avenue Road affair. But as to how Gamble had managed it, he was utterly at a loss to conceive. He kept an eye on him for some time, and whenever they met, Gamble winked at him derisively. The derision signified not so much a reference to what had just occurred as to the fact that Gamble was going on the straight, and giving Dickinson no chance to get at him. Dickinson, narrowly as he watched and listened, could hear nothing, until, suddenly, he missed his man. Gamble was no longer seen in his usual haunts – he made a complete disappearance. And it was not until he had been gone for some time, and Dickinson had failed to gain news of him, that he heard something from one of those strange individuals who hover between criminals and criminal-catchers, and who, being neither, have none of the honour which exists even amongst thieves. This man, being in conversation with Dickinson, suddenly turned to the subject which still rankled in the detective's mind.

'You ain't seen nothing of Jack Gamble of late, I reckon?' he observed. 'And you won't – no more. Made a clean wipe of the slate, Jack has; gone to Australia, he has, with a mate – horse-dealing – for good. On the straight, you understand?'

'That's it, is it?' remarked Dickinson.

'That's it, sir,' asserted the other, and laughed as at some pleasant thought. 'He done you a fair treat over that Avenue Road affair, didn't he, now? Of course, there was them as knew how it was done, me amongst 'em. And now that old Jack's t'other side of the world, I don't mind telling you, between you and me, private.

'It was like this here. When Jack came home after that last stretch, him and another mate of his looked round for some likely cribs to crack. One of 'em was that house in Avenue Road, and another was the judge's place near Wimbledon Common. They settled to do 'em the same night. Jack did the Avenue Road business, right enough; t'other man went to Wimbledon, and his job didn't come off. It was him – t'other man – as had all the adventures that Jack told in Court! He primed Jack with all the points next day, down to every detail, giving him that ticket, and it was agreed between 'em that if either of 'em got took in con-nection with the Avenue Road affair, which it was was to make use of the Wimbledon knowledge to get up an alibi. It happened to be Jack, and him having a particular good memory, he just reeled off all that had happened to the other chap as if it had been to himself, see? Nice, simple thing – what, Mr Dickinson?'

Mr Dickinson replied briefly that he had always known Jack Gamble to be a clever man, and retired – to visit Mr Justice Stapleton, and add to that learned gentleman's stock of knowledge.

BOOK FOUR

Antonia Fraser

THE CASE OF THE PARR CHILDREN

'I'VE COME ABOUT THE CHILDREN.'

The woman who stood outside the door of the flat, her finger poised to ring the bell again, looked desperate. She also looked quite unknown to the owner of the flat, Jemima Shore. It was ten o'clock on Sunday morning; an odd time for anyone to be paying a social call on the celebrated television reporter. Jemima Shore had no children. Outside her work she led a very free and very private existence. As she stood at the door, unusually dishevelled, pulling a dark blue towelling robe round her, she had time to wonder rather dazedly: Whose children? Why here? before she decided that the stranger had rung the wrong bell of the wrong flat, and very likely in the wrong house in Holland Park.

' I've come about the children.'

The woman before her was panting slightly as she repeated the words. But then Jemima Shore's flat was on the top floor. It was her appearance which on closer inspection was odd; she looked smudged and dirty like a charcoal drawing which had been abandoned. Her beltless mackintosh had presumably once been white, as had perhaps her ancient tennis shoes with their gaping canvas, and her thick woollen socks. The thin dark dress she wore beneath her mackintosh, hem hanging down, gave the impression of being too old for her until Jemima realized that it was the dress itself which was decrepit. Only her hair showed any signs of care: that had at least been brushed. Short and brown, it hung down straight on either side of her face: in this case the style was too young.

The woman before Jemima might have been a tramp. Then there was the clink of a bottle at her feet as she moved uneasily towards Jemima. In a brown paper bag were the remains of a picnic which had clearly been predominately alcoholic. The image of the tramp was confirmed.

'Jemima Shore, Investigator?' she gasped. 'You've *got* to help me.' And she repeated for the third time: 'You see, I've come about the children.'

Jemima recoiled slightly. It was true that she was billed by this title in her programmes of serious social reportage. It was also true that the general public had from time to time mistaken her for a real investigator as a result. Furthermore, lured by the magic spell of know-all television, people had on occasion brought her problems to solve; and she had on occasion solved them. Nevertheless, early Sunday morning, well before the first cup of coffee, seemed an inauspicious moment for such an appeal. In any case by the sound of it, the woman needed a professional social worker rather than an amateur investigator.

Jemima decided that the lack of coffee could at least be remedied. Pulling her robe still further around her, and feeling more than slightly cross, she lead the way into her elegant little kitchen. The effect of the delicate pink formica surfaces was to make the tramp-woman look grubbier than ever. At which point her visitor leant forward on her kitchen stool, covered in pretty rose-coloured denim, and started to sob loudly and uncontrollably into her hands. Tears trickled between her fingers. Jemima noticed with distaste that the finger nails were also dirty. Coffee was by now not so much desirable as essential. Jemima proceeded first to make it, and then to administer it.

Ten minutes later she found herself listening to a very strange story indeed. The woman who was telling it described herself as Mrs Catharine Parr.

'Yes, just like the wretched Queen who lost her head, and I'm just as wretched, I'm quite lost too.' Jemima raised her eyebrows briefly at the historical inaccuracy – hadn't Catharine Parr, sixth wife of Henry VIII, died in her bed? But as Mrs Parr rushed on with her dramatic tale, she reflected that here was a woman who probably embellished everything with unnecessary flourishes. Mrs Parr was certainly wretched enough; that went without question. Scotland. She had come overnight from Scotland. Hence of course both the mackintosh and the thin dress, even the picnic (although the empty wine bottles remained unexplained). Hence the early hour, for Mrs Parr had come straight from Euston Station, off her sleeper. And now it was back to the children again.

At this point, Jemima Shore managed at last to get a word in edgeways: 'Whose children? Your children?'

Mrs Parr, tears checked, looked at Jemima as though she must already know the answer to that question: 'Why the *Parr* children of course. Don't you remember the case of the Parr children? There was a lot about it on television,' she added reproachfully.

'The Parr children: yes, I think I do remember something – your children, I suppose.'

To Jemima's surprise there was a pause. Then Mrs Parr said with great solemnity:

'Miss Shore, that's just what I want you to find out. I just *don't* know whether they're my children or not. I just don't *know*.'

'I think,' said Jemima Shore, Investigator, resignedly drinking her third cup of coffee, 'You had better tell me all about it from the beginning.'

Oddly enough Jemima did genuinely remember something about the episode. Not from television, but from the newspapers where it had been much discussed, notably in the *Guardian*; and Jemima was a *Guardian* reader. It had been a peculiarly rancorous divorce case. The elderly judge had come down heavily on the side of the father. Not only had he taken the unusual step of awarding Mr Parr care and custody of the two children of the marriage – mere babies – but he had also summed up the case in full for the benefit of the press.

In particular he had dwelt venomously on the imperfections of Mrs Parr and her 'trendy amoral Bohemianism unsuitable for contact with any young creatures. This was because Mrs Parr had admitted having an affair with a gypsy or something equally exotic. She now proposed to take her children off with him for the glorious life of the open road; which, she suggested, would enable her children to grow up uninhibited loving human beings. Mr Parr responded with a solid bourgeois proposition, including a highly responsible Nannie, a general atmosphere of nursery tea now, private schools later. Columnists had had a field day for a week or two, discussing the relative merits of bourgeois and Bohemian life-styles for children. On the whole Jemima herself had sympathized with the warm-blooded Mrs Parr.

It transpired that Jemima's recollection of the case was substantially correct. Except that she had forgotten the crucial role played by the so-called Nannie; in fact no Nannie but a kind of poor relation, a trained nurse named Zillah. It was Zillah who had spoken with calm assurance of the father's love for his children, reluctantly of the

selfish flightiness of the mother. She had known her cousin Catharine
all her life, she said, although their material circumstances had been
very different. She pronounced with regret that in her opinion
Catharine Parr was simply not fitted to have sole responsibility for
young children. It was one of the reasons which had prompted
her to leave her nursing career in order to look after the Parr
babies.

Since Zillah was clearly a detached witness who had the welfare
of the children at heart, her evidence was regarded as crucial by the
judge. He contrasted Catharine and Zillah: ' Two young women so
outwardly alike so inwardly different'. He made this also a feature
of his summing-up. ' Miss Zillah Roberts, who has had none of the
benefits of money and education of the mother in the case, has nevertheless demonstrated the kind of firm moral character most
appropriate to the care of infants . . . etc etc.'

In vain Mrs Parr had exploded in court:

' Don't believe her! She's his mistress! They're sleeping together.
She's been jealous of me all her life. She always wanted everything
I had, my husband, now my children.' Such wild unsubstantiated
talk did Mrs Parr no good at all, especially in view of her own
admitted ' uninhibited and loving ' behaviour. If anything the judge's
summing-up gained in vinegar from the interruption.

Mrs Parr skated over the next part of the story. Deprived of her
children, she had set off for the south of Ireland with her lover.
Jemima had the impression, listening to her, that drink had played
a considerable part in the story – drink and perhaps despair too. Nor
did Mrs Parr enlarge on the death of her lover, except to say that
he had died as he had lived: ' violently '. As a result Jemima had
no idea whether Mrs Parr regretted her bold leap out of the bourgeois nest. All she discovered was that Mrs Parr had had no contact
whatsoever with her children for seven years. Neither sought nor proffered. Not sought because Mr Parr had confirmed Mrs Parr's
suspicions by marrying Zillah the moment his divorce became
absolute: ' and *she* would never have permitted it. Not Zillah.' Not
proffered, of course, because Mrs Parr had left no address behind
her.

' I had to make a new life. I wouldn't take any money from him.
They'd taken my children away from me and I had to make a new
life.'

It was only after the death of Mrs Parr's lover that, destitute and friendless, she had returned to England. Contacting perforce her ex-husband's lawyer for funds of some sort, she had discovered· to her astonishment that Mr Parr had died suddenly several months earlier. The lawyers had been trying in their dignified and leisurely fashion to contact his first wife, the mother of his children. In the meantime the second Mrs Parr, Zillah, the children's ex-Nannie and stepmother had taken them off to a remote corner of the Scottish Highlands. As she put it to the lawyer, she intended ' to get them and me away from it all '. The lawyer had demurred with the question of the children's future outstanding. But Zillah, with that same quiet air of authority which had swayed the divorce court judge, convinced him. It might be months before the first Mrs Parr was contacted, she pointed out. In the meantime they had her address. And the children's.

' And suddenly there I was!' exclaimed Mrs Catharine Parr to Jemima Shore, the vehemence returning to her voice. ' But it was too late.'

' Too late?'

' Too late for Zillah. You see, Miss Shore, Zillah was dead. She was drowned in a boating accident in Scotland. It was too late for Zillah.' Jemima sensing the depth of Mrs Parr's bitterness, realized that what she really meant was: Too late for vengeance.

Even then, Mrs Parr's troubles were not over. The encounter with the children had been even more upsetting. Two children, Tamsin nearly nine and Tara nearly eight, who confronted her with scared and hostile eyes. They were being cared for at the lodge which Zillah had so precipitately rented. A local woman from the village, responsible for the caretaking of the lodge, had volunteered. Various suggestions had been made to transfer the children to somewhere less lonely, attended by less tragic memories. However, Tamsin and Tara had shown such extreme distress at the idea of moving away from their belongings and the home they knew that the plan had been abandoned. In the meantime their real mother had also announced her arrival.

So Mrs Parr took the sleeper to Inverness.

' But when I got to Scotland I didn't recognize them!' cried Mrs Parr in a return to her dramatic style. ' So I want you to come back to Scotland with me and *interview* them. Find out who they are. You're an *expert* interviewer: I've seen you on television. That programme about refugee children. You talk to them. I beg you,

Miss Shore. You see before you a desperate woman and a fearful mother.'

'But were you likely to recognize them?' enquired Jemima rather dryly. 'I mean you hadn't seen either of them for seven years. How old was Tamsin then – eighteen months? Tara – what – six months?'

'It wasn't a question of *physical* recognition, I assure you. In a way, they *looked* more or less as I expected. Fair. Healthy. She'd looked after them all right, Zillah, whoever they are. She always looked after people, Zillah. That's how she got him of course.'

'Then why –?' began Jemima hastily.

Mrs Parr leant forward and said in a conspiratorial tone: 'It was spiritual recognition I meant. Nothing spoke to me and said: These are my children. In fact a voice deep in me cried out: Zillah! These are Zillah's children. This is Zillah's revenge. Even from the grave, she won't let me have my own children.' She paused for effect.

'You see, Zillah had this sister Kitty. We were cousins, I think I told you. Quite close cousins even though we had been brought up so differently. That's how Zillah came to look after the children in the first place: she wanted a proper home, she said, after the impersonality of nursing. But that didn't satisfy Zillah. She was always on at me to do something about this sister and her family – as though their awful lives were my fault!'

She went on: 'Kitty had two little girls, almost exactly the same ages as my two. Quite fair then, though not as fair as Zillah and not as fair as my children. But there was a resemblance, everyone said so. People sometimes took them for my children. I suppose our relationship accounted for it. Kitty was a wretched creature but physically we were not unlike. Anyway, Zillah thought the world of these babies and was always having them round. Kitty was unhappily married: I believe the husband ran off before the last baby was born. Suddenly, looking at this pair, I thought: little cuckoos. Zillah has taken her own nieces, and put them into my nest –'

'– Which you had left of your own accord.' But Jemima did not say the words aloud. Instead she asked with much greater strength: 'But *why*?'

'The money! That's why!' exclaimed Mrs Parr in triumph. 'The Parr money in trust for them. Parr Biscuits. Doesn't that ring a bell? The money only went to the descendants of Ephraim Parr. *She* wouldn't have got a penny – except what *he* left her. Her nieces had no Parr blood either. But my children, because they were Parrs, would have been, *are* rich. Maybe my poor little children died, ran away, maybe she put them in an orphanage – *I* don't know. Or ' – her voice suddenly changed totally, becoming dreamy, ' Or perhaps these are my children after all. Perhaps I'm imagining it all, after all I've been through. Miss Shore, this is just what I've come all the way from Scotland to beg you to find out.'

It was an extraordinary story. Jemima's original impulse had been to give Mrs Catharine Parr a cup of coffee and send her gently on her way. Now the overriding curiosity which was definitely her strongest attribute would not let her be. The appeals of the public to Jemima Shore Investigator certainly fell on compassionate ears; but they also fell on very inquisitive ones. In this instance she felt she owed it to the forces of common sense to point out first to Mrs Parr that lawyers could investigate such matters far more efficiently than she. To this Mrs Parr answered quite reasonably that lawyers would take an age, as they always did.

' And in the meantime what would happen to me and the children? We'd be getting to know each other, getting fond of each other. No, Miss Shore, *you* can settle it. I know you can. Then we can all get on with our lives for better or for worse.'

Then Jemima gave in and acceded to Mrs Parr's request.

It was in this way, for better or for worse as Mrs Parr had put it, that Jemima Shore Investigator found herself on the following night taking the sleeper back to Inverness. The sleeping-car attendant recognized Mrs Parr quite merrily:

' Why, it's you again, Mrs Parr. You'll keep British Rail in business with your travelling.' Then of course he recognized Jemima Shore with even greater delight. Later, taking her ticket, he was with difficulty restrained from confiding to her his full and rich life story which he was convinced would make an excellent television documentary. Staved off, he contented himself with approving Jemima's modest order of late night tea.

' You're not like your friend, Mrs Parr, then . . .' he made a significant drinking gesture. ' The trouble I had with her going north for the first time. Crying, and crying and disturbing all the passengers. However she was better the second time, and mebbe now you'll have a good influence on her, Miss Shore. I'll be seeing her now and asking her if this time she'll have a late night cup of tea.' He bustled off, leaving Jemima faintly disquieted. She hoped that Mrs Parr had no drink aboard. The north of Scotland with an alcoholic, probably a fantasist into the bargain . . .

Morning found her in a more robust mood, which was fortunate since Jemima's first sight of Kildrum Lodge, standing on the edge of a dark, seemingly endless loch, shut in by mountains, was once again disquieting. It was difficult for her to believe that Zillah could have brought the children to such a place out of sheer love for Scottish scenery and country pursuits such as fishing, swimming and walking. The situation of the lodge itself even for Scotland was so extremely isolated. Nor was the glen which led up to the lodge notably beautiful. A general lack of colour except blackness, in the water, reflected from the skies, made it in fact peculiarly depressing. There was a lack of vegetation even on the lower slopes of the mountains, which slid down straight into the loch. The single track road was bumpy and made of stones. It was difficult to imagine that much traffic passed that way. One could imagine a woman with something to hide – two children perhaps? – seeking out such a location, but not a warm comforting body hoping to cheer up her charges after the sudden death of their father.

The notion of Zillah's sinister purpose, far-fetched in London, suddenly seemed horribly plausible. And this was the loch, the very loch, in which Zillah herself had drowned. No, Kildrum to Jemima Shore did not have the air of a happy uncomplicated place. She looked across at Mrs Parr, in the passenger seat of the hired car. Mrs Parr looked pale. Whether she had passed the night consuming further bottles of wine or was merely dreading the next confrontation with the Parr children, the hands with which she was trying to light a cigarette were shaking. Jemima felt once more extremely sorry for her and glad that she had come to Kildrum.

They approached the lodge. It was surrounded by banks of dark green rhododendrons, growing unrestrained, which did nothing to cheer the surroundings. There was no other garden, only rough grass going down to the loch. The large windows of the lodge looked blank and unwelcoming. As Jemima drove slowly up the stony road, the front door opened and something white was glimpsed within. It was eerily quiet once the car's engine had stopped. Then the door opened further and the flash of white proved to be a girl wearing jeans and a blue jersey. She had extremely fair, almost lint-white hair in plaits. For a girl of eight she was quite well-built, even stocky.

'Tamsin,' said Mrs Parr. She pronounced the name as though

for Jemima's benefit; but it was once again disquieting that she made no move towards the child. The interior of the house, like the glen itself and the mountains, was dark. Most of the paintwork was brown and the chintz curtains were patterned in a depressing brown and green. Nevertheless some energy had obviously been spent recently in making it cosy. There were cheerful traces of childish occupation, books, a bright red anorak, shiny blue gumboots. Pot plants and an arrangement of leaves bore witness to the presence of a domestic spirit in the house – once upon a time.

In the large kitchen at the back of the house where Jemima insisted on repairing for coffee there was also an unmistakable trace of modern civilization in the shape of a television set. There was a telephone too – but that was black and ancient-looking. Tamsin went with them, still silent. In the kitchen they were immediately joined by Tara, equally silent, equally blonde.

The two sisters stared warily at the women before them as if they were intruders. Which in a sense, thought Jemima, we are. Her eyes caught and held by the two striking flaxen heads, she recalled Mrs Parr's words concerning Zillah's nephew and niece: ' Quite fair too then, but not as fair as Zillah and not as fair as my children . . .' Could children actually become fairer as the years went by? Impossible. No one became fairer with time except out of a bottle. Even these children's hair was darkening slightly at the roots. Jemima felt that she had a first very positive clue that the Parr children were exactly what they purported to be. She was so relieved that a feeling of bonhomie seized her. She smiled warmly at the children and extended her hand.

' I'm Jemima Shore –'

' Investigator!' completed Tamsin triumphantly. And from her back she produced a large placard on which the cheering words: 'Welcome Jemima Shaw Investogator' were carefully inscribed in a variety of lurid pentel colours.

' I did it,' exclaimed Tara.

' I did the spelling,' said Tamsin proudly.

Jemima decided it would be tactful to congratulate her on it. At least fame on the box granted you a kind of passport to instant friendship, whatever the circumstances. In the kitchen was another figure prepared to be an instant friend: Mrs Elspeth Maxwell, caretaker of the lodge and, since the death of Zillah, *in loco parentis* to the Parr children. Elspeth Maxwell, as Jemima quickly appreciated, was a woman of uncertain age but certain garrulity. Instinctively she summed people up according to whether they would make good or bad subjects for an interview. Mrs Parr, madness and melodrama and all, would not in the end make good television. She was perhaps too obsessional at centre. But Elspeth Maxwell, under her flow of anecdote, might give you just that line or vital piece of information you needed to illuminate a whole topic. Jemima decided to cultivate her, whatever the cost in listening to a load of irrelevant gossip.

As a matter of fact Elspeth Maxwell needed about as much cultivation as the rhododendrons growing wild outside the house. During the next few days, Jemima found that her great problem consisted in getting away from Elspeth Maxwell, occupying the kitchen, and into the children's playroom. Mrs Parr spent most of the time in her bedroom. Her public excuse was that she wanted to let Jemima get on with her task, which had been described to Tamsin and Tara as investigation for a programme about children living in the Highlands. Privately she told Jemima that she wanted to keep clear of emotional involvement with the children 'until I'm *sure*. One way or the other.' Jemima thought there might be a third reason: that Mrs Parr wanted to consume at leisure her daily ration of cheap red wine. The pile of empty bottles on the rubbish dump behind the rhododendrons continued to grow and there was a smell of drink upstairs emanating from Mrs Parr's bedroom. Whenever Mrs Parr chose to empty an ash-tray it was overflowing. On one occasion Jemima tried the door. It was locked. After a moment Mrs Parr called out in a muffled voice:

'Go away. I'm resting.'

It was conclusive evidence of Mrs Parr's addiction that no drink was visible in the rest of the house. Jemima was never offered anything alcoholic nor was any reference made to the subject. In her experience of alcoholics that was far more damning than the sight of a rapidly diminishing sherry bottle in the sitting-room.

Elspeth on the subject of the children was interminable:

'Ach, the poor wee things! Terrible for them, now, wasn't it? Their mother drowned before their very eyes. What a tragedy. Here in Kildrum.'

'Stepmother,' corrected Jemima. Elspeth swept on. But the tale was indeed a tragic one, whichever way you looked at it.

'A fearful accident indeed. Though there's other people been drowned in the loch, you know, it's the weeds, those weeds pull you

down, right to the bottom. And it's one of the deepest lochs in the
Highlands, deeper than Loch Ness, nearly as deep as Loch Morar,
did you know that, Miss Shore? Then their father not so long dead,
I believe, and this lady coming, their real mother, all on top of it.
Then you, so famous, from television . . .'

The trouble was that for all her verbiage, Elspeth Maxwell could
not really tell Jemima anything much about Zillah herself, still less
about her relationship with Tamsin and Tara. It was Elspeth
who had had the task of sorting out Zillah's effects and putting
them into suitcases, still lying upstairs, while some sort of
decision was reached as to what to do with them. These Jemima
made a mental note to examine as soon as possible. Otherwise Elspeth
had seen absolutely nothing of Zillah during her sojourn at Kildrum
Lodge.

' She wanted no help, she told the Estate office. She could perfectly
well take care of the lodge, she said, and the children. She was used
to it. And the cooking. She wanted peace and quiet, she said, and to
fish and walk and swim and go out in the boat –' Elspeth stopped.

Ah well, poor lady. But she certainly kept herself very close, herself
and the children. No one knew her in Kildrum. Polite mind you, a
very polite lady, they said at the Estate Office, wrote very polite
letters and notes. But very close.'

And the children? The verdict was more or less the same. Yes,
they had certainly seemed very fond of Zillah whenever glimpsed in
Kildrum. But generally shy, reserved. And once again polite. Elspeth
could only recall one conversation of any moment before Zillah's
death out of a series of little interchanges and that was when Tamsin,
in Kildrum Post Office referred to the impending arrival of Mrs
Parr. Elspeth, out of motherly sympathy for their apparent loneliness, had invited Tamsin and Tara to tea with her in the village.
Tamsin had refused:

' A lady's coming from London to see us. She says she's our
Mummy. But Billy and me think Zillah is our Mummy.' It was,
remarked Elspeth, an unusual burst of confidence from Tamsin. She
had put it down to Tamsin's distaste at the thought of the arrival of
' the lady from London ' – while of course becoming madly curious
about Tamsin's family history. As a result of a ' wee discussion ' of
the subject in her own home, she had actually put two and two
together and realized that these were the once famous Parr children.
Elspeth, even in Kildrum, had naturally had strong views on *that*

subject. How she would now have adored some contact with the household at Kildrum Lodge! But that was politely but steadfastly denied her. Until Zillah's death, ironically enough, brought to Elspeth exactly the involvement that she had so long desired.

' I did think: mebbe she has something to hide, and my brother-in-law, Johnnie Maxwell, the gillie, he thought mebbe the same. Keeping herself so much to herself. But all along, I dare say it was just the fear of the other mother, that one.' Elspeth rolled her eyes to the ceiling where Mrs. Parr might be supposed to be lying ' resting ' in her bedroom, ' Fear of her finding the children. Ah well, it's difficult to judge her altogether wrong. If you know what I mean. The dreadful case. All the publicity.'

But Elspeth looked as if she would readily re-hash every detail of the case of the Parr children, despite the publicity, for Jemima's benefit.

None of this was particularly helpful. Nor did inspection of Zillah's personal belongings, neatly sorted by Elspeth, bring any reward. It was not that Jemima expected to find a signed confession: ' Tamsin and Tara are imposters. They are the children of my sister . . .' Indeed, she was coming more and more to the conclusion that Mrs Parr's mad suspicions were the product of a mind disordered by alcohol. But Jemima did hope to provide herself with some kind of additional picture of the dead woman, other than the malevolent reports of the first Mrs Parr, and the second-hand gossip of Elspeth Maxwell. All she discovered was that Zillah, like Jemima herself, had an inordinate fondness for the colour beige, presumably for the same reason, to complement her fair colouring: and, like a good many other English women but unlike Jemima, bought her under-clothes at Marks & Spencer's (Jemima patronized Janet Reger). Jemima did not like to speculate where and when Mrs Parr might have last bought her underclothes.

There were various photographs of Tamsin and Tara but none pre-dating Scotland. There were also some photographs of Zillah's sister Kitty; she did look vaguely like Mrs Parr, Jemima noticed, but no more than that; their features were different; it was a question of physical type rather than strict resemblance. There were no photographs of Kitty's children. Was that sinister? Conceivably. Or maybe she had merely lost touch with them. Was it also sinister that Zillah had not preserved photographs of Tamsin and Tara in Sussex? Once again: conceivably. On the other hand Zillah might have packed

away all her Sussex mementoes (there were no photographs of Mr
Parr either). Perhaps she came into that category of grief-stricken
person who prefers not to be reminded of the past.

From the Estate Office Jemima drew another blank. Major Maclachlan, who had had the unenviable task of identifying Zillah's
body, was polite enough, particularly at the thought of a television
programme popularizing his corner of the Highlands. But he added
very little to the public portrait of a woman whose chief characteristic was her reserve and determination to guard her privacy – her
own and that of the children. However, her love of country sports,
especially fishing, had impressed him: Major Maclachlan clearly
found it unjust that someone with such admirable tastes should have
perished as a result of them.

Only Johnnie Maxwell, Elspeth's brother-in-law, who was in charge
of fishing on the loch, contributed anything at all vivid to her enquiries. For it was Johnnie Maxwell who had been the principal
witness at the inquest, having watched the whole drowning from the
bank of the loch. To the newspaper account of the tragedy, which
Jemima had read, he added some ghoulish details of the pathetic
cries of the ' wee girl ', unable to save Zillah. The children had
believed themselves alone on the loch. In vain Johnnie had called to
them to throw in the oar. Tamsin had merely screamed and screamed,
oar in hand, Tara had sat quite still and silent, as though dumb-
struck with horror. In their distress they did not seem to understand,
or perhaps they could not hear him.

Altogether it was a most unfortunate, if not unparalleled accident. One moment Zillah was casting confidently ('Aye, she was a
grand fisherwoman, the poor lady, more's the pity '), the next moment
she had overbalanced and fallen in the water. There was no one else
in the boat except the two children, and no one else to be seen on the
shores of the loch except Johnnie. By the time he got his own boat to
the children, Zillah had completely vanished and Tamsin was in
hysterics, while Tara was quite mute. Helpers came up from the
estate. They did not find the body till the next morning, when it
surfaced in the thick reeds at the shore. There were some bruises on
it, but nothing that could not be explained by a fall from the boat
and prolonged immersion.

That left the children. Jemima felt she owed it to Mrs Parr to
cross-examine them a little on their background. Confident that she
would turn up nothing to their disadvantage, she could at least

reassure Mrs Parr thoroughly as a result. After that she trusted that her eccentric new contact would settle into normal family life or the nearest approximation to it she could manage. Yes, the gentle, efficient cross-examination of Tamsin and Tara would be her final task and then Jemima Shore Investigator would depart for London, having closed the case of the Parr children once and for all.

But it did not work out quite like that.

The children, in their different ways, were friendly enough. Tamsin was even quite talkative once her initial shyness wore off. She had a way of tossing her head so that the blonde pigtails shook, like a show pony shaking its mane. Tara was more silent and physically frailer. But she sprang into life whenever Tamsin felt the need to contradict her, as being her elder and better. Arguing with Tamsin made even Tara quite animated. You could imagine both settling down quite easily once the double shock of Zillah's death and their real mother's arrival had been assimilated.

Nevertheless something was odd. It was instinct, not reason that guided her. Reason told her that Mrs Parr's accusations were absurd. But then nagging instinct would not leave her in peace. She had interviewed too many subjects, she told herself, to be wrong now. . . . Then reason reasserted itself once more, with the aid of the children's perfectly straightforward account of their past. They referred quite naturally to their life in Sussex.

' We went to a horrid school with nasty rough boys –' began Tara.

' It was a *lovely* school,' interrupted Tamsin. ' I played football with the boys in my break. Silly little girls like Tara couldn't do that.' All of this accorded with the facts given by the lawyer: how the girls had attended the local primary school which was fine for the tomboy Tamsin, not so good for the shrinking Tara. They would have gone to the reputedly excellent school in Kildrum when the Scottish term started had it not been for the death of Zillah.

Nevertheless something was odd, strange, not quite right.

Was it perhaps the fact that the girls never seemed to talk amongst themselves which disconcerted her? After considerable pondering on the subject, Jemima decided that the silence of Tamsin and Tara when alone – no happy or unhappy sounds coming out of their playroom or bedroom – which was the most upsetting thing about them. Even the sporadic quarrelling brought on by Tamsin's bossiness ceased. Yet Jemima's experience of children was that sporadic quarrels in front of the grown-ups turned to outright war in private.

But she was here as an investigator, not as a child analyst (who might
or might not have to follow later). Who was she to estimate the
shock effect of Zillah's death, in front of their own eyes? Perhaps
their confidence had been so rocked by the boating accident that they
literally could not speak when alone. It was, when all was said and
done, a minor matter compared to the evident correlation of the
girls' stories with their proper background.

And yet.... There was after all the whole question of Zillah's
absent nieces. Now was that satisfactorily dealt with or not? Torn
between reason and instinct Jemima found it impossible to make up
her mind. She naturally raised the subject, in what she hoped to be
a discreet manner. For once it was Tara who answered first:

'Oh, no we never see them. You see they went to America for
Christmas and they didn't come back.' She sounded quite blithe.

'Canada, silly,' said Tamsin.

'Same thing.'

'It's not, silly.'

'It is –'

'Christmas?' pressed Jemima.

'They went for a Christmas holiday to America. Aunt Kitty took
them and they never came back.'

'They went *forever*,' interrupted Tamsin fiercely. 'They went to
Canada and they went *forever*. That's what Zillah said. Aunt Kitty
doesn't even send us Christmas cards.' Were the answers, as corrected
by Tamsin, a little too pat?

A thought struck Jemima. Later that night she consulted Mrs
Parr. If Zillah's sister had been her next of kin, had not the lawyers
tried to contact her on Zillah's death? Slightly reluctantly Mrs Parr
admitted that the lawyers had tried and so far failed to do so. 'Oddly
enough it seemed I was Zillah's next of kin after Kitty,' she added.
But Kitty had emigrated to Canada (yes, Canada, Tamsin was right
as usual) several years earlier and was at present address unknown.
And she was supposed to have taken her two daughters with her.

It was at this point that Jemima decided to throw in her hand. In
her opinion the investigation was over, the Parr children had emerged
with flying colours, and as for their slight oddity, well, under the
circumstances that was really only to be expected, wasn't it? It was
time to get back to Megalith Television and the autumn series. She
communicated her decision to Mrs Parr, before nagging instinct
could resurrect its tiresome head again.

'You don't feel it then, Jemima?' Mrs Parr sounded for the first time neither vehement nor dreamy but dimly hopeful. 'You don't sense something about them? That they're hiding something? Something strange, unnatural . . .'

'No, I do not,' answered Jemima Shore firmly.

'And if I were you, Catharine' – they had evolved a spurious but convenient intimacy during their days in the lonely lodge – 'I would put all such thoughts behind you. See them as part of the ordeal you have suffered, a kind of long illness. Now you must convalesce and recover. And help your children, your own children, to recover too.' It was Jemima Shore at her most bracing. She hoped passionately not so much that she was correct about the children – with every minute she was more convinced of the rightness of reason, the false-ness of instinct – but that Mrs Parr would now feel able to welcome them to her somewhat neurotic bosom. She might even give up drink.

Afterwards Jemima would always wonder whether these were the fatal words which turned the case of the Parr children from a mystery into a tragedy. Could she even then have realized or guessed the truth? The silence of the little girls together: did she gloss too easily over that? But by that time it was too late.

As it was, immediately Jemima had spoken, Mrs Parr seemed to justify her decision in the most warming way. She positively glowed with delight. For a moment Jemima had a glimpse of the dashing young woman who had thrown up her comfortable home to go off with the raggle-taggle gypsies seven years before. This ardent and presumably attractive creature had been singularly lacking in the Mrs Parr she knew. She referred to herself now as 'lucky Catharine Parr', no longer the wretched Queen who lost her head. Jemima was reminded for an instant of one of the few subjects who had bested her in argument on television, a mother opposing organized schooling, like Catharine Parr, a Bohemian. There was the same air of elation. The quick change was rather worrying. Lucky Catharine Parr: Jemima only hoped that she would be third time lucky as the sleeping-car attendant had suggested. It rather depended on what stability she could show as a mother.

'I promise you,' cried Mrs Parr, interrupting a new train of thought, 'I give you my word. I'll never ever think about the past again. I'll look after them to my dying day. I'll give them all the love in the world, all the love they've missed all these years. Miss

Shore, Jemima, I told you I trusted you. You've done all I asked
you to do. Thank you, thank you.'

The next morning dawned horribly wet. It was an added reason
for Jemima to be glad to be leaving Kildrum Lodge. A damp
Scottish August did not commend itself to her. With nothing further
to do, the dripping rhododendrons surrounding the lodge were
beginning to depress her spirits. Rain sheeted down on the loch,
making even a brisk walk seem impractical. With the children, still
silent, in their playroom and Mrs Parr still lurking upstairs before
the kind of late morning rise she favoured, Jemima decided to make
her farewell to Elspeth Maxwell in the kitchen.

She was quickly trapped in the flood of Elspeth's reflections,
compared to which the rain outside seemed suddenly mild in contrast. Television intrigued Elspeth Maxwell in general, and Jemima,
its incarnation, intrigued her in particular. She was avid for every
detail of Jemima's appearances on the box, how many new clothes
she needed, television make-up and so forth. On the subject of hair,
she first admired the colour of Jemima's corn-coloured locks, then
asked how often she had to have a shampoo, and finally enquired
with a touch of acerbity:

' You'll not be putting anything on then? I'm meaning the colour,
what a beautiful bright colour your hair is, Miss Shore. You'll not be
using one of those little bottles?'

Jemima smilingly denied it. ' I'm lucky.' She wasn't sure whether
Elspeth believed her. After a bit Elspeth continued: ' Not like that
poor lady.' She seemed obsessed with the subject. Was she thinking
of dyeing her own hair? ' The late Mrs Parr, I mean, when I cleared
out her things, I found plenty of bottles, different colours, dark and
fair, as though she'd been making a wee experiment. And she had
lovely fair hair herself, or so they said, Johnnie and the men when
they took her out of the water. Just like the children. Look –'
Elspeth suddenly produced two bottles from out of the kitchen cupboard. One was called ' Goldilocks ' and the other ' Brown Leaf '.
Jemima thought her guess was right. Elspeth was contemplating her
own wee experiment.

' I'm thinking you'll not be needing this on your *natural* fair hair.'
There was a faint ironic emphasis in Elspeth's tone. ' And Tamsin
and Tara, they'll have lovely hair too when they grow up. They
won't need Goldilocks or such things. And who would want Brown
Leaf anyway with lovely fair hair like theirs? And yours. Brown

Leaf would only hide the colour.' Elspeth put the bottles back in the cupboard as though that settled the matter.

Irritated by her malice – there was nothing wrong with dyeing one's hair but Jemima just did not happen to do it – Jemima abandoned Elspeth and the kitchen for the nursery. Nevertheless, Elspeth's words continued to ring in her head. That and another remark she could not forget. Tamsin and Tara were both reading quietly, lying on their tummies on the floor. Tamsin looked up and smiled.

'When will the programme be, Miss Shore?' she asked brightly. 'When will you come back and film us? Oh, I'm so sad you're going away.'

Jemima was standing by the mantelpiece. It had a large mirror over it, which gave some light to the dark room. In the mirror she gazed back into the room, at the striking blonde heads of the two children lying on the floor. It was of course a mirror image, reversed. The sight was symbolical. It was as though for the first time she was seeing the case of the Parr children turned inside out, reversed, black white, dark fair. . . . Lucky children with their mother restored to them. A mother who drank and smoked and was totally undomesticated. But was still their mother. Zillah had done none of these things – but she had done worse: she had tried to keep the children from the mother who bore them. Lucky. Third time lucky.

Jemima stood absolutely still. Behind her back Tamsin smiled again that happy innocent smile. Tara was smiling too.

'Oh yes, Miss Shore,' she echoed, ' I'm so sad you're going away.' For once Tara was in total agreement with her sister. And in the mirror Jemima saw both girls dissolve into soundless giggles, hands over the mouth to stifle the noise. She continued to stare at the children's blonde heads.

With sudden horrible clarity, Jemima knew that she was wrong, had been wrong all along. She would have to tell the woman resting upstairs that the children were not after all her own. A remark that had long haunted her came to the front of her mind. Catharine Parr: ' Just like the wretched Queen who lost her head, and I'm just as wretched.' And now she knew why it had haunted her. Catharine Parr had not been executed by Henry VIII, but she had been childless by him. Now she would have to break it to Mrs Parr that she too was childless. Would be childless in the future.

It had to be done. There was such a thing as truth. Truth – and

justice. But first, however, dreadfully, she had to confront the children
with what they had done. She had to make them admit it.

Wheeling round, she said as calmly as possible to the little girls:
'I'm just going to drive to the telephone box to arrange with my
secretary about my return. This telephone is out of order with the
storm last night.' She thought she could trust Tamsin to accept that
story. Then Jemima added:

'And when I come back, we'll all go out in the boat. Will you
tell your – ' she paused in spite of herself. ' – Will you tell your
Mummy that?'

The children were not smiling now.

'The boat!' exclaimed Tamsin. 'But our Mummy can't swim.
She told us.' She sounded tearful. 'She told us not to go in the boat,
and anyway we don't want to. She told us we'd never ever have to
go in the boat again.'

'Oh, don't make us go in the horrid boat, Miss Shore,' Tara's
eyes were wide with apprehension. 'Please don't. We can't swim.
We never learnt yet.'

'I can swim,' replied Jemima. 'I'm a strong swimmer. Will you
give your Mummy my message?'

When Jemima got back, Mrs Parr was standing with Tamsin and
Tara by the door of the lodge, holding their hands (the first time
Jemima had glimpsed any sign of physical affection in her). She was
looking extremely distressed. She was wearing the filthy torn
mackintosh in which she had first appeared at Jemima's flat. Her
appearance, which had improved slightly over the last few days, was
as unkempt and desperate as it had been on that weird occasion.

'Miss Shore, you mustn't do this,' she cried, the moment Jemima
was out of the car. 'We can't go out in the boat. It's terrible for the
children after – after what happened. Besides, I can't swim –'

'I'm sorry, Catharine,' was all Jemima said. She did not relish
what she had to do.

Perhaps because she was childless herself, Jemima Shore believed
passionately that young children were basically innocent whatever
they did. After all, had the Parr children ever really had a chance in
life since its disturbed beginnings? And now she, the alleged protector of the weak, the compassionate social campaigner, was going
to administer the *coup de grâce*. She wished profoundly that she had
not answered the bell to Mrs Parr that fatal Sunday morning.

The rain had stopped. The weather was clearing above the

mountains in the west, although the sky over the loch remained sullen. In silence the little party entered the rowing boat and Jemima pushed off from the soft ground of the foreshore.

' Come on, Tamsin, sit by me. Row like you did that afternoon with Zillah.'

Mrs Parr gave one more cry:

' Miss Shore! No!' Then she relapsed with a sort of groan into the seat of the stern of the boat. Tara sat beside her, facing Jemima and Tamsin.

After a while Jemima rested on her oar. They were near the middle of the loch. The lodge looked small and far away, the mountains behind less menacing. Following the rain the temperature had risen. Presently the sun came out. It was quite humid. Flies buzzed round Jemima's head and the children. Soon the midges would come to torture them. The water had a forbidding look: she could see thick green weeds floating just beneath the surface. An occasional fish rose and broke the black surface. No one was visible among the reeds. They were, the silent boat load, alone on the loch.

Or perhaps they were not alone. Perhaps Johnnie Maxwell the gillie was somewhere amid the sedge, at his work. If so he would have seen yet another macabre sight on Loch Drum. He would have seen Jemima Shore, her golden hair illuminated by the sunlight, lean forward and grab Tara from her seat. He would have seen her hurl the little girl quite far into the lake, like some human Excalibur. He would have heard the loud splash, seen the spreading circles on the black water. Then he would surely, even at the edge of the loch – for the air was very still after the rain – heard Tara's cries. But even if Johnnie Maxwell had been watching, he would have been once again helpless to have saved the drowning person.

Mrs Parr gave a single loud scream and stood up at the stern of the boat. Jemima Shore sat grimly still, like a figure of vengeance. Tamsin got to her feet, wielded her oar and tried in vain to reach out to the child, splashing hopelessly now on, now under the surface of the loch. Jemima Shore continued to sit still.

Then a child's voice was heard, half choking with water:

' Zillah, save me! Zillah!'

It seemed as though the woman standing at the stern of the boat would never move. Suddenly, uncontrollably, she tore off her white mackintosh. And without further hesitation, she made a perfect racing dive onto the surface of the loch. Minutes later Tara, still sobbing and spluttering, but alive, was safely out of the water. Then for the first time since she had thrown Tara into the loch, Jemima Shore made a move – to pull the woman who had called herself Mrs Catharine Parr back into the boat again.

'The police are coming of course,' said Jemima. They were back in the garden of the house. ' You killed her, didn't you?'

Tamsin and Tara, in dry clothes, had been sent out to play among the patch of rhododendrons. The sun was gaining intensity. The loch had moved from black to grey to slate blue. Tara was bewildered. Tamsin was angry.

' Goodbye, *Mummy*,' she said fiercely to Zillah.

' Don't make her pretend any longer,' Jemima appealed to Zillah. And to Tamsin: ' I know, you see. I've known for some time.'

Tamsin then turned to her sister: ' Baby. You gave it away. You promised never to call her Zillah. Now they'll come and take Zillah away. I won't ever speak to you again.' And Tamsin ran off into the dark shrubberies.

Zillah Parr, wearing some of her own clothes fished out of Elspeth's packages, was sitting with Jemima by the playroom fire. She looked neat and clean and reassuring, a child's dream mother, as she must always have looked during the last seven years. Until she deliberately assumed the messy run-down identity of Mrs Parr, that is. How this paragon must have hated to dirty her finger nails! Jemima noticed that she had seized the opportunity to scrub them vigorously while she was upstairs in the bathroom changing.

Now the mirror reflected a perfectly composed woman, legs in nice shoes, neatly crossed, sipping the glass of whisky which Jemima had given her.

' Why not?' said Zillah coolly. ' I never drink you know, normally. Unlike *her*. Nor do I smoke. I find both things quite disgusting. As for pretending to be drunk! I used to pour all those wine bottles down the sink. But I never found a good way of producing cigarette stubs without smoking. Ugh, the smell. I never got used to it. But I feel I may need the whisky this afternoon.'

Silence fell between them. Then Zillah said, quite conversationally: ' By the way, how did you know?'

' A historical inaccuracy was your first mistake, replied Jemima. They might have been analysing a game of bridge. ' It always struck me as odd that a woman called Catharine Parr, an educated woman to boot, did not know the simple facts of her namesake's life. It was Catharine Howard who lost her head, not Catharine Parr.'

' Oh really.' Zillah sounded quite uninterested. ' Well I never had any education. I saw no use for it in my work either.'

' But you made other mistakes. The sleeping-car attendant: that was a risk to take. He recognized you because of all the drinking. He spoke of you being third time lucky, and at first I thought he meant your quick journey up and down from London to Inverness and back. But then I realized that he meant that this was your third journey *northwards*. He spoke of you " going north " the second time and how you weren't so drunk as the first time. She went up first, didn't she? You killed her. Then faked your own death, and somehow got down to London secretly, perhaps from another station. Then up and down again under the name of Catharine Parr.'

' That was unlucky,' Zillah agreed. ' Of course I didn't know that he'd met the real Catharine Parr when I travelled up under her name the first time. I might have been more careful.'

' In the end it was a remark of Elspeth Maxwell's which gave me the clue. That, and your expression.'

' That woman! She talks far too much,' said Zillah with a frown.

' The dyes: she showed me the various dyes you had used, I suppose to dye Mrs Parr's hair blonde and darken your own.'

' She dyed her own hair.' Zillah sounded positively complacent. ' I've always been good at getting people to do things. I baited her. Pointed out how well I'd taken care of myself, my hair was still blonde and thick, and what a mess she looked. Why, I looked more like the children's mother than she did. I knew that would get her. We'd once been awfully alike, you see, at least to look at. You never guessed that, did you? Kitty never really looked much like her, different nose, different shaped face. But as girls, Catharine and I were often mistaken for each other. It even happened one or twice when I was working for her. And how patronizing she was about it. ' Oh no, that was just Zillah,' she used to say with that awful laugh of hers when she'd been drinking, " Local saint and poor relation." I think that's why he – the children's father – first fell in love with me. I was like her but not like.' Zillah hesitated and then went on more briskly:

' I showed her the bottle of Goldilocks, pretended I used it myself and she grabbed it. " Now we'll see who the children's real mother is," she said, when she'd finished.'

'The bottle did fool me at first,' admitted Jemima. 'I thought it must be connected somehow with the children's hair. Then Elspeth gave me the key when she wondered aloud who would ever use Brown Leaf if they had fair hair: "It would only hide the colour."' She paused. 'So you killed her, blonde hair and all,' she said.

'Yes, I killed her.' Zillah was still absolutely composed. She seemed to have no shame or even fear. 'I drowned her. She was going to take the children away. I found out that she couldn't swim, took her out in the boat in the morning when I knew Johnnie Maxwell wasn't around. Then I let her drown. I would have done anything to keep the children,' she added.

'I told the children that she'd gone away,' she went on. 'That horrid drunken old tramp. Naturally I didn't tell them I'd killed her. I just said that we would play a game. A game in which I would pretend to fall into the lake and be drowned. Then I would dress up in her old clothes and pretend to *be* her. And they must treat me just as if I *was* her, all cold and distant. They must never hug me And if they played it properly, if they never talked about it to anyone, not even each other when they were alone, the horrid mother would never come back. And then I could be their proper mother, just as they had always wanted. "Zillah," they used to say with their arms around me, "we love you so much, won't you be our Mummy forever?" Her voice became dreamy and for a moment Zillah was reminded of the person she had known as Catharine Parr. 'I couldn't have any children of my own, you see; I had to have an operation when I was quite young. Wasn't it unfair? That she, who was such a terrible mother, could have them, and I couldn't. All my life I've loved other people's children. My sister's. Then his children.'

'It was the children all along, wasn't it? Not the money. The Parr Trust: that was a red herring.'

'The money!' exclaimed Zillah. Her voice was full of contempt. 'The Parr Trust meant nothing to me. It was an encumbrance if anything. Little children don't need money: they need love and that's exactly what I gave them. And she would have taken them away, the selfish good-for-nothing tramp that she was, that's what she threatened to do, take them away, and never let me see them again. She said in her drunken way, laughing and drinking together: "This time, my fine cousin Zillah, the law will be on my side." So I killed her. And so I defeated her. Just as I defeated her the last time when she tried to take the children away from me in court.'

'And from their father,' interposed Jemima.

'The judge knew a real motherly woman when he saw one,' Zillah went on as though she had not heard. 'He said so in court for all the world to hear. And he was right, wasn't he? Seven years she left them. Not a card. Not a present. And then thinking she could come back, just like that, because their father was dead, and claim them. All for an accident of birth. She was nothing to them, *nothing,* and I was everything.'

And Jemima herself? Her mission?

'Oh yes, I got you here deliberately. To test the children. I was quite confident, you see. I knew they would fool you. But I wanted them to know the sort of questions they would be asked – by lawyers, even perhaps the press. I used to watch you on television.' She added with a trace of contempt, 'I fooled that judge. He never knew about their father and me. I enjoy fooling people when it's necessary. I knew I could fool you.'

'But you didn't,' said Jemima Shore coldly. She did not like the idea of being fooled. 'There was one more clue. An expression. The expression on your face when I told you I was satisfied about the children and was going back to London. You dropped your guard for a moment. It reminded me of a woman who had once scored over me on television. I didn't forget that.' She added, 'Besides, you would never have got away with it.'

But privately she thought that if Zillah Parr had not displayed her arrogance by sending for Jemima Shore Investigator as a guinea pig she might well have done so. After all, no one had seen Catharine Parr for seven years; bitterly she had cut herself off completely from all her old friends when she went to Ireland. Zillah had also lead a deliberately isolated life after her husband's death; in her case she had hoped to elude the children's mother should she ever reappear. Zillah's sister had vanished to Canada. Elspeth Maxwell had been held at arm's length as had the inhabitants of Kildrum. Johnnie Maxwell had met Zillah once but there was no need for him to meet the false Mrs Parr, who so much disliked fishing.

The two women were much of an age and their physical resemblance in youth striking: that resemblance which Zillah suggested had first attracted Mr Parr to her. Only the hair had to be remedied, since Catharine's untended hair had darkened so much with the passing of the years. As for the corpse, the Parr family lawyer, whom Zillah had met face to face at the time of her husband's death, was, she knew, on holiday in Greece. It was not difficult to fake a resemblance sufficient to make Major Maclachlan at the Estate Office identify the body as that of Zillah Parr. The truth was so very bizarre: he was hardly likely to suspect it. He would be expecting to see the corpse of Zillah Parr, following Johnnie's account, and the corpse of Zillah Parr, bedraggled by the loch, he would duly see.

The unkempt air of a tramp was remarkably easy to assume: it was largely a matter of externals. After a while the new Mrs Catharine Parr would have discreetly improved her appearance. She would have left Kildrum - and who would have blamed her? - and started a new life elsewhere. A new life with the children. Her own children: at last.

As all this was passing through Jemima's head, suddenly Zillah's control snapped. She started to cry: ' My children, my children. Not hers, mine - '. And she was still crying when the police car came up the rough drive, and tall men with black and white check bands round their hats took her away. First they had read her the warrant: ' Mrs Zillah Parr, I charge you with the murder of Mrs Catharine Parr, on or about the morning of August 6, . . . at Kildrum Lodge, Inverness-shire.'

As the police car vanished from sight down the lonely valley, Tara came out of the rhododendrons and put her hand in Jemima's. There was no sign of Tamsin.

' She will come back, Miss Shore, won't she?' she said anxiously. ' Zillah, I mean, not that Mummy. I didn't like that Mummy. She drank bottles all the time and shouted at us. She said rude words, words we're not allowed to say. I cried when she came and Tamsin hid. That Mummy even tried to hit me. But Zillah told us she would make the horrid Mummy go away. And she did. When will Zillah come back, Miss Shore?'

Holding Tara's hand, Jemima reflected sadly that the case of the Parr children was probably only just beginning.

Sir Basil Thomson

THE HANOVER
COURT MURDER

A whole week had passed since Mr Pepper – and the small boy – had spoilt Mr Cohen's scheme; and no one had come near the office. My Chief spent the time in perfecting his scientific apparatus which had not been called into use since my short association with him. It was therefore with immense satisfaction that an opportunity for exercising Mr Pepper's higher art was thrown into my way.

An acquaintance at my club, finding me in the smoking-room when other people were working, took the chair opposite to mine and said, 'By the way, Jones, I hear that you dabble in detective work; that you have discovered a wonderful Yankee who wipes the eye of Scotland Yard. Why don't you make your name by solving this Hanover Court case?'

'I've never heard of it.'

'No; it hasn't got into the papers yet, but it will.'

He had himself heard of it only that morning. His landlord had a sister who let lodgings in Hanover Court. She had opened the luggage of a tenant who had gone abroad owing rent and had been horrified by finding in one of the trunks what appeared to be the remains of a dismembered human body. She had run at once to her brother, who consulted my friend as to what she ought to do. He took the usual course of advising that she should report the matter to the police, but, as far as he knew, she had not yet done so because she had made the discovery only that morning at breakfast-time. He gave me her address.

I seized my hat and took a taxi to Hanover Court. I found the poor landlady wringing her hands. 'You heard of the case through my brother, sir? Well, I am glad that you've come in time. I was just going off to the police, but it will ruin my business to have the police messing about the house, asking me a lot of questions and calling in the Coroner. They would make me appear as a witness at the inquest and the papers would publish the address. Then what chance would there be of the best class of people taking rooms where there's been a murder? It is not respectable. Now if you'll take away the trunk and take all responsibility I shall breathe more freely. Of course, if there *has* been a murder I must stand by it, but you will ferret it all out and I hope that I shall hear no more about it.'

I agreed to everything on the condition that she gave me all the information she possessed. She showed me the trunk which stood on the landing of the second floor. I opened it with trembling fingers. It contained a number of packages wrapped in dirty newspaper and enveloped in part of what appeared to be an old army blanket. I satisfied myself that they contained bones, probably human bones, and with her assistance carried the trunk downstairs for removal to our office. In the meantime she told me the story of her lodger.

' He was what they call an eccentric, sir – always going off without notice and writing letters asking me to reserve his room and take care of his luggage. He always sent me money for the rent while he was away. He would write from all sorts of places – Naples, Egypt, Athens, and one letter I had came from Peru. I never knew him pack anything for his journeys. All he said was that he was called away on business and would I be sure and feed his cat?'

' You haven't told me his name, Mrs Auger.'

' To tell you the truth, I had almost forgotten it. We always called him " The Doctor " because when he came to me five years ago he said something about being in the medical profession. But his real name was Allen – Henry Allen.'

' That sounds English enough.'

' Oh, there was nothing foreign about him except his hair. He never seemed to get it cut – his hair and his eccentricity – for foreigners *are* eccentric, don't you think so, Mr Meddlesome-Jones? His age? Well, that would be hard to say – something between thirty-five and fifty, I should say.'

' Had he no friends, no visitors?'

' That's the peculiar thing. He had none. No, I am wrong there. About three years ago a lady did call and ask for Dr Allen. I asked her what name I should give. She said, " Don't trouble; just tell me what floor he's on, and I'll find him myself." And up she walked, but of course he must have heard her voice. She soon came down again and said he wasn't there. Then I went up myself, and of course there he was, hiding under the bed. He said nothing to me, but I can't help thinking that that lady was his wife. She never came again, not to my knowledge.'

' Did he get no letters?'

' Yes, once a month, always on the second unless it was a Sunday, there would be a fat registered letter addressed " Henry Allen, Esq " – no doctor on the envelope. I think it was from a bank, but I don't remember which. He always paid his bill that morning for the whole month. He never had a meal in the house, not even his breakfast, but he used to bring back a little meat for his cat. Where did he go all day? Well, sir, that's more than I can tell you. On weekdays I would hear him coming downstairs regular at nine – I could have set my clock by him. If he passed me he would say " Good morning," but nothing else. On Sundays he would lie in bed all the morning, and go out punctually at twelve. Oh, he was eccentric, but not the sort to commit a cold-blooded murder; for it is cold-blooded, Mr Meddlesome-Jones, whatever you may say, to cut up a person into little bits like that, now isn't it? He had no books in his room and he didn't leave a scrap of writing behind him. What he did all day is a mystery to me.'

' When did you see him last?'

' It would be back in April. Yes, it is just three months. He just walked out of the house as usual and when I went up to do his room I found that he had packed everything away in his trunks. " Off again, I suppose," I said to myself, and I was right – only this time I had no letter and he hadn't paid me for the room. I didn't think very much of that – he had been behind with the rent before. I thought that the money would come. But then as the weeks went by and I had no letter I began to get anxious and I thought I had better see what he had left behind him. There wasn't a scrap of writing in any of the trunks – only old clothes and – and what you saw.'

' But the letters from the bank?'

' That's the peculiar thing. Whenever he went off those letters stopped coming. There hasn't been a letter since he left. Do you think he can have committed suicide after the murder?'

' We have got to find out first if there has been a murder, Mrs Auger. I suppose there has been no one missing in the neighbourhood?'

She thought for some moments and then shook her head. 'But I'm sure that lady who came to see him was his wife,' she said.

'Why?'

'Well, she had a masterful, disagreeable way with her and he got under the bed to hide from her. A man would never do that with anybody except his wife.' I forebore to evoke any confidences of Mrs Auger's own experience of the married state.

'And if she was his wife, what then?'

'Why, it might be her that's in the trunk.'

The taxi driver knew nothing of what his burden contained. For an extra shilling he helped me upstairs with it into the office where my Chief's face became a mark of interrogation until the man was gone. Then I told him the story and opened the trunk. I never saw him so much moved before. He laid the bones out on the table as if they were jewels, I noticed that desiccated flesh was adhering to some of them; it was quite inoffensive. At the bottom of the trunk was the skull carefully wrapped in newspaper by itself, We carried them into the laboratory and cleared a table for them. While he was arranging them in order I committed to paper what Mrs Auger had told me.

Now, if my Chief had a fault it was that he tried to do too much himself rather than call in the expert. My instinct would have been to call in a surgeon or an anatomist and let him express his opinion on the bones, but when I ventured to suggest this my Chief flew up in the air. 'What does your surgeon know of plastic reconstruction?' he said, and not knowing what plastic reconstruction was I said that I didn't know. 'Well,' he said, 'I am going to show you.'

It was a great opportunity for me. When I was admitted to the laboratory the bones were disposed on the table like a complete skeleton. My Chief's first words were disconcerting. 'Some of the bones are missing,' he said, 'but the curious thing is that the body was deformed. That ought to make our work easier, but it is a very remarkable case. This woman had the left leg three inches shorter than the right and the right arm two inches shorter than the left. She must have had a very odd appearance.

'We'll soon see what she looked like,' said my Chief, confidently, as he manipulated wax in a pan of warm water. The skull was secured in a wooden vice clamped to the table. With extraordinary dexterity he pinched off little cones from the lump of wax in the pan, warmed them over a spirit lamp, and stuck them all over the skull. Very gradually he began to build up a face; and after an hour's work it became under his skilled manipulation a human face certainly, but a face that one could only see in a nightmare. With her bodily deformities in addition she might have made a good living at a show.

'There,' he said, 'is the murdered woman as she was in life.' I had it on the tip of my tongue to say, 'Then she deserved to die,' but I restrained myself in time, and I suggested that Mrs Auger should be called to the office to identify her with Mrs Allen. But my Chief thought that the time had not come for that. 'Let us find the murderer and confront him with his victim,' he said. 'In nine cases out of ten he is so startled that he makes a full confession.'

'And if he does, what then? Surely we should have to hand him over to the police.'

'Yes,' he mused, 'but in the case of a felony it is the duty of any citizen to arrest the felon. You will make the arrest; I will call in the reporters, and then we will ring up your wonderful Scotland Yard.' There was the most subtle irony in his tone. He covered the remains with a sheet, and we sat down to consider the best way of finding Henry Allen. I was for advertising in the Agony Columns of *The Times*, the *Daily Telegraph* and the *Daily Mail*. 'Henry Allen. Come back and all will be forgiven.'

'He would plead at his trial that he had been promised a free pardon.'

'Then why not something like this? "If Henry Allen, late of 17 Hanover Court, will communicate with Pepper and Jones, Adelphi, London, he will hear of something to his advantage." ' My Chief snorted with contempt; I feared that it might be because for the first time I had dared to couple our two names.

'Do you really suppose that a man who goes in daily fear that his crime will be discovered would reply to an advertisement?'

'Well, you see them in the newspapers every day when lawyers want to get hold of a man. Someone must reply to them or they wouldn't put them in.'

'No, Mr Meddleston-Jones; if we use the newspapers we will proceed in quite a different way. I have there (he pointed to his card index cabinet) the names and addresses of the principal newspapers of every country in the world – daily and weekly. We would prepare a little news paragraph, a snappy little thing of how an Englishman named Henry Allen, had been named as residuary legatee to an eccentric lady who died leaving a million and a half, and that when the sole executor, Mr Pepper (there was no mention of " Meddleston-Jones " in the proposed paragraph) wrote to the happy legatee he found that he had gone abroad leaving no address and the letter was returned by the Post Office. Under the provisions of the will, if Henry Allen fails to claim his legacy within six months, the whole of the money goes to found a Home for Starving Cats in London. We would have this translated into every language and sent out through one of the press agencies. Everyone likes to read about unclaimed money.'

' Wouldn't you be inundated with false claimants?'

' All the better. We would confront them all with the corpse first, then with Mrs Auger, and they would be glad to get away alive.'

It seemed to me to be a very dilatory method of procedure, but my Chief must have adopted it because a week or so later reporters connected with the press agency began to hang about the office and stop me in the street. This annoyed my Chief very much. It appeared that he had made a confidential arrangement with the head of the Agency, that the paragraph should not be released to any newspaper in the United Kingdom, because he would have to confess that there was no eccentric millionaire lady in the case at all. But the paragraph must have appeared in foreign newspapers because later we received begging letters from abroad. An Englishwoman wrote from Leghorn to say that if Henry Allen failed to appear, there were more starving cats in Leghorn than there could possibly be in London, that they kept her awake at night by their me-owing, and that she would be glad to establish a home for them if she might have part of the money. A man signing himself ' Henry Allen ' wrote from Cooktown in Queensland, asking for the expenses necessary for him to come to England to establish his claim. Another wrote from Salt Lake City to say that though he was known locally as Richard Doherty, he was satisfied that as his mother's name was Allen he was the person named in the will, and he would be thankful if a payment could be made on account; and a lady, writing from Buenos Aires in the name of Mary Allen, claimed the legacy on the ground that when she was a girl her schoolfellows always called her ' Henry '. But of the real Henry Allen not a word.

My Chief was becoming impatient. He was engaged on several cases at the same time and the remains of the murdered woman, taking up nearly half the laboratory, were in his way. He had added chestnut hair to his reconstruction of the head, and colour to the cheeks; in her reconstructed state she must certainly have been very trying to live with, even when covered with a sheet. One morning he said to me, ' Mr Meddleston-Jones, we are not getting on with this Allen case. Why don't you bring the landlady down to identify the victim? Then we might get on.'

Mrs Auger did not take at all kindly to my suggestion. She reminded me that our agreement was that she should not be troubled with the case any more, and I had some difficulty in getting her to the office. When I drew back the sheet she uttered a piercing scream and fell into a chair. ' Oh! My heart!' she sobbed. ' My poor heart!' and she tried to clutch that organ in her anatomy.

' You recognize her, Mrs Auger? Is she like the wife?'

' She is like nothing on earth,' she gasped, ' and after seeing her I shall be ill for a week.' It was a great disappointment.

I persuaded my Chief at last to take a photograph of the head, and give it to an illustrated daily paper for circulation as a missing person about whom information was desired. He took the photograph, but ten minutes before I started with it for the newspaper office in Fleet Street, an event occurred which entirely changed the course of our enquiry. Mrs Auger reappeared.

She produced a picture postcard, bearing the Genoa postmark, from Henry Allen himself, saying that he would be in London within the week. ' And now,' she said, ' what am I to say to him when he asks for his trunk? I can't say that the police have taken it, can I? You had better pack up all those bones in the newspapers just as he left them and bring back the trunk.' To this proposition, of course, my Chief would not agree. He pointed out that, according to the law, Mrs Auger herself was bound to arrest him as soon as he set foot in her house.

' Arrest him?' she exclaimed aghast. ' How can a woman arrest a man?'

' The law knows no difference between men and women, Mrs Auger,' I said. ' Women serve on juries; there are women police. All you have to do is to lay your hand on his shoulder and say, " Henry Allen, I arrest you for the wilful murder of a woman unknown, and I must caution you that anything you say will be taken down in writing, and will be used against you at your trial." Then write down what he says, lock him up in his room, and telephone to Mr Pepper, Central 1202.'

'I could never do such a thing, Mr Meddlesome-Jones, were he a murderer three times over. You'll have to do this yourself.'

I looked at Mr Pepper and Mr Pepper looked at me. It seemed to me that this was the moment for calling in the regular police who are paid for doing these things, but I did not dare to say so. I had an uncomfortable feeling that I had read somewhere about a man being charged as an accessory after the fact, and I had a horrible presentiment that Pepper and I would find ourselves standing in the dock at the Old Bailey. We dismissed Mrs Auger with some difficulty on the plea that we had to consider our position. There were still four days before us. Mr Pepper was equally perturbed. The only solution which he could suggest was that I should wait at Mrs Auger's door day after day and as soon as Allen appeared accost him, and induce him to come to the office to be confronted with his victim. We would then be guided by events. If he displayed signs of guilt we might go so far as to telephone to the police. It was the first time I had ever known him to contemplate lowering his dignity as a scientific detective, and I honoured him for it though I cannot say that I liked the role he had assigned to me. An extraordinary coincidence saved me. I owed my rescue to the same club acquaintance who had first introduced me to the man whom I shall continue to regard as the greatest detective of the age.

My friend was lunching at a table for two. As I passed him he sprang up and introduced me to his guest, a middle-aged man with a beard turning grey, and asked me to join them. In the course of conversation it appeared that his guest was the head of a well-known medical school in London, and that he was at the moment of my appearance relating an unpleasant incident at the school. My friend asked him to begin the story again. 'Mr Meddleston-Jones,' he was good enough to say, 'is the very man to advise you. He is associated with the best detective brains in London, besides being himself a man of very wide experience in crime.' It was rather oddly expressed, but my friend meant well.

'But I don't want to call in the police – at any rate until we know more.'

'Bless you, Mr Meddleston-Jones has no connection with Scotland Yard. He is an " amateur " – if I may say so – a brilliant amateur.'

Thus reassured, the doctor told his story. A young man, an assistant to the custodian of the anatomical school, had disappeared two days before. His character was exemplary; he handled no money; as far as the custodian knew, he had no private worries. He had put away the 'subjects' on the Monday evening and had remarked to the custodian that he thought it looked like rain. At eight next morning he should have returned to work for he was always punctual. It was a busy day and when the students arrived at ten everything was late; some of them complained to him, the doctor, that if their 'subjects' were not arranged for them, they could not expect to do well in the approaching examination. He sent for the custodian, and it was thus for the first time that he learned that John was missing. They sent to his home to enquire the cause; he had not been home. The whole day passed without news of him. The obvious course was to report his disappearance to the police, but, as we could easily understand, it would be very disturbing to the young minds of the students then in the throes of preparing for examination, and destructive to the morale of the establishment to have detectives practically in charge of the place, questioning everybody and poking their noses into every part of the building. He wished to avoid it if possible. But there was one solution that had occurred to him – he scarcely liked to breathe it – which would make the intervention of the police inevitable – if the poor lad had been the victim of foul play, in the building itself – then –

'But why should you suspect that?'

'Well, I don't quite know. Perhaps it was that when I was going my rounds a few evenings ago I heard loud words coming from the laboratory. All the students had left for the day. I went to the door and I heard the custodian speaking very sharply to the boy, and he was answering much in the same tone. It was one of those quarrels about the details of duty in which a principal had better not interfere, and I went away. But I confess that it left a disagreeable impression on my mind. The custodian always seemed to me an excellent servant – been with us for years – but he is short-tempered and I confess that his language on the occasion was rather a shock to me. Perhaps his duties tend to make a man callous.'

'But there is a wide gap between bad language and murder.'

'I know, I know. Only it occurred to me – I may be unduly imaginative – that for a man in his position – alone in the building with this boy till a late hour, there are so many facilities for disposing of a body – the furnace and so forth – it is nothing more than a vague suspicion.'

We were silent for some time, leaving our food untasted. Then my friend said, ' Why don't you ask Jones to go back with you? He could look over the place and tackle the porter in a way you could not. Let him represent himself as employed to find the missing boy.'

' Will you?' said the doctor, turning to me. ' It would take a great load off my mind, but I scarcely liked to suggest it.'

We wasted no further time over luncheon. The doctor had his car waiting and drove me to the school. ' If you don't mind,' I said, ' I should like you to introduce me to the custodian and leave him to show me round. I can put the necessary questions to him as we go. It will seem less formal and official.' This being precisely what the doctor wanted, he took me straight to the laboratory, where a middle-aged man was moving about in his shirt sleeves. ' Stokes,' he said, ' this is Mr Meddleston-Jones, who is enquiring into the disappearance of young Sopwith. He would like you to show him round the premises. I'll leave him with you.' He shook hands with me and disappeared.

Stokes seemed quite glad to see me. ' We had better not disturb the students in the operating-room, sir. They'll all be gone at five and in the meantime we can go over the basement. Queer business, this of young Sopwith. A better lad never stepped, but I had noticed lately that things had been going wrong with him. He had lost interest in his work.'

' Had he anything on his mind?'

' That's just what I think. From things he let drop I think he was gone on some young woman who wouldn't have him. One day he said, "What's the least a young couple could live on in London, Mr Stokes?" And when I named two pounds a week, he just fell to pieces, as if I'd crushed him. He's never been the same lad since they refused him for the army. This is where they bring them in, sir.'

' Bring what in?'

' The subjects,' he said, in some surprise. We were in a vaulted tunnel in the basement. ' And this is the boiler house.' A furnace was glowing behind a red hot door.

' Whose duty is it to stoke the boiler?'

' That's just it, sir. It was young Sopwith's duty, but latterly he neglected it and it fell upon me. The same with the packing.'

' The packing?'

'Yes, packing the subjects into the coffins. Here is the packing room.' We were in a vaulted cellar. On one side was a pile of rough deal coffins stained black, on the other trays of bones and skulls with dried flesh adhering to them 'They come down here from the operating-room like that, sir, and it was young Sopwith's duty to sort them out into some sort of body for each coffin; that is to say, he was supposed to be careful that, as far as he could, there should be only one head, two arms and two legs in each coffin before it was nailed up and taken to the cemetery, but he was very careless latterly and I've had to see to it myself.'

'You mean he mixed up the bodies?'

'Oh, no one could help doing that, sir. You can't keep them distinct, but we keep a register of the names and each coffin has the name of one of the subjects tacked on to it for funeral purposes. But of course it may not be their remains. Probably there is something belonging to ten or a dozen in each coffin.'

While we were holding this cheerful conversation I was leaning on an enormous wooden box in the outer cellar. I ventured on a question.

'When they bring in the – the subjects, what is done with them?'

'If you will stand over there, sir, I'll show you. You are leaning on them.' I must have startled him by the speed of my movements. 'Oh, they won't bite, sir,' he said, smiling, as he lifted the heavy lid. I peeped over his shoulder. There on racks lay ten human bodies, old and young, stiff, nude and white, the debris of humanity, the homeless, and friendless, who lead their lives in the London work-houses and probably are sorry to leave them in spite of the misery they have known. In their death they do more for humanity than they have ever done in life, by furnishing material for each fresh generation of surgeons to work upon. 'We keep them fresh by injecting formalin,' he said, pointing to a wound in the neck of one of the corpses. He shut down the lid and looked at his watch. 'The students will be gone now, sir,' he said. 'I'll take you to the dissecting-room.' He led the way upstairs to a large room with high windows that ran the length of the building. A dozen tables, each covered with a sheet, held the subjects that were in the hands of the students. One attracted my attention on account of its great bulk in comparison with the rest. The sheet scarcely sufficed to cover it. 'Oh that. That's a young elephant that died in the Zoo. One of the students who is sure of his final had a fancy for it.'

At the end of the room were a number of iron doors labelled 'Head,' 'Arm,' 'Leg,' 'Pelvis,' and so on. I asked Stokes what was in them, for they were a possible hiding-place for the body of the missing youth. He threw open one of the iron doors disclosing iron racks, on which human remains were disposed in various stages of dissection.

'It's these that make our job of "assembling" so difficult downstairs. There's perhaps the arms of twenty people in there and there'll be twenty heads in the next cupboard but one. But it has to be like this so that a student can take up his work just where he left off.'

Something caught my attention and I was scarcely listening. These human arms with desiccated flesh adhering to the bones. Where had I seen them? Then it came upon me with a flash – the remains of the murdered woman in our office. I turned to Stokes.

'Do you ever lose any of these bodies?'

'Oh, now and again a student will take away a hand or a foot in his bag to work on at home, but if he did such a thing without reporting it to me there'd be trouble, sir. You see, they can't get past my system of booking in and out. I make 'em all sign for what they have. You, for instance, sir, suppose you were a new student. You come to me and you say, "Stokes, have you got a knee for me today?" "Yes," I says, "but you'll have to sign for a whole leg." And then you slip it into your bag and walk away with it. Then, the next morning you says, "Stokes, I think I'll work at the wrist and hand today. Have you got a nice fore-arm?" I look at my book and I say, "Mr Meddleston-Jones, not another bit do you get until I see that leg you had yesterday."' He became silent and thoughtful. 'Mind you, I don't say that I've never had them get by me. There was that Allen, for instance – I'll have something to say to *him* when he comes back, if he ever does.'

'Tell me about Allen,' I said, trying hard to keep my voice even and steady.

'Oh, you should ask the Principal about him. He'd have plenty to tell you. He got away with a whole body from me last year – more than a body – and I didn't find it out till I was going over my books afterwards. Cunning? I never knew a man to beat him. I'll tell you how he did it. On a Monday he'd ask for a head, and just before five I'd see him go to that locker with the head in his hand. Of course, I thought he'd put it back. On Tuesday I'd get a note from him to say he'd been called away. Would I keep the same head for him? He'd be away perhaps a week, and then he'd ask for an arm and so it went on. It wasn't for weeks that I found out what he'd been doing, and then it was too late: he'd gone abroad. He was always doing that – playing fast and loose with the institution. I can't understand why the Principal lets him come back time after time. Well, if he comes back after this he'll have some questions to answer. I've got them all booked up and I'd know them anywhere. Look here, sir, a page all to himself.'

He turned over the leaves of his ledger and there, under the name of Henry Allen, were the entries, ' 20 June. Head No. 128, male. 2 July. Forearm No. 43, female,' and so on.

'Would you know your – your specimens again if you saw them?'

'Know them? Yes, and could swear to every one of them. When Allen had a subject I put my private mark on it, so there should be no mistake. It's a theft, that's what it is, to say nothing of the trouble it meant for me if I couldn't make up the number of the funerals.'

I asked him whether the Principal was still in the building. If so I must see him before he left. He looked at his watch.

'You'll just catch him if you are quick, sir. He leaves sharp at six. It's the second door on the left as you go down the passage.'

I was just in time; the Doctor was brushing his hat, 'Well,' he said, ' any daylight?'

'I think I have cleared up one thing: young Sopwith has not been murdered on the premises.'

'And you think?'

'I think that you should report him to Scotland Yard as missing, giving his home address. It may be a case of suicide.' (I was justified next morning when Sopwith's body was found in the Thames, with a letter in the pocket addressed to the object of his affections.) 'But I came to ask you about another matter altogether. You had a student named Henry Allen!'

He threw down his hat and lifted his hands to heaven. 'Henry Allen! Has that fellow turned up again? I never met such a man in my life before. The most charitable view that one can take of Allen is to say that he was mad. Why, that man has been on our books for six years. He passed all his intermediate tests brilliantly, and I used to think that he would carry all before him in his final. Then, on the very eve of the examination I would get a note from him saying that he was called abroad on business and we might see nothing of him for six months. I don't know whether it was stage fright or simply a love of roving; perhaps a little of both. He was a good deal older than the ordinary run of pupils, and was an interesting person if one got him to talk. But he made no friends here. He paid his fees regularly and worked hard. You should get Stokes to tell you about him. He accuses him of stealing some of his subjects.'

' And I think he is right about that. But I can get them back for you if you think it worthwhile. I know where they are.'

' Is there anything in London that you don't know? Of course, we'd like them back.'

' Can Stokes come and identify them?'

' Of course he can. Arrange it with him – any time you like. And now I must be off – one of these horrible early public dinners. I cannot thank you enough for coming.'

I found Stokes in the laboratory just sitting down to his tea. ' Let me get you a cup, sir. A drop of tea helps one through the evening.' He pushed back a plate containing a human eye to make room for my cup, and I found my appetite had left me. I declined the tea, but we talked while he ate and drank. It was a creepy sort of place, this laboratory: bottles from ceiling to floor all alike and all containing the intimate machinery of the human machine – the watch-springs of the human body – bleached and half-floating in yellowish liquid. They did not disturb Stokes's appetite in the least.

' You said just now that you could identify the – er – specimens that Allen took away.'

' Try me, sir.'

' That's exactly what I want to do if you'll come with me now.'

' You know where they are!' he exclaimed in astonishment. ' I'll go whenever you like.'

It was past seven when we reached the office, but a light showing beneath the door proved that my Chief was still there. I asked Stokes to wait on the landing till I called him.

' I've been thinking over that Henry Allen case, Mr Meddleston-Jones,' said my Chief before I could speak. ' I've been waiting for you all the afternoon. I am now satisfied that in Allen we have got Jack the Ripper. That woman in there is one of his victims.' I was so much taken aback that I forgot all about Stokes. ' Yes,' my Chief continued, ' everything points to it – the man's personal habits – his secretiveness – his sudden disappearances. When you arrest him bear in mind that he has a knife about him.'

' Don't say any more, Mr Pepper, till you've heard what I've got to tell you. I have a man here who says he can identify the bones. They are surgical specimens which Allen stole from him.' I have never seen a face so transfigured with noble indignation. After all, I was belittling one of the most important cases in his experience.

'Bring him in,' he said faintly, and he lighted up the laboratory, into which I led Stokes. My Chief threw back the sheet while I watched Stokes. His was not usually an expressive face. First his eyes grew very round: then his whole frame was shaken with some strong emotion. He seemed quite unable to speak. When at last he found his voice it came harsh and loud. He picked up a thigh bone and said, 'You are right, sir; they're ours right enough. Here's my private mark,' and he showed me '128' scratched in minute figures on the bone. He looked hard at the face, and again his sturdy frame was shaken by a convulsive movement that began quite low down in his body and seemed to deprive him of speech. If his face had not been so impassive I should have said that his emotion was suppressed laughter. When at last he had recovered command of his voice he said, 'You've made a fine woman of No. 48, but what about his beard? He had a long grey beard when he was with us.' I did not dare to look at my Chief.

'I think,' I said very gently, 'that Mr Stokes had better take the bones away with him. They belong to his medical school, where Henry Allen was a student. They were, in fact, stolen, and the authorities may wish to prosecute.' My Chief made no sign, and Stokes began to pack up the specimens in the trunk.

'When Mr Henry Allen comes home,' he said, 'and asks for his trunk, you might refer him to the Principal, if you don't mind.' He took one long look at the head before he wrapped it up. 'I wouldn't damage this wax-work for the world: we'll put it in our museum.' As I was helping him down the stairs with the trunk, he said, 'Your friend must have been puzzled by the different sizes of the bones. One arm and one leg belonged to women.'

'He was a little puzzled. He thought that the murdered woman was deformed.'

'I suppose he didn't happen to notice that she had three hands. I see that he had put one of them where a foot was missing.'

When I reached Mrs Auger's door a man was ringing the bell. He was a thin, hunted-looking creature of about thirty, with three day's growth of beard. The door opened as I came up and Mrs Auger said, 'Oh, Mr Allen, where *have* you been?'

' I've been in Lisbon,' he said in a weak voice.

I laid my hand firmly on his shoulder and said, 'Henry Allen, you are wanted at the Medical School to explain why you are unlawfully in possession of certain anatomical specimens which are their property and I must caution you that anything you say will be taken down in writing and used against you at your trial.' He turned very white and Mrs Auger collapsed on her own doorstep.

But the Principal declined to prosecute.

Lawrence Treat

B AS IN BLUDGEON

ON HIS DAY OFF Inspector Mitch Taylor should have had more sense than to stay home. Because, right after Amy had gone out shopping and left him alone, the phone rang. And it had to be the dispatcher telling him something had turned up and they wanted him down at headquarters.

Only it wasn't the dispatcher. It was some dame all the way from Dallas, Texas, telling him he didn't have to worry about the shampoo soap in that tube, it couldn't hurt anybody, and besides, the company was giving up on lead and using aluminum.

Mitch said yeah a few times and figured either it was some crank or else the wires had got twisted, and he hung up. Then about five minutes later some other dame was calling from LA to tell the Taylor family pretty much the same stuff. This time Mitch managed to interrupt long enough to ask what it was all about, and it seemed that Amy had wanted to know whether you could get poisoned from using toothpaste out of a lead tube.

It was all news to Mitch, but it seemed Amy had got the big companies all het up about lead poisoning, because right after the LA dame, somebody called from Boston with pretty much the same pitch. Only this one, her voice was a little higher and she said there wasn't enough lead in a tube of ointment to kill a mouse.

That made three in a row and Mitch was thinking up a wisecrack or so for the next time around, and he had a pretty good one ready. He was going to ask why they were changing from lead if lead was okay. He figured that would shut them up, only he never got the chance to sound off. Because the next call was from the dispatcher telling him signal two-nine, which meant a homicide. It was up in the Short Hills section and a squad car would be waiting downstairs, so get going.

The cop who drove him, it was Malone from up in the Eighth

Precinct, and it seemed he knew all about lead poisoning. He had a brother-in-law who was a house painter, and after twenty years the white lead finally got to him. He ended up with brain damage that left his hands so weak he could hardly hold a spoon. And he had a grey line along his gums. You ought to see him.

After that they got talking about hospitals. Malone had just come out of one – he'd caught his hand in a car door on account he'd forgot to take it away when he'd slammed the thing shut. But the point was, the nurses weren't like they used to be. Now twenty years ago –

Mitch let him rattle on until they got to Short Hills, which was on the outskirts of the city and looked like real country except for that stucco apartment house. It was kind of like a concrete block in a bird bath – too big, and it didn't belong there.

The usual bunch of cars were there in front of it, precinct and headquarters and press cars, along with an ambulance and Jub Freeman's travelling laboratory truck. Upstairs on the second floor the place was jammed and they were all talking about what a beating this Marlie Pratt had taken before she'd died. Mitch managed not to get a look at the body – it would have left him seeing it every time he stopped talking.

He didn't get much in the way of details, because as soon as Lieutenant Decker spotted him, the Lieutenant told him to check the neighbourhood and see what he could dig up. The sort of woman Marlie had been, who her friends were, what they thought of her around here. And whether people had noticed anything yesterday afternoon, which was when the homicide had been committed. Any strangers, anything unusual – Mitch would know what to look for.

He was glad to get free of the mob, but before he left the place he got hold of Balenky who had been one of the first ones here and had the dope. It seemed that the dispatcher had got an anonymous call that there was a body in Marlie Pratt's apartment. The super, his name was Kutch and he had the apartment underneath Marlie's, had a key, so he unlocked the door for the police. Perkins was questioning him right now, and Balenky said it was even money Kutch had done it and that he'd confess before lunch.

'With all that blood around,' Mitch said, 'all you got to do is find the murderer's clothes, and you got him.'

'Where?' Balenky said. 'Where do you find 'em?' And when Mitch didn't answer, Balenky grinned and let the light hit that gold tooth of his. 'Besides,' he said, 'the killer washed and scrubbed up, but good. Water's all over the bathroom and even leaked downstairs.'

'Well,' Mitch said, 'I wish we could get this business over with. It's my day off and I want to get back home.'

'What were you doing?' Balenky asked.

'Loafing around, and thinking I ought to paint the ceiling,' Mitch grunted and added, 'So maybe I'm lucky after all. You paint the ceiling and breathe in all that lead, and it's no good.'

'Maybe,' Balenky said. 'But a lot of ceilings get painted. Matter of fact, I paint my own every couple of years.'

'Gets you in the head,' Mitch said, tapping his forehead and looking solemn, so Balenky wouldn't know he was being kidded. 'I been noticing you. You want to watch yourself.' And Mitch went off.

He had to shake loose from a couple of reporters on the way out, and he walked a block or so before he saw the shabby little store with a big awning that covered the news-stand and a soft-drink machine. The sign read JESSE'S, and a little guy with a long nose was standing or sitting at an open serving window. You could tell right off by the way he looked that he knew most of the neighbour-hood gossip and he'd tell you all about everything, and maybe he'd know what he was talking about and maybe he wouldn't.

Mitch fingered a paper, like he was a customer, before he started the conversation. 'You heard about what happened?' he said.

The little guy cranked himself up in a nasal voice. 'You kidding? All those cops and the TV truck, and then they had it on the radio. Marlie Pratt.'

'You knew her?'

'Was talking to her yesterday, and a nicer dame you don't want to meet. Except she had those way-out ideas.'

'What kind of ideas?'

'You know. Screwball stuff. Can't eat anything unless it's organic. Can't buy anything unless it's got some kind of a seal of approval. Won't use a spray can on account you breathe the stuff and maybe its poison. Same thing with that you buy in tubes. "They're lead tubes," she says, "and lead's a poison." '

'Where do you suppose she picked up an idea like that?' Mitch said, thinking mostly of Amy.

'I wouldn't know,' Jesse said, 'but I can tell you this – she don't know what she's talking about. And believe me, I got more sense than a lot of doctors do. You ask anybody around here and they'll tell you they come to Jesse's first, and then afterwards go to the doctor. Now the way I look at it, if you got something wrong with you, you got to have confidence that you're going to get better, and that's what I give them. Confidence. The body heals itself, so what can a doctor do that I can't, huh? Tell me that, Mister.'

' You got something there,' Mitch said, to kind of shove the guy along.

' You're a cop,' Jesse said. ' That's right, isn't it?'

' Sure.'

' I like cops. A couple of months ago a cop came in here with his family. They'd been out in the fields near here and his kid had got in some poison ivy. Been playing in it, so the cop asks me if I got something for poison ivy, and you know what I told him?' Mitch didn't answer because he didn't have to. ' I told him to go home and wash the kid with brown soap and hot water. Hot as he could stand it. That, and a tube of anti-itch, for a quarter.'

' About Marlie,' Mitch began, but Jesse wasn't ready to get around to her.

' I could have sold him anything I wanted to,' Jesse said. ' I could have sold him a bottle of something for a dollar, because I got a cure for anything. Take a look back there in the shop.'

Mitch stared into the shadows behind Jesse and saw long rows of shelves stocked with cans and bottles and packages. Mitch couldn't read any of the labels, but he got the idea that all that stuff had been there for a long time and it wasn't selling so fast. Meanwhile Jesse kept right on talking. ' I got things you can't buy anywhere else in town,' he said. ' Good old-fashioned items that I only sell to my regular customers.'

' Like Marlie?'

' Sure. Like Marlie. Maybe she didn't think the same way as me, but we got along.'

' You saw her yesterday. Was she alone?'

' No. She was with this guy, he comes to see her maybe once a month, and they stop in here for a paper.'

' Know his name?'

' She calls him Corny.'

' Cornelius,' Mitch said. ' Must be Cornelius.'

' That's it,' Jesse said. ' That's what she called him. They'd been scrapping about something and they were so mad they wouldn't hardly talk to each other. He dropped his dime and when he bent down to pick it up, and he was having trouble getting it, she tried to step on his hand. What do you think of a dame who'd do that huh?'

Mitch kind of muttered something and let the guy jabber on, but it was mostly a waste of time. Still, you had to listen, because you never knew when somebody was liable to come up with what you were really after.

After a while, though, Jesse ran out of steam, so Mitch paid for his paper and left. After that he spoke to a couple of kids and to a dame who took in washing, but he got nowheres.

By afternoon the homicide squad had about all they could find, so they turned things over to the guys in the Eighth and went back to headquarters. There, like always, they sat down in the squad room to see what they could figure out.

Decker led off. 'Let me sum up where we stand,' he said. 'The ME tells us Marlie was killed late yesterday afternoon or evening, and she was beaten with a wooden instrument similar to the cricket bats that were hanging up on the wall and are now missing. Anybody here play cricket?'

It seemed nobody did, so the boss explained that a cricket bat was something like a baseball bat with the fat part flattened out, so you could hit a home run every shot. Only Marlie, she'd been hit with the thin edge and it had broken her skull, and she'd been out cold right from the beginning.

'If she hadn't been,' Decker said, 'she'd have screamed her head off. And brother, that would have been fine for us, because somebody would have heard her and called us. And that would have been that.'

The Lieutenant wrinkled up his puss and took a deep breath, like he was thinking of Marlie and didn't want to blame her for not yelling. Then he pulled at the corners of his mouth and got back to his facts.

'The killer,' he said, 'then washed up thoroughly. His clothes must have been badly stained with blood, and he either took them with him or else dropped them down the incinerator. And then he left, probably wearing Marlie's white shirt and blue jeans.

'Next, about that anonymous call. The super, name of Kutch, admitted he made it. It seems that the water leaked down into the Kutch kitchen, so this morning he went upstairs to see what the trouble was. He opened the apartment with his passkey, but he wanted none of what he saw, so he put in that call. You talked to him, Perk. Anything else there?'

'Nothing more that I got,' Perks said, 'but I wouldn't cross him off the list. He claims he didn't hear anything because he was listening to a football game and he had the volume on high, but I've heard that one before.'

'The rest of you,' Decker said, 'checked up on the other tenants in the building. A couple of them say that late yesterday afternoon they saw a guy in a white shirt and blue jeans, walking down the street towards the bus stop. The bus drivers whose routes took them in the area around that time don't remember any such passenger.'

Decker looked at some notes. 'Marlie's married, but she's been separated from her husband for about two years. After the break-up she resumed her maiden name of Pratt. Her husband lives in Philadelphia, but we haven't been able to get in touch with him. Name's Cornelius Talbot. And that's where we stand now. Any ideas? Anything else we ought to know?'

Mitch piped up with what Jesse had told him, so it seemed Marlie had seen her husband yesterday afternoon and they'd had a scrap. But whatever else, the first order of business was to get hold of him.

The Lieutenant told Mitch to get in touch with Philadelphia and find out what he could, so Mitch was at the phone on and off for the next couple of hours. He was lucky too, on account he got hold of a Philadelphia cop named Epstein, and this Epstein was a wow. He checked up on Talbot and where he lived and what the neighbours knew about him and where he was, and it all added up.

It seemed that Talbot was in a hole, on account Marlie wanted dough and he didn't have it, so he'd gone to see her and talk it over. He was the kind of a guy who never had much anyhow. Give him a buck and it went to the first panhandler with an honest mug on him, or else to the first kid who looked like he wanted an ice-cream cone. Which made Talbot a real softie, right down to the holes in his socks. Except everybody said he had a temper, and when he got sore you'd better watch yourself.

With that information Mitch called the airlines and found out that Talbot had taken a nine am plane out of Philadelphia yesterday morning, and he had a reservation to come back at ten pm the same day, only he never showed up. So where was he?

With the case shaping up like that, it looked like it was just a matter of locating Talbot. Still, the Lieutenant had to go full steam ahead on all the other angles. It seemed that Jub Freeman had come up with a collection of hairs and assorted fibres. He had hair from two males and two females. One of the females was Marlie, the other one was a dame with light-brown hair that she was dyeing black. As for the males, they both had brownish hair, and from the descriptions of Talbot, that fitted him perfect.

On account of Mitch ought to have had the day off and here he'd turned in a pretty good job, Decker told him to go on home. If they got hold of Talbot, they'd let Mitch know.

He got back a little after five and naturally the big companies were calling long distance and trying to explain about lead in their toothpaste tubes.

'I'm sorry you were bothered,' Amy said, 'and maybe I shouldn't have sent those letters, but I did it because of a woman named Selma Cameron.'

'Who's she?'

'I don't know, but she got my name from some list and she phoned me and asked me to write those letters. She kept calling me every day and nagging me, and I finally wrote the letters. Then she phoned again yesterday to make sure I'd sent them. She's so persistent, and I don't know what to do about her.'

'If she calls again,' Mitch said, 'get hold of her number and then hang up. After that I'll handle her. I'll get her off your back.'

'I know you will,' Amy said, 'and I have her phone number right here.'

What with getting to the bottom of those long-distance calls this morning and feeling he'd got Amy settled down, Mitch felt pretty good. He slept fine and woke up with the feeling that the Marlie Pratt case was going to get wound up today. And when it was, he and Amy were going out and celebrate.

In the morning, though, things didn't look as good as Mitch had expected. Talbot hadn't gone back to Philadelphia and hadn't been located here. It looked more and more as if he was the guy they were after, because he'd been with Marlie and he had the motive and there was a half-empty bottle of bourbon with the label of a Philadelphia store that they'd found in her apartment. Then to pin it down, this Kutch who was the super, he said Marlie often went around in blue jeans and a white shirt. Which, Decker said, were no longer in her closet.

So the perpetrator must have left wearing her stuff instead of his own bloodstained clothes, and it all pointed to Talbot.

Still, they didn't have him in custody, not yet, and until they did they had to keep chasing down every clue they could get hold of. Which was why Decker started reading off the names in Marlie's address book and assigning them to the men to check up. But when he came to Selma Cameron, Mitch spoke up.

' I heard of her,' he said. ' She's a nut on food poisoning and stuff like that. Let me tackle her.'

Decker nodded that it was okay, and at the other end of the briefing session Mitch got his car, Number Four, and headed out for Jefferson Avenue, where the Cameron woman lived.

She wasn't tall, but she was the kind of a dame you don't tangle with unless you have to. The way she opened the door, she was ready to slam it back in your face and maybe throw you downstairs if she felt like it. Still, when Mitch showed his identification, she backed off and let him into her apartment.

The hallway where you came in, there wasn't too much light, but there was enough to show a bunch of photographs hanging on the walls. The pictures, they were teams, maybe women's soft ball and stuff like that. Then when Mitch stepped into the living room, the first thing he noticed was the pair of crossed cricket bats mounted over the fake fireplace. Then he took a good look at this female and he noticed she had black hair but you could see she'd dyed it because the roots were brownish and much lighter.

Mitch started easy, the way he always did. First off, he asked her whether she knew what had happened to Marlie and whether Marlie had been a friend of hers and when was the last time they'd seen each other. The Cameron answered straight out, nothing nervous about her. She said she hadn't seen Marlie for a week or so, although they usually saw each other pretty regular.

Along about then Mitch began to get the feeling that the Cameron dame was in this a lot deeper than she wanted him to think. So he fished around for a while, a little of this and a little of that, kind of trying to get the feel of things and wondering whether to bring up the Amy business. Only the Cameron dame did it for him.

' I think I've spoken to your wife,' she said.

' That's right, and you been pestering her for quite a while.'

' I talked to her about some consumer problems.'

' Look,' Mitch said. ' You been nagging her, but from now on you're going to lay off. Understand?'

' Don't threaten me with your Gestapo methods,' Cameron said.

Mitch figured she was just trying to get off the subject, so he came right back on. 'You and Marlie were pretty thick, weren't you?" he said.

'We were lovers,' Cameron answered. And the way she said it, kind of proud and daring him to fault her, it made him admire her.

'Sure,' he said. 'That's why you were so jealous of this guy she was going around with. That's what the fight was about.' And he waited to see how she'd react. Because he had nothing in particular in mind except to hope he could rile her. Only what happened was, she burst out laughing.

'Jealous of a *man*?' she said. 'Me?'

Mitch let that one go, and he pointed to the cricket bats. 'Where'd you get those?' he asked.

'I'm president of the American Women's Cricket Association. Since cricket bats cost so much, I import them wholesale and sell them here at cost, but I gave Marlie a pair free.'

'These?' Mitch said, pointing.

'Of course not. Do you mean to say —'

Mitch interrupted. 'I just want to know whether you hit her with these?'

'Me?' Cameron yelled. And Mitch had the feeling he was finally getting somewheres, so he kept pushing.

'Did you?' he demanded.

She practically spat out her answer. 'No,' she yelled. 'No – no – no!'

'Just take it easy and tell me where you were Sunday afternoon around five or six.'

'I was in the mayor's office, knitting him a pair of woollen pyjamas.'

'Look,' Mitch said. 'Either you answer straight or you're going down to headquarters in a patrol car.'

Her eyes, they'd been kind of brown and about normal in size, but now they narrowed and went black with gold dots in them. Mitch told himself that maybe that was the last thing Marlie ever saw, when Cameron was standing over her and beating her to a pulp.

With that he turned away and pointed to the bats. 'She was killed with one of those things,' he said. 'What did you do it for?'

He was still fishing. He figured he'd opened up a brand-new angle and right now he wasn't sure if it was Cameron or Talbot. But whatever he expected, what she did next just about knocked him for a loop. Because she crossed the room like she had a swarm of bees chasing her, and she grabbed the knob of the bedroom door and slapped it open.

'There!' she screamed. 'There's your murderer – Cornelius Talbot, and just look at him!'

The guy lying there on the bed kind of lifted up his head and then let out a sigh, like he'd done all he could to escape and he hadn't made it, so now he was giving up.

'Talbot?' Mitch asked. 'Are you Cornelius Talbot?' And the guy nodded weakly. Which was a break if there ever was one.

Still, Mitch wasn't any too sure who'd killed Marlie. Maybe it was Talbot and maybe it was Cameron. But whichever it was, Mitch was certain of one thing: Cameron had knowingly harboured a fugitive from justice, and if she kept bothering Amy, Mitch would slap down hard. And with that much settled, Mitch got down to the business in front of him, which was the kind of chance he didn't get any too often.

With the whole city looking for Talbot, Mitch had him along with a second suspect who was in this as deep as anybody. And while you usually don't let two suspects talk in front of each other, on account you don't want them to find out anything they didn't know before, still, with the pair of them here and all het up, this was the time to get them talking.

'How'd you get here?' Mitch asked Talbot.

'I hardly know. Marlie and I had an arrangement on Sunday, and after I left her I walked around. But then I decided we had to talk things over a little more quietly, so I went back. She was lying there in blood – blood –'

Talbot stuck his hands in front of his face, and kind of wagged his head, like he was still looking at Marlie and couldn't believe it. Which either was true, or else made him a damn good actor.

'So after you killed her, then what?' Mitch asked.

'I didn't kill her. I don't know who did. I can't even remember what I did after I saw her lying there, except that somehow I came here. Marlie had talked about Cameron, they were friends and I wanted to be with somebody who'd known her and loved her.'

'You lost your head and killed her,' Mitch said, still pushing it. 'Remember now?'

'I didn't – I couldn't. Even if we were separated and I wasn't in love with her any more, she was still my wife. We'd had some good years together, so how could I hurt her?'

'Then what did you run away for?'

'I don't know. It was a shock, and I was exhausted. I don't know where I went, but I must have been walking all night long. For hours and hours. I didn't eat. I just walked. I don't know where. I don't even remember getting here.'

'He killed her,' Cameron said flatly. 'I'm sure of it.'

Talbot shook his head, and his jaw dropped. 'I couldn't kill her. I couldn't kill anybody, even if I wanted to. My hands – they have no strength. I couldn't grip a bat no matter how hard I tried. Look!'

'How do I know –' Mitch began, but Talbot interrupted.

'Lead poisoning,' he said, 'from all the years I painted toys. The manufacturers bragged about them – expensive, hand-painted toys. Sure, with my hands! Let any doctor examine them.'

'We'll do just that,' Mitch said. 'We'll go down now to head-quarters and have a doctor look you over.' Then he turned to Cameron. 'And you better come along, too.'

'What for?'

'Harbouring a fugitive from justice,' Mitch said. 'You knew we were looking for Talbot, didn't you?'

'Yes. I thought he'd killed her, but I couldn't make him admit it. I wasn't going to let him go until he confessed. Then *you* came along and had to stick your nose in my business.'

'Not your business,' Mitch said. 'Ours.'

About half an hour later he got back to headquarters with Talbot and the Cameron dame. He figured there ought to be brass bands playing and a citation waiting for him, but it didn't exactly work out that way. Instead, as he came down the corridor to the door marked *Homicide Squad*, Lieutenant Decker happened to step out.

'Oh, Taylor,' he said casually. 'Glad you're back. We got a con-fession out of Jesse after a couple of witnesses showed up and said they'd seen him leave the apartment Sunday afternoon wearing a white shirt and blue jeans. Which explains why our guy in blue jeans never got to the bus station. It was Jesse, and he only had to go as far as his shop.'

'Why did he do it?' Mitch asked quietly.

'Marlie was ruining his business, with her talk about consumer education and how nobody should buy old stock, some of which had been condemned. That was about all Jesse had – junk he'd bought cheap because it had been banned by the food and drug people. So he went to see her on Sunday afternoon to ask her to lay off. They had an argument and he lost his head and beat her up. We found the cricket bat in the back of his store.' Decker frowned and glanced at Mitch's two prisoners. ' Who are they?'

' Cornelius Talbot,' Mitch said. ' And Miss Cameron, who was a friend of Marlie's.'

The Lieutenant nodded like this was pretty much what he'd expected. ' Mr Talbot,' he said. ' We've been looking for you, and we'll want a statement from you in a little while.' Then he turned to the Cameron dame, who let fly.

' This man,' she said. ' This dim-witted, misguided policeman who arrested me under false pretences and –'

Mitch kind of edged behind her, and as soon as he caught the Lieutenant's eye he gave him a wink. The Lieutenant nodded, okay, he'd cut her down to size, which he was good at. Only Cameron swung around and started after Mitch like she wasn't going to let him off so easy. So Mitch did the one thing that would get her off his back. He went into the Men's Room.

P.D. James

THE VICTIM

You know Princess Ilsa Mancelli, of course. I mean by that that you must have seen her on the cinema screen; on television; pictured in newspapers arriving at airports with her latest husband; relaxing on their yacht; bejewelled at first nights, gala nights, at any night and in any place where it is obligatory for the rich and successful to show themselves. Even if, like me, you have nothing but bored contempt for what I believe is called the international jet-set, you can hardly live in a modern world and not know Ilsa Mancelli. And you can't fail to have picked up some scraps about her past. The brief and not particularly successful screen career, when even her heart-stopping beauty couldn't quite compensate for the paucity of talent; the succession of marriages, first to the producer who made her first film and who broke a twenty-year-old marriage to get her; then to a Texan millionaire; lastly to a prince. About two months ago I saw a nauseatingly sentimental picture of her with her two-day-old son in a Rome nursing home. So it looks as if this marriage, sanctified as it is by wealth, a title and maternity may be intended as her final adventure.

The husband before the film producer is, I notice, no longer mentioned. Perhaps her publicity agent fears that a violent death in the family, particularly an unsolved violent death, might tarnish her bright image. Blood and beauty. In the early stages of her career they hadn't been able to resist that cheap, vicarious thrill. But not now. Nowadays her early history, before she married the film producer, has become a little obscure, although there is a suggestion of poor but decent parentage and early struggles suitably rewarded. I am the most obscure part of that obscurity. Whatever you know, or think you know of Ilsa Mancelli, you won't have heard about me. The publicity machine has decreed that I be nameless, faceless, unremembered, that I no longer exist. Ironically, the machine is right; in any real sense, I don't.

I married her when she was Elsie Bowman aged seventeen. I was assistant librarian at our local branch library and fifteen years older, a thirty-two-year-old virgin, a scholar manqué, thin-faced, a little stooping, my meagre hair already thinning. She worked on the cosmetic counter of our High Street store. She was beautiful then, but with a delicate, tentative, unsophisticated loveliness which gave little promise of the mature beauty which is hers today. Our story was very ordinary. She returned a book to the library one evening when I was on counter duty. We chatted. She asked my advice about novels for her mother. I spent as long as I dared finding suitable romances for her on the shelves. I tried to interest her in the books I liked. I asked her about herself, her life, her ambitions. She was the only woman I had been able to talk to. I was enchanted by her, totally and completely besotted.

I used to take my lunch early and make surreptitious visits to the store, watching her from the shadow of a neighbouring pillar. There is one picture which even now seems to stop my heart. She had dabbed her wrist with scent and was holding out a bare arm over the counter so that a prospective customer could smell the perfume. She was totally absorbed, her young face gravely preoccupied. I watched her, silently, and felt the tears smarting my eyes.

It was a miracle when she agreed to marry me. Her mother (she had no father) was reconciled if not enthusiastic about the match. She didn't, as she made it abundantly plain, consider me much of a catch. But I had a good job with prospects; I was educated; I was steady and reliable; I spoke with a grammar school accent which, while she affected to deride it, raised my status in her eyes. Besides, any marriage for Elsie was better than none. I was dimly aware when I bothered to think about Elsie in relation to anyone but myself that she and her mother didn't get on.

Mrs Bowman made, as she described it, a splash. There was a full choir and a peal of bells. The church hall was hired and a sit-down meal, ostentatiously unsuitable and badly cooked, was served to eighty guests. Between the pangs of nervousness and indigestion I was conscious of smirking waiters in short white jackets, a couple of giggling bridesmaids from the store, their freckled arms bulging from pink taffeta sleeves, hearty male relatives, red faced and with buttonholes of carnation and waving fern, who made indelicate jokes and clapped me painfully between the shoulders. There were speeches and warm champagne. And, in the middle of it all, Elsie my Elsie, like a white rose.

I suppose that it was stupid of me to imagine that I could hold her. The mere sight of our morning faces, smiling at each other's reflection in the bedroom mirror, should have warned me that it couldn't last. But, poor, deluded fool, I never dreamed that I might lose her except by death. Her death I dared not contemplate, and I was afraid for the first time of my own. Happiness had made a coward of me. We moved into a new bungalow, chosen by Elsie, sat in new chairs chosen by Elsie, slept in a befrilled bed chosen by Elsie. I was so happy that it was like passing into a new phase of existence, breathing a different air, seeing the most ordinary things as if they were newly created. One isn't necessarily humble when greatly in love. Is it so unreasonable to recognize the value of a love like mine, to believe that the beloved is equally sustained and transformed by it?

She said that she wasn't ready to start a baby and, without her job, she was easily bored. She took a brief training in shorthand and typing at our local Technical College and found herself a position as shorthand typist at the firm of Collingford and Major. That, at least, was how the job started. Shorthand typist, then secretary to Mr Rodney Collingford, then personal secretary, then confidential personal secretary; in my bemused state of uxorious bliss I only half registered her progress from occasionally taking his dictation when his then secretary was absent to flaunting his gifts of jewellery and sharing his bed.

He was everything I wasn't. Rich (his father had made a fortune from plastics shortly after the war and had left the factory to his only son), coarsely handsome in a swarthy fashion, big muscled, confident, attractive to women. He prided himself on taking what he wanted. Elsie must have been one of his easiest pickings.

Why, I still wonder, did he want to marry her? I thought at the time that he couldn't resist depriving a pathetic, under-privileged, unattractive husband of a prize which neither looks nor talent had qualified him to deserve. I've noticed that about the rich and successful. They can't bear to see the undeserving prosper. I thought that half the satisfaction for him was in taking her away from me. That was partly why I knew that I had to kill him. But now I'm not so sure. I may have done him an injustice. It may have been both simpler and more complicated than that. She was, you see – she still is – so very beautiful.

I understand her better now. She was capable of kindness, good humour, generosity even, provided she was getting what she wanted. At the time we married, and perhaps eighteen months afterwards, she wanted me. Neither her egoism nor her curiosity had been able to resist such a flattering, overwhelming love. But for her, marriage wasn't permanency. It was the first and necessary step towards the kind of life she wanted and meant to have. She was kind to me, in bed and out, while I was what she wanted. But when she wanted someone else, then my need of her, my jealousy, my bitterness, she saw as a cruel and wilful denial of her basic right, the right to have what she wanted. After all, I'd had her for nearly three years. It was two years more than I had any right to expect. She thought so. Her darling Rodney thought so. When my acquaintances at the library learnt of the divorce I could see in their eyes that they thought so too. And she couldn't see what I was so bitter about. Rodney was perfectly happy to be the guilty party; they weren't, she pointed out caustically, expecting me to behave like a gentleman. I wouldn't have to pay for the divorce. Rodney would see to that. I wasn't being asked to provide her with alimony. Rodney had more than enough. At one point she came close to bribing me with Rodney's money to let her go without fuss. And yet – was it really as simple as that? She had loved me, or at least needed me, for a time. Had she perhaps seen in me that father that she had lost at five years old?

During the divorce, through which I was, as it were, gently processed by highly paid legal experts as if I were an embarrassing but expendable nuisance to be got rid of with decent speed, I was only able to keep sane by the knowledge that I was going to kill Collingford. I knew that I couldn't go on living in a world where he breathed the same air. My mind fed voraciously on the thought of his death, savoured it, began systematically and with dreadful pleasure to plan it.

A successful murder depends on knowing your victim, his character, his daily routine, his weaknesses, those unalterable and betraying habits which make up the core of the personality. I knew quite a lot about Rodney Collingford. I knew facts which Elsie had let fall in her first few weeks with the firm, typing pool gossip. I knew the fuller and rather more intimate facts which she had disclosed in those early days of her enchantment with him, when neither prudence nor kindness had been able to conceal her obsessive preoccupation with her new boss. I should have been warned then. I knew, none better, the need to talk about the absent lover.

What did I know about him? I knew the facts that were common knowledge, of course. That he was wealthy; aged thirty; a notable golfer; that he lived in an ostentatious mock Georgian house on the banks of the Thames looked after by over-paid but non-resident staff; that he owned a cabin cruiser; that he was just over six feet tall; that he was a good business man but reputedly close-fisted; that he was methodical in his habits. I knew a miscellaneous and unrelated set of facts about him, some of which would be useful, some important, some of which I couldn't use. I knew – and this was rather surprising – that he was good with his hands and liked making things in metal and wood. He had built an expensively-equipped and large workroom in the grounds of his house and spent every Thursday evening working there alone. He was a man addicted to routine. This creativity, however mundane and trivial, I found intriguing, but I didn't let myself dwell on it. I was interested in him only so far as his personality and habits were relevant to his death. I never thought of him as a human being. He had no existence for me apart from my hate. He was Rodney Collingford, my victim.

First I decided on the weapon. A gun would have been the most certain, I supposed, but I didn't know how to get one and was only too well aware that I wouldn't know how to load or use it if I did. Besides, I was reading a number of books about murder at the time and I realized that guns, however cunningly obtained, were easy to trace. And there was another thing. A gun was too impersonal, too remote. I wanted to make physical contact at the moment of death. I wanted to get close enough to see that final look of incredulity and horror as he recognized, simultaneously, me and his death. I wanted to drive a knife into his throat.

I bought it two days after the divorce. I was in no hurry to kill Collingford. I knew that I must take my time, must be patient if I were to act in safety. One day, perhaps when we were old, I might tell Elsie. But I didn't intend to be found out. This was to be the perfect murder. And that meant taking my time. He would be allowed to live for a full year. But I knew that the earlier I bought the knife the more difficult it would be, twelve months later to trace the purchase. I didn't buy it locally. I went one Saturday morning by train and bus to a north-east suburb and found a busy ironmongers and general store just off the High Street. There was a variety of knives on display. The blade of the one I selected was about six inches long and was made of strong steel screwed into a plain wooden handle. I think it was probably meant for cutting lino. In the shop its razor edge was protected by a strong cardboard sheath. It felt good and right in my hand. I stood in a small queue at the pay desk and the cashier didn't even glance up as he took my notes and pushed the change towards me.

But the most satisfying part of my planning was the second stage. I wanted Collingford to suffer. I wanted him to know that he was going to die. It wasn't enough that he should realize it in a last second before I drove in the knife or in that final second before he ceased to know anything for ever. Two seconds of agony, however horrible, weren't an adequate return for what he had done to me. I wanted him to know that he was a condemned man, to know it with increasing certainty, to wonder every morning whether this might be his last day. What if this knowledge did make him cautious, put him on his guard? In this country, he couldn't go armed. He couldn't carry on his business with a hired protector always at his side. He couldn't bribe the police to watch him every second of the day. Besides, he wouldn't want to be thought a coward. I guessed that he would carry on, ostentatiously normal, as if the threats were unreal or derisory, something to laugh about with his drinking cronies. He was the sort to laugh at danger. But he would never be sure. And by the end, his nerve and confidence would be broken. Elsie wouldn't know him for the man she had married.

I would have liked to have telephoned him but that, I knew, was impracticable. Calls could be traced; he might refuse to talk to me; I wasn't confident that I could disguise my voice. So the sentence of death would have to be sent by post. Obviously, I couldn't write the notes or the envelopes myself. My studies in murder had shown me how difficult it was to disguise handwriting and the method of cutting out and sticking together letters from a newspaper seemed messy, very time consuming and difficult to manage wearing gloves. I knew, too, that it would be fatal to use my own small portable typewriter or one of the machines at the library. The forensic experts could identify a machine.

And then I hit on my plan. I began to spend my Saturdays and occasional half days journeying round London and visiting shops where they sold secondhand typewriters. I expect you know the kind of shop; a variety of machines of different ages, some practically obsolete, others hardly used, arranged on tables where the prospective purchaser may try them out. There were new machines too, and the proprietor was usually employed in demonstrating their merits or discussing hire-purchase terms. The customers wandered desultorily around, inspecting the machines, stopping occasionally to type out an exploratory passage. There were little pads of rough paper stacked ready for use. I didn't, of course, use the scrap paper provided. I came supplied with my own writing materials, a well-known brand sold in every stationers and on every railway bookstall. I bought a small supply of paper and envelopes once every two months and never from the same shop. Always, when handling them, I wore a thin pair of gloves, slipping them on as soon as my typing was complete. If someone were near, I would tap out the usual drivel about the sharp brown fox or all good men coming to the aid of the party. But if I were quite alone I would type something very different.

'This is the first comunication, Collingford. You'll be getting them regularly from now on. They're just to let you know that I'm going to kill you.'

'You can't escape me, Collingford. Don't bother to inform the police. They can't help you.'

'I'm getting nearer, Collingford. Have you made your will?'

'Not long now, Collingford. What does it feel like to be under sentence of death?'

The warnings weren't particularly elegant. As a librarian I could think of a number of apt quotations which would have added a touch of individuality or style, perhaps even of sardonic humour, to the bald sentence of death. But I dared not risk originality. The notes had to be ordinary, the kind of threat which anyone of his enemies, a worker, a competitor, a cuckolded husband, might have sent.

Sometimes I had a lucky day. The shop would be large, well supplied, nearly empty. I would be able to move from typewriter to typewriter and leave with perhaps a dozen or so notes and addressed envelopes ready to send. I always carried a folded newspaper in which I could conceal my writing pad and envelopes and into which I could quickly slip my little stock of typed messages.

It was quite a job to keep myself supplied with notes and I discovered interesting parts of London and fascinating shops. I particularly enjoyed this part of my plan. I wanted Collingford to get two notes a week, one posted on Sunday and one on Thursday. I wanted him to come to dread Friday and Monday mornings when the familiar typed envelope would drop on his mat. I wanted him to believe the threat was real. And why should he not believe it? How could the force of my hate and resolution not transmit itself through paper and typescript to his gradually comprehending brain?

I wanted to keep an eye on my victim. It shouldn't have been difficult; we lived in the same town. But our lives were worlds apart. He was a hard and sociable drinker. I never went inside a public house, and would have been particularly ill at ease in the kind of public house he frequented. But, from time to time, I would see him in the town. Usually he would be parking his Jaguar, and I would watch his quick, almost furtive, look to left and right before he turned to lock the door. Was it my imagination that he looked older, that some sort of confidence had drained out of him?

Once, when walking by the river on a Sunday in early Spring, I saw him manoeuvring his boat through Teddington Lock. Ilsa – she had, I knew, changed her name after her marriage – was with him. She was wearing a white trouser suit, her flowing hair was bound by a red scarf. There was a party. I could see two more men and a couple of girls and hear high female squeals of laughter. I turned quickly and slouched away as if I were the guilty one. But not before I had seen Collingford's face. This time I couldn't be mistaken. It wasn't, surely, the tedious job of getting his boat unscratched through the lock that made his face look so grey and strained.

The third phase of my planning meant moving house. I wasn't sorry to go. The bungalow, feminine, chintzy, smelling of fresh paint and the new shoddy furniture which she had chosen, was Elsie's home not mine. Her scent still lingered in cupboards and on pillows. In these inappropriate surroundings I had known greater happiness than I was ever to know again. But now I paced restlessly from room to empty room fretting to be gone.

It took me four months to find the house I wanted. It had to be on or very near a river within two or three miles upstream of Collingford's house. It had to be small and reasonably cheap. Money wasn't too much of a difficulty. It was a time of rising house prices and the modern bungalow sold at three hundred pounds more than I had paid for it. I could get another mortgage without difficulty if I didn't ask for too much, but I thought it likely that, for what I wanted, I should have to pay cash.

The house agents perfectly understood that a man on his own found a three bedroom bungalow too large for him and, even if they found me rather vague about my new requirements and irritatingly imprecise about the reasons for rejecting their offerings, they still sent me orders to view. And then, suddenly on an afternoon in April, I found exactly what I was looking for. It actually stood on the river, separated from it only by a narrow tow path. It was a one-bedroom shack-like wooden bungalow with a tiled roof, set in a small neglected plot of sodden grass and overgrown flower beds. There had once been a wooden landing stage but now the two remaining planks, festooned with weeds and tags of rotted rope, were half-submerged beneath the slime of the river. The paint on the small veranda had long ago flaked away. The wallpaper of twined roses in the sitting-room was blotched and faded. The previous owner had left two old cane chairs and a ramshackle table. The kitchen was pokey and ill-equipped. Everywhere there hung a damp miasma of depression and decay. In summer, when the neighbouring shacks and bungalows were occupied by holidaymakers and week-enders it would, no doubt, be cheerful enough. But in October, when I planned to kill Collingford, it would be as deserted and isolated as a disused morgue. I bought it and paid cash. I was even able to knock two hundred pounds off the asking price.

My life that summer was almost happy. I did my job at the library adequately. I lived alone in the shack, looking after myself as I had before my marriage. I spent my evenings watching television. The images flickered in front of my eyes almost unregarded, a monochrome background to my bloody and obsessive thoughts.

I practised with the knife until it was as familiar in my hand as an eating utensil. Collingford was taller than I by six inches. The thrust then would have to be upward. It made a difference to the way I held the knife and I experimented to find the most comfortable and effective grip. I hung a bolster on a hook in the bedroom door and lunged at a marked spot for hours at a time. Of course, I didn't actually insert the knife; nothing must dull the sharpness of its blade. Once a week, a special treat, I sharpened it to an even keener edge.

Two days after moving into the bungalow I bought a dark blue untrimmed track suit and a pair of light running shoes. Throughout the summer I spent an occasional evening running on the tow path. The people who owned the neighbouring chalets, when they were there which was infrequently, got used to the sound of my television through the closed curtains and the sight of my figure jogging past their windows. I kept apart from them and from everyone and summer passed into autumn. The shutters were put up on all the chalets except mine. The tow path became mushy with falling leaves. Dusk fell early, and the summer sights and sounds died on the river. And it was October.

He was due to die on Thursday 17 October, the anniversary of the final decree of divorce. It had to be a Thursday, the evening which he spent by custom alone in his workshop, but it was a particularly happy augury that the anniversary should fall on a Thursday. I knew that he would be there. Every Thursday for nearly a year I had padded along the two and a half miles of the footpath in the evening dusk and had stood briefly watching the squares of light from his windows and the dark bulk of the house behind.

It was a warm evening. There had been a light drizzle for most of the day but, by dusk, the skies had cleared. There was a thin white sliver of moon and it cast a trembling ribbon of light across the river. I left the library at my usual time, said my usual good-nights. I knew that I had been my normal self during the day, solitary, occasionally a little sarcastic, conscientious, betraying no hint of the inner tumult.

I wasn't hungry when I got home but I made myself eat an omelette and drink two cups of coffee. I put on my swimming trunks and hung around my neck a plastic toilet bag containing the knife. Over the trunks I put on my track suit, slipping a pair of thin rubber gloves into the pocket. Then, at about a quarter past seven, I left the shack and began my customary gentle trot along the tow path.

When I got to the chosen spot opposite to Collingford's house I could see at once that all was well. The house was in darkness but there were the customary lighted windows of his workshop. I saw that the cabin cruiser was moored against the boathouse. I stood very still and listened. There was no sound. Even the light breeze had died and the yellowing leaves on the riverside elms hung motionless. The tow path was completely deserted. I slipped into the shadow of the hedge where the trees grew thickest and found the place I had already selected. I put on the rubber gloves, slipped out of the track suit, and left it folded around my running shoes in the shadow of the hedge. Then, still watching carefully to left and right, I made my way to the river.

I knew just where I must enter and leave the water. I had selected a place where the bank curved gently, where the water was shallow and the bottom firm and comparatively free of mud. The water struck very cold, but I expected that. Every night during that autumn I had bathed in cold water to accustom my body to the shock. I swam across the river with my methodical but quiet breast stroke, hardly disturbing the surface of the water. I tried to keep out of the path of moonlight but, from time to time, I swam into its silver gleam and saw my red gloved hands parting in front of me as if they were already stained with blood.

I used Collingford's landing stage to clamber out the other side. Again I stood still and listened. There was no sound except for the constant moaning of the river and the solitary cry of a night bird. I made my way silently over the grass. Outside the door of his work-room, I paused again. I could hear the noise of some kind of machinery. I wondered whether the door would be locked, but it opened easily when I turned the handle. I moved into a blaze of light.

I knew exactly what I had to do. I was perfectly calm. It was over in about four seconds. I don't think he really had a chance. He was absorbed in what he had been doing, bending over a lathe, and the sight of an almost naked man, walking purposefully towards him, left him literally impotent with surprise. But, after that first paralys-ing second, he knew me. Oh yes, he knew me! Then I drew my right hand from behind my back and struck. The knife went in as sweetly as if the flesh had been butter. He staggered and fell. I had expected that and I let myself go loose and fell on top of him. His eyes were glazed, his mouth opened and there was a gush of dark red blood. I twisted the knife viciously in the wound, relishing the sound of tearing sinews. Then I waited. I counted five deliberately, then raised myself from his prone figure and crouched behind him before withdrawing the knife. When I withdrew it there was a fountain of sweet smelling blood which curved from his throat like an arch. There is one thing I shall never forget. The blood must have been red, what other colour could it have been? But, at the same time and for every day afterwards, I saw it as a golden stream.

I checked my body for blood stains before I left the workshop and rinsed my arms under the cold tap at his sink. My bare feet made no marks on the wooden block flooring. I closed the door quietly after me and, once again, stood listening. Still no sound. The house was dark and empty.

The return journey was more exhausting than I had thought possible. The river seemed to have widened and I thought that I should never reach my home shore. I was glad I had chosen a shallow part of the stream and that the bank was firm. I doubt whether I could have drawn myself up through a welter of mud and slime. I was shivering violently as I zipped up my track suit and it took me precious seconds to get on my running shoes. After I had run about a mile down the tow path I weighted the toilet bag containing the knife with stones from the path and hurled it into the middle of the river. I guessed that they would drag part of the Thames for the weapon but they could hardly search the whole stream. And, even if they did, the toilet bag was one sold at the local chain store which anyone might have bought, and I was confident that the knife could never be traced to me. Half an hour later I was back in my shack. I had left the television on and the news was just ending. I made myself a cup of hot cocoa and sat to watch it. I felt drained of thought and energy as if I had just made love. I was conscious of nothing but my tiredness, my body's coldness gradually returning to life in the warmth of the electric fire, and a great peace.

He must have had a lot of enemies. It was nearly a fortnight before the police got round to interviewing me. Two officers came, a Detective Inspector and a Sergeant, both in plain clothes. The Sergeant did most of the talking; the other just sat, looking round at the sitting room, glancing out at the river, looking at the two of us from time to time from cold grey eyes as if the whole investigation were a necessary bore. The Sergeant said the usual reassuring platitudes about just a few questions. I was nervous, but that didn't worry me. They would expect me to be nervous. I told myself that, whatever I did, I mustn't try to be clever. I mustn't talk too much. I had decided to tell them that I spent the whole evening watching television, confident that no one would be able to refute this. I knew that no friends would have called on me. I doubted whether my colleagues at the library even knew where I lived. And I had no telephone so I need not fear that a caller's ring had gone unanswered during that crucial hour and a half.

On the whole it was easier than I had expected. Only once did I feel myself at risk. That was when the Inspector suddenly intervened. He said in a harsh voice:

' He married your wife didn't he? Took her away from you some people might say. Nice piece of goods, too, by the look of her. Didn't you feel any grievance? Or was it all nice and friendly? You take her, old chap. No ill feelings. That kind of thing?'

It was hard to accept the contempt in his voice but if he hoped to provoke me he didn't succeed. I had been expecting this question. I was prepared. I looked down at my hands and waited a few seconds before I spoke. I knew exactly what I would say.

' I could have killed Collingford myself when she first told me about him. But I had to come to terms with it. She went for the money you see. And if that's the kind of wife you have, well she's going to leave you sooner or later. Better sooner than when you have a family. You tell yourself " good riddance ". I don't mean I felt that at first, of course. But I did feel it in the end. Sooner than I expected, really.'

That was all I said about Elsie then or ever. They came back three times. They asked me if they could look round my shack. They looked round it. They took away two of my suits and the track suit for examination. Two weeks later they returned them without comment. I never knew what they suspected, or even if they did suspect. Each time they came I said less, not more. I never varied my story. I never allowed them to provoke me into discussing my marriage or speculating about the crime. I just sat there, telling them the same thing over and over again. I never felt in any real danger. I knew that they had dragged some lengths of the river but that they hadn't found the weapon. In the end they gave up. I always had the feeling that I was pretty low on their list of suspects and that, by the end, their visits were merely a matter of form.

It was three months before Elsie came to me. I was glad that it wasn't earlier. It might have looked suspicious if she had arrived at the shack when the police were with me. After Collingford's death I hadn't seen her. There were pictures of her in the national and local newspapers, fragile in sombre furs and black hat at the inquest, bravely controlled at the crematorium, sitting in her drawing room in afternoon dress and pearls with her husband's dog at her feet, the personification of loneliness and grief.

' I can't think who could have done it. He must have been a madman. Rodney hadn't an enemy in the world.'

That statement caused some ribald comment at the library. One of the assistants said:

' He's left her a fortune I hear. Lucky for her she had an alibi. She was at a London theatre all the evening, watching *Macbeth*. Otherwise, from what I've heard of our Rodney Collingford, people might have started to get ideas about his fetching little widow.'

Then he gave me a sudden embarrassed glance, remembering who the widow was.

And so one Friday evening, she came. She drove herself and was alone. The dark green Saab drove up at my ramshackle gate. She came into the sitting room and looked around in a kind of puzzled contempt. After a moment, still not speaking, she sat down in one of the fireside chairs and crossed her legs, moving one caressingly against the other. I hadn't seen her sitting like that before. She looked up at me. I was standing stiffly in front of her chair, my lips dry. When I spoke I didn't recognize my own voice.

' So you've come back?' I said.

She glared at me, incredulous, and then she laughed :

' To you? Back for keeps? Don't be silly, darling! I've just come to pay a visit. Besides, I wouldn't dare to come back would I? I might be frightened you'd stick a knife into my throat.'

I couldn't speak. I stared at her, feeling the blood drain from my face. Then I heard her high, rather childish voice. It sounded almost kind.

' Don't worry, I shan't tell. You were right about him, darling, you really were. He wasn't at all nice really. And mean! I didn't care so much about your meanness. After all, you don't earn so very much do you? But he had half a million! Think of it, darling. I've been left half a million! And he was so mean that he expected me to go on working as his secretary even after we were married. I typed all his letters! I really did! All that he sent from home, anyway. And I had to open his post every morning, unless the envelopes had a secret little sign on them he'd told his friends about to show that they were private.'

I said through bloodless lips.

' So all my notes –'

' He never saw them darling. Well, I didn't want to worry him did I? And I knew they were from you. I knew when the first one arrived. You never could spell communication, could you? I noticed that when you used to write to the house agents and the solicitor before we were married. It made me laugh considering that you're an educated librarian and I was only a shop assistant.'

' So you knew all the time. You knew that it was going to happen.'

' Well, I thought that it might. But he really was horrible, darling.

You can't imagine. And now I've got half a million! Isn't it lucky that I have an alibi? I thought you might come on that Thursday. And Rodney never did enjoy a serious play.'

After that brief visit I never saw or spoke to her again. I stayed in the shack, but life became pointless after Collingford's death. Planning his murder had been an interest, after all. Without Elsie and without my victim there seemed little point in living. And, about a year after his death, I began to dream. I still dream, always on a Monday and Friday. I live through it all again; the noiseless run along the tow path over the mush of damp leaves, the quiet swim across the river; the silent opening of his door; the upward thrust of the knife; the vicious turn in the wound; the animal sound of tearing tissues; the curving stream of golden blood. Only the homeward swim is different. In my dream the river is no longer a cleansing stream, luminous under the sickle moon, but a cloying, impenetrable, slow moving bog of viscous blood through which I struggle in impotent panic towards a steadily receding shore.

I knew about the significance of the dream. I've read all about the psychology of guilt. Since I lost Elsie I've done all my living through books. But it doesn't help. And I no longer know who I am. I know who I used to be, our local Assistant Libarian, gentle, scholarly, timid, Elsie's husband. But then I killed Collingford. The man I was couldn't have done that. He wasn't that kind of person. So who am I? It isn't really surprising, I suppose, that the Library Committee suggested so tactfully that I ought to look for a less exacting job. A less exacting job than the post of Assistant Librarian? But you can't blame them. No one can be efficient and keep his mind on the job when he doesn't know who he is.

Sometimes, when I'm in a public house – and I seem to spend most of my time there nowadays since I've been out of work – I'll look over someone's shoulder at a newspaper photograph of Elsie and say:

'That's the beautiful Ilsa Mancelli. I was her first husband.'

I've got used to the way people sidle away from me, the ubiquitous pub bore, their eyes averted, their voices suddenly hearty. But sometimes, perhaps because they've been lucky with the horses and feel a spasm of pity for a poor deluded sod, they push a few coins over the counter to the barman before making their way to the door, and buy me a drink.

Elwyn Jones

TO PROTECT
THE INNOCENT

IT WAS A BRIGHT SUNNY DAY and Detective Inspector Tucker whistled merrily as he drove his 'master', Detective Chief Superintendent Barlow, along a quiet country road. His tune was 'A little grey home in the West' – which he thought appropriate since they were in the West Country and about to probe a little more deeply into the affairs of one Donald West, a man with a vast criminal reputation and no convictions recorded against him.

Barlow looked up from the map he was reading. 'Slow down. We should be able to see West's house round the next bend.' They could. It was set back half a mile or so from the road – a solid grey stone farmhouse with handsome out-buildings. The whole property looked trim and prosperous. 'That'll do,' said Barlow slowly. 'Move again. There's a glint, a reflection, in the bottom left-hand window. Somebody's watching with binoculars.'

'We're easy enough to spot,' grunted Tucker. 'This is a pretty conspicuous car.' It was a long bright red estate car. It looked aggressive somehow, arrogant and flaunting even, as Tucker parked it at the end of the village outside the small police station. A young constable came to greet them. 'Superintendent Summers is inside, gentlemen.'

He was tall, slow-spoken and not quite sure with what mixture of respect and authority he should treat Barlow. 'We could have provided better accommodation at headquarters,' he said. 'I'd prefer it, and so would the Chief Constable.' Barlow grinned as he looked around the box-like office with its desk, two chairs, filing cabinet, two telephones and nothing else. 'This is fine. I don't come here to pay social calls on the top brass. Now that back door?'

'Its own lock. And here's the key. A separate telephone line's been run in for you. And I've got a booster for the personal radio channel on its way over.'

'Fast work.'

Summers relaxed. ' Bit of local pull.'

Barlow encouraged him. ' So how about imparting some local knowledge?'

Summers obliged. ' Eight years ago the farmhouse was derelict. It's pretty spruce now. A lot of work put into it, a lot of money. The locals started saying, " Nothing but the best for Mr West." He paid for it, he got it.'

' And West himself?' Barlow asked carefully.

' I've met him twice,' Summers replied slowly. ' Met him socially you understand. He is, in my opinion, a hard case, a very hard case, a calculating man, wary, and cold.'

' He is that,' Barlow agreed. ' From all accounts. I've never met him. But I know a great deal about him. I know, Scotland Yard's Serious Crimes Squad know, Interpol knows. But nothing's ever been proved against him. It's why I thought it worthwhile asking you three months ago to cast a sharp eye on him.'

' Which I have done,' replied Summers. ' But with no result, until yesterday – when this arrived.' From his briefcase he produced a transparent plastic bag which contained an envelope and a sheet of paper. The envelope was addressed precisely to ' Superintendent J. H. Summers, MBE, Mid-Wessex Constabulary HQ ' and marked ' Personal '. All the letters had been cut from a newspaper. So had those to spell out the message enclosed: ' Tell Donald West to look to his daughter.'

A shade smugly Summers said ' It's Hamlet's advice to Polonius – " Look to your daughter." West has a daughter, thirteen years old, who goes to a boarding school in Suffolk. Except that she came home yesterday, even though it's the middle of term. West drove over to get her. I understand he told the school authority he needed her at home for a while.'

' Something's up then.' Barlow stared at the envelope and the message. ' Correct address, a literary quote . . .'

Summers had more to offer. ' And the words from a posh paper. The letters are all cut from *The Guardian*. Distinctive typography.' At Barlow's encouraging nod he went on. ' No fingerprints on the message. It was posted from Durham on Tuesday. Six prisoners were released from Durham jail on Tuesday, five on Monday. Here's the list of names. I've fed it to Central Criminal Records just in case, but no connection between any of them and West has been established yet.'

'A line worth following,' Barlow agreed. 'Now in the normal way, how would you have handled this matter?'

'Gone to see West I think. Sounding sympathetic, certainly curious. And since he's a prominent man I'd have telephoned first.'

'Then do that.'

But Summers had more to divulge. 'I only heard yesterday, but a week ago West had his telephone number changed. He'd complained to the Post Office that he was being pestered by unwanted calls in the middle of the night. So they intercepted his calls for three nights, then changed his number. It's ex-directory now. Of course I have it.'

'But don't show you have,' said Barlow shrewdly. 'Say you discovered the number was ex-directory and thought you'd better drive over to see him.'

Summers agreed. 'Gives me something to talk about. West is pretty tight-mouthed though. I don't see him volunteering anything.'

They were interrupted by a knock on the door. Barlow called 'Come in.' It was Tucker who closed the door carefully behind him. 'There's a man outside, sir, says he's Mr West. Mr Donald West. And he asked for Mr Barlow by name.'

'How could he know I was here?'

Summers protested. 'He didn't hear from us. Not even the local bobby was told your name.'

'But West does know,' Barlow said irritably.

'Better have him in. Though I'm not ready for him. Not equipped. Still, we'll try the radio. Channel Two.'

Swiftly Barlow opened the bottom drawer of the desk and put a personal radio inside it. The radio was on. The drawer was not completely closed. At a nod from Barlow, Tucker opened the door, formally announced 'Mr Donald West, sir,' and left.

West was not tall but he was wiry and looked fit. He was expensively, just a little loudly, dressed. His hands were powerful and restless, and Barlow braced himself as though for a wrestling match. 'Good morning, I'm Barlow.'

West nodded and asked amiably, 'What brings you here?'

Flatly Barlow said, 'Ditto. What brings you here?'

'I want to see you. And I want to see you alone.'

Summers said he had no objection. But Barlow raised a doubt. 'Why is Mr West reluctant to have a witness present I wonder? He could have something to hide. Or he could be waiting to make allegations about you, Mr Summers.'

West flushed angrily. ' I've nothing to hide. I've nothing to complain about Summers. I just want to tell you something.'

' But why me?' Barlow asked. ' And why me alone? Tell me, Mr Summers, he wouldn't have anything he'd want to try and bribe me about, would he?'

Almost desperately West said, ' I've got some information.'

Barlow beamed: ' We're all ears.'

It was a mistake which gave West the initiative. ' Even outside? I noticed your Inspector's radio on his desk. Yours in one of the drawers?'

Barlow shrugged defeat, pulled the radio out of the drawer and switched it off. ' It was worth trying. All right, Mr Summers. If you'll excuse us.'

Left alone he and West eyed each other coldly. ' No more electronic tricks,' said Barlow. ' I take it you're clean too?'

' This is too serious for tricks.' West sounded urgent again. ' I need help.'

Barlow was back in the match. Incredulously he asked, ' You're asking for help from the police? It must be your daughter, but I'm not really very good as a child guidance counsellor.'

West flushed angrily. ' Christine doesn't need guidance. She needs protection.'

' From whom?'

' I don't know. I wouldn't be here if I did. I'd be sorting him, then, in my own way.'

Barlow's voice was hard. ' As you have done before.'

West shrugged. ' Perhaps.'

' That's the root of our problem.' Barlow was bland once more. ' It's a little matter of candour, of frankness. Of getting at the truth.'

West replied, ' It's why I had to see you alone.'

Barlow looked at him with open hostility. ' So without witnesses, any admissions you make, deliberately or inadvertently, you can then deny. Why should I bother?'

' To help to protect a young girl.' West struggled with his thoughts. ' To help a young girl even though she's my daughter.'

' Then for her sake,' said Barlow, ' I wouldn't lift an eyebrow to protect you. On that basis start talking.'

As the minutes ticked by Superintendent Summers drank tea with Tucker in the outer office and grew impatient. ' You're very calm for a young 'un,' he said eventually. 'I'm bursting to know what they're talking about in there.'

'I'm keen to know too, sir. But I reckon I'll get told, told all I need to know. I've got a lot of faith in Mr Barlow, as a boss as well as a detective.'

'He's going to need all his skills with West.'

Tucker agreed. 'Struck me as a hard case too, sir. But we have got him at a bit of a disadvantage. We want him, certainly. But it looks as though he needs us – to help protect his daughter.'

As he spoke the door from the street swung open. Standing in the doorway was a young girl, dark-haired, wearing jodhpurs, and with a very assured manner. 'Good morning,' she said pleasantly. 'Would you tell my father I'm here please?'

Tucker looked at her. 'And who's your father?'

She flushed slightly. 'I thought everybody knew. I'm Christine West.'

Superintendent Summers introduced himself and Tucker and she said a polite 'Pleased to meet you,' before plunging on to ask 'My father's not in any kind of trouble is he?"

Tucker gave the time-honoured response. 'He's speaking to another officer at the moment.'

She, again politely, refused their offer of a cup of tea, but asked if she could wait. 'I don't suppose my father will be very long, do you?'

Tucker again was non-committal. 'Hard to say. You see, we don't know what your father and the other officer are talking about.'

'Me, probably,' Christine said calmly. 'My father's worried about me. I don't know why. But old people, sorry, older people do worry.'

'Is that why you're home from school?' asked Summers.

'I don't know why I'm home. My father doesn't tell me much, not about important things. He tells me a lot about, say, the milk yield, or how many fish he's caught, and how not to overfeed Bob – that's my pony.'

Gravely Tucker asked 'And how is Bob?'

'He's fine,' she said cheerfully. 'I came here on him, left him at the back, on that patch of green.'

Superintendent Summers gave a low groan. 'That's PC Leonard's attempt at a lawn.'

'Oh dear. Then I'd better move Bob.'

Tucker asked carefully, ' Is Bob gentle?' and took courage from her reply of ' Gentle as a lamb '. He volunteered to move him.

Christine smiled her thanks, adding a little anxiously, ' I don't suppose my father will be much longer.'

But in the inner office things were not going smoothly. Barlow agreed that West had given him grounds enough to believe that his daughter was under threat. But his tone was icy as he disclosed flatly ' I don't believe you don't know where or who the threat comes from. So I not only can't, I won't fight blindfold. If you were straight with me you'd list those with a grudge against you. A justifiable grudge or not. I could give you a list of people with a grudge against me.'

West tried a smile. ' Am I on it?'

Barlow did smile. ' At the end of the day you will be.'

' You're very confident, Chief Superintendent.'

Still with a smile Barlow answered, ' Pretty confident. And I'll tell you why: I've got an easy conscience. I've cheated sometimes, but I've always tried to be fair. And I'm on the side of the law.' He paused. ' There are no witnesses so I can say it. You're a crook. You are one of our few big operators, ranking second or third among the clever, effective, successful organizers of crime.'

West's grin did not deny the charge, but his expression changed as Barlow continued with savage calm. ' You're a crook, and your conscience is just not there. You present yourself as a big-hearted, concerned, ever-loving father – who is willing to risk his daughter for the sake of his own sleek, carefully tailored hide.'

West was on his feet spluttering with rage. ' I'm getting out of here.'

' Feel free,' snapped Barlow. ' Come back when you're willing to do something for your daughter.'

West hesitated. Barlow looked nonchalant. In the silence there came a heavy banging on the back door leading directly into the inner office. Angrily Barlow unlocked it and Tucker burst in with a minimum of apology. ' Had to come in this way.' He faced West. ' Your daughter's in the front office. Wait! She's all right. But she came on her pony. Which is outside, and very dead.'

An hour later Tucker was on watch in the West's living room. He had his personal radio and a pair of binoculars. He noted the number and description of every vehicle passing on the road. There were not many of them. He noted a milk lorry stop at the end of the driveway and watched the driver load full churns and replace them with empty ones. A little later he saw the farm cowman take up his tractor and trailer to bring back the empty churns. There was nothing unusual on the road.

A movement behind him caught him unawares. It was a sad-eyed Christine who attempted to smile. 'I wanted to ask you something. I'm not being hysterical any more so – how was Bob killed?' As Tucker hesitated she went on. 'I am nearly fourteen. He was my pony. And I'm not being weepy now.'

Tucker looked at her gravely. 'He didn't feel anything. It must have been very quick. The reports say less than four seconds. Somebody pumped air into his jugular vein.'

She stayed calm. 'And who did this horrible thing?'

'We don't know. Nobody saw anything. Nobody heard anything. The Sherlock Holmes stuff doesn't help either: no foot-prints, no special tyre marks.'

Christine had been listening carefully. 'Wouldn't Sherlock Holmes be looking for a motive? Are you and, what's his name, Mr Barlow? – looking for a motive?'

Tucker agreed they were, but hadn't found it yet. Christine was helpful. 'I think, I think whoever did this terrible thing to Bob wanted to frighten my father.'

'Were you frightened?'

'No.' She sounded very certain. 'I was upset, but I wasn't frightened. Do you think, please tell me, do you think my father is frightened?'

Tucker shrugged his shoulders. 'I don't think your father frightens easily. But he must be worried.'

In the room which was half farm office and half fisherman's den, West sat tensely facing Barlow who was substantially more relaxed. 'You've had time to think things out, Mr West. What are you going to do?'

The reply was defiant. 'What are you going to do?'

'All the serious, routine things have been done. The death of this pony is being treated like homicide, with searches and questions and statements. We have this house under surveillance. Inspector Tucker's here. I'm here. For how long is up to you.'

West announced flatly that he had made arrangements to hire a personal bodyguard. He was dismayed when Barlow guessed (if it was a guess) that he expected the arrival of the Marriott brothers, two London thugs. Barlow was even nearly ready to welcome them. ' They might be stupid enough to be carrying guns when they arrive.'

' No chance,' West protested. ' They know the law's here.'

Barlow beamed. ' And I suppose they also know that you have certificates for one sporting rifle and one shot gun. I know the certificates expire in four weeks. I also know that the local Chief Constable plans not to renew them.' He added helpfully: ' That's a decision you can always appeal against.'

West stared at him. ' You're trying to rile me.'

' In the absence of witnesses,' said Barlow, 'agreed. I think I'll succeed too. So I'll just have that drink you were about to offer me and Tucker and I'll get out of your hair.'

' You mean you'll just walk away from it all?'

' Drive away – or rather get driven. I don't want a breathalyser waved under my nose after my drink.'

West was hardly playing the gracious host. ' It's in the cupboard behind you.'

Barlow poured himself a generous measure of brandy and, as he closed the cupboard, again sounded chattily helpful. ' You'd better stock up on your brown ale. It's what the Marriott boys drink, in case you didn't know.'

' Do you know them well?'

' I've never met them, not even professionally. And they're certainly not members of my tight little social circle. But I know a lot about them, down to the butterfly tattooed on Billy Marriott's right shoulder to match the one tattooed on Tony Marriott's left shoulder. They are a bit of a duet.'

Barlow dropped his bantering tone. ' Keep them off hard liquor. Otherwise no woman is safe with them. Not even Christine would be.'

West bristled. ' If those dim thugs as much as –' He stopped himself.

' It's just a word to the wise,' said Barlow. ' It is up to you, Mr West, to " look to your daughter." '

West swung round. ' What did you say?'

' "Look to your daughter." It's Hamlet's advice to Polonius.'

' But why did you say it? Since when did you start spouting Shakespeare?'

' What makes you think all cops are illiterate?'

West struggled with his impatience. ' You're holding back on me.'

' Certainly. Just as you're holding back on me.'

Angrily West shouted, ' I have a right to know.'

Barlow was, if anything, angrier in his response. ' Don't talk to me about your rights. When it comes to locking you up I'll remind you of them. You have the right of any known criminal to stay silent, to refuse to answer questions.' He relaxed. ' I suppose you're exercising that right now. So be it. You are not legally obliged to say anything. In exactly the same way, exactly the same way, there is nothing in law which obliges me to share my confidences with you. So long as you're not helping me, then my conscience doesn't oblige me to help you either. Thanks for the drink.'

' You're not going?' West protested.

' Are you going to stop me?' Barlow jeered. ' I wish you'd try. Because you wouldn't succeed. And I'd get great pleasure from charging you with attempted assault. You wouldn't get further than the attempt.'

' You've got to tell me.'

' And you've got to be joking.'

The two men glared at each other. ' Stop concealing things,' said Barlow. ' Because " concealment like the worm in the back " could " feed on Christine's damask cheek." That's Shakespeare too, and very apt. Or does our mystery killer of ponies quote only from *Hamlet*?'

It was a taunt he regretted. West was quietly triumphant. ' So it was he who quoted from *Hamlet*.' Off-guard, Barlow stammered ' I didn't say so.'

West shook his head. ' But I don't hear you denying it.' He became acidly formal. ' Thank you very much, officer. You've been a great help. I'll make sure your courtesy and your thoroughness is brought to the attention of your superiors.'

Barlow stormed out of the room.

He passed a sullen, restless night and it took until the morning for him to stop being bad-tempered. When he and Superintendent Summers met in the village police station he was rueful.

' I think we'd have had to tell West, sir,' said Summers.

' Mebbe. But I'd liked to have chosen when and where. Instead I get smug – and West had me.'

' So West is hard and clever. We shall have to be harder and cleverer.'

Barlow shook his head. ' I don't think we can compete with him. I'm sure of that. He had a pretty good idea already. The bit about Shakespeare clinched it. Funny though. Somebody from his own world who quotes from the Bard. It's not likely is it? I've asked Criminal Intelligence to run through their list of West's associates with literature in mind. They weren't very hopeful. Neither am I.'

They were both getting gloomy. Nothing had emerged from the check on the prisoners released in Durham either.

Summers asked just what Barlow had learned about the threats offered to West. ' He had a telephone call a fortnight ago. A male voice he didn't recognize saying, ' I'm going to get your daughter.' Then, neatly spaced over four days he got four calls – at one am, two am, three am, and four am. No words were spoken – just the sound of laughter. So he had his number changed. Then on the same day as you got your little missive, West got a telegram. I'm having it checked but without much hope of result. It was sent from Trafalgar Square Post Office. It said " Christine will be removed in four days." And signed " *Guardian* ".'

' The right newspaper,' said Summers. ' And " removed " is a nice neutral word. West removed her from school the same day. But what brought him to us?'

Barlow said reluctantly, ' I'll have to change my car. I gather it's become conspicuous in West's circles. Odd, you see: he half-thought *we* were playing these threats on him. He's so unscrupulous himself he thinks we're as bad.'

' Does he know, or does he say, what the mystery man wants? Revenge? Or money? Or what?'

' According to West there's been no talk of ransom, no buying off the threat.'

' So we don't know his aims, let alone his identity.' Summers straightened up. ' Sir, will you define *our* aims in this?'

Barlow replied promptly. ' Two-fold. First " to protect the inno-cent " – which in this case is thirteen-year-old Christine. But second to hope, even to plan, that with villains falling out with each other we may get them, or some of them, or one of them. I'll admit it: I hope that West will involve himself, reveal himself, implicate him-self. Under stress he might.'

' He might.' Summers sounded doubtful. ' Meanwhile we're doing all we can. And your man Tucker has the house under surveillance. Actually it's time he was relieved.'

' I'll call him and cheer him up,' said Barlow. ' Maybe he'll cheer me up.' Into his personal radio he said, ' Barlow to Tucker. Routine check.'

The radio crackled Tucker's response. ' Not much to report, sir. Traffic on the road much the same as yesterday. Only one vehicle stopped near the farm. The milk lorry loaded with seven churns. Oh! The cowman's coming to get them now. He's got Christine with him.'

' She's probably getting restless tied to the house. You hang on a bit longer. Superintendent Summers is organizing a relief for you now.'

' Thank you, sir.'

Tucker heard Barlow switch off. Today he was watching the farmhouse from the outside, concealed behind a hedge on the other side of the road. Idly he watched the cowman expertly load the trailer with churns, turn the tractor and chug off to the house. Up front with him, Christine seemed to be chattering merrily.

There was no warning when one of the churns exploded with a heavy bang. The trailer seemed to leap into the air and the tractor overturned. Christine screamed shrilly.

Tucker began to run towards her but had the sense to pause and to say urgently into his radio, ' There's been an explosion. One of the milk churns. Get an ambulance. I'm off to assist.'

He was running again as he heard his message acknowledged. He tore up the drive to find Christine kneeling by the body of the cowman. It was very still. Quietly she said, ' I think poor Mr Jackson is dead.' Then she rushed into Tucker's arms wailing, ' Oh I wish it had been me. I wish it had been me.'

Tucker cradled her gently as West pounded down from the house followed by the easily identifiable ' bodyguards'. As West came towards them Tucker whispered to him, ' Watch it please. She'll crack under this strain.'

West glared at him. ' Copper, don't think I will.'

The ambulance came. The police cars came, with their uniformed men, and the forensic experts. Barlow got their preliminary reports then, with Tucker, faced West in his sanctum and said in an official tone :

' It's important you understand Mr West, that this is now a

formal investigation. Which is why Inspector Tucker is present and will be taking notes. We are now investigating a mysterious, violent death. The man Richard William Jackson was an employee of yours. What can you tell me about him?'

West shrugged. 'Nothing you don't know already. He was about fifty-five.'

'He was fifty-seven last March,' said Tucker.

Again West shrugged. 'Not far out, was I? Jackson had been working for me for seven years, as soon as I got the herd together. He was a good cowman. I understand he was a married man – separated. And with two daughters. I never met any of them.'

Barlow nodded. 'You last saw Jackson when?'

'I suppose about an hour and a half ago. I told him this morning to keep a look-out for strangers. I also told him that I didn't want Christine wandering about on her own. He asked me later if it was all right if she came with him to the gates to get the empty churns. I agreed.'

'And that was the last time you saw him?'

West could be formal too. 'I saw him after the big bang. He was dead then.'

'Mr West bent over the man, sir,' said Tucker. 'That was at 12.06, sir.'

West accepted that as an accurate timing. He seemed more relaxed now – until Barlow asked his next question. 'As far as you know, did Jackson have any enemies?' West gasped an incredulous 'What?' but Barlow went on. 'We're trying to discover who killed him. As far as you know did he have any enemies?'

As West shook his head, Barlow continued. 'We've not been able to discover any either.' He sounded genuinely puzzled. 'That's our problem you see. Who would want to kill a reliable, law-abiding, respectable cowman? Do you have any theories?'

Savagely West snapped, 'You're trying to rile me again.'

Barlow lifted an eyebrow. 'Again, sir? And how am I riling you? I'm puzzled. I've got problems. I ask very clearly and civilly if you have any theories. The Inspector will have noted all that. So, Mr West, do you have any theories? Can I have an answer please?'

'You know the answer.' West was taut with anger. Barlow was terribly bland. 'I'm counted a reasonable detective, but I'm not psychic. If you have any theories about the manner and cause of Jackson's death I'd be grateful if you'd share them.'

West was stung. He glared and said, 'You must be made of stone.'
At a nod from Barlow Tucker laid down his notebook..

Slowly Barlow quoted, ' " If you prick us, do we not bleed?" '

Helpfully Tucker said, 'From *The Merchant of Venice*, sir. By Shakespeare, sir.'

West was quaking. 'Have you heard anything else? Have you got any more of a lead?'

Barlow looked at him almost with sorrow. 'We'll postpone this interview. You're clearly overwrought. Mr Tucker, go and set down what you've got so far. And find out when the doctor thinks it will be sensible to get a formal statement from Christine.' Tucker left.

Alone with Barlow, West asked urgently, 'Have you anything else?'

'Only what you must have worked out for yourself. The explosion was cleverly contrived. The lorry was genuine. It was, I suppose the only word is hi-jacked, ten miles north of here; the driver replaced; one extra churn loaded on, and unloaded at your gate. The device was timed to go off seventeen minutes after it was set. It did. I've a feeling, it can only be a feeling, that it was meant to go off nearer the house, just to add to the confusion. I don't think it was intended for Christine.'

'Only to scare me,' said West dully.

'Or to get you to concede something. Is it much money?'

'It's not money.' West seemed to speak with absolute assurance.

'So what does he want "conceded"? Your legitimate betting shop? Your not-so-legitimate sex shop? Or your property companies?'

Levelly West replied, 'I'm admitting nothing. But any of the things you mention would mean money.'

'Man to man,' Barlow sounded as though he meant it, 'money you would pay?'

'I would.' West was definite.

'Then you're not all stone either. Let me put something to you.' Barlow was now deeply serious. 'You want to protect your daughter. So do I. I also want to lock up a ruthless, dangerous killer – who murdered an unfortunate cowman. You have theories. You have suspicions. Share them. Give us something to work on.'

Sullenly West asked, 'What about me?'

Barlow's tone was scornful. 'Try taking your own chances. Try risking your own skin, not your thirteen-year-old daughter's.'

West shook his head. ' I'm doing this for her.'

' What?' snapped Barlow, ' getting her pony killed? Nearly getting her blown up?'

All West muttered was, ' It's all for her.'

Barlow spoke with cruel deliberation. ' Then I hope she lives to enjoy it. I give up. I know when I'm beaten. Take the credit: you've licked me.'

He called loudly for Tucker and when he arrived said formally, ' We're leaving. Superintendent Summers of Mid-Wessex Constabulary will take charge of this enquiry. I'm sure he'll maintain the security check on the house and grounds, at least for the time being.'

As West sat slumped in an armchair Tucker reported that the doctor thought Christine would be fit to make a statement tomorrow, after a night's sleep.

' I hope she gets it,' said Barlow. To West he said, ' You get some sleep too.' Very savagely he added, ' " Sleep – perchance to dream." Call us if you get nightmares.'

He and Tucker were almost out of the room when in a strangled voice West uttered one word, ' Motamba.'

Barlow was puzzled. ' If that's some kind of blessing I'll say " Amen ".' But surprisingly, Tucker knew the name. ' Rolano Motamba, Minister of Finance of the Democratic Republic of Lowatenda. I saw him on television last night. He's very fluent, an Oxford graduate. Very literate.'

' He's a savage,' shouted West.

' A friend of yours?' Barlow asked politely.

West was shaking with rage. ' He'll be nobody's friend within twenty-four hours.'

Tucker had his notebook out. ' Sounds like a threat to me, sir. Better write it down.'

' Then write this down too,' said West. He pulled himself together and began to make the sort of stiff, careful statements issued at press conferences. ' I have reason to believe that Mr Rolano Motamba is in grave political trouble. His own finances are in better shape than those of his own country. He's going to be exposed.'

' Where do you fit in, sir?' asked Tucker.

' I don't.' West went on with his formal speech. ' I understand that Mr Motamba has had some dealings with a company with which I have some connection. Hence that company expects Mr

Motamba to make allegations against it. These are, of course, untrue. Anyway, I am in no way involved with that branch of the company's activities.'

Then what's the connection?' asked Tucker mildly.

'There's none.' West was not being formal now. 'It's all in that savage's crazy brain. He thinks it's my fault.'

It was Barlow's turn to ask, 'And what does he want from you? What concession?'

'I've no idea.'

Tucker took over again. 'What you've told us, sir – you know it from Mr Motamba himself?'

'I've only seen him twice in my life,' West protested. 'The last time over a year ago.'

'You may not have seen him, sir.' There was a roughness in Tucker's voice now. 'Have you heard from him?'

West paused. 'Not that I could swear to.'

'It was his voice on the telephone?' asked Barlow impatiently.

'I don't think so, officer.'

Barlow glared at West, who smiled in response. He stopped smiling when Tucker said, 'The party that Motamba belongs to is called " The Guardian Party ".'

'Bingo!' Barlow was beaming. 'West, this is your last chance. I'm not pussy-footing with you any more. I'm giving you a simple, formal caution. We believe you are deliberately impeding us in the execution of our duty, which here includes an enquiry into murder. You are holding back valuable information, misleading us, and thus compounding your offence. So get this. Tell us now what you know or you're going to be arrested.'

West shook his head. Barlow nodded to Tucker, who deliberately put his hand on West's shoulder as he recited, 'Donald West, I arrest you for impeding me in the course of my official duty. You are not obliged to say anything, but anything you do say will be taken down in writing and may be given in evidence.'

Incredulously West whispered, 'But what about Christine?'

Barlow was reassuring. 'I'll get a court order for her within an hour. She certainly needs care and protection. She'll get better care with us.'

West seemed dazed. 'I want to call my solicitor.'

'Feel free,' said Barlow casually. To Tucker he added, 'Let him make one call. Make sure it is to his solicitor. Then get him locked up. Don't do it yourself. I want you here. Christine is your responsibility.'

'What about you?' demanded West.

'Remember? I told you before. I'm not obliged to give you any information. Remember too, that I've got a clear conscience. And I'm not frightened.'

Indeed, Barlow seemed very relaxed late that evening as he sat in the inner office of the police station. By contrast Superintendent Summers was baffled. 'I don't understand, sir. On my own patch, and I don't understand what's happening. Tell me what you're doing.'

'Let me check some things first.' Barlow was very calm. 'West's daughter is legally in care, and in practice in our safe custody?'

'Yes, sir.'

'And West's arrest has been given as much publicity as possible?'

Summers lost his stiffness. 'All the publicity possible short of using the town crier and his bell. And as you instructed, this station is well-lit – every light is on. The electricity bill will be enormous.'

'Thank you.' Barlow smiled broadly. 'With all that done why haven't you offered me a drink?'

Summers was again taken off-guard. 'Why haven't I – ? Shall I send out for some, sir?'

'No need.' Barlow moved to his overcoat hanging on a peg behind the door and produced a handsome hip-flask. He apologized for having only the water glass to offer Summers. He himself used the small silver cup which covered the flask. 'This is good brandy. So let's sort of gather our roses while we may.'

They each took a sip, and Summers had just composed himself to ask for some explanation of Barlow's behaviour when there came a loud, deliberate knocking on the back door.

'Who can that – ?' began Summers, but Barlow was on his feet. 'I hope I know who it is.' He produced the personal radio from the desk drawer and switched it on. 'Leave me with him please. In case I'm right, or even more in case I'm wrong, keep a sharp ear open.'

As Summers left Barlow braced himself and unlocked the back door. Framed in the doorway was an enormous Negro, grave, and impeccably dressed in dark jacket and pin-striped trousers. He said, 'Mr Barlow I presume?'

Without a flicker came the reply, 'Mr Motamba I expect.'

The visitor stepped inside. 'Not an impressive room.'

Barlow agreed. 'Only an operational outpost. But if you'd come to the front door you would have been announced.'

'My dear fellow, announcements come later.' Motamba had a grand air to which Barlow responded. 'Do sit down. I'm short of glasses but – '

'It would be a privilege to share yours!'

Barlow poured a tot and handed it over. 'Be my guest.'

After sniffing it delicately Motamba swallowed the tot in one. 'That's exactly what I have in mind, old man: to be your country's guest.'

Barlow looked at him levelly. 'In prison?'

'For a while that may be necessary.' Motamba sounded very reasonable. 'I am here, sir, to claim political asylum.'

Barlow hesitated. 'Politics are not much in my line, Minister. But of course I will note your request.'

Motamba smiled. 'I assume my request has already been noted outside.' He glanced at Barlow's radio. 'Primitive apparatus. Not an impressive room.'

Barlow switched off the radio. 'I can do better at the Home Office. Would you like to go now?'

'Not to the Home Office. I thought you suggested prison.'

'Minister – it is likely to be for a long time.'

Motamba did not bat an eyelid. 'Very probably.'

Barlow fell back on formality. 'I need a witness to this conversation.'

'Feel free,' said Motamba with a wave of his hand.

Tucker entered as Barlow called for him. Introduced to Motamba he said cheerfully, 'I saw you on television last night, sir.'

Motamba gave a languid nod. 'Too black and badly lit. Which is my corruption of a phrase by the inestimable Oscar Wilde. He dismissed the countryside as "too green and badly lit".'

Barlow smiled. 'Wilde had two sons. He had no daughter to "look to".'

Motamba smiled. 'Well done. I need to know one thing please. West's arrest is, as you might say, for real?'

Tucker explained. 'He's been charged with impeding us in the execution of our duty.'

'I like "execution".' There was a sudden chill in the air as Motamba continued. 'It is otherwise a holding charge.'

Barlow shrugged. ' If we have anything else to hold him on.'

' Have no fear of that.' Motamba reached for the brandy flask and poured himself another tot. He drank it then composed himself. ' I am surrendering to you. So you will please agree an inventory of my possessions.' He produced them as he listed them. ' Item: one hundred and four pounds in pound notes, not new. Seventy-five pence in loose change. Item: one diplomatic passport. Item: one gold watch. Item: three diamond rings.' He lifted one of them to his lips before laying it on the desk and continuing: ' Then come two copies of one statement on how to kill a pony. Two copies of one statement on how to hi-jack a milk lorry. The statements contain the names of the perpetrators of both actions.

' Finally, one original document signed by Donald West which any intelligent police officer should be capable of making good use of, together with a certified cheque for one hundred thousand pounds made out to me by Donald West.'

Barlow stared at it. ' But this is dated only yesterday.'

' And I thought you were intelligent.' There was total scorn in Motamba's voice. ' It's very simple. West paid me. He thought I would take the money to keep quiet about him.' He took a deep breath. ' I am crooked. I have swindled and betrayed my own country, I did it with my eyes open. But not without guidance, not without prompting, not without West's expert help and urging. The scheme came unstuck. It was my scheme as much as West's. But I was prepared, I am prepared, to face the consequences. West is not. West is not an honourable man.'

' Does an honourable man kill?' asked Barlow.

' In my country, Chief Superintendent, we are not sensitive about animals.'

' But what about the cowman?' snapped Tucker.

Motamba shrugged. ' We are not sensitive about peasants either. Can't you both understand? I have nothing I wish to hide. I have everything to reveal. West was not honourable.' There was a long pause before Motamba went on solemnly. ' It is the cause. It is the cause my soul.'

' Get all this written down fast.' Barlow was urgent. ' Get it down fast.'

Motamba smiled. ' You understand at last.'

It was Tucker who stammered, ' Othello killed himself.'

Motamba smiled once more and reached for one of his diamond

rings. But his hand was already stiff – and he clattered heavily to the floor.

He was dead by the time the ambulance arrived. Summers watched the body taken away and muttered, 'A messy end. Very messy.' Tucker groaned. 'All the paper work.' Barlow gazed at them. 'West is locked up. Now who'll look to his daughter?'

John Wainwright

THE MAN WHO GRASSED

TUESDAY

11.35 pm.

The shooting took place in a basement club; an upholstered sewer one of the get-rich-quick boys had geared to trend-setters. No better, no worse, than a thousand others. A hole in the ground where the prophets of psychedelia gathered for their nightly lift-off; where LSD wasn't an overdraft; where fornication, pornography and perversion were solemnly discussed as art-forms.

That sort of club.

Nobody heard the shooting – the row from a score of loud-mouthed arguments backed by boosted high-powered jazz, was guaranteed to drown anything short of an atomic explosion . . . and the barrel was tucked into a cushion when the killer squeezed the trigger.

Nobody saw the shooting – the capricious shadows from the mobiles rippled darkness across the room and the lights were low wattage and coloured . . . it heightened the intimacy and hid the grime.

The killer almost got away with it. He was half-way to the door when he heard the scream. Not the hyena-shriek of a doped-up tart's appreciation of a risqué joke. Not the mock-modest yell of a street walker telling the world she's being seduced. A scream. A *real* scream. It held the terror from which nightmares bloom; it cut through the other noise like a violin note shattering a glass goblet.

It brought the manager to the door, with a pug-nosed bouncer at his elbow.

It turned the killer from his intended route and took him to where other members stared around and wondered.

It sent the bouncer scrambling up the stairs, into the rain-wet streets, looking for ' the law '.

11.45 pm.

Sergeant Hobson swung his cape back, across his shoulders, and said: 'Anybody left?'

'Not since we . . .' The manager had difficulty finding the right words. 'Not since she was – she was . . .'

'Stay here.' Hobson spoke to the constable. 'Nobody in. Nobody out.' The constable nodded.

'What other rooms?' asked Hobson. 'Apart from this main room, where else?'

'The – the store-room.' The manager's hand fluttered. 'The office. The toilets. That's all. I'll show you . . .'

'I'll find 'em.' Hobson turned to the bouncer and said: 'Can you use a telephone?'

The bouncer looked hurt.

'Dial nine-nine-nine,' said Hobson. 'Ask for "police". Tell 'em where you are – what's happened. Then get back here. Make sure nobody leaves.'

Sergeant Hobson moved into the crowd; deliberately and without apparent haste – middle-aged sanity elbowing its way through youthful eccentricity – uniformed phlegmatism soothing non-conformist nerves . . .

11.55 pm.

The bouncer had used the word 'murder'. The police machine had accepted the word at its face value and gone into action. It had been like pushing the throttles of an aeroplane through the safety-gate; a sudden upsurge of power, a shudder as the machine took the strain, then high-speed activity. The word was passed along radio waves; to patrol cars: to panda vans: to walkie-talkie sets. It was sent along telephone wires; to Hallsworth Hill DHQ: to Headquarters CID Office: to Detective Chief Superintendent Raff's bedside telephone. Police officers and vehicles converged on the club like iron filings moving towards a magnet. The area was cordoned-off; not merely the club – the whole block of which the club was a small part. The members had been herded into one corner, well away from the body. The subdued lighting had been swamped by harsh glare from unshaded bulbs – lighting installed for the benefit of cleaners, and rarely seen by customers – and the result was a visual hangover; the mobiles looked tatty and gimmicky; the alcoves looked like horse-boxes with grubby seats.

Hobson had remained in charge until the arrival of a uniformed inspector. The uniformed inspector had held the reins until the arrival of the Hallsworth Hill Divisional Detective Inspector – Detective Inspector Deverill. Deverill had had his few moments of glory then Raff arrived and, with Raff, Collins the Hallsworth Hill Divisional Superintendent.

Raff kept his hands in his pockets, eyed the corpse and said: ' She's dead? You've checked?'

' As mutton,' said Deverill.

' One of those beauties?' Raff glanced at the mob of gaping, muttering customers.

' Nobody's been allowed to leave.'

' Simple elimination,' murmured Collins.

Raff grunted, returned his attention to the body and said: ' Who is she?'

' Lilly Marsh. Known as " Lilly the Lush " – apparently for obvious reasons. Been a member about two years. Runs around with a gang – same clique all the time. Plays fast and loose. But – er – there's some talk of a special boy friend . . . Danny Shutt.'

' Again!' Raff's eyes widened into a glare.

Collins smiled and said: ' Knowing Shutt, that'll come as a surprise.'

' Is he here?' asked Raff.

' Yeah.' Deverill nodded. ' With the rest.'

Raff stared his disgust at the corpse for a second or two, sighed, then said: ' What about the brain-drain?'

' They've been told,' said Deverill. ' Fingerprints. Photography. Forensic Science. Map Drawing.'

' Ballistics?' asked Raff.

' No.'

' Better get 'em. It's a shooting. They'll sulk if they're not in on the act.' He turned his back on the corpse and said: ' An office . . . is there one?'

' The manager's,' suggested Deverill.

' That'll do. Feed 'em in, one at a time. Start with the manager – it's his office. Check on names – nobody leaves here till we know for sure who they are and where they live. Search 'em . . . and I *mean* search 'em. Get a couple of policewomen. Use the respective toilets. Not the pocket-patting routine. I want 'em searched to the skin.'

'They'll object,' said Deverill. 'Some of 'em . . . they're that kind.'

'Let 'em.'

'They won't all object, inspector.' Collins grinned and added: 'Some of them'll enjoy it.'

WEDNESDAY

4.00 am.

Raff said: 'All right . . . so, she was pregnant.' He blew out his cheeks and shook his head, wearily. 'She seems to have told everybody in the whole bloody club. I wonder she didn't put a notice in the local newsrag.'

'Modern morality,' drawled Collins.

'And motive for murder.'

'As always,' agreed Collins.

Sergeant Hobson sniffed and said: 'She was a tart . . . that's a fact.'

Collins said: 'Free love, sergeant. You're not with it.'

'Free *everything*,' grunted Raff.

Deverill poked his head round the door and said: 'Ready for the next one, sir?'

'Found anything yet?' asked Raff.

'No, sir – not yet.'

'There's a gun, somewhere.'

'Yeah . . . we'll find it.'

'Keep looking.' Raff swallowed a yawn and said: 'Who's next?'

'Danny Shutt.'

'My cup runneth over,' sighed Raff. 'Send him in.'

He had long blond hair and laughing, mocking eyes; his clothes were trendy, but expensive; his main occupation was driving policemen up the wall; he was a scoundrel, but a happy scoundrel – a likeable scoundrel.

He bounced into the room, beamed at the three officers and said: 'Hiya, Mister Raff.'

'Sit down.' Raff motioned to a chair. 'And let's try to keep things above the Keystone Cop level – eh?'

'Oh, sure. Sure, Mister Raff.' Solemnity dropped across his face like a curtain . . . with spy-holes from behind which his eyes twinkled.

'Daniel Shutt?' Raff asked the opening question in a flat, toneless voice.

'Yes, sir.'

'Twenty-two years? Single?'

'Yes, sir.'

'Address – forty-three, Parkside Avenue?'

'Yes, sir.'

'General dealer?'

'Yes, s . . .'

'What *is* a " general dealer "? ' asked Collins, innocently.

'Well – he's a . . . He's a dealer. That's all. He deals in anything. Everything. General.'

'Very lucid,' murmured Collins.

'It pays well?' asked Raff.

'I get by.'

'With other things?'

'Such as what, sir?'

'Such as women.'

'It has been known.'

'Lilly Marsh, for example?'

'The one out there?' Shutt jerked his head.

'That's why we aren't in bed,' said Collins.

'You knew her?' asked Raff.

'Sure – I knew her,' admitted Shutt.

Collins said: 'For the record. Explain what you mean by the word " knew ". In more detail than your definition of " general dealer ", please.'

'I knew her,' said Shutt. 'I've slept with her – plenty of times. We all have . . . most of us.'

'D'you put her in the family way?' asked Raff, quietly.

'I dunno. It's possible.'

'Is it?' Raff shifted an eyebrow a fraction of an inch higher.

'I'm being honest, Mister Raff.'

'Wise,' said Collins.

Raff added: ' And it makes a change.'

Shutt allowed the solemnity to slip a little and said: 'Ah . . . now you're getting at me.'

That was how the interrogation started; gently, as between friends, and with the mere feather-touch of officialdom. Archaeologists use the same technique; they move a hundred tons of rubble, a handful at a time, to reach one perfect relic; they use a camel-hair brush where less patient men would use a spade.

Raff and Collins were the archaeologists. They examined every word – put every nuance under a magnifying glass – in their dig for the truth. They were a good team. Hobson was their recorder and he, too, knew his job.

There was no chronological order to the questioning . . . only questions. Chronology pre-supposes the existence of time, and this was a murder inquiry. Time is a fantasy; a walled garden in which to luxuriate or suffer. It has boundaries . . . a place – a birth – a life – a death. Murder inquiries have no such boundaries; sleep is an irritating interruption; death is a mere change of interrogator. The questions are asked, and re-asked, and re-asked again until the truth is there . . . naked, vile and absolute.

6.00 am.
Shutt said: 'Don't we eat?'

He'd been questioned before. Many times. He was *always* being questioned. He was the gap-filler for every jack in the city . . . 'Nothing else to do? Okay – go lean on Danny Shutt. He might cough something.' He didn't mind. It was a game. He knew every copper on the force – was on first-name terms with some of them. He'd been questioned scores of times . . . and no hard feelings.

But not like this.

These two – Raff and Collins – played him like a ping-pong ball; patted him to each other with alternate questions. They didn't give him time to think. He was due to drop a stumer. He couldn't help himself. They'd already wheedled things out of him he shouldn't have said. He was worried.

He played for time and asked: 'Don't we eat?'

'Hungry?' Raff sounded surprised.

'Peckish.'

Collins smiled and said: 'They'll give you a good breakfast. Anything you want.'

'Not these days,' said Raff.

'Oh, no.' Collins sounded apologetic – as if he'd forgot something he should have remembered. 'Sorry . . . not these days.'

'Hey, what . . .' Shutt pressed his lips together to moisten them. 'What's that supposed to mean?'

'You're hungry,' Raff reminded him.

'Peckish,' corrected Collins.

Raff said: 'Let's forget food for a minute. Talk about murder.'

'Look, Mister Raff – I've told you all I know. I've been honest.'

'Nothing.'

'Eh?'

'Nothing,' repeated Raff. 'Nothing we didn't know. Nothing we couldn't have found out.'

'Now,' said Collins, quietly, 'we'll move on to things we don't know . . . things you can tell us.'

8.00 am.

Shutt was sweating. He knew it. He could taste the salt of sweat every time he licked his lips. He could feel it creeping down the side of his face – past his ear – like a thread of ice. He knew Raff and Collins could see the sweat; that, to them, it was liquid guilt oozing from his pores.

Raff said: ' She was carrying your child.'

'Oh no, Mister Raff – I didn't say that. Only that . . .'

'She might have been.' Collins ended the sentence for him.

'Yes, sir . . . she might have been.'

'Assuming she was.'

'No, sir. That . . .'

'Assuming she was,' insisted Raff. 'Would you have married her?'

Shutt stared – as if the question had overtones of insanity.

'It sometimes happens,' said Collins. 'In some circles it's even considered the right thing.'

'Did you . . .' Shutt hesitated, then said: ' Did you *know* her?'

'That's no answer,' said Raff.

'Yes, Mister Raff. It is!' He was panting a little; leaning forward in his chair; trying to force belief through to them. ' She – she was a bitch. A whore. A bag. She – she'd sleep with *anybody*. Christ! You don't marry people like that.'

'What do you do?' asked Raff. ' Shoot 'em?'

They waited for him to condemn himself. Calm. Stone-faced. Silent. They watched the one-word denial reach his eyes, but refuse to be uttered. They saw the panic, the conquering of the panic and the residue of fear. He wasn't cocky any more. The self-assurance had been wrung out of him. The friendliness was lickspittle; the humility was obsequiousness.

They'd crushed him . . . and they waited.

He swallowed and said: 'Mister Raff, I – I . . .' Then his throat dried up and the words ended in a whispered croak.

They waited.

He dropped his chin on to his chest. He couldn't meet their eyes when he mumbled: 'Honest, Mister Raff – *I* didn't shoot her.'

A grass-green recruit wouldn't have believed him.

Raff said: 'Caution him, sergeant.'

Hobson spoke as if he was reciting it from a book; no feeling – no meaning. 'Daniel Shutt, you're not obliged to say anything unless you wish to do so. What you say will be taken down in writing, and may be given in evidence.'

Shutt whispered: 'You bastards!'

10.30 am.

Deverill snarled: 'The bloody thing has to be *somewhere*.'

Raff didn't argue. He stood alongside the seat with the chalked outline of the body and watched the 'specialist services' go about their business. He wondered why the width of the bar-flap was important; the Map Drawing Section evidently thought it was . . . they seemed to be measuring it to the last thousandth of an inch.

A voice called: 'D'you mind, sir!'

Raff looked round. Photography Section wanted to take another shot; a thin faced, arty-arty type smiled apologetically from behind a tripod-mounted camera.

Raff said: 'Come on, inspector. We're in the way.'

'We've found everything.' Deverill's disgust reached caricature proportions. 'So help me, you name it – we've found it. Dope – every sort I know . . . and some I've never heard of. Flick-knives. Coshes. And pictures – my god, what pictures.'

'But no gun?' They reached a corner of the room and Raff strolled through an open door, into the store-room.

'No gun,' agreed Deverill.

'You've checked the toilets?'

'Superintendent Raff.' Deverill sounded offended. 'Wherever else, it's not in the toilets. That was the first place. We've been into, under, round and through everything. I've even had my hand down the bloody things.'

'I believe you,' said Raff. 'It's not in the toilets. What about this place?'

'Not here,' said Deverill, sadly. 'Not unless it's under the flag-stones . . . and nobody had time to do *that*. Y'see that door.' He nodded at the iron-plated fire exit. 'We've had a copper stationed outside there since ten minutes after it happened – in case somebody tried to nip out and sling it. Nothing!'

'And those ten minutes?' asked Raff.

'All right.' Deverill spread out his hands. 'Supposing – just *supposing*. He'd be a nutter. Those three bolts – top, bottom and middle. That damned great lock. They were all fastened when we arrived. I know . . . I checked 'em. So – *supposing* – that means he went outside, dumped the gun, then came back in again. He'd be a nutter.'

'He might have been missed.'

'In this dump?' The DI's indignation encompassed everything. 'You can hardly see anybody – much less miss anybody. And half of 'em are stoned out of their minds.'

'All right,' said Raff, 'he's a nutter. He went out. Dumped the gun. Came back. Locked and bolted the door. So?'

'He's catered for,' sighed Deverill. 'They're searching. A hundred-yard radius. Every street, every garden, every room, every gulley. Everywhere. They won't find anything . . . but they're searching.'

'The roofs? The spouting?'

'The lot,' said Deverill.

'What about an accomplice?' mused Raff. 'Somebody to lock and bolt the door, after he's scarpered?'

'No.' Deverill shook his head. 'That's out. Sergeant Hobson – PC Adams . . . they were first on the scene. They were on their toes. Nobody came in here. Nobody went out. They're sure. So is the manager. The time element kills it . . . nobody had *time*.'

'There is a gun,' said Raff.

'Yes, sir.' The DI knew what was coming; he didn't blame Raff – it was part of the system.

Raff said: 'Take a break – have a meal . . . then find it.'

12.30 pm.
Text books are written about murder inquiries. And other books; pseudo-realistic crime novels: 'Alone-I-Did-It' biographies and autobiographies of retired senior police officers. A few are good, some are bad, the majority are rambling and mediocre. They rarely

mention the unsolved killings – the failures. They never give the criminal's point of view.

He has one.

Daniel Shutt had one.

He sat on the bed-boards in a police cell and tried to figure his chances of getting away with it. They weren't healthy . . . not with a man like Raff treading on his tail.

He didn't hate Raff. He didn't even dislike him. Come to that, he didn't dislike *any* copper. Why the hell should he? It was as stupid as a punter hating a bookie. A man lived his own life; he went bent – he knew what he was doing. Nobody went bent by mistake. Nobody was forced to go bent . . . not really. If you got away with it, you were wide. If you didn't, you were a fink. And the coppers moved in on the finks.

It was what they were paid for – their job. It wasn't a crusade, for Christ's sake! A job. That's all. If nobody went bent they'd be on the bread-line.

That's why they were always friendly. A touch of schmaltz, here and there . . . but you could always tell kidology from the real thing. And nobody had ever laid a finger on him. Nobody had ever threatened him. *Ever*. Even when they knew, but couldn't prove it, and were choked to the eyeballs. They'd talked. They'd asked questions. They'd called him a liar – but politely . . . that's all.

And, what the hell? They'd been right!

So Danny Shutt didn't dislike coppers. Even now.

All right, so they pushed their weight around sometimes. But somebody else always pushed first. The yobs. The tearaways. The minders. A man airs his muscles – he shouldn't gripe if somebody has bigger muscles than this. That wasn't Danny Shutt's way. He knew his limitations. He kept his muscles tucked away under the padding of his jacket. That way, he didn't get hurt . . . only talked to.

Jesus wept, he even *liked* coppers!

They didn't double up on you. They stood there, in their big, size ten boots, and bawled you out – then handed you a snout . . . even when somebody was on their back and driving them like the clappers. They were overgrown kids. They felt sorry for you. You handled more lolly in a year than they handled in a lifetime . . . and they still felt sorry for you.

They were so bloody *innocent*!

A single tear left Daniel Shutt's eye and rolled slowly down his cheek. He was heartbroken.

Because he liked policemen . . . and knew he couldn't get away with it.

4.30 pm.

Raff tapped the Club Register and said: ' This is as useful as " The Daily Liar ". According to this, half the damned population are called " Smith ". The other half share " Brown " and " Jones " between 'em.'

' It's that sort of joint,' said Deverill, wearily.

' There are,' murmured Collins, ' odd flashes of humour. One member gives his – possibly her – name as " R. U. Gayme ".'

' Hilarious,' grunted Raff. He turned to Deverill and said: ' You've had – er – words with the manager?'

' He doesn't know whether it's punched, bored or counter-sunk,' growled Deverill.

' But he can't help?'

' No, sir. Those at the club, last night – we have them nailed . . . names, addresses, the lot. Those who weren't there . . .' He nodded at the register. ' Like you say – that doesn't help.'

' And no gun, yet?'

Deverill said: ' No, sir,' and left it at that.

They were in Collins's office at Hallsworth Hill DHQ. Raff, Collins, Deverill and Sergeant Hobson. It was not an arranged meeting. Collins, Deverill and Hobson worked from that building – it was their ' nick '. Raff was there from the Headquarters CID Office, to check on the inquiry; to see if he could help, if necessary, to ginger things up. They had met and an unofficial ' conference ' had developed in Collins's office.

Collins said: ' We have the pathologist's report. She was approximately four months pregnant. Oh, and – er – she died from a gunshot wound.'

' She's better off dead,' said Hobson, quietly.

Raff said: ' Nobody's better off dead, sergeant . . . not that way.'

' Ballistics say a .38,' murmured Deverill. ' Pretty well every pistol and revolver manufacturer makes a .38.'

' Some people get their money very easily,' said Raff, nastily.

There was a silence; as if frustration, disgust and annoyance had combined to smother conversation. It was not a pleasant silence – it was awkward and unhappy. Collins took a cigarette from his case, fitted it into a briar holder and lighted it.

He returned the lighter to his pocket and said: 'What about Shutt?'

'Has he said anything?' asked Raff.

'Not yet.'

'He knows the ropes,' said Deverill. 'He hasn't been charged, yet. He knows . . . we aren't dead sure, till we charge him.'

Raff said: 'We're light on evidence. We've motive and opportunity. We need means . . . we need the gun.'

Deverill was fed up with saying it, but he said it again. 'We're searching, sir. If it's there, we'll find it.'

Raff grunted.

'Then we can prove it was Shutt,' said Collins. It wasn't a question. It wasn't a statement of fact. It was a remark – with the hint of a question-mark tagged on to the last word.

'Can't we?' asked Raff.

Collins said: 'Probably. But it's not in character.'

'Okay – so he stepped out of character, and shot the Marsh woman . . . it's still murder.'

'We're all potential murderers,' said Deverill.

Collins said: 'Yes – I've read that, too . . . somewhere.'

'You saw him,' said Raff. 'You were there. Guilty as hell. That was my opinion.'

Hobson nodded.

'Certainly not innocent,' agreed Collins.

'So . . . guilty.'

Collins frowned and said: 'But, no admission.'

Deverill said: 'He's never admitted a thing in his life. *That* 'ud be out of character.'

'He's never faced murder before,' murmured Collins.

Raff watched the Hallsworth Hill superintendent's face and said: 'Motive. Opportunity. Means . . . when we find the gun. You're still not happy?' The question was flecked with impatience.

'I think it's possible,' said Collins. 'No more than that.'

'We don't decide.' Raff picked up some typed foolscap sheets from the desk top. 'They're all here. Ninety-odd . . . almost a hundred of 'em. Thrill-seekers. Dopies. Oddballs. Would-be intellectuals. All right – some of 'em *couldn't* commit murder. It needs guts . . . something some of 'em haven't got. But one of 'em *did*. We

don't decide. We pick who we think – stand him in front of a jury –
let them decide. I think Danny Shutt.' He dropped the sheets back
on to the desk top.

Collins shrugged.

The silence returned. This time it held pique and unreasonable
resentment.

Raff walked to the window. He pushed his hands into his pockets;
turned hunched shoulders on the other three officers. He watched the
rain; scowling – as if nature, too, was an illogical antagonist.

He stared at the weather and growled: 'Bring him up. We'll
charge him.'

4.50 pm.

Shutt seemed to have aged. The expensive clothes looked creased
and second-hand. The fancy hair style was like broken quills. He
walked into the office, and they knew he was licked; it was in his
stance: in his eyes: in his expression.

They were surprised . . . but not too surprised. They'd seen it
happen before. A man can stand interrogation; he can answer
questions for hours on end, and only give the answers he wants to
give – match cunning against cunning and personality against personality. But put him in a cell; let him live with himself a few hours;
let imagination and uncertainty crowd in from outside; let conscience
and guilty knowledge eat its way into his brain.

Then give him a chance to talk.

He'll answer questions before they're even asked!

Therefore, they were not too surprised . . . only surprised that it
had happened to Danny Shutt.

Raff said: 'Sit down, Shutt,' and his voice held gentle, but
solemn, authority.

Shutt nodded and folded himself into a chair. He sat forward,
with his hands clasped between his knees.

'You've already been cautioned,' said Raff. 'We'll repeat it, if
necessary – so you'll have no doubts.'

'No, sir. It doesn't matter.' The voice was heavy. Heartbroken.

'You have the right to call a solicitor.'

'I don't need a solicitor.'

'Think about it . . . we're going to charge you.'

Shutt looked up and said: 'I didn't do it, Mister Raff. On the
grave of my mother, I didn't do it.'

'We think you did, Danny,' said Deverill. 'You'd a reason.'

'Because she was expecting?'

Raff said: 'It's been good enough reason many times.'

'Oh, for Christ's sake!' Shutt shook his head at their stupidity –
at their unwillingness to see reason.

'I think you need a solicitor,' said Collins.

'*I* think I need my bloody head examining . . . for letting it go
this far.' The words were almost a snarl; self-disgust bonded to self-
pity. He said: 'You really are going to charge me, Mister Raff?'

'That's why you're here.'

'It isn't a come-on? You're not pulling a blinder?'

'It's murder, Danny. When it's murder, we don't bluff . . . believe
me.'

'That means you'll prove it.' Quietly spoken words and a sardonic
twist of the mouth. 'You'll prove black's white. You'll pull every
trick in the book . . . you'll prove I shot her.'

'We'll try,' agreed Raff.

'All right.' The sigh seemed to make his whole body shudder.
'I'll cough.'

'It is murder,' Collins reminded him. 'You may regret not having
a solic . . .'

'I don't need *anybody*!' The fury of self-hatred flared his nostrils
– blazed his eyes – brought spittle to his mouth corner. 'I'm going
to grass. For the first time in my life, I'm going to grass. I thought I
wouldn't have to. I thought I . . . Christ knows what I thought. But
I don't need a bloody audience.' He caught the anger; controlled it
until it was only a tremor in his voice. He said: 'I didn't shoot her.
He slipped into the store-room.'

Deverill said: 'Nobody went into the . . .'

'You weren't *there*.' The anger notched up again; silenced Deverill.
'The bint screamed . . . then everybody was looking at the body.
He – he thought nobody'd seen him.'

'Ah, but he was wrong,' said Raff. 'You'd seen him. Old Hawk-
eye Shutt . . . he'd seen everything.'

'Meaning you don't believe me?'

'What do you think?'

He met Raff's eyes and said: 'I think you're making a mistake,
sir. That's what I think. I think you'd be wise to forget this one.' He
was pleading but, in some odd way, not pleading for himself . . . not
only for himself.

Raff said: 'You must think we're soft in the head, Shutt.'

'No, sir.' He spoke softly – solemnly. 'You don't mean that, Mister Raff. You've known me a long time.'

'Too long.'

'I've never . . . Y'know what I mean – I've never done dirt on a copper in my life. Never wanted to. It's not . . .' His voice trailed off and he shook his head; he could con folding money from a sucker any day of the week, but he couldn't make these people understand.

Raff said: 'Are you telling us that you love all bobbies? That our policemen are wonderful?' The questions were heavy with sarcasm.

'Something like that,' muttered Shutt.

'Oh, for God's sake!'

'Not love them,' murmured Collins. 'But, at least, not dislike them.'

'Yes, sir.' There was eagerness in his voice; as if the Hallsworth Hill superintendent was a sudden and unexpected ally. He said: 'You know what I mean, sir. It ain't a war. Not unless you want it to be. Not unless you're crazy. We – we know each other . . . know what everybody's there for. So why gripe? Why *not* like each other?'

'Why not?' agreed Collins.

Raff said: 'So, now you like us.'

'Yes, sir.'

'Okay . . . tell us where the gun is.'

'Look, Mister Raff, I keep . . .'

'Stop wasting everybody's time. Cut the hearts and flowers – get down to how, and when, and why you killed her . . . then we'll *all* like each other.'

'I didn't kill her!' The desperation was back in his voice. 'I didn't have to kill her. She didn't try it on me. She'd more sense. Maybe it was my kid – I don't know . . . she didn't know.' He paused; looked at Collins: then Deverill: then Hobson: then back to Raff again, and said: 'She didn't want a husband . . . Christ Almighty, you don't think she wanted a husband! Pipe and slippers? All that crap? She didn't want a husband, Mister Raff. She wanted a schmoll – somebody she could put the black on. He . . . (He shrugged) I dunno – I think he'd have married her . . . whether it was his kid or not. He was cushy enough. But not her. She was too bloody twisted for that. She wanted somebody she could screw – for a long time . . . for the rest of her life, maybe. He had to kill her. She *made* him.'

'Danny.' Deverill spoke quietly – patiently. 'You don't know what you're saying.'

'So help me! I . . .'

'We've checked everybody in the club, last night. Checked and double-checked. Everybody. They're all there.' Deverill tapped the foolscap sheets with his forefinger.

'He was a loner,' said Shutt. 'He didn't belong. He didn't mix.'

Raff said: 'Forget it, Danny. He doesn't exist . . . and you know it.'

'You're wrong, Mister Raff.' He was suffering; his face was distorted – as if the words were pushing physical pain into his body. 'He was there. He shot her. He slipped into the store-room. Nobody saw . . .'

'Nobody went into that damned store-room,' interrupted Deverill. The patience had left his voice; he'd had enough – what with the blasted gun . . . and now this! He rasped: 'We're not mugs. When we say something, we're *sure*. Sergeant Hobson checked the store-room. I checked the bloody store-room . . . personally. It was empty. Nobody went in. Nobody came out.'

'He didn't come out,' whispered Shutt.

'How the hell can he . . .'

'I didn't want to do this, Mister Hobson.' Shutt wasn't listening to Deverill.

Sergeant Hobson nodded; a meaningless, heartbroken movement of the head.

'It's – it's . . . I liked him, Mister Hobson. He's a nice kid. And – I like *you*.'

'I'll fetch him. If you don't mind, sir. Not tell his mother. Not . . .' The voice choked and stopped. For the moment, they didn't recognize it as Hobson's voice. It was empty – lifeless. It said: 'I didn't know. I didn't even know he was a member. Not till . . . . Not till he was there. In the store-room. Then, I . . .' The voice stumbled, then stopped again.

Shutt closed his eyes and said: 'I'm sorry, Mister Hobson. Honest to God. . . . I'm sorry.'

'It's not . . .' Hobson tried to speak again, faltered then said: 'He was there. In the store-room. I – I locked the fire door after him. If I'd only . . .' His voice trailed off, then he spoke to Raff. 'Let me bring him in, sir. Please! Just me. He'll come. He'll bring the gun. He'll not – he'll not make things worse.'

Raff nodded.

They watched Hobson leave the office; slowly; brokenly; each step a mental agony. He closed the door gently – like the quiet ending of a life.

' His son?' asked Collins.

' Who else?' Shutt's voice was ugly and bitter. ' For Christ's sake, who else? Who else would he have done it for?' He took a deep breath, then sobbed: ' The bitch! The lousy, rotten *bitch*!'

Hulbert Footner

THE KING
OF THE GIGOLOS

WHEN MADAME STOREY AND I arrived at Monte Carlo she registered us at the Hôtel de Paris as Mrs Renfrew and Miss Renfrew. I was to pass as her sister-in-law for the time being. She wanted to avoid the attentions of society and the press.

But she couldn't get away with it. I noticed that the clerk looked at her hard and consulted a photograph under his desk. Presently an elegant gentleman came bustling up and introduced himself as *Monsieur le directeur*. Bowing like a jack-knife he ushered us with his own magnificent presence to a beautiful suite on the second floor. I am sure they were the best rooms in the house; imperial suite; millionaire's love-nest.

'*Ah, très belle!*' said Madame Storey, looking around her. 'But much too grand for me, monsieur. I can't afford it.'

'*Non! Non!*' he protested, waving his hands. 'You misunderstand, madame. Your privacy will be respected, but we know who you are. You shall be the guest of the principality of Monaco as long as you will honour us. His Highness the Prince has commanded it!'

'Nice of him!' said Madame Storey.

When the little man had vanished in a cloud of compliments, she said to me dryly, 'Something tells me there's a pickaninny in this elegant woodpile, my Bella!'

However, the rooms were lovely, a corner suite with windows on one side looking out on the Casino and the gardens, and on the other the ineffable blue sea. Whatever they may say, the old Paris is still one of *the* hotels in the world, and they went all out for us. Bellboys arrived in a procession bringing baskets of flowers, fruit, boxes of chocolates.

Presently, as if to give point to Madame Storey's words, another elegant gentleman arrived in our salon, less showy than the first, but better style. *Prominent Executive* was written all over him, or whatever the French equivalent may be; but I shall refer to our caller merely as Monsieur B.

He kissed our hands and when the inevitable compliments had been delivered, came right down to business. 'This lady,' he asked politely, looking at me, 'may I speak before her?'

'My secretary, Miss Brickley,' said Madame Storey. 'She is present at all interviews.'

'Nothing could be more opportune than your visit to Monte Carlo at this time,' said Monsieur B. enthusiastically. 'I have read so much of your successes in solving intricate crimes. Of all people in the world you are the one I most wish to consult with. Professionally, I mean.'

'But I'm on my vacation,' objected Madame Storey.

'No matter! No matter! You can deal with this affair without interfering in the least with your pleasures.'

'What is it?' she asked.

His face turned grave. 'There is a gang of young men operating here,' he said, 'what shall I say – gigolos. Every day ladies are being blackmailed and in some cases robbed. It culminated last week in the suicide of a lady of title here in one of our hotels.'

'I hadn't heard of it,' said Madame Storey.

'We kept it out of the papers,' he said, 'but of course it's a matter of common gossip. People say naturally that she lost all she possessed at the gaming tables. But that is not so. She was betrayed, robbed and blackmailed by these scoundrels, and the unfortunate lady could not face her family.'

Madame Storey was not attracted by the case. 'Gigolos?' she said, running up her eyebrows. 'Surely that's a matter for your police.'

'They are helpless,' said Monsieur B., spreading out his hands. 'When we make an arrest there is never any evidence because the victim will not testify. When these young men become known to us we can put them on the train. But soon they return. Or others take their places. We can forbid them to enter the Casino, the Sporting Club or the hotels under our management, but they pick up their victims outside. And if they suspect that the eye of the police is on them, they tempt the infatuated women to accompany them to Menton, or Nice, or Cannes, where they are out of our jurisdiction.'

Madame Storey sent a droll glance in my direction. Evidently Monte Carlo was losing business. That was the real rub.

'The gigolos, in themselves, they are nothing,' Monsieur B. went on, dismissing them with a gesture. 'What makes them dangerous is the fact that they are organized and directed by a subtle intelligence here in Monte Carlo. Find that man or that woman, madame; break up this ring, and you may ask what you will of us!'

She shook her head. 'I am on vacation,' she said. 'I am weary of crime. Better order me changed to a more modest suite, monsieur, and forget about me.'

'Never! Never!' he protested. 'In any case you remain our guest, madame.'

He brought up all the arguments he could muster. Would she not, as a woman, undertake to rescue her fellow woman from these birds of prey? Some of the victims had been American ladies. Did she not feel it her duty to . . . etc, etc. Madame Storey continued to smile, and to shake her head quite firmly; and being an experienced man he soon saw that it was useless. He left us.

A few minutes later Madame Storey and I, having changed our dresses, were seated on the terrace behind the Casino. It was in the middle of the afternoon. After the fogs and frost of Northern France, the hot and brilliant sunshine was like Paradise. Below us the calm sea was bluer than ultramarine. The fantastic architecture of the Casino; the gay clothes of the women; the profusion of flowers; the band playing a Strauss waltz: everything contributed to the holiday spirit. We dissolved in satisfaction.

'Let's do something foolish,' said Madame Storey.

Presently a young man came strolling by. One of the handsomest young men I have ever seen. He looked like a Spaniard or a South American: smooth, olive face; glowing dark eyes; slim and graceful as Mercury. He looked at Madame Storey out of the corner of his eyes, walked on a little way, and came back again.

'Here's one of them,' she murmured.

'Surely not!' I protested. 'That boy looks like one of the young angels painted by the Italian masters.'

'Quite!' she said dryly. 'But you can never tell about young men. They don't begin to show their real characters until they pass thirty.'

When he passed the second time he looked directly at Madame Storey with his velvety, compelling eyes. She smiled frankly, and he stopped.

'Charming afternoon,' he said, raising his hat. His English was as good as my own.

'Charming!' said Madame Storey. She glanced at the vacant seat beside her, and he dropped into it. He looked about twenty-four, but may have been older. He was dressed with the plainness that the most fashionable young men affect; everything about him was just right.

'You have just come,' he said.

'How did you guess it?'

His eyes were fixed on hers. 'The terrace has a brightness it never had before,' he said seriously.

She laughed delightedly. 'Well! You're what we call a fast worker in America!'

He did not smile. He wasn't looking at me, but I could feel the almost hypnotic effect of his eyes. 'I mean it,' he said. 'I have never seen anybody like you.'

'Compliments are so nice,' murmured Madame Storey, trying not to laugh. 'You see, they've gone out of fashion in my country.'

He glanced at me significantly and then back at her as much as to say that if she would get rid of me he would really tell her something. But Madame Storey made believe not to get it.

'A woman like you is wasted in a country of businessmen,' he said.

'Well, one can always get on a ship,' she said. 'Here I am!'

'I had a feeling when I got up this morning that something wonderful was going to happen today,' he murmured thrillingly.

Madame Storey could no longer hold in her laughter. It ran out delightedly. The young man turned angry. When she was able to speak she said – still rippling with laughter:

'I'm so sorry! I like you, really. You're so easy to look at. But I can't play up to you. Surely it must be a strain on you too, to be so romantic. Be yourself and let's enjoy the lovely weather.'

There was a struggle visible in his handsome face. He scowled, and rubbed his upper lip. Then suddenly he joined in her laughter. It changed the whole character of his face. Made him look like one of our nice American boys. He had beautiful white teeth. I began to like him.

'You're right,' he said, 'it *is* a strain. But . . .' He finished with an expressive shrug.

Madame Storey finished his sentence for him. 'You mean it's your job to be romantic. I know. And I ought to tell you that I am a very poor prospect. You'd better toddle along and look for some older lady who is starving for romance.'

His head went down, and a spasm of shame crossed his face. ' You see too much,' he murmured. ' You despise me.'

She shook her head. ' I never despise anybody.'

He raised his head. He was humbler now. ' I'd like to take a holiday from my job,' he murmured. ' If you would let me stay with you.'

' Why not?' she said. ' I'm sure you're the handsomest young man in Monte Carlo. What shall we do?'

' Do you like dancing?' he asked eagerly.

' I adore it!'

' There's a gala at the Sporting Club this afternoon.'

' Let's go . . . But we must introduce ourselves. I am Mrs Renfrew and this is Miss Renfrew, my sister-in-law.'

' I am Raoul d'Aymara,' he said as simply as if he had been a marquis. Perhaps he was.

' We must have another man,' he went on. ' There are several fellows I know along the terrace. . . . There's Nickol Copenhaver the Dane. Dumb, but he can dance.' Raoul signalled to an elegant young fellow who was loafing by the balustrade of the terrace, and the latter started towards us.

Raoul said hurriedly, half-ashamed, ' You understand, I shall have to play romantic when Nickol is in hearing. He wouldn't understand anything else.'

The new young man came up and was introduced. He fell to my share. Tall and blond, he seemed to be slightly in the gauze the whole time. I kept wondering if he had a real man's feelings inside his handsome shell.

It began to grow chilly on the terrace, and we adjourned to the Sporting Club. As the old Casino begins to grow out of date, the management has provided this gorgeous new palace of amusement to keep up the tone of Monte Carlo. There is nothing like it in our country. The ceiling of the restaurant must be forty feet high. One has a grand feeling of spaciousness. And what a floor! What music! What food!

The dumb Nickol danced like another Maurice. It was heavenly, but all the time I wondered if I was in the arms of a blackmailer and a robber. Well, danger added a spice to my pleasure. I envied the other couple a little. Raoul could not only dance, he could talk. He seemed to be filled with a kind of desperate gaiety.

When the four of us were together at the table it was funny to see him start making love to Madame Storey with a perfectly serious face. I suppose the boys spied on each other. However, as there were two orchestras, there was not much pause between dances.

Once or twice Raoul asked me to dance just for appearance's sake. When he was out of Nickol's hearing the poor lad was more frank and open. I liked him better and better. He said with a laugh:

'You know, I wouldn't be let in here alone.'

'Why not?' I asked.

He spun me around. 'Because of my fatal beauty. . . . You see the management employs dancing men of their own. There's one of them . . . there's another on your left. Nice lads but a bit *passé*. Beginning to be a little bald on the crown, and thick through the middle. Anything as fresh and willowy as me shows up the old boys at a disadvantage.'

In all his fun there was a bitter, reckless note that made me want to mother him.

Most of the time he talked about Madame Storey. 'Isn't she wonderful? I wouldn't have believed it possible that a woman of brains could be so . . . so . . . well, you know what I mean: so lovable!'

'Then you know who she is,' I said.

'Of course I know. Rosika Storey. Such a thing can't be hidden. I would be willing to bet that everybody here knows who she is. I can hear them murmuring when we dance around together.'

We danced for a while. Raoul's style was bolder and faster than Nickol's. He guided me as smoothly and surely through the crowding couples as a bird goes through the branches of a tree. Presently he said with the laugh that didn't hide the feeling in his voice:

'Meeting a woman like that has pulled me right up by the roots. I'll never be the same man again. What is it you say in America? I'm a dead pigeon!'

When the dance was over we strolled out into the beautifully lighted gardens. I saw that Madame Storey and Raoul had some sort of an understanding. They dropped Nickol politely at the foot of the hotel steps, but Raoul came up to our suite with us. There was a sharp mean look in the face of the young Dane as he turned away that I didn't like. Raoul didn't seem to care.

Up in our salon all Raoul's pumped-up gaiety dropped away. His smooth young face looked drawn and haggard.

'You said you had something to say to me,' said Madame Storey gravely.

'Yes. I'd better say it and go. . . .' It wasn't easy for him to get it out. He made a couple of false starts. 'Something has happened to me this afternoon. I . . . I . . . Oh well, never mind me. I don't mean anything in your life.'

'If you're up against it you do,' she said quickly. 'If you're sick of your crooked job here.'

He laughed. 'Sick of my job! Oh, God! Believe me, I've been sick of my job for a long time. But I kidded myself. Now I can't kid myself any longer. . . . No!' he cried out sharply. 'Leave me out of it! This is what I want to say. You must get out of Monte Carlo. At once. By the first train!'

'But why?' asked Madame Storey.

'I can't tell you that. I can only say that you're in danger. Horrible danger! You can't fight this thing. It's too well covered. They'll get you if you stay here!'

It was obvious that he thought Madame Storey had accepted the job of breaking the ring of blackmailers. She didn't undeceive him.

She said, 'If I were to leave now it would be suspected that you had warned me.'

He laughed a bitter note. 'I expect they know it already.'

'What will you do?' she said. 'You can't go on with your present life.'

'Never mind that. Only do what I say. You see that I'm in earnest. It's true I'm taking a risk in warning you. But let that go. It's the first decent act of my life. Let me feel that I've done some good. Will you do what I say? Will you go?'

'I don't know. I'll have to consider it,' said Madame Storey.

He turned to me in a kind of desperation. 'You persuade her,' he said. 'I can see that you're fond of her. Don't let her soil her hands with this pitch. Go away from here. There are plenty of places where you can amuse yourselves. If she stays here they'll get her!'

I could only spread out my hands helplessly. It was not for me to say anything.

'Raoul,' said Madame Storey frankly, 'come in with us. You're in wrong. Join up with us and get a fresh deal. With your aid I could smash these scoundrels!'

He shook his head. 'No,' he said gloomily. 'I couldn't betray my

mob. That's the right word, isn't it? I've done pretty nearly everything in my short life, but I've never been a traitor.'

'Then get out of Monte Carlo yourself,' she said. 'And keep on
going until you are out of reach of the ring. Go to America if
necessary. I'll stake you. Because I think you're worth saving.'

He stared at her, and a wonderful light broke in his face. He
seemed to be dazed by the offer. 'A fresh deal?' he stammered.
'Could I? . . . Could I?'

Madame Storey unlocked her writing case. 'You'd better get away
in a hurry,' she said.

He pulled himself together. 'Yes! I'll be followed from the
moment I leave here. But I think I can shake them off. I'll walk out
of town. The railway station will be watched. I'll pick up the
bus for Nice somewhere along the road, and take the train from
there.'

Madame Storey had taken a packet of bank notes from her case,
and was writing a card. 'Give this to my agent in Paris,' she said,
'and let me hear from you through him.'

Raoul thrust the notes and the card in his breast pocket. His face
was working strangely. 'I can't say anything,' he muttered.

'Don't try,' said Madame Storey.

When he had gone I dropped into a chair. I felt as if all the
strength had oozed out of my legs. 'What will you do?' I faltered.
'When he disappears they will suppose that he has confessed everything to you.'

'I reckon they will,' said Madame Storey coolly. She considered
for a moment. 'I don't know what I will do,' she said slowly. 'But
certainly I'm not going to let anybody run me out of Monte Carlo.'

I knew she was going to say it, but a little groan escaped me.

'But you don't have to stay here, Bella,' she added with quick
kindness. 'After all, this is a holiday. There is no need for you to be
frightened to death.'

'I stay where you are,' I said grimly.

After Raoul had gone Madame Storey looked over some mail that
had arrived during the afternoon. Amongst it was a note which had
been delivered by hand. It was signed *Amos Rudd*.

'Bless my fathers! Amos Rudd!' she exclaimed. 'He used to be a
great man in New York. President of the Madison National. Sold
out when his bank was merged. I thought he had passed out years

ago, and here he is risen like Lazarus in Monte Carlo. He must be about a hundred!'

Mr Rudd had written to ask her to dinner at his villa. He apologized for the shortness of the notice, saying that he had just heard of her arrival, and as he was entertaining some of his friends that night, he hoped she would waive ceremony and join them. He would be very glad to have her travelling companion also, he said.

'Let's go, Bella,' she said. 'If he's a resident here we may pick up some valuable information.'

I agreed, of course, but I had an uncomfortable feeling that she was about to be drawn into the ugly case of the gigolos in spite of herself.

So a telephone message was sent to Mr Rudd that we were coming, and we proceeded to get dressed.

Our host lived in almost feudal fashion in a sort of castle on the Cap Martin side. We were welcomed in a salon big enough for kings with a loggia opening on the moonlit sea. Rudd was a tiny man like a fledgling bird, all beak and eyes and with no feathers to speak of. Thus age returns to the semblance of youth. He had hardly a fledgling's innocence though. There was a fixed grin in his little withered face.

I disliked his wife at sight. Not the same wife he had left New York with, Madame Storey remarked later. A tall, luscious blonde with drooping lips and weary eyes. A woman of the highest fashion strung with jewels, she looked, to put it bluntly, capable of any crime.

Mr Rudd squeaked, 'Rosika! You were only a little girl when I saw you last! You've grown older and I've grown younger. He! He! He!' His wife drawled with infinite fatigue, 'Chawmed, Madame Storey. I hope you won't find Monte Carlo too boring.'

The company was a small one. There was a Prince Grimaldi, a tottering old beau with his hair plastered down. Several American women hung around him simply because the taste of his title (which they pronounced 'Prance') was like honey on their lips. There was a count who was a little younger but worse-favoured; and there was a bundle of wraps and veils enclosing an aged lady who was related to the late Sultan of Turkey. All we could see of her was a long and inquisitive nose.

Amongst the Americans there was a bloated couple who were always spoken of in hushed voices as the James Wentworth

Hawkinses. What they had done to deserve it I couldn't find out. The male Hawkins resembled a bulldog – but no dog could look so brutal. Something happens to Americans when they forsake their country for good. They hit the toboggan morally.

Madame Storey and I were much the youngest persons present. Amongst that crew my tall friend stood out like a lady in a museum. They all felt the contrast, I think. They all lavished compliments on her – and cordially disliked her.

Dinner was kept waiting by the non-arrival of somebody called Turner Moale. From the conversation I gathered that nothing in Monte Carlo was complete without Turner Moale. His name headed every subscription list. He gave the most delightful entertainments at his villa on the rock of Monaco.

Turner Moale; Turner Moale; the name rang through my head like some old rhyme. Suddenly it came to me that my mother used to talk about Turner Moale. When she was a girl he was the number one matinée idol of New York. Women used to mob the stage door in order to touch him as he passed.

Presumably he had been forced off the stage by age, and here he was established as the social arbiter of Monte Carlo. I wanted to change the ancient wheeze to run: When Americans die they rise up in Monte Carlo. I felt as if I were in a company of ghosts.

Presently he arrived, a very old man but marvellously preserved. I expect he had been in the hands of his valet for hours. Rosy and dignified, beautifully turned-out, he was certainly a personage. Everybody had to look when he came in. With his cool airs and affability he was like a little Highness.

He made directly for my employer and kissed her hand as if he were conferring an order upon her. 'Rosika Storey!' he exclaimed. 'The desire of my life is granted!' He drew her hand under his arm. 'I shall take you in to dinner. I don't care what anybody says. I shall fight for it!'

Everybody laughed. It appeared that Turner Moale must be allowed to do whatever he liked.

When we sat down at the table there was a burst of animation as if a large tap had been turned on. Everybody smirking, ogling, flirting, while they picked at the different courses which were whisked on and off. But while their lips smiled their eyes were ghastly. Madame Storey has taught me something about eyes. Every one of those dapper men and bejewelled women was frantic with boredom.

They hated each other; they hated themselves. People in that state are ripe for anything.

Except Turner Moale perhaps. He appeared to be serene. But perhaps it was only because he had a more perfect control over his eyes. He was no better than the others but he had a better style. He was like the popular ruler of some little country a long time ago who had nothing to fear. There are no rulers like that nowadays.

'I haven't been to America for years,' he said. 'I can't endure their barbarous customs. In America I am told that men wear dinner jackets when there are ladies present. I shall never go there.'

Madame Storey led up to what she had in mind by telling of our encounter with the good-looking young man on the terrace; just the beginning of it. They listened with smiles, but one could see that they disliked the subject. Madame Storey said with an innocent air:

'I suppose terrible things may happen to a woman who falls for those handsome rascals.'

Silence around the table.

She went on. 'In fact I have seen various references to women being robbed and blackmailed at Monte Carlo.'

Not a word. Mrs Hawkins tried to create a diversion by asking the prince if he liked Béarnaise sauce with his *entrecôte*. Madame Storey kept on:

'Mr Rudd, have you ever heard of these things?'

'Not I!' he said. 'I am of the wrong sex.'

His feeble joke produced a great laugh. Madame Storey, undiscouraged, blandly addressed Turner Moale at her side.

'What do you think, Mr Moale? Are these pleasant young fellows that one sees on the terrace dangerous criminals?'

'I hope so,' he said maliciously.

There were loud cries of protest from his admirers.

'It adds a zest to life,' he said. 'We are too far sunk in our creature comforts. Nothing like a good crime or two to rouse us.'

'I like to read about crimes in Chicago,' drawled Mrs Rudd, 'but not at my own front door.'

'The nearer, the more exciting,' said Turner Moale.

'No young man by himself is especially dangerous,' said Madame Storey. 'But suppose they combined to stand or fall together. Suppose they are only tools in the hands of a master who uses them for his own ends. That would be a dangerous racket. The boys, you see, would be comparatively innocent. All they would have to do would be to allow the women to make fools of themselves. Then the master would apply the screws.'

' Superb!' cried Turner Moale with his noiseless old man's laugh. ' You are wasted as an upholder of the law, Rosika. If you were a criminal you would go down in history!'

' Of course it's only the women in hotels who are victimized,' said Mrs Rudd languidly. ' It doesn't affect us who live here.'

The old Turkish woman shook with laughter inside her wrappings as if she knew some devilish joke of her own.

' Blackmail will soon become a lost art,' lisped the old prince. ' Because people are proud of being bad nowadays.'

' Then you can blackmail them for being found in church!' retorted Turner Moale.

' If you've got a good balance at the bank you don't need to care what anybody says about you,' put in Amos Rudd, grinning like a death's head.

His wife flashed a spontaneous look of hatred down the table.

' About those women who are blackmailed,' said Hawkins brutally, ' if they make fools of themselves I say they deserve no better than they get.'

Madame Storey took no further part in the discussion. She let them thrash it out amongst themselves as if she had learned what she wished to know.

When the party broke up we were besieged with invitations. These people did nothing in the world but give each other dinners every night. My heart sank. However, Madame Storey evaded them politely.

' I may be obliged to leave Monte Carlo tomorrow,' she said. ' I dare not make any engagements.'

How thankful I was to get back to our own quiet rooms! ' Pretty awful, wasn't it?' said Madame Storey, smiling. ' However, the evening was not entirely wasted.'

I looked at her inquiringly.

' Mrs Rudd possesses a photograph of Raoul,' she said, lighting a cigarette. ' Along with many other handsome young men.'

' What does that mean?' I said.

' I don't know. It's only a beginning.'

' Then you are going to take this case!' I exclaimed with a long face.

' I may be forced to,' she said enigmatically.

I spent a bad night, and got up ready to hate that gay and beautiful place. The air was like wine, the morning sunshine glorious, but I couldn't rise to it. Madame Storey was a little pale too. We ate our *petit déjeuner* by the open window in silence.

As we sat lingering over our cigarettes, an envelope was brought to her which bore the imprint of a café in Monte Carlo. No name was written on it, but only the number of our room. She read it and handed it over to me without any comment.

Dear R. S.,

I know that it is foolish of me to write to you, but it eases me so! They have me on the run, but so far I have been able to keep a jump or two ahead of them. I am waiting here for a friend who has promised to bring me a disguise. If I could only say some of the things that I feel! But I must not. I have no right. I can say this, though. Through you I have found myself. Whatever may happen to me now...

There was a break at this point, and the letter was carried on in a different hand, an uneducated hand, in French. Translated, it ran:

The gentleman told me who this was for. He had to leave in a hurry. I let him out through a back window.

PIERRE,
Waiter at Café des Arcades.

Madame Storey and I exchanged anxious glances. 'Let's go and see the Grand Vizier,' she said.

She was referring to M. le Président of the Society of the Baths of the Sea. I nodded, and we got ready immediately.

There was nothing frivolous about his suite. Very handsome and austere. As soon as we entered we perceived that something unusual was up. Excited-looking clerks were passing in and out. We had to wait until a couple of gaudy policeman made a report to Monsieur B. A presentiment of evil struck a slow chill through my veins.

When we were shown into his private office he still looked disturbed. In her forthright way Madame Storey said:

'What has happened, monsieur?'

'Why, nothing, nothing at all,' he replied quickly – too quickly.

Madame Storey merely looked at him in the way that draws things out of people.

'Well, a distressing accident,' he said, 'but nothing that need concern you or me, madame.'

She looked and waited for more.

'An unfortunate young man committed suicide last night by throwing himself over the cliffs of La Turbie.'

In spite of myself a little cry was forced from me.

'What's the matter with mademoiselle?' he asked, staring.

'She doubts if it was suicide,' said Madame Storey gravely.

'What else could it be?' he said irritably throwing up his hands. 'Some poor fool who has lost all at the gaming tables! He killed himself outside our borders anyway, but the French authorities seem to think we are responsible.'

'Who is he?'

'I do not know, madame. All marks of identification had been destroyed. An investigation is in progress.'

'Where is he?'

'At a mortuary in Beausoleil.'

Madame Storey's face was like marble. 'Is he . . . recognizable?'

'Yes, I am told that his face escaped mutilation though almost every bone in his body was broken.'

'I wish to see him.'

He jumped up waving his hands in distress. 'No! No! It is too horrible! Isn't there somebody who could act for you? Some man?'

'I am accustomed to acting for myself,' she said.

A moment or two later we were in Monsieur B.'s car, climbing through the narrow winding streets that lead to Beausoleil, the upper town. All Monte Carlo is built like a flight of steps up the side of a mountain. Beausoleil is in French territory.

The mortuary was a private one attached to an undertaking establishment. There is a stark, nightmare quality about such places in France. At the door of the inner room Madame Storey said kindly:

'You don't have to come in, Bella.'

I shook my head, and followed at her heels like a shadow. It would have been worse to wait outside for her.

A small bare room with whitewashed walls and cement floors. A smell of iodoform. In the middle there was a slab with a sheeted form upon it; a table at the side with the dead man's clothes under another sheet. An attendant standing beside the slab pulled down the sheet a little way and we saw – what we expected to see: Raoul's beautiful head.

He was no longer glad or sorry; neither proud nor shame-faced. Death had shaped a perfect mask of beauty. The rich-brown wavy hair; the clear olive skin; the lovely mouth; and so young! So pitifully young! I began to shake inside; the tears were running down my face without my knowing it. Madame Storey, as always when under strong emotion, was pale and cold.

She said, 'This man was murdered!'

'How do you know?' gasped Monsieur B.

'His lips were sealed with surgeon's tape. If you look closely you can see traces of the gum. . . . I wish to see his hands.'

The sheet was pulled down farther and I turned away. I could not bear any more. I heard her say:

'Observe those marks on his wrists, monsieur. He was bound and gagged when he was carried to La Turbie.'

Monsieur B. made incoherent sounds of distress.

When we returned to his car Madame Storey told him what we knew about the dead man. The name he had given us was no doubt an assumed one. Madame Storey said, 'I am now ready, monsieur, to undertake the work you offered me yesterday.'

Now that murder had come into it, he was not so eager. 'There must be no ugly publicity,' he muttered.

She looked at him coldly. 'It suits me to have as little publicity as possible,' she said. 'But I won't consent in advance to conceal anything.'

'An ugly murder! Just at the beginning of the season! Ruinous! Ruinous!' he cried.

'You can't clean up a mess without making a bad smell,' said Madame Storey bluntly.

'Ruinous! Ruinous!'

'Very well,' she said crisply, 'if you wish to withdraw your offer, that is quite all right. But in that case I must warn you that I shall go ahead on my own. Whatever happens, I am going to see that the murderer of this man – I mean the *real* murderer – is brought to justice.'

That brought him down on the run. 'No! No, madame! Of course not! Don't speak of such a thing, I beg! Certainly my offer of yesterday stands. I am anxious to co-operate with you in every way possible. No expense must be spared!' And so on. And so on.

We went right on to La Turbie in the car. Monsieur B. said we should find his chief of detectives on the spot. The road zigzagged endlessly back and forth across the face of the almost perpendicular mountain back of Monte Carlo. Though La Turbie almost overhangs the resort it is a half-hour's drive around those hairpin curves. We had no eye for the glorious views beneath us.

Like all the ancient villages thereabouts, La Turbie is almost a solid block of masonry tucked in a fold of the mountains. It is dominated by a huge ruined tower built by the Romans. Below the ancient part is a more modern esplanade ending in a sort of round bastion at the very edge of the cliffs. It was from this bastion that the body had been flung.

Madame Storey had the car stopped some distance short of the end of the road, hoping to find the tracks of the car that had preceded us some eight hours before. But the pavement was hard and so many people had shuffled back and forth that all marks of tyres were obliterated.

Within the circular parapet at the end, a knot of people were gathered, peering over, discussing the affair. The chief of detectives joined us. Madame Storey looked at him and looked at me ruefully. A worthy man! When Monsieur B. asked him what had developed he shrugged and spread his palms. Every soul in La Turbie had been asleep when it happened. Some perhaps had been wakened by the young man's cry, but they didn't know what had wakened them.

The village people drew back wonderingly at the sight of Madame Storey. They suspected a tragic romance. We looked over – not at the glorious panorama of mountain and sea, with the red-roofed town two thousand feet below, but straight down where we could see a dark stain on the rocks at the foot of the cliff. I shivered. I can't say how far down it was – hundreds of feet.

They told us that the spot where the body had fallen was inaccessible from below. Consequently, men had been lowered from the parapet to fetch it up. Indeed the ropes were still there, and the men who had gone down, telling the story to their neighbours over and over.

Madame Storey said: ' I will go down.'

There was a chorus of remonstrances from the Frenchmen. She merely waited with a cold smile until they talked themselves out.

' I will go for you,' said the detective.

She shook her head. ' I must use my own eyes.'

In the end, of course, she had her way. The men who manipulated the rope constructed a sort of sling for her. They helped her over the parapet, and presently I saw her swinging between rocks and sky, seated in the sling, clinging to the rope above her head with one hand and holding a cigarette in the other. It made me giddy, and I drew back. The village people were staring as at a marvel.

There was no accident. In half an hour they helped her over the parapet and she stood beside us safe and sound.

'Did you find anything?' asked the detective excitedly.

'No,' she said coolly. The village people were listening and gaping.

When we drove away in the car she opened her hand and showed us a brown button. Clinging to it was a scrap of frayed woollen cloth of the same colour.

'When they took off his bonds there was a brief struggle,' she said. 'He caught hold of a button on the coat of one of his assailants and it came away in his hand. Observe that the cloth is of the finest quality, and that the button is sewed on with silk thread.'

The French detective struck his fist into his palm. 'I will find the wearer of that coat, madame! You may leave it to me!'

'Quite!' she said dryly.

Back in the town we parted from our companions. The detective went off to set the usual machinery of the police in motion, while Madame Storey and I went in search of the 'Café des Arcades.'

There was none of the Monte Carlo glitter about this place. The sort of shabby and inviting little resort in a side street, where French people love to sit by the hour, talking, playing dominoes, writing letters. At this time of day it was almost empty. When we sat down a waiter assiduously wiped the marble table in front of us. He was a young man with a friendly smile, and all the stored-up wisdom of the café waiter in his wary eyes.

'Are you Pierre?' asked Madame Storey.

'But yes, madame,' he said, startled. 'How do you know my name?'

'You signed it to a letter that you sent me last night.'

'Yes! Yes!' he said. 'And you are the lady? Ahh!'

'What do you know about the young man who gave you that letter?'

Pierre spread out his hands expressively. 'I know nothing, madame. He is a customer. He is generous. I do not know his name.'

The proprietor was looking at us curiously from behind the

bar, and Madame Storey ordered aperitifs. Pierre flew to get them.

When he returned she asked: 'What made the young man leave so quickly last night?'

'I do not know,' said Pierre. 'He show me fifty-franc note. He say quiet: "Is there a way out at the back?" I say: "Follow me." I take him in the storeroom. He goes out through the window like a bird. Shove the letter in my hand. Say: "Send it to suite A, Hôtel de Paris." '

'He was waiting here for a friend. Did his friend come?'

'Ah, yes, the mademoiselle. She often met him here. Very pretty. She come and I say: "Your gentleman is gone." I didn't want to frighten her.' He gave us a good description of the girl.

'You must have some idea of the danger that threatened him,' said Madame Storey.

Pierre shrugged. 'Well, there were four young men waiting in the street,' he said. 'Afterwards they went away.'

'Could you identify them if you saw them again?'

An expression of prudence came over the waiter's face. 'Ah, no, madame,' he said quickly. 'It is impossible. It was dark in the street. Their hats were pulled over their eyes.'

'Pierre,' said Madame Storey gravely, 'they got him!'

'*Mon Dieu!*' he said softly. 'Is he dead?'

'He is dead!'

Pierre bustled away towards a table at a little distance, and fussed among a pile of magazines that lay upon it. He came back bringing one with his professional smile. This was for the watching proprietor's benefit. Pierre's eyes were full of tears.

'*Voilà!* L'Illustration, *madame,*' he said briskly. He leaned over and gave the table a swipe with his cloth. His back was turned towards his boss. 'I have something else for you,' he whispered. Digging into a pocket under his apron, he produced a tiny book in a pretty white binding. Madame Storey slipped it out of sight.

'He give me that with the letter,' whispered Pierre. 'He say: "If they get me you will hear of it, Pierre. If they get me I want the lady at the Hôtel de Paris to have this. If you hear nothing, throw it into the sea. It is dangerous to have on you." '

Somebody called him, and he hustled away. He could give us no further help.

Under cover of the magazine, we examined the little book. To our astonishment it was – a dictionary! The slip cover was a handsome affair of vellum decorated with gold, green and red bands, but it held just a common little five-franc English-French dictionary. Every traveller knows them.

Madame Storey ran over the pages hastily. They showed no marks of any sort.

'Just an ordinary dictionary!' I said disappointed.

'No!' she said thoughtfully. 'He had some special reason for sending it.' After a moment or two the explanation came to her. 'This is the code book used by the gang in exchanging messages. It is not the first time that a dictionary has been used for that purpose. It will come in useful later.'

We returned to our hotel. On the way Madame Storey telegraphed to Philippe Grandet in Paris, asking him to come to Monte Carlo – a clever man who had worked for her on several former occasions. I had an uncomfortable feeling that we were being followed through the streets but I couldn't spot anybody. When I suggested to Madame Storey that we ought to have protection, she merely shrugged.

'They would never dare murder us, Bella,' she said lightly. 'That would cause a sensation big enough to drive them out of business. . . . It would be one way of winning our case.'

A busy day followed. Madame Storey was in hourly consultation with the police. They were efficient enough as police go, but lacking in originality. I needn't put down everything we did, because in a case of this sort you have to start a hundred lines of investigation of which ninety-nine come to nothing. The chief of detectives did *not* find the coat from which the button had been torn; neither did he locate Raoul's little friend. Perhaps it was she who had betrayed Raoul.

During the afternoon Mr James Wentworth Hawkins called up. He wished to know if Madame Storey was still in Monte Carlo, and if she was available for dinner that night. The sound of his thick cruel voice over the wire made me shiver. Madame Storey declined. Awfully sorry, she said, but she had a business engagement she couldn't get out of.

'Business in Monte Carlo!' he said with an unpleasant laugh. 'That *is* uncommon!'

While the band was playing we sat down on the terrace for a breather, and there we had an odd experience. No handsome young man made eyes at us today, but one such sat down in a chair perhaps a hundred feet away, and my eyes almost popped out of my head when I saw him take a little white book with gold, green and red bands on the cover, and start reading it.

In a minute or two another young man approached him, showed him something in his hand – I had a glimpse of the red and green on white – and the first man made a somewhat lengthy communication. If we could have heard it! The second man strolled on, while the first remained sitting. Ten minutes later a third young man appeared, and the same performance was gone through with.

'The little book increases in importance,' said Madame Storey dryly. 'It is their code, and it is also the badge by which they know each other!'

She had not said anything to the police about this book. 'Shall you point out these men to the police?' I asked.

She shook her head. 'The police will accomplish nothing. And it is up to you and me to complete the case before we show our hands.'

When we returned to the hotel she looked at the little book thoughtfully. 'It would be unlucky if they discovered that we possessed this,' she said. 'It is possible that they have spies in the hotel. Our rooms may be searched while we are out.' She sealed it up, and posted it to herself in care of *Poste Restante, Nice,* where we could pick it up at any time.

We worked very late that night. The Commissaire de Police sent Madame Storey a bunch of reports from the various men who had been at work on the case during the day, and after studying them she had dictated suggestions for the work of the following day.

All this had been sealed up and sent off by a waiting messenger, and we were sitting in the salon of our suite, smoking, talking idly, letting ourselves relax in preparation for sleep. It was about half-past one I suppose, and a great silence had fallen on Monte Carlo, broken only by the occasional dull roar of a car on the main road at the top of the gardens.

Suddenly there was a discreet tap on the door. We had heard no one approach.

'Who is it?' asked Madame Storey coolly.

A low voice answered: 'A letter from the Commissaire de Police, madame.'

There was something not quite right about that voice, and Madame Storey's face turned grim. I was thankful that the door was a stout one, and securely bolted. ' Shove it under the door,' she said.

There was a silence. No letter appeared. Then the voice whined:
' It is too thick to go under the door, madame.'

' Then it must wait until morning,' she said coolly. ' I have
retired.'

Another pause. Though I put my head to the door I could not
hear a sound from the other side. But I had the feeling that there
was more than one man in the corridor, conferring. Then we heard
retreating footsteps.

I looked at Madame Storey questioningly. My heart was beating
like a motor. Still, the incident appeared to be over. She lit a fresh
cigarette, saying:

' They must think we are downy birds.'

There was another tap on the door.

' Well?' said Madame Storey.

' If you please, madame,' said the whining voice, ' the Commissaire
says it is very important.'

Madame Storey's lip curled in contempt. ' Go away!' she said.
' If you bother me again I shall telephone to the office.'

We were both facing the door listening for the sound of his footsteps. One of those mysterious intimations that come to us caused me
to turn my head. I saw four masked men. They had entered through
the balcony windows. One of them was wearing a brown suit with a
button missing. That was the thing which struck me.

Before I could scream a soft mass was thrown over my head and
drawn tight: a down coverlet. A bent arm was flung around my head,
drawing it back until I thought my neck would break, stifling any
cries. I was held thus while a rope was cast around and around my
body, binding my arms and legs fast. I guessed that Madame Storey
was being treated in the same way but I could hear nothing.

I struggled with all my might. I did my utmost to cry out. But it
did no good. The men who had hold of me knew just what they had
to do. I was like an infant in their hands. They worked with terrifying swiftness. Before I had recovered from the shock of being seized,
I was hoisted over the shoulder of one of them and run out through
the door.

All this time something hard, a towel I suppose, was pressing the
coverlet into my face and I was at the point of suffocation. Fiery
spots danced before my eyes, and my ears rang. My senses wavered.
Down the corridor; through another door and down a flight of steps.

Endless corridors, scraping against one side then the other. My senses weren't registering properly. We stopped, and I heard a voice say as from an immense distance: 'Open that door and look out.' Another answered: 'All clear.' I was shot into the open air and immediately flung into a car which started with the exhaust wide open. Then I passed out.

But only for a moment. When consciousness came back the exhaust was still roaring. I could breathe more freely now. The pressure had been removed from my face, but there was a rope drawing the coverlet into my mouth so that I could not cry out. I groaned, but that feeble sound was swallowed in the noise of the engine. Suddenly the exhaust was shut off, and I judged that we had passed out of town.

We slowed down for a sharp turn, passed it and increased speed again. We almost stopped, crawled around a complete half turn and speeded up again. Another turn, and I knew where we were. Climbing to La Turbie. I hope I may never know such another moment. Up to that moment I had been blindly resisting like an animal. Now I knew fear, and it drained all the blood from my heart.

I pictured the hideous cliff I had looked over that morning with the stain of blood on the rocks below. A phrase rang through my head: Broke every bone in his body! The prospect of such a death was worse than death. I died a thousand deaths on that mountain road.

I had no sense that Madame Storey was anywhere near me. So far as I could tell I was planted on the back seat of a closed car with a man on either side of me. They never spoke. Silent on each side of me they afflicted me with an unspeakable terror, like two death's heads conducting me to my death.

As we crawled around one of the close turns, I heard a speeding car above us, and then I knew why Madame Storey was not beside me. For a while I forgot myself in the horror of her death; a life like hers to be cut off!

When the car stopped, I went mad with fear again. I was all fear. In my imagination I was screaming at the top of my voice No! No! No! But I could make no sound, or almost none.

There was a pause while the two parties conferred together. A voice said: 'Send the little one first.' Another answered 'No, both together.'

Suddenly all fear left me. I suppose it is like that with men in battle when faced with inevitable death. The thought comes to you: Well, what's the difference?

One man took me by the shoulders, another by the ankles. They gave me a little shake as if to make sure of their grip. From the other party came the cold voice:

'Swing them well out. Three times. Let go when I say three.'

At that moment my whole life seemed to spread out before me. Every loved face that I had ever known passed before my eyes.

They began to swing me. One! Two! Three! They let go. . . . I knew nothing more.

After a while as it seemed to me, I began to dream. A delicious dream of running water; a swift little river in the American country-side with alders and willows growing overhead, the sunlight striking through and dappling the water.

Suddenly I realized that it was faintly light, and that Rosika was bending over me with a face of concern. She was bathing my temples with a wet handkerchief. For a moment I thought I had wakened to a new existence.

'Where are we?' I asked.

She smiled. 'In the same old wicked world, my dear!'

I was filled with a grinding confusion. 'But . . . but . . . but,' I stammered.

'Look around you!' she said.

Raising myself on my elbow I saw that I was lying in grass at the foot of a low stone wall. We *were* at La Turbie because I saw the ruined Roman tower against the pale morning sky. But it was *not* the hideous bastion on the edge of the cliffs. Below me were ghostly olive trees on their terraces.

'Look!' said Madame Storey. 'When I got clear of my bonds I found this pinned to my sleeve.' She held up a piece of paper on which some words had been roughly printed. I read:

THIS IS JUST TO SHOW YOU WHAT WE CAN DO WHEN WE WANT. WE DON'T LIKE KILLING WOMEN, BUT IF YOU DON'T TAKE WARN-ING FROM THIS, WE WON'T STOP NEXT TIME WITH GIVING YOU A FRIGHT.

Then the reaction set in. 'We're all right! We're all right!' I screamed, laughing and crying together. Then I was sick.

When I felt better Madame Storey helped me to my feet, and we climbed over the wall. The road lay on the other side of it. I was still pretty groggy.

'I'm sorry we have a long walk before us,' said Madame Storey.

'Fortunately it's downhill. Our abductors were wonderfully considerate. They brought our coats along, and flung them over the wall after us.'

I looked down at Monte Carlo, just beginning to show through the mist. 'Horrible, horrible place!' I said with a shiver. 'The hotel management must have been a party to what happened last night. To be kidnapped out of our own rooms!'

'Not at all!' said Madame coolly. 'You've lost your sense of proportion, Bella. We are up against a gang of clever and adventurous rogues, that's all. No doubt they hired the room over ours, and dropped down to our balcony with ropes. They were perfectly acquainted with the interior of the hotel. They carried us down the service stairs and through the service passages. At that hour of the night they would be deserted. If there was a watchman he was bribed.'

'And what are we going to do now?' I asked.

'We are going to act just as our enemies want us to act, like a pair of frightened women. We are going to take the first train out of Monte Carlo. It leaves at quarter to seven.'

A week later Madame Storey and I returned to Monte Carlo. It had been seven days filled with busy preparations, and our dearest friends would not have recognized us in our new character. Philippe Grandet had been brought back to Paris because he was too old for the particular work in hand, but we had a new emissary who had been sent on five days in advance of us. It had come about in this way.

Madame Storey and I had fled all the way to London. Satisfied, then, that we had left our spies in France, we returned to Paris on an unfashionable train and put up at a small hotel on the left bank. On our first day there we were walking through the Luxembourg gardens when we came upon a handsome young man seated on a bench in an attitude of complete dejection.

'There's our man!' said Madame Storey instantly.

He was blond and well-built, and there was a special attractiveness about him, compounded of good humour with a spice of the devil. He was an American, God bless him! And he was out of luck. His long legs were stretched in front of him, his hands thrust in his pockets, his chin resting on his breast.

Madame Storey stopped. 'You seem to be in bad, George,' she said with a cool and friendly smile.

'In bad!' he cried. Then he got a good look at her and sprang to his feet. 'Lady,' he said solemnly, 'I'm in so deep it would take a hundred-foot ladder to fetch me above ground! . . . My name is Charlie if it's just the same to you.'

We took to him instantly.

'Well, Charlie,' said Madame Storey, 'perhaps I can give you a job. Come along and have lunch with us at the Medici grill and we'll talk it over.'

Charlie was the lad for us all right. His other name was Raines, and his story was a simple one. The son of a rich man, he had been sent on a tour of Europe to complete his education, and had liked Paris so well that he had refused to go any farther. This had resulted in a break with the old man. Charlie thought that he could make his own way, but he had soon discovered that while Paris is Paradise for a young American with money, it is Hell for him who hath none. So here he was chucked out of his hotel, and too proud to cable home.

Madame Storey's intuition had not deceived her. Charlie looked on the affair as a big lark. She told him about Raoul, and warned him that if he were found out it would cost him his life. He waved it aside.

'All my life I've longed to have a real adventure!' he said.

He left for Monte Carlo that same night with a replenished wardrobe and a pocketbook stuffed with notes. He travelled under his own name with his own passport. His instructions were:

To put up at the Hôtel de Paris and start playing at the Casino or the Sporting Club. To begin to plunge until he lost or appeared to lose all his money. To get into a row with the hotel over his bill, and to move into a cheap lodging. To continue to wager a few francs daily at the Casino as if the madness had got him. To sell off his belongings and eat at the cheapest estaminets. After that he was to let things take their course. If a crooked proposition was put up to him he was to receive it indulgently.

'The lady in Monte Carlo who picks out the young men for this game is a connoisseur of manly good looks,' said Madame Storey dryly. 'I think I have gauged her taste correctly. Blonds are always in demand.'

'Spare my blushes, lady,' said Charlie grinning.

'When I get to Monte Carlo I shall be known as Lady Wedderminster,' Madame Storey went on. 'My arrival will be announced, and you can get in touch with me at the Hôtel de Paris. But don't put anything compromising in a letter. We will arrange a safer means of communicating.'

So Charlie had gone, and five days later Madame Storey and I followed him. During every spare moment of that time and all the way down in the train we rehearsed our new parts. Madame Storey is a past mistress of the art of disguise, but she never loses sight of the fact that acting is more important than disguise.

Lady Wedderminster is a real person, and a friend of Madame Storey's. It is one of the historic names of England, but the present bearer of it is a retiring person who goes very little into society. She had never been down to the French Riviera. English passports had been secured for us through influence in high places.

Madame Storey was turned out as one of those incredibly dowdy Englishwomen of high position. I don't know where they have their clothes made; perhaps by the village dressmaker. Such women care nothing for the styles of the moment, and they are hung all over with the strangest trimmings. And such hats; such feather boas; such shoes, miles too big, and turning up at the toes; a handbag grasped in one hand and an umbrella in the other.

Her face was in character. She was too wise to make up old. It won't pass muster in the sunlight. But any woman can make herself look like a fright. Madame Storey's hair was bleached to a sort of mousy colour and she had applied a wash to her complexion that made her look sallow and haggard. Her eyes were hollowed to give her a hungry and discontented look.

Such a woman nearly always has an unfortunate ' companion,' just to have somebody to order around, and I was her. My red locks were dyed a nondescript brown; I wore a pair of owlish glasses, and my nose was reddened. As for my clothes and hats – Ye Gods! All I need say is that they were supposed to be Lady Wedderminster's cast-offs and they looked it.

These extraordinary-looking women are very often wealthy. We telegraphed from Paris for a suite at the Hôtel de Paris and went down on the Blue Train. In the hotel Madame Storey was superb; complaining about everything, sending the servants scurrying in a dozen directions. The English are not loved in foreign hotels, but they get service.

As for myself, I am not a very good actress, but my part was a simple one. All I had to do was to look frightened, something I could very well get away with on returning to Monte Carlo.

We played a waiting game at first while Madame Storey's agent fed items to the *Paris Herald* concerning the arrival of Lady Wedderminster on the Riviera; the great wealth of the family; the part it had played in history, etc. As the *Herald* is the newspaper of the English-speaking contingent we knew that this stuff would be read in the right quarters. Meanwhile Lady Wedderminster was playing heavily at the Casino, and winning for the most part. She was invited to join the Sporting Club.

There had not been a word in the newspapers about the murder of Raoul d'Aymara or the activities of the police. As a matter of fact, after Madame Storey's disappearance, the case gradually petered out. There was never any inquiry for the poor lad. Like a trim yacht at sea he had appeared for a brief space out of the fog, and had been swallowed up in it again.

We were bothered about Charlie Raines. No communication was received from him. If he failed us, our whole elaborate plan collapsed. Moreover, we felt a very human anxiety as to the fate of that engaging young man.

Finally we saw him on the terrace all decked out in his new clothes. He was one of a quartet which included a dark, wicked-looking young man, an admirable foil for the gay Charlie, and two handsome, fashionably-dressed women. All eyes followed them as they strolled along laughing. A charming picture – if you didn't know the dark undercurrents of Monte Carlo.

This suggested that he had got a toe hold in the gigolo ring, and relieved us of a part of our anxiety.

During the afternoon of that day as Madame Storey and I were sitting on the terrace listening to the band, the same dark young man dropped in a chair alongside us. There was something vaguely familiar about him. My intuition told me that he was one of those who had entered our room that night, and the skin on the back of my neck crawled. But of course I could not have identified him.

He was a different type from the others; older, harder; with a wicked roll to his dark eyes. Well, many women are thrilled by that sort of thing. He said to Madame Storey in French:

'What trashy music they play!'

She did not answer him, but at the same time she contrived to look as if she wanted to. A nice piece of acting. The timid woman who is longing for an adventure.

'I beg your pardon,' he said. 'I spoke without thinking.'

'That's all right,' stammered Madame Storey. 'I . . . don't mind.'

He allowed a little more warmth to come into his voice. 'If they would only play good music! One gets so tired of the glitter and frivolity here. It doesn't satisfy you!'

'You must excuse me,' she murmured. 'My French is not very good.'

'So! Then I will talk English! . . . I felt at once that you were musical. One cannot be mistaken. The women one meets are so soulless! It is only once or twice in one's lifetime that one sees a woman with soul. You feel the mysterious currents of sympathy passing back and forth and then, *voilà!* you forget the conventions. Again, I must ask you to forgive me!'

So that was the line they took with a plain woman!

I realized that my presence was only obstructing the free development of the comedy, so I got up and strolled away along the terrace. When I got back half an hour later he had progressed from sympathy to the subject of dancing.

'I do not dance,' Madame Storey was saying in the awkward, wistful manner she had assumed.

'You *could* dance,' he murmured; 'a woman full of music like you!'

'I never had a chance,' she said, looking down at her hands.

'I understand,' he said sympathetically; 'and of course you do not like to begin on the public floor. . . . But you could dance with me,' he went on, lowering his voice, 'without any of the trouble of learning. Because we are in sympathy!'

Madame Storey said nothing.

'I have a friend who has a little studio of the dance on Avenue de Joffre,' he went on. 'Such a charming place! Would you like to come and see it?'

She shook her head.

'I am not a dancing teacher,' he said as if his feelings were wounded. 'My father allows me a sufficient income. I ask it for my own pleasure.'

She was obdurate in her refusal. 'I would like to dance,' she said, 'but I am not at ease with foreigners. If I could find an English teacher . . . or an American . . .'

The young man appeared to be crushed with disappointment. 'I am sorry,' he murmured. 'Very, very sorry that I have not had the happiness to please you.'

Madame Storey was giving an imitation of a woman who had never been made love to before. 'I . . . I like you,' she murmured, ' but you are strange to me.'

Soon after that he rose to go. 'If we meet on the terrace may I have the pleasure of talking with you again?' he asked.

'If you wish,' she said looking away. She would have blushed if she could, but that was impossible.

'I shall watch for you every afternoon!' he said eagerly. He placed his heels together and bowed. 'Permit me to introduce myself. Marcel Durocher.' He handed her his card.

'I am Mrs Bradford,' said Madame Storey in confusion. 'I'm sorry I haven't a card with me.'

'And this lady?' he said turning to me.

'Oh, Miss Toller, my companion!' she answered carelessly.

He left us.

When he was out of hearing Madame Storey murmured: 'Well, I planted a seed in his mind. Let us pray that it will sprout.'

On the following afternoon we were seated on the terrace when Madame Storey said suddenly: 'It *has* sprouted.'

Following the direction of her glance I saw Durocher coming along with Charlie Raines in tow. My heart began to pound against my ribs. Fortunately the scared red-nosed companion was not forced to take any part in the scene that followed.

Charlie had learned his lesson well. He never batted an eye when he was introduced.

They talked about all sorts of things. Lady Wedderminster appeared to warm towards the handsome young American. Marcel made believe to be jealous, but his wicked eyes were full of satisfaction. It was not necessary for anybody to steer the talk around to the subject of dancing. After a while it got there itself.

'Charlie is a wonderful dancer,' said Marcel jealously.

Lady Wedderminster looked at Charlie eagerly.

'Marcel mentioned that you would like to learn to dance,' said Charlie. 'I'd be tickled to death to teach you if you'll let me. There's a little studio on the Avenue de Joffre where we can practise. But I'll bet you anything you like, that inside an hour you'll be ready to take the floor at the Sporting Club.'

'I should like it,' murmured Lady Wedderminster, letting a world of meaning appear in her hungry hollow eyes.

'You go with him!' grumbled Marcel jealously. But his pleased eyes were saying: She's hooked! . . . It was a good comedy.

'Well, come on, let's go!' said Charlie.

We climbed the steps to the street and Marcel hailed a taxicab. Madame Storey said with the insulting indifference that she assumed towards me:

'Cora, you run off to the Café de Paris. Buy yourself a drink on the terrace and wait until I come back.'

This was about three o'clock. Shortly before five they returned. I was sitting with my drink before me when they got out of a taxi at the pavement. Marcel raised his hat and walked off; Madame Storey and Charlie came to my table. Charlie was saying: 'Thank God he's left us! I didn't dare come out of my part for a moment at the studio. That guy has eyes like a lynx and ears like nothing human!'

They sat down. 'Gee! What wonderful disguises!' Charlie went on. 'Both you and Bella. Marvellous! Even now I can't believe that you are really you.'

'Restrain your enthusiasm,' said Madame Storey in the dull manner of Lady Wedderminster. 'Marcel has gone, but there are other spies. Act towards me as if I were a difficult prospect that you were working on, and you can say what you like.'

Charlie passed a hand over his mouth. 'I can't help grinning when you and Bella and I are together,' he said apologetically.

'Why didn't you let me hear from you?' she asked.

'I couldn't. Until now I've been watched night and day. This is the first time Marcel has left me on my own.'

'Good! That means you have passed. . . . What has happened?'

'Well,' said Charlie, 'after I had been thrown up on the beach for a couple of days, this guy Marcel picked me up. Offered to share his room with me. Made out it was pure friendship. He has a swell room in a villa on the main street a little way out. We always ride in and out on the bus, though it isn't far.

'I haven't got any of the dope on the gang yet. Marcel admits, of course, that he's a gigolo, but makes out that he's on his own. He's training me as his side partner. He feeds me a line of cynical philosophy that would have corrupted the angel Gabriel when young. I appear to lap it up like milk. . . . One thing struck me as funny. He had me get my photograph taken in a photomat one day. Just for a joke, he made out.'

'He wanted to show it to his bosses,' said Madame Storey. 'Go on.'

'I haven't been told anything,' said Charlie, 'but I have put two and two together. There are a lot of these bozos in Monte Carlo. They live around in different places, and do not associate except when they need to help each other out. For an identification badge each one has a little white book to show, but I haven't been given one.'

'I know the book,' said Madame Storey dryly. 'What about the boss?'

'Haven't heard a whisper about him,' said Charlie, 'but I know there is a boss because Marcel gets orders from him in writing that he translates with the aid of the little white book. And he makes reports to his boss. But how he gets his orders or sends his reports I don't know.'

We sipped our *thé au rhum*, the gypsy orchestra played a *czardas*, and the people went hurrying along the pavement to the Casino. They always hurry when they go in.

'Now that you and I have joined up,' Madame Storey said to Charlie, 'we must pull off our trick swiftly. If there is any delay we are certain to be found out and then . . . good night! . . . Have you any idea of what their intentions are towards Lady Wedderminster?'

Charlie shook his head. 'Blackmail I reckon.'

'That's what I am afraid of,' she said. 'Blackmail is too complicated and too slow an operation. We must try to tempt them to rob me outright.'

'Robbery! Good God!' muttered Charlie, changing colour.

'When you make your report to Marcel about me,' Madame Storey went on, 'tell him that I confided to you that I had brought a large sum in cash to Monte Carlo because I didn't want my husband or my bankers to know that I was going to gamble. Tell him that I have almost doubled it since I came, and that I am carrying half a million francs around with me because I'm afraid to leave it in my room.'

'But . . . but,' stammered Charlie, 'they will attack you!'

'You are coming out of your part,' she warned. 'We will take care of that. . . . If I figure right,' she went on, 'as soon as Marcel gets this information he will report it to his boss, and will receive instructions how to act. Ah! If you could get me a copy of Marcel's instructions we would have them dead to rights!'

'I'll do my damnedest,' said Charlie.

The time that followed was hard on the nerves. Charlie reported to

Marcel that Lady Wedderminster was carrying around half a million francs on her person. Marcel transmitted the fact to his boss, and received instructions from him what to do. But Charlie was unable to find out what his orders were. Charlie said:

' While Marcel was decoding his letter from the boss he caught me looking at it. He didn't say anything, but his face turned ugly. When he had digested the contents he lit a match and burned it up.'

' H'm!' said Madame Storey grimly. ' Never allow yourself to look at one of the boss's letters again. Make no attempt to get hold of them. We don't want to lose you. I'll put out another line.'

' They write to each other on small pieces of paper,' said Charlie, ' and enclose their letters in little envelopes about two inches by three in size. There is no address on these envelopes. How they come to Marcel or how he sends them I can't guess. They don't go through the mail, and no messengers come to the house. Marcel goes out by himself about nine o'clock every morning, but I reckon it wouldn't be healthy for me to try to follow him.'

' It would not,' said Madame Storey. ' But you can bring me one of the envelopes they use if Marcel does not burn them.'

Thus we were in the position of expecting to be robbed at any moment without knowing when or where the blow would fall. Madame Storey did, as a matter of fact, carry around the half million with her. The bills were marked. What made the strain harder on me was that she took to going out by herself at all hours. That perpendicular line appeared between her brows which always warns me that the situation is serious. She never speaks of her plans in advance.

Marcel's instructions to Charlie were merely to ' keep the old girl going.' Sometimes when Charlie met us Marcel would be with him; sometimes Charlie came alone.

Meanwhile smart society in Monte Carlo, having been impressed by the social items in the *Paris Herald*, began to take notice of Lady Wedderminster. Amos Rudd sent her one of his characteristic notes asking her to dinner.

She answered it in the third person with that superb nonchalance of which only the English are capable.

Lady Wedderminster presents her compliments to Mr Rudd, and begs to thank him for his invitation. Lady Wedderminster never accepts invitations from those whom she has not had the pleasure of meeting.

So much for Amos!

Mr and Mrs James Wentworth Hawkins came to call. Their names were pronounced over the telephone with a certain awe.

'Why are they so famous?' I said.

'For no reason,' said Madame Storey, 'except that their names appear so often in the *Paris Herald*. That's what they live for.'

We went down to the hotel drawing room to receive them. I didn't like them any better at a second view. Like so many married couples they bore a strong resemblance to each other. Fat and brutalized by rich living they were the most useless cumberers of the earth I have ever encountered.

Madame Storey, alias Lady Wedderminster, polite and a little bored, forced them to make the running. They stumbled through it somewhat confused, but determined to see the visit to a finish. When they got up to go Mrs Hawkins said effusively:

'I hope you'll fix a night when we may have the pleasure of having you to dinner.'

'So kind of you,' drawled Lady Wedderminster playing with her bracelet. 'But I've come to Monte Carlo for a rest. I'm not accepting any invitations. I'm sure you'll understand.'

'Oh!' said Mrs Hawkins.

When they had gone Madame Storey said dryly, 'They won't be any the less anxious to have me because they were turned down once.'

One afternoon when Madame Storey sat down at a roulette table in the Sporting Club, she found herself almost directly opposite Turner Moale. I was standing meekly behind her chair.

Mr Moale paid no attention to us. The man's distinction was remarkable. He was beautifully dressed and he could gamble without losing his dignity. In his eyes showed that intensely withdrawn look that characterizes the born gambler. Well, if you require excitement there is nothing like roulette. I have enough excitement in my job.

The supposed Lady Wedderminster put a thousand francs on number thirty-three and won. An excited murmur went around the table. Turner Moale took notice of her. Presently she won again and refused to play any more for the moment.

'It is so tiresome when everybody follows one's play,' she said as we left the table.

We went into the café and ordered aperitifs. By and by Turner

Moale came strolling through the rooms, putting on his princely manner whether anybody was watching him or not. He stopped by our table.

'May I introduce myself?' he said with engaging affability. 'I am Turner Moale.'

Lady Wedderminster could afford to unbend with him because his style was so much better than the other Americans'. 'I have heard of you,' she said. 'Won't you sit down? I am Lady Wedderminster.'

'I know it,' he said, sitting.

'How did you know it?'

'I asked at the roulette table where you were both playing just now. Everybody around the table knew you. Everybody was talking of your luck.'

She frowned. 'How annoying!'

'Why?' he asked.

'Somebody may carry the news back to England.'

'What of it?' he said.

'I do not come of a gambling family,' she said dryly.

'Thank God I have no family!' he said with his calm assurance. 'And so I can say it openly. I love to gamble! When I gamble I am twenty-one again!'

Lady Wedderminster smiled. 'Sometimes one is dull in England,' she said, looking down at her hands.

'You like it here?' he asked.

She shrugged in a manner that allowed him to suppose anything he wished.

'How long shall you remain in Monte Carlo?'

'As long as my luck holds.'

'Ah, I wish I could catch a little luck from you, Lady Wedderminster. I always lose!' He said it with a wave of his hand that suggested he lost no sleep over it.

'I don't always win,' she said.

'But according to the gossip of the tables you are thousands and thousands ahead,' he said laughing. 'Do you know what they call you? The Golden Milady.'

Lady Wedderminster smiled.

Charlie came searching for us through the rooms, and she arose like a woman transformed. 'Charlie!' she murmured, slipping her hand under his arm. 'I was so afraid you weren't coming!'

Charlie was wise. He realized that a show was being put on for somebody, and played up to her. 'I am a bit late,' he said, patting her hand. 'So sorry!'

'Come,' she said. 'I have so much to tell you. I won a hundred thousand francs today.' Suddenly she appeared to recollect Mr Moale, and became the reserved Englishwoman again. 'Oh! Pardon! Au revoir, Mr Moale. I hope we may meet soon again.'

She moved away, leaning on Charlie's arm. Mr Moale returned to the gaming rooms treading like the prince of a small country, looking about him as if anxious not to miss anybody's bow. I paid the check.

On the following night Charlie turned up at the hotel resplendent in evening dress. My heart warmed to the boy, so handsome and droll; so essentially decent. He was very much upset. I could see the faint flush under his pale skin. He came alone and we received him in the parlour of our suite.

'Rosika,' he said in a voice that shook a little, 'I'm supposed to persuade you to dine with me tonight at a little place up in the mountains.'

'Well, I am persuaded,' she said smiling.

'But in the mountains!' he cried in distress. 'In a place chosen by themselves. I don't know what is going to happen. How can I go through with it?'

'But I wish to be robbed,' said Madame Storey. 'I am counting on it!'

'Don't joke about it! Suppose they were to hurt you!'

'They won't hurt me, because I'm going to squawk and give right up.'

'I'm to persuade you to leave Bella at home,' he said.

'Oh, no!' I exclaimed involuntarily.

'What, are you so anxious to be robbed?' asked Madame Storey teasingly.

'No! But it would be worse to be left here alone, and not to know what was happening. I couldn't bear it.'

She considered for a moment. 'I believe I'll take Bella,' she said. 'After all, it would be natural for the Englishwoman to have a spasm of propriety at the last moment, and insist on taking her companion.'

'I don't even know where the place is,' Charlie went on, pacing the room in his agitation. 'Only the chauffeur knows. You see, they don't trust me completely. It's supposed to be called Bruno's, and I was told to describe it to you as a very plain little place, but the last word in smartness. Only a few people know of it. All this is just a stall, I reckon.'

'It doesn't matter,' said Madame Storey.

'Just as I was leaving,' said Charlie, 'Marcel caught up my hand to compare my wrist watch with his. He said with a grin, "Dinner will be served at seven-thirty. When you hear the canary sing I suggest that you excuse yourself from the room for a moment. It will help to save your face later."'

'Good!' said Madame Storey. 'That is exactly what you must do.'

'I would feel like a cur if I walked out and left you to the mercy of those scoundrels!' cried poor Charlie.

'Your feelings do you credit,' she said, 'but you must suppress them and use your head.'

'All right,' he muttered. 'But it's not going to be easy!'

We set off at seven. The car we picked up at the hotel door appeared to be an ordinary taxi, but it had been planted there for Charlie. We climbed rapidly through the narrow twisting streets to the upper town. When we came out on the well-remembered road with the hairpin curves, I turned a little sick with apprehension. La Turbie again!

However, a mile short of that village we turned sharp to the right and sped around the side of the mountain in the opposite direction. The lights of Monte Carlo sparkled fifteen hundred feet below.

'This is the Grand Corniche road,' remarked Madame Storey. 'I have been looking at the map.'

After travelling for a mile or two, and putting a shoulder of the mountain between us and the friendly lights of town, we drew up before an ordinary little house on the outside of the road; a narrow one-storey house clinging to the steep mountainside like a limpet. The windows were shuttered tight.

'Is this the place?' asked Madame Storey, loud enough to carry to the chauffeur's ears.

'*Oui, madame; chez Bruno,*' he answered. '*Un bon restaurant!*'

Charlie whispered, 'Do you want to turn back? It would be natural.'

'No,' she said, 'I'm supposed to be an infatuated woman. Such a one would be blind.'

Certainly a more suitable place for the commission of a crime could scarcely have been found. The little house crouched alone under the stars, surrounded by dark mountain masses.

We got out, and the chauffeur drove on out of sight. The road was too narrow for him to turn around. He was supposed to return for us at eleven. Charlie rapped at the door.

We were admitted directly into a big kitchen with a white-clad chef presiding over the stove, an assistant and a waiter. They all had a self-conscious look as if they had been listening for us. There were no women visible. But the smell of the cooking was real.

'Anyhow they're going to feed us,' murmured Madame Storey, sniffing.

The men lined up bowing as the custom is. There was a look of animal greed in the chef's little eyes. He expressed surprise at the sight of me. 'Dinner was ordered for two persons,' he said respectfully.

'I brought my companion,' said Madame Storey in the cold English voice. 'Does it matter?'

'*Non, non, madame!* There is sufficient. Descend if you please.'

Owing to the manner of the house's construction, the dining room was below. We passed through a narrow hall to the stairs. There was a door opposite the kitchen which was standing open just an inch. The room inside it was dark. My skin prickled as I passed it. Instinct told me there were men in there listening.

Downstairs a small plain room with a table set for two, sideboard, sofa. The waiter followed us in and set a third place. He kept his eyes down the whole time and I could not read his expression. At the end of the room there was a glass door leading to a tiny terrace. From the terrace, steps rose to the kitchen above. The windows of the room looked down into a black abyss.

I cannot remember what we ate. Madame Storey said it was excellent. I shoved the food down my throat merely because I thought it would look suspicious if I sent it back untouched. Charlie had the hardest part to play, because he was supposed to make a noise as if we were having a good time. He drank a lot of wine.

In the beginning there was a good deal of running about and the sound of voices, as if there were parties dining in other rooms. Just stage business I assumed. It died away and silence filled the house except for the noise we made ourselves.

With the coffee and cointreau the waiter brought the bill. When Charlie paid it the man left the room with a furtive look. It was the first time I had seen his eyes. Presently we heard the main door of the house close, and a bar fell across it. Just for an experiment Madame Storey rang the bell. Nobody came.

'The staff has walked out on us,' she murmured.

Charlie had the liqueur glass at his lips when the bird whistle softly sounded upstairs. One of those lead whistles with a pea to imitate a trill. A cold perspiration broke out on me. Charlie turned pale and put his glass down.

'Must I go?' he murmured.

'Go!' said Madame Storey. 'There is no danger if you keep quiet.'

'Excuse me a minute,' he said, raising his voice, and dragged himself out of the room: started up the stairs.

He had no more than reached the upper floor when all the lights went out. It was so unexpected that a little cry broke from me. Hysteria gripped my throat; I clung to Madame Storey.

'Steady!' she whispered. 'There is no danger!'

That was all very well for a brave person, but my nerves were fluttering like aspen leaves.

We heard the door from the terrace open. A flashlight was switched on and cast into our eyes. In its light we clung together like any two frightened women. In the light reflected from the walls I could see that two dim shapes had entered. Their faces were indistinguishable. One was a powerful figure.

'Don't scream,' said the smaller man hoarsely.

'What do you want?' asked Madame Storey, letting a quaver come into her voice.

'The bundle of thousand-franc notes you have on your person,' he said. 'If you give them up you won't be harmed.' The voice was disguised, but I recognized it.

Madame Storey hesitated.

'Quick!' he said. 'Or I'll take them from you!'

She hastily unfastened the notes which she carried inside her dress, and threw them on the table. He put the light on them, and gave them a hasty examination.

'All right,' he said, thrusting them in his pocket.

Up to that moment everything had gone exactly as Madame Storey had foreseen. We would have been allowed to go, and there would have been no trouble, had it not been for one of those accidents that you cannot provide against.

I was wearing a string of common crystals around my neck. They were of no value, but I suppose in the flash of the electric torch they glittered like diamonds. The big man was a common fellow and he yielded to temptation. Slyly moving close to me, he put his two hands around my neck and jerked the string apart.

When his hands touched me I could not help myself; I screamed with all my might. The sound was too much for Charlie. There was the sound of a blow and fall from above, Charlie came leaping down the stairs shouting thickly:

'Keep your hands off them! Keep your hands off them!'

A scene of insane confusion followed. The smaller robber shouted, 'Silence that fool!' I had an impression that the big man drew a gun. Madame Storey leaped forward, and struck the flashlight out of the first man's hand. It went out and rolled away on the floor. We were left in complete darkness.

I heard the man scrabbling on the floor for his torch. The other kept shouting, 'Light! Light!' Somebody grabbed my wrist and pulled me violently towards the door at the foot of the stairs. There we met another man cascading down the stairs. There was a brief struggle. Somebody was thrown down with a groan. I was dragged on up the stairs. All this in the dark.

The kitchen was lighted with a candle. Just inside the door stood a fourth man with a chair raised over his head, prepared to smash the first who entered. Somehow we banged through the door across the landing, and got it shut behind us. It had both a bolt and a key. We leaned against it breathing heavily; Madame Storey, Charlie and I.

'You spoiled everything by your outbreak,' said Madame Storey sternly.

'How could I help it?' groaned Charlie.

'Never mind now. Listen!'

There was a furious pounding at the door, and we backed away from it. Marcel cried out – no longer taking any care to disguise his voice – 'Give us that fellow and we won't hurt you. He brought you here, didn't he? He betrayed you into our hands. Now he has betrayed us. Give him up to us and we'll let you go.'

No answer from our side of the door.

Marcel flung himself against it, cursing horribly. Luckily it was a heavy door. Several of them put their shoulders against it. It creaked dangerously, but held. Finally Marcel screamed in a voice breaking with rage.

' The axe! The axe!'

There was a pause. I felt like a rat in a trap. Madame Storey actually lit a cigarette. When the light flared up I saw that her face was calm. Inexplicable woman! Charlie went to a window which opened on the road.

' Don't open the shutters!' she said sharply.

' Can't we do something? Something?' I groaned.

' Wait!' she said.

Marcel aimed a blow at the door that split one of the panels but did not shatter it. Before he could strike another there was a crash from the kitchen and a rush of feet. An appalling struggle took place out there. Not a cry was raised; only the sound of blows and stamping feet, and one crash after another as the tables were overthrown, the crockery broken, the cooking utensils flung together.

' Let me get in this!' said Charlie thickly.

' There is no need,' said Madame Storey barring the way.

Suddenly it was over. We heard a low voice issuing commands. Then the voice was raised, calling:

' Lady Wedderminster! Lady Wedderminster!'

' Here!' said Madame Storey unlocking the door.

We followed her into the kitchen. They had got the lights turned on. It was like a battlefield. Against the far wall stood four sullen, beaten men handcuffed together. Six policemen took off their kepis and wiped their moist foreheads. Our old acquaintance the chief of detectives was in command.

' *Voilà, madame!*' he said. ' You see, we have them. You are a brave lady!'

Marcel, frantic with rage, spat out a stream of curses at the sight of Charlie. ' Traitor! Traitor! I'll get you yet!'

' Oh, I reckon you'll be put away for quite a spell,' drawled Charlie.

Marcel was wearing a brown suit. All the buttons were on it tonight. Madame Storey walked to him and examined it attentively.

' Chief,' she said, turning, ' one of the murderers of Raoul d'Aymara wore a suit of this material. You have the button that was pulled off his coat. It was the middle button on this coat. You can see where the hole in the cloth has been stopped. The present button has been sewed on with cotton thread, not silk like the others. This is your man.'

The chief's face was a study. ' But madame,' he stammered, ' how did you . . . how did you know about that affair?'

' All will be explained later,' she said.

He knew her then. His eyes almost started from his head. ' Incredible! Incredible!' he whispered.

And Marcel knew her. A wild terror came into his face. He had no more to say.

' Chief,' said Madame Storey, ' I beg that you will take these men into town, and lock them up quietly and secretly. If the news of their arrest should get about, their master will escape us.'

' I understand, madame,' he answered, bowing. ' It shall be done.'

Charlie could no longer hold himself in. ' How did the police get here?' he demanded to know.

' I gave them a tip,' said Madame Storey carelessly.

' How did you know where the place was? I didn't know.'

' I intercepted Marcel's instructions from his boss this morning.'

' Good God!' muttered Charlie. ' You might have let me know,' he added in a grumbling voice. ' It would have saved me a lot of mental agony.'

' Exactly,' she said smiling. ' That's why I didn't tell you. You were watched every minute. This was your first job, and if you had not appeared to be nervous their suspicions would have been aroused. . . . But I admit I should not have taken Bella,' she added teasingly. ' That was an error of judgement.'

I hung my head. ' If you had felt the man's fingers around your throat . . .'

She laughed.

Madame Storey accompanied the chief of detectives back to town in order to be present when he compared the button and its torn piece of cloth with Marcel's coat. She sent me direct to the hotel with Charlie, and I did not see her again that night.

Next morning when I got up she had already gone out. Shortly before ten she returned wearing an inscrutable smile. ' Get your hat, Bella, if you want to be in at the death,' she said.

The chief of detectives was waiting for us in the lobby of the hotel. The three of us crossed the street and entered the Casino, which had not yet opened its doors for the day. Our companion concealed himself in the room on the left, where you present your credentials and obtain cards for the gaming rooms, while we took up our position in the middle of the entrance hall. Through the glass we could see the most determined gamblers waiting on the steps for the doors to open.

'What are we waiting for?' I asked.

'The big boss,' she said smiling.

'How will we know him?'

'He will come out of the *vestiaire* – if he comes at all – carrying a swanky overnight bag of brown seal.'

At that moment the doors were opened and the waiting people swarmed through. They all made their way first into the cloakroom or *vestiaire* to leave their wraps. With the others there was a large personally conducted party of tourists and it made a lot of confusion. I could not possibly distinguish everybody.

'Never mind their faces,' said Madame Storey. 'Watch for the bag. I checked it here myself half an hour ago.'

She took pity on the torment of curiosity that my face must have expressed, and in a low voice explained what had happened, without ever ceasing to use her keen busy eyes on the people who passed to and fro in front of us.

'Their method of corresponding was as simple as it was ingenious. It was Marcel's habit of boarding a bus every morning at nine o'clock that gave me the lead. I noticed that he always took the same bus; number sixty-three. And occupied the last seat in the left-hand corner. He would slip his little envelope in the crack of the cushioned seat and leave it there. He always got out at the Casino gardens. Somewhere farther along the route the boss would get on and find his letter or leave one.

'Bus sixty-three was their post office. On its return trip Marcel boarded it to see if anything had been left for him. As soon as I got onto this, I boarded the bus as soon as Marcel got off; copied the note, enclosed it in a fresh envelope, replaced it and got off. If I had continued to the end of the line I might have been able to spot the boss, but the risk was too great. You see, it would have been entirely out of character for Lady Wedderminster to have been found riding in the street buses.'

'How could you read their letters?' I asked.

'With the dictionary it was easy. Without the dictionary their code would have baffled the greatest expert of them all. For any word beginning with A they would put down the first word that followed it in the dictionary. For a word beginning with B the second word that followed it, and so on through the alphabet. The

language used was English, and to make detection more difficult all
the little words such as pronouns, prepositions and articles were
written in correctly.'

'Where does the brown-seal bag come in?'

'In the boss's final instructions to Marcel yesterday, he told him
to put the half million francs in the bag, check it at the *vestiaire* of
the Casino, and send him the check in the usual manner. I found the
bag in Marcel's room and obeyed instructions.'

Time passed. The gamblers hurried past us with their curiously
intent expressions as if they were bound on errands of life and death.
The tourist party, having been taken for a tour of the rooms,
streamed out of the building gaping. A ceaseless procession
of motor-cars rolled up to the door, and discharged their
aristocratic freight. Beyond, the sunshine was glorious on a bed of
pink cyclamens.

The suspense was horrible. I was looking for something I had
never seen. Suppose our man had had a warning and never turned
up? One of the most difficult things in the world is to keep your
attention focused on individuals in a moving crowd. Scores of faces
passing one after another have a hypnotic effect. In spite of yourself
they begin to blur; they all look alike. I had a dread that I might
fail. I couldn't take things in quick enough. People passed with the
lower part of their bodies hidden. Stop! Stop! I cried in my mind –
but they were already gone.

In the end I was staring at the brown bag for a full second, I
suppose, before I realized with a terrific shock that *that* was what I
was waiting for. My heart began to pound; my eyes flew to the face
of the man who carried it. . . . It was Turner Moale.

I had a curiously gone feeling, as if the earth had dropped from
under me. Turner Moale! Walking out of the *vestiaire* as if he
owned all Monte Carlo! He was clad in a springtime symphony of
greys; hat, tie, suit, spats; with yellow gloves and a yellow carnation
in his buttonhole. Madame Storey dropped her umbrella on the floor
with a clatter, and the chief of detectives appeared from his place of
concealment.

'Lady Wedderminster!' cried Moale gaily. 'You *are* astir early!
And going to play at the Casino too!'

'Chief!' said Madame Storey a little grimly. 'There is your
man!'

That unhappy official turned as pale as paper. 'But madame!'

he protested. 'Surely there is a mistake. Monsieur Turner Moale is one of our most prominent citizens!'

'Oh, quite!' said Madame Storey. 'But in that bag you will find the half million francs that were stolen from me last night.'

The man's aplomb was perfect. He never turned a hair. 'Why, Lady Wedderminster, what is the matter?' he asked, laughing. 'You appear to be making a charge against me. How odd!'

'Monsieur, this lady is Madame Rosika Storey,' said the shaken chief.

This was a facer for Moale. The moment he was told who she was, he recognized her. He took it on the chin. 'So it is!' he cried gaily. 'But what has it got to do with me, monsieur?'

'Look in the bag,' suggested Madame Storey to the chief. 'Here is a key. I found it in Marcel's room.'

'Marcel's room!' repeated Moale sharply. His dark eyes rolled like those of a vicious horse.

'Marcel Durocher and the shock troops were arrested at Bruno's last night,' she said dryly.

The chief took a look in the bag, and his hesitation vanished. He placed a hand on Turner Moale's shoulder.

'Remove your hand!' said Moale with an air of outraged dignity. The policeman obeyed. Moale instantly recovered his affability. 'Let us not make a public scene,' he said. 'My car is here. Come to my house and we'll talk it over.'

'I suggest the police station,' said Madame Storey.

Driving away in the car Moale suddenly dropped his pretence of innocence. 'Lady, I salute you!' he said in his gay manner. 'How did you come to pick on me?'

Madame Storey loves a good loser. 'Have a cigarette,' she said. 'I suspected you because I couldn't figure out where a retired actor had found the money to entertain on such a princely scale.'

'You are marvellous!' he cried – but all the bravado had gone out of him. Suddenly he looked shrunken and old. I couldn't help but feel a kind of regret. It was like witnessing the destruction of a unique work of art.

Meanwhile Charlie had been sent to sit on the terrace, where he was told to read the little white book. It was the agreed signal between the gigolos. One by one they approached the reader. He sent them to Marcel's room on the pretext that they were to receive instructions there. Each one was arrested there as he came. Thus the whole bunch was rounded up in the course of the day. There was no evidence against these handsome good-for-nothings, and they were merely sent out of the principality with a warning not to return.

Mrs Rudd likewise escaped punishment, though she was certainly an accomplice of Moale's. It seemed that her wealthy husband kept too tight a hand on the purse strings. She presently ran away with a more open-handed man, and old Amos married again.

When the trial came on, Marcel Durocher gave evidence against his associates. The three men who were arrested with him at Bruno's were the same three who had assisted at the murder of Raoul d'Aymara. Marcel related his dealings with Turner Moale in detail. He swore that, until the moment that he was brought face to face with Moale in court, he had never laid eyes on him, and didn't know who he was.

Moale was sent to prison for life – not a long term in his case; Marcel got twenty years, and the three others lesser sentences.

As for Charlie Raines, having had the adventure of his life, he was perfectly content to sail for home and take a job in the old man's stove factory. From Cherbourg he sent me a postcard with a spirited sketch of himself balancing a kitchen stove on the tip of his nose. Underneath he had written: *Ex-gigolo juggling junk!*

F. Tennyson Jesse

LOT'S WIFE

THE HOTEL WAS FULL of just the sort of people you expect to find at hotels. There were the knitting women – grimmer than those harridans who knitted by the guillotine; there were Bright Young Things – to some minds grimmer still. There were family parties with small children who whooped up and down the corridors all day, and screamed when they had to go to bed. There were young men twirling Gallic moustaches and eyeing the smart ladies who sat about in bathing dresses, their slim brown legs unafraid of the eye of man or of the sun.

Solange decided that though within the hotel all was horrible, yet out of doors, in spite of endless motor cars along the highway, all was beautiful. After a winter in England most things would have been beautiful to Solange, but indeed the loveliness of this unspoiled Mediterranean Gulf would have pleased a far more exacting taste than was hers at the moment.

And then, as though to complete the charm, and reward Solange for sordid experiences of the immediate past, beauty was added even to life in the hotel. A young Scottish girl, Flora MacTavish, arrived with her mother, and Flora was one of those rare beings upon whom the eye can rest with endless enchantment. She was young and very fair without being insipid, high of cheek-bone, but with exquisitely tender and full lips. Her clear water-grey eyes were almond-shaped, with a fine line of fair brows set high above them. She was almost too thin for her height, and she more nearly resembled Botticelli's Venus than any human being Solange had ever known.

Foreheads were 'in' again, and Flora's was high, so high that it would have been thought incredibly dowdy, and would have been covered only a few years earlier. That high forehead, the almond-shaped eyes and long delicious nose, that tender mouth, pointed chin, and long thick neck were, so Solange told herself delightedly, not only complete Botticelli, but entirely the fashion of the moment as well. Flora MacTavish was one of those fortunate people who happen to be just right for the period in which they live.

Solange gazed, envied, and admired, for Flora, besides possessing that subtle disproportion which means beauty, had charm. She was not intellectual, but she had that fundamental mixture of sweetness and iron-hard determination possessed by all truly womanly women. Had her bones not been so small, she might have looked thin to angularity, and had her nature not been sweet and unselfish, her mind would have been thin to angularity also. Her ideas were very much at the mercy of any one whom she met; she was both fluid and obstinate. Compact of honey and rose and pearl, her fundamental sturdiness was only betrayed by her high cheek-bones and a certain way she had of setting her soft, full lips.

She was one of those girls who are perhaps ill-advised to travel with their mothers, for it was possible to see, almost lost in Mrs MacTavish's pink and white cushiony plumpness, in her large bosom and flat, dimpled hands, something of Flora's beauty. Flora, in fact, travelled about with her own future, but she was so enchanting that it took someone with an eye as well trained as was that of Solange to discover it.

Solange made friends with the MacTavishes, not because she thought they would interest her, but simply so that she could have an excuse for looking at Flora, and the more she grew to know her, the more delicious the girl appeared. Her high, clear, fluting voice, her swift rippling movements, the sudden stillnesses into which her long limbs fell, were in keeping with the sophisticated simplicity of her appearance. There was nothing of the ingénue, nothing of the pretty milkmaid, about Flora.

As the days went by, and Professor Fontaine's house, where he and Solange were hoping to spend the summer months, still remained impossible, owing to alterations in the bathroom and the dilatory habits of workpeople in the South, Solange grew more and more to depend for her daily interest on the intercourse with the MacTavishes. Flora MacTavish might not be a stimulating companion for the mind, but she was a delight for the eye. And then, almost before she realized it, Solange began to be aware that there was some strange undercurrent of feeling upsetting the minds of both mother and daughter, and at once her interest was alert. For several days Flora only appeared at dinner in the evening, and on those days Mrs Mac-

Tavish would ask Solange to lunch at her table. Flora was out with
a friend, she would say, the pursing of her lips not unlike Flora's
own little unconscious action. Almost without realizing the fact,
Solange knew that Mrs MacTavish disapproved of this friend. Flora
herself would flicker through the hotel like a lovely eager flame just
in time for dinner, her long, grey eyes shining, her pointed chin
tilted up on that long, thick neck of a Botticelli nymph, and during
dinner and afterwards she would be aloof and secret, yet alight.

One day Mrs MacTavish broke down, though with evident difficulty, her Scottish habit of reticence and confided her anxieties to
Solange over the luncheon table where Flora had left them to a
tête-à-tête meal.

'She is my only one, Miss Fontaine, and I am so worried I don't
know what to do. It is a man, of course. All the trouble in the world
is made by men. If I had my way, I really believe I'd shut them all
up in monasteries, or something.'

Solange, refraining from pointing out that had this excellent
method of settling the sex problem obtained some twenty years ago,
there would have been no Flora to worry a devoted mother, nodded
sympathy, and Mrs MacTavish, her plump face creased with worry,
poured out all her trouble. Flora was in love, and the man she loved
was, for all he knew to the contrary, a married man.

'How do you mean, "for all he knows to the contrary"?' asked
Solange, interested.

'His wife ran away,' said Mrs MacTavish. 'It's over a year ago
now, and although I believe he spent money like water trying to find
her, he hasn't succeeded. Not that he wants her back again, you
understand; he is in love with my Flora right enough. I never saw a
man so mad over a girl, but, naturally, if his wife's still alive, he
wants to know it and arrange a divorce; and if the poor thing's dead,
why, then I suppose he and Flora could marry right away. Not that
I'm keen on it. I'd sooner my girl didn't marry a widower. But then,'
added Mrs MacTavish, 'I don't suppose she'd be the first, even if he
hadn't been married, if you know what I mean.'

'What's the man like?' asked Solange. 'What does he do? Is he
a Frenchman?'

'No, he's an Englishman, though I will say he's a Scot on his
mother's side. His name's Angus Martin, and he's a painter, and
he's built a big house down on the shore near here. I don't know
that he does anything in particular except paint. He's travelled a lot.

He's very well off, and they all say he's very clever. Designed this house himself and supervised the building of it, which goodness knows you need to do in these parts if your house is ever to get finished at all. But he's forty if he's a day, which I think is too old for Flora, though she's always liked men a good bit older than herself, and been bored with boys, so perhaps that doesn't matter much. Oh, no; it's not his age or even his being a widower that I mind. It's that we don't know if he's a widower or not, and I feel he ought to leave Flora alone until he's made sure of his position; but she's mad about him and won't listen to anything I say.'

'But what does she hope to do? Obviously they can't be married until they can find proof that his wife's dead.'

'Exactly, Miss Fontaine, and why I've told you about it is that having got to know you has given Flora and Mr Martin an idea. In fact, when she told him you were here, he asked me to tell you all about it today. We are simple people, Miss Fontaine, and haven't mixed in what you might call the great world much, but we've heard of you and seen your name in the papers now and again. Mr Martin thinks that you will be able to find out whether his wife is alive or dead.'

'That's not my sort of work,' said Solange doubtfully. 'Do you know what there is to go on, Mrs MacTavish?'

'Very little, I believe. They had some kind of tiff. It appears they were quarrelling and she just went off one night. That's really all I know about it, but I expect he'll be able to tell you some more. Flora's going to ask him to come to dinner tonight.'

Solange had never met anyone who puzzled her so completely as did Angus Martin. Usually she either liked or disliked people, either responded warmly to all the good she felt in them, or was warned by that curious instinct of hers of some inherent evil which perhaps had remained undetected by anyone else for a lifetime.

Now she was at a loss and ruefully admitted it to herself. She could not say that she had with Angus Martin that overpowering awareness of something wrong which had so often warned her of a criminal, but neither did she feel the man was good and honest.

Angus was a tall, quiet, studious-looking individual, with a lean, interesting face. His dark-grey eyes were deep set, the eyes of a thinker, and would have been altogether pleasing had they not been set too close together. He had very beautiful hands, with long, finely shaped fingers, and his dark hair had that touch of silver at the temples which is supposed to be so fascinating to young women. Certainly Flora was fascinated, though whether by his distinguished personality or because she really knew some special fineness and goodness that was latent in his character, Solange could not guess.

Dinner might easily have been an awkward meal considering that all four of the diners knew of Angus Martin's invidious position, and of Mrs MacTavish's disapproval; and yet so charming in his quiet way – for there was nothing flamboyant about him – was Angus, so like a clear and flickering flame was Flora, that they both seemed to transcend any commonplace awkwardness that more ordinary people might have been unable to dispel.

There was no doubt, Solange admitted, that he was as madly in love with Flora as she was with him. The complete round of the love emotion is a very rare thing. To find passion, mental sympathy, and physical suitability in one relationship is asking a good deal of life, but that Angus and Flora, despite the dissimilarity of their ages, had found it, it was impossible to doubt. Then why is it, Solange asked herself disgustedly, that I feel there is something wrong somewhere? It was to be many months before she was to find the answer to that question.

Not until dinner was over and they were taking their coffee under the bottle-palms in the garden, did Angus refer to the reason of the meeting, and then so simply and quietly that Solange found herself forced into admiration. Forced, she thought to herself, that's what's so funny. I resent liking and admiring him.

'I want you to know my story, Miss Fontaine,' he said, as he leant forward and lit her cigarette for her, 'because I am sure you are the person to help me.'

He smiled suddenly at Solange, and his smile was so charming in his ordinarily sombre face that in a flash Solange could see why it was that the fastidious Flora loved him.

'If you have finished your coffee,' he went on, 'perhaps you will come and walk through the gardens with me? I think it is easier to talk, don't you, when there are only two of you, and when you are moving about? Sitting still is all right for ordinary conversation, but it is no good for confidences.'

Solange drew her silk Chinese shawl round her shoulders, and, with a little smile of reassurance at Flora, obeyed his request.

His face became grave again when they were alone together

amidst the pine trees. He told his story with the simplicity combined with attention to detail that shows a careful and acute mind.

He had married, when a young art student, a woman considerably older than himself, who had been his model. The marriage had not proved a happy one. He did not blame his wife in any way, he said; doubtless he was difficult to get on with, but the fact remained that they had been totally unsuited to each other. Things had not been so bad while they had been poor, but when some four or five years ago an unexpected legacy from a distant relation had made him a rich man, matters had gone from bad to worse. When she no longer had to do her own housework, Mrs Martin became thoroughly bored, and one of his reasons for completing his villa on this unfrequented part of the coast – for, a year ago, when he had been building, the place was practically undiscovered – had been that he preferred to keep his troubles to himself.

They moved into the villa when one wing of it was ready for occupation, and at first she had seemed pleased with her new home and had busied herself with putting it in order. However, one evening they had a terrible quarrel:

'Really, Miss Fontaine, I can't remember what it was about. I know it started over something absurdly small. I hadn't admired a new hat she'd bought, or she thought a criticism I had made of the dinner was levelled at her instead of at the cook. You know how these things start – a few drops of bitterness trickle out which seem negligible, and then suddenly one is overwhelmed by a dark and dreadful torrent.' His face had paled, and for a moment he placed his long, sensitive hand over his eyes.

'And then?' prompted Solange.

'Well, and then she went. It still seems incredible to me when I think of it. I didn't expect to see her early next morning; she always had breakfast in her room and never came downstairs till lunch-time. I slept late myself, for I was tired and upset. I waited lunch for her, and when she still didn't come I sent one of the maids up to her room. She was not there, the bed had not been slept in, and some of her clothes had gone.'

'Which clothes? The clothes she'd been wearing the night before?'

'Those and others as well. A travelling suit and a blouse and hat – all the usual sort of things women travel in.'

'Had the car been taken out of the garage?'

'No, I think she must have left by one of the motor buses that pass my garden gate at frequent intervals. By that she could have got to St Raphaël and there boarded a train.'

'But surely,' said Solange, 'if she had left that morning one of the servants would have seen her go out of the house?'

'The servants don't sleep in the villa, but in the *dépendance.*'

'The motor buses don't run at night, do they?'

'No, but there's one very early in the morning.'

'Had anyone seen her on it?'

'No one could remember her, but the bus was very full of people going in to market, and my wife spoke French perfectly. We had lived many years in Paris.'

'Did she ever write to you? Or ask for money?'

'Yes, she wrote asking for money to be sent in English banknotes to Poste Restante, Charing Cross. I sent her £100.'

'Did you take the numbers of the notes?'

'Yes, but you will be able to trace the transaction at the bank at St Raphaël. They got the notes for me.'

'Did she acknowledge them?'

'Yes, and a couple of months later I got a note from her written from a house in Hereford Road, Bayswater, where she said she was very ill in lodgings. I had by then just met Flora. You can see what she is, Miss Fontaine, and won't be surprised to know that I loved her at once. I am not a man who has frittered himself away in light emotions, and I may say I had never loved before or realized in the least what it could be. I can only tell you that life will have no meaning for me if I can't marry Flora.

'When I got this letter from my wife I set off at once for the address she had given me, and arrived in London the following evening. I found my wife looking ill, but not desperately ill, though she had a nasty cough. I was sorry to see her so run down, and told her so. I offered to make, within reason, any settlement she liked if she would let me divorce her, or would divorce me. She promised to think it over and asked me to come again two days later. I trusted her, paid a lot of money – a thousand pounds – into her bank, and tried to possess my soul in patience for forty-eight hours.

'When I returned to Hereford Road she had gone, having closed her banking account and drawn all the money out of her bank. She must have bribed the landlady well, or won her sympathy in some way, for she refused to give me the slightest idea where she had gone; in fact, she said she didn't know, which may have been true, but my opinion is that landladies are an invariably curious sort of people and study addresses on labels and that sort of thing. I went nearly distracted, and when I got back to my hotel I found a letter from my wife. It bore the Portsmouth postmark, and simply said she had no intention of doing me such a good turn as setting me free to marry another woman; the money I'd given her would last a nice time, and that when she wanted more she would communicate with me again.

'Well, I have lived in hopes that she would. I have more money than I know what to do with now that it's no good to me, but I have never heard from that day to this. That is my story, Miss Fontaine, and if you can prove that my wife is dead – which I think must be the case; or she'd have tried to get more money from me – you can name your own fee. If she is alive, perhaps she will consent to the divorce by now. Anyway, I want the matter settled one way or another. I can't go on like this.'

Solange studied him and saw that that was true. His face seemed to have set into lines of suffering, as he told his story, and his hand was shaking a little as he took a cigarette out of his case.

'But what do you want me to do?' she asked.

'I want you to go and see what you can get out of the landlady. I believe she knows something, and though *I* can't get it out of her, *you* might be able to. I need hardly tell you that the question of expense doesn't enter in. For Heaven's sake, find out where my wife is!'

They were walking slowly back towards the hotel by now, and already Solange could see Flora approaching them between the trees, her frock gleaming through the dusk. Solange glanced at Angus and saw that his eyes were fixed on Flora with such a look of hunger in them as startled her. It was so avid, so naked, so primitive in such a quiet and highly civilized being. She felt extremely interested in both him and Flora, and made up her mind swiftly.

'Give me the name and address of the landlady, and a description of your wife, and I can start tomorrow,' she said, not without a feeling of relief that she was going to have a respite from the hotel and its denizens.

Solange found the Hereford Road landlady less adamant than had Angus Martin. Perhaps this was because Solange represented herself as being Mrs Martin's niece, anxious to find her and do her best for her. Perhaps it was because of the two ten-pound notes that she crackled between her fingers alluringly, or perhaps it was because of the bottle of port that she sent out to fetch from the nearest public house on making the discovery that the landlady, being a teetotaller, could only drink port.

'Poor lady,' observed Mrs Smithson pityingly, as she finished her third glass. 'If I ever saw death in any woman's face, it was in hers, miss. I don't need any doctors to tell me what I can see for myself. *I know.* Wasting away with consumption she was, and of course, London wasn't the best place for her. " I'll never get better, Mrs Smithson," she says to me, for she treated me very friendly and like a sister, as you might say, " I'll never get better, and I'm bound to get worse, but at least I'm going to do it in the best surroundings," and so off she went, and I packed for her with my own hands. The boxes were labelled for Portsmouth, but more than that I couldn't tell the gentleman, because I didn't know any more, and I couldn't tell you any more either, miss, only that I had a postcard from her yesterday, and I think, perhaps, in spite of my having promised not to tell, I really ought to, for her own sake.'

Yesterday! Solange felt she was indeed in luck. Chance, without which a detective is so often powerless, seemed to be on her side.

'Indeed, I ought to know where my aunt is, Mrs Smithson,' she said smoothing out the ten-pound notes on her knee, and gazing at them reflectively. 'Perhaps you would let me have a look at the postcard and then you wouldn't feel you had broken your word.'

This compromise at once satisfied any scruples that Mrs Smithson might have had, and she handed over the postcard. It was addressed in an educated hand, the postmark was the Isle of Wight, and the picture represented children playing on the beach at Ventnor. Across the sky was written:

Just a little line to let you know I am comfortable, though much weaker, and to thank you again for all you did for me. I have a nice little bedroom facing south, with a balcony, and lie out on it in the sun whenever there is any.

Yours affectionately,
G. M.

'No address, you see,' said Mrs Smithson, hastily pocketing the twenty pounds in case her information should be considered inadequate.

'That doesn't matter,' said Solange absently. 'She'll be easy enough to trace at Ventnor as she's living under her own name. Well, thank you very much, Mrs Smithson. I'll be sure and recommend your lodgings to anyone who wants rooms in London.'

'Thank you, dearie, and bless you,' said Mrs Smithson, whose teetotal liquor had begun to affect her tearducts, 'and I only hope you'll find the blessed angel a bit better.'

This pious wish was not to be fulfilled. The landlady had been right, and death was indeed stamped on the face of Gertrude Martin when Solange succeeded in finding her. She was lying out on a long chair on the balcony, and the pillow was hardly whiter than the face against it. She must have been a beautiful woman once. Her features, though wasted, still retained an exquisite fineness of contour. The great dark eyes, though sunken, were still brilliant. She did not hold out her hand to Solange after the latter had introduced herself, but lay looking at her with a whimsical smile on her pale mouth.

'I thought Angus would manage it,' she said. 'My congratulations to him. Of course, you come from him?'

'Yes,' replied Solange, 'I do. He'll be very sorry to hear you are like this.'

'Don't you believe it,' flashed the invalid. 'This is what he's been wanting. I'm only good for a few weeks more at the outside. Even the doctor admits that, and if you ask me I think it will be days. You're only just in time, Miss Fontaine – ' She broke off and gave a little elfin chuckle. 'Oh, Lord, it would have upset Angus if he hadn't got his proofs. However, there's no need to worry about that. Here I am, and here you are. If you like to wait till I die, you can, and then go back and tell him all about it.'

She was interrupted by a fit of coughing, which left her shaken and exhausted. She motioned with her hand towards a medicine bottle half-full of brandy standing on a little table. Solange poured some out and brought it to her. The sick woman's hand felt burning hot as it closed over hers round the tumbler.

Solange chatted with the landlady, a very much nicer woman than she of Hereford Road, and also went to see the invalid's doctor. He was a pleasant, straightforward, sensible man, and he told her candidly that Mrs Martin had very little longer to live.

Solange wired to Angus, although Gertrude Martin had told her that she would not see him, even were he to come over. Nevertheless, he came, as Solange felt that he would. Solange was as puzzled by the wife as by the husband. She had imagined from his account that

she would find a vulgar, common woman, instead of which Gertrude
was evidently possessed of a brilliant if caustic wit, and, so far as
Solange could see, of a remarkably sound philosophy. It was hard to
believe that this woman had ever ramped or raved over petty household details. But Solange knew from past experience that it is impossible for an outsider to gauge how hardly the presence of one
human being in a house may press upon another. This woman, who
showed traces of beauty and wit and now displayed such courage
and philosophy, might indeed have raved like a vulgar termagant
against her husband. Marriage was a relationship that did queer
things to people.

What she and Angus said to each other Solange never knew. To
all appearances, he was the devoted husband. He took up his quarters
at the nearest hotel; every day he called in to inquire, and sent her
flowers and fruit and champagne. But Gertrude only saw him twice,
once on his arrival and once a fortnight later, on the day she died.
He made no pretence of affection in his talks with Solange, but he
was obviously anxious to conform to all the decencies of life.

'What do you think of my husband?' Gertrude asked Solange
abruptly one day. Solange hesitated. 'You don't know what to think,
is that it?' asked the dying woman shrewdly.

'I feel I know him better than I did,' said Solange, 'but there's
something about him that makes him very difficult for me to know.
I don't think I can even explain what it is.'

'I suppose you mean that everything seems all right, and yet you
have some sort of a feeling that it isn't?'

Solange had never in all her life felt so startled. She had been
lying back in her chair, but now she sat up suddenly and stared at
Gertrude. She went swiftly in her own mind over her acquaintanceship with Angus Martin. She had nothing against him. His conduct
towards the dying woman, towards Flora, towards herself, was in
every degree what it should be, yet somehow she liked Gertrude
better than Angus. Indeed, it was for Gertrude's sake she had stayed
on in Ventnor, a place she abominated, after the job she had con-
tracted to do – the finding of Mrs Martin – was completed. The two
women had a queer sort of liking and respect for each other, and to
Solange there was the added fascination that Gertrude puzzled her.
Why was there sometimes that odd look of compunction in Gertrude's
eyes when she was talking to her?

'You're the only person who's made me feel mean over the whole business,' said Mrs Martin one day. Solange stared at her, uncomprehending. 'Oh, never mind. It doesn't matter. But you are good to me. I like you. We could have been friends. I haven't met many people as decent as you in my life. Ah, well, it can't be helped.'

That was the last day she spoke really sensibly. Next evening she was wandering in her talk, and repeated several times, 'I hope he'll play straight, as I have. Mind that he plays straight.' Twice she mentioned a name, but it was not that of Angus; it was 'Davie.' She lingered over her last pronunciation of the name very softly, and so died.

Solange stayed for the funeral, saw Angus give the order for the simple headstone:

> IN MEMORY OF GERTRUDE MARTIN,
> WIFE OF ANGUS MARTIN.
> DIED JUNE 3RD, 1929

and then travelled with him as far as Paris, where she was going to stay. He thanked her very warmly when they parted.

It was odd, she told herself, completely unreasonable, that she should still have that little feeling of dissatisfaction. It's as though the pattern weren't quite right, somehow, she thought, and yet really the pattern is perfect. I found Gertrude Martin. She wanted to die. He, of course, wanted her to die, and dead she is. I've done my job successfully. I've got a nice cheque. Why aren't I quite pleased? I don't know. I suppose it's because, like Mrs MacTavish, I feel he doesn't really deserve Flora, although he loves her so devotedly. The funny thing is I feel he didn't quite deserve Gertrude, either. Oh well, it's none of my business any longer.

And that was where Solange made one of the many mistakes that she made in this particular case.

It was some six months later that Solange again met Angus and Flora. It was a rainy, stormy autumn for the South of France, and Solange, who was staying in her own little house in the mountains behind Cannes, was becoming thoroughly bored and was glad when an invitation came from Flora to go and stay at the Villa Sans Souci.

The first evening passed happily enough. Solange arrived too late to see the garden, but the house itself was charming. Angus had been his own architect. He was a man of amazing versatility and, besides being a portrait painter, he was a brilliant musician and architect. The house, though built in the Provençal style, was not a slavish imitation. Solange thought she had never seen a more delightful room than the drawing-room, with its patine walls of parchment colour, rubbed through with silver, the brilliant vermilion of its tiled floor, its silvery ceiling and beaten-silver electric-light fittings. The furniture was of green lacquer, except for two rounded corner cupboards of yellow Italian lacquer, and the curtains were of green and silver brocade. The whole house was at once gay and restful, and suited Flora marvellously well. She looked more like a Botticelli than ever, and just as virginal as when Solange had first met her.

She lay curled up, a mere wisp of silver, on the green divan, one of those rare creatures who could have had dozens of lovers, and husbands, and yet remain in appearance the eternal virgin – the most fascinating type in the world, and one to which, strangely enough, sometimes the most depraved of women can belong.

The next day the storm that had raged all night had beaten itself out, and the sun was shining, although the sea still ran with crests of foam upon the little beach at the bottom of the big garden. They all bathed, for the sea was still warm with the stored heat of the summer. Angus and Flora stayed in longer than Solange, who ran up to the house, her towel wrapped round her, glowing with a sense of physical well-being. All was for the best. Angus was just one of those people who were rather difficult to know, but the nicest fellow in the world. Flora would always be radiantly happy, the house was perfection, and the garden a dream of loveliness with its cypresses and roses.

The short cut into the house for her room was, Flora had told her, through a pillared pergola covered with roses, and into a sort of garden room, whence a flight of stairs led up to the bedrooms. Towards this pergola ran Solange, singing happily as she went. She only sang when by herself; she had no ear whatever and could not sing two notes in tune, but she herself enjoyed the performance very much, and it was always with her a sign of high spirits.

The pergola was made of square concrete pillars, which, with the cross beams above them, were painted the same soft jade green as the shutters of the house. A riot of late roses hung all about the pergola, which ran all along that wing of the building. That's the most effective thing in the whole house, thought Solange, as she moved towards it.

She was passing under the shadow-net thrown by the leaves, when suddenly she stopped. For a moment she thought she must be going to be ill. Perhaps she had swum too far in the rough sea. Her skin felt cold, her heart fluttered, and seemed to fade away in her breast, then started to race as though it would choke her. So sudden was the impact of the sensation that she stood still for half a minute, hoping she was not going to faint. Then she went on indoors, and sat down in a deep garden chair, leaning her head back. The horrible sensation passed away in a few moments, and she went up to her room and dressed. When she left her room she came down again to the garden room, and, looking out, saw Angus and Flora just coming up from the beach. They were making for the ordinary entrance to the big hall when Flora caught sight of her and came towards her. Angus hesitated for a moment, then went on into the hall.

'Ready for a cocktail?' called Flora. She ran under the showering roses and came into the garden room. 'Angus will make them in a few minutes.'

'I'd love one. Where do you have them? Under the pergola?'

'Funnily enough, we never do. I don't know why. It's the nicest place of all to sit in, I think, but Angus never will. He says it's draughty. I love it, don't you? It's just the right mixture of sun and shade, and I love those great square pillars. But we always have drinks on the terrace when it's fine. I shan't be more than a few moments.' And she went on into the house. Solange stepped out into the pergola.

Curious – the heat seemed to have gone out of the sun; Angus must be right, and there must be a draught in the pergola. But it was not a draught that seemed to stir the hair of her bare head, or make her skin prickle as if she had gooseflesh. She did not feel physically ill as she had when passing through, but she shivered, nevertheless. She turned her head and looked suddenly over her shoulder. She had the absurd feeling that she was not alone, that something venomous was close to her. She recognized the sensation of that tingling sense of evil that some people gave her, and she stared down the length of the pergola either way, and peered into the garden. There was no one to be seen. Yet she was still cold, so cold that now her teeth actually chattered a little. I stayed in too long, that's it, she thought angrily. But she had not stayed in as long as Angus and Flora. She forced herself to remain where she was and looked about her more curiously, with an eye attentive to detail.

There were eight pillars in all, each about two and a half feet square and ten feet high. Red and pale-yellow roses grew round them and clambered over the beams laid across their tops. One pillar had been newly repainted. She could see the paint on it glistening in the sun, and the roses, which looked sickly and drooping, had been cut away to allow of the paint being put on over a large surface. She went towards it and touched it. Yes, the paint was wet in a big patch.

And then the 'feeling' took Solange and shook her as never before. She stared wide-eyed, her heart beating fast in pure terror. For she had never had the 'feeling' in her life except for people. She had once had it in the presence of the dead, when she had gone into the room where the sinister Mr Brownlie lay smiling over his base secret, but never had a place given it to her. I must ask if this house is haunted, she thought, with a contemptuous smile at her own idea. And then remembered, with a little sense of shock, that the house was new, that Angus had built it himself. But there's no feeling of anything unpleasant in the house itself, she thought; it's only out here. Perhaps something awful happened just here – before the house was built, of course.

Gradually her nerves quietened down, as though the strength of whatever strange message had come to her had exhausted itself for the time being, and she went out into the sunshine with a sigh of relief. Of course, it was all nerves. She had been working too hard, that was what it was. Nevertheless, she avoided the pergola for the next few days. She thought of asking Angus, who also, according to Flora, seemed to dislike the place, whether he had heard of anything odd that had taken place there, but something prevented her – that odd little feeling of not quite liking or trusting Angus which she always had.

Charming host as he was, Solange was guiltily conscious of feeling pleased when he had to go to Paris on business connected with a picture show and she and Flora were left alone.

'Let's have tea under the pergola,' she suggested, determined to master her qualms, on the first afternoon that they were by themselves; 'there can't be a draught today, there's no wind at all. And it does seem a shame to waste the last of the roses.'

'I'd love to,' said Flora. 'I never can persuade Angus. He had to paint over that pillar that always gets damp the other day, and he said it would be smelling of paint, but it must be all right now.'

'Why is one pillar always damp?' asked Solange.

'Angus says its the fault of the masons,' answered Flora. 'They must have used some sea-water in mixing the concrete, with the result that it will never dry out completely. I don't think it matters a bit. It just makes it look nice and odd. It doesn't worry me at all, but Angus fusses about it dreadfully, and keeps a pot of green paint handy so that he can paint it over whenever it gets really bad.'

Tea was not a success. In spite of telling herself that she was an idiot, Solange could not be at ease under the pergola. It was quite absurd, but there it was.

'Had this piece of land any history, do you know, Flora?' she asked. 'Before Angus built on it, I mean. Is there any ghost story connected with it, or was a crime committed here?'

'Not that I have ever heard of,' said Flora. 'Of course, it must have been a very lonely strip of shore until people began to build on it, so I suppose anything might have happened here, but I never heard that anything did. Why, Solange, you're shivering; don't you feel well?'

'I believe Angus must be right,' said Solange, laughing; 'there must be a draught here, or perhaps there's a spring underneath and the damp strikes up, but it isn't a nice place to sit, somehow. Come on, Flora, show me all over the house. You know you promised you'd show me Angus's painting room when he was away. I haven't seen any of his work yet.'

'Angus hates showing people his work,' said Flora. 'It's been difficult to persuade him to have this show in Paris, but his things are so good, he really ought to be better-known. Come along, we'll go and look now while the light's still good.'

Angus Martin's studio ran along the north side of the house at the back. It was reached by an outside stairway of stone. In front of it, over the bedrooms, was a flat, stone roof with a balustrade round it.

'He comes and walks about here when he's got really stuck in his work,' explained Flora. 'I love the studio, but I seldom go up there because he has to be alone to paint, except, of course, for his models.'

They went into the big, bare, empty room with its sloping north light – obviously the room of a worker and not of an amateur. There were none of the rich hangings, the divans, and the bronzes, so often described as making up the studios of the fashionable painters. At one end of the room was a low wooden model throne. A lay figure sprawled dejectedly in a chair, bald head lolling and still hands hanging down towards the floor. An unfinished canvas was on the easel, a carefully cleaned palette was on a scrubbed wooden table.

There was a sink in one corner of the room, and all round the wall the canvases were stacked with their backs to the room.

Solange glanced around her and felt she liked Angus Martin better than she ever had before. Then she stepped up to the canvas on the easel and stood looking at it. It was the picture of an old tramp, and if ever an evil and mean life showed in any man's face, it did in his. He was a bleary-eyed, sly, dissolute looking old fellow, with a loose, cunning mouth, and long, dirty hands folded over the top of his stick. The picture was a brilliant piece of work, unfinished as it was.

'But how magnificent!' said Solange. 'Of course he ought to have a show if he can do things like this. But what a dreadful man. I wonder you could bear to have him in the house.'

'Oh, but there's the outside staircase,' said Flora. 'So many of Angus's models are so terrible, you couldn't have them going through the house. He only seems to like doing very ugly and wicked-looking people. I think that old man has a dreadful face, don't you? He's an awful old man, called Matthieu, who is well known in the country-side here. He just wanders about and makes himself such a nuisance that people pay him money to get rid of him, and then he goes and spends it in an estaminet. Angus began that picture months ago, before he went to England, but he's never had him here since. I think they quarrelled.'

She began to pull out some of the canvases from the wall, so that Solange could see them. They were all brilliant, all interesting, but even in the landscapes, showing grim piles of rocks and distorted trees, Angus seemed unable to show anything but the repulsive side of Nature; something cruel and sad had left its impression on them. They looked the work of a man whose soul was sick. That's it, thought Solange, suddenly. I don't feel he's evil. I have never thought that, only that something's happened to him that's made him all wrong somehow. His soul is sick.

She turned several more canvases to the light and studied them. They were all bold and cunning.

'Oh,' she said suddenly, turning towards the window the portrait of a woman, 'this is the most terrifying of the lot.'

The picture represented a woman of about fifty, with a thin shrew's face. Her greyish-sandy hair was unkempt about her peering eyes, her twisted mouth was indescribably bitter. Solange found herself flushing as she looked at the thing, it was so cruel, such an outrage on the privacies and decencies of Nature. It had been painted by sheer hate. She felt that, however foul the woman was, no man should, in common decency, have depicted her so brutally.

Flora was silent for a moment. Then:

' It's hateful, isn't it?' she said. ' When I first found that, I almost felt I disliked Angus. Of course, I don't mean that really but somehow it seemed so dreadful that, however awful she was, he should have shown her up like that. I think that's what they finally quarrelled about; she must have come up here and found it. I don't really blame her for running away after that, do you?'

The blood hummed in Solange's head, and she waited a moment to control her voice before she spoke.

' You haven't told me who it is,' she said at last.

' Oh, I thought you would recognize it. Don't you think it's like her, then? It's Gertrude, Angus's first wife. Was she very changed when she was dying?'

' Yes,' said Solange, ' yes, she was very changed . . .'

Gertrude Martin — what a gullible fool she had been — but how diabolically ingenious the plot that Angus had woven to obtain freedom to marry Flora! He couldn't be free to marry again unless he could prove his first wife's death. She ran her mind swiftly over the past year. She remembered how Angus had asked Flora to tell her the story of their frustrated love, how he had enlisted her help, how he had given her the clue of the London lodging house. Clever, oh, how clever! So much better to let a third person discover the dying wife, instead of doing it himself! She understood now many sardonic phrases of the false Gertrude which had puzzled her at the time. Gertrude — she would always think of her by that name — what had her motive been? Money to die in comfort? Somehow, that didn't fit in with the stoical, philosophical woman she had grown to know so well, and for whom she had such an admiration. And then there came to her in a flash the dying woman's last words, ' I hope he'll play straight, as I have . . .' And then, that softly breathed ' Davie . . .' Yes, it was for some one else that she had lent herself to that carefully planned deception. It was to get money for somebody — a husband, perhaps, or a son.

Everything was accounted for — even her own feeling that all was not quite straight with Angus. Of course, it had been an awful situation for him! That woman in the picture would be quite capable of staying away without letting him know her whereabouts, or whether she were even alive or not, just because she knew he wanted to marry someone else. It was a jealous and vindictive, as well as a bestial, face.

And then there came to Solange, mechanically stacking canvases so as to keep her face turned away from Flora, another thought. Why had not a woman such as the one shown on the canvas turned up again since his re-marriage? That was not the sort of woman to let him enjoy felicity with her successor. Only death could be keeping such a woman from disturbing his happiness. Had he heard of her death since her impersonator had died at Ventnor? Or – or had she died before? But then he would only have had to bring proofs of her death if he had known of it. *Unless her death had been such a one that it could not be revealed.* I mustn't leap to conclusions, she told herself; after all, it's always possible that she did die, but that he has never heard of it. She may have had an accident soon after she left him, or died of flu; anything may have happened, and he may never have been able to trace it. That is the only solution . . . that, or the other one . . .

The picture – why, in Heaven's name, had a man who had so carefully planned an elaborate fraud kept the one thing that betrayed him? Criminals – luckily for the police – nearly always did something of the sort. There are dozens of cases where they had carefully destroyed all the evidence against themselves, except the one fatal thing that, for sentiment's sake or by sheer oversight, they had kept. The vanity of the artist might have absolutely inhibited Angus Martin from destroying the most brilliant, if the most cruel, of all his works, or perhaps more strange and subtle motives had been at work. He might like to look at it and remind himself of what he had escaped, to add to his present happiness. Perhaps he was of that deep egoism that cannot bear to destroy relics of the past because, by so doing, something of himself would die.

Solange was startled to see whither her thoughts were leading her. True the elaborate deception practised by Angus had been a crime of a sort, but she knew nothing worse of him. Yet she felt a deep unease in her heart.

When, a couple of days later, Angus returned from Paris in high spirits, having fixed up his show on very satisfactory terms, she tried to tell herself that any dark suspicions of him were unjustified. She had deliberated over her own duty in the matter and decided, with rather a feeling that she was being a coward, against any action.

What could ensue but endless worry if she told Angus that she knew he had lied, that he had staged an elaborate comedy to deceive her? He would merely reply, Yes, I didn't know where my wife was; I thought she must be dead, but had no chance of ever proving it, and I was made to marry Flora. I admit I did a wrong thing, but what do you propose to do about it? Tell Flora, and break her heart? What is there to be gained by it? Besides, between the two of us, she will probably believe me if I deny your whole story. And she will certainly stick to me, even if I admit it.

Yes, that would be true, Solange knew. Flora would feel that Angus had risked even his soul for her, and only love him the more. Passionate and very feminine women did not take very seriously a technical offence against the law. The best woman in the world didn't think she was doing any wrong in smuggling, or cheating the income tax, and it would seem a small thing to Flora that, for love of her, Angus had deceived the registrar of deaths, especially as by so doing he had eased the last weeks of a dying woman.

But was that elaborate comedy of deception the extent of his criminality? Back and back to that nagging question Solange always came. But I know nothing, nothing; there has never been any hint of a worse crime, no suspicion of it in any quarter whatsoever. I must mind my own business, and just bring my visit to an end as soon as possible. A wire calling me to Paris . . .

The wire arrived. Flora bewailed it, but Angus, though he said everything that was charming and polite, did not seem too desolated. Solitude with his Flora was evidently enough for him. In reply to Flora's affectionate requests that she should stay one day longer, she at length acceded so much, and then, with a lighter heart, her decision taken, spent her last day but one happily enough in the winter sunlight amid the pine-woods. Angus looked a little out of place at a picnic, but Flora shone with a new grace; she seemed the spirit of the woods incarnate, running like a child hither and thither, singing little snatches of song in her small, though true and bird-like voice.

She was a little tired when they returned, and went to her room to lie down till dinner, at the anxious solicitation of her husband. He himself went up to his studio, and Solange went down to the sea, regretting that she would soon be exchanging it for the murky Seine. Soon the swift dusk of the South would fall, but the beach got the western sun, and she lay on the sand absorbing the last of the blessed warmth.

A dark figure came plodding noiselessly towards the little break-water, and only the sound of feet scrambling up its side made Solange sit up. A face was looking at her over the cement path that ran along the top of the breakwater, a dreadful face . . . where had she seen it before . . . that sly and brutal countenance with the sloppy mouth and rheumy eyes? Of course . . . the old model, the man whose portrait had been upon the easel the other day in the studio.

The old man stayed a moment, staring goatishly at her, then, in reply to her crisp and angry French, touched his decrepit hat and apologized. He was only on his way up to the studio of the English painter, he whined. With many smirks and would-be ingratiatory smiles, he shuffled past her and took the little path that led up to the side of the house and the outer stairway. Solange watched him go, her very flesh creeping with distaste. Here was a foul thing that crawled on the fair surface of the earth and made the daylight abominable. Odd that the fastidious Angus could bear him near him, even as a model, even granting that he apparently liked to paint the shocking secrets of base souls. And then she remembered that Flora had said Angus had quarrelled with the old man, had forbidden him in the house. And Angus was not a man who changed his mind, whose emotions were brief and passing in quality.

Solange rose to her feet, and in her turn went up the path to the outside stairway. At its foot she stood hesitating for a moment. What could she say if she were discovered spying? She did not even know quite why she was doing it herself. She only knew that in this house of strangeness her senses were on the alert, and that her senses had warned her of something very terrible in that old goatish man. Now, as she stood on the stairs, her every nerve warned her of danger, some dreadful danger that was imminent. Whom it threatened she did not know, or where evil lay, but that danger and evil were wrapped up in the very fabric of that house, she was at last certain. Softly, she went up the stairs in her soundless, string-soled shoes, and stood outside the door of the studio.

Low, angry, rapid French came to her ears; she bent nearer to the door and blessed Heaven that, in that land of scamped workman-ship and wood not properly seasoned, the door had shrunk so that there was a gap between it and the post. As she listened her pale face grew paler; she realized that this was what, in the back of her mind, she had suspected ever since she had visited the studio three days ago.

Oh, what was the good of this old tramp thinking he could blackmail a man like Angus Martin, a man with his deadly determination, his powers of planning, his lack of scruples? You're signing your death warrant, she wanted to call to him. He was a foul old man – a blot on humanity – but it was not in Solange to treat any human life as without value, unsentimental as she was. This old man's life would be in danger now, in deadly and immediate danger. Fool, fool, fool, why did he threaten a man like Angus Martin?

The voice of Angus replied to the threats, calm, cold, but deadly.

' I will not have you coming here in the day-time. I've told you so. If you do this again, you shall not get one penny more from me. I'll give you the sum you want, but I shall have to get it first, and you will come here after dark or not at all.'

' After dark . . . after dark. I know the sort of thing you do here after dark!'

' Don't be a fool. The house is full of people now. It was empty that time you came before . . . and found me.'

' All the same, I'd rather you met me at the inn or at the harbour.'

' Thanks, and be seen by all the world handing money to a foul old brute like you, whom no one will touch. You will come here or not get it at all.'

' Well, I shall come in the day-time. Everyone knows you have painted me. No one will think anything if they see me coming here. They will only think I have come to sit to you again. I won't come in the dark. I'll tell the whole story to the police first.'

There was a little silence, then Martin's voice said flatly:

' Very well, as you will. Come at five o'clock tomorrow afternoon. I shall have to go into St Raphaël first to get the money.'

The footsteps of the old man began to shuffle towards the door, and Solange fled down the stairs. Without noticing where she was going, she ran on, only eager to get out of sight and, turning the corner of the house, took refuge in the pergola. She heard the footsteps of the old man move away through the pines; then there came to her ears a remote and muffled bang which she guessed was Angus shutting the door of the studio after his unwelcome guest.

The old man had gone, but was to return the next day at five o'clock. She herself was leaving on a train that drew out of St Raphaël at 4.08 pm. The house would be free of her presence, but surely Flora would be there? No, for Flora would come in to see her off. But then she would be back soon after five. If Angus contemplated anything against the old tramp, surely it would not be with

Flora in the house. Yet, knowing what she now knew, Solange would give very little for the chances of old Matthieu's life. No one went to the studio without the permission of Angus. A body could be concealed there till nightfall made its disposal possible. It was true that old Matthieu was a condoner of crime and blackmailer – a breed of whom Solange thought worse than she necessarily did of murderers – but that did not allow her to leave him to his death without making an effort to save his worthless life.

The swift darkness had fallen as she stood thinking, and she felt very cold. She came to herself and to the present moment with a little shiver, and suddenly realized where she was – a sentence she had heard of Matthieu's came back to her. That was why she had felt that awful chill as from another clime in this spot; she knew now. And as she stood, less fearful now she knew all, it seemed to her that through the darkness came a little stuffless laugh, a dreadful laugh of enjoyment.

Did the mortal remains of Gertrude Martin, that sheath of flesh and bones that had housed so much malice in life, still hold its evil thoughts and sensation now that it was dead and corrupt and sealed within a painted pillar? Did what men call the soul, that quality or essence that neither Solange nor any explorer into the nature of man had ever located in the laboratory, cling about what had been its mortal habitation and spread its old accustomed influence, in this case such a malignant influence, around it? She was not afraid of poor Gertrude Martin, her thoughts were too occupied with practical questions, but her flesh revolted from the place where she stood, and she went out into the garden and thence into the house.

Angus made no attempt to go into St Raphaël next day to get money, which did not surprise Solange. It was not money that would be awaiting old Matthieu when he arrived at the studio that evening. Solange herself borrowed the car and spent the morning making artless but acute inquiries into the past of Matthieu – and heard enough to make her very pleased with her morning's work.

When the time came for her to leave to catch her train, Angus excused himself from accompanying her. Flora's lovely eyes showed a hurt surprise – Angus was going to let her have the dull drive back alone! But when he held her close and told her that he wanted to work, she gave him her lips sweetly, the gracious, yielding creature that she always was. No wonder, thought Solange, watching, that he loved Flora after having been married to Gertrude.

Flora had a lot of shopping to do in St Raphaël, things that Angus had asked her to buy, quite a long list of them. He doesn't mean her to get home until well after five o'clock, thought Solange. The problem was how she herself was to evade Flora and get back to Sans Souci in time to spy upon or, if necessary, to show herself, at the interview with old Matthieu. .

'Don't come and see me off, Flora darling,' she said, as the car ran down the steep hill between Fréjus and St Raphaël. 'I hate people hanging about on platforms to watch trains go out. It always seems hours. I don't care how fond you are of the person, there never seems anything to say.'

'Well, I *have* a lot of shopping to do,' said Flora, 'so if you're sure you don't mind . . .'

'Not a bit, I'd rather.'

She kissed Flora good-bye in the station entrance and waited till the car was out of sight, then she put her luggage in the cloakroom and went on foot to a little garage she knew of, where she had ordered a racing Bugatti to be ready for her. She tucked her little red-felt hat down behind the seat, and pulled on a leather motoring helmet that she carried in her bag, complete with racing goggles. The red-leather coat was reversible, being lined with dark-blue leather. Solange now turned it inside out, and when the Bugatti a moment later started back for Sans Souci, it would have been impossible to recognize the Solange who had left to catch the Paris train.

She did the distance in thirty minutes, and it was only a quarter to five when she ran the car over a rough cart track into the pine woods on the other side of the road from the villa. Still keeping on her goggles, she looked quite like a stranded lady motorist in need of help as she went though the trees by a circuitous way towards the outside staircase of Sans Souci.

Under the staircase she knew there was a door opening into a place where garden tools were kept. She slipped through the door and kept it a crack open, so that she could watch for old Matthieu's appearance. After about ten minutes' wait in the stuffy darkness, she heard shuffling footsteps and, peering out cautiously, saw the old man reach the foot of the stairs. Then she heard his feet on the steps that sloped above her head. She waited a moment and then followed him up the staircase, and once again applied first her ear and then her eye to the gaping crack in the doorway.

She heard the voice of Angus, calm and unemotional, give the

old man a brusque greeting, and then, as she peered through, she could
see him point contemptuously to a wooden chair set just by the
electric lamp, which was lit, for it was already dusk out of doors. Old
Matthieu dropped into the chair with a grumbling remark about the
steepness of the stairs.

'I never wanted you to come up them,' retorted Angus bitterly,
'and the sooner you go down them again, the better I shall be pleased,
but as you won't go down without your money, here it is.'

He was fumbling in a drawer in the bureau behind Matthieu's
back, and Solange heard the rustling of notes. Angus had his back to
her, and very gently she pushed the door a little way open. She
saw Angus take a packet of notes in his left hand, and, with his right,
take out of the drawer, a heavy revolver. He held it by the barrel, so
evidently it was unloaded and he meant to use it as a club.

'Here's your money,' he said abruptly, his voice rather strained
and high. Old Matthieu swung round and held out his hand, but
Angus threw the notes onto the table. 'Count them,' he ordered.

'But these are only fifty-franc notes,' cried Matthieu, bending to
his task. 'There's nothing like enough here.'

'Go on,' said Angus. 'The thousand-franc notes are underneath,'
and he pointed with his left hand over Matthieu's shoulder while
bringing his right arm up to strike the blow.

'Angus!' said Solange sharply, stepping into the studio and flinging
the door wide-open.

Old Matthieu made a grab at the notes. Angus stood like a man
turned to stone, his right hand still upraised and his left hand pointing; only his head moved and turned towards Solange. His face was
so drained of colour that it seemed the face of a dead man.

'It's no good, Angus,' said Solange. 'You can't cover up one
crime by another.'

'Shut the door,' ordered Angus sharply.

'I prefer it to remain open. I hate firearms as a rule, they always
make me feel a fool, but I've got one with me now,' and she levelled
her little revolver at him as she spoke. 'Yours isn't loaded, so you'd
better keep where you are.'

'No, it's not loaded,' said Angus. 'May I put it down?'

'Yes, put it down, and I think you'd better go and sit on that
chair the other side of the table. Matthieu, drop those notes. They're
not for you.'

The man whose life she had saved was as angry as the man whom

she had prevented in the commission of a crime. Matthieu snarled at
her as he reluctantly withdrew his dirty, yellowish talons from the
pile of notes. A filthy old man, she thought; a blackmailer and much
better out of the way, but she had had to follow the law that says life
must be saved, however vile it may be.

'Where's Flora?' asked Angus, in a shaking voice. 'For heaven's
sake, don't say Flora's come back with you!'

'No, that's all right. She doesn't know I've come back. I overheard you and Matthieu yesterday; I know all about it, how he
came up to the studio just after you had killed your wife, and then
hung round and saw you cementing her up in the pillar of the pergola that night. You can't go on paying blackmail, Angus; it's too
stupid.'

'I know it is,' he answered grimly. 'That's why I was going to
do this instead.'

'More stupid still!'

'As things are,' he admitted, 'if I'd known you knew – but you
see, I didn't.'

'I suppose now,' remarked Solange, 'you want to kill me, but
you can't go on for ever like this, you know, Angus. You're a very
clever man, and I admit you lay your plans remarkably well, but
there's a limit to what even you can do.'

'Oh, my God!' he groaned, suddenly breaking down and burying
his haggard face in his hands. 'Don't I know it? You needn't think I
should ever have been happy again if I had succeeded in knocking this
old ruffian on the head. I was going to take his body out to sea
tonight, in the canoe, and tip it overboard in the mouth of the gulf.
Nobody'd have missed him, and it would have been a good riddance.
But God knows I didn't want to kill him. He's brought it on himself,
but I didn't want it. There wasn't anything else to be done.'

'Nothing else to suit your convenience, you mean. That's what
the murderer always thinks. I suppose you killed your wife for the
same reason?'

He looked up at that, and met her eyes squarely.

'I didn't kill her on purpose, that I swear to you! She came up
here and found me working on a picture of her. We had an awful
quarrel. She wanted me to destroy it, and I said it was the best thing
I'd done, and I'd never destroy it. She made a dash at it and tried
to get hold of it, and in getting away from her, I knocked her over.
She fell with her head against the radiator, and she never moved

again. I was horribly frightened at first, I didn't mean it to happen, didn't want it. Then I began to be glad – I know it sounds horrible; why should I pretend? I had spent abominable years with her. I knew it would sound altogether too thin to tell the truth and say it was an accident. I'd been amusing myself working with the masons. We were building the pergola just then. I don't know if you know anything about building? No? Well, when you make concrete pillars, you build up a shuttering of wooden planks with thin, steel rods set just inside the shuttering.

'I waited till it was fairly dark – the moon was half-full that night – and then I went down to the pergola. There were no other houses anywhere near in those days, and I had only two servants, who slept in the *dépendance*, right away from the villa. I mixed a lot of concrete; it's made of gravel and sand and cement, and you make it with water on a platform on the ground. Then I went upstairs and fetched her; I carried her down over my shoulder. She was in a sort of evening wrap, but I got her travelling clothes and hat, because I wanted them to disappear as well.

'I climbed up the step-ladder and rammed her down between the steel rods in the shuttering. They gave a funny little clang; I remember how it startled me, as I jammed her in. And then I poured in the concrete. It was a hot night and the sweat ran off me. It seemed as if I were working for hours – and I was, too. I rammed the stuff down with the long-handled iron ram that the workmen had left, and then I found I hadn't enough concrete. I went down the ladder again and found that, although I had gravel and cement, I hadn't any sand. I had to make some more as the stuff was only up to her shoulders in the pillar. I got the wheelbarrow and went down to the beach and brought it back full of sea-sand. That's why the pillar has never dried out properly, but what else could I do? I had to stand a lot of chaff from the workmen afterwards; they offered to do it again for me.

'Just as I was finishing, it was beginning to grow light with dawn, and I saw that one of her shoes, which must have fallen off, was lying on the ground. I went down the ladder to pick it up, and I suddenly heard a sneeze. It may sound quite funny to you now, but it was the most awful thing I ever heard in my life.'

The low voice paused, and Angus wiped the sweat from his high, glistening forehead.

'It sounds more absurd still, but I thought it had come from inside the pillar. And then I saw the bushes behind the pergola move a little, and I dashed into them and dragged out this creature here. I nearly killed him on the spot; I wish I had, but he swore he would always keep my secret if I made him an allowance for the rest of his life. I didn't want to kill him. You won't believe me, I know, but I didn't – any more than I wanted to tonight, so I believed him and let him go. But first I made him take the shoe, and put it in the pillar and concrete it up himself. I wanted him to have a hand in it. I thought it might frighten him; he is afraid of the law and the police. Well, that's all. The first thing was an utter accident, and everything I have done since has been for Flora. Now, I suppose it's all no good and you'll give me up.'

'Wait,' said Solange. She kept her revolver pointed at the table mechanically, her hand alert, in case of any movement on the part of either man, but her brain busy thinking out the problem of her own conduct.

She felt sure that what Angus had told her was the truth. He was not a born killer. That was why she had never felt with him that overpowering sense of evil which she had always experienced at meeting a true killer. He was something almost as dangerous: he was a man of one passionately fixed idea, a man capable of any act for the furtherance of that idea, and his idea was Flora – Flora, and her happiness mingled with his own. He was, of course, the complete egoist and he had the ruthlessness of egoism, but he was not a pre-destined killer. Flora . . . What utter ruin would this bring into her life, how completely it would lay all waste about her.

Solange thought of the long, drawn-out months in a French prison, of a French trial, a trial of which anything might be the outcome. That dreadful night's work on the concrete pillar would damn him utterly, would show him to the world as a cold-blooded murderer, when he was, she felt convinced, merely a very level-headed man who had made the best of a horrible accident. That coolness of his, that iron determination, that cunning of mind and hand, were not amiable traits, but that was not her affair.

Still keeping the little revolver pointed at Angus, she turned her face towards old Matthieu and let loose upon him a flood of extremely scathing French. She told him of her connection with the police, she hinted at all the information she had gathered about him that morning, and implied that she knew a great deal more. Little matters of illicit business in the contraband line, a more serious affair when a

traveller had been found stunned and robbed by the highway. . . .
There were quite a lot of little things with which she taunted Matthieu,
and she ended up by assuring him that as he had kept silence all this
time, and had helped with the concreting of the pillar, he would
probably, if the whole story came out, spend his few remaining years
in a convict prison.

Matthieu wilted in his chair, his loose mouth slobbered and
quivered, his pale, rheumy eyes rolled affrightedly. 'At least,' he
whined, 'I may take these with me?'

'Not a single fifty-franc note,' said Solange, 'and if ever you
breathe a word of what you know, or come to this house again, your
allowance will be stopped, and I will witness against you at your
trial. Get out.'

She moved away from the door, and the old man, shuffling and
panting, got past her as quickly as he could and went down the
stairs. They could hear him drawing frightened, sobbing breaths, and
Solange felt a twinge of pity. He was utterly base, but he had probably had no chance in life. She turned and looked at the man to
whom many talents had been given, and her eyes were hard.

'How you're going to arrange your future life,' she said, 'I don't
know. I shall have nothing to do with it. I shall have to give up my
friendship with Flora, which will hurt her feelings very much, but it
can't be helped. I warn you that if old Matthieu comes to any unnatural end, I shall investigate the affair myself, that's all.'

Angus raised his face from his hands and gazed at her.

'Of course, you're doing this for Flora,' he said, 'but I thank you
all the same.'

'Chiefly for Flora, but not entirely. The lives of most human
creatures are a bad mess, and unless the ends of justice are to be
served, I don't see much point in making a worse mess of any one
of them. If I were you, I should sell this house and go away.'

'I daren't. Do you think I haven't often wanted to? And then I
imagine somebody getting to hate the sight of that pillar with its
damnable patch of wet, and having the thing pulled down.' He
broke off, shuddering.

'Well, that's your affair. You've got your punishment, whether
you stay here or go away. There's one thing I should like to know:
Who was *my* Gertrude Martin?'

'She'd been a fellow student of mine in Paris. She was a plucky
girl, though she was delicate even then. Just before the . . . the

accident happened to my wife, I had gone up to Paris and had run into her again by chance. She was dying of tuberculosis, but what was worrying her was that she was miserably poor. She had a little annuity which would stop with her death, and her son David was just growing up. After everything had happened here and after I had met Flora, I remembered her and I went again to Paris to see her. I'd tried to get her to take money before, but she was always proud, and said she couldn't take money when she could do nothing in return. I told her my wife had disappeared and that I wanted to marry again, and couldn't because I had no proof of her death. She agreed to my plan if I would start the boy off in life – if I would keep him at the Varsity and settle five thousand pounds on him.

'The rest you know. I did the thing thoroughly, with great attention to detail, and so did she. I wired her from here that she was to send the postcard to the Hereford Road lodgings. I had actually sent her the hundred pounds in banknotes, and paid into her account the one thousand pounds I told you of. I was determined that everything should be traceable.'

'She said,' remarked Solange, 'when she was dying: "I hope he'll play straight, as I have. Mind that he plays straight." Have you?'

Angus, the man who could work all night at walling up a woman, and who had planned the deliberate and cold-blooded murder of an old man, looked, and was, genuinely shocked.

'Of course I have,' he replied stiffly. 'I will send you my passbook if you like, or you can go to England and find David Grimshaw for yourself. He has just gone to Cambridge. He thinks his mother died on a sea-voyage and was buried at sea.'

Solange knew he was speaking the truth. It would have been impossible for Angus Martin to have cheated any one of sixpence. She slipped the revolver into the pocket of the leather coat, and as she did so he heard the hoot of the horn as Flora's car came up into the drive.

'That's Flora,' said Angus, starting up. Solange moved aside, and let him pass her.

At the head of the stairs he paused and looked round at her.

'I suppose you wouldn't . . .' he asked, and held out his hand.

'No, thank you,' said Solange.

The rebuff glanced off him and left him unhurt. He turned and ran swiftly down the stairs with no thought, Solange was sure, but that of relief and joy at meeting Flora in his mind.

Solange went through the trees, and when she was at a safe distance, turned and looked back at the house. A light had sprung up in the drawing-room, and she saw Angus and Flora standing together, his arms round her and their lips meeting. A very dangerous man, thought Solange. I'm sure his show in Paris will be a great success, but I don't envy him, all the same.

The picture of him and Flora clasped together in the lovely lighted drawing-room remained in her mind, but side by side with it was another picture – that of a damp-stained pillar. Flora might be happy in her ignorance, but for him there would always be a perpetual reminder – that pillar of salt in which the other woman stayed for ever, to nag and mock at him in death as she had done in life. In the warm and lighted house, Flora; but outside, in the dampness and the dark, there would always be, for his heart's undoing, the sly eyes and vindictive smile of his first wife.

Ellery Queen

THE BLACK
CATS VANISHED

THE TINKLY BELL QUAVERED over the door of Miss Curleigh's Pet Shoppe on Amsterdam Avenue, and Mr Ellery Queen wrinkled his nose and went in. The instant he crossed the threshold he was thankful it was not a large nose, and that he had taken the elementary precaution of wrinkling it. The extent and variety of the little shop's odours would not have shamed the New York Zoological Park itself. And yet it housed only creatures, he was amazed to find, of the puniest proportions; who, upon the micrometically split second of his entrance, set up such a chorus of howls, yelps, snarls, yawps, grunts, squeaks, caterwauls, croaks, screeches, chirrups, hisses and growls that it was a miracle the roof did not come down.

'Good afternoon,' said a crisp voice. 'I'm Curleigh. What can I do for you, please?'

In the midst of raging bedlam Mr Ellery Queen found himself gazing into a pair of mercurial eyes. There were other details – she was a trim young piece, for example, with masses of Titian hair and curves and at least one dimple – but for the moment her eyes engaged his earnest attention. Miss Curleigh, blushing, repeated herself.

'I beg your pardon,' said Ellery hastily, returning to the matter in hand. 'Apparently in the animal kingdom there is no decent ratio between lung-power and – ah – aroma on the one hand and size on the other. We live and learn! Miss Curleigh, would it be possible to purchase a comparatively noiseless and sweet-smelling canine with frizzy brown hair, inquisitive ears at the half-cock, and crooked hind legs?'

Miss Curleigh frowned. Unfortunately, she was out of Irish terriers. The last litter had been gobbled up. Perhaps a Scottie – ?

Mr Queen frowned. No, he had been specifically enjoined by Djuna, the martinet, to procure an Irish terrier; no doleful-looking sawed-off substitute, he was sure, would do.

'I expect,' said Miss Curleigh professionally, 'to hear from our Long Island kennels tomorrow. If you'll leave your name and address?'

Mr Queen, gazing into the young woman's eyes, would be delighted to. Mr Queen, provided with pencil and pad, hastened to indulge his delight.

As Miss Curleigh read what he had written the mask of business fell away. 'You're not Mr *Ellery* Queen!' she exclaimed with animation. 'Well, I declare. I've heard *so* much about you, Mr Queen. And you live practically around the corner, on Eighty-seventh Avenue. This is really thrilling. I never expected to meet –'

'Nor I,' murmured Mr Queen. 'Nor I.'

Miss Curleigh blushed again and automatically prodded her hair. 'One of my best customers lives right across the street from you, Mr Queen. I should say one of my most frequent customers. Perhaps you know her? A Miss Tarkle – Euphemia Tarkle? She's in that large apartment house, you know.'

'I've never had the pleasure,' said Mr Queen absently. 'What extraordinary eyes you have! I mean – Euphemia Tarkle? Dear, dear, this is a world of sudden wonders. Is she as improbable as her name?'

'That's unkind,' said Miss Curleigh severely, 'although she *is* something of a character, the poor creature. A squirrelly-faced old lady, *and* an invalid. Paralytic, you know. The queerest, frailest tiniest little thing. Really, she's quite mad.'

'Somebody's grandmother, no doubt,' said Mr Queen whimsically, picking up his stick from the counter. 'Cats?'

'Why, Mr Queen, however did you guess?'

'It always is,' he said in a gloomy voice, 'cats.'

'You'd find her interesting, I'm sure,' said Miss Curleigh with eagerness.

'And why I, Diana?'

'The name,' said Miss Curleigh shyly, 'is Marie. Well, she's so strange, Mr Queen. And I've always understood that strange people interest you.'

'At present,' said Mr Queen hurriedly, taking a firmer grip on his stick, 'I am enjoying the fruits of idleness.'

'But do you know what Miss Tarkle's been doing, the mad thing?'

'I haven't the ghost of a notion,' said Mr Queen with truth.

'She's been buying cats from me at the rate of about one a week for weeks now!'

Mr Queen sighed. 'I see no special cause for suspicion. An ancient and invalid lady, a passion for cats – oh, they go together, I assure you. I once had an aunt like that.'

'That's what's so strange about it,' said Miss Curleigh triumphantly. 'She doesn't like cats!'

Mr Queen blinked twice. He looked at Miss Curleigh's pleasant little nose. Then he rather absently set his stick on the counter again. 'And how do you know that, pray?'

Miss Curleigh beamed. 'Her sister told me. Hush, Ginger! You see, Miss Tarkle is absolutely helpless with her paralysis and all, and her sister Sarah-Ann keeps house for her; they're both of an age, I should say, and they look so much alike. Dried-up little apples of ladies, with the same tiny features and faces like squirrels. Well, Mr Queen, about a year ago Miss Sarah-Ann came into my shop and bought a black male cat – she hadn't much money, she said, couldn't buy a really expensive one; so I got just a – well, just a cat for her, you see.'

'Did she ask for a black tomcat?' asked Mr Queen intently.

'No. Any kind at all, she said; she liked them all. Then only a few days later she came back. She wanted to know if she could return him and get her money back. Because, she said, her sister Euphemia couldn't stand having a cat about her; Euphemia just detested cats, she said with a sigh, and since she was more or less living off Euphemia's bounty she couldn't very well cross her, you see. I felt a little sorry for her and told her I'd take the cat back; but I suppose she changed her mind, or else her sister changed her mind, because Sarah-Ann Tarkle never came back. Anyway, that's how I know Miss Euphemia doesn't like cats.'

Mr Queen gnawed a fingernail. 'Odd,' he muttered. 'A veritable saga of oddness. You say this Euphemia creature has been buying 'em at the rate of one a week? What kind of cats, Miss Curleigh?'

Miss Curleigh sighed. 'Not very good ones. Of course since she has pots of money – that's what her sister Sarah-Ann said, anyway – I tried to sell her an Angora – I had a beauty – and a Maltese that took a ribbon at one of the shows. But she wanted just cats, she said, like the one I sold her sister. Black ones.'

'Black. . . . . It's possible that –'

'Oh, she's not at all superstitious, Mr Queen. In some ways she's a very weird old lady. Black tomcats with green eyes, all the same size. I thought it very queer.'

Mr Ellery Queen's nostrils quivered a little, and not from the racy odour in Miss Curleigh's Pet Shoppe, either. An old invalid lady named Tarkle who bought a black tomcat with green eyes every week!

'Very queer indeed,' he murmured; and his grey eyes narrowed. 'And how long has this remarkable business been going on?'

'You are interested! Five weeks now, Mr Queen. I delivered the sixth one myself only the other day.'

'Yourself? Is she totally paralysed?'

'Oh yes. She never leaves her bed; can't walk a step. It's been that way, she told me, for ten years now. She and Sarah-Ann hadn't lived together up to the time she had her stroke. Now she's absolutely dependent on her sister for everything – meals, baths, bed . . . all sorts of attention.'

'Then why,' demanded Ellery, 'hasn't she sent her sister for the cats?'

Miss Curleigh's mercurial eyes wavered. 'I don't know,' she said slowly. 'Sometimes I get the shivers. You see, she's always telephoned me – she has a phone by her bed and can use her arms sufficiently to reach for it – the day she wanted the cat. It would always be the same order – black, male, green eyes, the same size as before, and as cheap as possible.' Miss Curleigh's pleasant features hardened. 'She's something of a haggler, Miss Euphemia Tarkle is.'

'Fantastic,' said Ellery thoughtfully. 'Utterly fantastic. There's something in the basic situation that smacks of lavenderish tragedy. Tell me; how has her sister acted on the occasions when you've delivered the cats?'

'Hush, Ginger! I can't tell you, Mr Queen, because she hasn't been there.'

Ellery started. 'Hasn't been there! What do you mean? I thought you said the Euphemia woman is helpless – '

'She is, but Sarah-Ann goes out every afternoon for some air, I suppose, or to a movie, and her sister is left alone for a few hours. It's been at such times, I think, that she's called me. Then, too, she always warned me to come at a certain time, and since I've never seen Sarah-Ann when I made the delivery I imagine she's planned to keep her purchases a secret from her sister. I've been able to get in because Sarah-Ann leaves the door unlocked when she goes out.

Euphemia has told me time and again not to breathe a word about the cats to anyone.'

Ellery took the pince-nez off his nose and began to polish the shining lenses – an unfailing sign of emotion. ' More and more muddled,' he muttered. ' Miss Curleigh, you've stumbled on something – well, morbid.'

Miss Curleigh blanched. ' You don't think – '

' Insults already? I do think; and that's why I'm disturbed. For instance, how on earth could she have hoped to keep knowledge of the cats she's bought from her sister! Sarah-Ann isn't blind, is she?'

' Blind? Why, of course not. And Euphemia's sight is all right, too.'

' I was only joking. It doesn't make sense, Miss Curleigh.'

' Well,' said Miss Curleigh brightly, ' at least I've given the great Mr Queen something to think about. . . . I'll call you the moment an Ir – '

Mr Ellery Queen replaced his glasses on his nose, threw back his square shoulders and picked up the stick again. ' Miss Curleigh, I'm an incurable meddler in the affairs of others. How would you like to help me meddle in the affairs of the mysterious Tarkle sisters?'

Scarlet spots appeared in Miss Curleigh's cheeks. ' You're not serious?' she cried, excitement in her voice.

' Quite.'

' I'd love to! What am I to do?'

' Suppose you take me up to the Tarkle apartment, and introduce me as a customer. Let's say that the cat you sold Miss Tarkle the other day had really been promised to me, that as a stubborn fancier of felines I won't take any other, and that you'll have to have hers back and give her another. Anything to permit me to see and talk to her. It's mid-afternoon, so Sarah-Ann is probably in a movie theatre somewhere. What do you say?'

Miss Curleigh flung him a ravishing smile. ' I say it's – it's too magnificent for words. One minute while I powder my nose and get someone to tend the shop; Mr Queen. I wouldn't miss this for anything!'

Ten minutes later they stood before the front door to Apartment 5-C of the Amsterdam Arms, a rather faded building, gazing in silence at two full bottles of milk on the corridor floor. Miss Curleigh looked troubled, and Mr Queen stooped. When he straightened he looked troubled, too.

'Yesterday's and today's,' he muttered, and he put his hand on the doorknob and turned. The door was locked. 'I thought you said her sister leaves the door unlocked when she goes out.'

'Perhaps she's in,' said Miss Curleigh uncertainly. 'Or, if she's out, that she's forgotten to take the latch off.'

Ellery pressed the bell-button. There was no reply. He rang again. Then he called loudly: 'Miss Tarkle, are you there?'

'I can't understand it,' said Miss Curleigh with a nervous laugh. 'She really should hear you. It's only a three-room apartment, and both the bedroom and the living-room are directly off the sides of a little foyer on the other side of the door. The kitchen's straight ahead.'

Ellery called again, shouting. After a while he put his ear to the door. The rather dilapidated hall, the ill-painted door. . . .

Miss Curleigh's extraordinary eyes were frightened silver lamps. She said in the queerest voice: 'Oh, Mr Queen. Something dreadful's happened.'

'Let's hunt up the superintendent,' said Ellery quietly.

They found *Potter, Sup't* in a metal frame before a door on the ground floor. Miss Curleigh was breathing in little gusts. Ellery rang the bell.

A short fat woman with enormous forearms flecked with suds opened the door. She wiped her red hands on a dirty apron and brushed a strand of bedraggled grey hair from her sagging face. 'Well?' she demanded stolidly.

'Mrs Potter?'

'That's right. We ain't got no empty apartments. The doorman could ' a ' told you – '

Miss Curleigh reddened. Ellery said hastily: 'Oh, we're not apartment-hunting, Mrs Potter. Is the superintendent in?'

'No, he's not,' she said suspiciously. 'He's got a part-time job at the chemical works in Long Island City and he never gets home till ha'past three. What do you want?'

'I'm sure you'll do nicely, Mrs Potter. This young lady and I can't seem to get an answer from Apartment 5-C. We're calling on Miss Tarkle, you see.'

The fat woman scowled. 'Ain't the door open? Generally is this time o' day. The spry one's out, but the paralysed one – '

'It's locked, Mrs Potter, and there's no answer to the bell or to our cries.'

'Now ain't that funny?' shrilled the fat woman, staring at Miss Curleigh. 'I can't see – Miss Euphemia's a cripple; she never goes out. Maybe the poor thing threw a fit!'

'I trust not. When did you see Miss Sarah-Ann last?'

'The spry one? Let's see, now. Why two days ago. And, come to think of it, I ain't seen the cripple for two days, neither.'

'Heavens!' whispered Miss Curleigh, thinking of the two milk-bottles. 'Two days!'

'Oh, you do see Miss Euphemia occasionally?' asked Ellery grimly.

'Yes, sir.' Mrs Potter began to wring her red hands as if she were still over the tub. 'Every once in a while she calls me up by phone in the afternoon, if her sister's out, to take somethin' out to the incinerator, or do somethin' for her. She – she gives me somethin' once in a while. But it's been two days now. . . .'

Ellery pulled something out of his pocket and cupped it in his palm before the fat woman's tired eyes. 'Mrs Potter,' he said sternly, 'I want to get into that apartment. There's something wrong. Give me your master-key.'

'P-p-police!' she stammered, staring at the shield. Then suddenly she fluttered off and returned to thrust a key into Ellery's hand. 'Oh, I wish Mr Potter was home!' she wailed. 'You won't – '

'Not a word of this to anyone, Mrs Potter.'

They left the woman gaping loose-tongued and frightened after them, and took the self-service elevator back to the fifth floor. Miss Curleigh was white to the lips; she looked a little sick.

'Perhaps,' said Ellery kindly, inserting the key into the lock, 'you had better not come in with me, Miss Curleigh. It might be unpleasant I –' He stopped abruptly, his figure crouching.

Somebody was on the other side of the door.

There was the unmistakable sound of running feet, accompanied by an uneven scraping, as if something were being dragged. Ellery twisted the key and turned the knob in a flash, Miss Curleigh panting at his shoulder. The door moved a half-inch and stuck. The feet retreated.

'Barricaded the door,' growled Ellery. 'Stand back, Miss Curleigh.' He flung himself sidewise at the door. There was a splintering crash and the door shot inward, a broken chair toppling over backward.

'Too late – '

'The fire-escape!' screamed Miss Curleigh. 'In the bedroom. To the left!'

He darted into a large narrow room with twin beds and an air of disorder and made for an open window. But there was no one to be seen on the fire-escape. He looked up; an iron ladder curved and vanished a few feet overhead.

'Whoever it is got away by this room, I'm afraid,' he muttered, pulling his head back and lighting a cigarette.

'Smoke? Now, then, let's have a look about. No bloodshed apparently. This may be a pig-in-the-poke after all. See anything interesting?'

Miss Curleigh pointed a shaking finger. 'That's her – her bed. The messy one. But where is she?'

The other bed was neatly made up, its lace spread undisturbed. But Miss Euphemia Tarkle's was in a state of turmoil. The sheets had been ripped away and its mattress slashed open; some of the ticking was on the floor. The pillows had been torn to pieces. A depression in the centre of the mattress indicated where the missing invalid had lain.

Ellery stood still, studying the bed. Then he made the rounds of the closets, opening doors, poking about, and closing them again. Followed closely by Miss Curleigh, who had developed an alarming habit of looking over her right shoulder, he glanced briefly into the living room, the kitchen and the bathroom. But there was no one in the apartment. And, except for Miss Tarkle's bed, nothing apparently had been disturbed. The place was ghastly, somehow. It was as if violence had visited it in the midst of a cloistered silence; a tray full of dishes, cutlery, and half-finished food lay on the floor, almost under the bed.

Miss Curleigh shivered and edged closer to Ellery, 'It's so – so deserted here,' she said, moistening her lips. 'Where's Miss Euphemia? And her sister? And who was that – that creature who barred the door?'

'What's more to the point,' murmured Ellery, gazing at the tray of food, 'where are the seven black cats?'

'Sev – '

'Sarah-Ann's lone beauty, and Euphemia's six. Where are they?'

'Perhaps,' said Miss Curleigh hopefully, 'they jumped out the window when that man – '

'Perhaps. And don't say "man". We just don't know.' He looked irritably about him. 'If they did, it was a moment ago, because the catch on the window has been forced indicating that the window has been closed and consequently that the cats might have – ' He stopped short. 'Who's there?' he called sharply, whirling.

'It's me,' said a timid voice, and Mrs Potter appeared hesitantly in the foyer. Her tired eyes were luminous with fear and curiosity. 'Where's – '

'Gone.' He stared at the slovenly woman. 'Nothing to worry about. You're sure you didn't see Miss Euphemia or her sister today?'

'Nor yesterday. I – '

'There was no ambulance in this neighbourhood within the past two days?'

Mrs Potter went chalky. 'Oh, no, sir! I can't understand how she got out. She couldn't walk a step. If she'd been carried, someone would have noticed. The doorman, sure. I just asked him. But nobody did. I know everythin' goes on – '

'Is it possible your husband may have seen one or both of them within the past two days?'

'Not Potter. He saw 'em night before last. Harry's been makin' a little side-money, sort of, see, sir. Miss Euphemia wanted the landlord to do some decoratin' and paperin', and a little carpentry, and he wouldn't do it. So, more'n a month ago, she asked Harry if he wouldn't do it on the sly, and she said she'd pay him, although less than if a regular decorator did it. So he's been doin' it spare time, mostly late afternoons and night – he's handy, Potter is. He's most done with the job. It's pretty paper, ain't it? So he saw Miss Euphemia night before last.' A calamitous thought struck her, apparently, for her eyes rolled and she uttered a faint shriek. 'I just. . . . If – if anythin's happened to the cripple, we won't get paid! All that work. . . . And the landlord – '

'Yes, yes,' said Ellery impatiently. 'Mrs Potter, are there mice or rats in this house?'

Both women looked blank. 'Why, not a one of 'em,' began Mrs Potter slowly. 'The exterminator comes – ' when they all spun about at a sound from the foyer. Someone was opening the door.

'Come in,' snapped Ellery, and strode forward; only to halt in his tracks as an anxious face poked timidly into the bedroom.

'Excuse me,' said the newcomer nervously, starting at the sight of Ellery and the two women. 'I guess I must be in the wrong apartment. Does Miss Euphemia Tarkle live here?' He was a tall, needle-thin man with a scared, horsy face and stiff tan hair. He wore a rather rusty suit of old-fashioned cut and carried a small handbag.

'Yes, indeed,' said Ellery with a friendly smile. 'Come in, come in. May I ask who you are?'

The young man blinked. 'But where's Aunt Euphemia? I'm Elias Morton, Junior. Isn't she here?' His reddish little eyes blinked from Ellery to Miss Curleigh in a puzzled, worried way.

'Did you say " Aunt " Euphemia, Mr Morton?'

'I'm her nephew. I come from out of town – Albany. Where – '

Ellery murmured. 'An unexpected visit, Mr Morton?'

The young man blinked again; he was still holding his bag. Then he dumped it on the floor and eagerly fumbled in his pockets until he produced a much-soiled and wrinkled letter. 'I – I got this only a few days ago,' he faltered. 'I'd have come sooner, only my father went off somewhere on a – I don't understand this.'

Ellery snatched the letter from his lax fingers. It was scrawled painfully on a piece of ordinary brown wrapping paper; the envelope was a cheap one. The pencilled scribble, in the crabbed hand of age, said:

Dear Elias

You have not heard from your Auntie for so many years, but now I need you, Elias, for you are my only blood kin to whom I can turn in my Dire Distress! I am in great danger, my dear boy. You must help your poor Invalid Aunt who is so helpless. Come at once. Do not tell your Father nor anyone, Elias! When you get here make believe you have come just for a visit. Remember. Please, please do not fail me. Help me, please!

Your loving Aunt,
Euphemia Tarkle.

'Remarkable missive,' frowned Ellery. 'Written under stress, Miss Curleigh. Genuine enough. Don't tell anyone, eh? Well, Mr Morton, I'm afraid you're too late.'

'Too – but – ' The young man's horse-face whitened. 'I tried to come right off, b-but my father had gone off somewhere on a – on one of his drunken spells and I couldn't find him. I didn't know what to do. Then I came. T-t-to think – ' His buck teeth were chattering.

'This is your aunt's handwriting?'

'Oh, yes. Oh, yes.'

'Your father, I gather, is not a brother of the Tarkle sisters?'

'No, sir. My dear mother w-was their sister, God rest her.' Morton groped for a chair-back. 'Is Aunt Euphemia – d-dead? And where's Aunt Sarah?'

'They've both gone.' Ellery related tersely what he had found. The young visitor from Albany looked as if he might faint. 'I'm – er – unofficially investigating this business, Mr Morton. Tell me all you know about your two aunts.'

'I don't know m-much,' mumbled Morton. 'Haven't seen them for about fifteen years, since I was a kid. I heard from my Aunt Sarah-Ann once in a while, and only twice from Aunt Euphemia. They never – I never expected – I do know that Aunt Euphemia since her stroke became . . . funny. Aunt Sarah wrote me that. She had some money – I don't know how much – left her by my grandfather, and Aunt Sarah said she was a real miser about it. Aunt Sarah didn't have anything; she had to live with Aunt Euphemia and take care of her. She wouldn't trust banks, Aunt Sarah said, and had hidden the money somewhere about her, Aunt Sarah didn't know where. She wouldn't even have doctors after her stroke, she was – is so stingy. They didn't get along; they were always fighting, Aunt Sarah wrote me, and Aunt Euphemia was always accusing her of trying to steal her money, and she didn't know how she stood about it. That's – that's about all I know, sir.'

'The poor things,' muttered Miss Curleigh with moist eyes. 'What a wretched existence! Miss Tarkle can't be responsible for – '

'Tell me, Mr Morton,' drawled Ellery. 'It's true that your Aunt Euphemia detested cats?'

The lantern-jaw dropped. 'Why, how'd you know? She hates them. Aunt Sarah wrote me that many times. It hurt her a lot, because she's so crazy about them she treats her own like a child, you see, and that makes Aunt Euphemia jealous, or angry, or something. I guess they just didn't – don't get along.'

'We seem to be having a pardonable difficulty with our tenses,' said Ellery. 'After all, Mr Morton, there's no evidence to show that your aunts aren't merely off somewhere on a vacation, or a visit, perhaps.' But the glint in his eyes remained. 'Why don't you stop at a hotel somewhere nearby? I'll keep you informed.' He scribbled the name and address of a hotel in the Seventies on the page of a notebook, and thrust it into Morton's damp palm. 'Don't worry. You'll hear from me.' And he hustled the bewildered young man out of the apartment. They heard the click of the elevator-door a moment later.

Ellery said slowly: 'The country cousin in full panoply. Miss Curleigh, let me look at your refreshing loveliness. People with faces like that should be legislated against.' He patted her cheek with a frown, hesitated, and then made for the bathroom. Miss Curleigh blushed once more and followed him quickly, casting another apprehensive glance over her shoulder.

'What's this?' she heard Ellery say sharply. 'Mrs Potter, come out of that – By George!'

'What's the matter now?' cried Miss Curleigh, dashing into the bathroom behind him.

Mrs Potter, the flesh of her powerful forearms crawling with goose-pimples, her tired eyes stricken, was glaring with open mouth into the tub. The woman made a few inarticulate sounds, rolled her eyes alarmingly, and then fled from the apartment.

Miss Curleigh said: 'Oh, my God,' and put her hand to her breast. 'Isn't that – isn't that horrible!'

'Horrible,' said Ellery grimly and slowly, 'and illuminating. I didn't see it when I glanced in here before. I think . . .' he stopped and bent over the tub. There was no humour in his eyes or voice now; only a sick watchfulness. They were both very quiet. Death lay over them.

A black tomcat, limp and stiff and boneless, lay in a welter and smear of blood in the tub. He was large, glossy, black, green-eyed, and indubitably dead. His head was smashed in and his body seemed broken in several places. His blood had clotted in splashes on the porcelain sides of the tub. The weapon, hurled by a callous hand, lay beside him: a blood-spattered bath-brush with a heavy handle.

'That solves the mystery of the disappearance of at least one of these seven,' murmured Ellery, straightening. 'Battered to death with the brush. He hasn't been dead more than a day or so, either, from the looks of him. Miss Curleigh, we're engaged in a tragic business.'

But Miss Curleigh, her first shock of horror swept away by rage, was crying: 'Anyone who would kill a puss so brutally is – a monster!' Her silvery eyes were blazing. 'That terrible old woman – '

'Don't forget,' sighed Ellery, 'she can't walk.'

'Now this,' said Mr Ellery Queen some time later, putting away his cunning and compact little pocket-kit, 'is growing more and more curious, Miss Curleigh. Have you any notion what I've found here?'

They were back in the bedroom again, stooped over the bedtray which he had picked up from the floor and deposited on the night-table between the missing sisters' beds. Miss Curleigh had recalled that on all her previous visits she had found the tray on Miss Tarkle's bed or on the table, the invalid explaining with a tightening of her pale lips that she had taken to eating alone of late, implying that she and the long-suffering Sarah-Ann had reached a tragic parting of the ways.

'I saw you mess about with powder and things, but – '

'Fingerprint test.' Ellery stared enigmatically down at the knife, fork, and spoon lying awry in the tray. 'My kit's a handy gadget at times. You saw me test this cutlery, Miss Curleigh. You would say these implements had been used by Euphemia in the process of eating her last meal here?'

'Why, of course,' frowned Miss Curleigh. 'You can still see the dried food clinging to the knife and fork.'

'Exactly. The handles of knife, fork, and spoon are not engraved as you see – simple silver surfaces. They should bear fingerprints.' He shrugged. 'But they don't.'

'What do you mean, Mr Queen? How is that possible?'

'I mean that someone has wiped this cutlery free of prints. Odd, eh?' Ellery lit a cigarette absently. 'Examine it, however. This is Euphemia Tarkle's bedtray, her food, her dishes, her cutlery. She is known to eat, and alone. But if only Euphemia handled the cutlery, who wiped off the prints? She? Why should she? Someone else? But surely there would be no sense in someone else's wiping off Euphemia's prints. Her fingerprints have a right to be there. Then, while Euphemia's prints were probably on these implements someone else's prints were also on them, which accounts for their having been wiped off. Someone else, therefore, handled Euphemia's cutlery. Why, I begin,' said Ellery in the grimmest of voices, 'to see daylight. Miss Curleigh, would you like to serve as handmaiden to Justice?' Miss Curleigh, overwhelmed, could only nod. Ellery began to wrap the cold food left-overs from the invalid's tray. 'Take this truck down to Dr Samuel Prouty – here's his address – and ask him to analyse it for me. Wait there, get his report, and meet me back here. Try to get in here without being observed.'

'The food?'

'The food.'

'Then you think it's been – '

'The time for thinking,' said Ellery Queen evenly, 'is almost over.'

When Miss Curleigh had gone, he took a final look around, even to the extent of examining some empty cupboards which had a look of newness about them, set his lips firmly, locked the front door behind him – pocketing the master-key which Mrs Potter had given him – took the elevator to the ground floor, and rang the bell of the Potter apartment.

A short, thickset man with heavy, coarse features opened the door; his hat was pushed back on his head. Ellery saw the agitated figure of Mrs Potter hovering in the background.

'That's the policeman!' shrilled Mrs Potter. 'Harry, don't get mixed up in – '

'Oh, so you're the dick,' growled the thickset man, ignoring the fat woman. 'I'm the super here – Harry Potter. I just get home from the plant and my wife tells me there's something wrong up in the Tarkle flat. What's up, for God's sake?'

'Now, now, there's no cause for panic, Potter,' murmured Ellery. 'Glad you're home, though; I'm in dire need of information which you can probably provide. Has either of you found anywhere on the premises recently – any dead cats?'

Potter's jaw dropped, and his wife gurgled with surprise. 'Now that's damn' funny. We sure have. Mrs Potter says one of 'em's dead up in 5-C now – I never thought those two old dames might be the ones – '

'Where did you find them, and how many?' snapped Ellery.

'Why, down in the incinerator. Basement.'

Ellery smacked his thigh. 'Of course! What a stupid idiot I am. I see it all now. The incinerator, eh? There were six, Potter, weren't there?'

Mrs Potter gasped: 'How'd you know that, for mercy's sake?'

'Incinerator,' muttered Ellery, sucking his lower lip. 'The bones, I suppose – the skulls?'

'That's right,' exclaimed Potter; he seemed distressed. 'I found 'em myself. Empty out the incinerator every mornin' for ash-removal. Six cats' skulls and a mess o' little bones. I raised hell around here with the tenants, lookin' for the damn' fool who threw 'em down the chute, but they all played dumb. Didn't all come down the same time. It's been goin' on now maybe four-five weeks. One a week, almost. The damn' fools. I'd like to get my paws on – '

' You're certain you found six?'

' Sure.'

' And nothing else of a suspicious nature?'

' No, sir.'

' Thanks. I don't believe there will be any more trouble. Just forget the whole business.' And Ellery pressed a bill into the man's hand and strolled out of the lobby.

He did not stroll far. He strolled, in fact, only to the side-walk steps leading down into the basement and cellar. Five minutes later he quietly let himself into Apartment 5-C again.

When Miss Curleigh stopped before the door to Apartment 5-C in late afternoon, she found it locked. She could hear Ellery's voice murmuring inside and a moment later the click of a telephone receiver. Reassured, she pressed the bell-button; he appeared instantly, pulled her inside, noiselessly shut the door again, and led her to the bedroom, where she slumped into a rosewood chair, an expression of bitter disappointment on her pleasant little face.

' Back from the wars, I see,' he grinned. ' Well, sister, what luck?'

' You'll be dreadfully put out,' said Miss Curleigh with a scowl. ' I'm sorry I haven't been more helpful – '

' What did good Dr Prouty say?'

' Nothing encouraging. I like your Dr Prouty, even if he is the Medical Examiner or something and wears a horrible little peaked hat in the presence of a lady; but I can't say I'm keen about his reports. He says there's not a thing wrong with that food you sent by me! It's a little putrefied from standing, but otherwise it's pure enough.'

' Now isn't that too bad?' said Ellery cheerfully. ' Come, come, Diana, perk up. It's the best news you could have brought me.'

' Best n – ' began Miss Curleigh with a gasp.

' It substitutes fact for theory very nicely. Fits, lassie, like a brassière. We have,' and he pulled over a chair and sat down facing her, ' arrived. By the way, did anyone see you enter this apartment?'

' I slipped in by the basement and took the elevator from there. No one saw me, I'm sure. But I don't underst – '

' Commendable efficiency. I believe we have some time for expatiation. I've had an hour or so here alone for thought, and it's been a satisfactory if morbid business.' Ellery lit a cigarette and crossed his legs lazily. 'Miss Curleigh, you have sense, plus the advantage of an innate feminine shrewdness, I'm sure. Tell me, why should a wealthy old lady who is almost completely paralysed stealthily purchase six cats within a period of five weeks?'

Miss Curleigh shrugged. 'I told you I couldn't make it out. It's a deep, dark mystery to me.' Her eyes were fixed on his lips.

'Pshaw, it can't be as completely baffling as all that. Very well, I'll give you a rough idea. For example, so many cats purchased by an eccentric in so short a period suggests – vivisection. But neither of the Tarkle ladies is anything like a scientist. So that's out. You see?'

'Oh, yes,' said Miss Curleigh breathlessly. 'I see now what you mean. Euphemia couldn't have wanted them for companionship, either, because she hates cats!'

'Precisely. Let's wander. For extermination of mice? No, this is from Mrs Potter's report a pest-free building. For mating? Scarcely; Sarah-Ann's cat was a male, and Euphemia also bought only males. Besides, they were nondescript tabbies, and people don't play Cupid to nameless animals.'

'She might have bought them for gifts,' said Miss Curleigh with a frown. 'That's possible.'

'Possible, but I think not,' said Ellery dryly. 'Not when you know the facts. The superintendent found the skeletal remains of six cats in the ashes of the incinerator downstairs, and the other one lies, a very dead pussy, in the bathtub yonder.' Miss Curleigh stared at him, speechless. 'We seem to have covered the more plausible theories. Can you think of some wilder ones?'

Miss Curleigh paled. 'Not – not for their fur?'

'Bravo,' said Ellery with a laugh. 'There's a wild one among wild ones. No, not for their fur; I haven't found any fur in the apartment. And besides, no matter who killed Master Tom in the tub, he remains bloody but unskinned. To frighten Sister Sarah-Ann? Hardly; Sarah is used to cats and loves them. To scratch Sarah-Ann to death? That suggests poisoned claws. But in that case there would be as much danger to Euphemia as to Sarah-Ann; and why six cats? As – er – guides in eternal dark? But Euphemia is not blind, and besides she never leaves her bed. Can you think of any others?'

'But those things are ridiculous!'

'Don't call my logical meanderings names. Ridiculous, perhaps, but you can't ignore even apparent nonsense in an elimination.'

'Well, I've got one that isn't nonsense,' said Miss Curleigh suddenly. 'Pure hatred. Euphemia loathed cats. So, since she's cracked, I suppose, she's bought them just for the pleasure of exterminating them.'

'All black tomcats with green eyes and identical dimensions?' Ellery shook his head. 'Her mania could scarcely have been so exclusive. Besides, she loathed cats even before Sarah-Ann bought her distinctive tom from you. No, there's only one left that I can think of, Miss Curleigh.' He sprang from the chair and began to pace the floor. 'It's not only the sole remaining possibility, but it's confirmed by several things. . . . Protection!'

'Protection!' Miss Curleigh's devastating eyes widened. 'Why, Mr Queen. How could that be? People buy dogs for protection, not cats.'

'I don't mean that kind of protection,' said Ellery impatiently. 'I'm referring to a compound of desire to remain alive and an incidental hatred for felines that makes them the ideal instruments towards that end. This is a truly horrifying business, Marie. From every angle. Euphemia Tarkle was afraid. Of what? Of being murdered for her money. That's borne out amply by the letter she wrote to Morton, her nephew; and it's bolstered by her reputed miserliness, her distrust of banks, and her dislike of her own sister. How would a cat be protection against intended murder?'

'Poison!' cried Miss Curleigh.

'Exactly. As a food-taster. There's a reversion to medievalism for you! Are there confirming data? A-plenty. Euphemia had taken to eating alone of late; that suggests some secret activity. Then she re-ordered cats five times within a short period. Why? Obviously, because each time her cat, purchased from you, had acted in his official capacity, tasted her food, and gone the way of all enslaved flesh. The cats were poisoned, poisoned by food intended for Euphemia. So she had to re-order. Final confirmation; the six feline skeletons in the incinerator.'

'But she can't walk,' protested Miss Curleigh. 'So how could she dispose of the bodies?'

'I fancy Mrs Potter innocently disposed of them for her. You'll recall that Mrs Potter said she was often called here to take garbage to the incinerator for Euphemia when Sarah-Ann was out. The " garbage ", wrapped up, I suppose, was a cat's dead body.'

'But why all the black, green-eyed tomcats of the same size?'

'Self-evident. Why? Obviously, again, to fool Sarah-Ann. Because Sarah-Ann had a black tomcat of a certain size with green eyes. Euphemia purchased from you identical animals. Her only reason for this could have been, then, to fool Sarah-Ann into believing that the black tom she saw about the apartment at any given time was her own, the original one. That suggests, of course, that Euphemia used Sarah-Ann's cat to foil the first attempt, and Sarah-Ann's cat was the first poison-victim. When he died, Euphemia bought another from you – without her sister's knowledge. How Euphemia suspected she was slated to be poisoned, of course, at the very time in which the poisoner got busy, we'll never know. It was probably the merest coincidence, something psychic – you never know about slightly mad old ladies.'

'But if she was trying to fool Sarah-Ann about the cats,' whispered Miss Curleigh, aghast, 'then she suspected – I mean, she thought – '

'Precisely. She suspected her sister of trying to poison her.'

Miss Curleigh bit her lip. 'Would you mind giving me a – a cigarette? I'm – ' Ellery silently complied. 'It's the most terrible thing I've ever heard of. Two old women, sisters, practically alone in the world, one dependent on the other for attention, the other for subsistence, living at cross-purposes – the invalid helpless to defend herself against attacks . . .' She shuddered. 'What's happened to those poor creatures, Mr Queen?'

'Well, let's see. Euphemia is missing. We know that there were at least six attempts to poison her, all unsuccessful. It's logical to assume that there was a seventh attempt, then, and that – since Euphemia is gone under mysterious circumstances – the seventh attempt was successful.'

'But how can you know she's – she's dead?'

'Where is she?' asked Ellery dryly. 'The only other possibility is that she fled. But she's helpless, can't walk, can't stir from bed without assistance. Who can assist her? Only Sarah-Ann, the very one she suspects of trying to poison her. The letter to her nephew shows that she wouldn't turn to Sarah-Ann. So flight is out and, since she's missing, she must be dead. Now, follow. Euphemia knew she was the target of poisoning attacks via her food, and took precautions against them; then how did the poisoner finally penetrate her defences – the seventh cat? Well, we may assume that Euphemia made the seventh cat taste the food we found on the tray. We know that food was not poisoned, from Dr Prouty's report. The cat, then, didn't die of poisoning from the food itself – confirmed by the fact that he was beaten to death. But if the cat didn't die of poisoned food, neither did Euphemia. Yet all the indications are that she must have died of poisoning. Then there's only one answer: she died of poisoning not in eating but in the process of eating.'

' I don't understand,' said Miss Curleigh intently.

' The cutlery!' cried Ellery. ' I showed you earlier this afternoon that someone other than Euphemia had handled her knife, spoon, and fork. Doesn't this suggest that the poisoner had poisoned the cutlery on his seventh attempt? If, for example, the fork had been coated with a colourless, odourless poison which dried, Euphemia would have been fooled. That cat, flung bits of food by hand – for no one feeds an animal with cutlery – would live; Euphemia, eating the food with the poisoned cutlery, would die. Psychologically, too, it rings true. It stood to reason that the poisoner, after six unsuccessful attempts one way, should in desperation try a seventh with a variation. The variation worked and Euphemia, my dear, is dead.'

' But her body – where – '

Ellery's face changed as he whirled noiselessly toward the door. He stood in an attitude of tense attention for an instant and then, without a word, laid violent hands upon the petrified figure of Miss Curleigh and thrust her rudely into one of the bedroom closets, shutting the door behind her. Miss Curleigh, half-smothered by a soft sea of musty-smelling feminine garments, held her breath. She had heard that faint scratching of metal upon metal at the front door. It must be – if Mr Queen acted so quickly – the poisoner. Why had he come back? she thought wildly. The key he was using – easy – a duplicate. Earlier, when they had surprised him and he had barricaded the door, he must have entered the apartment by the roof and fire-escape window because he couldn't use the key . . . someone must have been standing in the hall. . . .

She choked back a scream, her thought snapping off as if a switch had been turned. A hoarse, harsh voice – the sounds of a struggle – a crash . . . they were fighting!

Miss Curleigh saw red. She flung open the door of the closet and plunged out. Ellery was on the floor in a tangle of threshing arms and legs. A hand came up with a knife. . . . Miss Curleigh sprang and kicked in an instantaneous reflex action. Something snapped sharply, and she fell back, sickened, as the knife dropped from a broken hand.

'Miss Curleigh – the door!' panted Ellery, pressing his knee viciously downward. Through a dim roaring in her ears Miss Curleigh heard pounding on the door, and tottered toward it. The last thing she remembered before she fainted was a weird boiling of blue-clad bodies as police poured past her to fall upon the struggling figures.

'It's all right now,' said a far-away voice, and Miss Curleigh opened her eyes to find Mr Ellery Queen, cool and immaculate, stooping over her. She moved her head dazedly. The fireplace, the crossed swords on the wall. . . . 'Don't be alarmed, Marie,' grinned Ellery; 'this isn't an abduction. You have achieved Valhalla. It's all over, and you're reclining on the divan in my apartment.'

'Oh,' said Miss Curleigh, and she swung her feet unsteadily to the floor. 'I – I must look a sight. What happened?'

'We caught the bogey very satisfactorily. Now you rest, young lady, while I rustle a dish of tea – '

'Nonsense!' said Miss Curleigh with asperity. 'I want to know how you performed that miracle. Come on, now, don't be irritating!'

'Yours to command. Just what do you want to know?'

'Did you know that awful creature was coming back?'

Ellery shrugged. 'It was a likely possibility. Euphemia had been poisoned, patently, for her hidden money. She must have been murdered at the very latest yesterday – you recall yesterday's milk-bottle – perhaps the night before last. Had the murderer found the money after killing her? Then who was the prowler whom we surprised this afternoon and who made his escape out of the window after barricading the door? It must have been the murderer. But if he came back after the crime, then he had not found the money when he committed the crime. Perhaps he had so much to do immediately after the commission of the crime that he had had no time to search. At any rate, on his return we surprised him – probably just after he had made a mess of the bed. It was quite possible that he had still not found the money. If he had not, I knew he would come back – after all, he had committed the crime for it. So I took the chance that he would return when he thought the coast was clear, and he did. I phoned for police assistance while you were out seeing Dr Prouty.'

'Did you know who it was?'

'Oh yes. It was demonstrable. The first qualification of the poisoner was availability; that is, in order to make those repeated poisoning attempts, the poisoner had to be near Euphemia or near her food at least since the attempts began, which was presumably five weeks ago. The obvious suspect was her sister. Sarah-Ann had motive — hatred and possibly cupidity; and certainly opportunity, since she prepared the food herself. But Sarah-Ann I eliminated on the soundest basis in the world.

'For who had brutally beaten to death the seventh black tomcat? Palpably, either the victim or the murderer in a general sense. But it couldn't have been Euphemia, since the cat was killed in the bathroom and Euphemia lay paralysed in the bedroom, unable to walk. Then it must have been the murderer who killed the cat. But if Sarah-Ann were the murderer, would she have clubbed to death a cat — she, who loved cats? Utterly inconceivable. Therefore Sarah-Ann was not the murderer.'

'Then what —'

'I know. What happened to Sarah-Ann?' Ellery grimaced. 'Sarah-Ann, it is to be feared, went the way of the cat and her sister. It must have been the poisoner's plan to kill Euphemia and have it appear that Sarah-Ann had killed her — the obvious suspect. Sarah-Ann, then, should be on the scene. But she isn't. Well, her disappearance tends to show — I think the confession will bear me out — that she was accidentally a witness to the murder and was killed by the poisoner on the spot to eliminate a witness to the crime.'

'Did you find the money?'

'Yes. Lying quite loosely,' shrugged Ellery, 'between the pages of a Bible Euphemia always kept in her bed.'

'And,' quavered Miss Curleigh, 'the bodies . . .'

'Surely,' drawled Ellery, 'the incinerator? It would have been the most logical means of disposal.'

'But that means — Who was that fiend on the floor? I never saw him before. It couldn't have been Mr Morton's f-father . . . ?'

'No, indeed. Fiend, Miss Curleigh?' Ellery raised his eyebrows. 'There's only a thin wall between sanity and —'

'You called me,' said Miss Curleigh, 'Marie, before.'

Ellery said hastily: 'No one but Sarah-Ann and Euphemia lived in the apartment, yet the poisoner had access to the invalid's food for over a month — apparently without suspicion. Who could have had such access? Only one person: the man who had been decorating the apartment in the late afternoons and evenings — around dinner-time — for over a month; the man who worked in a chemical plant and therefore, better than anyone, had knowledge of and access to poisons; the man who tended the incinerator and therefore could dispose of the bones of his human victims without danger to himself. In a word,' said Ellery, ' the superintendent of the building, Harry Potter.'

Other titles available from Robinson Publishing

Honour the Dead (hardback) Steven Saylor **£16.99** [ ]
Based on a string of horrifying crimes that took place more than a century ago,
Honour the Dead vividly evokes a fledging American South in the aftermath of the
civil war. This enthralling Texas-based historical thriller is an exciting new departure
from Steven Saylor's internationally popular series of Roman detective stories.

At End of Day (hardback) George V. Higgins **£17.99** [ ]
Based around the true story of two gangsters and their unusual relationship with the
city's top FBI men, *At End of Day* is packed with characters displaying a broad range
of human nature illustrating the power of corruption and greed. A last novel by a rich
and complex literary talent.

The Friends of Eddie Coyle George V. Higgins **£6.99** [ ]
This fast-paced, dialogue-driven story established George V. Higgins as the unrivalled
chronicler of American low-life. Made into a classic film of the same name starring
Robert Mitchum, *The Friends of Eddie Coyle* has previously been chosen as one of the
top 50 post-war American novels.

The Crimes of Charlotte Brontë James Tully **£7.99** [ ]
The story of the lives of the Brontë family is as haunting and tragic as their novels:
three sisters and an alcoholic brother shut in the bleak and claustrophobic parsonage at
Haworth. Noted criminologist James Tully became fascinated by the inconsistencies of
their lives and deaths and decided to tell the story in the form of a novel.

*Robinson books are available from all good bookshops or can be ordered direct from
the Publisher. Just tick the title you want and fill in the form below.*

TBS Direct
Colchester Road, Frating Green, Colchester, Essex CO7 7DW
Tel: +44 (0) 1206 255777
Fax: +44 (0) 1206 255914
Email: sales@tbs-ltd.co.uk

UK/BFPO customers please allow £1.00 for p&p for the first book, plus 50p for the
second, plus 30p for each additional book up to a maximum charge of £3.00.
Overseas customers (inc. Ireland), please allow £2.00 for the first book, plus £1.00 for
the second, plus 50p for each additional book.

Please send me the titles ticked above.

NAME (block letters) . . . .
ADDRESS . . . .
. . . .
POSTCODE . . . .

I enclose a cheque/PO (payable to TBS Direct) for . . . .
I wish to pay by Switch/Credit card
Number . . . .
Card Expiry Date . . . .
Switch Issue Number . . . .